This book belongs to

READER'S DIGEST

BEST LOVED
BOOKS

FOR YOUNG
READERS

READER'S DIGEST

BEST LOVED
BOOKS

FOR YOUNG
READERS

selected and condensed by
the Editors of The Reader's Digest

◈

VOLUME TWO

THE READER'S DIGEST ASSOCIATION
PLEASANTVILLE, NEW YORK

Contents

7

THE SCARLET PIMPERNEL
by Baroness Orczy

141

The Adventures of
TOM SAWYER
by Mark Twain

275

THE GOOD EARTH
by Pearl S. Buck

447

The Merry Adventures of
ROBIN HOOD
by Howard Pyle

THE SCARLET PIMPERNEL

a
condensation
of
the
book
by

BARONESS ORCZY

illustrated by
STANLEY MELTZOFF

BARONESS EMMUSKA ORCZY used to say that *The Scarlet Pimpernel* was born in a subway station. Waiting in the London Underground one day, and worrying about a newspaper commission for a serial, she saw a man whose appearance immediately suggested to her the role of the Scarlet Pimpernel. She hurried home and started to write, and the story, later published as a book, became such an enormous success that she continued to write about the adventures of the Scarlet Pimpernel and his league of faithful followers at the rate of two books a year.

Baroness Orczy was born in Hungary in 1863, the daughter of a feudal landowner who was also a fine pianist. In 1880 Baron Felix Orczy was exiled from his homeland and took refuge, with his wife and daughter, in England, where he taught piano. The young baroness met her husband-to-be, Montagu Barstow, when they were both studying art. After their marriage they went to Paris and lived in the bohemian Latin Quarter, struggling along for some years on Barstow's sparse earnings as an artist, although he later became famous and successful. With such a background it is not surprising that Baroness Orczy should show such evident sympathy for aristocratic exiles—and such knowledge of France and her people.

In 1898 she and her husband returned to England, and it was then that chance turned Baroness Orczy to writing. Their landlord's daughter won a short-story competition, and the winning piece was read aloud to the assembled boarders. Later the baroness declared to her husband, "Why, I could write a better story than that!"

The French Revolution has inspired many novelists, but perhaps no character has caught the imagination of readers in quite the same way as the baroness' gallant, daring adventurer who rescued condemned French aristocrats from beneath the knife of the guillotine.

A SURGING, SEETHING, murmuring crowd of beings that are human only in name, for to the eye and ear they seem naught but savage creatures, animated by vile passions and by the lust of vengeance and of hate. The hour, some little time before sunset, and the place, the West Barricade.

During the greater part of the day the guillotine had been kept busy at its ghastly work: all that France had boasted of in past centuries, of ancient names and blue blood, had paid toll to her desire for liberty and for fraternity. The carnage had only ceased at this late hour of the day because there were other more interesting sights for the people to witness, a little while before the final closing of the barricades for the night.

And so the crowd rushed from the Place de Grève and made for the various barricades to watch this amusing sight.

It was to be seen every day, for those aristos were such fools! They were traitors, of course. Their ancestors had crushed the people under the scarlet heels of their dainty buckled shoes, and now the people had become the rulers of France and crushed their former masters—not beneath their heels, for they went shoeless mostly in these days—but beneath the knife of the guillotine.

This was as it should be: for two hundred years now the people had sweated and toiled and starved to keep a lustful court in lavish extravagance; now the descendants of those who made those courts brilliant had to fly for their lives to avoid the vengeance of the people. And they did try to fly: that was just the fun of the thing. Every afternoon before the gates closed and the market carts went out, some aristo endeavored to evade the clutches of the Committee of Public Safety. In various disguises, they tried to slip through the barriers which were so well guarded by citizen soldiers of the Republic. Men in women's clothes, women in male attire, children disguised in beggars' rags: there were some of all sorts, *ci-devant* counts, marquises, even dukes, who wanted to fly to England or some other equally accursed country, and there try to rouse feeling against the glorious revolution.

But they were nearly always caught at the barricades. Sergeant Bibot especially, at the West Gate, had a wonderful nose for scenting an aristo in the most perfect disguise. Oh! It was well worth hanging around that barricade to see him catch an aristo in the very act of trying to flee.

On this fine afternoon in September the crowd around Bibot's gate was eager and excited. The lust of blood grows with its satisfaction: the crowd had seen a hundred noble heads fall beneath the guillotine today, it wanted to make sure that it would see another hundred fall on the morrow.

Bibot was sitting on an overturned cask close by the gate of the barricade; a small detachment of *citoyen* soldiers was under his command. Every day lately Bibot had had the satisfaction of unmasking some fugitive royalists and sending them back to be tried by the Committee of Public Safety. Robespierre and Danton both had commended Bibot for his zeal, and Bibot was proud of the fact that he had sent at least fifty aristos to the guillotine.

But today all the sergeants at the barricades had had special orders. Recently a great number of aristos had succeeded in escaping and reaching England in safety. There were curious rumors about these escapes; they had become singularly daring: Sergeant Grospierre had been sent to the guillotine for allowing a whole family to slip out of the North Gate under his very nose. It was asserted that these escapes were organized by a band of daring

Englishmen under the leadership of a man whose pluck and audacity were almost fabulous. Strange stories were afloat of how he and those aristos whom he rescued became suddenly invisible and escaped out of the gates by sheer supernatural agency.

No one had seen these Englishmen; and their leader was never spoken of save with a superstitious shudder. The Committee of Public Safety would receive from some mysterious source a scrap of paper, which contained a brief notice that the band of Englishmen were at work, and it was always signed with a device drawn in red—a little star-shaped flower which we in England call the Scarlet Pimpernel. Within a few hours of the receipt of this impudent notice, the committee would hear that so many royalists were safely on their way to England.

The guards at the gates had been doubled, the sergeants in command had been threatened with death, while a sum of five thousand francs was promised to the man who laid hands on the elusive Scarlet Pimpernel. Everyone felt that Bibot would be that man, and so, day after day, people came to the West Gate to be present when he laid hands on that mysterious Englishman.

"Bah!" he said to his trusted corporal. "Citoyen Grospierre was a fool! Had it been me, now, at that North Gate last week . . ."

Citoyen Bibot spat on the ground to express his contempt.

"How did it happen, citoyen?" asked the corporal.

"Grospierre was at the gate," began Bibot pompously, as the crowd closed in, listening eagerly. "The market carts were going through; there was one laden with casks, driven by an old man. Grospierre thought himself very clever; he looked into the casks— most of them, at least—and saw they were empty, and let the cart go through."

A murmur of wrath went around the group.

"Half an hour later," continued the sergeant, "up comes a captain of the guard with some dozen soldiers. 'Has a cart gone through?' he asks Grospierre breathlessly. 'Yes,' says Grospierre, 'not half an hour ago.' 'And you have let them escape,' shouts the captain furiously. 'That cart held concealed the ci-devant Duc de Chalis and all his family!' 'What!' thunders Grospierre, aghast.

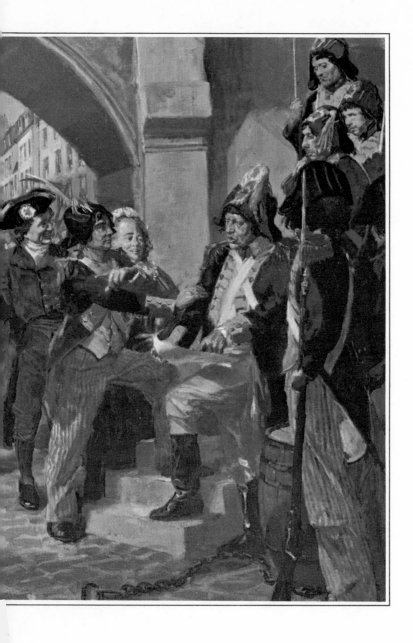

'Aye! And the driver was none other than that cursed Englishman, the Scarlet Pimpernel.'"

A howl of execration greeted this tale. Citoyen Grospierre had paid for his blunder on the guillotine, but oh, what a fool!

"'After them, my men,' shouts the captain," Bibot continued, "'they cannot have gone far!' And with that he rushes through the gate, followed by his soldiers."

"But it was too late!" shouted the crowd excitedly.

"Curse that Grospierre for his folly."

These sallies seemed to amuse Bibot exceedingly; he laughed until his sides ached. "Nay, nay!" he said at last. "Those aristos weren't in the cart; the driver was not the Scarlet Pimpernel!"

"What?"

"No! The captain of the guard was that damned Englishman in disguise, and every one of his soldiers aristos!"

The crowd this time said nothing: the story certainly savored of the supernatural. Truly that Englishman must be the devil himself.

The sun was sinking low in the west. Bibot prepared to close the gates. "*En avant* the carts," he said.

Some dozen covered carts were drawn up in a row, ready to leave town in order to fetch country produce for market the next morning. They were mostly well-known to Bibot, as they went through his gate twice every day, but he was at great pains to examine the inside of the carts. The women who drove them usually spent their day on the Place de Grève beneath the platform of the guillotine, knitting and gossiping while they watched the rows of tumbrils arriving with the victims of the Reign of Terror. Bibot, during the day, had been on duty in the Place. He recognized most of the *tricoteuses*, as they were called, who sat knitting while head after head fell beneath the knife.

"*Hé! La mère!*" said Bibot to one of these horrible hags. "What have you got there?"

He had seen her earlier in the day, with her knitting, her cart close beside her. Now she had fastened a row of curly locks to her whip handle, and she stroked them with her huge, bony fingers as she laughed at Bibot.

"I made friends with Madame Guillotine's lover," she said with a coarse laugh. "He cut these off for me from the heads as they rolled down. He has promised me some more tomorrow, but I don't know if I shall be at my usual place."

"Ah! How is that, la mère?" asked Bibot, who, hardened soldier though he was, could not help shuddering at the loathsomeness of this woman with her ghastly trophy.

"Some say my grandson has got the plague," she said, with a jerk of her thumb toward the inside of her cart. "If it is so, I shan't be allowed to come into Paris tomorrow."

At the mention of the plague Bibot stepped hastily back. "Curse you!" he muttered, while the whole crowd avoided the cart.

The old hag laughed. "Curse you, citoyen, for being a coward," she said. "Bah! What a man to be afraid of sickness."

"*Morbleu!* The plague!"

Everyone was filled with horror for the loathsome malady, the one thing which could arouse terror in these brutalized creatures.

"Get out with you and with your plague-stricken brood!" shouted Bibot hoarsely. And with another rough laugh the old hag whipped up her lean nag and drove out of the gate.

This incident had spoiled the afternoon. The people hung about the barricades, silent and sullen, eyeing one another suspiciously, as if the plague lurked already in their midst. Presently a captain of the guard appeared. But he was known to Bibot, and there was no fear of his turning out to be a sly Englishman in disguise.

"A cart . . ." he shouted breathlessly.

"What cart?" asked Bibot roughly.

"Driven by an old hag . . ."

"There were a dozen . . ."

"Who said her son had the plague?"

"Yes . . ."

"You have not let them go?"

"Morbleu!" said Bibot, whose purple cheeks had suddenly become white with fear.

"The cart contained the ci-devant Comtesse de Tournay and her two children, all of them traitors and condemned to death."

"And their driver?" muttered Bibot, as a superstitious shudder ran down his spine.

"*Sacré tonnerre*," said the captain, "but it is feared that it was that accursed Englishman himself—the Scarlet Pimpernel."

✿

DOVER: THE FISHERMAN'S REST

IN THE KITCHEN Sally was extremely busy—saucepans and frying pans were standing in rows on the gigantic hearth, and the jack slowly turned a noble sirloin of beef. Two little kitchen maids bustled around, hot and panting, with cotton sleeves tucked up above dimpled elbows, giggling whenever Miss Sally's back was turned. And stolid old Jemima kept up a subdued grumble while she stirred the stockpot over the fire.

"What ho, Sally!" came in cheerful accents from the coffee room close by, and a chorus of pewter mugs, tapped impatiently against oak tables, accompanied the shouts for mine host's buxom daughter. "Are ye goin' to be all night with that there beer?"

"I do think Father might get the beer for them!" exclaimed Sally, as Jemima began filling tankards with some of that home-brewed ale for which The Fisherman's Rest had been famous since the days of King Charles. " 'E knows 'ow busy we are."

"Your father is too busy discussing politics with Mr. 'Empseed to worry 'isself about you and the kitchen," grumbled Jemima.

Sally had gone to a small mirror and was hastily setting her frilled cap at its most becoming angle over her dark curls; then she took up the tankards by their handles, and laughing, grumbling, blushing, carried them through into the coffee room.

The coffee room of The Fisherman's Rest in the year of grace 1792 was an old place even then, for the oak rafters and beams were already black with age—as were the paneled seats with their tall backs, and the long polished tables between. That the landlord of The Fisherman's Rest at Dover was a prosperous man was clear to the most casual observer. The pewter on the fine old dressers, the brass above the gigantic hearth, shone like silver and gold.

The red tiled floor was as brilliant as the scarlet geraniums on the windowsill, and this meant that his servants were good and plentiful, that the custom was constant and necessitated a high standard of elegance and order.

As Sally came in she was greeted with shouts and applause.

"Why, here's Sally! Hurrah for pretty Sally!"

"All ri'! All ri'!" Sally laughed as she deposited the tankards upon the tables. "Why, what a 'urry, to be sure!" But it was clear that a young man with fair curly hair and eager, bright blue eyes was engaging most of Sally's attention.

Facing the hearth, his legs wide apart, a long clay pipe in his mouth, stood mine host himself, worthy Mr. Jellyband, landlord of The Fisherman's Rest, as his father and grandfather had been before him. Portly in build, jovial in countenance and somewhat bald of pate, Mr. Jellyband was a typical rural John Bull. He wore the scarlet waistcoat with shiny brass buttons, the corduroy breeches, the gray stockings and buckled shoes that characterized every self-respecting innkeeper in Great Britain in those days. While pretty, motherless Sally had need of four pairs of hands to do all the work that fell on her shapely shoulders, Jellyband discussed the affairs of nations with his guests.

They were mostly fishermen who patronized Mr. Jellyband's coffee room. But the London and Dover coach started from the hostel daily, and passengers who had come across the Channel, and those who started for the grand tour, all became acquainted with Mr. Jellyband, his French wines and his home-brewed ales.

It was toward the close of September and the hot weather had suddenly broken up; for two days torrents of rain had deluged the south of England, doing its level best to ruin what chances the apples and pears had of becoming really fine. Even now it was beating against the leaded windows and tumbling down the chimney, making the cheerful wood fire sizzle in the hearth.

"Lud! Did you ever see such a wet September, Mr. Jellyband?" asked Mr. Hempseed.

He sat in one of the seats inside the hearth, did Mr. Hempseed, for he was an important personage at The Fisherman's Rest, where

Mr. Jellyband always selected him as a foil for political arguments.

"No," replied Mr. Jellyband sententiously, "I dunno, Mr. 'Empseed, as I ever did. But what can you expect, Mr. 'Empseed, I says, with a government as we've got?"

Mr. Hempseed shook his head with an infinity of wisdom tempered by deeply rooted mistrust of the British climate and the British Government. "I don't expect nothing, Mr. Jellyband," he said, "and it's not often as I do complain. But when it comes to sich wet weather in September, and all me fruit a-rottin' and a-dyin'—"

"That's quite right, Mr. 'Empseed," assented Jellyband, "and as I says, what can you expect? There's all them Frenchy devils over the Channel yonder a-murderin' their nobility, and Mr. Pitt and Mr. Fox and Mr. Burke a-fightin' and a-wranglin' between them. 'Let 'em murder!' says Mr. Pitt. 'Stop 'em!' says Mr. Burke."

"And let 'em murder, says I, and be demmed to 'em," said Mr. Hempseed emphatically, for he had but little liking for his friend Jellyband's political arguments. "But don't let's 'ave sich rain in September—"

"Lud! Mr. 'Arry, 'ow you made me jump!"

It was unfortunate for Sally and her flirtation with young Harry Waite that her remark occurred at the precise moment when Mr. Hempseed was collecting his breath, for it brought down upon her pretty head the full flood of her father's wrath.

"Now then, Sally me girl, now then!" he said. "Stop that fooling with that young jackanapes and get on with my Lord Tony's supper, for if it ain't the best we can do, and 'e not satisfied, see what you'll get, that's all."

Reluctantly Sally obeyed.

"Is you expecting special guests then tonight, Mr. Jellyband?" asked one of his customers.

"Aye! That I be," replied Jellyband. "Dukes and duchesses from over the water, whom my Lord Tony and his friend, Sir Andrew Ffoulkes, and other young noblemen have helped out of the clutches of them murderin' devils."

But this was too much for Mr. Hempseed's querulous philosophy. "Lud!" he said. "What they do that for, I wonder? I don't 'old with interferin' in other folks' ways."

"Maybe, Mr. 'Empseed," said Jellyband sarcastically, "maybe you've made friends with some of them French chaps 'oo come over here o' purpose to make us Englishmen agree with their murderin' ways. There was my friend Peppercorn, a true and loyal Englishman, 'e made friends with some o' them Frogeaters—immoral God-forsaking furrin spies. Well! And what happened? Peppercorn 'e now ups and talks of revolutions and liberty and down with the aristocrats."

At one table two customers—gentlemen apparently by their clothes—had pushed aside their half-finished game of dominoes and were listening with amusement to Mr. Jellyband.

"You seem to think, my honest friend," one of them now said quietly, "that these Frenchmen—spies I think you called them—are mighty clever fellows to have made mincemeat of your friend Mr. Peppercorn's opinions. How did they accomplish that?"

"Lud, sir! I suppose they talked 'im over. Those Frenchies, I've 'eard it said, 'ave got the gift of the gab."

"Faith, then," said the stranger, "let us hope these clever spies will not succeed in upsetting your extremely loyal opinions."

This was too much for Mr. Jellyband. He burst into uproarious laughter. "Ha-ha-ha! Ho-ho-ho!" He laughed until his eyes streamed. "Why, Lud love you, sir, I wouldn't so much as drink a glass of ale with one o' them murderin' Frenchmen, and nothin'd make me change my opinions."

"Aye, my honest friend," assented the stranger cheerfully, "I see that you are a match for any twenty Frenchmen! And here's to your very good health, my worthy host, if you'll do me the honor to finish this bottle of wine with me."

"I am sure you're very polite, sir," said Mr. Jellyband, wiping his eyes, "and I don't mind if I do."

The stranger poured out a couple of tankards full of wine, and having offered one to mine host he took the other himself. "Loyal Englishmen as we all are," he said, "we must admit that this at least is one good thing which comes to us from France."

"Aye! We'll none of us deny that, sir," assented mine host.

"And here's to the best landlord in England—Mr. Jellyband," said the stranger loudly.

"Hip, hip, hurrah!" exclaimed the whole company present, with loud clapping of hands and rattling of tankards.

✿

THE REFUGEES

FEELING IN EVERY PART of England ran high against the French. Snatches of the news from over the water made every honest Englishman's blood boil at those murderers who had imprisoned their king and his family and were now loudly demanding the blood of all the Bourbons. The daily executions of royalists seemed to cry for vengeance to the whole of Europe.

Yet no one dared to interfere. Burke had exhausted all his eloquence in trying to induce the British Government to fight the revolutionary government of France, but Mr. Pitt, with charac-teristic prudence, did not feel that his country was fit to embark on another costly war. It was for Austria to take the initiative; Austria, whose fairest daughter, Marie Antoinette, was even now a dethroned queen, imprisoned and insulted by a howling mob.

As for Mr. Jellyband and his fellow John Bulls, they were royal-ists and anti-revolutionists to a man, and were furious with Pitt for his caution, although they naturally understood nothing of the diplomatic reasons which guided that great man's policy.

But now Sally came running back, excited and eager. "I think I seed my Lord Antony's horse in the yard, Father," she said, and she ran across the room to greet the visitor. But already the front door had been thrown open, and the next moment an arm, covered in drab cloth and dripping with the rain, was around Sally's waist, while a hearty voice echoed along the polished rafters.

"Aye, and bless your brown eyes for being so sharp, my pretty Sally." And worthy Mr. Jellyband came bustling forward, alert and fussy, as became the advent of one of his most favored guests.

"Lud, I protest, Sally," added Lord Antony, as he deposited a kiss on Miss Sally's blooming cheeks, "but you are growing prettier every time I see you."

Lord Antony Dewhurst was a perfect type of young English gentleman. Tall, broad of shoulder and merry of face, a good sportsman, courteous, he was a favorite in London drawing rooms or village inns. At The Fisherman's Rest everyone knew him—for he was fond of a trip to France, and always spent a night under Mr. Jellyband's roof on his way.

He nodded to Waite, Hempseed and the others as he crossed over to the hearth to warm and dry himself; he cast a quick, somewhat suspicious glance at the two strangers, who had quietly resumed their game of dominoes, and a look of anxiety clouded his young face. But only for a moment; the next he had turned to Mr. Hempseed, who was respectfully touching his forelock.

"Well, Mr. Hempseed, and how is the fruit?"

"Badly, my lord, badly," replied Mr. Hempseed, "but what can you expect with this 'ere government favoring them rascals over in France who would murder their king and all their nobility?"

"Od's life!" retorted Lord Antony. "So they would, honest Hempseed. But we have got some friends coming here tonight who have evaded their clutches."

"Thanks to you, my lord, and to your friends, so I've heard it said," said Mr. Jellyband.

Lord Antony's hand fell warningly on mine host's arm. "Hush!" he said, looking again toward the strangers.

"Oh! Lud love you, they are all right, my lord," said Jellyband. "That gentleman over there is as true and loyal a subject of King George as you are yourself, my lord. He is but lately arrived in Dover, and is settling down to business in these parts."

"Oh, that's all right, then, if we are among friends," said Lord Antony. "But you have no one else staying here, have you?"

"No one, my lord, and no one coming, either, save Sir Percy Blakeney and his lady, who will be here presently."

"Lady Blakeney?" queried Lord Antony in some astonishment.

"Aye, my lord. Briggs, Sir Percy's skipper, was here just now. My lady's brother is crossing over to France today in the *Day*

Dream, which is Sir Percy's yacht, and Sir Percy and my lady will come as far as here with him. It don't put you out, do it, my lord?"

"Not unless that supper is not the very best which Miss Sally can cook. My friends will be tired, and, I hope, hungry."

"You need have no fear of that, my lord," said Sally, who had been setting the table with bright pewter goblets and blue china. "Here they are, I do believe," she added excitedly, as a clatter of horses and wheels could now be heard drawing rapidly nearer.

There was general commotion in the coffee room. Everyone was curious to see Lord Antony's friends from over the water. Mr. Jellyband bustled out to welcome his distinguished guests. Only the two strangers in the corner did not participate in the excitement.

The door was thrown wide open, and a party of four—two ladies and two gentlemen—entered the coffee room.

"Welcome! Welcome to old England!" said Lord Antony effusively, as he came forward with both hands outstretched.

"Ah, you are Lord Antony Dewhurst, I think," said one of the ladies, speaking with a strong foreign accent.

"At your service, madame," he replied. He kissed the hands of the ladies, then turned and shook the men warmly by the hand.

Sally helped the ladies to take off their traveling cloaks, and both turned, with a shiver, toward the brightly blazing hearth.

"Ah, messieurs! What can I say?" said the elder of the two, as she stretched her hands to the warmth of the blaze and looked with gratitude first at Lord Antony, then at one of the young men who was busy divesting himself of his heavy, caped coat.

"Only that you are glad to be in England, Comtesse," replied Lord Antony, "and that you have not suffered too much from your trying voyage."

"Indeed, indeed, we are glad to be in England," she said, while her eyes filled with tears. Her voice was low, and there was dignity and suffering in the handsome, aristocratic face, with snow-white hair dressed high after the fashion of the times.

"I hope my friend, Sir Andrew Ffoulkes, proved an entertaining traveling companion, madame?"

"Ah, indeed, Sir Andrew was kindness itself. How could my

children and I ever show enough gratitude to you all, messieurs?"

Her companion, a dainty, girlish figure pathetic in its fatigue and sorrow, had said nothing as yet, but her large, brown eyes looked up with unconcealed admiration at Sir Andrew Ffoulkes. "So this is England," she said, as she looked around at the open hearth, the oak rafters and the rubicund British countenances.

"A bit of it, Mademoiselle Suzanne," replied Sir Andrew, smiling, "but all of it at your service."

The girl blushed and a sweet smile illumined her face. She said nothing, and Sir Andrew, too, was silent, yet they understood one another, as young people have a way of doing the world over.

The next moment Sally returned from the kitchen, carrying a gigantic tureen from which rose a savory odor. "Od's my life, supper at last!" ejaculated Lord Antony merrily, as he gallantly offered his arm to the comtesse and led her toward the table.

Mr. Hempseed and the fisherfolk had gone to make way for "the quality." Only the two strangers stayed on, quietly playing their game of dominoes and sipping their wine.

Sally bustled around the table, and the susceptible young Vicomte de Tournay could hardly take his eyes off her pretty face. He was scarce nineteen, elegantly, even foppishly dressed, and once safely landed in England he was evidently ready to forget the horrors of the Revolution in the delights of English life.

"*Pardi*, if zis is England," he said, as he continued to ogle Sally, "I am of it satisfied."

✣

THE LEAGUE OF THE SCARLET PIMPERNEL

THEY LOOKED A MERRY PARTY, the five of them, as they sat around the table. In the corner the two strangers had finished their game; one of them rose, and standing with his back to the table he adjusted with much deliberation his triple-caped coat. As he did so, he glanced around him. Everyone was busy laughing and chatting, and he murmured, "All safe!" His companion, with the alertness born of long practice, slipped to his knees and crept

23

noiselessly under the oak bench. Then the stranger, with a loud "Good night," walked out of the coffee room.

Not one of those at the supper table had noticed the curious maneuver, but when the stranger closed the door behind him they all instinctively sighed with relief.

"Alone, at last!" said Lord Antony jovially.

Then the young vicomte rose, glass in hand, and said in broken English, "To His Majesty George Three of England. God bless him for his hospitality to us all, poor exiles from France."

"His Majesty the King!" echoed Lord Antony and Sir Andrew, as they drank loyally to the toast.

"To His Majesty King Louis of France," added Sir Andrew. "May God protect him, and give him victory over his enemies."

Everyone rose and drank this toast in silence.

"And to Monsieur le Comte de Tournay de Basserive," said Lord Antony. "May we welcome him in England before many days are over."

"Ah, monsieur," said the comtesse, with a heavy sigh, "I trust in God, but I scarcely dare to hope . . ."

"Aye, madame!" interposed Sir Andrew Ffoulkes. "Trust in God by all means, but believe also in your English friends, who have sworn to bring the count safely across the Channel, even as they have brought you today."

"Indeed, indeed, monsieur," she replied. "I have the fullest confidence in you and in your friends. But my husband"—the comtesse paused—"he is in such deadly peril. I never would have left him, only . . . there were my children. But, oh! Now that I am here—in this beautiful, free England—I think of him, flying for his life. . . . Ah! I should not have left him. . . ." The poor woman had completely broken down from fatigue, sorrow and emotion. Suzanne ran to her and tried to kiss away her tears.

"As for me, monsieur," Suzanne said as she looked across at Sir Andrew, "I trust you absolutely, and I know that you will bring my dear father safely to England." This was said with so much confidence that it seemed as if by magic to dry her mother's eyes and to bring a smile upon everybody's lips.

"Nay! You shame me, mademoiselle," replied Sir Andrew with warmth. "I am but a tool in the hands of our great leader, who organized and effected your escape."

"Your leader, monsieur?" said the comtesse eagerly. "Ah! Of course, you must have a leader. But tell me, where is he? I must thank him for all that he has done for us."

"Alas, madame!" said Lord Antony. "That is impossible. The Scarlet Pimpernel works in the dark, and his identity is only known under a solemn oath of secrecy to his immediate followers."

"The Scarlet Pimpernel?" said Suzanne, with a merry laugh. "Why, what a droll name! What is the Scarlet Pimpernel, monsieur?" She looked at Sir Andrew with eager curiosity. The young man's eyes shone with enthusiasm and admiration for his leader.

"The Scarlet Pimpernel, mademoiselle," he said, "is the name of a humble English wayside flower; but it is also the name chosen to hide the identity of the best and bravest man in all the world, so that he may better succeed in accomplishing his noble task."

"Ah, yes," here interposed the young vicomte. "I have heard speak of this Scarlet Pimpernel. A little flower—red? Yes! They say in Paris that every time a royalist escapes to England that devil, the Public Prosecutor, receives a paper with that little flower upon it. . . . Yes?"

"Yes, that is so," assented Lord Antony.

"Ah, monsieur," sighed the comtesse, "I cannot understand it all. Tell me, why should you and your leader risk your lives for us French men and women who are nothing to you?"

"Sport, Madame la Comtesse," asserted Lord Antony. "We are a nation of sportsmen, you know, and this is the finest sport I have yet encountered."

But the comtesse shook her head incredulously. To her it seemed preposterous that these young men, all rich and wellborn, should for no other motive than sport run such risks. In France, she knew, anyone found assisting royalists would be executed, whatever his nationality. And these Englishmen had snatched away condemned victims almost from the very foot of the guillotine. With a shudder she recalled the events of the last few days.

She and her husband had been placed on the list of "suspected persons," which meant that their death was but a matter of days—of hours perhaps. Then came the mysterious epistle signed with the enigmatical scarlet device; the clear directions; the parting from the comte; the flight with her two children; that awful hag driving the cart, who looked like some evil demon, with the ghastly trophy on her whip handle! Every moment, lying amid turnips and cabbages in that cart while the mob howled "*À la lanterne les aristos!*" she had expected arrest and condemnation, and these young Englishmen, under the guidance of their mysterious leader, had risked their lives to save them. And all only for sport? Impossible!

Suzanne's eyes plainly told Sir Andrew that she thought that *he* at any rate had a nobler motive. "How many are there in your league, monsieur?" she asked timidly.

"Twenty all told, mademoiselle," he replied, "one to command and nineteen to obey. All pledged to rescue the innocent."

"May God protect you," said the comtesse. "It is wonderful that you English should be so brave, while in France treachery is rife. There was that woman, Marguerite Saint-Just, for instance," she added bitterly. "She denounced the Marquis de Saint-Cyr and all his family to the awful tribunal of the Terror."

"Marguerite Saint-Just?" said Lord Antony, as he shot a quick and apprehensive glance across at Sir Andrew. "Surely . . ."

"Yes!" replied the comtesse. "Surely you know her. She was a leading actress of the Comédie Française, and she married an Englishman not long ago. You must know her—"

"Know her?" said Lord Antony. "Know Lady Blakeney—the most fashionable woman in London—the wife of the richest man in England? Of course, we all know Lady Blakeney."

"She was a schoolfellow of mine at the convent in Paris," interposed Suzanne. "I was very fond of Marguerite, and I cannot believe that she ever did anything so wicked."

"It seems incredible," said Sir Andrew. "You say that *she* denounced the Marquis de Saint-Cyr? There must be some mistake."

"No mistake is possible, monsieur," rejoined the comtesse

coldly. "Marguerite Saint-Just's brother is a noted republican. There was some talk of a feud between him and my cousin, the Marquis de Saint-Cyr. You have not heard this story?"

"Faith, madame, I did hear some vague rumors of it, but in England no one would credit it. Sir Percy is a man of high social position, the intimate friend of the Prince of Wales; and Lady Blakeney leads both fashion and society in London."

"That may be, monsieur, but I pray God that while I remain in this beautiful country I may never meet Marguerite Saint-Just."

The proverbial wet blanket seemed to have fallen over the company. Suzanne looked sad and silent; Sir Andrew fidgeted uneasily with his fork, while the comtesse sat rigid in her straight-backed chair. As for Lord Antony, he looked extremely uncomfortable.

"At what time do you expect Sir Percy and Lady Blakeney?" he contrived to whisper unobserved to mine host.

"Any moment, my lord," whispered Jellyband in reply.

Even as he spoke, a distant clatter was heard of an approaching coach; then the rattle of horses' hoofs on the uneven cobblestones. The next moment a stableboy threw open the door, shouting excitedly, "Sir Percy Blakeney and my lady, they're just arriving!"

And with shouting, jingling of harness and the clatter of iron hoofs a magnificent coach, drawn by four superb bays, halted outside the porch of The Fisherman's Rest.

✤

MARGUERITE

In a moment the pleasant coffee room of the inn became the scene of confusion and discomfort. Lord Antony, with a fashionable oath, had jumped up and was giving directions to poor bewildered Jellyband.

"For goodness' sake, man," admonished his lordship, "try to keep Lady Blakeney talking outside for a moment while the ladies withdraw. Zounds!" he added. "This is most unfortunate."

"Quick, Sally! The candles!" shouted Jellyband, as he ran hither and thither.

The comtesse, too, had risen to her feet; rigid and erect, she repeated mechanically, "I will not see her! I will not see her!"

Then suddenly a singularly sweet voice, with a soupçon of foreign intonation, was heard through all the din.

"B-r-r-r-r! I am as wet as a herring! *Dieu!* Has anyone ever seen such a contemptible climate?"

Inside, everyone paused. Sally was holding the candles at the door which led upstairs, and the comtesse was in the act of beating a hasty retreat; Suzanne reluctantly was preparing to follow her mother, while hoping still to see her erstwhile schoolfellow.

"Suzanne, come with me at once," said the comtesse.

"Oh, *Maman!*" pleaded Suzanne.

Jellyband threw open the door, still hoping to avert the catastrophe which he felt was in the air. "My lady . . . er . . . my lady!" he said, clumsily trying to bar the way.

"*Pardieu*, my good man," said Lady Blakeney with some impatience, "why are you dancing about like a turkey with a sore foot? Let me get to the fire, I am perished with the cold." And the next moment she had swept into the room.

Marguerite Blakeney was then scarcely five-and-twenty, and her beauty was at its most dazzling. Tall, with magnificent, regal presence, it is small wonder that even the comtesse paused for a moment in involuntary admiration. The large hat, with its waving plumes, threw a soft shadow across the classic brow with the aureole of auburn hair—free at the moment from powder; the childlike mouth, the straight chiseled nose, round chin and delicate throat all seemed set off by her rich velvet robe, which molded the graceful contour of her figure, while one tiny hand held a fashionable tall stick adorned with ribbons.

With a quick glance around the room Marguerite Blakeney had taken stock of everyone there. She nodded pleasantly to Sir Andrew, while extending a hand to Lord Antony. "My Lord Tony— what are *you* doing here in Dover?" she said merrily.

Then, without waiting for a reply, she turned and faced the comtesse and Suzanne. Her whole face lighted up as she stretched out both arms toward the young girl. "Why! If that isn't my little

Suzanne! Pardieu, citizeness, how came you to be in England? And madame, too!"

She went up effusively to them both, with not a single touch of embarrassment. Lord Tony and Sir Andrew watched the scene with apprehension. They realized the bitter hatred with which the old French noblesse viewed all those who had helped to contribute to their downfall. Armand Saint-Just, the brother of beautiful Lady Blakeney, was an ardent republican. His feud with the ancient family of Saint-Cyr—the rights and wrongs of which no one ever knew—had culminated in the almost total extinction of the latter. Here in England, face to face with these three refugees, stood a fair scion of those same republicans who had hurled down a throne and uprooted an aristocracy. She stood before them and stretched out her hands as if she would, by that one act, bridge over the conflict and bloodshed.

"Suzanne, I forbid you to speak to that woman," said the comtesse sternly in English, as she placed a restraining hand upon her daughter's arm.

Marguerite's sweet face became as white as the soft fichu which swathed her throat, and a keen observer might have noted that the hand which held the tall, beribboned stick was clenched, and trembled somewhat. But the next instant the delicate eyebrows were raised slightly, the lips curved sarcastically, and the clear blue eyes looked straight at the erect and defiant comtesse.

"Hoity-toity, citizeness," she said, with a slight shrug of the shoulders, "what fly stings you, pray?"

"We are in England now, madame," rejoined the comtesse coldly, "and I am at liberty to forbid my daughter to touch your hand in friendship. Come, Suzanne." Without another look at Marguerite Blakeney, but with a deep, old-fashioned curtsy to the two young men, she sailed majestically out of the room.

There was silence in the old inn parlor for a moment. Marguerite followed with hard eyes the upright figure as it disappeared through the doorway, but as Suzanne was obediently about to follow her mother a wistful look stole into Lady Blakeney's eyes. Suzanne caught that look; her sweet nature went out to the beau-

30

tiful woman scarce older than herself. She turned, ran back to Marguerite, and putting her arms around her kissed her effusively. Then only did she follow her mother.

Suzanne's sweet impulse had relieved the tension. Marguerite kissed her hand to the ladies. "So that's it, is it?" she said gaily. "La! Sir Andrew, did you ever see such an unpleasant person?"

She gathered up her skirts and stalked toward the fireplace.

"'Suzanne,'" she said, mimicking the comtesse's voice, "'I forbid you to speak to that woman.'"

The laugh which accompanied this sally sounded perhaps a little forced, but the mimicry was so perfect that both the young men joined in a hearty, cheerful "Bravo!"

"Ah, Lady Blakeney!" added Lord Tony. "How they must miss you at the Comédie Française, and how the Parisians must hate Sir Percy for having taken you away."

"Lud, man," rejoined Marguerite, with a shrug of her graceful shoulders, "'tis impossible to hate Sir Percy for anything. His sallies would disarm even Madame la Comtesse herself."

The young vicomte, who had not elected to follow his mother, now made a step forward, ready to champion the comtesse. But before he could utter a word of protest, a pleasant though distinctly inane laugh was heard from outside, and an unusually tall and very richly dressed figure appeared in the doorway.

❉

AN EXQUISITE OF '92

Sir Percy Blakeney was, in this year of grace 1792, still a year or two on the right side of thirty. Tall above the average, even for an Englishman, broad-shouldered and massively built, he would have been called unusually good-looking but for a certain lazy expression in his deep-set blue eyes and that perpetual laugh which seemed to disfigure his strong, clearly cut mouth.

It was nearly a year ago now that Sir Percy Blakeney had astonished society in London and Bath by bringing home a beautiful, fascinating, clever French wife. He, the sleepiest, and to some the dullest, most British Britisher that had ever set a pretty woman yawning, had secured a brilliant matrimonial prize for which there had been many competitors.

Marguerite Saint-Just had made her debut in artistic Parisian circles when the greatest social upheaval ever known was taking place. Scarcely eighteen, lavishly gifted with beauty and talent, chaperoned only by a devoted brother, she had soon gathered around her in her charming apartment in the rue Richelieu a coterie as brilliant as it was exclusive—exclusive, that is to say, only from one point of view. Marguerite Saint-Just was by conviction a republican. Equality of birth was her motto—the only inequality she admitted was that of talent and intellect. Thus her salon was reserved for clever men and talented women, and entrance into it came to be looked upon as the seal to an artistic career.

Then one fine day, without any warning to her friends, without a *dîner de fiançailles* or other appurtenance of a fashionable French wedding, Marguerite Saint-Just married Sir Percy Blakeney. How that "demmed idiot" ever came to be admitted within the intellectual circle which revolved around "the cleverest woman in Europe" no one could understand. Her friends laughed to scorn the idea that Marguerite Saint-Just had married a fool for the sake of his wealth and title, but the real motive remained a mystery.

As for Sir Percy, London society thought that, considering his own intellectual limitations, it would have been wiser had he bestowed those worldly advantages upon a less brilliant wife.

Sir Percy had spent most of his early life abroad: he had just been born when his mother fell prey to hopeless insanity. His father, the late Sir Algernon Blakeney, took his afflicted wife abroad, and there Percy grew up. Shortly after he attained his majority the death of both his parents left him a free man, and he traveled for several years before he at last returned home to England, bringing with him his beautiful young French wife.

The fashionable circles of the time were ready to receive them both with open arms. Sir Percy was rich, his wife accomplished, the Prince of Wales took a great liking to them both. Within six months Sir Percy's coats were the talk of the town, his inanities were quoted at Almack's or the Mall. Everyone thought him hopelessly stupid, and as for his marriage with "the cleverest woman in Europe," well! He got no pity, because he seemed to require none—he seemed, in fact, proud of his clever wife, and to care little that she took no pains to disguise the good-natured contempt she evidently felt for him. In his beautiful house at Richmond he played second fiddle to her with imperturbable bonhomie, while she dispensed the hospitality of his home with the same graciousness with which she had welcomed the intellectual coterie of Paris.

Sir Percy was undeniably handsome—always excepting the lazy, bored look habitual to him. He was always impeccably dressed, and on this September evening, in spite of the long journey by coach, in spite of rain and mud, his coat sat irreproachably across his fine shoulders; his white hands emerged through frills of finest Mechlin lace. The short-waisted satin coat, wide-lapelled waistcoat and tight-fitting striped breeches set off his massive figure to perfection.

He had lolled into the inn parlor, shaking the wet off his coat; then, putting up a gold-rimmed eyeglass to his lazy blue eye, he surveyed the company, upon whom an embarrassed silence had fallen. "How do, Tony! How do, Ffoulkes!" he said, recognizing the two young men and shaking them by the hand. "Zounds, did you ever see such a beastly day? La!" he added after a moment's silence. "How sheepish you all look. . . . What's up?"

"Oh, nothing to disturb you, Sir Percy," replied Marguerite, with forced gaiety. "Only an insult to your wife."

"La, m'dear!" Sir Percy rejoined placidly. "You don't say so. Begad! Who was the bold man who dared to tackle you—eh?"

The young vicomte quickly stepped forward. "Monsieur," he said, prefixing his little speech with an elaborate bow. "My mother, the Comtesse de Tournay de Basserive, has offended madame, who, I see, is your wife. I am ready to offer you the usual reparation between men of honor." The young man proudly drew up his slim stature to its full height as he gazed at six-foot-odd of gorgeousness in the person of Sir Percy Blakeney, Bart.

33

"Lud, Sir Andrew," said Marguerite, with one of her infectious laughs, "look on that pretty picture—the English turkey and the French bantam."

The simile was quite perfect, and the English turkey looked down with bewilderment upon the threatening little French bantam. "La, sir!" said Sir Percy at last, putting up his eyeglass. "Where, in the cuckoo's name, did you learn to speak English? I vow I can't speak the French lingo like that. What?"

"Nay, I'll vouch for that!" rejoined Marguerite. "Sir Percy has a British accent you could cut with a knife."

"Monsieur," interposed the vicomte, "I fear you have not understood. I offer you the only possible reparation among gentlemen."

"What the devil is that?" asked Sir Percy blandly.

"My sword, monsieur, a duel," replied the vicomte, who was beginning to lose his temper.

Blakeney stared sleepily down on the choleric little man before him; not for a second did he lose his imperturbable good humor. He laughed and said, "A duel? Od's fish! You are a bloodthirsty young ruffian. I never fight duels." He sat down and stretched his long legs out before him. "Demmed uncomfortable things, duels."

Now the vicomte had no doubt heard that in England dueling among gentlemen had been suppressed by law; still, to a Frenchman's code of honor the spectacle of a gentleman actually refusing to fight a duel was little short of an enormity. He vaguely pondered whether he should strike that long-legged Englishman when Marguerite happily interposed.

"I pray you, Lord Tony," she said in her musical voice, "I pray you play the peacemaker. The child is bursting with rage and," she added with a soupçon of sarcasm, "might do Sir Percy an injury."

"Sir Percy is in the right, Vicomte," said Lord Antony, laying a friendly hand on the young Frenchman's shoulder. "It would hardly be fitting to commence your career in England by provoking him to a duel."

The vicomte hesitated; then, with a slight shrug of the shoulders, he said with becoming dignity, "Ah, well! If monsieur is satisfied,

I have no griefs. You, milor', are our protector. If I have done wrong, I withdraw myself."

"Aye!" rejoined Blakeney, with a sigh of satisfaction. "Withdraw yourself over there. Demmed excitable little puppy," he added under his breath. "Faith, Ffoulkes, if that's a specimen of the goods you and your friends bring over from France, my advice is, drop 'em mid-Channel, or I shall have to get Pitt to put you in the stocks."

"La, Sir Percy, your chivalry misguides you," said Marguerite coquettishly. "You forget that you yourself have imported one bundle of goods from France."

Blakeney slowly rose to his feet and, making a deep bow before his wife, he said with consummate gallantry, "I had the pick of the market, madame, and my taste is unerring." Then, in a change of tone, "Od's fish, we must have a bowl on that!" and he tapped vigorously on the table near him. "Hey! Jelly! A bowl of punch, hot and strong!"

"Nay, there is no time, Sir Percy," interposed Marguerite. "The skipper will be here directly and my brother must get on board, or the *Day Dream* will miss the tide."

"I think, your ladyship," said Jellyband respectfully, "that the young gentleman is coming along now with Sir Percy's skipper."

"Then Armand can join us," said Blakeney. "Think you, Tony," he added, turned toward the vicomte, "that that jackanapes of yours will join us in a glass? Tell him that we drink in token of reconciliation."

"You are all such merry company," said Marguerite, "that I trust you will forgive me if I bid my brother good-by in another room."

It would have been bad form to protest. Lady Blakeney's love for her brother, Armand Saint-Just, was deep. He had spent a few weeks with her in her English home, and was going back to serve his country.

Sir Percy made no attempt to detain his wife. With that somewhat affected gallantry which characterized his every movement he opened the coffee-room door for her and made her a most elaborate bow as she sailed out of the room without bestowing on him more than a passing glance. Only Sir Andrew Ffoulkes noted the curious look of intense, hopeless longing with which Sir Percy followed the retreating figure of his wife.

ARMAND SAINT-JUST

ONCE OUTSIDE THE NOISY coffee room Marguerite Blakeney heaved a deep sigh, like one who had long been oppressed with constant self-control, and a few tears fell down her cheeks. The rain had ceased. Marguerite stepped onto the porch and looked out to sea. There was the *Day Dream*, ready to take Armand Saint-Just back to France into the midst of that bloody revolution.

Two figures were approaching The Fisherman's Rest: one, an oldish man who walked with the rolling gait of a sailor; the other, a young, slight figure in a many-caped overcoat.

"Armand!" said Marguerite, and a happy smile shone through her tears. A minute later brother and sister were in each other's arms. "How much time have we got," Lady Blakeney asked the skipper, "before Monsieur Saint-Just need go on board?"

"We ought to weigh anchor before half an hour, your ladyship," replied the old man, pulling at his gray forelock.

Linking her arm in his, Marguerite led her brother toward the cliffs. "Half an hour more," she said, looking wistfully out to sea, "and you'll be far from me, Armand! Oh! I can't believe that you are going! These last few days—while Percy has been away, and I've had you to myself—have slipped by like a dream."

"I am not going far, sweet one," said Armand gently. "A narrow channel to cross—a few miles of road. I can soon come back."

"Nay, 'tis not the distance, Armand, but that awful Paris, just now . . ." They had reached the edge of the cliff. The gentle sea breeze blew Marguerite's hair about her face. "They are going too far, Armand," she said vehemently. "We are republicans; we have the same enthusiasm for liberty and equality. But even *you* must think that they are going too far. . . ."

"Hush!" said Armand instinctively, as he threw a quick, apprehensive glance around him.

"Ah! You see: you don't think that it is safe to speak of these things even here in England!" She clung to him suddenly. "Don't go back, Armand!" she begged. "What should I do if . . . if . . ." Her voice was choked with sobs.

"You would remember," he said gently, "that when France is in peril, it is not for her sons to turn their backs on her."

That sweet smile crept back into her face. "Oh! Armand! You *will* be prudent? Remember, I have only you . . . to care for me."

"Nay, sweet one. Percy cares for you. . . ."

With a look of wistfulness she murmured, "He did, once. . . ."

"Listen, dear," he said, "I have not spoken of this to you before; something always seemed to stop me. But I feel I could not go away without asking you . . . Does Sir Percy know the part you played in the arrest of the Marquis de Saint-Cyr?"

She laughed a mirthless laugh. "That I denounced the marquis to the tribunal that sent him and his family to the guillotine? Yes, he knows. I told him after I married him."

"You told him all the circumstances—which so completely exonerated you from any blame?"

"It was too late to plead extenuating circumstances: he had already heard the story from others; my confession came too tardily. I could not demean myself by trying to explain— And now I have the satisfaction of knowing that my husband has complete contempt for his wife." She spoke with bitterness, and Armand Saint-Just felt he had placed a clumsy finger upon an aching wound.

"But Sir Percy loved you, Margot," he repeated gently.

"Loved me? Well, Armand, I thought at one time that he did, or I should not have married him. He seemed to worship me with a passion which went straight to my heart. It had always seemed to me that it would be *heavenly* to be loved blindly, passionately— and I was ready to respond, Armand; I would have given infinite tenderness in return."

She sighed—and there was a world of disillusionment in that sigh. Armand had allowed her to speak without interruption; but it was terrible to see a young and beautiful woman standing almost at the threshold of her life, bereft of hope and illusions. Yet even now his own sister puzzled him. Could it be that with the waning of her husband's love Marguerite's heart had awakened with love for him? But he could not broach that subject with her. He knew that reserve which lurked behind her frank, open ways.

They had always been together, these two, for their parents had died when Armand was still a youth and Marguerite but a child. He, some eight years her senior, had chaperoned her during those brilliant years in the rue Richelieu and had seen her enter upon this new life of hers with some foreboding.

This was Armand's first visit to England since her marriage. And now he was going away, Marguerite feared for his safety; she felt lonely and unhappy. She led him gently along the cliffs, then down to the beach. She would not spoil these last few sadly sweet moments by speaking more about herself.

✥

THE ACCREDITED AGENT

THE *Day Dream* HAD SET SAIL, and Marguerite stood alone on the edge of the cliff watching those dim white sails which bore so swiftly away the only being who really cared for her. Some little distance away the lights of The Fisherman's Rest glittered yellow.

Sir Percy had had the delicacy to leave her alone. Marguerite was grateful for this; she always tried to be grateful for his constant thoughtfulness and generosity. She tried to curb the bitter thoughts of him which made her—in spite of herself—say cruel things to wound him. Yes! For she often wished to make him feel that she too held him in contempt, that she too had forgotten that once she had almost loved him. Loved that inane fop! And yet, vague, sweet memories came back to her: of the time when there had been an intensity in his love which had fascinated her.

Then suddenly that love, that devotion seemed to vanish. Twenty-four hours after the simple little ceremony at old Saint-Roch, the Marquis de Saint-Cyr and his family had been sent to the guillotine. She hated the marquis. Years ago, her dear Armand had loved Angèle de Saint-Cyr, but Saint-Just was a plebeian and the marquis full of the arrogant prejudices of his caste. One day Armand ventured on sending a small poem—ardent, passionate—to the idol of his dreams. The next night he was waylaid by the valets of the marquis and ignominiously thrashed like a dog.

Marguerite remembered it all: what her brother must have suffered in his manhood and his pride and what she had suffered through him. Then the day of retribution came. Armand and Marguerite adopted with the enthusiasm of their youth the utopian doctrines of the Revolution, while the Marquis de Saint-Cyr and his family fought for the retention of those privileges which placed them socially above their fellowmen. Marguerite, impulsive, not calculating the consequence, still smarting under the insult to her brother, happened to hear—and repeated—that the Saint-Cyrs were in treasonable correspondence with Austria.

In those days one denunciation was sufficient: Marguerite's thoughtless words bore fruit within twenty-four hours, and the Marquis de Saint-Cyr was arrested. Letters from the Austrian emperor, promising to send troops to quell the growing revolution in France, were found in his desk. He was arraigned for treason and sent to the guillotine, his wife and son sharing this awful fate.

Marguerite, horrified at the terrible consequences of her action, tried in vain to save them; her own coterie acclaimed her as a heroine.

When she married Sir Percy, she made confession to him, trusting to his blind love to make him forget what might have sounded unpleasant to an English ear. But never after that could she detect the slightest sign of that love which had been wholly hers. She tried to arouse him by sharpening her ready wit against his reserve; endeavored to excite his jealousy, if she could not arouse his love. But he remained the same, always passive, drawling, courteous. She had all that the world and a wealthy husband can give to a pretty woman, yet this evening, with the *Day Dream* finally hidden from sight, she felt more lonely than ever in her life.

With a heavy sigh, Marguerite Blakeney walked slowly back toward The Fisherman's Rest. Realizing the loneliness of the dark road, she quickened her steps. The next moment she perceived a stranger coming rapidly toward her. He paused just as she was about to slip past him, and said very quietly, "Citoyenne Saint-Just."

Marguerite uttered a little cry of astonishment at hearing her maiden name. She looked up at the stranger and put out her hands toward him. "Chauvelin!" she exclaimed.

"Himself, citoyenne, at your service," said the man, gallantly kissing the tips of her fingers.

Marguerite surveyed with delight the not very prepossessing little figure before her. Chauvelin was then near forty—clever, shrewd-looking, with a curious, foxlike expression in the sunken eyes. He was the same stranger who, an hour or two previously, had joined Mr. Jellyband in a friendly glass of wine.

"Chauvelin . . . my friend," said Marguerite, happy to see a face that brought back memories of that time in the rue Richelieu. "I am mightily pleased to see you. But tell me, what in the world are you doing here in England?"

Chauvelin turned and walked beside her. "I might return the compliment, fair lady," he said. "What of yourself?"

"Oh, I?" she said with a shrug. "*Je m'ennuie, mon ami*, that is all."

They reached the porch of The Fisherman's Rest, but Marguerite seemed loath to go within. The evening air was lovely after the storm, and she had found a friend who exhaled the breath of Paris. She lingered on, while Chauvelin stood beside her, his shrewd eyes fixed on her pretty face.

"You surprise me, citoyenne," he said quietly, as he took a pinch of snuff.

"Do I now?" she retorted gaily. "Faith, my little Chauvelin, I should have thought that you would have guessed that an atmosphere composed of fogs and virtues would never suit Marguerite Saint-Just."

"Dear me! Is it as bad as that?" he asked, in mock consternation. "And within a year of a romantic love match!"

"Yes! . . . That's just the difficulty."

"Ah! That idyllic folly," said Chauvelin, "did not then survive the lapse of . . . weeks?"

"Idyllic follies never last, Chauvelin. They come upon us like the measles . . . and are as easily cured."

Chauvelin took another pinch of snuff. "No wonder," he said gallantly, "that the cleverest woman in Europe is troubled with ennui." His keen eyes darted a quick glance at Marguerite. "Yet I have a perfect prescription against the worst form of ennui, my dear lady. It is called by a very plebeian name, work!"

"Work?"

Chauvelin looked at Marguerite long and scrutinizingly. He took a step or two from the porch, looked around him; then, seeing that no one was within earshot, he came back close to her.

"Will you render France a service, citoyenne?" he asked, with sudden earnestness.

"La, man!" she replied flippantly. "How serious you look. . . . Indeed, I do not know; it depends upon the kind of service."

"Have you ever heard of the Scarlet Pimpernel, Citoyenne Saint-Just?" asked Chauvelin, abruptly.

"Faith, man," she retorted with a merry laugh, "we talk of nothing else. . . . We have hats à la Scarlet Pimpernel; our horses are called Scarlet Pimpernel; at the Prince of Wales' supper party the other night we had a soufflé à la Scarlet Pimpernel!"

But while she laughed, Chauvelin remained serious as he said, "Then, citoyenne, you must also know that the man who hides his identity under that pseudonym is the most bitter enemy of France, of men like Armand Saint-Just."

"La!" she said. "France has many bitter enemies these days."

"But you, citoyenne, should be ready to help her in a moment of deadly peril."

"My brother Armand devotes his life to France," she retorted proudly. "As for me, I can do nothing, here in England."

"Here, in England," he urged, "you alone can help us. Listen! I have been sent by the Republican Government. One of my duties is to find out all about this League of the Scarlet Pimpernel, which is pledged to help our cursed aristocrats escape from the punishment they deserve. You know as well as I do, citoyenne, that once they are here they try to arouse public feeling against the Republic. . . . Now, even within the last month, scores of emigrés have succeeded in crossing the Channel. Their escape in each instance was effected by this society of young English jackanapes, headed by a man whose brain seems as resourceful as his identity is mysterious. He is a young buck in English society, of that I feel sure. Find that man for me, citoyenne! Find him for France."

Marguerite had listened to Chauvelin's impassioned speech without uttering a word. Before this, her heart had been stirred by the thought of the brave man who had rescued hundreds from a terrible fate. She had little real sympathy with those haughty French aristocrats, but, republican though she was from principle, she loathed the methods which the young republic had chosen for establishing itself. Her very soul recoiled from the horrors of the Reign of Terror, which had culminated in the September Massacres. Her thoughts went wandering in search of the Scarlet Pimpernel. Ah! There was a man she might have loved. Everything in him appealed to her: his personality, his strength, his bravery and above all that anonymity which crowned him with romantic glory.

"Find him for France, citoyenne!"

Chauvelin's voice close to her ear roused her from her dreams.

"La, man!" she said with a return of her assumed flippancy. "You are astonishing. Where in the world am I to look?"

"You go everywhere, citoyenne," whispered Chauvelin insinuatingly. "Lady Blakeney is the pivot of social London, so I am told. . . . You see everything, you *hear* everything."

"Easy, my friend," retorted Marguerite. "You seem to forget that Sir Percy Blakeney and a long line of ancestors stand between Lady Blakeney and such a thing. Besides, this Scarlet Pimpernel is an Englishman. You could do nothing to him!"

"We could send him to the guillotine first to cool his ardor," said Chauvelin with a rasping little laugh. "Then, when there is a diplomatic fuss about it, we can apologize—humbly—to the British Government."

"What you propose is horrible, Chauvelin," she said, drawing away from him as from some noisome insect. "Whoever the man may be, he is brave and noble. Never would I lend a hand to such villainy."

"You prefer to be insulted by every French aristocrat who comes to this country?"

Chauvelin had taken sure aim when he shot this tiny shaft. Marguerite's cheeks became a thought more pale and she bit her lip. "That is beside the question," she said at last. "I can defend myself, but I refuse to do any dirty work for you—or for France."

And without another look at Chauvelin, Marguerite Blakeney turned her back on him and walked straight into the inn.

"That is not your last word, citoyenne," said Chauvelin, as a light from the passage illumined her elegant, richly clad figure. "We meet in London, I hope!"

"We meet in London," she said, speaking over her shoulder, "but that is my last word."

She threw open the coffee-room door and disappeared, but he remained on the porch for a moment or two, taking a pinch of snuff. He looked neither abashed nor disappointed; on the contrary, a satisfied smile played around the corners of his thin lips.

❧

THE OUTRAGE

A BEAUTIFUL NIGHT had followed on the day of incessant rain. The magnificent coach, drawn by four of the finest Thoroughbreds in England, had driven off along the London road, with Sir Percy Blakeney on the box holding the reins in his slender hands, and beside him Lady Blakeney wrapped in costly furs. A long drive on a starlit night! Marguerite was delighted at the notion of it. . . . Sir Percy was a dexterous whip; he was very fond of driving by night, and she had quickly adopted his fancy.

At The Fisherman's Rest Mr. Jellyband was putting out the lights. Upstairs in the snug bedrooms were his important guests: the Comtesse de Tournay with Suzanne and the vicomte; and two rooms were ready for Sir Andrew and Lord Antony. For the moment these two young gallants were comfortably installed in the coffee room before the huge log fire.

"I say, Jelly, can we talk here undisturbed for half an hour?" asked Lord Tony, as the landlord busied himself clearing away glasses and mugs.

"At your service, my lord. I'll leave your candles on the dresser."

"All right, Jelly. You can put the lamp out—the fire'll give us all the light we need. And let's have a bottle of wine."

The room now was quite dark, save for the light formed by the brightly blazing logs in the hearth.

"Is that all, gentlemen?" asked Jellyband, as he placed a bottle of wine and a couple of glasses on the table.

"That'll do nicely, thanks," said Lord Tony. "Good night."

"Good night, my lord! Good night, sir!"

The heavy tread of Mr. Jellyband along the passage and staircase died out, and The Fisherman's Rest seemed wrapped in sleep. For a while no sound was heard save the ticking of the old grandfather clock and the crackling of the burning wood.

"All right again this time?" asked Lord Antony at last.

Sir Andrew had been dreaming—no doubt of a pretty, piquant face with large brown eyes, and a wealth of dark curls.

"Yes!" he said. "All right!"

Lord Antony laughed as he poured a glass of wine. "I need not ask, I suppose, whether you found the journey pleasant?"

"No, friend, you need not ask," replied Sir Andrew, gaily.

"Then, here's to her very good health," said Lord Tony. "She's a bonnie lass, though she *is* a French one. May your courtship flourish." He drained his glass to the last drop.

"Well! You'll be doing the journey next, Tony," said Sir Andrew, rousing himself from his meditations.

The two young men drew their chairs closer together, and instinctively their voices sank to a whisper.

"I saw the Scarlet Pimpernel alone for a few moments in Calais," said Sir Andrew. "He crossed over to England two days before we did. He had escorted the party all the way from Paris, dressed—you'll never credit it!—as an old market woman, and driving the covered cart in which the Comtesse de Tournay, Mademoiselle Suzanne and the vicomte lay concealed among the turnips and cabbages. Of course, they never suspected who their driver was. He drove them right through a mob screaming '*À bas les aristos!*' and the Scarlet Pimpernel, in shawl, petticoat and hood, yelled '*À bas les aristos!*' louder than anybody. Faith, he's a marvel! His cheek is preposterous, I vow—and that's what carries him through. He wants you and Hastings to meet him at Calais on the second of next month. That will be next Tuesday."

"Yes."

"It is, of course, the case of the Comte de Tournay, this time; a dangerous task, for the comte is under sentence of death. It will be rare sport to get *him* out of France. Saint-Just has actually gone to meet him—of course, no one suspects Saint-Just as yet. But after that . . . to get them both out of the country! I' faith, 'twill be a tough job."

"Have you any special instructions for me?" said Lord Tony.

"Yes. The Republican Government have sent an agent over to England, a man named Chauvelin, who is determined to discover the identity of our leader so that he may have him kidnaped the next time he sets foot in France. This Chauvelin has brought a whole army of spies with him, and until the chief has sampled the lot, he thinks we should meet as seldom as possible on the business of the league, and on no account in public places. When he wants to speak to us, he will contrive to let us know."

The two young men were bent over the fire, for the blaze had died down and only a red glow from the embers cast a lurid light on a narrow semicircle in front of the hearth; the rest of the room lay in complete gloom. Sir Andrew had taken a paper from his pocketbook, and together they tried to read it by the dim firelight. So intent were they upon this document, which came from the very hand of their adored leader, that they were unaware of the sounds around them, of the monotonous ticking of the clock, of the soft rustle of something on the floor behind them. A figure had emerged from under one of the benches; with snake-like movements it crept closer to the two young men.

"You are to read these instructions and commit them to memory," said Sir Andrew, "then destroy them."

He was about to replace the pocketbook in his pocket when a tiny slip of paper fluttered from it to the floor. Lord Antony picked it up and glanced at it. "It is from the chief," he said.

Both stooped to try and decipher this scrap of paper on which a few words had been hastily scrawled, when a slight noise from the passage attracted their attention.

"What's that?" said both instinctively. Lord Antony crossed the room and threw open the door, and at that very moment he received a stunning blow between the eyes which threw him back into the room. Simultaneously the crouching figure in the gloom had hurled itself from behind upon Sir Andrew. Before either had time to utter a cry or to struggle, they were each seized by two men, a muffler was tied around their mouths and they were pinioned to one another back to back, their arms, hands and legs securely fastened. One man had quietly shut the door; he wore a mask and stood motionless while the others completed their work.

"All safe, citoyen!" said one of the men, as he took a final survey of the bonds which secured the two young men.

"Good!" replied the man at the door. "Now search their pockets and give me all the papers you find."

This was promptly and quietly done. The masked man, having taken possession of all the papers, listened for a moment; evidently satisfied that this outrage had remained unheard, he opened the door. The four men lifted Sir Andrew and Lord Antony from the ground, and as noiselessly as they had come they bore the two pinioned young gallants out of the inn and into the gloom beyond.

In the coffee room the masked leader was quickly glancing through the stolen papers. "Not a bad day's work on the whole," he muttered, as he took off his mask, and his foxlike eyes glittered in the red glow of the fire.

He noted the scrap of paper which the two young men had only just had time to read; but one letter from Sir Andrew's pocketbook signed *Armand Saint-Just* seemed to give him strange satisfaction.

"Armand Saint-Just a traitor after all," he murmured. "Now, fair Marguerite Blakeney," he added viciously, "I think that you will help me to find the Scarlet Pimpernel."

✳

IN THE OPERA BOX

It was the first gala night of the autumn season at Covent Garden Theatre, in this memorable year of grace 1792. The house was packed with a gaily dressed and brilliant throng to hear Gluck's *Orfeo ed Euridice*. As the curtain came down after the glorious finale to the second act, the audience seemed to breathe a long sigh of satisfaction previous to letting loose its frivolous tongues. In the smart orchestra boxes many well-known faces were to be seen. Mr. Pitt, overweighted with cares of state, was finding brief relaxation in tonight's musical treat; the Prince of Wales, jovial, somewhat coarse in appearance, moved from box to box, visiting his more intimate friends.

In Lord Grenville's box a curious personality attracted attention: a thin figure with shrewd, sarcastic face and deep-set eyes keenly critical of the audience, dressed in immaculate black, with dark hair free from any powder. Lord Grenville—the Foreign Secretary—paid him marked though frigid deference.

Here and there, among distinctly English types of beauty, foreign faces stood out in contrast: the haughty aristocratic countenances of the French royalists who had found a refuge in England. Among these was the Comtesse de Tournay de Basserive, in heavy black silk, with only a white lace kerchief to relieve her mourning; she sat beside Lady Portarles, who was vainly trying to bring a smile to the comtesse's sad mouth. Behind her sat Suzanne and the vicomte, both somewhat shy among so many strangers.

"Ah, Lord Grenville," said Lady Portarles, as the Foreign Secretary appeared in the doorway of the box, "you could not arrive more apropos. Here is Madame la Comtesse de Tournay, positively dying to hear the latest news from France."

The distinguished diplomat came forward and greeted the ladies. "Alas," he said sadly, "it is of the very worst! The massacres continue and the guillotine claims a hundred victims a day."

The comtesse was listening. "Ah, monsieur!" she said. "It is dreadful for me to be here while my husband is in such peril."

"Lud, madame!" said bluff Lady Portarles. "Your sitting in a convent won't make your husband safe, and your children are too young to be dosed with premature mourning."

The comtesse smiled through her tears. Lady Portarles had a heart of gold hidden beneath her somewhat coarse manners.

"Besides which, madame," added Lord Grenville, "has not the Scarlet Pimpernel pledged to bring Monsieur le Comte safely to England?"

"Ah, yes!" replied the comtesse. "I saw Lord Hastings yesterday—he reassured me again."

"Then I am sure you need have no fear. Ah!" added the old diplomatist with a sigh. "If I were but a few years younger . . ."

"La, man!" interrupted honest Lady Portarles. "You are still young enough to turn your back on that French scarecrow that sits enthroned in your box tonight."

"I wish I could, but Monsieur Chauvelin is the accredited agent of his government, and it has not been thought advisable as yet," said the minister guardedly, "for England to break off diplomatic relations with France."

"Diplomatic relations be demmed, my lord! That sly little fox over there is nothing but a spy, I'll warrant!"

But what Lord Grenville thought of this matter remained unspoken, for the curtain had just risen on the third act of *Orfeo*, so he took a hasty farewell of the ladies and slipped away.

M. Chauvelin had sat all through this *entr'acte*, his eternal snuffbox in his hand, and his keen eyes intently fixed upon a box opposite to him where, with much laughter and general stir among the audience, Marguerite Blakeney had just entered accompanied by Sir Percy. She looked divinely pretty, her golden, reddish curls slightly besprinkled with powder, her head and neck encircled with magnificent diamonds and rubies. Always in the latest fashion,

Marguerite alone that night had discarded the crossover fichu and broad-lapelled overdress of the last two or three years. She wore the short-waisted, classical-shaped gown which so soon was to become the approved mode in every country in Europe. It shimmered with rich gold embroidery and suited her graceful figure to perfection. She leaned for a moment out of the box, taking stock of all those whom she knew. Many bowed to her, and from the royal box there came a gracious salute.

Sir Percy stayed in the box just as long as convention demanded. Then he strolled off, making way for his Royal Highness and for the host of admirers who came to pay homage to the queen of fashion. Marguerite had a little court around her, but after a while she dismissed them all, wishing to be alone with Gluck.

She was passionately fond of music. *Orfeo* charmed her tonight. The joy of living was writ plainly upon the sweet young face; she was but five-and-twenty, adored, feted, cherished. And the *Day Dream* had returned from Calais, bringing word that her idolized brother had safely landed, that he would be prudent for her sake.

A discreet knock at the door roused her from her enjoyment.

"Come in," she said with some impatience, without turning to look at the intruder.

Chauvelin had noted that she was alone; now he slipped into the box. "A word with you, citoyenne," he said quietly.

Marguerite turned quickly in alarm. "Lud, man! You frightened me," she said. "Your presence is entirely inopportune. I want to listen to Gluck, and have no mind for talking."

"But this is my only opportunity," he said, and he drew a chair so close that he could whisper in her ear without being seen in the dark of the box. "Lady Blakeney is always so surrounded by her court that a mere old friend has but very little chance."

"Faith, man!" she said. "You must seek for another opportunity then. I am going to Lord Grenville's ball tonight after the opera. So are you, probably. I'll give you five minutes then. . . ."

"Three minutes in the privacy of this box are sufficient," he rejoined placidly, "and you would be wise to listen to me, Citoyenne Saint-Just."

Marguerite instinctively shivered. Chauvelin had not raised his voice above a whisper, yet something seemed to freeze the blood in her veins. "Is that a threat, citoyen?" she asked.

"Nay, fair lady," he said gallantly, "only an arrow shot into the air." He paused a moment, like a cat ready to spring. Then he said quietly, "Your brother, Saint-Just, is in peril."

He could only see the beautiful face in profile, for Marguerite seemed to be watching the stage intently, but he noticed the sudden hardening of the mouth, the tension of the graceful figure.

"Well?" she said at last, with feigned unconcern.

"I have news for you which, I think, will interest you, but first let me explain. The other day, citoyenne, I asked for your help. France needed it, but you gave me your answer. . . ."

"To the point, I pray you, citoyen," she said lightly.

"One moment, citoyenne. Less than an hour after I had the honor of meeting you at Dover, I obtained possession of some papers which revealed another subtle scheme for the escape of French aristocrats—that traitor Tournay among others—organized by that archmeddler, the Scarlet Pimpernel. Lord Antony Dewhurst and Sir Andrew Ffoulkes were at The Fisherman's Rest that same night. They were already known to my spies as members of that accursed league. When the two gentlemen were alone in the coffee room, my spies pinioned them and seized their papers, which they gave to me. Those papers have told me enough, I think, to thwart the league's projected coup for the moment, but they still leave me in ignorance of the identity of the Scarlet Pimpernel."

"La! My friend," she said, "then you are where you were before, and you can let me enjoy the music. Faith!" she added, smothering an imaginary yawn. "Had you not spoken about my brother—"

"I am coming to him now, citoyenne. Among the papers there was a letter to Sir Andrew Ffoulkes written by your brother, Saint-Just. That letter shows him to be a helper, if not actually a member, of the League of the Scarlet Pimpernel."

The blow had been struck at last. Marguerite knew that Chauvelin had spoken the truth; the man was too blindly devoted to his cause to stoop to purposeless falsehoods. A letter of Armand's—

foolish, imprudent Armand—was in Chauvelin's hands, and Chauvelin would hold it until it suited him to make use of it. But she was determined not to show fear.

"La, man!" she said, looking him squarely in the face. "Another of your imaginary plots! Armand in league with the Scarlet Pimpernel! Armand helping those aristocrats whom he despises! Faith, the tale does infinite credit to your imagination!"

"Let me make my point clear, citoyenne," said Chauvelin. "Saint-Just is compromised beyond the slightest hope of pardon."

Inside the orchestra box all was silent for a moment or two. Marguerite sat rigid trying to realize what had best be done. "Chauvelin," she said at last, without bravado, "shall we try to understand each other? Tell me, you are very anxious to discover the identity of the Scarlet Pimpernel, isn't that so? And you would now force me to do some spying work for you in exchange for my brother Armand's safety? Is that it?"

"Fie! Ugly words, fair lady," protested Chauvelin urbanely. "My intention is that you yourself win a free pardon for Armand Saint-Just by doing a small service for France."

"What is it?"

"Only watch for me tonight, citoyenne," he said eagerly. "Among the papers which were taken from Sir Andrew Ffoulkes there was a tiny note. See!" He handed her a scrap of paper.

It was the same scrap of paper which, a few days ago, the two young men had been reading when they were attacked by Chauvelin's minions. Marguerite took it mechanically. There were only three lines, written in a distorted, evidently disguised handwriting:

> Remember we must not meet more often than is strictly necessary. You have all instructions for the 2nd. If you wish to speak to me again, I shall be at G.'s ball.

"What does it mean?" she asked. "There is a device here in the corner, a small red flower. . . ."

"Yes."

"The Scarlet Pimpernel," she said eagerly, "and *G.'s ball* means my Lord Grenville's ball tonight."

"That is how I interpret the note, citoyenne," concluded Chauvelin blandly. "Lord Antony Dewhurst and Sir Andrew Ffoulkes were carried to a lonely house on the Dover road, where they remained close prisoners until this morning. But, having found this scrap of paper, I intended that they should go to Lord Grenville's ball. Therefore, this morning, they found their jailers disappeared and two good horses standing ready, saddled, in the yard. I have not seen them yet, but I think we may safely conclude that they did not draw rein until they reached London. They must have a great deal to say to their chief . . . and they will have an opportunity of speaking to him tonight. Now you see how simple it all is, citoyenne! I offer you a chance of saving the brother you love from the consequences of his own folly."

Marguerite's face softened, her eyes grew moist. "But what do you want me to do, Chauvelin?" she said in a tear-choked voice. "In my present position, it is well-nigh impossible!"

"Nay, citoyenne," he said relentlessly, "as Lady Blakeney, no one suspects you, and with your help I may succeed in finally establishing the identity of the Scarlet Pimpernel. You are going to the ball anon. Watch for me there, and listen. Note everyone to whom Sir Andrew or Lord Antony will speak. Find out who the Scarlet Pimpernel is, and I will pledge the word of France that your brother shall be safe."

Marguerite felt herself entangled in a web from which she could hope for no escape. But—womanlike—she still hoped to temporize. "If I promise to help you in this matter, Chauvelin," she said pleasantly, "will you give me that letter of Saint-Just's?"

"If you render me useful assistance tonight," he replied with his sarcastic smile, "I will give you that letter . . . tomorrow."

"I may be powerless to help you, were I ever so willing."

"That would be terrible indeed," he said quietly, "for you . . . and for Saint-Just."

Marguerite shuddered. From this hated man she could expect no mercy. All-powerful, he held the beloved life in the hollow of his hand. She felt cold in spite of the oppressive air of the opera house. The music seemed to reach her from a distance, and her thoughts wandered to that other man who had a claim on her confidence and her affection. She longed to seek comfort and advice; Sir Percy had loved her once; he was her husband. He showed very little intelligence, to be sure, but he had plenty of pluck and muscle; surely, if she provided the thought, together they could outwit the astute diplomatist and save the hostage without imperiling the noble leader of that band of heroes. Sir Percy seemed attached to Saint-Just—she was sure that he could help.

A rap at the door roused Marguerite. It was Percy Blakeney, tall, sleepy, good-humored, and wearing that smile which seemed to irritate her every nerve. "Er, your chair is outside, m'dear," he said, with his usual exasperating drawl. "I suppose you will want to go to that demmed ball. Excuse me—er—Monsieur Chauvelin—I had not observed you."

He extended two slender white fingers toward Chauvelin, who had risen when Sir Percy entered the box.

"Are you coming, m'dear?"

Marguerite sighed and wrapped her cloak around her. "I am ready," she said, taking his arm. At the door of the box she turned and looked straight at Chauvelin, who was preparing to follow.

"It is only au revoir, Chauvelin," she said pleasantly. "We shall meet at my Lord Grenville's ball anon."

With a smile, the Frenchman took a pinch of snuff. Then, having adjusted his lace jabot, he rubbed his bony hands contentedly together.

❈

LORD GRENVILLE'S BALL

THE HISTORIC BALL given by Lord Grenville was the most brilliant function of the year. Everybody who was anybody had contrived to be there. The Prince of Wales was coming on presently from the opera. Lord Grenville himself had listened to the first two acts of *Orfeo* before preparing to receive his guests. At ten o'clock— an unusually late hour in those days—the grand rooms of the Foreign Office, exquisitely decorated with exotic palms and flowers,

53

were filled to overflowing. The strains of the minuet made a soft accompaniment to the gay chatter of the company.

In the small chamber facing the top of the fine stairway, the host stood receiving his guests. Distinguished men, beautiful women, notabilities from every European country, had already exchanged elaborate bows and curtsies with him and dispersed in the ball, reception and card rooms beyond.

Standing not far from Lord Grenville, Chauvelin had noted that Sir Percy and Lady Blakeney had not yet arrived, and his keen eyes glanced quickly at every newcomer. In his irreproachable black he stood somewhat isolated: the envoy of the revolutionary government of France was not popular in England at a time when the news of the September Massacres was still fresh.

In his official capacity he had been received courteously by his English colleagues, but London society ignored him altogether. Chauvelin was not the man to trouble himself about this; he was blindly enthusiastic for the revolutionary cause, he had a burning love for his country and he despised all social inequalities. Above all, Chauvelin believed that the French aristocrat was the most bitter enemy of the new France; he looked upon every one of them who had escaped as so much prey of which the guillotine had been cheated. Small wonder, therefore, that the mysterious Scarlet Pimpernel was an object of hatred to him.

Suddenly there was a great stir; all conversation stopped as the majordomo's voice outside announced: "His Royal Highness the Prince of Wales and suite, Sir Percy Blakeney, Lady Blakeney."

Lord Grenville went quickly forward to receive his exalted guest. The Prince of Wales, dressed in a salmon-colored velvet richly embroidered with gold, entered with Marguerite Blakeney on his arm, and on his left, Sir Percy, in bronze satin coat and cream satin breeches, priceless lace at his neck and wrists.

After a few words of greeting, Lord Grenville said to his royal guest, "Will your Highness permit me to present Monsieur Chauvelin, the accredited agent of the French Government?"

Chauvelin stepped forward and bowed very low.

"Monsieur," said his Royal Highness coldly, "we will try to

forget the government that sent you, and look upon you merely as our guest. As such you are welcome, monsieur."

"Ah! My little Chauvelin!" said Marguerite gaily, extending her hand to him. "Monsieur and I are old friends, your Highness."

"Ah, then," said the prince, this time very graciously, "you are doubly welcome, monsieur."

"I would crave permission also to present to your Highness Madame la Comtesse de Tournay de Basserive and her family, who have but recently come from France," said Lord Grenville.

"By all means! They are among the very lucky ones, then!"

Lord Grenville turned in search of the comtesse, who sat at the farther end of the room.

"Lud love me!" whispered his Royal Highness to Marguerite, as he caught sight of the comtesse. "She looks very virtuous and very melancholy."

"Faith, your Royal Highness," she rejoined with a smile. "Virtue is like precious odors, most fragrant when it is crushed."

"Virtue, alas," sighed the prince, "is most unbecoming to your charming sex, madame."

"Madame la Comtesse de Tournay de Basserive," said Lord Grenville, introducing the lady.

"This is a pleasure, madame; my royal father, as you know, is ever glad to welcome those whom France has driven from her shores."

"Your Royal Highness is most gracious," replied the comtesse, with becoming dignity. "May I present my daughter, Suzanne, Monseigneur," she said.

"Ah! Charming, charming!" said the prince. "And now allow me, Comtesse, to introduce to you Lady Blakeney. You and she will have much to say to one another, I vow. Every compatriot of Lady Blakeney's is doubly welcome for her sake."

Marguerite's blue eyes twinkled; the Comtesse de Tournay, who lately had so flagrantly insulted her, was here receiving a public lesson. But the comtesse was too well schooled in courtly etiquette to show the slightest sign of embarrassment as the two ladies curtsied ceremoniously to one another.

The prince in the meanwhile was speaking to the vicomte. "I am happy to know you. I knew your father well, monsieur, when he was ambassador to London," he said.

"Ah, Monseigneur!" replied the vicomte. "I owe the honor of this meeting to our protector, the Scarlet Pimpernel."

"Hush!" said the prince quickly, as he indicated Chauvelin, who stood on one side.

"Nay, Monseigneur," said the French envoy, as if in direct response, "pray do not check this gentleman's display of gratitude; the name of that interesting red flower is well-known to me—and to France."

The prince looked at him keenly. "Faith, then, monsieur," he said, "perhaps you know more about our national hero than we do ourselves. Perchance you know who he is. You would render yourself popular among the fair sex if you were to gratify their curiosity."

"Ah, Monseigneur," said Chauvelin, "rumor has it in France that your Highness could give the truest account of that enigmatical flower!" He looked at Marguerite as he spoke; but she betrayed no emotion.

"Nay, man," said the prince, "the members of the league jealously guard the secret of their chief. We know not if he be tall or short, fair or dark, handsome or ill formed; but we know that he is the bravest gentleman in the world, and we feel a little proud, monsieur, that he is an Englishman."

"Ah, Monsieur Chauvelin," added Marguerite, looking almost with defiance at the Frenchman, "his Royal Highness should add that we ladies think of him as a hero of old. We wear his badge. We tremble for him when he is in danger, and exult with him in the hour of his victory."

Chauvelin did no more than bow; he felt that both speeches were intended to convey contempt or defiance. The pleasure-loving, idle prince he despised; the beautiful woman he held in the hollow of his hand. He could afford to remain silent and await events.

An inane laugh broke the silence which had fallen. "And we

poor husbands," came in slow, affected accents from Sir Percy, "have to stand by while they worship a demmed shadow."

Everyone laughed—the prince more loudly than anyone. The tension was relieved, and the gay crowd dispersed.

✳

THE SCRAP OF PAPER

MARGUERITE SUFFERED INTENSELY. Though she laughed and chatted, though she was more courted than any woman there, she felt like one condemned to death. Her tension had increased a hundredfold during that brief hour which she had spent in her husband's company between the opera and the ball. The hope that she might find in him a friend and adviser had vanished as quickly as it had come. Good-humored contempt made her turn away from the man who should have been her moral support in this heartrending crisis.

A crowd of empty-headed young fops were repeating with the keenest enjoyment a doggerel couplet which Sir Percy had just given forth. Everywhere the absurd, silly words met her.

> *"We seek him here, we seek him there,*
> *Those Frenchies seek him everywhere.*
> *Is he in heaven? Is he in hell?*
> *That demmed, elusive Pimpernel."*

"All done in the tying of a cravat," Sir Percy had declared to his clique of admirers, and his bon mot had quickly gone the round of the crowded rooms. The prince was enchanted. He vowed that life without Blakeney would be but a desert. Then he led him to the cardroom and engaged him in a game of hazard.

Sir Percy, whose chief interest seemed to center around the card tables, usually allowed his wife to flirt, dance or amuse herself as she liked. And tonight he had left Marguerite surrounded by admirers. She would not allow herself time to think. She was something of a fatalist, and felt that events would shape themselves.

Later in the evening she caught sight of Sir Andrew Ffoulkes and Lord Antony Dewhurst, who had just arrived. Both young men looked a little haggard and anxious, but otherwise they gave no sign of the catastrophe which hovered around them and their chief. Sir Andrew immediately made for Suzanne de Tournay.

As she looked around the gaily lit ballroom, a burning curiosity seized Marguerite to know the mysterious Scarlet Pimpernel. She looked at the aristocratic Norman faces, the fair, squarely built Saxon, the more humorous Celt, wondering which of these betrayed the power, the energy, the cunning which had imposed its leadership upon a number of highborn English gentlemen among whom, rumor asserted, was his Royal Highness himself.

Sir Andrew Ffoulkes? Surely not, with his gentle blue eyes looking longingly after little Suzanne, who was led away from their pleasant tête-à-tête by her stern mother. Marguerite watched from across the room as he strolled toward a small sitting room, then paused at the doorway, looking anxiously around.

Marguerite contrived to evade her attentive cavaliers and, skirting the fashionable crowd, to draw nearer to Sir Andrew. Why, she could not have said: perhaps she was impelled by that all-powerful fatality which so often seems to rule the destinies of men.

Suddenly she stopped; her very heart seemed to stand still: Sir Andrew was still in the same listless position by the door, but Marguerite had distinctly seen that Lord Hastings—a young buck, a friend of her husband's—had, as he brushed past him, slipped something into his hand. For one moment longer Marguerite paused; the next, she resumed her walk across the room—but this time more quickly toward that doorway whence Sir Andrew had now disappeared.

Now Lady Blakeney had ceased to exist. It was Marguerite Saint-Just who was there: she had forgotten everything save that Armand stood in peril of his life, and that in the hands of Sir Andrew Ffoulkes might be the talisman which would save her brother.

When she reached the sitting room, Sir Andrew was standing with his back to her and close to a table upon which stood a massive silver candelabra. A slip of paper was in his hand, and he was in the very act of perusing its contents.

Unperceived, her soft clinging robe making not the slightest sound upon the heavy carpet, not daring to breathe, Marguerite slipped close behind him. At that moment he looked around and saw her; she uttered a groan, passed her hand across her forehead and murmured faintly, "The heat in the room was terrible . . . I felt so faint . . . Ah! . . ." She tottered as if she would fall, and Sir Andrew, quickly recovering himself and crumpling in his hand the tiny note, was just in time to support her.

"You are ill, Lady Blakeney?" he asked with concern. "Let me—"

"No, no, nothing—" she interrupted quickly. "A chair—quick."

She sank into a chair by the table and, throwing back her head, closed her eyes. "There!" she murmured, still faintly. "The giddiness is passing off. . . . Do not heed me, Sir Andrew."

From the ballroom the sweet notes of the gavotte, the froufrou of rich dresses, the talk and laughter of the crowd, came as a weird accompaniment to the drama which was being enacted. Sir Andrew had not uttered another word, but an extra sense became potent in Marguerite Blakeney. She could not see, for her eyes were closed; she could not hear, for the noise from the ballroom drowned the soft rustle of that momentous scrap of paper; nevertheless she knew that Sir Andrew was even now holding the paper to the flame of one of the candles. At that exact moment she opened her eyes, raised her hand and took the burning scrap of paper from the young man's hand. Then she blew out the flame, and held the paper to her nostril.

"How thoughtful of you, Sir Andrew," she said with perfect composure. "Surely 'twas your grandmother who taught you that the smell of burned paper was a sovereign remedy for giddiness."

She sighed with satisfaction, holding the paper tightly between her jeweled fingers. Sir Andrew was staring at her, too dazed for the moment to realize what had happened.

"Why do you stare at me?" she said playfully. "I assure you I feel much better; your remedy has proved most effectual. This room is delightfully cool, and the sound of the gavotte is soothing."

She prattled on, while Sir Andrew, in an agony of mind, was racking his brains as to the quickest method of getting that bit of paper out of the beautiful woman's hand.

"What? Still dreaming and staring?" she said, standing up with a merry laugh. "You are most ungallant, Sir Andrew; and now I come to think of it, you seemed more startled than pleased when you saw me just now. I do believe it was not concern for my health that caused you to burn this scrap of paper. I vow it must have been your ladylove's last cruel epistle you were trying to destroy!"

"Whatever it is, Lady Blakeney," said Sir Andrew, at last recovering his self-possession, "this little note is mine, and—"

Not caring whether his action would be thought ill-bred, the young man made a bold dash for the note; but Marguerite's thoughts flew quicker than his own. She took a quick step backward and knocked over the small table, which fell with a crash, together with the massive candelabra upon it.

She gave a cry of alarm: "The candles, Sir Andrew—quick!"

There was not much damage done; one or two of the candles had blown out as the candelabra fell; others had merely sent some grease upon the valuable carpet. Sir Andrew dexterously replaced the candelabra and the table; but this took him a few seconds, and those seconds were all that Marguerite needed to cast a quick glance at the paper and to note its contents—a dozen words in the same distorted handwriting she had seen before, signed with the same red, star-shaped flower.

When Sir Andrew once more looked at her, he only saw on her face alarm at the untoward accident, while the tiny note had apparently fluttered to the ground. Eagerly the young man picked it up.

"For shame, Sir Andrew," she said, shaking her head, "making havoc in the heart of some impressionable duchess, while conquering the affections of my sweet little Suzanne."

"You will forgive me, Lady Blakeney," said Sir Andrew, now as calm as she was herself, "if I resume the interesting occupation which you had interrupted?"

"By all means, Sir Andrew, burn your love token!"

Sir Andrew had already twisted the paper into a spill, and was once again holding it to a candle which had remained alight. He did not notice the strange smile on the face of his fair vis-à-vis, but watched the fateful note as it curled under the flame. Soon the last fragment fell to the floor, and he placed his heel upon the ashes.

"And now, Sir Andrew," said Marguerite Blakeney, with the most winning of smiles, "will you venture to excite the jealousy of your fair lady by asking me to dance the minuet?"

✢

ONE O'CLOCK PRECISELY

THE FEW WORDS on the scorched piece of paper seemed literally to be the words of Fate. *Start myself tomorrow* . . . Marguerite had read quite distinctly, then came a smoky blur; but right at the bottom there was another sentence, which was now standing in her mind in letters of fire: *If you wish to speak to me again, I shall be in the supper room at one o'clock precisely.*

It was now close upon eleven; the hands of the handsome Louis XV clock seemed to move along with maddening rapidity. Two hours more and she must make up her mind whether she would keep the knowledge so cunningly gained to herself and leave her brother to his fate, or whether she would willfully betray a brave man who was noble, generous and, above all, unsuspecting. It was monstrous. Armand, too, was noble, brave and unsuspecting.

These conflicting thoughts raged in Marguerite's brain while, with a smile upon her lips, she glided through the intricate figures of the last minuet before supper. She noted that she had succeeded in completely allaying Sir Andrew's fears. Her self-control had been perfect—she was a finer actress at this moment than she had ever been upon the boards of the Comédie Francaise; but then a beloved brother's life had not depended upon her histrionic powers. She was too clever to overdo her part, but when the minuet was over she asked Sir Andrew to take her into the next room.

"I have promised to go down to supper with his Royal Highness," she said, "but before we part, tell me . . . shall I welcome you at my water party on Tuesday?"

"I am not sure, Lady Blakeney," he replied evasively. "I may have to leave London tomorrow." And he had led her to a room beyond, where already his Royal Highness was waiting for her.

"Madame, supper awaits us," said the prince, offering his arm to Marguerite. "The goddess Fortune has frowned so persistently on me at hazard that I look for the smiles of the goddess of Beauty."

"Your Highness has been unfortunate at the card tables?" asked Marguerite, as she took the prince's arm.

"Aye! Most unfortunate. Blakeney, not content to be the richest of my father's subjects, has also the most outrageous luck."

SUPPER HAD BEEN EXTREMELY GAY. Never had Lady Blakeney been more adorable or that "demmed idiot," Sir Percy, more amusing. His Royal Highness had laughed until the tears streamed down his cheeks at Blakeney's repartees. His verse, *We seek him here, we seek him there*, was sung to the tune of "Ho! Merry Britons!" and to the accompaniment of glasses knocked loudly against the table.

Marguerite was in her most brilliant mood, and surely not a soul in that crowded supper room had an inkling of the struggle raging within her. The clock was ticking mercilessly on. It was long past midnight. Soon the destinies of two brave men would be pitted against one another—the beloved brother and the unknown hero.

After supper, dancing was resumed. His Royal Highness had left, and there was talk of departing among the older guests—but the young ones had started to dance a gavotte. Marguerite did not feel equal to another dance. Escorted by a cabinet minister, she had once more found her way to the tiny sitting room. She knew Chauvelin must be lying in wait for her somewhere, ready to seize the first opportunity for a tête-à-tête. His eyes had met hers for a moment after the 'fore-supper minuet, and she knew that the keen diplomatist had divined that her work was accomplished.

Fate had willed it so. Marguerite had resigned to its decrees. But Armand must be saved at any cost; to think of him dying on the guillotine was too horrible. As for the stranger, the hero . . . well! Let the cunning Scarlet Pimpernel extricate himself. She thought of all this as she sat listening to the witty discourse of the cabinet minister. Suddenly she saw the foxlike face of Chauvelin peeping through the curtained doorway.

"Lord Fancourt," she said to the minister, "will you see if my husband is still in the cardroom? And if he is, will you tell him I am very tired, and would be glad to go soon? We shall not—if we do not hurry—get back to Richmond before daybreak."

"I am entirely at your ladyship's service," replied Lord Fancourt, rising at once.

The moment he had disappeared, Chauvelin slipped into the room. "You have news for me?" he said.

Though Marguerite's cheeks glowed with fire, she felt chilled and numbed. "Nothing of importance," she said, staring mechanically before her, "but it might prove a clue. I contrived—no matter how—to detect Sir Andrew Ffoulkes in the act of burning a paper at one of these candles. I succeeded in holding that paper for two minutes, and in casting my eyes on it for ten seconds."

"Time enough to learn its contents?" asked Chauvelin.

She nodded. "In the corner of the paper there was the small star-shaped flower. I read two lines, everything else was scorched. One was, *Start myself tomorrow*. The other—*If you wish to speak to me again, I shall be in the supper room at one o'clock precisely*."

Chauvelin looked up at the clock just above the mantelpiece. "Then I have plenty of time," he said placidly.

"What are you going to do?" she asked. She was pale as a statue; her head and heart throbbed with the awful strain.

"Nothing for the present," he replied. "After that it will depend on whom I see in the supper room at one o'clock precisely."

"You will see the Scarlet Pimpernel, but you do not know him."

"No. But I shall presently."

"Sir Andrew will have warned him."

"I think not. When you parted from him after the minuet he watched you for a moment or two, which gave me to understand that something had happened between you. It was only natural, was it not, that I should make a shrewd guess as to the nature of that 'something'? I thereupon engaged the young gallant in an animated conversation until a lady claimed his arm for supper."

"Since then?"

"I did not lose sight of him through supper. When we all came upstairs again, Lady Portarles buttonholed him and started on the subject of pretty Mademoiselle Suzanne de Tournay, which will not be exhausted for another quarter of an hour at least, and it is five minutes to one now."

He went to the doorway and, drawing aside the curtain, he pointed out the figure of Sir Andrew Ffoulkes in conversation with Lady Portarles. "I think," he said triumphantly, "that I may safely expect to find the person I seek in the supper room."

"There may be more than one."

"Whoever is there, as the clock strikes one, will from then on be shadowed by one of my men; of them, one will leave for France tomorrow. I also, fair lady, will leave for France tomorrow. The papers found at Dover upon the person of Sir Andrew Ffoulkes speak of an inn near Calais called *Le Chat Gris*, and of the Père Blanchard's hut somewhere on the coast. These are the points where this meddlesome Englishman has bidden the traitor Tournay and others to meet his emissaries. But it seems that he has decided he will start himself tomorrow. Now, one of those persons whom I shall see in the supper room will be journeying to Calais, and I shall follow that person to where those fugitive aristocrats await him; for that person, fair lady, will be the man whom I have sought for nearly a year—the mysterious Scarlet Pimpernel."

"And Armand?" she pleaded.

"I promise you that the day the Scarlet Pimpernel and I start for France, I will send you that imprudent letter of his by special courier. More than that—the day I lay hands on that elusive Englishman, Saint-Just will be safe." And with a deep bow and another look at the clock, Chauvelin glided out of the room.

It seemed to Marguerite, as she lay back in her chair, that through all the noise she could hear his catlike tread go down the massive staircase and reach the supper room. Fate *had* decided, had made her do an abominable thing, for the sake of the brother she loved.

WHEN CHAUVELIN REACHED the supper room it had a forsaken appearance: chairs were turned toward one another, in groups of twos and threes, that recalled pleasant, animated discussions over the latest scandals; or in rows that looked like starchy dowagers.

He smiled benignly, and rubbing his long, thin hands together he looked around the room, whence even the last flunky had retired.

Chauvelin tried to peer into the future. What would this man be like, whom he had sworn to bring to his death? Everything about him was mysterious: his personality, which he had so cunningly concealed; the power he wielded over nineteen English gentlemen, who seemed to obey his every command blindly and enthusiastically; and above all his marvelous audacity, the impudence which had caused him to beard his enemies within the very walls of Paris. Chauvelin felt a strange feeling of awe creeping down his spine. But his plans were well laid. Fortunately the supper room was deserted: this would make his task all the easier when presently that unsuspecting enigma should enter it alone.

Stay! As he surveyed the room with a satisfied smile, the cunning French agent became aware of the monotonous breathing of one of my Lord Grenville's guests, who, no doubt, had supped well and was enjoying a quiet sleep. Chauvelin looked around once more, and there, on a sofa in the dark angle of the room, his mouth open, his eyes shut, reclined the gorgeously appareled, long-limbed husband of the cleverest woman in Europe.

Chauvelin looked at him, and a smile that was almost one of pity softened for a moment the hard lines of the Frenchman's face. Evidently the slumberer, deep in dreamless sleep, would not interfere with Chauvelin's trap. Again he rubbed his hands together, and following the example of Sir Percy Blakeney he too stretched himself out on another sofa, shut his eyes, opened his mouth, gave forth sounds of peaceful breathing and . . . waited!

✿

DOUBT

MARGUERITE BLAKENEY WAITED in the small sitting room, anxious and weary. Her mind conjured up the vision of what was, perhaps at this very moment, passing downstairs. The deserted supper room, the fateful hour—Chauvelin on the watch! Then, precise to the moment, the entrance of the Scarlet Pimpernel—

"Faith! Your ladyship must have thought me remiss," said Lord Fancourt's voice suddenly, close to her elbow. "I had a deal of difficulty in delivering your message, for I could not find Blakeney anywhere. . . . I did find him at last, and he said that he would give orders at once for the horses to be put to."

Marguerite had forgotten all about her husband and her message to him. "Ah!" she said. "You gave my husband my message?"

"Yes; he was in the supper room fast asleep."

"Thank you very much," she said mechanically, trying to collect her thoughts.

"Will your ladyship honor me with the *contredanse* until your coach is ready?" asked Lord Fancourt.

"No, I thank you, my lord, but—and you will forgive me—I really am too tired."

This long interval of waiting was intolerable. Why did not Chauvelin come and tell her the result of his watch?

Lord Fancourt was very attentive, but it was quite clear that the fair lady's thoughts were far away, and at length she startled him by asking abruptly, "Lord Fancourt, did you perceive who was in the supper room just now besides Sir Percy Blakeney?"

"Only the agent of the French Government, Monsieur Chauvelin, equally fast asleep in another corner," he said.

"Did you notice the time when you were there?"

"It must have been about five or ten minutes past one."

Had Chauvelin failed? For one instant that possibility rose before her as a hope—the hope that the Scarlet Pimpernel had been warned by Sir Andrew, and that Chauvelin's trap had failed to catch his bird! But then—what of Armand!

"Shall I find out if your ladyship's coach is ready?" Lord Fancourt said at last.

"Oh, thank you. . . . I fear I am but sorry company."

She was longing to be rid of him, for she hoped that Chauvelin would be prowling around, thinking to find her alone. But Lord Fancourt went, and still Chauvelin did not come. Oh! What had happened? She felt Armand's fate trembling in the balance. She feared now that Chauvelin *had* failed, and she knew that she need hope for no mercy from him. Yet she had done her best, had strained every nerve for Armand's sake.

Lord Grenville himself came presently to tell her that her coach was ready, and that Sir Percy was waiting for her. The minister took leave of beautiful Lady Blakeney at the top of the stairs, and it was then, suddenly, that she saw Chauvelin: he was coming up the stairs slowly, rubbing his hands together. There was a puzzled look on his face, and as his eyes met Marguerite's they became sarcastic.

"Monsieur Chauvelin," she said as he reached her, "my coach is outside; may I claim your arm?"

Gallantly he offered her his arm and led her downstairs through the great crowd of departing guests.

"Chauvelin," she said at last, desperately, "I must know what has happened."

"What has happened, dear lady?" he said, with affected surprise. "Where? When?"

"You are torturing me, Chauvelin," she said in a whisper. "What happened in the supper room at one o'clock?"

"Quiet and peace reigned supreme, fair lady; at that hour I was asleep on one sofa and Sir Percy Blakeney on another."

"Nobody came into the room at all?"

"Nobody."

"Then we have failed, you and I? . . ."

"We have failed—perhaps."

"But Armand?"

"Ah! Armand Saint-Just's chances hang on a thread. . . ."

"Chauvelin, I worked for you . . . remember. . . ."

"I remember my promise," he said quietly. "The day the Scarlet Pimpernel and I meet on French soil, Saint-Just will be in the arms of his charming sister. Surely you must hope, as I do, that the Scarlet Pimpernel will start for Calais today."

Downstairs she was soon surrounded. Lady Blakeney never stepped from any house into her coach without an escort of fluttering human moths around the dazzling light of her beauty. But before she turned away from Chauvelin, she held out a hand to him.

"Give me some hope, Chauvelin," she pleaded.

With perfect gallantry he bowed over that tiny hand in its black lace mitten. "Pray heaven that the thread may not snap," he said, with his enigmatic smile. And, stepping aside, he allowed the moths to flutter more closely around the candle.

RICHMOND

A FEW MINUTES LATER Marguerite was sitting, wrapped in furs, next to Sir Percy on the box seat of his magnificent coach, and the four splendid bays were thundering down the quiet street. Soon London was left behind. These drives after balls and suppers in London were a delight to Marguerite, and she appreciated the eccentricity which caused her husband to take her to their beautiful home in Richmond instead of a stuffy London house. The drive was less than an hour when the bays were fresh and Sir Percy gave them full rein. Tonight he seemed to have a very devil in his fingers, and the coach seemed to fly along the road beside the river, which looked like a silver serpent beneath the moon.

As usual, Sir Percy did not speak to her. Marguerite looked at him tentatively once or twice; the face in the moonlight looked singularly earnest, and recalled to Marguerite's aching heart those happy days of courtship, before he had become the lazy, effete fop, whose life seemed spent in cards and supper rooms.

But now she could not catch the expression of the blue eyes; she could only see the outline of the firm chin, the corner of the strong mouth, the well-cut forehead; truly, nature had meant well by Sir Percy; his faults must all be laid at the door of that poor, half-crazy mother. Marguerite suddenly felt intense sympathy for her husband. The moral crises she had just gone through made her feel indulgent toward the faults of others. Had anyone told her a week ago that she would betray a brave and unsuspecting man into the hands of a relentless enemy, she would have laughed the idea to scorn. The Marquis de Saint-Cyr had perished through a thoughtless word of hers; but in that case she was morally innocent. This time she had deliberately done a base thing. As she felt her husband's strong arm beside her, she also felt how much more he would despise her if he knew of this night's work.

Buried in her thoughts, Marguerite had found the drive all too brief; and it was with disappointment that she realized that the bays had turned into the massive gates of her home. Sir Percy Blakeney's palatial house on the river stood in the midst of exquisitely laid out gardens. Built in Tudor days, the old masonry of the walls looked eminently picturesque in the midst of the moonlit lawn. Great trees lent cool shadows to the grounds, and on this autumn night the garden looked singularly poetic and peaceful.

In spite of the lateness of the hour, an army of grooms seemed to emerge from the very ground as Sir Percy brought the four bays to a standstill in front of the entrance. He jumped down quickly, then helped Marguerite to alight. She lingered a moment, then skirted the house and stepped onto the lawn, looking out dreamily into the silvery landscape. She could hear the ripple of the river, the horses being led to their stables. The house was now quite still. In two separate apartments, just above the magnificent reception rooms, lights were burning; they were her rooms and his, divided from each other by the whole width of the house, as far apart as their own lives had become. Involuntarily she sighed. Never had she felt so lonely, so in want of comfort and sympathy. With another sigh she started back toward the house, wondering if, after such a night, she could find rest.

But before she reached the terrace she heard a firm step upon the gravel, and the next moment her husband's figure emerged from the shadow. He still wore his heavy driving coat, but he had thrown it well back, burying his hands in the pockets of his satin breeches; the ivory costume looked strangely ghostly against the dark background of the house. He apparently did not notice her, for after a moment's pause he too turned back toward the terrace.

"Sir Percy!"

At her voice he started, then looked searchingly into the shadows. She came forward quickly into the moonlight, and he said with his usual gallantry, "At your service, madame!" But his foot was on the terrace steps, and in his whole attitude there was a suggestion that he wished to go, and had no desire for an interview.

"The air is deliciously cool," she said, "and the garden inviting. Will you not stay in it awhile? Or is my company so distasteful?"

"Nay, madame," he rejoined placidly, "but 'tis on the other foot the shoe happens to be, and I'll warrant you'll find the midnight air more agreeable without my company."

"I protest you mistake me, Sir Percy," she said hurriedly. "The estrangement, which, alas, has arisen between us, was none of my making, remember."

"Begad! You must pardon me there, madame!" he protested coldly. "My memory was always of the shortest."

Her eyes softened as she came closer to him at the foot of the terrace steps. "Of the shortest, Sir Percy? Faith! How it must have altered! Was it three years ago or four that you saw me for one hour in Paris, on your way to the East? When you came back two years later you had not forgotten me."

She looked divinely pretty as she stood there in the moonlight, with the fur cloak sliding off her beautiful shoulders, the gold embroidery on her dress shimmering around her, her blue eyes turned up to him. For a moment he stood rigid, but for the clenching of his hand against the stone balustrade of the terrace.

"You desired my presence, madame," he said frigidly. "I take it that it was not with a view to indulging in tender reminiscences."

His voice was cold and uncompromising; his attitude unbending. Womanly decorum suggested that Marguerite return coldness for coldness, and sweep past without another word. But womanly instinct suggested that she remain. She stretched out her hand to him. He bent and kissed the tips of her fingers ceremoniously.

"Is it possible that love can die?" she said with unreasoning vehemence. "Methought the passion you felt for me would outlast the span of human life. Is there nothing left of that love, Percy . . . which might help . . . to bridge over our sad estrangement?"

His massive figure seemed, while she spoke, to stiffen still more, the strong mouth hardened, a look of relentless obstinacy crept into the habitually lazy blue eyes.

"With what object, I pray you, madame?" he asked with sudden

72

bitterness. "My dull wits are unable to grasp the cause of this, your ladyship's new mood. Is it that you wish to see me once more a lovesick suppliant at your feet, so you might have the pleasure of kicking me aside like a troublesome lapdog as you did last year?"

"Percy! I entreat you!" she said, while a tone of tenderness crept into her voice. "Oh! I was vain and frivolous; your wealth and position allured me: I married you, hoping that your great love for me would beget in me a love for you . . . but, alas! . . ."

The moon had sunk low behind a bank of clouds. In the east a soft gray light was beginning to chase away the night.

"Twenty-four hours after our marriage, madame, the Marquis de Saint-Cyr and all his family perished on the guillotine, and the popular rumor reached me that it was the wife of Sir Percy Blakeney who helped to send them there."

"Nay! I myself told you the truth of that odious tale."

"Not till after it had been recounted to me by strangers."

"And you believed them," she said bitterly, "without proof or question—you believed that I, whom you vowed to love more than life, could do a thing so base as these *strangers* chose to recount. You thought I meant to deceive you about it—that I ought to have spoken before I married you; yet I would have told you that up to the very morning of our marriage I was using all the influence I possessed to save Saint-Cyr and his family, and pride sealed my lips when your love seemed to perish."

Her voice became choked with tears. She paused for a moment, trying to gain some sort of composure, and looked appealingly at him, almost as to a judge. He had allowed her to speak, offering no comment, but Marguerite could see that the lazy good-natured face looked strangely altered: a look of intense passion seemed to glow from beneath his drooping lids.

Marguerite knew in a moment that for the past few months she had been mistaken; that this man who stood before her loved her as he had loved her a year ago; that his love might have been dormant, but that it was there, as strong, as intense as when first her lips met his. Pride had kept him from her, and, womanlike, she meant to win back that conquest which had been hers. Suddenly it

73

seemed that the only happiness life could hold for her again would be in feeling that man's kiss once more upon her lips.

"Listen to the tale, Sir Percy," she said, and her voice now was low, sweet, tender as she told him of her closeness to Armand and of her suffering at his humiliation by the Marquis de Saint-Cyr. "When the opportunity occurred," she went on, "I took my revenge. But I only thought to bring humiliation to that proud marquis. He had plotted against his own country. Knowledge of this came to me; I spoke of it, but how could I guess what would happen? When I realized what I had done, it was too late."

"It is a little difficult, madame," said Sir Percy, after a moment of silence, "to go back over the past. I have confessed that my memory is short, but the thought lingered in my mind that, at the time of the marquis's death, I entreated you for an explanation of these rumors. I fancy that, beyond a bald confession of the horrible facts, you refused me *all* explanation, and demanded of my love a humiliating allegiance it was not prepared to give."

"I wished to test your love for me."

"And to test that love, you demanded that I should forfeit mine honor, that I should accept without question every action of my mistress. My heart was overflowing with love; had you spoken but one word of explanation I would have believed it."

She need not complain now that he was cold and impassive; his voice shook with an intensity of passion which he was making superhuman efforts to keep in check.

"Aye! The madness of my pride!" she said sadly. "I soon repented, but already you had put on that mask of indifference which you have never laid aside until . . . until now."

She was so close to him that her soft hair was wafted against his cheek; her eyes, glowing with tears, maddened him, the music in her voice sent fire through his veins. But he would not yield to the magic charm of this woman he so deeply loved and at whose hands his pride had suffered so bitterly. He closed his eyes to shut out the vision of that sweet face and graceful figure, around which the faint light of dawn was beginning to hover.

"Nay, madame, it is no mask," he said icily. "I swore to you once that my life was yours. For months now it has been your plaything. . . . It has served your purpose."

But now she knew that that coldness *was* a mask. The crisis she had gone through last night suddenly came back to her mind, but now with a feeling that this man, who loved her, would help her to bear the burden. "Sir Percy," she asked impulsively, "you spoke of my new mood just now. We will call it that, if you will. I wish to speak to you . . . because . . . because I am in trouble . . ."

"I pray you, madame," he said, while his voice now shook almost as much as hers, "in what way can I serve you?"

"Percy—Armand is in deadly danger. A letter of his . . . rash, impetuous, written to Sir Andrew Ffoulkes, has fallen into the hands of a fanatic. Armand is hopelessly compromised. Tomorrow, perhaps, he will be arrested . . . after that the guillotine, unless— Oh! It is horrible!" she said with sudden anguish. "And I have no one to whom I can turn for help, or even sympathy." Her struggle, the awful uncertainty of Armand's fate, now overwhelmed her. She tottered, and leaning against the stone balustrade she buried her face in her hands and sobbed bitterly.

At first mention of Armand Saint-Just's name and of the peril in which he stood, Sir Percy's face had become a shade more pale, and his look of determination and obstinacy more marked than ever. He watched her as her delicate frame was shaken with sobs.

"And so," he said with sarcasm, "the murderous dog of the Revolution is turning upon the hands that fed it? Begad, madame," he added gently, as Marguerite continued to sob, "will you dry your tears? I never could bear to see a pretty woman cry, and I . . ."

Instinctively he stretched out his arms, and would have seized her and held her to him, protected from every evil with his very life. . . . But pride had the better of him once again; he restrained himself with a tremendous effort of will and said, "Will you not tell me in what way I may have the honor to serve you?"

She tried to control herself, and turning her tear-stained face to him she once more held out her hand, which he kissed with the same punctilious gallantry; but Marguerite's fingers, this time, lingered in his hand for a second or two longer than was absolutely necessary, because she felt that it trembled and was burning hot, while his lips were as cold as marble.

"Can you do aught for Armand?" she said, sweetly and simply. "You have so much influence at court . . . so many friends . . ."

"Nay, madame, should you not rather seek the influence of your French Republican friend, Monsieur Chauvelin?"

"I cannot ask him, Percy. . . . Oh! I wish I dared to tell you, but . . . he has put a price on my brother's head, which . . ."

She would have given worlds to have had the courage then to tell him everything: how she had suffered and how her hand had been forced. But she dared not make another confession to him, when she was just beginning to feel that he still loved her. He might not understand her struggles and temptation.

Perhaps he divined what was passing in her mind. His whole attitude was one of longing for that confidence which her foolish pride withheld from him. When she remained silent he sighed, and said, "Faith, madame, since it distresses you, we will not speak of it. . . . As for Armand, I pray you, have no fear. I pledge you my word that he shall be safe. Now, have I your permission to go? The hour is getting late."

"You will at least accept my gratitude?" she said tenderly.

"It is too soon, madame!" he said quietly. "I have done nothing as yet. The hour is late, and you must be fatigued."

He stood aside to allow her to pass. She sighed, a quick sigh of disappointment. Pride had conquered—an impassable barrier which neither of them cared to be the first to demolish. He bent in a low bow as she began to mount the terrace steps.

Her gold-embroidered gown swept the dead leaves off the steps as she glided up, the rosy light of the rising sun making her hair an aureole of gold around her head, and causing the rubies and diamonds to sparkle. Before entering the house she paused to look at him, hoping against hope to hear his voice calling her back. But his massive figure looked the personification of unbending pride. Hot tears again surged to her eyes; she turned quickly within, and ran as fast as she could up to her own rooms.

Had she but turned back then, she would have seen that which would have made her sufferings easy to bear: pride had given way at last; he was but a man blindly, passionately in love, and as soon as her light footsteps had died away, he knelt on the terrace steps and kissed one by one the places where her small foot had trodden, and the stone balustrade where her tiny hand had rested last.

✿

FAREWELL

WHEN MARGUERITE REACHED her room, she found her maid anxiously waiting for her. "Your ladyship will be so tired," said the woman, whose own eyes were half closed with sleep. "It is past five o'clock."

"Ah, yes, Louise, I daresay I shall be tired presently," said Marguerite kindly, "but you are very tired now, so go to bed at once. Give me a wrap, and leave me alone."

Louise, only too glad to obey, brought her mistress a soft billowy gown. When she was gone, Marguerite drew aside the curtains and threw open the windows. To the east, the rising sun had changed the rose to vivid gold. The lawn was deserted now, and Marguerite looked down upon the spot where she had stood a few moments ago trying to win back a man's love.

How strange it all was! She loved him. And now that she looked back upon the last few months of misunderstandings and loneliness, she realized that she had always loved him; that deep down in her heart she had always felt that his foolish inanities, his lazy nonchalance were nothing but a mask behind which the real man, strong, passionate, lay hidden. And she meant to capture that obstinate heart again; for this much was certain: there was no longer any happiness for her without it.

Absorbed in her thoughts and emotions, she allowed time to slip by; perhaps she sank into a troubled sleep. Suddenly she was roused by footsteps outside her door. She jumped up and listened: the house itself was as still as ever; the footsteps had retreated. The morning sun was flooding her room with light. She looked up at the clock; it was half past six. Gently, on tiptoe, she crossed the room and opened the door to listen. But at her feet she saw something white—a letter! It certainly was not there when she came upstairs.

She stooped to pick it up, and, amazed, she saw that the letter was addressed to herself in her husband's large, businesslike hand. She tore open the envelope and read:

A most unforeseen circumstance forces me to leave for the North immediately, so I beg your ladyship's pardon if I do not avail myself of the honor of bidding you good-by. My business may keep me employed for about a week, so I shall not have the privilege of being present at your ladyship's party on Tuesday. I remain, your ladyship's most humble and obedient servant,

Percy Blakeney

Marguerite read this mysterious epistle again and again, her nerves strained with a presentiment she could not have explained.

Sir Percy owned considerable property in the North and he had often before gone there for a week at a time; but it seemed very strange that circumstances should have arisen between five and six o'clock in the morning that compelled him to start in this extreme hurry. An unconquerable desire seized her to see her husband again, if he had not already started. Forgetting that she was only lightly clad, she flew down the stairs, through the hall toward the front door, which was still barred and bolted. Her keen ears had detected the sound of a horse's hoof against the flagstones. With trembling fingers Marguerite undid the heavy, stiff bolts, and at last she had thrown open the door.

Her ears had not deceived her. A groom was standing close by, holding a couple of horses; one of these was Sultan, Sir Percy's favorite and swiftest horse, saddled ready for a journey. The next moment Sir Percy himself came quickly around the corner of the house toward the horses. He had changed his ball costume, but was as usual irreproachably appareled in a suit of fine cloth, high top boots and riding breeches.

Marguerite went forward a few steps. He looked up and saw her. A slight frown appeared between his eyes.

"You are going?" she said quickly. "Whither?"

"As I have had the honor of informing your ladyship, urgent, most unexpected business calls me to the North this morning," he said, in his usual cold manner.

"But your guests tomorrow . . . surely the business is not so urgent . . . and you said nothing about it—just now."

"My business, madame, is as unexpected as it is urgent. . . . May I therefore crave your permission to go?" He was trying to get away, while she was straining every nerve to keep him back.

"Percy," she said, "will you not tell me why you go today? You have *not* been called away to the North. I know it. There were no letters, no couriers, nothing was waiting for you when we returned from the ball. . . . There is some mystery."

"Nay, there is no mystery, madame," he replied, with slight impatience. "My business has to do with Armand. As you say, I have some influence; my intention is to exert it, before it be too late. Now, have I your leave to depart?"

"Will you allow me to thank you at least?"

"Nay, madame," he said. "My life is at your service, and I am already more than repaid."

"And mine will be at yours, Sir Percy, if you will but accept it, in exchange for what you do for Armand," she said, as, impulsively, she stretched out her hands to him. "There! I will not detain you. My thoughts go with you. Farewell."

How lovely she looked in this morning sunlight, with her hair streaming around her shoulders. He bowed very low and kissed her hand; she felt the burning kiss and her heart thrilled with joy and hope. "You will remember?" she asked tenderly.

"I will always remember, madame, that you have honored me by commanding my services."

The words were cold and formal, but they did not chill her this time. Her woman's heart had read in his eyes the longing beneath the impassive mask his pride still forced him to wear.

He bowed to her again, jumped onto Sultan's back; then, as he galloped out of the gates, she waved him a final adieu. A bend in the road soon hid him from view. Marguerite, with a sigh that was

almost a happy one, turned and went within. Her heart seemed to be at peace. All would be well now: she would crush her own pride, tell him everything, trust him.

She had no more fear of Chauvelin. He had not discovered the identity of the Scarlet Pimpernel, of that she felt sure: no one had been in the dining room at one o'clock except the Frenchman himself and Percy. The unknown hero would not fall into Chauvelin's trap. Armand was still in danger, but she felt no longer anxious about him. Percy had pledged his word that Armand would be safe, and somehow, as Marguerite had seen him riding away, the possibility that he could fail in whatever he undertook never even remotely crossed her mind. She went to bed at last, and, like a wearied child, soon fell into a peaceful and dreamless sleep.

THE DAY WAS WELL ADVANCED when Marguerite woke, refreshed. Thoughts crowded thick and fast in her mind as with hearty appetite she partook of some fresh milk and a dish of fruit. Most of these thoughts went galloping after her husband. In answer to her eager inquiries, Louise brought the news that the groom had come home with Sultan, having left Sir Percy in London where he was about to board his schooner, lying just below London Bridge.

This news puzzled Marguerite more than ever. Where could Sir Percy be going just now in the *Day Dream?* On Armand's behalf, he had said. Well! Sir Percy had influential friends everywhere. Perhaps he was going to Greenwich, or . . . But Marguerite ceased to conjecture; all would be explained anon.

An idle day lay before Marguerite. She was expecting the visit of Suzanne de Tournay. Mischievously she had tendered her request for Suzanne's company to the comtesse in the presence of the Prince of Wales last night. His Royal Highness had loudly applauded the notion and declared that he would call on the two ladies in the course of the afternoon; the comtesse had not dared to refuse. Marguerite longed for a chat about old school days; she felt that she would prefer Suzanne's company to that of anyone else. But Suzanne had not come yet, and Marguerite prepared to go downstairs.

81

She crossed the landing outside her apartments and stood for a moment at the head of the fine oak staircase. On her left was her husband's suite of rooms, which she practically never entered. It consisted of bedroom, dressing and reception room, and a small study which, when Sir Percy did not use it, was always kept locked. His confidential valet, Frank, had charge of this room. No one else was allowed inside. Marguerite had often chaffed her husband about the secrecy which surrounded his private study. Laughingly she had declared that a comfortable armchair for Sir Percy's sweet slumbers was, no doubt, its most conspicuous piece of furniture.

This bright October morning Frank was evidently busy with his master's rooms, for the doors stood open. A burning curiosity seized Marguerite to have a peep at Sir Percy's sanctum. She hoped that the valet would be busy in one of the other rooms.

On tiptoe, she crossed the landing and, like Bluebeard's wife, trembling with excitement and wonder, she paused a moment on the threshold. The door was ajar; she pushed it open tentatively: there was no sound; Frank was not there, and she walked boldly in. At once she was struck by the severe simplicity of everything around her. The dark hangings, the massive oak furniture, the maps on the wall in no way recalled the dandified leader of fashion that was the outward representation of Sir Percy Blakeney. Facing the window, and well into the center of the room, stood a business-like desk. On the wall to the left of it was a magnificent full-length portrait of a woman, signed with the name of Boucher. It was Percy's mother. She had been a very beautiful woman, and Marguerite could not but be struck by the extraordinary resemblance between mother and son. There was the same low, square forehead crowned with thick, fair hair; the same deep-set, somewhat lazy blue eyes with the same latent passion which used to light up Percy's face before his marriage, and which Marguerite had noted today at dawn.

Marguerite studied the portrait; then she looked at the desk. It was covered with papers, which looked like accounts and receipts, all neatly tied and docketed. Since she had entered this orderly room, she had been taken so much by surprise that this proof of her husband's strong business capacities did not cause her more than passing wonder. But it strengthened her in the now certain knowledge that his foppish ways and foolish talk were not only a mask, but that he was playing a deliberate and studied part. Why should he—obviously a serious, earnest man—wish to appear before his fellowmen as a nincompoop? He may have wished to hide his love for a wife who held him in contempt, but surely such an object could have been gained at less sacrifice.

A nameless dread had begun to seize upon her. There were no pictures on the walls save the fine Boucher portrait, only a couple of maps of France, one of the north coast and the other of the environs of Paris. What did Sir Percy want with those, she wondered. Her head began to ache; she turned away from this strange Bluebeard's chamber, which she did not understand. She did not wish Frank to find her here, and she turned to the door. As she did so, her foot knocked against a small object which had been lying close to the desk and which now went rolling across the room. She stooped to pick it up. It was a solid-gold ring, with a flat shield on which was engraved a small device. Marguerite turned it over in her fingers, and then studied the engraving on the shield. It represented a small flower, of a shape she had seen distinctly twice before: once at the opera, and once at Lord Grenville's ball.

�֍

THE SCARLET PIMPERNEL

AT WHAT PARTICULAR MOMENT the doubt first crept into Marguerite's mind she could not herself afterward have said. With the ring tightly clutched in her hand she had run out of the room, down the stairs and out into the garden, where, in complete seclusion, she could study that device more closely.

Now, sitting beneath the shade of a sycamore, she was looking at the plain gold shield with the star-shaped little flower engraved upon it. Bah! It was ridiculous! Was not everybody affecting the device of that mysterious Scarlet Pimpernel? Did she not herself wear it set in gems in her hair? What was there strange in the fact that Sir Percy should have chosen to use it as a seal ring? And what connection could there be between her exquisite dandy of a husband and the daring plotter who rescued victims from beneath the very eyes of the leaders of a bloodthirsty revolution?

Her thoughts were in a whirl. She did not see anything around her and was quite startled when a fresh young voice called to her across the garden.

"*Chérie—chérie!* Where are you?" and Suzanne, eyes dancing and brown curls fluttering, came running across the lawn. "They told me you were in the garden," she went on, throwing herself into Marguerite's arms, "so I ran out to give you a surprise."

Marguerite, who had hastily concealed the ring in the folds of her kerchief, tried to respond gaily to the girl's impulsiveness. "Indeed, sweet one," she said with a smile, "it is delightful to have you all to myself for a whole day. You won't be bored?"

"Oh! Bored! Margot, how *can* you say such a wicked thing! Why! In the convent we were always happy to be together."

"And to talk secrets."

The two linked arms and began wandering around the garden. "Oh! How lovely your home is, Margot, darling," said Suzanne enthusiastically, "and how happy you must be!"

"Aye, indeed! I ought to be happy—oughtn't I, sweet one?" said Marguerite, with a wistful sigh.

"How sadly you say it, chérie. Ah, well, I suppose now that you are a married woman you won't care to talk secrets with me."

"And now you have one all-important secret, no?" said Marguerite. "Nay, you need not blush. Faith, he is a noble and true man, one to be proud of as a lover and . . . as a husband."

"Indeed, chérie," rejoined Suzanne softly; "it makes me very proud to hear you speak so well of him. But, of course, nothing is to be thought of until Papa is safe. . . ."

Marguerite started. Suzanne's father! The Comte de Tournay! One of those whose life would be jeopardized if Chauvelin succeeded in establishing the identity of the Scarlet Pimpernel. While Suzanne went prattling on, Marguerite's thoughts went back to the events of the past night—Armand's peril, Chauvelin's threat, and her own work in the matter. She had heard nothing more from Chauvelin. She had concluded that he had failed, and yet she had not felt anxious about Armand, because her husband had promised that Armand would be safe.

But now, suddenly, an awful horror came upon her for what she had done. She remembered how evil Chauvelin had looked when she took final leave of him after the ball. Had he already laid his plans for catching the Scarlet Pimpernel red-handed and sending him to the guillotine? Marguerite's hand convulsively clutched the ring in her kerchief.

"You are not listening, chérie," said Suzanne reproachfully.

"Yes, yes, darling—indeed I am," said Marguerite, forcing herself to smile. "Your happiness makes me so very glad. Have no fear, we will propitiate Maman. But now, tell me, what is the latest news about your father?"

"Oh!" said Suzanne with glee. "The best we could possibly hear. My Lord Hastings came to see Maman this morning. He said that we may safely expect him in England in less than four days."

"Yes," said Marguerite, whose eyes were fastened on Suzanne as she continued.

"The noble Scarlet Pimpernel himself has gone to save Papa. He was in London this morning; he will be in Calais, perhaps, to-morrow, where he will meet Papa, and then . . ."

The blow had fallen. Marguerite had expected it, though she had tried for the last half hour to delude herself. He had gone to Calais, had been in London this morning. . . . He . . . the Scarlet Pimpernel . . . Percy Blakeney . . . her husband . . . whom she had betrayed last night to Chauvelin. Oh! How could she have been so blind? She understood it all, now . . . that part he played to throw dust in everybody's eyes while he was saving people from death—and all for the love of the thing, the excitement.

Perhaps he had meant to tell her when they were first married; and then the story of the Marquis de Saint-Cyr had come to his ears and he had suddenly turned from her, thinking, no doubt, that she might someday betray him and his comrades. So he had tricked her, as he tricked all others. The mask of the inane fop had been a good one, and the part consummately well played. Even last night, when Chauvelin went to Lord Grenville's supper room to seek the Scarlet Pimpernel, he saw only the indolent Sir Percy Blakeney fast asleep on a sofa. Had his astute mind guessed the secret, then? Here lay the whole horrible puzzle. In betraying a nameless stranger in order to save her brother, had Marguerite Blakeney sent her husband to his death? No! No! No! Surely Fate could not deal a blow like that.

"But what is it, chérie?" said Suzanne, now genuinely alarmed, for Marguerite's color had become ashen. "Are you ill?"

"It is nothing, child," Marguerite murmured as in a dream. "Wait a moment. . . . You said the Scarlet Pimpernel had gone today? I must be alone a minute."

Suzanne felt her friend's trouble, and with infinite tact she did not try to pry. She was about to leave her when a groom came running toward his mistress. He carried a sealed letter. Suzanne hesitated; here perhaps was further ill news for her poor Margot.

"This has just come by runner, my lady," the groom said.

Marguerite took the letter mechanically and turned it over in her trembling fingers. "Who sent it?" she said.

"The runner said, my lady," replied the groom, "that your ladyship would understand from whom it came."

Marguerite tore open the envelope. Already her instinct had told her what it contained: it was the letter written by Armand Saint-Just to Sir Andrew Ffoulkes, which Chauvelin had held as a rod over her to enforce her obedience. Now he had kept his word—he had sent her back the compromising letter, for he was on the track of the Scarlet Pimpernel.

Marguerite's senses reeled; she tottered and would have fallen but for Suzanne's arm around her waist. With a violent effort she regained control over herself—there was much to be done.

"Bring that runner here," she said to the servant. Then she turned to Suzanne. "Chérie, I fear you must go home. Pray run in and tell my maid to prepare a traveling dress and cloak for me."

"Don't think of me," Suzanne replied. "My maid and I will go back together." Impulsively she threw her arms around Marguerite and kissed her tenderly. Then she hurried back across the lawn, overawed by the misery in her friend's face.

A minute later the groom returned, followed by the runner.

"Who gave you this packet?" asked Marguerite.

"A gentleman, my lady," replied the man, "at The Rose and Thistle, opposite Charing Cross. He said you would understand."

"At The Rose and Thistle? What was he doing?"

"He was waiting for the coach, your ladyship, which he had ordered. I understood that he was posting to Dover."

"That's enough. You may go." Then she turned to the groom: "My coach and the four swiftest horses in the stables, to be ready at once."

The groom and runner went quickly to obey. Marguerite remained standing for a moment on the lawn, her hands tightly clasped across her breast. Her lips moved as she murmured pathetically, "What's to be done? Where to find him?—O God, grant me light!"

She had done—unwittingly—a terrible thing. How could she imagine that a man who could love as Percy Blakeney had loved her once could be the brainless idiot he chose to appear? But there was no time now to go over the past. By her blindness she had sinned; now she must repay by prompt and useful action.

Percy had started for Calais utterly unconscious of the fact that his most relentless enemy was on his heels. He had set sail early that morning from London Bridge. Provided he had a favorable wind, he would no doubt be in France within twenty-four hours.

Chauvelin, on the other hand, would post to Dover, charter a vessel there, and undoubtedly reach Calais about the same time. Once in Calais, Percy would meet those who were eagerly waiting for the brave Scarlet Pimpernel to rescue them. With Chauvelin's eyes now fixed upon his every movement, Percy would thus not only be endangering his own life but that of the Comte de Tournay, and even of Armand, who had gone to meet Tournay.

These lives and that of her husband lay in Marguerite's hands; these she must save, if human pluck and ingenuity were equal to the task. Unfortunately, she could not do all this alone. Once in

Calais she would not know where to find her husband, while Chauvelin, in stealing the papers at Dover, had obtained the whole plan. Above everything, she wished to warn Percy. She knew enough about him by now to understand that he would never abandon those who trusted in him. But if he were warned he might form new plans, and he might yet succeed. Her body stiffened with firm resolution. Her eyes sparkled with joy at the thought of meeting him again soon, of sharing his dangers, of helping him, perhaps—of being with him at the last, if she failed.

Already her plans were formed. She would go and find Sir Andrew Ffoulkes first; he was Percy's friend, and Marguerite remembered with what blind enthusiasm the young man always spoke of his mysterious leader. He would help her. Her coach was ready. A change of raiment and she could be on her way. Without hesitation now she walked quietly into the house.

✺

THE FRIEND

LESS THAN HALF AN HOUR LATER Marguerite, buried in thoughts, sat inside her coach, which was bearing her swiftly to London. She had sent a courier with a respectful letter of excuse to his Royal Highness, begging for a postponement of the august visit. Then she had changed to a dark traveling costume and mantle, had provided herself with money and had started on her way.

She did not attempt to delude herself; as Chauvelin had sent her Armand's compromising letter, there was no doubt that he was quite satisfied that Percy Blakeney was the man whose death he had sworn to bring about. If Chauvelin succeeded in trapping him, his death would be at her door. His death! When she would have given willingly her life for his.

She had ordered her coach to drive her to The Crown Inn; once there she told her coachman to give the horses food and rest. Then she ordered a chair and had herself carried to the house in Pall Mall where Sir Andrew Ffoulkes lived. There she was shown into a small dining room. A moment or two later Sir Andrew appeared.

He had evidently been much startled when he heard who his visitor was, for he looked anxiously at her as he bowed.

Marguerite returned the young man's salute and began very calmly: "Sir Andrew, I have no desire to waste valuable time in much talk. Your leader and comrade, the Scarlet Pimpernel—my husband, Percy Blakeney—is in deadly peril."

Had she had the remotest doubt of the correctness of her deductions, she would have had them confirmed now, for Sir Andrew, completely taken by surprise, had grown very pale.

"No matter how I know this, Sir Andrew," she continued quietly. "Thank God that I do, and that perhaps it is not too late to save him. Unfortunately, I cannot do this alone."

"Lady Blakeney," said the young man, trying to recover himself, "I . . ."

"Will you hear me first?" she interrupted. "When the agent of the French Government stole your papers that night in Dover, he found among them certain plans to carry out the rescue of the Comte de Tournay and others. The Scarlet Pimpernel—my husband—has gone on this errand himself today. Chauvelin knows that the Scarlet Pimpernel and Percy Blakeney are the same person. He will follow him to Calais, and there will lay hands on him. You know the fate that awaits him at the hands of the revolutionary government of France. No interference from England—from King George himself—would save him. But not only that, the trusted leader will also have been unconsciously the means of revealing the hiding place of the Comte de Tournay and of all those who, even now, are placing their hopes in him."

She had spoken quietly and with resolution. Her purpose was to make that young man trust and help her, for she could do nothing without him. "You must know that I am speaking the truth, Sir Andrew," she continued. "Percy has sailed for Calais, and Chauvelin is on his track. *He* has posted for Dover and will cross the Channel, probably tonight. What do you think will happen?"

The young man was silent.

"Percy will arrive at his destination. Unconscious of being followed, he will seek out Tournay and the others—among these is my brother—not knowing that the sharpest eyes in the world are watching his every movement. The doors of the trap will close upon him and he will end his noble life upon the guillotine."

Still Sir Andrew was silent.

"You do not trust me," she said passionately. "O God! Cannot you see that I am in deadly earnest?" She seized the young man by the shoulder. "Tell me, do I look like that vilest thing on earth—a woman who would betray her own husband?"

"God forbid, Lady Blakeney, that I should attribute such evil motives to you," Sir Andrew said at last. "But will you tell me whose hand helped to guide Monsieur Chauvelin to the knowledge which you say he possesses?"

"Mine," she said quietly. "I own it—I will not lie to you, for I wish you to trust me absolutely. But I had no idea—how *could* I have—of the identity of the Scarlet Pimpernel . . . and my brother's safety was to be my prize if I succeeded."

"In helping Chauvelin to track the Scarlet Pimpernel?"

She nodded. "Armand is more than a brother to me, and . . . how *could* I guess? But we waste time, Sir Andrew, every second is precious. In the name of God! My husband is in peril. Help me to save him!"

Sir Andrew felt his position to be a very awkward one. The oath he had taken before his leader was one of obedience and secrecy, and yet this beautiful woman, who was asking him to trust her, was undoubtedly in earnest.

"Lady Blakeney," he said at last, "God knows you have perplexed me, so that I do not know which way my duty lies. Tell me what you wish me to do. There are nineteen of us ready to lay down our lives for the Scarlet Pimpernel if he is in danger."

"There is no need for lives just now, my friend," she said, "but I must know where to find him." Her eyes filled with tears. "I have owned my fault to you; shall I confess my weakness? My husband and I have been estranged, because he did not trust me, and I was too blind to understand. You must confess that the bandage which he put over my eyes was very thick. It has now fallen from my eyes. If you will not help me, Sir Andrew, I would still strive to save my husband, but I might arrive too late, and nothing would be left for you but lifelong remorse, and, for me, a broken heart."

"Lady Blakeney," said the young man simply, "you cannot possibly journey to Calais alone. If you *will* go yourself, you must command me—I await your orders."

"Listen, then. My coach is ready to take me to Dover. Follow me as swiftly as horses will take you. We meet at nightfall at The Fisherman's Rest. Chauvelin would avoid it, as he is known there. I will gladly accept your escort to Calais. We'll charter a schooner at Dover and cross over during the night. Disguised, if you agree to it, as my lackey, you will I think escape detection."

"I am entirely at your service, madame. I trust to God that you will sight the *Day Dream* before we reach Calais. With Chauvelin at his heels, every step the Scarlet Pimpernel takes on French soil is fraught with danger."

"God grant it, Sir Andrew. Farewell. We meet at Dover!"

He kissed her hand and then escorted her to her chair. A quarter of an hour later she was back at The Crown Inn, where her coach and horses were ready and waiting for her. The next moment they thundered along the London streets and on to the Dover road.

✹

SUSPENSE

IT WAS LATE INTO THE NIGHT when Marguerite reached The Fisherman's Rest. She had done the whole journey in less than eight hours, thanks to innumerable changes of horses. The arrival of Lady Blakeney alone at this extraordinary hour caused a considerable flutter. Sally jumped hastily out of bed, and Mr. Jellyband was at great pains to make his important guest comfortable; but these good folk were too well drilled to exhibit surprise.

Mr. Jellyband hastily relit the lamp, rekindled a cheerful bit of fire in the great hearth of the coffee room, and then wheeled a comfortable chair by it into which Marguerite gratefully sank.

"Will your ladyship stay the night?" asked pretty Miss Sally.

"No," replied Marguerite. "I shall not want any room but this, if I can have it to myself for an hour or two."

"It is at your ladyship's service," said honest Jellyband.

"I shall be crossing over at the first turn of the tide," said Marguerite, "and in the first schooner I can get. But my coachman and men will stay the night, and probably several days longer, so I hope you will make them comfortable."

"Yes, my lady; I'll look after them. Shall Sally bring your ladyship some supper?"

"Yes, please. Put something cold on the table, and as soon as Sir Andrew Ffoulkes comes, show him in here."

"Yes, my lady."

Honest Jellyband's face now expressed distress in spite of himself. He had great regard for Sir Percy Blakeney, and did not like to see his lady running away with Sir Andrew. Still, Lady Blakeney would pay handsomely for the accommodation, and it certainly was no business of his. Sally arranged a simple supper; then with a respectful curtsy she retired, wondering why her ladyship looked so serious when she was about to elope with her gallant.

Then commenced a period of weary waiting for Marguerite. She knew that Sir Andrew—who would have had to provide himself with clothes befitting a lackey—could not reach Dover for an hour or so. As for Chauvelin, he had been ahead of her all the time, and she wondered whether he had chartered a vessel and was now himself on the way to France. That thought gripped her heart as with an iron vise. If indeed she should be too late already!

Loneliness overwhelmed her, and Marguerite had need of all her courage through this weary waiting. The beautiful October's day had turned into a rough, cold night, and she was glad of the cheerful blaze in the hearth. As time wore on the weather became more rough, and the sound of the great breakers against the distant Admiralty Pier came to her as the noise of muffled thunder. The wind was rattling the leaded windows and the massive doors of the old house; it roared down the vast chimney.

A sudden commotion outside roused her; it was Sir Andrew Ffoulkes, and she heard Mr. Jellyband bidding him welcome. The awkwardness of her position struck Marguerite: having an assignation at this hour with a young cavalier in disguise! But there was such contrast between the seriousness of her errand and the construction which would naturally be put on her actions by honest Jellyband that, for the first time in many hours, a little smile played around her mouth. When Sir Andrew, in his lackey's garb, entered the coffee room, she was able to greet him with a merry laugh. "Faith, my lackey," she said, "I am satisfied with your appearance!"

Mr. Jellyband had followed Sir Andrew; the young gallant's disguise had confirmed his worst suspicions. Without a smile he drew the cork from the bottle of wine, set the chairs ready and prepared to wait.

"Thanks, honest friend," said Marguerite, who was still smiling at the thought of what the worthy fellow must be thinking, "we shall require nothing more; and here's for all the trouble you have been put to." And she handed him two or three gold pieces.

"Stay, Lady Blakeney," interposed Sir Andrew, as Jellyband was about to retire, "I am afraid we shall require something more of my friend Jelly's hospitality. I am sorry to say we cannot cross over tonight. There is a nasty storm blowing, the wind is dead against us, we cannot possibly sail until it has changed."

Marguerite became deadly pale. "But we must go! We must!" she repeated persistently. "Can't you find a way?"

"I have been down to the shore already," he said. "Every sailor has assured me that no one"—he looked significantly at Marguerite—"*no one* could possibly put out of Dover tonight."

Marguerite at once understood. *No one* included Chauvelin as well as herself. She nodded pleasantly to Jellyband. "Well, then, I must resign myself," she said to him. "Have you a room for me?"

"Oh, yes, your ladyship. And another for Sir Andrew."

"That's brave now, mine honest Jelly," said Sir Andrew gaily, clapping his worthy host vigorously on the back. "You unlock both those rooms, and leave our candles here on the dresser. Have no fear," he went on, no doubt guessing the worthy innkeeper's suspicions, "Sir Percy Blakeney will reward you doubly, if you see well to her ladyship's privacy and comfort."

Jellyband's countenance brightened at mention of Sir Percy's name. "I'll go and see to it at once, sir," he said with alacrity.

"Now," Marguerite said eagerly, as soon as Jellyband had gone from the room, "tell me all your news."

"There is nothing else much to tell you, Lady Blakeney," replied the young man. "The storm makes it quite impossible for us to put out of Dover tonight. But Chauvelin is in the same quandary. The sailors I spoke to all assured me that no schooner had put out of Dover for several hours; but I ascertained that a stranger had arrived by coach this afternoon, and had made some inquiries about crossing over to France."

"Then Chauvelin is still in Dover?"

"Undoubtedly."

Sir Andrew then persuaded Marguerite to partake of some supper and a little wine. He made her almost happy by talking to her about the daring escapes the brave Scarlet Pimpernel had contrived for the poor French fugitives. He even made her laugh as he described Blakeney's appearance as a hideous old market woman, in filthy cap and straggling gray locks, when the Comtesse de Tournay and her children had made their escape. Thus an hour wore on. Marguerite wondered where Percy was now. The *Day Dream* was a well-built, seagoing yacht. Perhaps she had not ventured into the open, but was lying quietly at Gravesend. Briggs was an expert skipper, and there was no danger for them from the storm.

It was long past midnight when Marguerite retired. Sleep avoided her eyes, and her thoughts were of the blackest during those long, weary hours while the storm raged which was keeping her away from Percy.

✿

CALAIS

THE WEARIEST NIGHTS, the longest days must perforce come to an end. Marguerite had spent over fifteen hours in acute mental torture. After a sleepless night, she rose early, dying to start on her journey, terrified lest further obstacles lay in her way.

Downstairs, she found Sir Andrew Ffoulkes in the coffee room. He had gone earlier to the Admiralty Pier, only to find that no vessel could put out of Dover yet. The storm was then at its fullest, and they would perforce have to wait another ten or twelve hours until the next tide, before a start could be made.

How they spent that day at Dover Marguerite could never afterward say. She and Sir Andrew sat hour after hour with nothing to do but to conjecture and only occasionally to hope.

There had been one happy interval in this weary day, when Sir Andrew went down again to the pier and presently came back to tell Marguerite that he had chartered a quick schooner whose skipper was ready to put to sea the moment the tide was favorable.

From that moment the hours seemed less wearisome. The storm slowly abated, the wind changed, and at last, at five in the afternoon, Marguerite, closely veiled and followed by Sir Andrew as her lackey, found her way to the pier. Once on board, the fresh sea air revived her; the strong breeze swelled the sails of the *Foam Crest* as she cut her way toward the open.

The sunset was glorious after the storm, and Marguerite, as she watched the white cliffs of Dover gradually disappearing from view, felt once more almost hopeful. Gradually the gray coast of France began to emerge from the fast-gathering evening mists.

Shortly after nightfall, Marguerite landed upon the French shore. She was back in that country where at this very moment men slaughtered their fellow creatures by the hundreds. The aspect of even this remote seacoast town spoke of that seething revolution, three hundred miles away, in Paris. The men wore red caps with the tricolor cockade pinned on the left-hand side. Marguerite noticed that instead of the laughing countenances habitual to her countrymen, their faces now wore a look of sly distrust.

Every man nowadays was a spy upon his fellows: the most innocent word uttered in jest might at any time be brought up as a proof of treachery against the people. All watched Marguerite as she and Sir Andrew stepped on shore, and murmured: "*Sacrés aristos!*" or "*Sacrés Anglais!*" Otherwise their presence excited no further comment, for even in these days English merchants were often to be seen on this coast. Marguerite, however, wondered how her husband's tall, massive figure could have passed through Calais unobserved, what disguise he assumed to do his noble work.

Sir Andrew led her right across the town, toward Cap Gris-Nez. The streets were narrow, tortuous and evil smelling. There had been heavy rain during the storm and sometimes Marguerite sank ankle deep in mud. But she did not heed any of these discomforts: "We may meet Blakeney at Le Chat Gris," Sir Andrew had said, and she was walking as if on rose leaves.

At last they reached their destination. Sir Andrew had walked unerringly in the dark, and had not asked his way from anyone. Le Chat Gris was evidently a small wayside inn on the outskirts of Calais, on the way to Gris-Nez. It lay some little distance from the coast, for the sound of the sea seemed to come from afar.

Sir Andrew knocked at the door, and from within Marguerite heard the muttering of oaths as shuffling steps drew near. The door was thrown open, and Marguerite found herself on the threshold of the most dilapidated, most squalid room she had ever seen in her life. The paper, such as it was, was hanging from the walls in strips; most of the chairs had broken backs, others had no seats to them; one corner of the table was propped up with a bundle of fagots. High up on one wall there was a loft before which hung a tattered blue-and-white-checked curtain. A rickety set of steps led up to it. On the filthy walls, above the torn paper, there were chalked up at intervals the words: *Liberté—Egalité—Fraternité*. An oil lamp hung from the rafters. It all looked so sordid, so dirty and uninviting, that Marguerite hardly dared to cross the threshold.

Sir Andrew, however, stepped unhesitatingly forward. "English travelers, citoyen!" he said boldly, speaking in French.

The individual who had come to the door and who, presumably, was the landlord of Le Chat Gris, was an elderly peasant dressed in a dirty blue blouse, heavy sabots, shabby blue trousers and the inevitable red cap with the tricolor cockade. He looked with suspicion at the two travelers, muttered, "Sacrés Anglais!" and spat upon the ground. But he stood aside to let them enter, well aware that these same "sacrés Anglais" always had well-filled purses.

"Oh, Lud!" said Marguerite, as she advanced into the room, holding her handkerchief to her dainty nose. "What a dreadful hole! Are you sure this is the place?"

"Aye! 'Tis the place, sure enough," replied the young man as he dusted a chair for Marguerite to sit on; "but I vow I never saw a more villainous hole."

The landlord, Brogard, took no further notice of his guests; it was not for a free citizen to show deference to anyone.

By the huge hearth sat the huddled-up figure of a woman, clad mostly in rags. She was mumbling to herself, and from time to time stirring the brew in her stockpot.

"Hey, my friend!" said Sir Andrew at last. "We should like some supper. . . . The citoyenne there," he added, pointing to the bundle of rags, "is concocting some delicious soup, I'll warrant, and my mistress has not tasted food for several hours."

"Sacrés aristos!" murmured Brogard, and once more spat upon the ground. Then he went very slowly up to a dresser, took an old pewter tureen and, without a word, he handed it to his better half, who began filling it with soup. Marguerite watched these preparations with horror.

"Faith! Our host and hostess are not cheerful people," said Sir Andrew, seeing the look on Marguerite's face. "But I think you will find the soup eatable and the wine good; these people wallow in dirt but live well as a rule."

"I pray you, Sir Andrew," she said gently, "be not anxious about me. My mind is scarce inclined to dwell on thoughts of supper."

Brogard produced a bottle of wine and some bread, and Marguerite drew her chair to the table to make some pretense at eating. Sir Andrew, as befitting his role of lackey, stood behind her chair.

"Nay, madame," he said, seeing that Marguerite seemed quite unable to eat, "I beg of you to try and swallow some food— remember you have need of all your strength."

The soup certainly was not bad; it smelled and tasted good. Marguerite might have enjoyed it but for the surroundings.

"Faith, Sir Andrew," she said. "You have need of food just as much as I have. This creature will only think that I am an eccentric

97

Englishwoman eloping with her lackey, if you'll sit down and partake of this semblance of supper beside me."

"Confound the brute!" said Sir Andrew, sitting down, as Brogard leaned against the table, smoking an evil-smelling pipe and looking down superciliously at these two sacrés Anglais.

"I pray you," said Marguerite, "keep the creature in a good temper, so that he may answer the questions we must put to him."

"I'll do my best, but, begad! I'd sooner scrag him than question him. Hey! My friend," he said pleasantly in French, "do you see many English travelers along these parts?"

Brogard puffed at his pipe, then muttered: "*Heu*—sometimes!"

"Ah!" said Sir Andrew carelessly. "English travelers always know where they can get good wine, eh, my friend? Now, tell me, my lady was desiring to know if by any chance you happen to have seen a friend of hers, a tall English gentleman, who often comes to Calais on business."

Marguerite tried not to look at Brogard, lest she should betray before him the burning anxiety with which she waited for his reply. Brogard took his time, then he said very slowly, "Tall Englishman? Today! Yes." He took Sir Andrew's hat from a chair close by, put it on his own head and generally tried to express in pantomime that the individual in question wore very fine clothes. "Sacré aristo!" he muttered. "That tall Englishman!"

"It's Sir Percy right enough," Marguerite murmured, "and not even in disguise!" She smiled at the thought of Percy running into the wildest dangers, with the latest cut coat upon his back and the laces of his jabot unruffled. "Quick, Sir Andrew!" she said. "Ask the man when he went."

"Ah, yes," said Sir Andrew, addressing Brogard, "the tall Englishman you saw was certainly my lady's friend. He has gone, you say?"

"He went, yes, but he's coming back—he ordered supper."

Sir Andrew put his hand with a quick gesture of warning upon Marguerite's arm; her mad joy would have betrayed her.

"Where is the English gentleman now?" she asked Brogard.

"He went to get a horse and cart," said Brogard.

"At what time did he go?"

But Brogard had evidently had enough of these questionings. "I don't know," he said rudely. "I have said enough, *voyons, les aristos!*" And with this parting assertion of his rights, Brogard shuffled through to the inner room with his wife, banging the door after him.

✦

HOPE

"FAITH, MADAME!" said Sir Andrew. "We shall not get anything more out of him."

"What care I," she replied lightly, "now I know that my husband is safe, and that I shall see him almost directly!"

"Hush!" he said in genuine alarm. "The very walls have ears in France these days."

He rose and walked around the squalid room, listening attentively at the door through which Brogard had disappeared. He also ran up the rickety steps to the attic, to assure himself that there were no spies about the place.

"Are we alone, monsieur my lackey?" said Marguerite gaily, as the young man once more sat down. "Faith, but you wear a glum face! *I* could dance with joy! Surely there is no longer any cause for fear. My husband will be here, under this very roof, within the next half hour perhaps, and Chauvelin has not yet arrived."

"Nay, madame; that, I fear, we do not know. I did not speak of it before, for I feared to alarm you—I saw him on the beach at Dover not five minutes before we embarked. He was disguised as a curé, and I heard him bargaining for a vessel to take him swiftly to Calais. He must have set sail less than an hour after we did."

Marguerite's face quickly lost its joy. The terrible danger in which Percy now stood became suddenly clear to her. Chauvelin was close upon his heels; here in Calais, a word from him and Percy could be tracked down and brought to the guillotine. Armand Saint-Just, the Comte de Tournay and other fugitive royalists were to have met two of the Scarlet Pimpernel's emissaries on this day, the second of October, at a place alluded to as "the Père Blanchard's hut." Armand, whose connection with the Scarlet Pimpernel was still unknown to his countrymen, had left England a little more than a week ago to convey the other fugitives to this place of safety. They would be at the appointed time and place, not knowing the danger which now awaited their brave rescuer.

Marguerite knew, too, that Sir Percy, aware that his plans had been stolen by Chauvelin and unable to communicate in time with the fugitives, would not allow his younger comrades to run the risk of almost certain capture. Hence his hurried note to them at Lord Grenville's ball—*Start myself tomorrow*. And now, his identity known, he would be tracked down by Chauvelin's emissaries to the Père Blanchard's hut, and there the trap would be closed.

There was but one hour in which to warn Percy of his danger and to persuade him to give up the expedition. She turned to Sir Andrew. "We have an hour's start of Chauvelin," she said, "and Percy will be here directly. We shall be mid-Channel ere Chauvelin has realized we have slipped through his fingers."

Sir Andrew shook his head sadly. "Faith, madame, in making your rose-colored plans you are forgetting the most important factor. Do you think that Blakeney would leave Calais without having accomplished what he set out to do? There's the Comte de Tournay, and Saint-Just, and others. . . ."

"My brother!" she said, with a sob of anguish. "Heaven help me, but I fear I had forgotten." With the sublime selfishness of a woman who loves with her whole heart, she had had no thought save for her husband.

"Sir Percy Blakeney would not be the honored leader of a score of English gentlemen," said Sir Andrew proudly, "if he abandoned those who placed their trust in him. As for breaking his word, the very thought is preposterous!"

There was silence for a moment or two. Marguerite had buried her face in her hands. The young man's heart ached for this beautiful woman in her grief.

"Faith, Sir Andrew," said Marguerite at last, drying her tears, "you are right, and I would not now shame myself by trying to dissuade him from doing his duty. God grant him strength and ability," she added fervently and resolutely, "to outwit his pursuers. But I think we should lose no time. I still believe that his safety depends upon his knowing that Chauvelin is on his track."

"Undoubtedly. As soon as he is aware of his danger he will exercise more caution; his ingenuity is a veritable miracle."

"Then, what say you to a voyage of reconnaissance while I wait here against his coming! You might come across Percy's track and thus save valuable time."

"But this is such a villainous hole for you to wait in."

"Nay, that I do not mind! But you might ask our surly host if he could let me wait in another room, where I could be safer from the prying eyes of any chance traveler. Offer him some ready money, so that he should not fail to give me word the moment the tall Englishman returns."

Sir Andrew obeyed her without further comment. He went to the door of the inner room and knocked. "Hey! Friend Brogard!" he said peremptorily. "My lady would wish to rest here awhile alone. Could you give her the use of another room?"

He took some money out of his pocket and allowed it to jingle significantly in his hand. Brogard had opened the door with surly apathy. At sight of the gold, however, he took his pipe from his mouth and shuffled in. He then pointed at the attic. "She can wait up there!" he said with a grunt. "I have no other room."

"Nothing could be better," said Marguerite in English; she at once realized the advantages such a position hidden from view would give her. "Give him the money, Sir Andrew; up there I shall be able to see everything without being seen."

"May I entreat you, madame," said Sir Andrew, "not to reveal yourself to Sir Percy, unless you are absolutely certain that you are alone with him."

"Nay," she said, "that can I faithfully promise you. I would not thus jeopardize my husband's life, nor yet his plans."

"I pray you be of good cheer, madame," said Sir Andrew. "If I do not come across Blakeney in half an hour, I shall return, expecting to find him here."

"Yes. Chauvelin cannot possibly be here before half an hour. God grant that either you or I may have seen Percy by then. Good luck to you, friend!"

Lightly she mounted the rickety wooden steps that led to the attic. Sir Andrew watched her reach the loft and pull the tattered curtains across. He noted that she was singularly well placed for seeing and hearing, while remaining unobserved. He had paid Brogard well; the innkeeper would have no object in betraying her. At the door Sir Andrew looked up once again. Through the ragged curtains Marguerite's smiling face was peeping down at him. With a final nod of farewell to her, he walked out into the night.

✿

THE CURÉ

THE NEXT QUARTER OF AN HOUR went by swiftly. Downstairs, Brogard was rearranging the table for another guest. Evidently he had a certain amount of respect for the tall Englishman, as he produced what actually looked like a tablecloth, although it was full of holes; then he got out a serviette, also old and ragged, and carefully wiped the glasses, spoons and plates. When the table was set—such as it was—Brogard surveyed it with evident satisfaction. He then dusted one of the chairs with the corner of his blouse, gave a stir to the stockpot, threw a fresh bundle of fagots onto the fire and slouched out of the room.

Marguerite was left alone with her reflections. She had spread her traveling cloak over some straw and was sitting fairly comfortably, as the straw was fresh. She was almost happy, because soon, very soon, Percy would be here, and they would be together. She would run down the ladder, and he would take her in his arms, and she would let him see that she would gladly die for him.

And then what would happen? She could not even remotely conjecture. She knew, of course, that Sir Andrew was right, that Percy would do everything he had set out to accomplish; that she could do nothing beyond warning him that Chauvelin was on his track. Then she would perforce have to see him go off upon his daring mission. She would have to wait in indescribable agony while he, perhaps, went to his death. But even that seemed less terrible to bear than the thought that he should never know how much she loved him—that at any rate would be spared her.

Suddenly her oversensitive ears caught the sound of distant footsteps drawing near; her heart gave a wild leap of joy! Was it Percy at last? No; she could hear two sets of footsteps. The next moment the door was violently thrown open from the outside, while a rough, commanding voice shouted, "Hey! Citoyen Brogard! *Holà!*"

Marguerite could not see the newcomers, but through a hole in one of the curtains she could observe a portion of the room below. She heard Brogard's shuffling footsteps; then he paused in the middle of the room, within range of her vision, looked at the strangers with withering contempt and muttered, "Sacré soutane!"

One of the newcomers took a quick step toward Brogard. He was dressed in the soutane, broad-brimmed hat and buckled shoes habitual to the French curé, but he threw open his soutane for a moment, displaying the tricolor scarf of officialism, which transformed Brogard's attitude into cringing obsequiousness.

At the sight of this curé Marguerite's heart seemed to stop beating. She could not see his face, which was shaded by his hat, but she recognized the thin, bony hands, the slight stoop, the whole gait of the man! It was Chauvelin! The awful disappointment, the dread of what was to come, made her very senses reel.

"A plate of soup and a bottle of wine," said Chauvelin imperiously to Brogard, "then clear out of here—understand?"

Silently Brogard obeyed. Chauvelin sat down at the table which had been prepared for the tall Englishman, and the innkeeper busied himself dishing up the soup and pouring out the wine. The man who had entered with Chauvelin and whom Marguerite could not see stood close by the door. Brogard hurried back to the inner room, and Chauvelin now beckoned to the other man. Marguerite at once recognized Desgas, Chauvelin's secretary, whom she had often seen in Paris in the days gone by. For a second she dreaded lest Chauvelin should order Desgas to search the place; what would happen if she were to be discovered she hardly dared to imagine.

Fortunately, however, Chauvelin seemed more impatient to talk to his secretary than afraid of spies.

"The English schooner?" he asked.

"She was lost sight of at sundown, citoyen," replied Desgas, "but was then making west, toward Cap Gris-Nez."

"Ah—good! And now, what did Captain Jutley say?"

"He assured me that all the orders you sent him last week have been implicitly obeyed. All the roads have been patrolled night and day ever since, and the beach and cliffs have been most rigorously searched and guarded."

"Does he know where this Père Blanchard's hut is?"

"No, citoyen, nobody seems to know of it. There are any amount of fishermen's huts along the coast."

"Go back to Captain Jutley and tell him to send reinforcements to the patrols, especially to those along the beach."

Chauvelin spoke curtly, and every word struck at Marguerite's heart like the death knell of her fondest hopes.

"The men," he continued, "are to keep the sharpest possible lookout tonight for any stranger who may be walking, riding or driving along the road or the beach, more especially for a tall stranger, who will probably be disguised, but he cannot conceal his height except by stooping. As soon as any of the men have sighted a stranger, two of them are to keep him in view. The man who loses sight of him will pay for his negligence with his life; but one man is to ride straight here and report to me. Is that clear?"

"Absolutely clear, citoyen," replied Desgas.

"Very well, then. Go and see Jutley at once. See the reinforcements start off, then ask him to let you have half a dozen more men and bring them here. You can be back in ten minutes. Go!"

Desgas saluted and went to the door.

As Marguerite, sick with horror, listened to Chauvelin's directions, the plan for the capture of the Scarlet Pimpernel became appallingly clear to her. Chauvelin wished that the fugitives should be left in false security, waiting in their hidden retreat until Percy joined them. Then he was to be surrounded and caught red-handed in the very act of aiding and abetting royalists, who were traitors to the Republic. Thus even the British Government could not legally protest; since he had plotted with the enemies of the French Government, France had the right to put him to death.

Desgas was about to go, but Chauvelin called him back. Marguerite could just see his face as he turned to speak to Desgas. There was at that moment such malice in it that she felt that from this man she could expect no mercy.

"I had forgotten," said Chauvelin, as he rubbed his hands with a gesture of fiendish satisfaction. "The tall stranger may show fight. No shooting, remember, except as a last resort. I want that tall stranger alive . . . if possible."

Marguerite now felt as if all that she had suffered was nothing compared with this. Chauvelin's plans were well laid—every road guarded, every corner watched, and in that lonely hut somewhere on the coast a small band of fugitives waited for their rescuer. And she, his wife, who loved him, could do nothing to help him.

Desgas departed, and Chauvelin sat closer to the table; he had taken off his hat, and Marguerite could now see his thin profile as he bent over his meager supper.

Suddenly, as she watched him, a sound caught her ear which turned her very heart to stone. And yet that sound was not calculated to inspire anyone with horror, for it was merely the sound of a gay, fresh voice singing lustily, *"God save the King!"*

✷

THE TRAP

MARGUERITE SEEMED TO FEEL her very life standing still. In the singer she had recognized her husband. Chauvelin darted a quick glance toward the door, then hurriedly clapped on his hat.

The voice drew nearer; for one brief second the wild desire seized Marguerite to rush down the steps and fly across the room, to beg the singer to fly for his life before it be too late. She checked the impulse just in time. Chauvelin would stop her before she reached the door, and, moreover, if he had soldiers within his call, her impetuous act might prove her husband's death signal.

"*Long to reign over us, God save the King,*" sang the voice more lustily than ever. The next moment the door was thrown open and there was dead silence.

Marguerite could not see the door. She held her breath, trying to imagine what was happening.

Percy Blakeney, on entering, had at once caught sight of the curé at the table; his hesitation lasted less than five seconds; the next moment Marguerite saw his tall figure crossing the room, while he called cheerfully, "Hello, there! Where's that fool Brogard?"

He wore the magnificent coat and riding suit which he had on when Marguerite last saw him at Richmond. His getup was immaculate, and he carried his eyeglass with his usual affected gesture. In fact, Sir Percy Blakeney, Bart., might have been on his way to a garden party instead of deliberately running his head into a trap set for him by his deadliest enemy.

He paused in the middle of the room; then he walked to the table and, jovially clapping the curé on the back, said in his drawly way, "Od's fish! ... er ... Monsieur Chauvelin ... I vow I never thought of meeting you here."

Chauvelin, who had been in the act of conveying soup to his mouth, fairly choked. His face became purple, and a violent fit of coughing saved the cunning representative of France from betraying boundless surprise. There was no doubt that this bold move on the part of the enemy completely nonplussed him for the moment. Blakeney had evidently guessed that he had not taken the precaution of having the inn surrounded with soldiers, and no doubt his resourceful brain would turn this unexpected interview to account.

Marguerite, paralyzed with horror, had not moved. She had made a solemn promise to Sir Andrew not to speak to her husband before strangers. To sit still and watch these two men together was a terrible trial of fortitude. She knew that if Percy now left Le Chat Gris, he could not go far without being sighted by one of Captain Jutley's patrols. On the other hand, if he stayed, then Desgas would come back with the half dozen men Chauvelin had ordered.

The two men looked a strange contrast, and of the two it was Chauvelin who exhibited a slight touch of fear. Marguerite knew

that Chauvelin would willingly have braved perilous encounters for the sake of the cause he had at heart, but what he did fear was that this impudent Englishman would, by knocking him down, double his own chances of escape; Chauvelin's underlings might not succeed so well in capturing the Scarlet Pimpernel when not directed by his shrewd brain.

Evidently, however, he had nothing to fear for the moment. Blakeney, with his most inane laugh, was patting him on the back. "I am so demmed sorry. . . . I seem to have upset you. . . . Nasty, awkward thing, soup . . . er . . . Begad! A friend of mine died once . . . er . . . choked . . . with a spoonful of soup."

And he smiled good-humoredly down at Chauvelin. "Od's life!" he continued, as soon as the latter had somewhat recovered himself. "Beastly hole this . . . ain't it now? La! You don't mind?" he added, apologetically, as he sat down and drew the soup tureen toward him. "That fool Brogard seems to be asleep."

There was a second plate on the table, and he calmly helped himself to soup, then poured himself a glass of wine. Chauvelin recovered himself and said pleasantly, "I am charmed to see you, Sir Percy. You must excuse me—h'm—I thought you the other side of the Channel. Surprise almost took my breath away."

"La!" said Sir Percy, with a grin. "It did that quite, didn't it?" He was calmly eating his soup, as if he had come all the way to Calais for the express purpose of enjoying supper at this filthy inn in the company of his archenemy.

Marguerite wondered why Percy did not knock the little Frenchman down, for every now and then his lazy eyes seemed to flash ominously as they rested on the slight figure of Chauvelin. But the keen brain, which had carried through so many daring plots, was too farseeing to take unnecessary risks. So while he ate and chatted, he thought and planned, and up in the loft the poor anxious woman racked her brains as to what she should do.

"I didn't know," Blakeney was saying jovially, "that you . . . er . . . were in holy orders."

"I . . . er . . . hem . . ." stammered Chauvelin.

"But, la! I should have known you anywhere," continued Sir

Percy, as he poured himself another glass of wine. "Although the wig and hat have changed you a bit. Begad! I hope you don't mind my having made the remark? Demmed bad form. . . ."

"No, no, not at all—hem! I hope Lady Blakeney is well," said Chauvelin, hurriedly changing the topic of conversation.

Blakeney, with much deliberation, finished his plate of soup, drank his glass of wine, and it seemed to Marguerite as if he glanced all around the room. "Quite well, thank you," he said at last, dryly. There was a pause, during which the two measured themselves against one another, and Marguerite indulged in the luxury dear to every woman's tender heart, of looking at the man she loved, in whose lazy blue eyes and behind whose foolish smile she could now so plainly see the strength, energy and resourcefulness of the Scarlet Pimpernel.

Chauvelin, who was trying to conceal his impatience, took a quick look at his watch. Desgas should not be long: another two or three minutes and this impudent Englishman would be secure in the keeping of half a dozen soldiers.

"You are on your way to Paris, Sir Percy?" he asked carelessly.

"Od's life, no," replied Blakeney with a laugh. "Only as far as Lille—beastly uncomfortable place, Paris, just now."

"Not for an Englishman like yourself, Sir Percy," rejoined Chauvelin sarcastically, "who takes no interest in the conflict that is raging there."

"La! It's no business of mine. You are in a hurry, sir," he added, as Chauvelin once again took out his watch. "An appointment, perhaps . . . I pray you take no heed of me. . . ."

He rose from the table and dragged a chair to the hearth. "Begad, sir," he continued, as Chauvelin surreptitiously looked at his watch for the third time, "that watch of yours won't go any faster. You are expecting a friend, maybe?"

"Aye—a friend!"

"Not a lady—I trust, Monsieur l'Abbé," laughed Blakeney. "Surely the holy Church does not allow? . . . Eh? But I say, come by the fire . . . it's getting demmed cold."

He kicked the logs, making them blaze. He seemed unconscious of his immediate danger. He dragged another chair to the fire, and Chauvelin, whose impatience was now beyond control, sat down beside the hearth so as to command a view of the door. Desgas had been gone nearly a quarter of an hour. It was quite plain to Marguerite that, as soon as he arrived, Chauvelin would abandon all his other plans and capture this impudent Scarlet Pimpernel at once.

"Tell me, I pray you, Monsieur Chauvelin, is your friend pretty?" the latter was saying as he carelessly strode back toward the supper table. "But I protest I need not ask."

But Chauvelin's every faculty was now concentrated on that door through which Desgas would enter. And Marguerite's ears had suddenly caught, through the stillness of the night, the sound of measured treads some distance away.

It was Desgas and his men. Another three minutes and they would be here! She dared not move; for, while she heard the soldiers approaching, she was watching Percy's every movement. He was standing by the table whereon the remnants of the supper were scattered. His back was turned to Chauvelin and he was still prattling along in his affected way, but from his pocket he had taken his snuffbox and quickly he emptied the contents of the pepper pot into it. Then he again turned with a laugh to Chauvelin: "Eh? Did you speak, sir?"

Chauvelin had been too intent on listening to the sound of those approaching footsteps to notice what his adversary had been doing. He now pulled himself together. "No," he said, "that is—as you were saying, Sir Percy?"

"I was saying," said Blakeney, going up to Chauvelin by the fire, "that my man in Piccadilly has sold me better snuff this time than I have ever tasted. Will you honor me, Monsieur l'Abbé?"

He stood carelessly holding out his snuffbox to his archenemy.

Chauvelin, who had seen a trick or two in his day, had never dreamed of this one. With one eye on the door, lulled into false security by the Englishman's airy manner, he took a pinch of snuff.

Only he who has ever by accident sniffed vigorously a dose of pepper can have the faintest conception of the hopeless condition to which it can reduce any human being. Chauvelin felt as if his head would burst—sneeze after sneeze seemed nearly to choke him; he was blind, deaf and dumb for the moment, and during that moment Blakeney quietly, without haste, took up his hat, left some money on the table and calmly stalked out of the room!

❧

THE JEW

IT TOOK MARGUERITE SOME TIME to collect her scattered senses; this last episode had taken place in less than a minute, and Desgas and the soldiers were still about two hundred yards away from Le Chat Gris. When she realized what had happened, a mixture of joy and wonder filled her heart. It all was so neat, so ingenious. Chauvelin was helpless, and his adversary had slipped through his fingers.

Blakeney was gone, obviously to try and join the fugitives at the Père Blanchard's hut. But all the roads and the beach were patrolled. How far could he go thus arrayed in his gorgeous clothes without being sighted? Now she blamed herself terribly for not having gone down to give him that word of warning and of love which, perhaps, after all, he needed. Even now she heard Desgas's voice shouting "Halt!" to his men outside the inn.

Chauvelin had partially recovered, and now he struggled to his feet. He managed to throw open the door, and before his secretary could say a word he stammered between two sneezes, "The tall stranger—quick—did any of you see him?"

"Where, citoyen?" asked Desgas in surprise.

"Here, man! Through this door! Not five minutes ago."

"We saw nothing, citoyen! The moon is not yet up, and . . ."

"And you are just five minutes too late, my friend," said Chauvelin, with concentrated fury.

Desgas turned a little pale. "He cannot go far, citoyen. Captain Jutley sent forty men as reinforcements for the patrol duty, twenty went down to the beach. No stranger could possibly reach a boat without being sighted."

"That's good. Do the men know their work?"

"They have had very clear orders, citoyen. They are to shadow— as secretly as possible—any stranger they may see."

"In no case to detain such a person, of course," said Chauvelin eagerly. "We must let that impudent Scarlet Pimpernel get to the Père Blanchard's hut now; there surround and capture him."

"The men understand that, citoyen, and also that, as soon as a stranger has been sighted, one man is to turn straight back and report to you."

"That is right," said Chauvelin, rubbing his hands.

"I have further news for you, citoyen. A tall Englishman had a conversation about three quarters of an hour ago with a Jew, Reuben by name, about hiring a horse and cart, which was to have been ready for him by eleven o'clock."

"It is past that now. Where does that Reuben live?"

"A few minutes' walk from this door."

"Send to find if the stranger has driven off in Reuben's cart."

"Yes, citoyen."

Desgas left. Every word he and Chauvelin had spoken seemed to strike at Marguerite's heart with dark foreboding. Chauvelin was moodily pacing up and down now, evidently devoured with impatience.

After about five minutes Desgas returned, followed by an elderly Jew in a dirty, threadbare gaberdine. His red hair, which he wore with corkscrew curls each side of his face, was sprinkled with gray; his cheeks and his chin were coated with grime. He had the habitual humble stoop his race had affected since before the dawn of free- dom of faith, and he walked behind Desgas with a shuffling gait.

Chauvelin motioned to the fellow to keep a respectful distance. The three men were standing just underneath the hanging oil lamp, and Marguerite had a clear view of them.

"Is this the man?" asked Chauvelin.

"No, citoyen," replied Desgas. "Reuben could not be found, but this man seems to know something which he is willing to sell for a consideration."

The Jew stood on one side, leaning on a knotted staff, his greasy, broad-brimmed hat casting a deep shadow over his face.

"The citoyen tells me," said Chauvelin curtly, "that you know something of the tall Englishman whom I desire to meet."

"Yes, your Excellency," replied the Jew, who spoke with that peculiar lisp which denotes Eastern origin, "I and Reuben Goldstein met a tall Englishman close by here this evening. He wanted to know if he could hire a horse and cart to go to a place he wanted to reach tonight."

"What did you say?"

"I did not say anything," said the Jew in an injured tone. "When I was about to offer my horse and cart, Reuben Goldstein, that accursed traitor, took the words out of my mouth, your Excellency, and offered his half-starved nag and his broken-down cart."

"And what did the Englishman do?"

"He listened to Reuben, your Excellency, and showed a handful of gold to that descendant of Beelzebub, telling him that it would be his if the horse and cart were ready by eleven o'clock."

"And the horse and cart were ready? They have started?"

"Yes, about five minutes ago. I was disgusted with that stranger's folly. He ought to have known Reuben's nag was not fit to drive. Did I not repeat to him a dozen times that my horse and cart would take him quicker, and more comfortably than Reuben's bag of bones. . . ."

"Do you happen to know which way my friend went?"

The man rubbed his dirty chin. Marguerite's heart was beating well-nigh to bursting. She watched anxiously as he slowly put his hand in his pocket and drew out a number of silver coins. He gazed at them thoughtfully, then remarked, "The tall stranger gave me twenty francs for holding my tongue about him."

Chauvelin shrugged impatiently, took a few pieces of gold out of his own pocket and allowed them to jingle in the palm of his hand. "Are there enough gold pieces in my hand to loosen your tongue?" he asked.

The Jew shot a keen glance at the gold. "What does your Excellency wish to know?"

"Whether your horse and cart can take me to where I can find the tall stranger who has driven off in Reuben Goldstein's cart."

"My horse and cart can take your Honor there, when you please."

"To a place called Père Blanchard's hut?"

"Your Honor has guessed?" said the Jew in astonishment.

"You know the place? Which road leads to it?"

"The Saint-Martin road, then a footpath to the cliffs."

Chauvelin without another word threw the gold pieces before the Jew, who knelt down and struggled to collect them. When he was again on his feet, Chauvelin said, "How soon can your horse and cart be ready?"

"They are ready now, your Honor. Not ten paces from this door. And I am sure that not two leagues from here we shall come across that wily Reuben, his nag, his cart and the tall stranger all in a heap in the middle of the road."

"If you have deceived me," said Chauvelin, "I shall tell two of my most stalwart soldiers to give you such a beating that your breath will perhaps leave your ugly body forever. But if we find the tall Englishman, on the road or at the Père Blanchard's hut, there will be ten more gold pieces for you. Do you accept the bargain?"

The Jew again rubbed his chin. He looked at the money, then at his stern interlocutor. After a pause he said deliberately, "I accept."

"Go and wait outside then," said Chauvelin, "and remember to stick to your bargain, or, by heaven, I will keep to mine."

With a final abject bow, the old man shuffled out of the room. Chauvelin seemed pleased. "My coat and boots," he said to Desgas.

Desgas went to the door and presently a soldier entered, carrying Chauvelin's coat, boots and hat. He took off his soutane, beneath which he was wearing close-fitting breeches and a cloth waistcoat, and began changing his attire.

"You, citoyen," he said to Desgas, "go back to Captain Jutley as fast as you can and tell him to let you have another dozen men, and bring them with you along the Saint-Martin road, where I daresay you will soon overtake the Jew's cart with myself in it. There will be hot work presently in the Père Blanchard's hut. We shall corner our game there, I'll warrant. They will be a band of desperate men at bay, but we shall be five against one at least.

You can follow the cart closely with your men. The Englishman is ahead of us, and not likely to look behind him."

While he gave these curt orders, he had completed his change and was once more dressed in his usual dark clothes.

"I shall have an interesting prisoner to deliver into your hands," he said with a chuckle, as he led Desgas toward the door. "We won't kill him outright, eh, friend Desgas? Choose your men well. We must see that Scarlet Pimpernel shrink and tremble, eh? . . . before we finally . . ." he made an expressive gesture, while he laughed a low, evil laugh, which filled Marguerite's soul with horror, and led his secretary finally out of the room.

✢

ON THE TRACK

NEVER FOR A MOMENT did Marguerite Blakeney hesitate. The last sounds outside Le Chat Gris had died away. She had heard Desgas giving orders to his men and then starting off toward the fort to get reinforcements. She heard the Jew's voice shouting to his nag, then the rumble of cart wheels bumping over the rough road.

Inside the inn, everything was still. Brogard and his wife, terrified of Chauvelin, had given no sign of life. Marguerite waited a moment, then quietly climbed down the broken stairs, wrapped her dark cloak closely around her and slipped out of the inn.

Thus she started on the last stage of her journey, alone, at night, and on foot. The Jew's half-starved nag could not get on very fast, and though Marguerite was weary she knew that she could keep up with it. The road lay some distance from the sea, bordered by shrubs and stunted trees bent by a perpetual wind.

Fortunately, the moon showed no desire to peep between the clouds, and Marguerite, hugging the road close to the low line of shrubs, was fairly safe from view. The air was keen and full of brine; after that enforced period of inactivity inside the squalid inn, she would have enjoyed this autumnal night and the distant melancholy moan of the waves; but her heart was too full of ache and longing. Already the few dim lights of Calais lay far behind, and on this road there was not a sign of human habitation; away on her right was the edge of the cliff, and ahead the rumble of the wheels bearing an implacable enemy to his triumph.

On ahead, jolted in the Jew's vehicle, Chauvelin was nursing comfortable thoughts. His capture of the audacious Englishman would be the finest leaf in Citoyen Chauvelin's wreath of glory. But the Jew's lean nag did little more than walk, and her driver had to give her frequent rests.

"Are we a long way yet from the footpath?" asked Chauvelin after a time.

"Not very far, your Honor," was the placid reply.

"We have not yet come across your friend and mine, lying in a heap in the roadway," was Chauvelin's sarcastic comment.

"Patience, noble Excellency, they are ahead of us. I can see the imprint of the cart wheels, driven by that son of the Amalekite. Hark! What was that?" said the Jew suddenly.

Through the stillness there could now be heard distinctly the sound of horses' hoofs on the muddy road.

"Stop a moment, I want to hear," said Chauvelin.

Marguerite had also heard the galloping hoofs. She had been on the alert, thinking Desgas and his squad would soon overtake them, but this came from the opposite direction. She trembled in every limb; for she had guessed what news these horsemen would bring. Had the tall stranger been sighted at last?

The cart had come to a standstill; Marguerite slipped nearer to it in the darkness. She heard the challenge: "Liberté, Egalité, Fraternité!" then Chauvelin's quick query: "What news?"

Two men on horseback had halted beside the vehicle. And now, behind her, some distance off, Marguerite could hear the measured tread of a body of advancing men: Desgas and his soldiers.

"You have seen the stranger?" Chauvelin eagerly asked the two mounted men.

"No, citoyen, but about a couple of leagues from here, on the cliffs, we saw what looked like the wooden hut of a fisherman, where he might keep his nets. At first we thought there was nothing suspicious about it, until we saw some smoke issuing through an aperture at the side. I dismounted and climbed down to it. It was then empty, but in one corner of the hut there was a charcoal fire. We decided that my comrades should take cover with the horses, and that I should remain on watch."

"Well! And did you see anything?"

"About half an hour later I heard voices, and two men came along the edge of the cliff. One was young, the other quite old."

Marguerite's heart almost stopped beating as she listened. Was the young one Armand and the old one Tournay?

"The two men climbed down the cliffs and went into the hut," continued the soldier, "and I crept nearer to it then. The hut is roughly built, and I caught snatches of their conversation."

"Yes? What did you hear?"

"The old man asked the young one if he were sure that was the right place. 'Oh, yes,' he replied, ''tis the place sure enough. Here is the plan which he gave me before I left London. We were to adhere strictly to it unless I had contrary orders.'"

"Well—and?" asked Chauvelin impatiently.

"There were six of us patrolling that part of the beach, so we thought it best that four should remain and keep the hut in sight, and I and my comrade rode back at once to report."

"There is not a moment to lose," said Chauvelin savagely. "You say that hut is two leagues from here? You can find it again?"

"I have absolutely no doubt, citoyen," replied the soldier firmly.

"Fall in behind then. Let your comrade take both your horses back to Calais. You won't want them. Keep beside the cart, and show the Jew where to drive."

While Chauvelin spoke, Desgas and his men were fast approaching. Behind the shrubs at the edge of the road, Marguerite seemed suddenly to have lost all faculty even for suffering: her heart, her nerves, her brain were numb after all the hours of ceaseless anguish culminating in this awful despair. For now there was not the faintest hope. Within two short leagues of this spot the fugitives were waiting for their brave deliverer, and presently he would join them. Then two dozen men, led by one whose hatred was as deadly as his cunning, would close around them. They would all be captured.

Armand, according to Chauvelin's pledged word, would be restored to her, but her adored husband, Percy, would fall into the hands of a remorseless enemy.

Desgas and his men came up and fell in behind the cart, and they all started down the dark road. Marguerite waited until they were well ahead; then she, too, in the darkness which suddenly seemed to have become more intense, crept noiselessly along.

✣

THE PÈRE BLANCHARD'S HUT

As IN A DREAM, Marguerite followed on. Despairingly she gazed around her into the darkness, and wondered whence her husband would presently come, to fall into the deathtrap. Her feet were sore. Her knees shook under her. For days she had lived in a wild turmoil of excitement; she had not had a quiet rest for three nights; now she had walked for more than two hours, and yet her determination never swerved for a moment.

Suddenly her ears told her that the cart had stopped and that the soldiers had halted. No doubt somewhere close was the footpath that led to the edge of the cliff and the hut. Chauvelin and Desgas, followed by the soldiers, turned sharply to the right, apparently onto the footpath. The Jew remained on the road with his cart.

Marguerite, with infinite caution, crawling on her hands and knees, also turned off to the right through the rough shrubs, tearing her face and hands against the dry twigs, intent only upon hearing without being seen or heard. The footpath was bordered by a low hedge, behind which was a dry ditch filled with coarse grass. In this Marguerite managed to find shelter; she was quite hidden from view, yet could contrive to get within three yards of where Chauvelin stood giving orders to his men. What little chance she yet had of being useful to Percy consisted in hearing absolutely every word of his enemy's plans.

"Now," Chauvelin was saying, "where is the Père Blanchard's hut?"

"About eight hundred meters from here, along the footpath,"

said the soldier who had lately been directing the party, "and halfway down the cliff."

"Very good. You shall lead us. You shall creep down first to the hut, as noiselessly as possible, and ascertain if the traitor royalists are there. Do you understand?"

"I understand, citoyen."

"Now listen attentively, all of you," continued Chauvelin. "You who have crept up to the hut will peep inside. If a tall Englishman is there with those two traitors, or a man who stoops as if he would disguise his height, then give a sharp whistle as a signal to your comrades. All of you then quickly surround and rush into the hut and seize the men there, before they have time to draw their fire-arms; if any of them struggle, shoot at their legs or arms, but on no account kill the tall man. He is probably also very strong; it will take four or five of you to overpower him."

There was a little pause, then Chauvelin said, "If the royalist traitors are still alone, then warn your comrades, and all of you take cover around the hut and wait until the tall Englishman arrives; then only rush the hut, when he is safely within its doors. But remember, you must be silent. I do not wish those royalists to be on the alert—the firing of a pistol or a call on their part would be sufficient to warn the tall personage to keep clear, and," he added emphatically, "it is the tall Englishman whom it is your duty to capture tonight."

"You shall be implicitly obeyed, citoyen."

"Then get along, and I will follow you."

"What about the Jew, citoyen?" asked Desgas, as, silently, like shadows, the soldiers began to creep along the narrow footpath.

"Ah, yes!" said Chauvelin, turning toward the road. "Here, you . . . whatever your confounded name may be."

"Benjamin Rosenbaum, so it please your Honor," he replied humbly.

"It does not please me to hear your voice, but it does please me to give you certain orders, which you will find it wise to obey. You shall stay here with your horse and cart until our return. You are on no account to utter the faintest sound, and if, when I do return,

I do not find you here, I most solemnly assure you that I shall find you and punish you. Do you hear me?"

"I hear, your Honor," protested the Jew, "and I swear by Abraham, Isaac and Jacob that I would obey your Honor most absolutely, but I am a poor old man; my nerves are not as strong as those of a young soldier. If midnight marauders should come prowling around this lonely road, I might scream or run in my fright! Is my life to be forfeit for that which I cannot help?"

The Jew seemed in real distress; he was shaking from head to foot. And he spoke truly; he might, in sheer terror, utter the shriek that might prove a warning to the wily Scarlet Pimpernel.

Chauvelin reflected for a moment. "Well, you lazy old coward," he said at last, "we shall want you to drive back the wounded presently, so you had better shuffle along behind us. Here, Citoyen Desgas, tie this handkerchief tightly around the fellow's mouth."

Chauvelin handed a scarf to Desgas, and meekly Benjamin Rosenbaum allowed himself to be gagged. He evidently preferred this to being left alone on the dark Saint-Martin road. Then the three men fell in line, and their footsteps soon died away along the path.

Marguerite had not lost a single word of Chauvelin's commands, but for the moment she could do nothing but follow him and the soldiers. She feared to lose her way, or she would have rushed forward and found that wooden hut, and perhaps been in time to warn the fugitives and their brave deliverer.

The thought flashed through her mind to shriek a warning to the Scarlet Pimpernel and his friends—in the wild hope that they would yet have time to escape. But she was still far from the cliff; her effort might be premature, and she would never be allowed another.

Like a ghost, then, she flitted noiselessly behind the hedge: she had taken her shoes off, and her stockings were by now torn off her feet. She felt no soreness; indomitable will to reach her husband killed all sense of bodily pain within her. Suddenly, the moon, which had proved a friend to her by remaining hidden behind a bank of clouds, emerged and flooded the weird and lonely landscape with a rush of brilliant light. Two hundred yards ahead was the edge of the cliff, and below, stretching away to free and happy

England, the sea rolled on smoothly and peaceably. Marguerite's gaze rested for an instant on the silvery waters, and her numbed heart softened and her eyes filled with hot tears: not two miles away a graceful schooner lay in wait. Marguerite had guessed rather than recognized her. It was the *Day Dream*, Percy's yacht; her sails, glistening in the moonlight, conveyed a message to Marguerite of joy and hope which yet she feared could never be. She waited for her master like a beautiful white bird ready to take flight.

The sight of the schooner seemed to infuse into the poor wearied woman the superhuman strength of despair. There was the edge of the cliff, and some way below was the hut where, presently, her husband would meet his end. But the moon was out; she could see her way, now: she would locate the hut, run to it and warn them.

She stumbled on behind the hedge in the thick grass of the ditch. She must have outdistanced Chauvelin and Desgas, for presently she reached the edge of the cliff, and heard their footsteps behind her. She peeped down the great rugged cliffs—the descent would be easy enough, as they were not precipitous—and she saw on her left, about midway down, a rough wooden construction through the walls of which a tiny red light glimmered like a beacon. At once she began the descent, creeping from boulder to boulder, caring nothing for the enemy behind or for the soldiers, who evidently had all taken cover, since the tall Englishman had not yet appeared. On she pressed, stumbling, half dazed . . . when, suddenly, a crevice, or slippery bit of rock, threw her violently to the ground. She struggled to her feet and started forward once more. But now steps quicker than her own were close at her heels. The next instant a hand dragged at her skirt and she was on her knees, while something was wound around her mouth to prevent a scream.

Bewildered, half frantic, she looked around helplessly. Quite close to her she saw a pair of keen, malicious eyes. She knelt in the shadow of a great boulder; Chauvelin could not see her features, but he passed his thin, white fingers over her face.

"A woman!" he whispered. "By all the saints in the calendar. I wonder now . . ." After a few seconds of deadly silence he gave a long, low, curious chuckle, while again Marguerite felt, with a horrible shudder, his fingers wandering over her face. "Dear me!" he whispered, with affected gallantry. "This is indeed a charming surprise," and her hand was raised to Chauvelin's mocking lips.

The situation was indeed grotesque, had it not been at the same time so tragic: the weary woman receiving on her knees the banal gallantries of her deadly enemy. Half choked with the bandage around her mouth, full of blank despair, she had no strength to move or to utter the faintest sound. Then she felt herself lifted, and a pair of strong arms carried her toward that tiny red light which she had looked upon as the last glimmer of hope.

For a few moments she lost all notion of time and space. When she once more became conscious, she felt that she was placed upon a man's coat, with her back resting against a rock. The moon was hidden again behind some clouds, and the darkness seemed intense. The sea was roaring some two hundred feet below her, and she could no longer see the glimmer of red light.

That the end of the journey had been reached, she gathered from the rapid questions and answers whispered quite close to her.

"There are four men in there, citoyen; they seem to be waiting."

"The hour?"

"Nearly two o'clock."

"The tide?"

"Coming in quickly."

"The schooner?"

"Obviously an English one, lying some three kilometers out. But we cannot see her boat."

"Have the men taken cover? They will not blunder?"

"They will not stir until the tall Englishman comes, then they will surround and overpower the five men."

"Right. And the lady?"

"Still dazed, I fancy. She's close beside you, citoyen."

"And the Jew?"

"He's gagged, and his legs and arms strapped."

"Good. Now get close to the hut and leave me to look after the lady."

Marguerite heard Desgas creeping away along the stony cliffs,

then she felt a pair of thin, talonlike hands take both of her own and hold them in a grip of steel.

"Before that handkerchief is removed from your pretty mouth, fair lady," whispered Chauvelin close to her ear, "I think it right to give you one small word of warning. What has procured me the honor of being followed across the Channel by so charming a companion I cannot, of course, conceive, but I think that I am right in surmising that the first sound which your pretty lips would utter, as soon as the cruel gag is removed, would perhaps be a warning to the cunning man whom I have been at such pains to track down."

He paused a moment, while the steellike grasp seemed to tighten around her wrist. "Inside that hut, if I am not mistaken," he went on, "your brother, Armand Saint-Just, waits with that traitor Tournay and two other men for the arrival of the Scarlet Pimpernel. No doubt if you scream, if there is a scuffle, if shots are fired, the same long legs that brought this scarlet enigma here will as quickly take him to some place of safety. The purpose, then, for which I have traveled all these miles will remain unaccomplished. On the other hand, it only rests with yourself that your brother shall be free to go with you tonight, to any place of safety."

Marguerite could not utter a sound, but no doubt her hand gave a responsive appeal to this last suggestion, for presently Chauvelin continued, "What I want you to do to ensure Armand's safety is a very simple thing, dear lady. It is to remain on this spot, without uttering a sound, until I give you leave to speak. Ah! But I think you will obey," he added, as Marguerite seemed to stiffen, "for if you utter one sound, or attempt to move from here, my men will seize Saint-Just, Tournay and their two friends, and shoot them here before your eyes."

Marguerite had listened to her enemy's speech with increasing terror. She yet had sufficient mental vitality to realize the full horror of this "either-or." It meant that she should keep still and allow the husband she worshiped to walk unconsciously to his death, or that she should, by trying to give him a word of warning, give the signal for her own brother's death, and that of three other men.

"Nay, fair lady," Chauvelin added urbanely, "you can have no interest in anyone save Saint-Just, and all you need do for his safety is to remain where you are, and to keep silent. My men have strict orders to spare him in every way. As for that enigmatic Scarlet Pimpernel, what is he to you? Now, dear lady, let me remove this unpleasant coercion from your pretty mouth. You see, I wish you to be perfectly free in the choice which you are about to make."

Chauvelin removed the handkerchief. She certainly did not scream; she had not strength to do anything but sit upright, her temples aching, her nerves paralyzed, and to force herself to think. The minutes flew on. More and more unreal did the whole situation seem. It was impossible that she, Marguerite Blakeney, the queen of London society, should be sitting here on this bit of lonely coast in the middle of the night side by side with a bitter enemy. And oh! It was not possible that, not many hundred feet away, the being who became more and more dear was walking to his doom.

Why did she not scream out a warning to him to retrace his steps? Oh! That fiend in human shape next to her knew human—female—nature well. He had gauged her very thoughts to a nicety. She could not give that signal—for she was weak, and she was a woman. How could she deliberately order Armand to be shot before her eyes? Suddenly from somewhere, not very far away, a cheerful, strong voice was heard singing, *"God save the King!"*

✦

THE SCHOONER

MARGUERITE'S ACHING HEART stood still. She felt, more than she heard, the men on watch preparing for the fight.

The voice came nearer; in the vast immensity of these lonely cliffs it was impossible to say how near or yet from which direction came that cheerful singer who sang to God to save his king, while he himself was in such deadly danger. The voice grew louder. Marguerite heard the click of Desgas's gun close to her. . . .

No! No! No! O God in heaven! This cannot be! Let Armand's blood then be upon her head! But, O God! Save him whom she loved at any cost!

With a wild shriek, she sprang to her feet and darted around the rock. She saw the hut, ran up and fell against it, hammering with clenched fists while she shouted, "Armand! Armand! For God's sake fire! Your leader is near! He is betrayed!"

She was seized and thrown to the ground. She lay there, bruised but still half sobbing, half shrieking, "Percy, my husband, for God's sake fly! Armand! Why don't you fire?"

"One of you stop that woman screaming," hissed Chauvelin.

Something was thrown over her face; she could not breathe, and perforce she was silent. The bold singer, too, had become silent, warned, no doubt, by Marguerite's frantic shrieks. The men had sprung to their feet.

Chauvelin, with a muttered oath, hastily shouted, "Into it, my men, and let no one escape from that hut alive!"

The moon had again emerged from between the clouds, shedding once more a brilliant, silvery light. The soldiers rushed to the rough wooden door of the hut. It was partially open; one of the soldiers pushed it farther; within, the charcoal fire gave only a dim red light. The soldiers paused. Chauvelin, who was prepared for vigorous resistance from the four fugitives, was for the moment paralyzed with astonishment when he saw the soldiers standing there, while not a sound proceeded from the hut.

Filled with foreboding, he too went to the door, and peering into the gloom he asked quickly, "What is the meaning of this?"

"I think, citoyen, that there is no one there now," replied one of the soldiers imperturbably.

"You have not let those four men go?" thundered Chauvelin. "I ordered you to let no man escape alive! Quick, after them!"

The men rushed down the rocky incline toward the beach.

"You and your men will pay with your lives for this blunder, citoyen sergeant," said Chauvelin viciously.

"You ordered us to wait, citoyen, until the tall Englishman arrived and joined the four men in the hut. No one came," said the sergeant sullenly.

"But I ordered you just now, when the woman screamed, to rush in and let no one escape."

"But, citoyen, the four men who were there before had been gone some time, I think. . . ."

"And you let them go. . . ." said Chauvelin furiously.

"You ordered us to obey your commands on pain of death," protested the sergeant. "I heard the men creep out of the hut not many minutes after we took cover, and long before the woman screamed."

"Hark!" said Desgas suddenly.

In the distance the sound of firing was heard. Chauvelin tried to peer along the beach below, but the fitful moon once more hid her light and he could see nothing. "One of you go into the hut and strike a light," he stammered at last.

Stolidly the sergeant obeyed: he lit the small lantern he carried in his belt from the charcoal fire in the hut. Then he came back. "They went straight down the cliff," said the sergeant, "then disappeared behind some boulders."

"Hush! What was that?"

All three men listened attentively. In the far distance could be heard faintly the splash of oars.

"The schooner's boat!" Chauvelin gasped.

Evidently Armand Saint-Just and his three companions had managed to creep along the side of the cliffs while the well-drilled soldiers had with blind obedience obeyed Chauvelin's orders—to wait for the tall Englishman, who was the important capture. The fugitives had no doubt reached one of the points which jut far out to sea on this coast at intervals; behind this, the boat of the *Day Dream* must have been on the lookout for them; and they were by now safely on the way to the British schooner.

Presently the dull boom of a gun was heard from out at sea.

"The schooner, citoyen," said Desgas quietly. "She's off."

It needed all Chauvelin's presence of mind not to give way to useless rage. There was no doubt now that once again that accursed British head had completely outwitted him. How he had contrived to reach the hut without being seen by one of the soldiers was more than Chauvelin could conceive. That he had done so before his men had arrived on the cliff was, of course, fairly clear, but how he had come over in Reuben Goldstein's cart without being sighted by the patrols was impossible of explanation. It really seemed as if some potent Fate watched over that daring Scarlet Pimpernel.

But Chauvelin and his men had heard that hated voice singing *God save the King* fully half an hour after they had taken cover around the hut; by that time the four fugitives must have reached the point, and the nearest point was a mile from the hut. Where had the singer got to? He could not have covered that mile on a rocky cliff in five minutes; and only five minutes had elapsed between his song and the sound of the boat's oars away at sea. He must have remained behind and was even now hiding somewhere about the cliffs. Chauvelin felt hopeful once again, just as one of the men who were slowly working their way up the cliff reached his side.

"We were too late, citoyen," the soldier said. "When we got to the beach the boat was already making quickly for the schooner. We fired after her, but it was no good. She must have shoved off some minutes before the woman began to scream."

Some minutes before the woman began to scream! Then the Scarlet Pimpernel was still on shore, and all the roads were patrolled. All was not yet lost. "Bring the light in here!" Chauvelin commanded as he entered the hut.

The sergeant brought his lantern, and with a rapid glance Chauvelin noted the contents of the place: the caldron containing the last dying embers of charcoal, a couple of stools, the fisherman's tools and nets lying in one corner, and beside them something small and white. It was a crumpled piece of paper, evidently forgotten there by the fugitives. "Pick that up and read it, sergeant," said Chauvelin curtly.

The sergeant picked up the paper and, by the light of his lantern, began deciphering the few hastily scrawled words.

"I cannot reach you without risking your lives and endangering your rescue. When you receive this, wait two minutes, then creep out of the hut one by one, turn to your left and creep cautiously down the cliff; keep to the left till you reach the first rock, which you see jutting far out to sea—behind it in the cove the boat is on the lookout for you—give a long whistle—she will come up—my men will row you to the schooner. Once on board the *Day Dream* send the boat back for me. I shall be at the point which is in a direct line opposite Le Chat Gris near Calais as soon as possible. My men know it. They must wait for me at a safe distance offshore, till they hear the usual signal.

Then there is the signature, citoyen," added the sergeant.

One phrase of the momentous scrawl had caught Chauvelin's ear: *I shall be at the point which is in a direct line opposite Le Chat Gris near Calais.* That phrase might yet mean victory for him.

"Which of you knows this coast well?" he shouted to his men, who now were assembled once more around the hut.

"I do, citoyen," said one of them. "I was born in Calais, and know every stone of these cliffs."

"There is a point in a direct line from Le Chat Gris?"

"There is, citoyen. I know it well."

"The Englishman is hoping to reach that point. He does *not* know every stone of these cliffs; there is a chance to get him yet. A thousand francs to each man who gets to that point before that long-legged Englishman."

"I know a shortcut across the cliffs," said the soldier, and with an enthusiastic shout he started to climb upward, followed by his comrades.

Desgas stood close to Chauvelin, waiting for further orders, while two soldiers knelt beside the prostrate form of Marguerite. Chauvelin gave his secretary a vicious look. His well-laid plan had failed, its sequel was problematical; there was still a chance that the Scarlet Pimpernel might escape, and Chauvelin was longing to vent his rage on somebody.

Marguerite lay in a dead swoon. Her eyes were circled by deep purple lines, her hair matted and damp, her lips parted in physical pain. The elegant and fashionable Lady Blakeney presented a pathetic picture, which would have appealed to any but the vengeful heart of her baffled enemy.

"It is no use mounting guard over a woman who is half dead," he said spitefully to the soldiers, "when you have allowed five men who were very much alive to escape."

The soldiers rose to their feet.

"Where is the Jew?" asked Chauvelin.

"Close by here, citoyen," said Desgas.

From the immediate vicinity, a plaintive moan reached Chauvelin's ears. His secretary led the way to the other side of the hut where, with his legs tightly pinioned together and his mouth gagged, lay the unfortunate Benjamin Rosenbaum. His face in the silvery light of the moon was ghastly with terror and his whole body was trembling. The rope around his shoulders and arms had given way, but he had not made the slightest attempt to move from the place where Desgas had originally put him.

"Remove the gag," Chauvelin commanded Desgas.

Chauvelin felt exceedingly vicious, and this son of a despised race would prove an excellent butt. When his order had been obeyed, he said with biting sarcasm to the wretched old man, "I suppose you have a good memory for bargains?"

"Yes, your Honor," stammered poor Benjamin.

"You remember, then, the one you and I made together, that you would overtake Reuben Goldstein and my friend the tall stranger?"

"Y . . . yes . . . your Honor!"

"What was the bargain?" The unfortunate man said nothing. "I must needs refresh your memory," said Chauvelin sarcastically. "It was agreed that if we overtook my friend the tall stranger before he reached this place, you were to have ten pieces of gold."

A low moan escaped from the Jew's trembling lips.

"But," added Chauvelin, with slow emphasis, "if you deceived me in your promise, you were to have a sound beating."

"Your Honor . . ." the Jew ventured imploringly.

"You did not fulfill your share of the bargain, but I am ready to fulfill mine." Turning to the soldiers, Chauvelin said, "The buckle end of your two belts to this confounded Jew."

As the soldiers unbuckled their heavy leather belts, the Jew set up a great howl.

"I think I can rely on you, citoyen soldiers," said Chauvelin maliciously, "to give him the soundest beating he has ever experienced. But don't kill him," he added dryly.

"We will obey, citoyen," replied the soldiers.

"When that lumbering coward has had his punishment," Chauvelin said to Desgas, "the men can drive us in the cart back to Calais. The Jew and the woman can look after each other," he added roughly, "until we can send somebody for them in the morning. They can't run away very far, in their present condition."

Chauvelin had not given up all hope. But he felt less sure now: the Englishman's audacity had baffled him once, while the wooden-headed stupidity of the soldiers and the interference of a woman had turned his winning hand into a losing one. The howls of the Jew behind him, undergoing his punishment, sent a balm through his heart, overburdened as it was with vengeful malice.

He turned and took a last look at the lonely bit of coast where stood the wooden hut, the scene of the greatest discomfiture ever experienced by a leading member of the Committee of Public Safety. Against a rock lay the unconscious figure of Marguerite Blakeney, while farther on the unfortunate Jew was receiving on his broad back the blows of two stout leather belts, wielded by two sturdy soldiers of the Republic. The howls of Benjamin Rosenbaum were fit to make the dead rise from their graves.

"That will do," commanded Chauvelin, as the fellow's moans became more feeble, "we don't want to kill him."

Obediently the soldiers buckled on their belts, one of them viciously kicking the old man to one side.

"Leave him there," said Chauvelin. "Lead the way to the cart."

He walked up to Marguerite and looked down into her face. She was recovering consciousness and making feeble efforts to rise. Her blue eyes were looking around her with terror; they rested with a mixture of horror and pity on the Jew; then she caught sight of Chauvelin. He stooped and raised her icy hand to his lips.

"I much regret, fair lady," he said in his most suave tones, "that circumstances over which I have no control compel me to leave you here for the moment. But our friend Benjamin, though a trifle the worse for wear, will prove a gallant defender of your fair person, I have no doubt. At dawn I will send an escort for you."

Marguerite only had the strength to turn her head away. Her

heart was broken with anguish. One awful thought had returned to her mind: What has become of Percy? What of Armand?

"I myself," concluded Chauvelin, "must now leave you. Au revoir, fair lady."

And with a last ironical smile and bow he disappeared up the footpath in the wake of the soldiers, followed by Desgas.

✦

THE ESCAPE

ALL NATURE WAS SO STILL that Marguerite, lying with her ear close to the ground, could distinctly trace the sound of their retreating footsteps, and presently the faint echo of cart wheels. How long she lay there she knew not. Dreamily she looked up at the moonlit sky and listened to the monotonous roll of the waves. Her brain only remained conscious of its intolerable torture of uncertainty.

She did not know whether Percy was even now in the hands of the soldiers of the Republic. She did not know, on the other hand, whether Armand's lifeless body did not lie there in the hut, while Percy had escaped only to hear that his wife had guided the human bloodhounds to the murder of Armand and his friends. The physical pain of utter weariness was so great that she hoped her tired body could rest here forever. All was so solitary, so silent.

Suddenly . . . a sound . . . the strangest, undoubtedly, that these lonely cliffs of France had ever heard, broke the silence. So strange a sound was it that Marguerite thought that the approach of death was playing a weird trick on her half-sleeping senses.

It was the sound of a good, solid, absolutely British *damn!*

The sea gulls in their nests awoke and looked around in astonishment; the tall cliffs frowned down at the unheard-of sacrilege.

Half raising herself on her hands, Marguerite strained every sense to see or hear, to know the meaning of this very earthly sound. Then she heard it again and this time her heart stood still; she looked around her, not daring to trust to her other sense.

"Od's life! But I wish those demmed fellows had not hit quite so hard!"

This time it was unmistakable; only one pair of essentially British lips could have uttered those words in sleepy, affected tones.

"Zounds!" said those same British lips emphatically. "But I'm as weak as a rat!"

In a moment Marguerite was on her feet. Once again she heard the same very earthly sounds of good, honest British language, not the least akin to whisperings from paradise. She looked eagerly at the tall cliffs, the lonely hut. Somewhere above or below her, hidden from her longing eyes, must be the owner of that beloved voice.

"Percy! Percy!" she shrieked hysterically, tortured between doubt and hope. "Come to me! Where are you? Percy!"

"It's all very well calling me, m'dear!" said the same sleepy, drawly voice. "But od's life, those demmed Frogeaters have trussed me like a goose on a spit, and I can't get away."

And still Marguerite did not realize whence came that voice, so drawly, so dear, but, alas! with a strange accent of weakness. There was no one within sight . . . except by that rock. . . . Great God! . . . The Jew! . . . Was she mad or dreaming?

His back was against the pale moonlight, he was half crouching, trying vainly to raise himself, with his legs tightly pinioned. Marguerite ran up to him, took his head in both her hands . . . and looked straight into a pair of blue eyes, good-natured, even a trifle amused—shining out of the distorted mask of the Jew.

"Percy! . . . Percy! . . . My husband!" she gasped, faint with the fullness of her joy. "Thank God! Thank God!"

"La, m'dear!" he rejoined good-humoredly. "We will both do that anon, if you think you can loosen these demmed ropes."

Her fingers were numb and weak, but she worked away with her teeth while great welcome tears poured from her eyes.

"Od's life!" he said. "But I marvel whether an Englishman ever allowed himself to be licked by a demmed foreigner and made no attempt to give as good as he got."

It was obvious that he was exhausted from sheer physical pain, and when at last the rope gave way he fell in a heap against the rock. Marguerite looked helplessly around. "Oh, for a drop of water!" she cried in agony, seeing that he was ready to faint.

"Nay, m'dear," he murmured with a smile. "I should prefer a drop of good French brandy! If you'll dive in the pocket of this dirty garment, you'll find my flask. . . ."

He forced Marguerite to drink some brandy, too.

"La! That's better now, eh, little woman!" he said with a sigh of satisfaction. "Heigh-ho! But this is a queer rig-up for Sir Percy Blakeney, Bart., to be found in by his lady, and no mistake. Begad! I must look a disgusting object. As for these curls . . ."

And laughingly he took off the disfiguring wig and stretched out his long limbs, which were cramped from many hours' stooping. Then he bent forward and looked long and searchingly into his wife's blue eyes.

"Percy," she whispered, while a deep blush suffused her delicate cheeks and neck, "if you only knew . . ."

"I do know, dear . . . everything," he said with infinite gentleness.

"And can you ever forgive?"

"I have naught to forgive, sweetheart; your heroism, your devotion, which I, alas! so little deserved, have more than atoned for that unfortunate episode at the ball."

"Then you knew?" she whispered. "All the time . . ."

"Yes," he replied tenderly. "I knew . . . all the time. . . . But begad! Had I but known what a noble heart yours was, my Margot, I should have trusted you, and you would not have had to undergo the terrible sufferings of the past hours."

They were sitting side by side against a rock, and he had rested his head on her shoulder. She certainly now deserved the name of "the happiest woman in Europe."

"It is a case of the blind leading the lame, sweetheart, is it not?" he said with his good-natured smile of old. "Od's life! But I do not know which are the more sore, my shoulders or your little feet." He bent forward to kiss them, for they peeped out through her torn stockings and bore pathetic witness to her endurance and devotion.

"But Armand . . ." she said, with sudden terror and remorse, as the image of her brother rose now before her.

"Have no fear for Armand, sweetheart," he said tenderly. "He and the others are even now on board the *Day Dream*."

"But how?" she gasped. "I do not understand."

"Yet 'tis simple enough, m'dear. When I found that that brute Chauvelin meant to stick to me like a leech, I thought the best thing I could do was to take him along with me. I had to get to Armand and the others somehow, and all the roads were patrolled. I knew that when I slipped through Chauvelin's fingers at Le Chat Gris he would lie in wait for me here. I wanted to keep an eye on him, and a British head is as good as a French one any day."

Indeed it had proved to be infinitely better, and Marguerite was filled with joy as he recounted the daring manner in which he had snatched the fugitives from under Chauvelin's very nose.

"Dressed as the old Jew," he said gaily, "I knew I should not be recognized. I had met Reuben Goldstein in Calais earlier in the evening. For a few gold pieces he supplied me with this rig-out and his cart and nag and undertook to bury himself out of sight."

"But if Chauvelin had discovered you," she gasped.

"Od's fish!" he rejoined quietly. "Then the game would have been up. I could but take the risk. I know human nature pretty well by now, and when I heard Chauvelin giving his orders to the soldiers, I reckoned on their blind obedience. Chauvelin had ordered them, on pain of death, not to stir until the tall Englishman came. Desgas had thrown me down close to the hut; the soldiers took no notice of the Jew. I managed to free my hands. I always carry pencil and paper with me, and I hastily scrawled a few important instructions; then I crawled to the hut under the very noses of the soldiers, dropped my little note through a chink in the wall, and waited. In this note I told the men to creep out of the hut and down the cliffs, keep to the left until they came to the first point, to give a certain signal, when the boat of the *Day Dream* would pick them up. They obeyed implicitly. The soldiers who saw them were equally obedient to Chauvelin's orders. They did not stir! I waited for nearly half an hour; when I knew that the men were safe I gave the signal which caused so much ado."

And that was the whole story. It seemed so simple, and Marguerite could but marvel at the wonderful ingenuity, the boundless audacity which had carried out this daring plan.

"But those brutes struck you!" she gasped in horror.

"Well, that could not be helped," he said gently. "I had to remain here by my little wife's side."

Marguerite laughed. It was so good to be beside him, to hear his cheery voice, to watch the twinkle in his blue eyes. Suddenly, however, she started. She had heard a stealthy footfall overhead, and a stone rolled down from the top of the cliffs.

"What's that?" she whispered in alarm.

"Oh, nothing, m'dear!" he said with a laugh. "Only a trifle you have forgotten. . . . My friend, Ffoulkes. . . ."

"Sir Andrew!" she gasped.

Indeed, she had wholly forgotten the devoted friend and companion who had stood by her during all these hours of anxiety and suffering. She remembered him now with a pang of remorse.

"Aye! You had forgotten him, m'dear," said Sir Percy merrily. "Fortunately, I met him not far from Le Chat Gris, before I had that interesting supper party with my friend Chauvelin. . . . I told him of a long, circuitous road which Chauvelin's men would never suspect, that would bring him here just about now, when we are ready for him. He was not in the way when I did not want him, and now he arrives in the nick of time. Ah! He will make pretty little Suzanne a most admirable and methodical husband."

In the meanwhile Sir Andrew Ffoulkes had cautiously worked his way down the cliffs. "Blakeney!" he ventured to say cautiously. "Blakeney! Are you there?"

The next moment he rounded the rock against which Sir Percy and Marguerite were leaning, and seeing the weird figure clad in the Jew's gaberdine he paused in sudden bewilderment. But already Blakeney had struggled to his feet.

"Here I am, friend," he said. "Though I do look a begad scarecrow in these demmed things."

"Zooks!" ejaculated Sir Andrew as he recognized his leader. "Of all the . . ." The young man had seen Marguerite, and happily checked the forcible language that rose to his lips at sight of the exquisite Sir Percy in this dirty garb.

"Yes!" said Blakeney calmly. "Of all the . . . hem! . . . My friend!

I have not yet had time to ask you what you were doing in France. Insubordination? Wait till my shoulders are less sore and, begad, see the punishment you'll get."

"Od's fish! I'll bear it," said Sir Andrew with a merry laugh, "seeing that you are alive to give it. . . . Would you have had me allow Lady Blakeney to do the journey alone?"

"Now you are here, Ffoulkes," said Sir Percy, with sudden earnestness, "we must lose no more time: that brute Chauvelin may send someone to look after us."

At mention of Chauvelin's name Marguerite started in alarm. "But how can we get back!" she gasped. "The roads are full of soldiers between here and Calais and . . ."

"We are not going back to Calais, sweetheart," he said, "but just the other side of Gris-Nez, not half a league from here. The boat of the *Day Dream* will meet us there."

"The boat of the *Day Dream?*"

"Yes!" he said, with a merry laugh. "Another little trick of mine. I should have told you before that when I slipped that note into the hut, I also added another for Armand, which I directed him to leave behind, and which has sent Chauvelin and his men running back full tilt to Le Chat Gris after me; but the first little note contained my real instructions, including those to old Briggs. He had my orders to go farther toward the west. Then he will send the galley to a little cove just beyond Gris-Nez. The men will look out for me—and we will all be safely aboard while Chauvelin and his men watch the point which is 'just opposite Le Chat Gris.'"

"The other side of Gris-Nez? But I . . . I cannot walk, Percy."

"I will carry you, dear," he said simply.

Sir Andrew was ready, too, to help, but Sir Percy would not entrust his beloved to any arms but his own.

"When you and she are both safely on board the *Day Dream*," he said to his young comrade, "then it will be my turn to rest."

And his arms closed around Marguerite and lifted her gently. His shoulders must have been very sore, but the man seemed made of steel, his energy almost supernatural. It was a tramp of half a league along the cliffs, but never for a moment did he yield to fatigue. On he tramped with his precious burden, and . . . no doubt, as she lay, quiet and happy, watching the pleasant, cheerful face with the lazy blue eyes, she whispered many things which helped to shorten the road.

Dawn was breaking when at last they reached the point beyond Gris-Nez. The galley lay in wait; in answer to a signal from Sir Percy she drew near, and two sturdy British sailors had the honor of carrying my lady into the boat. Half an hour later they were on board the *Day Dream*. Armand Saint-Just, Tournay and the other fugitives were eagerly awaiting their rescuer; he would not stay to hear their gratitude, but found his way to his private cabin, leaving Marguerite in the arms of her brother.

Everything on board the *Day Dream* was fitted with that luxury so dear to Sir Percy Blakeney's heart, and by the time they all landed at Dover he had changed into the sumptuous clothes which he loved. The difficulty was to provide Marguerite with a pair of shoes, and great was one little middy's joy when my lady found that she could put foot on English shore in his best pair.

The rest is silence! Silence and joy for those who had endured so much suffering, yet found at last a great and lasting happiness. But it is on record that at the brilliant wedding of Sir Andrew Ffoulkes, Bart., with Mlle. Suzanne de Tournay de Basserive, a function at which H.R.H. the Prince of Wales and all the elite of fashionable society were present, the most beautiful woman there was unquestionably Lady Blakeney, while the clothes Sir Percy Blakeney wore were the talk of the jeunesse dorée of London for many days.

It is also a fact that M. Chauvelin, the accredited agent of the French Republican Government, was not present at that or any other social function in London after that memorable evening at Lord Grenville's ball.

The Adventures of
TOM SAWYER

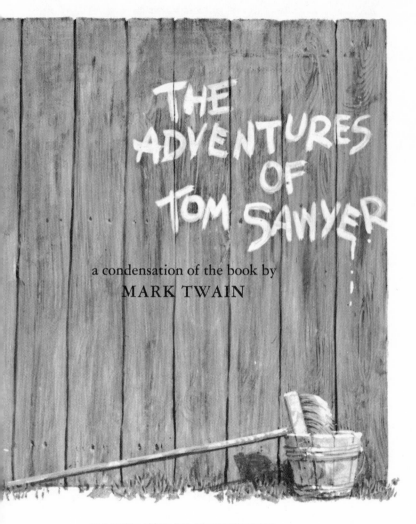

THE ADVENTURES OF TOM SAWYER

a condensation of the book by

MARK TWAIN

ILLUSTRATED BY JOHN FALTER

FOR TOM SAWYER, adventure was always just around the corner. Sometimes, tired of being the respectable boy his kindly but harassed Aunt Polly felt he should be, he sneaked out in the dark of night to seek excitement with his wonderful *un*respectable friend, Huck Finn. Sometimes adventure came to him by accident—when he witnessed a murder in a lonely cemetery, was surprised by "ghosts" in a haunted house, and got lost in a labyrinthine cave with the bewitching Becky Thatcher. His was a joyous life, filled with feuds and friendships, with crazy jokes, narrow escapes and splendid schemes.

Mark Twain, author of this classic story of American boyhood, said in a preface to the 1876 edition: "Most of the adventures recorded in this book really occurred: one or two were experiences of my own, the rest those of boys who were schoolmates of mine. Huck Finn is drawn from life; Tom Sawyer also, but not from an individual—he is a combination of the characteristics of three boys whom I knew. . . . The odd superstitions touched upon were all prevalent among children and slaves in the West at the period of this story."

Born in Florida, Missouri, in 1835, Mark Twain grew up in Hannibal, a sleepy little town on the banks of the Mississippi River very like Tom's St. Petersburg. His real name was Samuel Langhorne Clemens; and he took his pen name from the call of the steamboat hands that meant "two fathoms" on the sounding line. In his long and varied career he was a printer, a steamboat pilot, a silver miner, a journalist, and finally a successful writer and lecturer.

Mark Twain traveled far from Hannibal, and the mane of white hair that characterized him in his later years was as well known in Vienna and London as in the cities of the United States. He died, at the age of seventy-five, in his home in Redding, Connecticut. But when one thinks of him today, one thinks of the Middle West before the Civil War, of *The Adventures of Tom Sawyer*, of its equally famous sequel, *The Adventures of Huckleberry Finn*, and of *Life on the Mississippi*, in all of which a way of life now past is vividly immortalized.

CHAPTER I

"Tom!"

No answer.

"Tom!"

No answer.

"What's gone with that boy, I wonder? You TOM!"

No answer.

The old lady pulled her spectacles down and looked over them about the room; then she put them up and looked out under them. She seldom or never looked *through* them for so small a thing as a boy; they were her state pair, the pride of her heart, and were built for "style," not service—she could have seen through a pair of stove lids just as well. She looked perplexed, and then said, not fiercely but still loud enough for the furniture to hear:

"Well, I lay if I get hold of you I'll—"

She did not finish, for by this time she was punching under the bed with the broom, and needed breath to punctuate the punches with. She resurrected nothing but the cat.

"I never did see the beat of that boy!" She went to the open door and lifted up her voice: "Y-o-u-u *Tom!*"

There was a slight noise behind her and she turned just in time to seize a small boy by the slack of his roundabout. "There! I might 'a' thought of that closet. What you been doing in there?"

"Nothing."

"Nothing! Look at your hands. And your mouth. What *is* that truck?"

"*I* don't know, Aunt."

"Well, *I* know. It's jam. Forty times I've said if you didn't let that jam alone I'd skin you. Hand me that switch."

The switch hovered in the air—the peril was desperate—

"My! Look behind you, Aunt!"

The old lady whirled round. The lad fled, on the instant, scrambled up the high board fence and disappeared over it. His Aunt Polly stood surprised a moment, and then broke into a laugh.

"Hang the boy, can't I never learn anything? Ain't he played me tricks enough like that for me to be looking out for him by this time? But my goodness, he never plays tricks alike, two days, and how is a body to know what's coming? And he 'pears to know that if he can put me off for a minute or make me laugh, it's all down again and I can't hit him a lick. I ain't doing my duty by that boy, and that's the truth. But laws-a-me! He's my own dead sister's boy, and I ain't got the heart to lash him, somehow. Every time I let him off, my conscience does hurt me so, and every time I hit him my old heart 'most breaks. Now he'll play hookey this afternoon, and I'll be obleeged to make him work tomorrow to punish him. It's mighty hard to make him work Saturdays, but he hates work more than he hates anything else, and I've *got* to do some of my duty by him or I'll be the ruination of the child."

Tom did play hookey, and he had a very good time. He got back home barely in season to help Jim, the small colored boy, split the kindlings before supper—at least he was there in time to tell his adventures to Jim while Jim did three fourths of the work. Tom's younger brother (or rather, half brother), Sid, was already through with his part of the work (picking up chips), for he was a quiet boy, and had no adventurous, troublesome ways.

While Tom was eating his supper, Aunt Polly asked him questions that were full of guile, and very deep—for she wanted to trap him into damaging revealments. Said she:

"Tom, it was powerful warm in school today, warn't it?"

"Yes'm."

"Didn't you want to go in a-swimming, Tom?"

A bit of a scare shot through Tom—a touch of uncomfortable suspicion. He searched Aunt Polly's face, but it told him nothing. So he said, "No'm—well, not very much."

The old lady reached out and felt Tom's shirt, and said, "But you ain't too warm now, though." It flattered her to reflect that she had discovered that the shirt was dry without anybody knowing that that was what she had in her mind. But in spite of her, Tom knew where the wind lay, now. So he forestalled what might be the next move:

"Some of us pumped on our heads—mine's damp yet. See?"

Aunt Polly was vexed to think she had overlooked that bit of circumstantial evidence. Then she had a new inspiration: "Tom, you didn't have to undo your shirt collar where I sewed it, to pump on your head, did you? Unbutton your jacket!"

The trouble vanished out of Tom's face. He opened his jacket. His shirt collar was securely sewed.

"Bother! Well, go 'long with you. I'd made sure you'd played hookey and been a-swimming. But I forgive ye, Tom. I reckon you're a kind of a singed cat, as the saying is—better'n you look. *This* time." She was half sorry her sagacity had miscarried, and half glad that Tom had stumbled into obedient conduct for once.

But Sidney said, "Well, now, if I didn't think you sewed his collar with white thread, but it's black."

"Why, I did sew it with white! Tom!"

But Tom did not wait for the rest. As he went out at the door he said, "Siddy, I'll lick you for that."

In a safe place Tom examined two large needles which were thrust into the lapels of his jacket, and had thread bound about them—one needle carried white thread and the other black. He said, "She'd never noticed if it hadn't been for Sid. Confound it! Sometimes she sews it with white, and sometimes with black. I wish to geeminy she'd stick to one or t'other—*I* can't keep the run of 'em. But I'll lam Sid for that. I'll learn him!"

Within two minutes, or even less, he had forgotten all his

troubles. Not because his troubles were one whit less heavy and bitter to him than a man's are to a man, but because a powerful new interest bore them down and drove them out of his mind for the time—just as men's misfortunes are forgotten in the excitement of new enterprises. This new interest was a valued novelty in whistling, which he had just acquired and was suffering to practice. It consisted in a peculiar birdlike turn, a sort of liquid warble, produced by touching the tongue to the roof of the mouth at short intervals. Diligence and attention soon gave him the knack of it, and he strode down the street with his mouth full of harmony.

The summer evenings were long. It was not dark, yet. Presently Tom checked his whistle. A stranger was before him—a boy a shade larger than himself. A newcomer of any age or either sex was an impressive curiosity in the poor little village of St. Petersburg. This boy was well dressed, too—well dressed on a weekday. This was simply astounding. His cap was a dainty thing, and his close-buttoned blue cloth roundabout was new and natty. He had shoes on—and it was only Friday. He had a citified air about him that ate into Tom's vitals. The more Tom stared at the splendid marvel, the higher he turned up his nose at his finery and the shabbier and shabbier his own outfit seemed to him to grow. Neither boy spoke. If one moved, the other moved—but only sidewise, in a circle; they kept face to face and eye to eye all the time. Finally Tom said, "I can lick you!"

"I'd like to see you try it."

"Well, I can do it."

"No you can't, either."

"Yes I can."

"You can't."

"Can!"

"Can't!"

An uncomfortable pause. Then Tom said, "What's your name?"

"'Tisn't any of your business."

"Well I 'low I'll *make* it my business."

"Well why don't you?"

"If you say much, I will."

"Much—much—*much*. There now."

"Oh, you think you're mighty smart, *don't* you? Smarty! Oh, what a hat!"

"You can lump that hat if you don't like it."

"By jingo! For two cents I'd lick you till you couldn't stand up."

The new boy took two coppers out of his pocket and held them out with derision. Tom struck them to the ground. In an instant both boys were rolling and tumbling in the dirt, gripped together like cats, and for the space of a minute they tugged and tore at each other's hair and clothes, punched and scratched each other's noses, and covered themselves with dust and glory. Presently the confusion took form, and through the fog of battle Tom appeared, seated astride the new boy, and pounding him with his fists.

"Holler 'nuff!" said he.

The boy only struggled to free himself. He was crying—mainly from rage.

"Holler 'nuff!"—and the pounding went on.

At last he got out a smothered "'Nuff!" and Tom let him up and said, "Now that'll learn you. Better look out who you're fooling with next time."

The new boy went off, snuffling, and occasionally looking back and threatening what he would do to Tom "next time." To which Tom responded with jeers. As soon as his back was turned the new boy snatched up a stone, threw it and hit him between the shoulders and then turned tail and ran like an antelope. Tom chased the traitor home, and thus found out where he lived. He then held a position at the gate for some time, daring the enemy to come outside, but the enemy only made faces at him through the window. At last the enemy's mother appeared, and called Tom a bad, vicious, vulgar child and ordered him away. So he went away, but he "'lowed" to "lay" for that boy.

He got home pretty late that night, and when he climbed cautiously in at the window, he uncovered an ambuscade in the person of his aunt; and when she saw the state his clothes were in her resolution to turn his Saturday holiday into captivity at hard labor became adamantine in its firmness.

CHAPTER II

SATURDAY MORNING WAS COME, and all the summer world was bright and fresh. There was a song in every heart; and if the heart was young the music issued at the lips. There was cheer in every face and a spring in every step. The locust trees were in bloom and their fragrance filled the air. Cardiff Hill, beyond the village and above it, was green with vegetation and seemed a Delectable Land, dreamy, reposeful and inviting.

Tom appeared on the sidewalk with a bucket of whitewash and a long-handled brush. He surveyed the fence, and all gladness left him. Thirty yards of board fence nine feet high. Life seemed hollow, existence but a burden. Sighing, he dipped his brush and passed it along the top; repeated the operation; did it again; compared the insignificant whitewashed streak with the far-reaching continent of unwhitewashed fence, and sat down on a tree box discouraged. Jim came skipping out at the gate with a tin pail, singing "Buffalo Gals." Bringing water from the town pump had always been hateful work in Tom's eyes, before, but now he remembered that there was company at the pump. Boys and girls were always there waiting their turns, trading playthings, quarreling, skylarking. And he remembered that although the pump was only a hundred and fifty yards off, Jim never got back with a bucket of water under an hour. Tom said:

"Say, Jim, I'll fetch the water if you'll whitewash some."

Jim shook his head and said, "Can't, Marse Tom. Ole Missis, she say she spec' Marse Tom gwine to ax me to whitewash, an' so she tole me go 'long an' 'tend to my own business."

"Oh, never you mind what she said, Jim. Gimme the bucket— *She* won't ever know."

"Oh, I dasn't, Marse Tom."

"Jim, I'll give you a marvel. I'll give you a white alley!"

Jim began to waver.

"White alley, Jim! And it's a bully taw."

"My! Dat's a mighty gay marvel, *I* tell you! But Marse Tom—"

"And besides, if you will I'll show you my sore toe."

Jim was only human—this attraction was too much for him. He put down his pail and bent over the toe with interest while the bandage was being unwound. In another moment he was flying down the street with his pail and a tingling rear, Tom was whitewashing with vigor and Aunt Polly was retiring from the field with a slipper in her hand and triumph in her eye.

But Tom's energy did not last. He began to think of the fun he had planned for this day, and his sorrows multiplied. Soon the free boys would come tripping along on all sorts of delicious expeditions, and they would make a world of fun of him for having to work. He got out his worldly wealth and examined it—bits of toys, marbles and trash; enough to buy an exchange of *work*, maybe, but not half enough to buy so much as half an hour of pure freedom. So he returned his straitened means to his pocket, and gave up the idea of trying to buy the boys. At this dark moment a magnificent inspiration burst upon him!

He took up his brush and went tranquilly to work. Ben Rogers hove in sight presently—the very boy, of all boys, whose ridicule he had been dreading. Ben's gait was the hop-skip-and-jump—proof enough that his heart was light and his anticipations high. He was eating an apple, and giving a long, melodious whoop, at intervals, followed by a deep-toned ding-dong-dong, ding-dong-dong, for he was personating a steamboat. As he drew near he slackened speed, took the middle of the street, leaned far over to starboard and rounded to ponderously—for he was personating the *Big Missouri*, and considered himself to be drawing nine feet of water. He was boat and captain and engine bells combined, so he had to imagine himself standing on his own hurricane deck giving the orders and executing them:

"Stop her, sir! Ting-a-ling-ling! Ship up to back! Ting-a-ling-ling! Set her back on the stabboard! Ting-a-ling-ling! Chow! Ch-chow-wow! Chow!" His right hand, meantime, describing stately circles.

Tom went on whitewashing—paid no attention to the steamboat. Ben stared a moment and then said, "Hi-*yi!* *You're* up a stump, ain't you!"

No answer. Tom surveyed his last touch with the eye of an artist, then he gave his brush another gentle sweep and surveyed the result, as before. Ben ranged up alongside of him. Tom's mouth watered for the apple, but he stuck to his work. Ben said, "Say—*I'm* going in a-swimming, *I* am. Don't you wish you could? But of course you'd druther *work*—wouldn't you?"

Tom contemplated the boy a bit, and said, "What do you call work?"

"Why, ain't *that* work?"

Tom resumed his whitewashing and answered carelessly, "Well, maybe it is, and maybe it ain't. All I know is, it suits Tom Sawyer."

"Oh come, now, you don't mean to let on that you *like* it?"

The brush continued to move.

"Like it? Well, I don't see why I oughtn't to like it. Does a boy get a chance to whitewash a fence every day?"

That put the thing in a new light. Ben stopped nibbling his apple. Tom swept his brush daintily back and forth—stepped back to note the effect—added a touch here and there—criticized the effect again—Ben watching every move. Presently he said, "Say, Tom, let *me* whitewash a little."

Tom considered. "No—no—I reckon it wouldn't hardly do, Ben. You see, Aunt Polly's awful particular about this fence— right here on the street, you know— It's got to be done very careful. I reckon there ain't one boy in a thousand can do this fence the way it's got to be done."

"Oh come, now—I'd let *you*, if you was me."

"Ben, I'd like to, honest injun; but Aunt Polly—well, Jim wanted to do it, but she wouldn't let him; Sid wanted to do it, and she wouldn't let Sid. If you was to tackle this fence and anything was to happen to it—"

"Oh, shucks, I'll be just as careful. Now lemme try. Say—I'll give you the core of my apple."

"Well, here— No, Ben, I'm afeard—"

"I'll give you *all* of it!"

Tom gave up the brush with reluctance in his face, but alacrity in his heart. And while the late steamer *Big Missouri* worked and sweated in the sun, the retired artist sat on a barrel in the shade close by, dangled his legs, munched his apple and planned the slaughter of more innocents. There was no lack of material; boys happened along every little while; they came to jeer, but remained to whitewash. By the time Ben was fagged out, Tom had traded the next chance to Billy Fisher for a kite; and when *he* played out, Johnny Miller bought in for a dead rat and a string to swing it with—and so on. And when the middle of the afternoon came, from being a poverty-stricken boy in the morning, Tom was literally rolling in wealth. He had, beside the things before mentioned, twelve marbles, part of a Jew's harp, a fragment of chalk, a glass stopper of a decanter, a tin soldier, a kitten with one eye, a brass doorknob, a dog collar—but no dog—four pieces of orange peel and a dilapidated old window sash. He had had a nice, good, idle time all the while—plenty of company—and the fence had three coats of whitewash on it! If he hadn't run out of whitewash, he would have bankrupted every boy in the village.

Tom had discovered a great law of human action, without knowing it—namely, that in order to make a man or a boy covet a thing, it is only necessary to make the thing difficult to attain. If he had been a great philosopher, like the writer of this book, he would have comprehended that Work consists of whatever a body is *obliged* to do, and that Play consists of whatever a body is not obliged to do. And this would help him to understand why constructing artificial flowers or performing on a treadmill is work, while rolling tenpins or climbing Mont Blanc is only amusement.

The boy mused awhile over the substantial change which had taken place in his worldly circumstances, and then wended toward headquarters to report. Aunt Polly was knitting by an open window in a pleasant rearward apartment, which was bedroom, breakfast room, dining room and library combined. She had thought that of course Tom had deserted long ago, and she wondered at seeing him place himself in her power again in this intrepid way. He said, "Mayn't I go and play now, Aunt?"

"What, a'ready? How much have you done?"

"It's all done, Aunt."

"Tom, don't lie to me—I can't bear it."

"I ain't, Aunt; it *is* all done."

Aunt Polly went out to see for herself; and she would have been content to find twenty percent of Tom's statement true. When she found the entire fence not only whitewashed but elaborately coated and recoated, her astonishment was almost unspeakable. She said, "Well, I never! There's no getting round it, you *can* work when you're a mind to, Tom. Well, go 'long and play; but mind you get back sometime in a week, or I'll tan you."

She was so overcome by the splendor of his achievement that she took him into the closet and selected a choice apple and delivered it to him, along with an improving lecture upon the added value and flavor a treat took to itself when it came through virtuous effort. And while she closed with a happy scriptural flourish, he "hooked" a doughnut. Then he skipped out over the fence and was gone. There was a gate, but as a general thing he was too crowded for time to make use of it.

Skirting the block, Tom hastened toward the public square of the village, where two "military" companies of boys had met for conflict, according to appointment. Tom was General of one of these armies, Joe Harper (a bosom friend) General of the other. These two great commanders did not condescend to fight in person, but sat together on an eminence and conducted the field operations by orders delivered through aides-de-camp. Tom's army won a great victory, after a hard-fought battle. Then the dead were counted, prisoners exchanged, the terms of the next disagreement agreed upon and the day for battle appointed; after which the armies marched away, and Tom turned homeward alone.

As he was passing by the house where Jeff Thatcher lived, he saw a new girl in the garden—a lovely little blue-eyed creature with yellow hair plaited into two long tails, white summer frock and embroidered pantalets. The fresh-crowned hero fell without firing a shot. A certain Amy Lawrence vanished out of his heart and left not even a memory of herself behind. He had regarded his passion for Amy as adoration; he had been months winning her; he had been the proudest boy in the world only seven short days, and here in one instant of time she had gone out of his heart like a casual stranger whose visit is done.

He worshiped this new angel with furtive eye, till he saw that she had discovered him; then he pretended he did not know she was present, and began to "show off" in all sorts of absurd ways, in order to win her admiration. While he was in the midst of some dangerous gymnastic performances, he saw that the little girl was wending her way toward the house. Tom came up to the fence and leaned on it, grieving. But his face lit up, right away, for she tossed a pansy over the fence a moment before she disappeared.

The boy ran around and stopped within a foot of the flower, and then shaded his eyes with his hand and began to look down the street as if he had discovered something of interest going on in that direction. Presently he began trying to balance a straw on his nose, with his head tilted far back; and as he moved from side to side, in his efforts, he edged nearer and nearer to the pansy; finally his bare foot rested upon it, his pliant toes closed upon it, and he hopped away with the treasure and disappeared round the corner. There he buttoned the flower inside his jacket, next his heart—or next his stomach, possibly, for he was not much posted in anatomy, and not hypercritical, anyway.

Finally he returned home, with his head full of visions. All through supper his spirits were so high that his aunt wondered "what had got into the child." He tried to steal sugar under his aunt's very nose, and got his knuckles rapped for it. He said, "Aunt, you don't whack Sid when he takes it."

"Well, Sid don't torment a body the way you do."

Presently she stepped into the kitchen, and Sid, happy in his immunity, reached for the sugar bowl—a sort of glorying over Tom which was well-nigh unbearable. But Sid's fingers slipped and the bowl dropped and broke. Tom was in ecstasies, but he controlled his tongue and was silent. He said to himself that even when his aunt came in he would sit perfectly still till she asked who did it; and then he would tell, and see that pet model "catch it." He was

full of exultation when the old lady came back and stood above the wreck discharging lightnings of wrath. He said to himself, Now it's coming! And the next instant he was sprawling on the floor! The potent palm was uplifted to strike again when Tom cried out, "Hold on, now, what're you belting *me* for? Sid broke it!"

Aunt Polly paused, perplexed, and Tom looked for healing pity. But when she got her tongue again, she only said, "Umf! Well, you didn't get a lick amiss, I reckon. You been into some other audacious mischief when I wasn't around, like enough."

Then her conscience reproached her, and she yearned to say something kind and loving; but she judged that this would be construed into a confession that she had been in the wrong, and discipline forbade that. So she kept silence, and went about her affairs with a troubled heart. Tom sulked in a corner and exalted his woes. He knew that in her heart his aunt was on her knees to him, and he was morosely gratified. He knew that a yearning glance fell upon him, now and then, through a film of tears, but he refused recognition of it. He pictured himself lying sick unto death and his aunt bending over him beseeching one little forgiving word, but he would turn his face to the wall, and die with that word unsaid. Ah, how would she feel then? And he pictured himself brought home from the river, dead, with his curls all wet, and his sore heart at rest. How she would throw herself upon him, and how her tears would fall like rain, and her lips pray God to give her back her boy! And such a luxury to him was this petting of his sorrows, that he could not bear to have any worldly cheeriness intrude upon it; it was too sacred for such contact; and so, presently, when his cousin Mary danced in, all alive with the joy of seeing home again after an agelong visit of one week to the country, he got up and moved in clouds and darkness out at one door as she brought song and sunshine in at the other.

He wandered far from the accustomed haunts of boys, and sought desolate places in harmony with his spirit. A log raft in the river invited him, and he seated himself on its edge and contemplated the dreary vastness of the stream, wishing he could be drowned, all at once and unconsciously, without undergoing the uncomfortable routine devised by nature. Then he got out his flower, rumpled and wilted, and wondered if *she* would pity him if she knew? At last he rose up sighing and departed in the darkness.

About ten o'clock he came along the deserted street to where the Adored Unknown lived. A candle was casting a dull glow upon the curtain of a second-story window. Was the sacred presence there? He climbed the fence, threaded his stealthy way through the plants, till he stood under that window; he looked up at it with emotion; then he laid him down on the ground under it, disposing himself upon his back, with his hands clasped upon his breast and holding his poor wilted flower. And thus he would die—with no shelter over his homeless head, no loving face to bend pityingly over him when the great agony came! And thus *she* would see him when she looked out upon the glad morning!

The window went up, a maidservant's discordant voice profaned the holy calm, and a deluge of water drenched the martyr's remains! The strangling hero sprang up with a relieving snort. There was a whiz as of a missile in the air, mingled with the murmur of a curse, a sound as of shivering glass followed, and a small, vague form went over the fence and shot away in the gloom.

CHAPTER III

THE SUNDAY SUN ROSE upon a tranquil world and beamed down upon the village like a benediction. Breakfast over, Aunt Polly had family worship; it began with a prayer built from the ground up of solid courses of scriptural quotations, welded together with a thin mortar of originality; and from the summit of this she delivered a grim chapter of the Mosaic law, as from Sinai.

Then Tom girded up his loins, so to speak, and went to work to "get his verses." Sid had learned his lesson days before. Tom bent all his energies to the memorizing of five verses, and he chose part of the Sermon on the Mount, because he could find no verses that were shorter. At the end of half an hour he had a vague general idea of his lesson, but no more, for his mind was traversing the whole field of human thought, and his hands were busy with distracting recreations. Mary took his book to hear him recite, and he tried to find his way through the fog:

"Blessed are the—a—a—"

"Poor—"

"Yes—poor. Blessed are the poor—a—a—"

"In spirit—"

"In spirit. Blessed are the poor in spirit, for they—they—"

"*Theirs*—"

"For *theirs*. Blessed are the poor in spirit, for *theirs* is the kingdom of heaven. Blessed are they that mourn, for they—they—"

"S, h, a—"

"For they s, h— Oh, I don't know what it is!"

"*Shall!*"

"Oh, *shall!* For they shall—a—a—shall *what?* Why don't you tell me, Mary?"

"Oh, Tom, you poor thickheaded thing, you must go learn it again. Don't be discouraged, Tom, you'll manage it—and if you do, I'll give you something nice."

"All right! What is it, Mary? Tell me what it is."

"Never you mind, Tom. You know if I say it's nice, it *is* nice."

"You bet you that's so, Mary. All right, I'll tackle it again."

And he did "tackle it again"—and under the double pressure of curiosity and prospective gain, he did it with such spirit that he accomplished a shining success. Mary gave him a brand-new Barlow knife worth twelve and a half cents; and the delight that swept his system shook him to his foundations. True, the knife would not cut, but it was a "sure enough" Barlow, and Tom contrived to scarify the cupboard with it, and was arranging to begin on the bureau, when he was called off to dress for Sunday school.

Mary gave him a tin basin of water and a piece of soap, and he went outside with it. Then Mary got out a suit of his clothing that had been used only on Sundays during two years—they were simply called his "other clothes"—and so by that we know the size of his wardrobe. The girl "put him to rights" after he had more or less washed and dressed himself; she buttoned his roundabout up to his chin, turned his vast shirt collar down over his shoulders, brushed him off and crowned him with his speckled straw hat. He now looked exceedingly improved and uncomfortable. He hoped that Mary would forget his shoes, but the hope was blighted; she brought them out. He lost his temper and said he was always being made to do everything he didn't want to do. But Mary said, persuasively, "Please, Tom—that's a good boy."

So he got into the shoes, snarling. Mary was soon ready, and the three children set out for Sunday school—a place that Tom hated with his whole heart; but Sid and Mary were fond of it. Sunday school was from nine to half past ten; and then church service.

The church was a small, plain affair, with a sort of pine-board tree box on top of it for a steeple. At the door Tom dropped back a step and accosted a comrade. "Say, Billy, got a yaller ticket?"

"Yes."

"What'll you take for her?"

"What'll you give?"

"Piece of lickrish and a fishhook."

"Let's see 'em."

Tom exhibited. They were satisfactory, and the property changed hands. Then Tom traded a couple of white alleys for three red tickets, and some small trifle or other for a couple of blue ones. He waylaid other boys as they came, and went on buying tickets of various colors ten or fifteen minutes longer. He entered the church, now, with a swarm of clean and noisy boys and girls, proceeded to his seat and started a quarrel with the first boy that came handy. The teacher, a grave, elderly man, interfered; then turned his back a moment and Tom pulled a boy's hair in the next bench. Tom's whole class were of a pattern—restless, noisy, and troublesome.

When they came to recite their lessons, not one of them knew his verses perfectly. However, they worried through, and each got his reward—in small blue tickets, each with a passage of Scripture on it; each blue ticket was pay for two verses of the recitation. Ten blue tickets equaled a red one, ten red tickets equaled a yellow one; for ten yellow tickets the superintendent gave a very plainly bound Bible (worth forty cents in those times) to the pupil. Only the older pupils managed to keep their tickets and stick to their tedious work long enough to get a Bible, and the successful pupil was so conspicuous for that day that every scholar's heart was fired with a fresh ambition that often lasted a couple of weeks. It is possible that Tom's mental stomach had never really hungered for one of those prizes, but unquestionably his entire being had for many a day longed for the glory that came with it.

In due course the superintendent stood up in front of the pulpit and commanded attention. This superintendent, Mr. Walters, was a slim creature of thirty-five, with a sandy goatee and short sandy hair; and he wore a stiff standing collar whose upper edge almost reached his ears. He was very earnest of mien, and he held sacred things in such reverence, and so separated them from worldly matters, that unconsciously to himself his Sunday-school voice had acquired a peculiar intonation which was wholly absent on week-days. He began after this fashion:

"Now, children, I want you all to sit up just as straight and pretty as you can and give me all your attention. I see one little girl who is looking out of the window—I am afraid she thinks I am out there somewhere—perhaps up in one of the trees making a speech to the little birds. [Applausive titter.] I want to tell you how good it makes me feel to see so many bright, clean little faces assembled in a place like this, learning to do right and be good." And so forth and so on. The latter third of the speech was marred by the resumption of fights and other recreations among certain of the bad boys, and by fidgetings and whisperings that extended far and wide, washing even to the bases of isolated and incorruptible rocks like Sid and Mary. But now every sound ceased suddenly, with the subsidence of Mr. Walters' voice, and the conclusion of the speech was received with a burst of silent gratitude.

A good part of the whispering had been occasioned by the entrance of visitors: Lawyer Thatcher with a portly, middle-aged gentleman with iron-gray hair, and a dignified lady who was doubtless the latter's wife. The lady was leading a child. When Tom saw this small newcomer his soul was at once ablaze with bliss. The next moment he was "showing off" with all his might—cuffing boys, pulling hair, making faces—in a word, using every art that seemed likely to fascinate a girl and win her applause.

The visitors were given the highest seat of honor, and Mr. Walters introduced them to the school. The middle-aged man turned out to be no less than the County Judge—altogether the most august creation these children had ever looked upon. He was from Constantinople, twelve miles away—so he had traveled, and seen the world—these very eyes had looked upon the county courthouse, which was said to have a tin roof. The awe which these reflections inspired was attested by the ranks of staring eyes. This was the great Judge Thatcher, brother of their own lawyer, who was Jeff Thatcher's father. Jeff Thatcher immediately went forward, to be familiar with the great man and be envied by the school. It would have been music to his soul to hear the whisperings:

"Look at him, Jim! He's a-going up there. Say! By jings, don't you wish you was Jeff?"

Mr. Walters fell to "showing off" with all sorts of official bustlings and activities, giving orders, delivering judgments, discharging directions here, there, everywhere. The librarian "showed off"—running hither and thither with his arms full of books. The young lady teachers "showed off"—bending sweetly over pupils that were lately being boxed—and the little boys "showed off" with such diligence that the air was thick with paper wads and the murmur of scufflings. And above it all the great man beamed a majestic smile upon all the house, and warmed himself in the sun of his own grandeur—for he was "showing off," too.

There was only one thing wanting to make Mr. Walters' ecstasy complete, and that was a chance to deliver a Bible prize and exhibit a prodigy. Several pupils had a few tickets, but none had enough.

And now at this moment, when hope was dead, Tom Sawyer came forward with nine yellow tickets, nine red tickets and ten blue ones, and demanded a Bible. This was a thunderbolt out of a clear sky. Walters was not expecting an application from this source for the next ten years. But there was no getting around it—here were the certified checks. Tom was therefore elevated to a place with the Judge and the other elect, and the great news was announced. It was the most stunning surprise of the decade. The boys were all eaten up with envy—but those that suffered the bitterest pangs were those who perceived that they themselves had contributed to this hated splendor by trading tickets to Tom for the wealth he had amassed in selling whitewashing privileges.

The prize was delivered to Tom with as much effusion as the superintendent could pump up under the circumstances; but it lacked the true gush, for the poor fellow's instinct taught him that there was a mystery here that could not well bear the light. Tom was then introduced to the Judge; but his tongue was tied, his heart quaked—partly because of the awful greatness of the man, but mainly because he was *her* parent. The Judge put his hand on Tom's head and called him a fine little man, and asked him what his name was. The boy stammered, gasped, and got it out:

"Tom."

"Oh, no, not Tom—it is—"

"Thomas."

"Ah, that's it. But you've another one I daresay."

"Tell the gentleman your other name, Thomas," said Walters, "and say *sir*. You mustn't forget your manners."

"Thomas Sawyer—sir."

"That's a good boy. Fine, manly little fellow. Two thousand verses is a great many—very, very great many. And you never can be sorry for the trouble you took to learn them; for knowledge is worth more than anything in the world; it's what makes great men and good men; you'll be a great man and a good man yourself, someday, Thomas, and then you'll look back and say, 'It's all owing to the precious Sunday-school privileges of my boyhood!' And now, Thomas, you wouldn't mind telling me and this lady some of the things you've learned, for we are proud of little boys that learn. Now, no doubt you know the names of the twelve disciples. Won't you tell us the names of the first two that were appointed?"

Tom was tugging at a buttonhole. He blushed, and his eyes fell. Mr. Walters' heart sank within him. Yet he felt obliged to speak up and say, "Answer the gentleman, Thomas—don't be afraid."

Tom still hung fire.

"Now I know you'll tell *me*," said the lady. "The names of the first two disciples were—"

"DAVID AND GOLIATH!"

Let us draw the curtain of charity over the rest of the scene.

ABOUT HALF PAST TEN the cracked bell of the small church rang, and the people began to gather for the sermon. The Sunday-school children distributed themselves about the house and occupied pews with their parents, so as to be under supervision. Aunt Polly came, and Tom and Sid and Mary sat with her—Tom being placed next the aisle, in order that he might be as far away from the open window and the seductive outside scenes as possible. The crowd filed up the aisles: the aged postmaster; the mayor and his wife; the justice of the peace; the Widow Douglas, fair, smart and forty, a good-hearted soul and well-to-do, her hill mansion the only palace in the town, and the most hospitable in the matter of festivities that St. Petersburg could boast; then, all the young clerks in town in a body—for they had stood in the vestibule, sucking their cane heads, till the last girl had run their gantlet.

The congregation being fully assembled, the bell rang once more, and a solemn hush fell upon the church. The minister gave out the hymn, and after it had been sung, he turned himself into a bulletin board, and read off "notices." And now he prayed. A good, generous prayer it was: it pleaded for the church, and the little children of the church; for the other churches of the village; for the village itself; for the county, the state, the state officers, the United States, the churches of the United States, Congress, the President; for poor sailors, tossed by stormy seas; for oppressed millions groaning under the heel of despotisms; for such as have the light and the good tidings, and yet have not eyes to see nor ears to hear withal; for the heathen in the far islands of the sea; and closed with a supplication that the words he was about to speak might find grace and favor, and be as seed sown in fertile ground, yielding in time a grateful harvest of good. Amen.

The boy whose history this book relates was restive all through the prayer, for he was not listening, but knew the ground of old.

In the midst of it a fly had lit on the pew in front of him and tortured his spirit by calmly rubbing its hands together, embracing its head with its arms, and polishing it so vigorously that it seemed to almost part company with the body; scraping its wings with its hind legs and smoothing them as if they had been coattails; going through its whole toilet as tranquilly as if it knew it was perfectly safe. As indeed it was; for as sorely as Tom's hands itched to grab for it they did not dare—he believed his soul would be instantly destroyed if he did such a thing while the prayer was going on. But with the closing sentence his hand began to steal forward; and the instant the "Amen" was out the fly was a prisoner of war. His aunt detected the act and made him let it go.

The minister gave out his text and droned along. Tom counted the pages of the sermon; after church he always knew how many pages there had been, but he seldom knew anything else about it. Presently he bethought him of a treasure he had and got it out. It was a large black beetle with formidable jaws—a "pinch bug," he called it. It was in a percussion-cap box. The first thing the beetle did was to take him by the finger. A natural fillip followed, the beetle went flying into the aisle and lit on its back, and the hurt finger went into the boy's mouth. The beetle lay there working its helpless legs, unable to turn over. Tom eyed it, and longed for it; but it was safe out of his reach. Other people, uninterested in the sermon, found relief in the beetle, and they eyed it too.

Presently a vagrant poodle dog came idling along, sad at heart, sighing for change. He spied the beetle; the drooping tail lifted and wagged. He surveyed the prize; walked around it; smelled at it from a safe distance; walked around it again; grew bolder, and took a closer smell; then lifted his lip and made a gingerly snatch at it, just missing it; made another; subsided to his stomach with the beetle between his paws, and continued his experiments; grew weary at last, and then indifferent. For a time he followed an ant around, with his nose close to the floor, and wearied of that; yawned, forgot the beetle entirely, and sat down on it. Then there was a wild yelp of agony and the poodle dog went sailing up the aisle; he crossed the house in front of the altar; he flew down the other aisle; his anguish grew with his progress, till he was but a woolly comet moving in its orbit with the speed of light. At last the frantic sufferer sheered from its course, and sprang into its master's lap; his master flung it out of the window, and the voice of distress quickly died in the distance.

By this time the whole church was red-faced and suffocating with suppressed laughter, and the sermon had come to a dead standstill. It was resumed presently, but it went lame and halting, for even the gravest sentiments were received with a smothered burst of unholy mirth. It was a genuine relief to the whole congregation when the ordeal was over and the benediction pronounced.

Tom Sawyer went home quite cheerful, thinking to himself that there was some satisfaction about divine service when there was a bit of variety in it. He had but one marring thought; he was willing that the dog should play with his pinch bug, but he did not think it was upright in him to carry it off.

CHAPTER IV

Monday morning found Tom Sawyer miserable. Monday morning always found him so—because it began another week's slow suffering in school. He generally began that day with wishing he had had no intervening holiday, it made the going into captivity again so much more odious.

Tom lay thinking. Presently it occurred to him that he wished he was sick; then he could stay home from school. He canvassed his system. No ailment was found, and he investigated again. Suddenly he discovered something. One of his upper front teeth was loose. But when he went downstairs and complained that the tooth ached, his aunt called Mary. "Mary, get me a silk thread, and a chunk of fire out of the kitchen stove."

Tom said, "Oh, Auntie, don't pull it out. It don't hurt anymore. Please don't, Auntie. *I* don't want to stay home from school."

"Oh, you don't, don't you? So all this row was because you thought you'd get to stay home from school?" By this time the dental instruments were ready. The old lady made one end of the thread fast to Tom's tooth with a loop and tied the other to the bedpost. Then she seized the chunk of fire and suddenly thrust it almost into the boy's face. The tooth hung dangling by the bedpost.

But all trials bring their compensations. As Tom wended to school he was the envy of every boy he met because the gap in his teeth enabled him to expectorate in a new and admirable way; he gathered quite a following of lads interested in the exhibition.

Shortly Tom came upon the juvenile pariah of the village, Huckleberry Finn, son of the town drunkard. Huckleberry was cordially hated and dreaded by all the mothers of the town, because he was idle and lawless and vulgar and bad—and because all their children admired him so, and delighted in his forbidden society. Tom envied Huckleberry his gaudy outcast condition, and was under strict orders not to play with him. So he played with him every time he got the chance.

Huckleberry was always dressed in the cast-off clothes of full-grown men. His hat was a vast ruin with a wide crescent lopped out of its brim; his coat, when he wore one, hung nearly to his heels, and but one suspender supported his trousers. Huckleberry came and went at his own free will. He slept on doorsteps in fine weather and in empty hogsheads in wet; he did not have to go to school or to church; he could go fishing or swimming when and where he chose; he was the first boy that went barefoot in the spring and the last to resume leather in the fall; he never had to wash; he could swear wonderfully. In a word, everything that goes to make life precious, that boy had. So thought every harassed, hampered, respectable boy in St. Petersburg.

Tom hailed the romantic outcast: "Hello, Huckleberry!"

"Hello yourself, and see how you like it."

"What's that you got?"

"Dead cat."

"Lemme see, Huck. He's pretty stiff. Where'd you get him?"

"Bought him off'n a boy."

"What did you give?"

"I give a bladder that I got at the slaughterhouse."

"Say—what is dead cats good for, Huck?"

"Good for? Cure warts with."

"No! Is that so? I know something that's better. Spunkwater."

"Spunkwater! I wouldn't give a dern for spunkwater."

"You wouldn't, wouldn't you? D'you ever try it?"

"No, I hain't. But Bob Tanner did."

"Tell me how Bob Tanner done it, Huck."

"Why, he took and dipped his hand in a rotten stump where the rainwater was."

"In the daytime?"

"Certainly."

"Did he *say* anything?"

"I don't reckon he did. I don't know."

"Aha! Talk about trying to cure warts with spunkwater such a blame-fool way as that! Why, you got to go to the stump at night, and just as it's midnight you back up against the stump and jam your hand in and say,

> *Barleycorn, Barleycorn, injun-meal shorts,*
> *Spunkwater, spunkwater, swaller these warts,*

and then walk away quick, eleven steps, and then turn around three times and walk home without speaking to anybody. Because if you speak the charm's busted."

"Well, that sounds like a good way, but that ain't the way Bob Tanner done."

"No, sir, you can bet he didn't, becuz he's the wartiest boy in this town; and he wouldn't have a wart on him if he'd knowed how to work spunkwater. I've took thousands of warts off that way, Huck. I play with frogs so much that I've always got considerable many warts. But say—how do you cure 'em with dead cats?"

"Why, you take your cat and go in the graveyard 'long about midnight when somebody that was wicked has been buried; and when it's midnight a devil will come, or maybe two or three, but you can't see 'em, you can only hear something like the wind, or maybe hear 'em talk; and when they're taking that feller away, you heave your cat after 'em and say, 'Devil follow corpse, cat follow devil, warts follow cat, *I'm* done with ye!' That'll fetch *any* wart."

"Sounds right. D'you ever try it, Huck?"

"No, but old Mother Hopkins told me."

"Well, I reckon it's so, then. Becuz they say she's a witch."

"Say! Why, Tom, I *know* she is. She witched Pap one day and he rolled off'n a shed wher' he was a-layin' drunk, and broke his arm."

"Why, that's awful. How did he know she witched him?"

"Lord, Pap can tell, easy. Pap says when they keep looking at you right stiddy, they're a-witching you. Specially if they mumble. When they mumble they're saying the Lord's Prayer backwards."

"Say, Hucky, when you going to try the cat?"

"Tonight. I reckon they'll come after old Hoss Williams tonight."

"But they buried him Saturday. Didn't they get him Saturday night?"

"Why, how you talk! How could their charms work till midnight? And *then* it's Sunday. Devils don't slosh around much of a Sunday, I don't reckon."

"I never thought of that. That's so. Lemme go with you?"

"Of course—if you ain't afeard."

"Afeard! 'Tain't likely. Will you meow?"

"Yes—and you meow back. Last time, you kep' me a-meowing around till old Hays went to throwing rocks at me and says 'Dern that cat!'"

"I couldn't meow that night, becuz Auntie was watching me, but I'll meow this time."

The boys separated. When Tom reached the little isolated frame schoolhouse, he strode in briskly, with the manner of one who had come with all honest speed. He hung his hat on a peg and flung himself into his seat with businesslike alacrity. The master, throned on high in his great armchair, was dozing, lulled by the drowsy hum of study. The interruption roused him.

"Thomas Sawyer!"

Tom knew that when his name was pronounced in full, it meant trouble.

"Sir!"

"Come up here. Now, sir, why are you late again, as usual?"

Tom was about to take refuge in a lie, when he saw two long tails of yellow hair hanging down a back that he recognized; and by that form was *the only vacant place* on the girls' side of the schoolhouse. He instantly said:

"I STOPPED TO TALK WITH HUCKLEBERRY FINN!"

The master stared. The buzz of study ceased. The pupils wondered if this foolhardy boy had lost his mind. The master said:

"You—you did what?"

"Stopped to talk with Huckleberry Finn."

"Thomas Sawyer, this is the most astounding confession I have ever listened to. No mere ferule will answer for this offense. Take off your jacket."

The master's arm performed until it was tired. Then the order followed: "Now, sir, go and sit with the *girls!* And let this be a warning to you."

The titter that rippled around the room appeared to abash the boy, but in reality that result was caused rather more by his worshipful awe of his unknown idol. He sat down upon the end of the pine bench, and the girl hitched herself away from him. Nudges and winks and whispers traversed the room, but Tom sat still, with his arms upon the desk before him, and seemed to study his book.

By and by attention ceased from him, and the accustomed school murmur rose once more. Presently the boy began to steal furtive glances at the girl. She observed it, "made a mouth" at him and gave him the back of her head. When she cautiously faced around again, a peach lay before her. She thrust it away. Tom gently put it back. She thrust it away again, but with less animosity. Tom patiently returned it. Then she let it remain. Tom scrawled on his slate, *Please take it—I got more.* The girl glanced at the words, but made no sign. Now the boy began to draw something, hiding his work with his left hand. For a time the girl refused to notice; but her human curiosity presently began to manifest itself. At last she gave in and hesitatingly whispered:

"Let me see it."

Tom uncovered a dismal caricature of a house with two gable

ends and a corkscrew of smoke issuing from the chimney. The girl gazed a moment, then whispered, "It's nice—make a man."

The artist erected a man in the front yard, that resembled a derrick. He could have stepped over the house; but the girl was not hypercritical; she was satisfied with the monster, and whispered, "It's ever so nice—I wish I could draw."

"It's easy," whispered Tom, "I'll learn you."

"Oh, will you? When?"

"At noon. Do you go home to dinner?"

"I'll stay if you will."

"Good—that's a go. What's your name?"

"Becky Thatcher. What's yours? Oh, I know. It's Thomas Sawyer."

"That's the name they lick me by. I'm Tom when I'm good. You call me Tom, will you?"

"Yes."

Now Tom began to scrawl something on the slate, hiding the words from the girl. But she was not backward this time. She begged to see. Tom said, "Oh, it ain't anything."

"Yes it is."

"No it ain't. You don't want to see it."

"Yes I do. Please let me." And she put her small hand upon his and a little scuffle ensued, Tom pretending to resist but letting his hand slip by degrees till these words were revealed: *I love you.*

"Oh, you bad thing!" And she hit his hand a smart rap, but reddened and looked pleased, nevertheless.

Just at this juncture the boy felt a slow, fateful grip closing on his ear, and a steady lifting impulse. In that vise he was borne across the house and deposited in his own seat, under a peppering fire of giggles. Then the master stood over him during a few awful moments, and finally moved away to his throne without saying a word. But although Tom's ear tingled, his heart was jubilant.

As the school quieted down Tom made an honest effort to study, but the turmoil within him was too great. In turn he took his place in the reading class and made a botch of it; then in the geography class and turned lakes into mountains, mountains into rivers and rivers into continents, till chaos was come again; then in the spelling class, and got "turned down," by a succession of mere baby words, till he brought up at the very foot. But at last school broke up at noon. Tom flew to Becky Thatcher, and whispered in her ear.

"Put on your bonnet and let on you're going home; and when you get to the corner, give the rest of 'em the slip and come back. I'll go the other way and come it over 'em the same way."

So the one went off with one group of scholars, and the other with another. In a little while the two met at the bottom of the lane, and when they reached the school they had it all to themselves. Then they sat together, with a slate before them, and Tom gave Becky the pencil and held her hand in his, guiding it, and so created another surprising house. When the interest in art began to wane, the two fell to talking. Tom was swimming in bliss. He said:

"Do you love rats?"

"No! I hate them!"

"Well, I do, too—*live* ones. But I mean dead ones, to swing round your head with a string."

"No, I don't care for rats much, anyway. What *I* like is chewing gum."

"Oh, I should say so. I wish I had some now."

"Do you? I've got some. I'll let you chew it a while, but you must give it back to me."

That was agreeable, so they chewed it turn about, and dangled their legs against the bench in excess of contentment.

"Was you ever at a circus?" said Tom.

"Yes, and my pa's going to take me again, if I'm good."

"I been to the circus three or four times—lots of times. Church ain't shucks to a circus. I'm going to be a clown when I grow up."

"Oh, are you! That will be nice. They're so lovely, all spotted up."

"Yes. And they get slathers of money—'most a dollar a day, Ben Rogers says. Say, Becky, was you ever engaged?"

"What's that?"

"Why, engaged to be married."

"No."

"Would you like to?"

"I reckon so. I don't know. What is it like?"

"Like? Why it ain't like anything. You only just tell a boy you won't ever have anybody but him, ever ever *ever*, and then you kiss and that's all. Anybody can do it."

"Kiss? What do you kiss for?"

"Why, that, you know, is to—well, they always do that."

"Everybody?"

"Why yes, everybody that's in love with each other. Do you remember what I wrote on the slate?"

"Ye—yes."

"What was it?"

"I shan't tell you."

"Shall I tell *you?*"

"Ye—yes—but some other time."

"Oh, no, *now*. Please, Becky—I'll whisper it, ever so easy."

Becky hesitating, Tom took silence for consent, and passed his arm about her waist and whispered the tale ever so softly, with his mouth close to her ear. And then he added, "Now you whisper it to me—just the same."

She resisted, for a while, and then said, "You turn your face away so you can't see, and then I will."

He turned his face away. She bent timidly around till her breath stirred his curls and whispered, "I—love—you!"

Then she sprang away and ran around and around the desks and benches, with Tom after her, and took refuge in a corner at last, with her little white apron to her face. Tom clasped her about her neck and pleaded, "Now, Becky, it's done—all over but the kiss. Don't be afraid of that—it ain't anything at all. Please, Becky." And he tugged at her apron.

By and by she let her hands drop; her face, all glowing with the struggle, came up and submitted. Tom kissed the red lips and said, "Now it's all done, Becky. And always after this, you know, you ain't ever to love anybody but me, and you ain't ever to marry anybody but me, never never and forever. Will you?"

"No, I'll **never** love anybody but you, Tom, and I'll **never** marry anybody but you—and you ain't to ever marry anybody but me, either."

"Certainly. Of course. That's *part* of it. And always coming to school, you're to walk with me, when there ain't anybody looking—and you choose me and I choose you at parties, because that's the way you do when you're engaged."

"It's nice. I never heard of it before."

"Oh, it's ever so gay! Why, me and Amy Lawrence—"

The big eyes told Tom his blunder and he stopped, confused.

"Oh, Tom! Then I ain't the first you've ever been engaged to!"

The child began to cry. Tom said, "Oh, don't cry, Becky, I don't care for her anymore."

"Yes, you do, Tom—you know you do."

Tom tried to put his arm about her neck, but she pushed him away and turned her face to the wall, and went on crying. Tom tried again, and was repulsed again. Then his pride was up, and he strode outside. He stood about, restless and uneasy, hoping she would repent and come to find him. But she did not. He finally went back to her and stood a moment, not knowing exactly how to proceed. She was still in the corner, sobbing. Then he said hesitatingly, "Becky, I—I don't care for anybody but you. Becky, won't you say something?"

No reply—but sobs. Tom got out his chiefest jewel, a brass knob from an andiron, and passed it around her so that she could see it, and said:

"Please, Becky, won't you take it?"

She struck it to the floor. Then Tom marched out of the house and over the hills and far away, to return to school no more that day. Presently Becky began to suspect. She ran to the door; he was not in sight; she flew around to the play yard; he was not there. Then she called, "Tom! Come back, Tom!"

She listened intently, but there was no answer. So she sat down to upbraid herself; and by this time the scholars began to gather again, and she had to hide her griefs and take up the cross of a long, dreary afternoon, with none among the strangers about her to exchange sorrows with.

CHAPTER V

AT HALF PAST NINE that night, Tom and Sid were sent to bed as usual. Sid was soon asleep, and Tom lay awake and waited, in restless impatience. When it seemed to him that it must be nearly daylight, he heard the clock strike ten! This was despair. He would have tossed and fidgeted, but he was afraid he might wake Sid. Everything was dismally still. At last he was satisfied that time had ceased and eternity begun; he began to doze, in spite of himself; the clock chimed eleven, but he did not hear it. And then there came, mingling with his half-formed dreams, a most melancholy caterwauling. The raising of a neighboring window disturbed him. A cry of "Scat! you devil!" and the crash of an empty bottle brought him wide awake, and a minute later he was dressed and out the window and creeping along the roof of the "ell." He meowed with caution, then jumped to the roof of the woodshed and thence to the ground. Huckleberry Finn was there, with his dead cat. The boys disappeared in the gloom. At the end of half an hour they were wading through the tall grass of the graveyard.

The graveyard was on a hill about a mile and a half from the village. It had a crazy board fence around it, which leaned inward in places, and outward the rest of the time, but stood upright nowhere. Grass and weeds grew rank. All the old graves were sunken in, and round-topped, worm-eaten boards staggered over them, leaning for support and finding none. "Sacred to the memory of" so-and-so had been painted on them once, but it could no longer have been read on most of them, even if there had been light.

A faint wind moaned through the trees. The boys talked little, for the place oppressed their spirits. They found the sharp new heap they were seeking, and ensconced themselves within the protection of three great trees a few feet from the grave.

They waited for a long time. The hooting of an owl was all that troubled the dead stillness. At last Tom said in a whisper, "Hucky, do you believe the dead people like it for us to be here?"

Huckleberry whispered, "I wisht I knowed. It's awful solemn."

The boys canvassed this matter inwardly. Then Tom whispered, "Say, Hucky—do you reckon Hoss Williams hears us talking?"

"O' course he does. Least his sperrit does."

Tom, after a pause: "I wish I'd said *Mister* Williams. But I never meant any harm. Everybody calls him Hoss."

"A body can't be too particular how they talk 'bout these yer dead people, Tom."

This was a damper, and conversation died again.

Presently Tom seized his comrade's arm and said, "*Sh!*"

"What is it, Tom?" And the two clung together.

"Sh! There 'tis again! Didn't you hear it?"

"Lord, Tom, they're coming, sure! What'll we do?"

"I dono. Think they'll see us?"

"Tom, they can see in the dark, same as cats. I wisht I hadn't come."

"*I* don't believe they'll bother us. We ain't doing any harm. If we keep perfectly still, maybe they won't notice us at all. . . . Listen!"

The boys scarcely breathed. A muffled sound of voices floated up from the far end of the graveyard.

"Look! See there!" whispered Tom. "What is it?"

"It's devil-fire. Oh, Tom, this is awful."

Some vague figures approached through the gloom, swinging an old-fashioned tin lantern that freckled the ground with innumerable little spangles of light. Presently Huckleberry whispered with a shudder, "It's the devils, sure enough. Three of 'em! Lordy, Tom, we're goners! Can you pray?"

"I'll try. 'Now I lay me down to sleep, I—' What is it, Huck?"

"They're *humans!* One of 'em is, anyway. One of 'em's old Muff Potter's voice. Drunk, the same as usual, likely—blamed old rip!"

"Say, Huck, I know another o' them voices; it's Injun Joe."

"That's so—that murderin' half-breed! I'd druther they was devils a dern sight. What kin they be up to?"

The whispers died wholly out, now, for the three men had reached the grave and stood within a few feet of the boys' hiding place.

"Here it is," said the third voice; and the owner of it held the lantern up and revealed the face of young Dr. Robinson.

Potter and Injun Joe were carrying a handbarrow with a rope and a couple of shovels on it. They cast down their load and began to open the grave. The doctor put the lantern at the head of the grave and came and sat down with his back against one of the trees. He was so close the boys could have touched him.

"Hurry, men!" he said in a low voice. "The moon might come out any moment."

They growled a response and went on digging. For some time there was no noise but the grating sound of the spades. It was very monotonous.

Finally a spade struck upon the coffin with a dull woody accent, and within another minute or two the men had hoisted it out. They pried off the lid and dumped the body rudely on the ground. The moon drifted from behind the clouds and exposed the pallid face. The corpse was placed on the barrow, covered with a blanket and bound to its place with the rope.

Potter took out a large spring knife and cut off the dangling end of the rope and then said, "Now the cussed thing's ready, Sawbones, and you'll just out with another five, or here she stays."

"That's the talk!" said Injun Joe.

"Look here, what does this mean?" said the doctor. "You required your pay in advance, and I've paid you."

"Yes, and you done more than that," said Injun Joe, approaching the doctor. "Five years ago you drove me away from your father's kitchen one night, when I asked for something to eat, and you said I warn't there for any good; and when I swore I'd get even with you, your father had me jailed for a vagrant. Did you think I'd forget? The Injun blood ain't in me for nothing. And now I've *got* you, and you got to *settle!*"

He was threatening the doctor, with his fist in his face, by this time. The doctor struck out suddenly and stretched the ruffian on the ground. Potter dropped his knife, and exclaimed:

"Here, now, don't you hit my pard!" and the next moment he had grappled with the doctor and the two were struggling with might and main, trampling the grass and tearing the ground with their heels.

Injun Joe sprang to his feet, his eyes flaming, snatched up Potter's knife and went creeping, catlike and stooping, round and round the combatants, seeking an opportunity. All at once the doctor flung himself free, seized the heavy headboard of Williams' grave and felled Potter with it—and in the same instant the half-breed saw his chance and drove the knife to the hilt in the young man's breast. He reeled and fell partly upon Potter, flooding him with his blood, and in the same moment the clouds blotted out the dreadful spectacle and the two frightened boys went speeding away in the dark.

Presently, when the moon emerged again, Injun Joe was standing over the two forms. The doctor gave a long gasp or two and was still. The half-breed muttered:

"*That* score is settled—damn you."

Then he robbed the body. After which he put the fatal knife in Potter's open right hand, and sat down on the coffin.

Three—four—five minutes passed, and then Potter began to stir and moan. His hand closed upon the knife; he raised it, glanced at it, and let it fall, with a shudder. Then he sat up, pushing the body from him, and gazed at it, and then around him, confusedly. His eyes met Joe's.

"Lord, how is this, Joe?" he said.

"It's a dirty business," said Joe, without moving. "What did you do it for?"

"I! I never done it!"

"Look here! That kind of talk won't wash."

Potter trembled and grew white.

"I thought I'd got sober. I'd no business to drink tonight. But it's in my head yet—worse'n when we started here. I'm all in a muddle; can't recollect anything of it, hardly. Tell me, Joe—*honest*, now, old feller—did I do it? Joe, I never meant to—'pon my soul and honor! Oh, it's awful—and him so young and promising. Joe, don't tell! Say you won't tell, Joe! I always liked you, Joe, and stood up for you. You *won't* tell, *will* you, Joe?" And the poor creature dropped on his knees before the stolid murderer, and clasped his appealing hands.

"No, you've always been fair and square with me, Muff Potter, and I won't go back on you. There, now, that's as fair as a man can say."

"Oh, Joe, I'll bless you for this the longest day I live." And Potter began to cry.

"Come, now, this ain't any time for blubbering. You be off yonder way and I'll go this. Move, now, and don't leave any tracks."

Potter started on a trot that quickly increased to a run. The half-breed stood looking after him. He muttered:

"If he's as much stunned with the lick and fuddled with the rum as he had the look of being, he won't think of the knife till he's gone so far he'll be afraid to come back after it to such a place by himself—chickenheart!"

Two or three minutes later the murdered man, the blanketed corpse, the lidless coffin and the open grave were under no inspection but the moon's.

The stillness was complete again, too.

CHAPTER VI

THE TWO BOYS FLEW ON AND ON, toward the village, speechless with horror. They glanced backward over their shoulders from time to time, apprehensively, as if they feared they might be followed. Every stump that started up in their path seemed a man and an enemy, and made them catch their breath; and as they sped by some outlying cottages near the village, the barking of the aroused watchdogs seemed to give wings to their feet.

"If we can only get to the old tannery before we break down!" whispered Tom, in short catches between breaths. "I can't stand it much longer."

Huckleberry's hard pantings were his only reply. The boys gained steadily on their goal, and at last they burst through the open door of the tannery and fell grateful and exhausted in the sheltering shadows beyond. By and by their pulses slowed down, and Tom whispered:

"Huck, what do you reckon'll come of this?"

"If Dr. Robinson dies, I reckon hanging'll come of it."

"Do you though?"

"Why, I *know* it, Tom."

Tom thought awhile, then he said:

"Who'll tell? We?"

"What are you talking about? S'pose something happened and Injun Joe *didn't* hang? Why he'd kill us some time or other, just as dead sure as we're a-laying here."

"That's just what I was thinking to myself, Huck."

"If anybody tells, let Muff Potter do it, if he's fool enough. He's generally drunk enough."

Tom said nothing—went on thinking. Presently he whispered:

"Huck, Muff Potter don't *know* it. How can he tell?"

"What's the reason he don't know it?"

"Because he'd just got that whack when Injun Joe done it. D'you reckon he could see anything? D'you reckon he knowed anything?"

"By hokey, that's so, Tom!"

"And besides, looky here—maybe that whack done for *him!*"

"No, 'tain't likely, Tom. He had liquor in him; I could see that. But if a man was dead sober, I reckon maybe that whack might fetch him; I dono."

After another reflective silence, Tom said:

"Hucky, you sure you can keep mum?"

"Tom, we *got* to keep mum. *You* know that. That Injun devil wouldn't make any more of drownding us than a couple of cats, if we was to squeak 'bout this and they didn't hang him. Now, looky here, Tom, let's take and swear to one another—that's what we got to do—swear to keep mum."

"I'm agreed. It's the best thing. Would you just hold hands and swear that we—"

"Oh, no, that wouldn't do for this. That's good enough for little rubbishy common things—specially with gals, cuz *they* go back on you anyway, and blab if they get in a huff—but there orter be writing 'bout a big thing like this. And blood."

Tom's whole being applauded this idea. It was deep, and dark, and awful; the hour, the circumstances, the surroundings, were in keeping with it. He picked up a clean pine shingle that lay in the moonlight, took a little fragment of "red keel" out of his pocket, got the moon on his work, and painfully scrawled these lines, emphasizing each slow downstroke by clamping his tongue between his teeth, and letting up the pressure on the upstrokes:

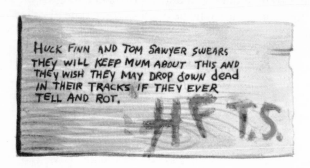

Huckleberry was filled with admiration for the sublimity of Tom's language. He at once took a pin from his lapel, and each boy pricked his thumb and squeezed out a drop of blood. In time, after many squeezes, Tom managed to sign his initials. Then he showed Huckleberry how to make an H and an F, and the oath was complete. They buried the shingle close to the wall, with some dismal incantations, and the fetters that bound their tongues were considered to be locked and the key thrown away.

A figure crept stealthily through a break in the other end of the ruined building, now, but they did not notice it.

"Tom," whispered Huckleberry, "does this keep us from *ever* telling—*always?*"

"Of course it does. We'd drop down dead if we tell—don't *you* know that?"

"Yes, I reckon that's so."

Presently, just outside, a dog set up a long, lugubrious howl. The boys clasped each other suddenly, in an agony of fright.

"Which of us does he mean?" gasped Huckleberry. "Which does he mean is gonna die?"

"I dono—peep through the crack. Quick!"

"No, *you*, Tom!"

"I can't—I can't *do* it, Huck!"

"Please, Tom. Maybe it ain't a stray. There 'tis again!"

Tom, quaking with fear, put his eye to the crack. His whisper was hardly audible when he said, "Oh, Huck, IT IS A STRAY!"

"Quick, Tom, quick! Who does he mean?"

"Huck, he must mean us both—we're right together."

"Oh, Tom, I reckon we're goners! And I reckon there ain't no mistake about where *I'll* go to, I been so wicked."

"Dad fetch it! I might 'a' been good, like Sid, if I'd 'a' tried—but no, I wouldn't, of course. But if I get off this time, I lay I'll just *waller* in Sunday schools!" And Tom began to snuffle.

"*You* bad!" and Huckleberry began to snuffle too. "Confound it, Tom Sawyer, you're just old pie, 'longside o' what *I* am!"

Tom choked off: "Look, Hucky! He's got his *back* to us!"

Hucky looked, with joy in his heart. "Well, he has, by jingoes! Did he before?"

"Yes, he did. But I never thought. Oh, this is bully, you know. *Now* who can he mean?"

The howling stopped. Tom pricked up his ears. "Sh! What's that?" he whispered.

"Sounds like—like hogs grunting. No—it's somebody snoring, Tom. I bleeve it's down at t'other end."

The spirit of adventure rose in the boys' souls once more.

"Hucky, do you dast to go if I lead?"

"I don't like to, much. Tom, s'pose it's Injun Joe!"

Tom quailed. But the temptation rose up strong again and the boys agreed to try, with the understanding that they would take to their heels if the snoring stopped. So they went tiptoeing stealthily down. When they had got to within five steps of the snorer, Tom stepped on a stick, and it broke with a snap. The man writhed a little, and his face came into the moonlight. It was Muff Potter.

The boys' hearts had stood still when the man moved, but their fears passed away now. They tiptoed out, through the broken weatherboarding, and stopped to exchange a parting word. That long howl rose on the night air again! They turned and saw the strange dog standing within a few feet of where Potter was lying, and *facing* Potter, with his nose pointing heavenward.

"Oh, geeminy, it's *him!*" exclaimed both boys, in a breath.

"Say, Tom—they say a stray dog come howling around Johnny Miller's house, 'bout midnight, two weeks ago; but there ain't anybody dead there yet."

"Well, I know that. And suppose there ain't. Didn't Gracie Miller fall in the kitchen fire and burn herself terrible the very next Saturday?"

"Yes, but she ain't *dead*. She's getting better."

"All right, you wait and see. She's a goner, just as sure as Muff Potter's a goner."

Then they separated. When Tom crept in at his bedroom window the night was almost spent. He fell asleep congratulating himself that nobody knew of his escapade. He was not aware that the gently snoring Sid was awake, and had been for an hour.

When Tom awoke, Sid was dressed and gone. There was a late look in the light, and he was startled. Why had he not been called— persecuted till he was up, as usual? The thought filled him with bodings. Within five minutes he was dressed and downstairs, feeling sore and drowsy. The family were still at table. There was no voice of rebuke; but there were averted eyes; there was a silence and an air of solemnity that struck a chill to the culprit's heart. He sat down and tried to seem gay, but it was uphill work; it roused no smile, no response.

After breakfast his aunt took him aside, and Tom almost brightened in the hope that he was going to be flogged; but it was not so. His aunt wept over him and asked him how he could break her old heart so; and finally told him to go on, and ruin himself, and bring her gray hairs with sorrow to the grave, for it was no use for her to try anymore. This was worse than a thousand whippings. Tom cried, he pleaded for forgiveness, and when he received his dismissal, was too miserable even to feel revengeful toward Sid.

He moped to school, gloomy and sad, and took his flogging for playing hookey the day before, with the air of one whose heart was busy with heavier woes and wholly dead to trifles. Then he betook himself to his seat, rested his elbows on his desk and his jaws in his hands, and stared at the wall with the stony stare of suffering. His elbow was pressing against some hard substance. After a long time he slowly and sadly changed his position, and took up this object. It was in a paper. He unrolled it. A long, lingering sigh followed, and his heart broke. It was his brass andiron knob!

This final feather broke the camel's back.

CHAPTER VII

CLOSE UPON NOON the whole village was suddenly electrified with the ghastly news. No need of the as yet undreamed-of telegraph; from house to house the tale flew with telegraphic speed. Of course the schoolmaster gave holiday for that afternoon; the town would have thought strangely of him if he had not.

A gory knife had been found close to the murdered man, and it had been recognized as belonging to Muff Potter—so the story ran—and a belated citizen had come upon Potter washing himself in the "branch"—suspicious circumstances—for washing was not a habit with Potter. It was said that the town had been ransacked for this "murderer" (the public are not slow in the matter of sifting evidence and arriving at a verdict) but that he could not be found. Horsemen had departed in every direction and the sheriff "was confident" that he would be captured before night.

All the town was drifting toward the graveyard. Tom's heartbreak vanished and he joined the procession, not because he would not a thousand times rather go anywhere else but because an awful, unaccountable fascination drew him. Arrived at the dreadful place, he wormed his small body through the crowd and saw the dismal spectacle. Somebody pinched his arm. He turned, and his eyes met

Huckleberry's. Then both looked elsewhere at once, and wondered if anybody had noticed anything in their glances. But everybody was intent upon the spectacle before them. "Poor young fellow!" "This ought to be a lesson to grave robbers!" "Muff Potter'll hang for this!" Such was the drift of remark; and the minister said, "It was a judgment; His hand is here."

Now Tom shivered from head to heel; for his eye fell upon the stolid face of Injun Joe. At this moment the crowd began to struggle, and voices shouted, "It's him! It's Muff Potter! He's coming!"

The crowd fell apart, now, and the sheriff came through, ostentatiously leading Potter by the arm. The poor fellow's face was haggard and fearful. When he stood before the murdered man, he shook as with a palsy and burst into tears. "I didn't do it," he sobbed; "'pon my honor I never done it."

"Who's accused you?" shouted a voice.

This shot seemed to carry home. Potter lifted his face with pathetic hopelessness. He saw Injun Joe, and exclaimed, "Oh, Injun Joe, you promised me—"

"Is that your knife?" and it was thrust before him by the sheriff.

Potter would have fallen if they had not caught him. Then he said, "Something told me t' come back and get—" He shuddered, then said, "Tell 'em, Joe, tell 'em—it ain't any use anymore."

Then Huckleberry and Tom stood dumb and staring, and heard the stonyhearted liar reel off his serene statement of Potter's guilt, they expecting every moment that the clear sky would deliver God's lightnings upon his head. And when he had finished and still stood alive and whole, their wavering impulse to break their oath and save the poor betrayed prisoner's life vanished away, for plainly this miscreant had sold himself to Satan and it would be fatal to meddle with the property of such a power as that.

"Why didn't you leave? What did you want to come here for?" somebody said.

"I couldn't help it—" Potter moaned. "I couldn't seem to come anywhere but here." And he fell to sobbing again.

Injun Joe repeated his statement, just as calmly, a few minutes afterward at the inquest, under oath. He was now become, to the boys, the most balefully interesting object they had ever looked upon, and they could not take their fascinated eyes from his face. They inwardly resolved to watch him, nights, when opportunity should offer, in the hope of getting a glimpse of his dread master.

TOM'S FEARFUL SECRET disturbed his sleep for a week after this; and at breakfast one morning Sid said, "Tom, you talk in your sleep so much that you keep me awake."

Tom blanched and dropped his eyes.

"It's a bad sign," said Aunt Polly gravely. "What you got on your mind, Tom?"

"Nothing. Nothing 't I know of." But the boy's hand shook so that he spilled his coffee.

"And you do talk such stuff," Sid said. "Last night you said, 'It's blood, it's blood, that's what it is!' And you said, 'Don't torment me so—I'll tell!' Tell *what?*"

Everything was swimming before Tom. There is no telling what might have happened, now, but luckily Aunt Polly came to Tom's relief without knowing it. She said, "Sho! It's that dreadful murder. I dream about it 'most every night myself. Sometimes I dream it's me that done it."

Mary said she had been affected much the same way. Sid seemed satisfied. After that Tom complained of toothache for a week, and tied up his jaws every night. His distress of mind wore off gradually and the toothache grew irksome and was discarded.

Every day or two, Tom watched his opportunity and went to the little grated jail window and smuggled such small comforts through to the "murderer" as he could get hold of. The jail was a trifling little brick den that stood in a marsh at the edge of the village, and no guards were afforded for it; indeed it was seldom occupied. These offerings greatly helped to ease Tom's conscience.

The villagers had a strong desire to tar and feather Injun Joe and ride him on a rail for body snatching, but nobody was willing to take the lead in the matter, so it was dropped. He had been careful to begin both of his inquest statements with the fight, without confessing the grave robbery that preceded it; therefore it was deemed wisest not to try the case in the courts at present.

Then Tom's mind found a new and weighty interest. Becky Thatcher had stopped coming to school. She was ill. What if she should die! Tom began to hang around her father's house, nights, and feel miserable. He no longer took an interest in war, and he put his hoop away, and his bat; there was no joy in them anymore.

His aunt was concerned. She began to try all manner of remedies on him. She was one of those people who are infatuated with patent medicines and all newfangled methods of producing health or mending it. The water treatment was new, now, and Tom's low condition was a windfall to her. She had him out at daylight every morning, stood him up in the woodshed and deluged him with cold water; then she scrubbed him down with a towel like a file; then she rolled him up in a wet sheet and put him away under blankets till she sweated his soul clean. Notwithstanding all this, the boy grew more and more melancholy and pale. She added hot baths, sitz baths and shower baths. The boy remained as dismal as a hearse. She began to assist the water with a slim oatmeal diet and blister plasters, and calculating his capacity as she would a jug's, she filled him up every day with quack cure-alls.

Tom had become indifferent to persecution by this time. This filled the old lady with consternation. This indifference must be broken up at any cost. Now she heard of Pain-killer for the first time. She ordered a lot, tasted it and was filled with gratitude. It was simply fire in a liquid form. She gave Tom a teaspoonful and watched anxiously for the result. Her soul was instantly at peace; for the boy could not have shown a wilder, heartier interest if she had built a fire under him.

Tom had felt that it was time to wake up; this sort of life might be romantic, but it was getting to have too much distracting variety. So he had thought over various plans for relief, and had hit upon that of professing to be fond of Pain-killer. He asked for it so often that his aunt ended by telling him to help himself and quit bothering her. She watched the bottle clandestinely, and found that the medicine did really diminish. But it did not occur to her that the boy was mending the health of a crack in the floor with it.

One day Tom was dosing the crack when his aunt's yellow cat came along, purring, eyeing the teaspoon avariciously and begging for a taste. Tom said, "Don't ask for it unless you want it, Peter."

But Peter signified that he did want it.

"You better make sure."

Peter was sure.

"Now you've asked for it, and if you find you don't like it, you mustn't blame anybody but your own self."

Peter was agreeable. So Tom pried his mouth open and poured down the Pain-killer. Peter sprang a couple of yards in the air, and then delivered a war whoop and set off round the room, banging against furniture and upsetting flowerpots. Next he rose on his hind feet and pranced around, in a frenzy of enjoyment, his voice proclaiming happiness. Aunt Polly entered in time to see him throw a few double somersets, deliver a final mighty hurrah and sail through the open window, carrying the rest of the flowerpots with him. The old lady stood petrified with astonishment, peering over her glasses; Tom lay on the floor expiring with laughter.

"Tom, what on earth ails that cat?"

"*I* don't know, Aunt," gasped the boy.

"Why, I never see anything like it. What *did* make him act so?"

"'Deed I don't know, Aunt Polly; cats always act so when they're having a good time."

"They do, do they?" The old lady bent down. The handle of the telltale teaspoon was visible under the bed valance. Aunt Polly held it up. Tom winced and dropped his eyes. Aunt Polly cracked his head soundly with her thimble.

"Now, sir, why did you want to treat that poor dumb beast so?"

"I done it out of pity for him—because he hadn't any aunt."

"Hadn't any aunt! What has that got to do with it?"

"Heaps. Because if he'd 'a' had one she'd 'a' burned him out herself! She'd 'a' roasted his bowel out of him 'thout any more feeling than if he was a human!"

Aunt Polly felt a sudden pang of remorse. This was putting the thing in a new light; what was cruelty to a cat *might* be cruelty to a boy, too. She put her hand on Tom's head and said gently,

"I was meaning for the best, Tom. And, Tom, it *did* do you good."

Tom looked up in her face with just a perceptible twinkle peeping through his gravity. "I know you was meaning for the best, Auntie, and so was I with Peter. It done *him* good, too. I never see him get around so since—"

"Oh, go 'long with you, Tom. You try and be a good boy, for once, and you needn't take any more medicine."

Tom reached school ahead of time, a strange thing that had been occurring every day latterly. And now, as usual of late, he hung about the gate of the school yard instead of playing with his comrades. He was sick, he said, and he looked it. He tried to seem to be looking everywhere but whither he really was looking—down the road—hoping whenever a frisking frock came in sight, and hating the owner of it as soon as he saw she was not the right one.

At last frocks ceased to appear, and he dropped hopelessly into the "dumps." Then one more frock passed in at the gate, and Tom's heart gave a great bound. The next instant he was "going on" like an Indian; yelling, laughing, chasing boys, throwing handsprings, doing all the heroic things he could conceive of. But Becky Thatcher seemed to be unconscious of it all; she never looked. Was it possible that she was not aware that he was there? He carried his exploits to her immediate vicinity; war-whooped, snatched a boy's cap, hurled it away, broke through a group of boys and fell sprawling under Becky's nose, almost upsetting her— and she turned, with her nose in the air, and he heard her say: "Mf! Some people think they're mighty smart—always showing off!"

Tom's cheeks burned. He gathered himself up and sneaked off, crushed and crestfallen.

CHAPTER VIII

TOM'S MIND WAS MADE UP. He was a forsaken, friendless boy; nobody loved him; when they found out what they had driven him to, perhaps they would be sorry; he had tried to do right and get along, but they would not let him. Yes, they had forced him to it at last: he would run away, become a pirate and lead a life of crime.

By this time he was far down Meadow Lane, and the bell for school to "take up" tinkled faintly upon his ear. He sobbed, now, to think he should never, never hear that old familiar sound anymore; since he was driven out into the cold world, he must submit—but he forgave them. Then the sobs came thick and fast.

Just at this point he met his soul's sworn comrade, Joe Harper. Tom, wiping his eyes with his sleeve, began to blubber out something about a resolution to escape from hard usage and lack of sympathy at home by roaming abroad into the great world; and ended by hoping that Joe would not forget him.

But it transpired that this was a request which Joe had just been going to make of Tom, and had come to hunt him up for that purpose. His mother had whipped him for drinking some cream which he had never tasted and knew nothing about; it was plain that she was tired of him and wished him to go; if she felt that way, there was nothing for him to do but succumb; he hoped she would be happy, and never regret having driven her poor boy out into the unfeeling world to suffer or die.

As the two boys walked sorrowing along, they made a new compact to stand by each other till death relieved them of their troubles. Then they began to lay plans. Joe was for being a hermit, and living on crusts in a remote cave; but after listening to Tom, he conceded that there might be some advantages about a life of crime, and so he consented to be a pirate.

Below St. Petersburg, where the Mississippi was a trifle over a mile wide, there was a long, narrow, wooded island, with a shallow bar at the head of it. It was not inhabited; it lay close to the further shore, abreast a dense forest. So Jackson's Island was chosen. Who were to be the subjects of their piracies was a matter that did not occur to them. Then they hunted up Huckleberry Finn, and he joined them promptly, for all careers were one to him.

They presently separated, to meet at a spot on the riverbank two miles above the village at the favorite hour—midnight. There was a small log raft there which they meant to capture. Each would bring hooks and lines, and such provision as he could steal in the most dark and mysterious way—as became outlaws. Before the afternoon was done, they had all managed to enjoy the sweet glory of spreading the fact that pretty soon the town would "hear something." All who got this vague hint were cautioned to "be mum and wait."

About midnight Tom arrived with a boiled ham and a few trifles, and stopped in a dense undergrowth on a small bluff overlooking the meeting place. It was starlight, and very still. The mighty river lay like an ocean at rest. Tom listened a moment. Then he gave a low, distinct whistle. It was answered from under the bluff, and a guarded voice said, "Who goes there?"

"Tom Sawyer, the Black Avenger of the Spanish Main. Name your names."

"Huck Finn the Red-Handed, and Joe Harper the Terror of the Seas." Tom had furnished these titles from his favorite literature.

" 'Tis well. Give the countersign."

Two hoarse whispers delivered the same awful word simultaneously to the brooding night: "BLOOD!"

Then Tom let himself down over the bluff, tearing skin and clothes to some extent in the effort. There was an easy, comfortable path along the shore under the bluff, but it lacked the advantages of difficulty and danger so valued by a pirate.

The Terror of the Seas had brought a side of bacon, and had about worn himself out with getting it there. Finn the Red-Handed had stolen a skillet and a quantity of half-cured leaf tobacco, and had brought a few corncobs to make pipes with, though none of the pirates smoked but himself. The Black Avenger of the Spanish Main said it would never do to start without some fire. That was a wise thought; matches were hardly known there in that day. They saw a fire smoldering upon a great raft a hundred yards above, and they went stealthily thither and helped themselves to a chunk. They made an imposing adventure of it, saying, "Hist!" every now and then, and halting with finger on lip, hands on imaginary dagger hilts; and giving whispered orders that if "the foe" stirred, to "let him have it to the hilt." They knew the raftsmen were all at the village laying in stores or having a spree, but that was no excuse for conducting this thing in an unpiratical way.

They shoved off, presently, Tom in command, Huck at the after oar and Joe forward. Tom stood gloomy-browed, with folded arms, and gave his orders. "Luff, and bring her to the wind!"

"Aye, aye, sir!"

"Steady, steady-y-y-y!"

"Steady it is, sir!"

As the boys were monotonously driving the raft toward midstream it was understood that these orders were given only for "style," and were not intended to mean anything in particular.

"What sail's she carrying?"

"Courses, tops'ls and flying jib, sir."

"Send the r'yals up! Lively, now!"

"Aye, aye, sir!"

When the raft drew beyond the middle of the river, the boys pointed her head right, and then lay on their oars to travel with the current. Hardly a word was said during the next hour. Now the raft was passing the distant town. Two or three glimmering lights showed where it lay, peacefully sleeping, beyond the vague vast sweep of star-gemmed water. The Black Avenger stood still with folded arms, "looking his last" upon the scene of his former joys and his later sufferings, and wishing "she" could see him now, abroad on the wild sea, facing peril and death with a grim smile on his lips. It was but a small strain on his imagination to remove Jackson's Island beyond eyeshot of the village, and so he "looked his last" with a broken and satisfied heart.

About two o'clock in the morning the raft grounded on the bar above the head of the island, and they waded back and forth until they had landed their freight. Part of the raft's belongings consisted of an old sail, and this they spread over a nook in the bushes for a tent to shelter their provisions; but they themselves would sleep in the open air, as became outlaws.

They built a fire against the side of a great log in the forest, and then cooked some bacon in the frying pan for supper, and used up half of the corn-pone stock they had brought. It seemed glorious sport to be feasting in that wild free way in the virgin forest of an unexplored island, while the climbing fire lit up their faces, and they said they never would return to civilization. When the last crisp slice of bacon was gone, they stretched themselves out on the grass, filled with contentment. "*Ain't* it gay?" said Joe.

"It's *nuts!*" said Tom. "What would the boys say if they could see us?"

"Say? Well, they'd just die to be here—hey, Hucky!"

"I reckon so," said Huckleberry; "anyways, *I'm* suited. I don't want nothing better. I don't ever get enough to eat, gen'ally—and here they can't come and pick at a feller."

"It's just the life for me," said Tom. "You don't have to get up, mornings, and you don't have to go to school, and wash, and all that foolishness. You see a pirate don't have to do *anything*, Joe, when he's ashore, but a hermit *he* has to be praying considerable."

"Yes, that's so," said Joe, "but I hadn't thought much about it, you know. I'd a good deal rather be a pirate, now that I've tried it."

"And then," said Tom, "a hermit's got to sleep on the hardest place he can find, and put sackcloth and ashes on his head, and—"

"What does he put sackcloth and ashes on his head for?" inquired Huck.

"*I* dono. But they've *got* to. You'd have to if you was a hermit."

"Dern'd if I would," said Huck. "I'd run away." He had now finished gouging out a cob, and when he had fitted a weed stem to it, he loaded it with tobacco and pressed a coal to it. As he blew out a cloud of fragrant smoke the other pirates envied him this majestic vice, and secretly resolved to acquire it shortly. Presently Huck said, "What does pirates have to do?"

Tom said, "Oh, they have a bully time—take ships and burn them, and get the money and bury it, and kill everybody in the ships—make 'em walk a plank."

"And they carry the women to their island," said Joe; "they don't kill the women."

"No," assented Tom, "they don't kill the women—they're too noble. And the women's always beautiful, too."

"And they wear the bulliest clothes! All gold and silver and di'monds," said Joe.

"Who?" said Huck.

"Why, the pirates."

Gradually drowsiness began to steal upon them. The pipe dropped from the fingers of the Red-Handed, and he slept the sleep of the conscience-free and the weary. The Terror of the Seas and the Black Avenger of the Spanish Main had more difficulty in getting to sleep. They said their prayers inwardly, and lying down, since there was nobody there to make them kneel and recite aloud; in truth, they had a mind not to say them, but they were afraid lest they call down a special thunderbolt from heaven. Then they hovered upon the verge of sleep—but an intruder came, now, that would not "down." It was conscience. They thought of the stolen meat, and tried to argue it away by reminding conscience that they had purloined sweetmeats and apples scores of times; but conscience was not to be appeased by such thin plausibilities; it seemed to them, in the end, that there was no getting around the stubborn fact that taking sweetmeats was only "hooking," while taking bacon and hams and such valuables was plain *stealing*—and there was a command against that in the Bible. So they inwardly resolved that their piracies should not again be sullied with the crime of stealing. Then conscience granted a truce, and these curiously inconsistent pirates fell peacefully to sleep.

WHEN TOM AWOKE in the morning, he wondered where he was. He sat up and rubbed his eyes and looked around. Then he comprehended. It was the cool gray dawn, and there was a delicious sense of repose in the deep pervading silence of the woods. Not a leaf stirred; beaded dewdrops stood upon the leaves and grasses. A white layer of ashes covered the fire, and a thin blue breath of smoke rose straight into the air. Joe and Huck still slept.

Now, far away in the woods a bird called; another answered; presently the hammering of a woodpecker was heard. Gradually the cool dim gray of the morning whitened, and as gradually sounds multiplied and life manifested itself. The marvel of nature shaking off sleep unfolded itself to the musing boy. A little green worm came crawling over a dewy leaf, lifting two-thirds of his body into the air from time to time and "sniffing around," then proceeding again—for he was measuring, Tom said. Now a procession of ants appeared, from nowhere in particular; and now a brown-spotted ladybug climbed the dizzy height of a grass-blade, and Tom bent down close to it and said, "Ladybug, ladybug, fly away home, your house is on fire, your children's alone," and she took wing and went off to see about it—which did not surprise the boy, for he knew of old that this insect was credulous about conflagrations.

When long lances of sunlight began to pierce through the foliage, Tom stirred up the other pirates, and in a minute or two they all were stripped and tumbling over each other in the shallow limpid water of the white sandbar. A vagrant current in the river had carried off their raft, but this only gratified them, since its going was something like burning the bridge between them and civilization.

They came back to camp wonderfully refreshed and ravenous; and they soon had the campfire blazing up again. Huck found a spring of clear water close by, and the boys made cups of hickory leaves, and felt that water, sweetened with such a wildwood charm as that, would be a good-enough substitute for coffee. While Joe was slicing bacon for breakfast, Tom and Huck stepped to a nook in the riverbank and threw in their lines. Joe had not had time to get impatient before they were back again with some handsome bass, a couple of sun perch and a small catfish. They fried the fish with the bacon, and no fish had ever seemed so delicious before.

After breakfast they went off through the woods on an exploring expedition. They tramped gaily along, over decaying logs, through underbrush, among solemn monarchs of the forest hung with a drooping regalia of grapevines. Now and then they came upon snug nooks carpeted with grass and jeweled with flowers.

They found plenty of things to be delighted with, but nothing to be astonished at. They discovered that the island was about three miles long and a quarter mile wide, and that it was only separated from the eastern shore by a narrow channel hardly two hundred yards wide. They took a swim about every hour, so it was the middle of the afternoon when they got back to camp. Then they fared sumptuously upon cold ham, and threw themselves down in the shade to talk. But the talk soon began to drag. The solemnity that brooded in the woods, and the sense of loneliness, began to tell upon their spirits. They fell to thinking. A sort of undefined longing crept upon them. This took dim shape, presently—it was budding homesickness. Even Finn the Red-Handed was dreaming of his doorsteps and empty hogsheads. But they were all ashamed of their weakness, and none spoke his thought.

For some time, now, the boys had been dully conscious of a peculiar sound in the distance, just as one sometimes is of the ticking of a clock which he takes no distinct note of. But now this sound became pronounced, and forced a recognition. The boys started, glanced at each other, and then assumed a listening attitude. There was a long silence; then a deep, sullen boom.

"What is it!" exclaimed Joe, under his breath.

"I wonder," said Tom in a whisper. They waited a time that seemed an age, listening, and then the same muffled boom troubled the solemn hush. "Let's go and see."

They hurried to the shore toward the town, parted the bushes on the bank and peered out over the water. The little steam ferryboat was about a mile below the village, drifting with the current. Her deck seemed crowded with people. There were also a great many skiffs rowing about or floating with the stream. Presently a great jet of white smoke burst from the ferryboat's side, and as it expanded and rose in a lazy cloud, that same dull throb of sound was borne to the listeners again.

"I know now!" exclaimed Tom. "Somebody's drownded!"

"That's it," said Huck; "they done that when Bill Turner got drownded; they shoot a cannon over the water, and that makes him come up to the top."

"By jings, I wish I was over there, now," said Joe.

"I do too," said Huck. "I'd give heaps to know who it is."

The boys still listened and watched. Presently a revealing thought flashed through Tom's mind, and he exclaimed:

"Boys, I know who's drownded—it's us!"

They felt like heroes in an instant. Here was a gorgeous triumph; they were missed; they were mourned; tears were being shed; and best of all, the departed were the talk of the town, and the envy of

all the boys, as far as this dazzling notoriety was concerned. This was fine. It was worthwhile to be a pirate, after all.

As twilight drew on, the ferryboat and the skiffs disappeared. The pirates returned to camp. Jubilant over their new grandeur, they caught fish, cooked supper and ate it, and then fell to guessing at what the village was saying about them. But when the shadows of night closed them in, they gradually ceased to talk, and sat gazing into the fire, with their minds evidently wandering elsewhere. The excitement was gone, now, and Tom and Joe could not keep back thoughts of certain persons at home who were not enjoying this fine frolic as much as they were. Misgivings came; and a sigh or two escaped unawares.

By and by, as the night deepened, Huck began to nod, and presently to snore. Joe followed next. Tom lay upon his elbow motionless for some time, watching the two. At last he got up cautiously, on his knees, and went searching in the grass. He picked up and inspected several semicylinders of the thin white bark of a sycamore, and finally chose two. Then he knelt by the fire and painfully wrote something upon each of these with his "red keel"; one he rolled up and put in his jacket pocket, and the other he put in Joe's hat. And he also put into the hat certain schoolboy treasures of almost inestimable value—a lump of chalk, an India-rubber ball and three fishhooks. Then he tiptoed his way among the trees till he felt that he was out of hearing, and straightway broke into a run in the direction of the sandbar.

A FEW MINUTES LATER Tom was in the shoal water of the bar, wading toward the Illinois shore. Before the depth reached his middle he was halfway over; and he struck out confidently to swim the remaining hundred yards. He swam quartering upstream, reached the shore finally and drew himself out. He put his hand on his jacket pocket, found his piece of bark safe, and then struck through the woods, following the shore. Shortly before ten o'clock he came out into an open place opposite the village, and saw the ferryboat lying in the shadow of the high bank. Everything was quiet under the stars. He crept down the bank, watching with all his eyes, slipped into the water, and climbed into the skiff that was tied to the ferryboat's stern. He laid himself down under the thwarts and waited, panting.

Presently the bell tapped and a voice gave the order to "cast off." A minute later the skiff's head was standing high up against the boat's swell, and the voyage was begun. Tom felt happy in his success, for he knew it was the boat's last trip for the night. At the end of fifteen minutes the wheels stopped, and Tom slipped overboard and swam ashore, landing fifty yards downstream, out of danger of possible stragglers.

He flew along unfrequented alleys, and shortly found himself at his aunt's back fence. He climbed over, and approached the sitting-room window, where a light was burning. There sat Aunt Polly, Sid, Mary, and Joe Harper's mother, talking. They were by the bed, and the bed was between them and the door. Tom went to the door and began to softly lift the latch; then he pressed gently, and the door yielded a crack; he continued pushing, quaking every time it creaked, till he judged he might squeeze through on his knees; so he put his head through and began, warily.

"What makes the candle blow so?" asked Aunt Polly. "Why that door's open, I believe. Go 'long and shut it, Sid."

Tom disappeared under the bed just in time. He lay and "breathed" himself for a time, and then crept to where he could almost touch his aunt's foot.

"But as I was saying," said Aunt Polly, "he warn't *bad*, so to say—only mischee*v*ous. He warn't any more responsible than a colt. *He* never meant any harm, and he was the best-hearted boy that ever was"—and she began to cry.

"It was just so with my Joe—always up to every kind of mischief, but he was just as unselfish and kind as he could be—and laws bless me, to think I went and whipped him for taking that cream, never once recollecting that I throwed it out myself because it was sour, and I never to see him again in this world, never, never, never, poor abused boy!" And Mrs. Harper sobbed as if her heart would break.

"I hope Tom's better off where he is," said Sid, "but if he'd been better in some ways—"

"*Sid!*" said Aunt Polly. "Not a word against my Tom, now that he's gone! God'll take care of *him*—never you trouble *yourself*, sir! Oh, Mrs. Harper, I don't know how to give him up! He was such a comfort to me, although he tormented my old heart out of me, 'most."

At this the old lady broke entirely down. Tom was snuffling now, himself, more in pity of himself than anybody else. He began to have a nobler opinion of himself than ever before. Still, he was sufficiently touched by his aunt's grief to long to rush out from under the bed and overwhelm her with joy—but he resisted.

He went on listening, and gathered by odds and ends that it was conjectured at first that the boys had got drowned while taking a swim; then the small raft had been missed; next, certain boys said the missing lads had promised that the village should "hear something" soon; the wiseheads had "put this and that together" and decided that the lads had gone off on that raft and would turn up at the next town below; but toward noon the raft had been found, lodged against the Missouri shore some five miles below the village—and then hope perished; they must be drowned, else hunger would have driven them home. It was believed that the drowning must have occurred in mid-channel, since the boys, being good swimmers, would otherwise have escaped to shore. This was Wednesday night. If the bodies continued missing until Sunday, all hope would be given over, and the funerals would be preached on that morning. Tom shuddered.

Mrs. Harper gave a sobbing good-night and rose to go. The two women flung themselves into each other's arms and had a good, consoling cry, and then parted. Aunt Polly was tender far beyond her wont, in her good-night to Sid and Mary. Sid snuffled a bit and Mary went off, crying with all her heart.

Aunt Polly knelt down and prayed for Tom so touchingly, so appealingly, and with such measureless love in her words and her old trembling voice, that he was soon weltering in tears again.

He had to keep still long after she went to bed, for she kept tossing unrestfully. But at last she was quiet, only moaning a little in her sleep. Now the boy stole out, rose gradually by the bedside, shaded the candlelight with his hand and stood regarding her. His heart was full of pity for her. He took out his sycamore scroll and placed it by the candle. But something occurred to him, and he lingered, considering. His face lighted with a happy solution of his thought; he put the bark hastily in his pocket. Then he bent over and kissed the faded lips, and straightway made his stealthy exit.

He threaded his way back to the ferry landing and walked boldly on board the boat, for he knew she was tenantless except for a watchman who always turned in and slept. He untied the skiff at the stern, slipped into it, and was soon rowing cautiously upstream. When he had pulled a mile above the village, he started across. He hit the landing on the other side neatly, for this was a familiar bit of work to him. Then he stepped ashore and entered the wood.

It was broad daylight before he found himself fairly abreast the island bar. He plunged into the stream. A little later he paused, dripping, upon the threshold of the camp, and heard Joe say:

"No, Tom's true-blue, Huck. He won't desert. He's up to something. Now I wonder what?"

"Well, the things is ours, anyway, ain't they?"

"Pretty near, but not yet. The writing says they are if he ain't back here to breakfast."

"Which he is!" exclaimed Tom, with fine dramatic effect, stepping grandly into camp.

A sumptuous breakfast of bacon and fish was shortly provided, and as the boys set to work upon it, Tom recounted (and adorned) his adventures. They were a vain and boastful company of heroes when the tale was done. Then Tom hid himself away in a shady nook to sleep, and the other pirates got ready to fish and explore.

CHAPTER IX

AFTER DINNER ALL THE GANG turned out to hunt for turtle eggs on the bar. They poked sticks into the sand, and when they found a soft place they dug with their hands. The eggs were round white things a trifle smaller than an English walnut. They had a famous fried-egg feast that night, and another on Friday morning.

After breakfast they went whooping and prancing out on the bar, and chased each other round and round, shedding clothes as they went, until they were naked, and then continued the frolic far away up the shoal water, against the stiff current, which latter tripped their legs from under them from time to time and greatly increased the fun. And now and then they stooped and splashed water in each other's faces, finally gripping and struggling till the best man ducked his neighbor, and then they all went under in a tangle of white legs and arms, and came up sputtering, laughing, and gasping for breath. When they were well exhausted, they would run out and sprawl on the dry, hot sand, and by and by break for the water again and go through the performance once more.

Finally they drew a ring in the sand and had a circus—with three clowns in it. Next they got their marbles and played knucks and ringtaw and keeps till that amusement grew stale. But by this time they all were tired. They gradually wandered apart, dropped into the "dumps," and fell to gazing across the river to where the village lay drowsing in the sun. Tom found himself writing *Becky* in the sand with his big toe. He scratched it out, and was angry with himself for his weakness. But he wrote it again, nevertheless; he could not help it. He erased it once more and then took himself out of temptation by driving the other boys together and joining them.

But Joe's spirits had gone down almost beyond resurrection. He was so homesick that he could hardly endure the misery of it. Huck was melancholy, too. Tom was downhearted, but tried not to show it. He had a secret which he was not ready to tell, yet, but if this mutinous depression was not broken up soon, he would have to bring it out. He said, with a great show of cheerfulness:

"I bet there's been pirates on this island before, boys. We'll explore it again. They've hid treasures here somewhere. How'd you feel to light on a rotten chest full of gold—hey?"

But it roused only a faint enthusiasm, which faded out, with no reply. Joe sat poking up the sand with a stick and looking very gloomy. Finally he said, "Oh, boys, let's give it up. I want to go home. It's lonesome."

"Joe, you'll feel better by and by," said Tom. "Just think of the fishing that's here."

"I don't care for fishing. I want to go home."

"But, Joe, there ain't such another swimming place anywhere."

"Swimming's no good. I don't seem to care for it, somehow, when there ain't anybody to say I shan't go in."

"Oh, shucks! Baby! You want to see your mother, I reckon."

"Yes, I *do* want to see my mother—and you would, too, if you had one." And Joe snuffled a little.

"Well, we'll let the crybaby go home to his mother, *won't* we Huck? *You* like it here, *don't* you, Huck?"

Huck said, "Y-e-s"—without any heart in it.

"I'll never speak to you again as long as I live," said Joe, rising. "There now!" And he moved moodily away and began to dress.

"Who cares!" said Tom. But he was uneasy, nevertheless, and alarmed to see Huck eyeing Joe's preparations so wistfully, and keeping up such an ominous silence. Presently, without a parting word, Joe began to wade off toward the Illinois shore. Tom's heart sank. He glanced at Huck, but Huck dropped his eyes. Then he said:

"I want to go, too, Tom. It was getting so lonesome, and now it'll be worse. Let's us go, too, Tom."

"I won't! You can all go, if you want to. I mean to stay."

"Tom, I better go."

"Well, go 'long—who's hendering you?"

Huck began to pick up his clothes. He said, "Tom, I wisht you'd come, too. We'll wait for you when we get to shore."

"Well, you'll wait a blame long time, that's all."

Huck started sorrowfully away, and Tom stood looking after him, with a strong desire tugging at him to yield his pride and go along too. He hoped the boys would stop, but they waded on. It suddenly dawned on Tom that it was very lonely and still. He made one final struggle with his pride, and then darted after his comrades, yelling, "Wait! Wait! I want to tell you something!"

They stopped and turned. When he got to where they were, he unfolded his secret, and when they saw the point he was driving at, they set up a war whoop, and said it was "splendid!" and said if he had told them at first, they wouldn't have started away. He made a plausible excuse; but his real reason had been the fear that not even the secret would keep them with him for long, and so he had held it in reserve as a last seduction.

The lads came gaily back, chattering about Tom's stupendous plan. After a dainty egg-and-fish dinner, Tom said he wanted to learn to smoke, now. Joe caught at the idea and said he would like to try, too. So Huck made pipes and filled them. These novices had never smoked anything before but cigars made of grapevine, and they "bit" the tongue, and were not considered manly anyway.

Now they stretched themselves out on their elbows and began to puff charily. The smoke had an unpleasant taste, and they gagged a little, but Tom said, "Why, it's just as easy! If I'd 'a' knowed *this* was all, I'd 'a' learnt long ago."

"So would I," said Joe. "It's just nothing."

"Why, many a time I've looked at people smoking, and thought well I wish I could do that; but I never thought I could," said Tom.

"That's just the way with me. I bleeve I could smoke this pipe all day," said Joe. "*I* don't feel sick."

"Neither do I," said Tom. "*I* could smoke it all day. But I bet you Jeff Thatcher couldn't."

"Jeff Thatcher! Why, he'd keel over just with two draws."

"I bet he would, Joe. Say—I wish the boys could see us now."

"So do I."

"Say—boys, don't say anything about it, and sometime when they're around, I'll come up to you and say, 'Joe, got a pipe? I want a smoke.' And then you'll out with the pipes, and we'll light up just as ca'm, and then just see 'em look!"

"By jings, that'll be gay, Tom!"

So the talk ran on. But presently it began to flag a trifle. The silences widened; the expectoration marvelously increased. Both boys were looking very pale and miserable, now. Joe's pipe dropped from his fingers. Tom's followed. Joe said feebly, "I've lost my knife. I reckon I better go and find it."

Tom said, with quivering lips, "I'll help you. You go that way

and I'll hunt around by the spring. No, you needn't come, Huck—
we can find it."

Huck waited an hour. Then he went to find his comrades. They
were wide apart in the woods, both very pale, both fast asleep. But
something informed him that if they had had any trouble they
had got rid of it.

They were not talkative at supper that night. They had a humble
look, and when Huck prepared his pipe after the meal and was
going to prepare theirs, they said no, they were not feeling very
well—something they ate at dinner had disagreed with them.

About midnight Joe awoke, and called the boys. There was a
brooding oppressiveness in the air that seemed to bode something. The boys huddled together near the fire, though the dull
dead heat of the atmosphere was stifling. Beyond the light of the
fire everything was swallowed up in darkness. Presently there
came a quivering glow that vaguely revealed the foliage for a
moment and then vanished. By and by another came, a little
stronger. Then another. Then a faint moan came sighing through
the branches of the forest and the boys felt a fleeting breath upon
their cheeks, and shuddered with the fancy that the Spirit of the
Night had gone by. Now a weird flash turned night into day and
showed every little grass-blade, separate and distinct, that grew
about their feet. And it showed three white, startled faces, too. An
instant crash followed that seemed to rend the treetops right over
the boys' heads. A few big raindrops fell pattering upon the leaves.

"Quick, boys! Go for the tent!" exclaimed Tom.

They sprang away, stumbling over roots in the dark. A furious
blast roared through the trees, making everything sing as it went.
One blinding flash after another came, and peal on peal of deafen-
ing thunder. And now a drenching rain poured down and the
rising hurricane drove it in sheets along the ground. One by one
the boys straggled under the tent, cold, scared, and streaming
with water. The old sail flapped furiously, the tempest rose higher
and higher, and presently the sail tore loose from its fastenings
and went winging away. The boys seized each other's hands and
fled, to the shelter of a great oak that stood upon the riverbank.

Under the ceaseless conflagration of lightning that flamed in the skies, everything below stood out in shadowless distinctness: the bending trees, the river white with foam. Every little while some giant tree fell crashing; and the unflagging thunderpeals came now in earsplitting bursts, unspeakably appalling.

The storm culminated in one matchless effort that seemed likely to tear the island to pieces, drown it to the treetops, blow it away, and deafen every creature in it. But at last it retired, and its threatenings and grumblings grew weaker and weaker. The boys went back to camp, a good deal awed; but they found there was still something to be thankful for, because the great sycamore, the shelter of their beds, was a ruin now, blasted by the lightnings, and they were not under it when the catastrophe happened.

Everything in camp was drenched, the fire as well; for they had made no provision against rain. Here was a matter for dismay, for they were soaked through and chilled. But they presently discovered that the fire had eaten so far up under the great log it had been built against, that a handbreadth of it had escaped wetting; so they patiently wrought until, with shreds and bark gathered from the undersides of logs, they coaxed the fire to burn again. Then they piled on boughs till they had a roaring furnace, and were gladhearted once more. They dried their ham and had a feast, and after that they sat by the fire and glorified their midnight adventure until morning, for there was not a dry spot to sleep on.

As the sun began to steal in upon the boys, drowsiness came over them and they went out on the sandbar and lay down to sleep. They got scorched out by and by, and drearily set about getting breakfast. After the meal they felt rusty, and stiff-jointed, and a little homesick once more. Tom saw the signs, and fell to getting them interested in a new device. This was to knock off being pirates, for a while, and be Indians. They were attracted by this idea; so it was not long before they were stripped, and striped from head to heel with black mud, like so many zebras—all of them chiefs, of course—and then they separated into three hostile tribes, and killed and scalped each other by thousands. It was a gory day. Consequently it was an extremely satisfactory one.

They assembled in camp toward suppertime, hungry and happy; but now a difficulty arose—hostile Indians could not break the bread of hospitality together without first making peace, and this was a simple impossibility without smoking a pipe of peace. Two of the savages almost wished they had remained pirates. However, there was no other way; so with such show of cheerfulness as they could muster they called for the pipe and took their whiff as it passed, in due form.

And behold, they were glad they had gone into savagery, for they had gained something; they found that they could now smoke a little without having to go and hunt for a lost knife. They practiced more after supper, with right fair success, and so spent a jubilant evening. We will leave them to smoke and chatter and brag, since we have no further use for them at present.

BUT THERE WAS NO HILARITY in the little town that same tranquil Saturday afternoon. The Harpers, and Aunt Polly's family, were being put into mourning, with great grief and many tears. The villagers conducted their concerns with an absent air, and talked little; but they sighed often. The Saturday holiday seemed a burden to the children. They had no heart in their sports, and gradually gave them up. Becky Thatcher moped about the deserted schoolhouse yard, but she found nothing there to comfort her. She soliloquized, "Oh, if I only had his brass andiron knob again! But I haven't got anything now to remember him by." She choked back a sob, and the tears rolled down her cheeks. "Oh, if it was to do over again, I wouldn't say that! But he's gone now; and I'll never never see him anymore!"

The next morning, when the Sunday-school hour was finished, the bell began to toll instead of ringing in the usual way. It was a very still Sabbath, and the mournful sound seemed in keeping with the musing hush that lay upon nature. The villagers began to gather, loitering a moment in the vestibule to converse in whispers. But there was no whispering in the church; only the funereal rustling of dresses as the women gathered to their seats. Then Aunt Polly entered, and Sid and Mary and the Harper family, all in deep black; and the whole congregation, the old minister as well, rose reverently and stood until the mourners were seated in the front pew. And then the minister spread his hands abroad and prayed. A moving hymn was sung, and the text followed: "*I am the resurrection and the life . . .*"

As the service proceeded, the clergyman drew such pictures of the graces, the winning ways and the rare promise of the lost lads, and related so many touching incidents from their lives, that every soul there, thinking he recognized these pictures, felt a pang that he had persistently blinded himself to them always before, and had as persistently seen only faults and flaws in the poor boys. The congregation became more and more moved as the pathetic tale went on, till at last the whole company broke down and joined the mourners in a chorus of anguished sobs, the preacher himself giving way to his feelings, and crying in the pulpit.

There was a rustle in the gallery; a moment later the church door creaked; the minister raised his streaming eyes above his handkerchief, and stood transfixed! First one and then another pair of eyes followed the minister's, and then almost with one impulse the congregation rose and stared while the three dead boys came marching up the aisle, Tom in the lead, Joe next, and Huck sneaking sheepishly in the rear! They had been hid in the gallery listening to their own funeral sermon!

Aunt Polly, Mary and the Harpers threw themselves upon their restored ones and smothered them with kisses, while poor Huck stood abashed and uncomfortable. He wavered, and started to slink away, but Tom seized him and said, "Aunt Polly, it ain't fair. Somebody's got to be glad to see Huck."

"And so they shall. *I'm* glad to see him, poor motherless thing!" And the loving attentions which Aunt Polly then lavished upon Huckleberry were the one thing capable of making him more uncomfortable than he had been before.

Suddenly the minister shouted at the top of his voice: "*Praise God from whom all blessings flow*—SING!" And they did. "Old Hundred" swelled up with a triumphant burst, and while it shook the rafters Tom Sawyer the Pirate looked around upon the envying juveniles about him and confessed in his heart that this was the proudest moment of his life.

Tom got more cuffs and kisses that day—according to Aunt Polly's varying moods—than he had earned before in a year; and he hardly knew which expressed the most gratefulness to God and affection for himself.

CHAPTER X

THAT HAD BEEN TOM'S great secret—the scheme to return home with his brother pirates and attend their own funerals. They had paddled over to the Missouri shore on a log, at dusk on Saturday, landing five or six miles below the village; they had slept in the woods at the edge of the town till nearly daylight, and had then crept through back lanes and finished their sleep in the unused gallery of the church among a chaos of invalided benches.

At breakfast, Monday, Aunt Polly and Mary were very loving and attentive to Tom. There was an unusual amount of talk. In the course of it Aunt Polly said, "Well, I don't say it wasn't a fine joke to keep everybody suffering 'most a week so you boys had a good time, but it is a pity you could let *me* suffer so. If you could come over on a log to go to your funeral, you could have come over and give me a hint someway that you warn't *dead*."

"Yes, you could have done that, Tom," said Mary; "and I believe you would if you had thought of it."

"Would you, Tom, if you'd thought of it?" said Aunt Polly, her face lighting wistfully.

"I—well, I don't know. 'Twould 'a' spoiled everything."

"Tom, I hoped you loved me that much," said Aunt Polly, with a grieved tone. "It would have been something if you'd cared enough to *think* of it, even if you didn't *do* it."

"I dreamed about you anyway, Auntie," said Tom, feeling repentant. "That's something, ain't it?"

"It's better than nothing. What did you dream?"

"Why, Wednesday night I dreamed that you was sitting over

there by the bed, and Sid was sitting by the woodbox, and Mary next to him. And Joe Harper's mother was here."

"Why, she *was* here! Did you dream any more?"

"Oh, lots. But it's so dim, now."

"Well, *try* to recollect—can't you?"

"Somehow it seems to me that the wind—the wind blowed the—the—" Tom pressed his fingers on his forehead and then said, "I've got it now! It blowed the candle! And you said, 'Why, I believe that that door—that door is open.'"

"As I'm sitting here, I did! Didn't I, Mary! Go on!"

"And then—and then—well I won't be certain, but it seems like as if you made Sid go and—and—shut it."

"Well, for the land's sake! I never heard the beat of that. Don't tell *me* there ain't anything in dreams. Go on, Tom!"

"Oh, it's all getting bright as day, now. Next you said I warn't *bad*, only mischeevous, and not any more responsible than—than— I think it was a colt. And then you began to cry."

"So I did. Not the first time, neither. And then—"

"Then Mrs. Harper she began to cry, and said Joe was just the same, and she wished she hadn't whipped him for taking cream when she'd throwed it out her own self—"

"Tom! The sperrit was upon you! Land alive, go on, Tom!"

"And after a while there was a lot of talk 'bout dragging the river for us, and 'bout having the funeral, and then you and old Mrs. Harper hugged and cried, and she went."

"It happened just so!"

"Then I thought you prayed for me—and you went to bed, and I was so sorry, that I took and wrote on a piece of sycamore bark, 'We ain't dead, we are only off being pirates,' and put it on the table by the candle; and then you looked so good, laying there asleep, that I thought I leaned over and kissed you on the lips."

"Did you, Tom, *did* you! I just forgive you everything for that!" And she seized the boy in a crushing embrace that made him feel like the guiltiest of villains.

"It was very kind, even though it was only a—dream," Sid soliloquized just audibly.

"Shut up, Sid! A body does just the same in a dream as he'd do if he was awake. Here's the big apple I've been saving for you, Tom. Now go 'long to school. I'm thankful to the good God and Father of us all I've got you back. Go 'long, Sid, Mary, Tom— you've hendered me long enough."

The children left for school. What a hero Tom was become, now! He did not go skipping and prancing, but moved with a dignified swagger as became a pirate who felt that the public eye was on him. As indeed it was; he tried not to seem to see the looks or hear the remarks as he passed along, but they were food and drink to him. Smaller boys than himself flocked at his heels; and at school the children made so much of him and of Joe Harper that the two heroes were not long in becoming insufferably stuck-up. The very summit of glory was reached when they began to tell their adventures to hungry listeners—but they only began; it was not a thing likely to have an end, with imaginations like theirs to furnish material.

Tom decided now that he could be independent of Becky Thatcher. Now that he was distinguished, maybe she would be wanting to "make up." Well, let her—she should see that he could be as indifferent as some other people. Presently she arrived. Tom pretended not to see her. He moved away and joined a group of boys and girls and began to talk. Soon he observed that she was tripping gaily back and forth with flushed face and dancing eyes, pretending to be busy chasing schoolmates, and screaming with laughter when she made a capture; but he noticed that she always made her captures in his vicinity, and that she cast a conscious eye in his direction at such times, too. It gratified all the vicious vanity that was in him; and so, instead of winning him, it only "set him up" the more and made him the more diligent to avoid betraying that he knew she was about.

Presently she gave over skylarking, and moved irresolutely about, sighing once or twice and glancing furtively and wistfully toward Tom. Then she observed that now Tom was talking more particularly to Amy Lawrence than to anyone else. She felt a sharp pang and tried to go away, but her feet were treacherous, and carried her to the group instead. She said to a girl almost at Tom's elbow—with sham vivacity, "Why, Mary Austin! You bad girl, why didn't you come to Sunday school?"

"I did come—didn't you see me? I saw *you*."

"Did you? Well, I wanted to tell you about the picnic. My ma's going to let me have one."

"Oh, goody; I hope she'll let *me* come."

"She will. The picnic's for me. She'll let anybody come that I want, and I want you."

"That's ever so nice. When is it going to be?"

"By and by. Maybe about vacation."

"You going to have all the girls and boys?"

"Yes, everyone that's friends to me—or wants to be," and she glanced at Tom, but he talked right along to Amy Lawrence about the terrible storm on the island, and how the lightning tore the great sycamore tree "all to flinders" while he was "standing within three feet of it."

"Oh, may I come?" said Gracie Miller.

"Yes."

"And me, too?" said Susy Harper. "And Joe?"

"Yes."

And so on, till all the group had begged for invitations but Tom and Amy. Then Tom turned coolly away, still talking, and took Amy with him. Becky's lips trembled and the tears came to her eyes; she hid these signs and went on chattering, but the life had gone out of the picnic, now; she got away as soon as she could and hid herself and had what her sex call a good cry. Then she sat moody, with wounded pride, till the bell rang. She roused up, now, and gave her plaited tails a shake and said she knew what *she'd* do.

At recess Tom continued his flirtation with Amy with jubilant self-satisfaction. And he kept drifting about to find Becky and lacerate her with the performance. At last he spied her, but there was a sudden falling of his mercury. She was sitting cozily on a little bench behind the schoolhouse looking at a picture book with Alfred Temple—and so absorbed were they, and their heads so close together over the book, that they did not seem to be conscious of anything in the world besides.

Jealousy ran red-hot through Tom's veins. He began to hate himself for throwing away the chance Becky had offered for a reconciliation. Amy chatted happily along, as they walked, but Tom's tongue had lost its function. Soon her happy prattle became intolerable. Tom hinted at things he had to attend to, and leaving her, he hastened away.

Any other boy! Tom thought, grating his teeth. Any boy but that St. Louis smarty! Oh, all right, I licked you the first day you ever saw this town, mister, and I'll lick you again. You just wait till I catch you out!

At noon Tom fled home; his jealousy could bear no more. Becky resumed her picture inspections with Alfred, but as the minutes dragged along and no Tom came to suffer, her triumph began to cloud and she lost interest. When poor Alfred, seeing that he was losing her, he did not know how, kept exclaiming, "Oh, here's a jolly one! Look at this!" she lost patience at last, and said, "Oh, don't bother me! I don't care for them!" and burst into tears, and got up and walked away.

Alfred went musing into the deserted schoolhouse. He was humiliated and angry. He easily guessed his way to the truth— the girl had simply made a convenience of him to vent her spite upon Tom Sawyer. He was far from hating Tom the less when this thought occurred to him. He wished there was some way to get that boy into trouble without much risk to himself. Tom's spelling book fell under his eye. Here was his opportunity. He gratefully opened to the lesson for the afternoon and poured ink upon the page.

Becky, glancing in at a window behind him at the moment, saw the act, and moved on. She started homeward, now, intending to find Tom and tell him; Tom would be thankful and their troubles would be healed. Before she was halfway home, however, she had changed her mind. The thought of Tom's treatment of her when she was talking about the picnic came scorching back and filled her with shame. She resolved to let him get whipped on the damaged spelling book's account, and to hate him forever, into the bargain.

Poor girl, she did not know how fast she was nearing trouble herself. The master, Mr. Dobbins, had reached middle age with an unsatisfied ambition. The darling of his desires was to be a doctor, but poverty had decreed that he should be nothing higher than a village schoolmaster. Every day he took a mysterious book out of his desk and absorbed himself in it when no classes were reciting. He kept that book under lock and key. Every boy and girl in school had a theory about the nature of that book; but no two theories were alike, and there was no way of getting at the facts in the case.

Now, as Becky returned to school and was passing by Mr. Dobbins' desk, which stood near the door, she noticed that the key was in the lock! It was a precious moment. She glanced around, found herself alone, and the next instant she had the book in her hands. The title page—Professor Somebody's *Anatomy*—carried no information to her mind; so she began to turn the leaves. She came at once upon a handsomely engraved and colored frontispiece—a human figure, stark naked. At that moment Tom Sawyer stepped in at the door and caught a glimpse of the picture. Becky snatched at the book to close it, and had the hard luck to tear the pictured plate half down the middle. She thrust the volume into the desk, turned the key, and burst out crying with vexation.

"Tom Sawyer, you are just as mean as you can be, to sneak up on a person and look at what they're looking at."

"How could *I* know you was looking at anything?"

"You ought to be ashamed, Tom Sawyer; you know you're going to tell on me, and oh, what shall I do! I'll be whipped, and I never was whipped in school." Then she stamped her little foot and said, "*Be* so mean if you want to! Hateful, hateful, hateful!" And she flung out of the house with a new explosion of crying.

Tom stood still, rather flustered by this onslaught. Presently he said to himself:

What a curious kind of a fool a girl is! Never been licked in school! Shucks. What's a licking! Well, of course *I* ain't going to tell old Dobbins on this little fool, because there's other ways of getting even on her that ain't so mean; but what of it? Old Dobbins will ask who it was tore his book. Nobody'll answer. Then he'll ask first one and then t'other, and when he comes to the right girl he'll know it. Girls' faces always tell. She'll get licked. Well, there ain't any way out of it for Becky Thatcher. Tom conned the thing a moment longer and then added: All right, though; she'd like to see me in just such a fix—let her sweat it out!

In a few moments the master arrived and school "took in." Tom did not feel a strong interest in his studies. Every time he stole a glance at the girls' side of the room Becky's face troubled him. Presently the spelling-book discovery was made, and Tom's mind was entirely full of his own matters for a while after that. Becky roused up from her lethargy of distress and showed good interest in the proceedings. She did not expect that Tom could get out of his trouble by denying that he spilled the ink himself; and she was right. The denial only seemed to make the thing worse for Tom. Becky tried to believe she was glad of it, but she found she was not certain. When the worst came to the worst, she had an impulse to get up and tell on Alfred Temple, but she forced herself to keep still—because, said she to herself, he'll tell about me tearing the picture sure. I wouldn't say a word, not to save his life!

Tom took his whipping and went back to his seat not at all brokenhearted, for he thought it was possible that he had unknowingly upset the ink himself, in some skylarking bout—he had denied it for form's sake and because it was custom, and had stuck to the denial from principle.

A whole hour drifted by, the master sat nodding in his throne, the air was drowsy with the hum of study. By and by, Mr. Dobbins straightened himself up, yawned, then unlocked his desk and reached for his book, but seemed undecided whether to take it out or leave it. Most of the pupils glanced up languidly, but there were two among them that watched his movements with intent eyes. Mr. Dobbins fingered his book absently for a while, then took it out and settled himself in his chair to read!

Tom shot a glance at Becky. He had seen a hunted and helpless rabbit look as she did, with a gun leveled at its head. Instantly he forgot his quarrel with her. Quick—something must be done! He would run and snatch the book, spring through the door and fly! But his resolution shook for one little instant, and the chance was lost—the master opened the volume.

The next moment the master faced the school. Every eye sank under his gaze. There was that in it which smote even the innocent with fear. There was silence while one might count ten, the master was gathering his wrath. Then he spoke:

"Who tore this book?"

There was not a sound. One could have heard a pin drop. The master searched face after face for signs of guilt.

"Benjamin Rogers, did you tear this book?"

A denial. A pause.

"Joseph Harper, did you?"

Another denial. Tom's uneasiness grew more and more intense. The master scanned the ranks of boys—considered awhile, then turned to the girls:

"Amy Lawrence?"

A shake of the head.

"Gracie Miller?"

Another negative.

"Rebecca Thatcher [Tom glanced at her face—it was white with terror]—did you tear—no, look me in the face—did you tear this book?"

A thought shot like lightning through Tom's brain. He sprang to his feet and shouted—"*I* done it!"

The school stared in perplexity at this incredible folly. But as Tom stepped forward to go to his punishment the surprise, the gratitude, the adoration that shone upon him out of poor Becky's eyes seemed pay enough for a hundred floggings. Inspired by the splendor of his own act, he took without an outcry the most merciless flaying that even Mr. Dobbins had ever administered; and also received with indifference the added cruelty of a command to remain two hours after school—for he knew who would wait for him outside till his captivity was done.

Tom went to bed that night planning vengeance against Alfred Temple; for with shame and repentance Becky had told him all; but even the longing for vengeance had to give way, soon, to pleasanter musings, and he fell asleep at last, with Becky's latest words lingering dreamily in his ear—

"Tom, how *could* you be so noble!"

VACATION WAS APPROACHING. The schoolmaster, always severe, grew more severe than ever, for he wanted the school to make a good show on Examination Day. His rod and his ferule were seldom idle now. Mr. Dobbins' lashings were very vigorous ones, too; for although he carried, under his wig, a perfectly bald and shiny head, there was no sign of feebleness in his muscle.

As the great day approached, he seemed to take a vindictive pleasure in punishing the least shortcomings. The consequence was that the boys spent their nights in plotting revenge. At last they hit upon a plan that promised victory. They swore in the sign painter's boy, told him the scheme, and asked for his help. He had reasons for being delighted, for the master boarded in his father's family and had given the boy ample cause to hate him. The master always prepared himself for great occasions by getting pretty well fuddled, and when the dominie reached the proper condition on Examination Evening the sign painter's boy said he would "manage the thing" while the master napped in his chair; then he would be awakened at the right time and hurried to school.

In the fullness of time the interesting occasion arrived. At eight in the evening the schoolhouse was brilliantly lighted, and adorned with festoons of flowers. The master sat throned in his chair upon a raised platform, with his blackboard behind him. He was looking tolerably mellow. Rows of benches in front of him were occupied by the dignitaries of the town and by the parents of the pupils. To his left were seated the scholars who were to take part; the rest of the house was filled with nonparticipating scholars.

The exercises began. A very little boy stood up and sheepishly recited, "You'd scarce expect one of my age to speak in public on the stage," etc.—accompanying himself with the painfully exact and spasmodic gestures which a machine might have used—supposing the machine to be a trifle out of order. But he got through safely, though cruelly scared, and got a round of applause.

A little shamefaced girl lisped "Mary had a little lamb," etc., performed a compassion-inspiring curtsy, got her meed of applause and sat down flushed and happy.

Tom Sawyer stepped forward with conceited confidence and soared into the indestructible "Give me liberty or give me death" speech, with fine fury and frantic gesticulation, and broke down in the middle of it. A ghastly stage fright seized him, and his legs quaked. True, he had the manifest sympathy of the house—but he had the house's silence, too, which was even worse than its sympathy. Tom struggled awhile and then retired, utterly defeated. There was a weak attempt at applause, but it died early.

"The Boy Stood on the Burning Deck" followed: also "The Assyrian Came Down," and other declamatory gems. Then there were reading exercises and a spelling fight. The Latin class recited with honor. The feature of the evening was in order now—original "compositions" by the young ladies. Each in her turn stepped forward, cleared her throat, held up her manuscript (tied with dainty ribbon) and proceeded to read, with labored attention to "expression." The themes were the same that had been illuminated by their mothers and grandmothers before them. "Friendship," "Memories of Other Days," "Forms of Political Government Compared and Contrasted," "Melancholy," "Filial Love," etc. It may also be remarked that the number of compositions in which the word "beauteous" was overfondled and human experience referred to as "life's page" was up to the usual average.

When the last composition had been read, the master, mellow almost to the verge of geniality, put his chair aside, turned his back to the audience and began to draw a map of America on the blackboard, to exercise the geography class upon. But he made a sad business of it with his unsteady hand, and a smothered titter rippled over the house. He knew what the matter was and set himself to right it. He sponged out lines and remade them; but the tittering was only more pronounced. He threw his entire attention

upon his work, now, as if determined not to be put down by the mirth. Yet the tittering continued; it even manifestly increased.

And well it might. There was a garret above, pierced with a scuttle over his head; and down through this scuttle came a cat, suspended around the haunches by a string; she had a rag tied about her head and jaws to keep her from mewing; as she slowly descended she curved upward and clawed at the string, she swung downward and clawed at the intangible air.

The tittering rose higher and higher—the cat was within six inches of the absorbed teacher's head—down, down, a little lower, and she grabbed his wig with her desperate claws, clung to it, and was snatched up into the garret in an instant with her trophy still in her possession! And how the light did blaze abroad from the master's bald pate—for the sign painter's boy had *gilded* it!

That broke up the meeting. The boys were avenged. Vacation had come.

CHAPTER XI

TOM PRESENTLY WONDERED to find that his coveted vacation was beginning to hang heavily on his hands. Becky Thatcher was gone to her Constantinople home to stay with her parents during vacation—so there was no bright side to life anywhere.

The dreadful secret of the murder was a chronic misery.

Tom attempted a diary—but nothing happened during three days, and so he abandoned it.

Even the Glorious Fourth was in some sense a failure, for it rained hard, and there was no procession in consequence.

Then came the measles.

During two long weeks Tom lay a prisoner. He was very ill, he was interested in nothing. When he got upon his feet at last and moved feebly downtown, a melancholy change had come over everything and every creature. There had been a "revival," and everybody had "got religion." Tom found Joe Harper studying a Testament, and turned sadly away. He sought Ben Rogers, and found him visiting the poor with a basket of tracts. And when, in desperation, he flew for refuge to Huckleberry Finn and was received with a scriptural quotation, his heart broke and he crept home realizing that he alone of all the town was lost forever.

The next day the doctors were back; Tom had relapsed. The three weeks he spent on his back this time seemed an entire age. When he got abroad at last he was hardly grateful that he had been spared, remembering how companionless and forlorn he was. He drifted listlessly down the street and found Joe Harper and Huck Finn up an alley eating a stolen melon. Poor lads! They—like Tom—had suffered a relapse.

Then at last the sleepy atmosphere was stirred—and vigorously: the murder trial came on in the court.

The murder became the absorbing topic of village talk immediately. Tom could not get away from it. Every reference sent a shudder to his heart; he did not see how he could be suspected of knowing anything about the murder, but still he could not be comfortable in the midst of the gossip. It kept him in a cold shiver all the time. He took Huck to a lonely place to have a talk with him. It would be some relief to divide his burden of distress with another sufferer. Moreover, he wanted to assure himself that Huck had remained discreet.

"Huck, have you ever told anybody about—that?"

"Course I haven't. What makes you ask?"

"Well, I was afeard."

"Why, Tom Sawyer, we wouldn't be alive two days if that got found out. *You* know that."

Tom felt more comfortable. After a pause: "Huck, they couldn't anybody get me to tell."

"Well, that's all right, then. I reckon we're safe as long as we keep mum. But let's swear again, anyway. It's more surer."

"I'm agreed."

So they swore again with dread solemnities.

"What is the talk around you, Huck? I've heard a power of it."

"Talk? It's just Muff Potter, Muff Potter all the time. It keeps me in a sweat, constant, so's I want to hide som'ers."

"That's just the same way they go on round me. I reckon he's a goner. Don't you feel sorry for him, sometimes?"

"Most always. He ain't no account; but then he hain't ever done anything to hurt anybody. Just fishes a little, to get money to get drunk on—and loafs. But he give me half a fish, once, when there warn't enough for two; and lots of times he's kind of stood by me when I was out of luck."

"Well, he's mended kites for me, Huck, and knitted hooks onto my line. I wish we could get him out of there."

"My! We couldn't get him out, Tom. And besides, 'twouldn't do any good; they'd ketch him again."

"Yes, they would. But I hate to hear 'em abuse him so like the dickens when he never done—that."

"I do too, Tom. Lord, I hear 'em say he's the bloodiest-looking villain in this country, and they wonder he wasn't ever hung before."

The boys' talk brought them little comfort. As the twilight drew on, they did as they had often done before—went to the cell grating of the little isolated jail and gave Potter some tobacco and matches. His gratitude for their gifts had always smote their conscience before—it cut deeper than ever, this time. They felt cowardly and treacherous to the last degree when Potter said:

"You've been mighty good to me, boys—better'n anybody else in this town. And I don't forget it. Often I says to myself, says I, 'I used to mend all the boys' kites and things, and now they've all forgot old Muff when he's in trouble; but Tom don't, and Huck don't—*they* don't forget him,' says I, 'and I don't forget them.' Well, boys, I done an awful thing—drunk and crazy at the time—and now I got to swing for it, and it's right, I reckon—hope so, anyway. Well, we won't talk about that. Stand a little furder west—so—that's it; it's a prime comfort to see faces that's friendly. Git up on one another's backs and let me shake hands—that's it—yourn'll come through the bars, but mine's too big. Little hands, and weak—but they've helped Muff Potter a power, and they'd help him more if they could."

Tom went home miserable, and his dreams that night were full of horrors. The next day and the day after, he hung about the courtroom, drawn by an almost irresistible impulse to go in, but forcing himself to stay out. Huck was having the same experience. They studiously avoided each other. Tom kept his ears open, but invariably heard distressing news—the toils were closing relentlessly around poor Potter. At the end of the second day the village talk was to the effect that Injun Joe's evidence stood firm and unshaken, and that there was not the slightest question as to what the jury's verdict would be.

All the village flocked to the courthouse on the third morning, for this was to be the great day. After a long wait the jury filed in; shortly afterward, Potter, pale, timid and hopeless, was brought in, with chains upon him, and seated where all the curious could stare at him; no less conspicuous was Injun Joe, stolid as ever. There was another pause, and then the Judge arrived and the sheriff proclaimed the opening of the court.

Now a witness was called who testified that he found Muff Potter washing in a brook, at an early hour of the morning the murder was discovered, and that he immediately sneaked away. After some further questioning, counsel for the prosecution said, "Take the witness."

The prisoner raised his eyes for a moment, but dropped them again when his own counsel said, "I have no questions to ask him."

The next witness proved the finding of the knife near the corpse. Counsel for the prosecution said, "Take the witness."

"I have no questions to ask him," Potter's lawyer replied.

A third witness swore he had often seen the knife in Potter's possession. Again counsel for Potter declined to question. The faces of the audience began to betray annoyance. Did this attorney mean to throw away his client's life without an effort?

Several witnesses deposed concerning Potter's guilty behavior when brought to the scene of the murder. They were allowed to leave the stand without being cross-questioned. The perplexity and dissatisfaction of the house expressed itself in murmurs and provoked a reproof from the bench. Counsel for the prosecution now said, "By the oaths of citizens whose word is above suspicion, we have fastened this awful crime, beyond all possibility of question, upon the unhappy prisoner at the bar. We rest our case here."

A groan escaped from poor Potter, and he put his face in his hands and rocked his body softly to and fro. Many men in the courtroom were moved, and many women's compassion testified itself in tears. Counsel for the defense rose and said:

"Your Honor, in our remarks at the opening of this trial, we foreshadowed our purpose to prove that our client did this fearful deed while under the influence of a blind and irresponsible delirium produced by drink. We have changed our mind. We shall not offer that plea." Then to the clerk: "Call Thomas Sawyer!"

A puzzled amazement awoke in every face in the house, not even excepting Potter's. Every eye fastened itself upon Tom as he took his place upon the stand. The boy looked wild enough, for he was badly scared. The oath was administered.

"Thomas Sawyer, where were you on the seventeenth of June, about the hour of midnight?"

Tom glanced at Injun Joe's iron face and his tongue failed him. The audience listened, breathless, but the words refused to come. After a few moments, however, the boy managed to make part of the house hear:

"In the graveyard!"

"A little louder, please. Don't be afraid. You were—"

"In the graveyard."

A contemptuous smile flitted across Injun Joe's face.

"Were you anywhere near Horse Williams' grave?"

"Yes, sir."

"Speak up—just a trifle louder. How near were you?"

"Near as I am to you."

"Were you hidden, or not?"

"I was hid."

"Where?"

"Behind the trees that's on the edge of the grave."

Injun Joe gave a barely perceptible start.

"Anyone with you?"

"Yes, sir. I went there with—"

"Wait—wait a moment. Never mind mentioning your companion's name. We will produce him at the proper time. Did you carry anything there with you?"

Tom hesitated and looked confused.

"Speak out, my boy. What did you take there?"

"Only a—a—dead cat."

There was a ripple of mirth, which the court checked.

"We will produce the skeleton of that cat. Now, my boy, tell us everything that occurred—in your own way; don't be afraid."

Tom began—hesitatingly at first, but as he warmed to his subject his words flowed more easily; every sound ceased but his own voice, and with bated breath the audience hung upon his words, rapt in the ghastly fascinations of the tale. The strain upon pent emotion reached its climax when the boy said:

"—and as the doctor fetched the board around and Muff Potter fell, Injun Joe jumped with the knife and—"

Crash! Quick as lightning the half-breed sprang for a window, tore his way through all opposers, and was gone!

CHAPTER XII

TOM WAS A GLITTERING HERO once more—the pet of the old, the envy of the young. His name even went into immortal print, for the village paper magnified him. There were some that believed he would be President, yet, if he escaped hanging.

As usual, the fickle, unreasoning world took Muff Potter to its bosom and fondled him as lavishly as it had abused him before. But that sort of conduct is to the world's credit; therefore it is not well to find fault with it.

Tom's days were days of splendor to him, but his nights were seasons of horror. Injun Joe infested all his dreams, and always with doom in his eye. Hardly any temptation could persuade the boy to stir abroad after nightfall. Poor Huck was in the same state, for Tom had told the whole story to Muff Potter's lawyer, and Huck was sore afraid that his share in the business might leak out yet, notwithstanding Injun Joe's flight had saved him the suffering of testifying in court. He had got the attorney to promise secrecy, but what of that? Since Tom's harassed conscience had managed to drive him to the lawyer's house and wring a dread tale from lips that had been sealed with the dismalest of oaths, Huck's confidence in the human race was well-nigh obliterated.

Rewards had been offered, the country had been scoured, but no Injun Joe was found. Half the time Tom was afraid Injun Joe would never be captured; the other half he was afraid he would be. He felt sure he never could draw a safe breath again until that man was dead and he had seen the corpse.

The slow days drifted on, and each left behind it a slightly lightened weight of apprehension.

Meanwhile, one day, Tom found himself with a sudden raging desire to go somewhere and dig for hidden treasure. This desire is one which usually comes at some time or other in every rightly constructed boy's life. He sallied out to find Huck Finn the Red-Handed, and opened the matter to him. Huck was willing. "Where'll we dig?" said Huck.

"Oh, most anywhere."

"Why, is it hid all around?"

"No indeed it ain't. It's hid in mighty particular places—sometimes on islands, sometimes in rotten chests under the end of a limb of an old dead tree, just where the shadow falls at midnight; but mostly under the floor in ha'nted houses."

"Who hides it?" Huck asked.

"Why, robbers, of course—who'd you reckon? Sunday-school sup'rintendents?"

"I don't know. If 'twas mine I wouldn't hide it; I'd spend it."

"So would I. But robbers don't do that way. They always hide it. They think they will come after it, but they generally forget the marks, or else they die. Anyway, it lays there a long time and gets rusty; and by and by somebody finds an old yellow paper that tells how to find the marks—a paper that's got to be ciphered over about a week because it's mostly hi'roglyphics."

"Hiro—which?"

"Hi'roglyphics—pictures and things, you know, that don't seem to mean anything."

"Have you got one of them papers, Tom?"

"No."

"Well then, how you going to find the marks?"

"I don't want any marks. We've tried Jackson's Island a little, and we can try it again; and there's the old ha'nted house up the Still-House branch, and there's lots of dead-limb trees—dead loads of 'em."

"How you going to know which one to go for?"

"Go for all of 'em!"

"Why, Tom, it'll take all summer."

"Well, what of that? Suppose you find a brass pot with a hundred dollars, or a rotten chest full of di'monds. How's that?"

Huck's eyes glowed. "That's bully. Just you gimme the hundred dollars and I don't want no di'monds."

"All right. But I bet you *I* ain't going to throw off on di'monds. Some of 'em's worth twenty dollars apiece—there ain't any, hardly, but's worth six bits or a dollar. Kings have slathers of them."

"Well, all right. But say, Tom—where you going to dig first?"

"S'pose we tackle that old dead-limb tree on the hill t'other side of Still-House branch?"

"I'm agreed."

So they got a crippled pick and a shovel, and set out on their three-mile tramp. They arrived hot and panting, and threw themselves down in the shade of a neighboring elm to rest.

"Say, Huck," said Tom, "if we find a treasure here, what you going to do with your share?"

"Well, I'll have pie and a glass of soda every day, and I'll go to every circus that comes along. I'll have a gay time."

"Ain't you going to save any of it?"

"Save it? What for?"

"Why, so as to have something to live on, by and by."

"Oh, that ain't any use. Pap would come back to town someday and get his claws on it, and I tell you he'd clean it out pretty quick. What you going to do with yourn, Tom?"

"I'm going to buy a new drum, and a sword, and a red necktie and a bull pup, and get married."

"Married! Tom, you—why, you ain't in your right mind! Look at Pap and my mother. Fight! Why, they used to fight all the time."

"That ain't anything. The girl I'm going to marry won't fight."

"Tom, they're all alike. They'll all comb a body. Now you better think 'bout this awhile. What's the name of the gal?"

"I'll tell you sometime—not now."

"All right. Only if you get married I'll be more lonesomer than ever."

"No you won't. You'll come and live with me. Now stir out of this and we'll go to digging."

They worked and sweated for half an hour. No result. They toiled another half hour. Still no result. Huck said, "Do they always bury it as deep as this?"

"Not generally. I reckon we haven't got the right place."

So they chose a new spot and began again. After some time Huck leaned on his shovel, swabbed his brow with his sleeve, and said, "Where you going to dig next, after we get this one?"

"I reckon maybe we'll tackle the old tree that's over yonder on Cardiff Hill back of the widow's."

"I reckon that'll be a good one." The work went on. By and by Huck said, "Blame it, we must be in the wrong place again."

"It *is* mighty curious, Huck. I don't understand it. Oh, *I* know! What blamed fools we are! You got to find out where the shadow of the limb falls at midnight, and that's where you dig!"

"Then confound it, we got to come back in the night. Can you get out?"

"I bet I will."

"Well, I'll come around and meow tonight."

"All right."

That night, about the appointed time, they sat in the shadow waiting. Spirits whispered in the rustling leaves, ghosts lurked in the murky nooks, and the deep baying of a hound floated up out of the distance. The boys talked little. By and by they judged that twelve had come; they marked where the shadow fell, and began to dig. Their hopes commenced to rise, and their interest grew stronger. The hole deepened, but every time their hearts jumped to hear the pick strike something, they suffered a new disappointment. At last Tom said, "It ain't any use, Huck, we're wrong again."

"We *can't* be wrong. We spotted the shadder to a dot."

"I know it, but we only guessed at the time. Like enough it was too late or too early."

Huck dropped his shovel. "That's the very trouble," he said. "We can't ever tell the right time, and besides, I been creeping all over, ever since I got here. Let's try somewheres else."

Tom considered awhile, and then said, "The ha'nted house. That's it!"

"Blame it, I don't like ha'nted houses. Those ghosts come sliding around in a shroud, when you ain't noticing, and peep over your shoulder and grit their teeth. I couldn't stand such a thing, Tom."

"Yes, but, Huck, ghosts don't travel around except at night. They won't hender us from digging there in the daytime."

"Well, that's so. But you know mighty well people don't go about that ha'nted house in the day nor the night."

"Well, nothing's ever been seen in that house except in the night—just blue lights slipping by the windows—no regular ghosts."

"Well, where you see one of them blue lights flickering around, Tom, you can bet there's a ghost mighty close behind it. *You* know that they don't anybody but ghosts use 'em."

"Yes, that's so. But anyway they don't come around in the daytime, so what's the use of our being afeard?"

"Well, all right. We'll tackle the ha'nted house if you say so—but I reckon it's taking chances. Let's hide the tools in the bushes."

They had started down the hill by this time. There in the middle of the moonlit valley below them stood the "ha'nted" house, utterly isolated, its fences gone long ago, rank weeds smothering the doorsteps, a corner of the roof caved in. The boys gazed awhile, half expecting to see a blue light flit past a window; then they struck far off to the right, to give the haunted house a wide berth, and took their way homeward through the woods that adorned the rearward side of Cardiff Hill.

About noon the next day the boys arrived at the dead tree; they had come for their tools. Tom was impatient to go to the haunted house; Huck was also—but suddenly said, "Looky here, Tom, do you know what day it is?"

Tom was startled. "My! I never thought of it, Huck!"

"Well, I didn't neither, but all at once it popped onto me that it was Friday."

"Blame it, a body can't be too careful, Huck. We might 'a' got into an awful scrape, tackling such a thing on a Friday."

"*Might!* Better say we *would!* There's some lucky days, maybe, but Friday ain't."

"Well, Huck, we'll drop this thing for today, and play. Do you know Robin Hood?"

"No. Who's Robin Hood?"

"Why, he was one of the greatest men that was ever in England. He was a robber. He robbed sheriffs and rich people and such like. But he never bothered the poor. He always divided up with 'em."

"Well, he must 'a' been a brick."

"I bet you he was, Huck. He could lick any man in England; and he could take his yew bow and plug a ten-cent piece at a mile and a half. We'll play Robin Hood—it's nobby fun. I'll learn you."

"I'm agreed."

So they played Robin Hood all afternoon, now and then casting an eye down upon the haunted house and passing a remark about the morrow's prospects there. As the sun began to sink into the west they took their way homeward. On Saturday, shortly after noon, they were back. They dug a little in their last hole at the dead tree, not with great hope, but merely because Tom said there were so many cases where people had given up a treasure after getting down within six inches of it, and then somebody else had turned it up with a single thrust of a shovel. The thing failed this time, however, so the boys shouldered their tools and went away feeling that they had fulfilled all the requirements that belong to the business of treasure hunting.

When they reached the haunted house there was something so

weird and grisly about the dead silence that reigned there under the baking sun that they were afraid, for a moment, to venture in. Then they crept to the door and took a trembling peep. They saw a weed-grown, floorless room, an ancient fireplace, vacant windows, a ruinous staircase; and everywhere hung ragged and abandoned cobwebs.

They presently entered, softly, with quickened pulses and muscles tense and ready for instant retreat. In a little while familiarity modified their fears and they gave the place an interested examination, rather wondering at their own boldness. Next they wanted to look upstairs. This was something like cutting off retreat, but they got to daring each other, and of course there could be but one result—they threw their tools into a corner and made the ascent. Up there were the same signs of decay. In one corner they found a closet that promised mystery, but there was nothing in it. Their courage was up now and well in hand. They were about to go down and begin work when—

"Sh!" said Tom.

"What is it?" whispered Huck, blanching with fright.

"Sh! . . . There! . . . Hear it?"

"Yes! . . . Oh, my! Let's run!"

"Keep still! They're coming right toward the door."

The boys stretched themselves upon the floor with their eyes to knotholes, and lay waiting, in a misery of fear.

"They've stopped . . . no—coming . . . here they are. Don't whisper another word, Huck. My, I wish I was out of this!"

Two men entered. Each boy said to himself, There's the old deaf and dumb Spaniard that's been about town once or twice lately—never saw t'other man before.

"T'other" was a ragged, unkempt creature, with nothing very pleasant in his face. The Spaniard was wrapped in a serape; he had bushy white whiskers; long white hair flowed from under his sombrero, and he wore green goggles. When they came in, "t'other" was talking in a low voice; they sat down on the ground, with their backs to the wall, and the speaker's words became more distinct.

"No," said he, "I don't like it. It's dangerous."

"Dangerous!" grunted the "deaf and dumb" Spaniard to the vast surprise of the boys. "Milksop!"

This voice made the boys gasp and quake. It was Injun Joe's! After a silence Joe said, "What's any more dangerous than that job up yonder—but nothing's come of it."

"That's different. Not another house about."

"Well, what's more dangerous than coming here in the daytime! Anybody would suspicion us that saw us."

"*I* know that. But there warn't any other place as handy. I want to quit this shanty. I wanted to yesterday, only it warn't any use trying to stir out of here with those infernal boys playing over there on the hill right in full view."

"Those infernal boys" quaked again, and thought how lucky it was that they had remembered it was Friday and concluded to wait a day. They wished in their hearts they had waited a year.

The two men got out some food and made a luncheon. After a long and thoughtful silence, Injun Joe said, "Look here, lad—you go back up the river where you belong. Wait there till you hear from me. I'll take the chances on dropping into this town just once more. We'll do that 'dangerous' job after I've spied around a little and think things look right for it. Then for Texas! We'll leg it, together!"

This was satisfactory. Both men presently fell to yawning, and Injun Joe said, "I'm dead for sleep! It's your turn to watch."

He curled down in the weeds and soon began to snore. His comrade became quiet and presently began to nod; his head dropped lower, and now both men were snoring. The boys drew a long breath. Tom whispered, "Now's our chance—come!"

Huck said, "I can't—I'd die if they was to wake."

Tom urged—Huck held back. At last Tom started alone. But the first step he made wrung such a hideous creak from the floor that he sank down almost dead with fright. He never made a second attempt. The boys lay there counting the dragging moments till it seemed to them that time must be done and eternity growing gray; and then they were grateful to note that at last the sun was setting.

Now one snore ceased. Injun Joe sat up, stared around, stirred his comrade with his foot and said, "Here! *You're* a watchman, ain't you! All right, though—nothing's happened."

"My! Have I been asleep?"

"Oh, partly, partly. Nearly time for us to be moving, pard. What'll we do with what little swag we've got left?"

"Leave it here, I reckon. No use to take it away till we start south. Six hundred and fifty in silver's something to carry."

"Yes, but look here; it may be a good while before I get the right chance at that job; accidents might happen; 'tain't in such a very good place; we'll just regularly bury it."

"Good idea," said the comrade, who walked across the room, knelt down, raised one of the hearthstones and took out a bag that jingled pleasantly. He subtracted from it twenty or thirty dollars for himself and as much for Injun Joe and passed the bag to the latter, who was in the corner, now, digging with his bowie knife.

The boys forgot all their fears in an instant. With gloating eyes they watched every movement. Luck! The splendor of it was beyond imagination! Six hundred dollars was money enough to make half a dozen boys rich! Here was treasure-hunting under the happiest auspices—there would not be any bothersome uncertainty as to where to dig. They nudged each other every moment—eloquent nudges easily understood, for they simply meant—Oh, but ain't you glad *now* we're here!

Joe's knife struck upon something. "Hello!" said he.

"What is it?" said his comrade.

"Half-rotten plank—no, it's a box! Here—I've broke a hole." He reached his hand in. "Man, it's money!"

The two men examined the handful of coins. They were gold. The boys above were as excited as themselves, and as delighted.

Joe's comrade said, "We'll make quick work of this. There's an old rusty pick over in that corner—I saw it a minute ago."

He brought the boys' pick and shovel. Injun Joe took the pick, looked it over critically, shook his head, and then began to use it. The ironbound box was soon unearthed. The men contemplated the treasure in it.

"Pard, there's thousands of dollars here," said Injun Joe.

" 'Twas always said that Murrel's gang used to be around here one summer," the stranger observed.

"I know it," said Injun Joe; "and this looks like it."

"*Now* you won't need to do that job."

The half-breed frowned. Said he, "You don't know all about that thing. 'Tain't robbery—it's *revenge!*" and a wicked light flamed in his eyes. "I'll need your help in it. When it's finished—then Texas. Go home to your Nance and your kids, and stand by till you hear from me."

"Well—if you say so. What'll we do with this—bury it again?"

"Yes. [Ravishing delight overhead.] *No!* By the great Sachem, no! [Profound distress overhead.] I'd nearly forgot. That pick had fresh earth on it! [The boys were sick with terror in a moment.] What business has a pick and shovel here? Who brought them here—and where are they gone? What! Bury it again and leave them to come and see the ground disturbed? Not exactly. We'll take it to my den."

"Why, of course! You mean Number One?"

"No—Number Two—under the cross. The other place is too common."

"All right. It's nearly dark enough to start."

Injun Joe got up and went about from window to window peeping out. Presently he said, "Who could have brought those tools here? Do you reckon they can be upstairs?"

The boys' breath forsook them. Injun Joe put his hand on his knife, halted a moment, undecided, and then turned toward the stairway. The boys thought of the closet, but their strength was gone. The steps came creaking up the stairs—the intolerable distress of the situation woke the stricken resolution of the lads— they were about to spring for the closet, when there was a crash of rotten timbers and Injun Joe landed on the ground amid the debris of the ruined stairway. He gathered himself up cursing, and his comrade said:

"Now what's the use of all that? If anybody's up there, let them *stay* there—who cares? If they want to jump down, now, and get into trouble, who objects? It will be dark in fifteen minutes—and then let them follow us if they want to. In my opinion, whoever hove those things in here caught a sight of us and took us for ghosts or something. I'll bet they're running yet."

Joe grumbled awhile; then he agreed with his friend. Shortly afterward they slipped out of the house in the twilight, and moved toward the river with their precious box.

Tom and Huck rose up, weak but vastly relieved, and stared after them through the chinks between the logs of the house. Follow? Not they. They were content to reach ground again without broken necks, and take the townward track over the hill. They did not talk much. They were too much absorbed in hating themselves—hating the ill luck that made them take the spade and the pick there. But for that, Injun Joe never would have suspected. He would have hidden the silver with the gold to wait there till his "revenge" was satisfied, and then he would have had the misfortune to find that money turn up missing.

They resolved to keep a lookout for that Spaniard when he should come to town spying out for chances to do his revengeful job, and follow him to "Number Two," wherever that might be. Then a ghastly thought occurred to Tom. "Revenge. What if he means *us*, Huck!"

"Oh, don't!" said Huck, nearly fainting.

They talked it all over, and as they entered town they agreed to believe that he might possibly mean somebody else—might at least mean nobody but Tom, since only Tom had testified.

Very, very small comfort it was to Tom to be alone in danger! Company would be a palpable improvement, he thought.

CHAPTER XIII

THE ADVENTURE OF THE DAY mightily tormented Tom's dreams that night. In the morning it even occurred to him that the great adventure itself might have been a dream! There was one very strong argument in favor of this idea—namely, that the quantity of coin he had seen was too vast to be real. He had never seen as much as fifty dollars in one mass before, and he was like all boys of his age and station in life, in that he imagined that all references to "hundreds" and "thousands" were mere fanciful forms of speech, and that no such sums really existed in the world. This uncertainty must be swept away. He snatched a hurried breakfast and went to find Huck. Huck was sitting on the gunwale of a flatboat, dangling his feet in the water and looking very melancholy.

"Hello, Huck!"

"Hello, yourself." Silence for a minute. "Tom, if we'd 'a' left the blame tools at the dead tree, we'd 'a' got the money. Oh, ain't it awful!"

"'Tain't a dream, then! Somehow I most wish it was."

"What ain't a dream?"

"That thing yesterday."

"Dream! If them stairs hadn't broke down you'd 'a' seen how much dream it was! I've had dreams enough all night—with that patch-eyed Spanish devil going for me all through 'em—rot him!"

"No, not rot him. *Find* him! Track the money!"

"Tom, we'll never find him. A feller don't have only one chance for such a pile—and that one's lost. I'd feel mighty shaky if I was to see him, anyway."

"Well, so'd I; but I'd like to see him, anyway—and track him out—to his Number Two."

"Number Two—yes. I ben thinking 'bout that. What do you reckon it is?"

"I dono. Say, Huck—maybe it's the number of a house!"

"Goody! . . . No, Tom, that ain't it. If it is, it ain't in this one-horse town. They ain't no numbers here."

"Well, that's so. Lemme think a minute. Here—the number of a room—in a tavern?"

"Oh, that's the trick! They ain't only two taverns. We can find out quick."

"You stay here, Huck, till I come."

Tom was off at once, and was gone half an hour. He found that in the best tavern, Number Two had long been occupied by a young lawyer. In the less ostentatious Temperance Tavern,

Number Two was a mystery. The tavern keeper's young son said it was kept locked all the time, and he never saw anybody go in or out of it except at night; he did not know any particular reason for this; had had some curiosity, but had entertained himself with the idea that room was "ha'nted."

"That's what I've found out, Huck. I reckon that's the very Number Two we're after."

"I reckon it is, Tom. Now what you going to do?"

Tom thought. Then he said, "I'll tell you. The back door of that Number Two comes out into that little close alley between the tavern and the old brick store. Now you get hold of all the door keys you can find, and I'll nip all of Auntie's, and the first dark night we'll go there and try 'em. And mind you, keep a lookout for Injun Joe, because he said he was going to drop into town once more. If you see him, you just follow him; and if he don't go to that Number Two, that ain't the place."

"Lordy, I don't want to foller him by myself!"

"Why, it'll be night, sure. He mightn't ever see you—and if he did, maybe he'd never think anything."

"Well, I dono. If it's pretty dark—I'll try."

"You bet *I'll* follow him, if it's dark, Huck. Why, he might 'a' found out he couldn't get his revenge, and be going right after that money."

"It's so, Tom. I'll foller him; I will, by jingos!"

"Now you're *talking!* Don't you weaken, Huck, and I won't."

THAT NIGHT TOM AND HUCK were ready for their adventure. They hung about the tavern until after nine, one watching the alley and the other the tavern door. Nobody entered the alley or left it; nobody resembling the Spaniard entered or left the tavern door. The night promised to be a fair one; so Tom went home with the understanding that if a considerable degree of darkness came on, Huck was to come and "meow," whereupon he would slip out and try the keys. But the night remained clear, and Huck retired to bed in an empty sugar hogshead about twelve.

Tuesday the boys had the same ill luck. Also Wednesday. But

Thursday night promised better. Tom slipped out with his aunt's old tin lantern, and a large towel to blindfold it with. He hid the lantern in Huck's sugar hogshead and the watch began. An hour before midnight the tavern lights (the only ones thereabouts) were put out. No Spaniard had been seen. Nobody had entered or left the alley. Darkness reigned. Everything was auspicious.

Tom got his lantern, lit it, wrapped it in the towel, and the two adventurers crept in the gloom toward the tavern. Huck stood sentry and Tom felt his way into the alley. Then there was a season of waiting anxiety that weighed upon Huck's spirits like a mountain. Momentarily he expected catastrophe, and it seemed as if his heart would soon wear itself out, the way it was beating. Suddenly there was a flash of light and Tom came tearing by him. "Run!" said he. "Run for your life!"

He needn't have repeated it; once was enough; Huck was making thirty or forty miles an hour before the repetition was uttered. The boys never stopped till they reached the shed of a deserted slaughterhouse at the lower end of the village. As soon as Tom got his breath he said:

"Huck, it was awful! I tried two of the keys, just as soft as I could; but they made a power of racket. They wouldn't turn in the lock, either. Well, without noticing what I was doing, I took hold of the knob, and open comes the door! It warn't locked! I hopped in, and shook off the towel, and, *great Caesar's ghost!*"

"What—what'd you see, Tom?"

"Huck, I most stepped onto Injun Joe's hand! He was laying there, sound asleep on the floor, with his old patch on his eye and his arms spread out."

"Lordy, what did you do? Did he wake up?"

"No, never budged. Drunk, I reckon. I just grabbed that towel and started!"

"I'd never 'a' thought of the towel, I bet!"

"Well, *I* would. My aunt would make me mighty sick if I lost it."

"Say, Tom, did you see that box?"

"Huck, I didn't wait to look around. I didn't see anything but a bottle and a tin cup on the floor by Injun Joe; yes, and I saw two barrels and lots more bottles. Don't you see, now, what's the matter with that ha'nted room?"

"How?"

"Why, it's ha'nted with whiskey! Maybe *all* the Temperance Taverns have got a ha'nted room, hey, Huck?"

"I reckon maybe that's so. Who'd 'a' thought such a thing? But say, Tom, now's a mighty good time to get that box, if Injun Joe's drunk."

"It is that! You try it!"

Huck shuddered. "Well, no—I reckon not."

"Only one bottle alongside of Injun Joe ain't enough, Huck. If there'd been three, he'd be drunk enough and I'd do it."

There was a long pause for reflection, and then Tom said, "Looky here, Huck, let's not try that thing anymore till we know Injun Joe's not in there. Now, if we watch every night, we'll be dead sure to see him go out, sometime or other, and then we'll snatch that box quicker'n lightning."

"Well, I'm agreed. I'll watch the whole night long, and I'll do it every night, too, if you'll do the other part of the job."

"All right, I will. All you got to do is to trot up Hooper Street a block and meow."

"Agreed, and good as wheat!"

"Now, Huck, I'll go home. It'll begin to be daylight in a couple of hours. You go back and watch, will you?"

"I'll ha'nt that tavern every night for a year, Tom! I'll sleep all day and I'll stand watch all night."

"That's all right. Now, where you going to sleep?"

"In Ben Rogers' hayloft."

"Well, if I don't want you in the daytime, I'll let you sleep. I won't come bothering around. Anytime you see something's up, in the night, just skip right around and meow."

THE FIRST THING TOM HEARD on Friday morning was a glad piece of news—Judge Thatcher's family had come back to town. Both Injun Joe and the treasure sank into secondary importance for a moment, and Becky took the chief place in the boy's interest. He saw her, and they had an exhausting good time playing "hi-spy" and "gully-keeper" with a crowd of their schoolmates.

The day was crowned in a peculiarly satisfactory way: Becky teased her mother to appoint the next day for the long-promised picnic, and she consented. The invitations were sent out before sunset, and straightway the young folks of the village were thrown into a fever of pleasurable anticipation. Tom's excitement enabled him to keep awake until a late hour, and he had good hopes of hearing Huck's "meow," and of having his treasure to astonish Becky and the picnickers with, next day; but he was disappointed; no signal came that night.

Morning came, eventually, and by eleven o'clock a giddy and rollicking company were gathered at Judge Thatcher's. It was not the custom for elderly people to mar picnics with their presence. The children were considered safe enough under the wings of a few young ladies of eighteen and a few young gentlemen of twenty-three or thereabouts. The old steam ferryboat was chartered for the occasion; presently the gay throng filed up the main street laden with provision baskets. Sid was sick and had to miss the fun; Mary remained at home to entertain him. The last thing Mrs. Thatcher said to Becky was, "You'll not get back till late. Perhaps you'd better stay all night with one of the girls that live near the ferry landing, child."

"Then I'll stay with Susy Harper, Mamma."

"Very well. Mind and behave yourself."

Three miles below town the ferryboat stopped at the mouth of a woody hollow and tied up. The crowd swarmed ashore and soon the forest distances and craggy heights echoed with shoutings and laughter. All the different ways of getting hot and tired were gone through with, and by and by the rovers straggled back to camp fortified with responsible appetites, and then the destruction of the good things began. After the feast there was a refreshing season of rest and chat in the shade. By and by somebody shouted, "Who's ready for the cave?"

Everybody was. Candles were procured, and straightway there

was a general scamper up the hill. The mouth of the cave was up the hillside—an opening shaped like a letter A. Its massive oaken door stood unbarred. Within was a small chamber, chilly as an ice-house, and walled with limestone that was dewy with a cold sweat.

It was romantic and mysterious to stand here in the gloom and look out upon the green valley shining in the sun. But the impressiveness of the situation quickly wore off, and the romping began again. By and by the procession went filing down the steep descent of the main avenue, the flickering rank of lights dimly revealing the lofty walls of rock almost to their point of junction sixty feet overhead. This main avenue was not more than eight or ten feet wide.

Every few steps other lofty and still narrower crevices branched from it on either hand—for McDougal's Cave was but a vast labyrinth of crooked aisles that ran into each other and out again and led nowhere. It was said that one might wander days and nights together through its tangle of rifts and chasms, and never find the end; and that he might go down and down, into the earth, and it was just the same—labyrinth underneath labyrinth, and no end to any of them. No man "knew" the cave. Most of the young men knew a portion of it, and it was not customary to venture much beyond this known portion. Tom Sawyer knew as much of the cave as anyone.

The procession moved along the main avenue some three quarters of a mile, and then groups and couples began to slip aside into branch avenues, fly along the dismal corridors, and take each other by surprise at points where the corridors joined again. Parties were able to elude each other for the space of half an hour without going beyond the "known" ground.

By and by, one group after another came straggling back to the mouth of the cave, panting, hilarious, smeared with tallow drippings and daubed with clay. Then they were astonished to find that they had been taking no note of time and that night was at hand. The clanging bell had been calling for half an hour. However, this sort of close to the day's adventures was romantic and therefore satisfactory. When the ferryboat with her wild freight pushed into the stream, nobody cared sixpence for the wasted time but the captain of the craft.

Huck was already upon his watch when the ferryboat's lights went past the wharf. He heard no noise on board, for the young people were as subdued as people usually are who are nearly tired to death. He wondered what boat it was, and then he dropped it out of his mind and put his attention upon his business. The night was growing cloudy and dark. Ten o'clock came, and the noise of vehicles ceased, scattered lights began to wink out, the village betook itself to its slumbers and left the small watcher alone with the silence. Eleven o'clock came, and the tavern lights were put out; darkness everywhere, now. Huck waited what seemed a weary long time, but nothing happened. His faith was weakening. Was there any use? Why not give it up and turn in?

A noise fell upon his ear. He was all attention in an instant. The alley door closed softly. He sprang to the corner of the brick store. The next moment two men brushed by him, and one seemed to have something under his arm. It must be that box! So they were going to remove the treasure. Why call Tom now? It would be absurd—the men would get away with the box and never be found again. No, he would follow them; he would trust to the darkness for security from discovery. So Huck stepped out and glided along behind the men, catlike, with bare feet, allowing them to keep just far enough ahead not to be invisible.

They moved up the river street, then turned left and went straight ahead to the path that led up Cardiff Hill. This they took, climbing up toward the summit. Presently they plunged into a narrow path between tall sumac bushes, and were at once hidden in the gloom. Huck shortened his distance, now, for they would never be able to see him. He trotted along awhile; then slackened his pace, fearing he was gaining too fast; then stopped altogether; listened; no sound save the beating of his own heart. The hooting of an owl came from over the hill. But no footsteps. Heavens, was everything lost! He was about to spring with winged feet, when a man cleared his throat not four feet from him! Huck's heart shot into his throat, but he swallowed it again; then he stood there shaking as if a dozen agues had taken charge of him. He knew where he was. He was within five steps of the stile leading into Widow Douglas's grounds. Very well, he thought, let them bury it there; it won't be hard to find.

Now there was a voice—a very low voice—Injun Joe's:

"Damn her, maybe she's got company—there's lights, late as it is."

"I can't see any."

This was the stranger's voice—the stranger of the haunted house. A deadly chill went to Huck's heart—this, then, was the "revenge" job! His thought was to fly. Then he remembered that the Widow Douglas had been kind to him more than once, and maybe these men were going to murder her. He wished he dared venture to warn her; but he didn't dare—they might come and catch him. He thought all this in the moment that elapsed between the stranger's remark and Injun Joe's next—which was—

"Because the bush is in your way. Now—this way—now you see, don't you?"

"Yes. Well, there *is* company, I reckon. Better give it up."

"Give it up, and I just leaving this country forever! Give it up and never have another chance! I tell you, I don't care for her swag—you can have it. But her husband was rough on me many times—he was the justice of the peace that jugged me for a vagrant. And that ain't all. He had me horsewhipped! *Horsewhipped!* In front of the jail—with all the town looking on! Then he took advantage of me and died. But I'll take it out of *her*."

"Oh, don't kill her! Don't do that!"

"Kill? Who said anything about killing? I would kill *him* if he was here, but not her. When you want to get revenge on a woman you don't kill her—bosh! You go for her looks. You slit her nostrils—you notch her ears like a sow!"

"By God, that's—"

"Keep your opinion to yourself! I'll tie her to the bed. If she bleeds to death, is that my fault? You'll help in this thing, my friend, that's why you're here—I mightn't be able alone. If you flinch, I'll kill you. Do you understand?"

"Well, if it's got to be done, let's get at it. The quicker the better—I'm all in a shiver."

"Do it *now?* And company there? No—we'll wait till the lights are out."

Huck held his breath and stepped gingerly back; planted his foot carefully, after balancing, one-legged, in a precarious way and almost toppling over. He took another step back, with the same elaboration and the same risks; then another and another, and—a twig snapped under his foot! His breath stopped and he listened. There was no sound. His gratitude was measureless. Now he turned in his tracks, between the walls of sumac bushes—turned himself as carefully as if he were a ship—and then stepped quickly but cautiously along. When he felt secure he picked up his nimble heels and flew. Down, down he sped, till he reached a house belonging to an old Welshman, halfway down the hill. He banged at the door, and presently the heads of the old man and his two stalwart sons were thrust from windows.

"What's the row there? What do you want?"

"Let me in—quick! It's me—Huckleberry Finn!"

"Huckleberry Finn, indeed! It ain't a name to open many doors! But let him in, lads, and let's see what's the trouble."

"Please don't ever tell *I* told you," were Huck's first words when he got in. "Please don't—I'd be killed, sure—but the widow's been good friends to me, and I want to tell—I *will* tell if you'll promise you won't ever say it was me."

"By George, he *has* got something to tell, or he wouldn't act so!" exclaimed the old man. "Out with it, and nobody here'll ever tell, lad."

Three minutes later the old man and his sons, well armed, were up the hill and entering the sumac path on tiptoe, their weapons in their hands. Huck accompanied them no farther. He hid behind a boulder and fell to listening. There was a lagging, anxious silence, and then all of a sudden there was an explosion of firearms and a cry.

Huck waited for no particulars. He sprang away and sped down the hill as fast as his legs could carry him.

CHAPTER XIV

As THE EARLIEST SUSPICION of dawn appeared on Sunday morning, Huck rapped gently at the old Welshman's door. The inmates were asleep, but it was a sleep that was set on a hair trigger. A call came from a window: "Who's there!"

Huck's scared voice answered, "It's only Huck Finn!"

"It's a name that can open this door night or day, lad—and welcome!"

These were strange words to the vagabond boy's ears. He could not recollect that the closing word had ever been applied in his case before. The door was unlocked, and he entered. He was given a seat, and the old man and his tall sons dressed speedily.

"Now, my boy, I hope you're good and hungry, because breakfast will be ready soon! I and the boys hoped you'd stop here last night."

"I was awful scared," said Huck. "I took out when the pistols went off, and I didn't stop for three mile. I've come now becuz I wanted to know about it, and I come before daylight becuz I didn't want to run acrost them devils, even if they was dead."

"You do look as if you've had a hard night—but there'll be a bed here for you when you've had your breakfast. No, they ain't dead, lad—we are sorry for that. We crept along on tiptoe till we got within fifteen feet of them—dark as a cellar that sumac path was—and just then I found I was going to sneeze. I tried to keep it back, but no use! The sneeze started those scoundrels a-rustling, so I sung out, 'Fire, boys!' and blazed away at the place where the rustling was. So did the boys. But they were off in a jiffy, those villains, and we after them, down through the woods. I judge we never touched them. They fired a shot apiece as they started, but their bullets whizzed by us. As soon as we lost the sound of their feet we went and stirred up the constables. They got a posse together, and went off to guard the riverbank, and as soon as it is light the sheriff and a gang are going to beat up the woods. My boys will be with them presently. I wish we had some sort of description of those rascals. But you couldn't see what they were like in the dark, lad, I suppose?"

"Oh, yes, I saw them downtown and follered them. One's the old deaf and dumb Spaniard that's ben around here once or twice, and t'other's a mean-looking, ragged—"

"That's enough, lad, we know the men! Happened on them in the woods one day, and they slunk away. Boys, tell the sheriff—get your breakfast tomorrow morning!"

The Welshman's sons departed at once. As they were leaving Huck exclaimed, "Oh, please don't tell *anybody* it was me that blowed on them! Oh, please!"

"All right if you say it, Huck, but you ought to have the credit of what you did."

When the young men were gone, the old Welshman said, "They won't tell—and I won't. But how did you come to follow these fellows, lad? Were they looking suspicious?"

Huck was silent while he framed a duly cautious reply. Then he said, "Well, you see, I'm a kind of a hard lot—least everybody says so—and sometimes I can't sleep much on account of thinking about it and sort of trying to strike out a new way of doing. That was the way of it last night. I couldn't sleep, and so I come along up street 'bout midnight, a-turning it all over, and just when I got to that old brick store by the Temperance Tavern along comes these two chaps, slipping along close by me. They had something under their arm, and I reckoned they'd stole it. Then they went on, and I follered 'em. I wanted to see what was up—they sneaked along so. I dogged 'em to the widder's stile, and stood in the dark and heard the ragged one beg for the widder, and the Spaniard swear he'd spile her looks just as I told you and your two—"

"What! The *deaf and dumb* man said all that!"

Huck had made a terrible mistake! He was trying his best to keep the old man from getting the faintest hint of who the Spaniard might be, and yet his tongue seemed determined to get him into trouble. He made several efforts to creep out of his scrape, but the old man's eye was upon him and he made blunder after blunder.

Presently the Welshman said, "My boy, don't be afraid of me. I wouldn't hurt a hair of your head for all the world. You know something about that Spaniard that you want to keep dark. Now tell me what it is, and trust me—I won't betray you."

Huck looked into the old man's honest eyes a moment, then bent over and whispered, "'Tain't a Spaniard—it's Injun Joe!"

The Welshman almost jumped out of his chair. In a moment he said, "It's all plain enough, now. When you talked about notching ears and slitting noses I judged that that was your own embellishment, because white men don't take that sort of revenge. But an Injun! That's a different matter altogether."

During breakfast the talk went on, and in the course of it the old man said that the last thing which he and his sons had done, before going to bed, was to get a lantern and examine the stile and its vicinity for marks of blood. They found none, but captured a bulky bundle of—

"Of WHAT?"

If the words had been lightning they could not have leaped with a more stunning suddenness from Huck's blanched lips. His eyes were staring wide, now, and his breath suspended—waiting for the answer. The Welshman started—stared in return—then replied, "Of burglar's tools. Why, what's the *matter* with you?"

Huck sank back, unutterably grateful. The Welshman eyed him curiously. "That appears to relieve you a good deal. What were *you* expecting we'd found?"

Huck was in a close place—the inquiring eye was upon him—a senseless reply offered—at a venture he uttered it: "Sunday-school books, maybe."

The old man laughed, loud and joyously, and ended by saying that such a laugh was money in a man's pocket, because it cut down the doctor's bills. Then he added, "Poor old chap, you're white and jaded—you ain't well—no wonder you're a little flighty. But rest and sleep will fetch you out all right, I hope."

Huck was irritated to think he had betrayed such a suspicious excitement, for before this he had all but dropped the idea that the parcel brought from the tavern was the treasure. But on the whole he felt glad the little episode had happened, for now he knew beyond all question that that bundle was not *the* bundle, and so his mind was at rest. The treasure must be still in Number Two, the men would be captured and jailed that day, and he and Tom could seize the gold that night without any fear of interruption.

Just as breakfast was completed there was a knock at the door. Huck jumped for a hiding place, for he had no mind to be connected even remotely with the late event. The Welshman admitted several ladies and gentlemen, among them the Widow Douglas, and noticed that groups of citizens were climbing up the hill—to stare at the stile. So the news had spread.

The Welshman had to tell the story of the night to the visitors. He told all, save Huck's role in the affair. The widow's gratitude for her preservation was outspoken. "I went to sleep reading in bed and slept straight through all the noise," she said. "Why didn't you come and wake me?"

"We judged it warn't worthwhile. Those fellows warn't likely to come again—and what was the use of waking you up and scaring you to death? My three Negro men stood guard at your house the rest of the night. They've just come back."

More visitors came, and the story had to be told and retold for a couple of hours more.

There was no Sabbath school during day-school vacation, but everybody was early at church. The stirring event was well canvassed. News came that not a sign of the two villains had been yet discovered. When the sermon was finished, Judge Thatcher's wife dropped alongside of Mrs. Harper as she moved down the aisle with the crowd and said, "Is my Becky going to sleep all day? I just expected she would be tired to death."

"Your Becky?"

"Yes"—with a startled look. "Didn't she stay with you last night?"

"Why, no."

Mrs. Thatcher turned pale, and sank into a pew, just as Aunt Polly passed by. Aunt Polly said, "Good morning, Mrs. Thatcher, Mrs. Harper. I've got a boy that's turned up missing. I reckon my

Tom stayed at your house last night—one of you. And now he's afraid to come to church. I've got to settle with him."

Mrs. Thatcher shook her head and turned paler than ever. "He didn't stay with us," said Mrs. Harper, beginning to look uneasy. A marked anxiety came into Aunt Polly's face.

"Joe Harper, have you seen my Tom this morning?"

"No'm."

"When did you see him last?"

Joe tried to remember, but was not sure he could say. People had stopped moving out of church, and uneasiness took possession of every countenance. Children were anxiously questioned, and young teachers. They all said they had not noticed whether Tom and Becky were on board the ferryboat on the homeward trip; it was dark; no one thought of inquiring if anyone was missing. One young man finally blurted out his fear that they were still in the cave! Mrs. Thatcher swooned away. Aunt Polly fell to crying and wringing her hands.

The alarm swept from lip to lip, from group to group, and within five minutes the bells were wildly clanging and the whole town was up! The widow's burglars were forgotten, horses were saddled, the ferryboat was ordered out, and before the horror was half an hour old two hundred men were pouring down highroad and river toward the cave.

All the long afternoon the village seemed empty and dead. Many women visited Aunt Polly and Mrs. Thatcher and tried to comfort them. All the tedious night the town waited for news; but when the morning dawned at last, all the word that came was, "Send more candles—and send food." Judge Thatcher sent hopeful messages from the cave, but they conveyed no real cheer.

The old Welshman came home toward daylight, spattered with candle grease and worn out. He found Huck still in the bed that he had provided for him, and delirious with fever. The physicians were all at the cave, so the Widow Douglas came and took charge of the patient. Mr. Jones said Huck had good spots in him, and the widow said, "You can depend on it. That's the Lord's mark. He puts it somewhere on every creature that comes from His hands."

Early in the forenoon parties of jaded men began to straggle into the village, but the strongest of the citizens continued searching. All the news that could be gained was that remotenesses of the cavern were being ransacked that had never been visited before; that wherever one wandered through the maze of passages, lights were to be seen flitting hither and thither in the distance, and shoutings and pistol shots sent their hollow reverberations down the somber aisles. In one place, far from the section usually traversed by tourists, the names *Becky & Tom* had been found traced upon the rocky wall with candle smoke, and near at hand a grease-soiled bit of ribbon. Mrs. Thatcher recognized the ribbon and cried over it.

Three dreadful days and nights dragged their tedious hours along, and the village sank into a hopeless stupor. No one had heart for anything. The tremendous discovery, just made, that the proprietor of the Temperance Tavern kept liquor on his premises, scarcely fluttered the public pulse. In a lucid interval, Huck feebly led up to the subject of taverns, and asked—dimly dreading the worst—if anything had been discovered at the Temperance Tavern.

"Yes," said the widow.

Huck started up in bed, wild-eyed. "What! What was it?"

"Liquor! And the place has been shut up. Lie down, child— What a turn you did give me!"

"Only tell me just one thing—just one—please! Was it Tom Sawyer that found it?"

The widow burst into tears. "Hush, child, hush! I've told you before, you must *not* talk. You are very, very sick!"

Then nothing but liquor had been found; there would have been a great powwow if it had been the gold. So the treasure was gone forever—gone forever! But what could she be crying about?

These thoughts worked their dim way through Huck's mind, and under the weariness they gave him he fell asleep. The widow said to herself, There—he's asleep, poor wreck. Tom Sawyer find it! Pity but somebody could find Tom Sawyer! Ah, there ain't many left, now, that's got hope enough, or strength enough, either, to go on searching.

CHAPTER XV

Now to return to Tom and Becky's share in the picnic. They tripped along the murky aisles with the rest of the company, visiting the familiar wonders of the cave—wonders dubbed with rather overdescriptive names, such as The Drawing Room, The Cathedral, Aladdin's Palace and so on. Presently the hide-and-seek frolicking began, and Tom and Becky engaged in it with zeal until the exertion began to grow a trifle wearisome; then they wandered down a sinuous avenue holding their candles aloft and reading the tangled webwork of names, dates and mottoes with which the rocky walls had been frescoed (in candle smoke). Still drifting along and talking, they scarcely noticed that they were now in a part of the cave whose walls were not frescoed. They smoked their own names under an overhanging shelf and moved on.

Presently they came to a place where a little stream of water, trickling over a ledge and carrying a limestone sediment with it, had, in the slow-dragging ages, formed a laced and ruffled Niagara in gleaming stone. Tom squeezed his small body behind it in order to illuminate it for Becky's gratification. He found that it curtained a sort of steep natural stairway which was enclosed between narrow walls, and at once the ambition to be a discoverer seized him. Becky responded to his call, and they made a smoke mark for future guidance and started upon their quest. They wound this way and that, far down into the secret depths of the cave, made another mark, and branched off in search of novelties to tell the upper world about. In one place they found a spacious cavern, from whose ceiling depended a multitude of shining stalactites of the length and circumference of a man's leg; they walked all about it, wondering and admiring, and presently left it by one of the numerous passages that opened into it.

This shortly brought them to a cavern whose walls were supported by many fantastic pillars, formed by the joining of great stalactites and stalagmites together. Under the roof vast knots of

bats had packed themselves together, thousands in a bunch; the lights disturbed the creatures, and they came flocking down by hundreds, squeaking and darting furiously at the candles. Tom knew their ways and the danger of this sort of conduct. He seized Becky's hand and hurried her into the first corridor that offered; and none too soon, for a bat struck Becky's light out with its wing while she was passing out of the cavern. The bats chased the children a good distance; but the fugitives plunged into every new passage that offered, and at last got rid of the perilous things.

Tom found a subterranean lake, shortly, which stretched its dim length away until its shape was lost in the shadows. He wanted to explore its borders, but concluded that it would be best to sit down and rest awhile, first. Now, for the first time, the deep stillness of the place laid a clammy hand upon the spirits of the children. Becky said, "Why, I didn't notice, but it seems ever so long since I heard any of the others."

"Come to think, Becky, we are away down below them—and I don't know how far away north, or south, or east, or whichever it is. We couldn't hear them here."

Becky grew apprehensive. "I wonder how long we've been down here, Tom. We better start back."

"Yes, I reckon we better."

"Can you find the way, Tom? It's all a mixed-up crookedness to me."

"I reckon I could find it—but then the bats. If they put both our candles out it will be an awful fix. Let's try not to go through there."

They started through a corridor, and traversed it in silence a long way, glancing at each new opening to see if there was anything familiar about the look of it; but they were all strange. Every time Tom made an examination, Becky would watch his face for an encouraging sign, and he would say cheerily, "Oh, it's all right. This ain't the one, but we'll come to it right away!"

But he felt less and less hopeful with each failure, and presently began to turn off into diverging avenues at sheer random. He still said it was "all right," but there was such a leaden dread at his heart that the words had lost their ring and sounded just as if he had said, All is lost! Becky clung to his side in an anguish of fear. At last she said, "Oh, Tom, never mind the bats, let's go back that way! We seem to get worse off all the time."

Tom stopped. "Listen!" said he.

Profound silence; silence so deep that even their breathings were conspicuous. Tom shouted. The call went echoing down the aisles and died out in the distance in a faint sound that resembled a ripple of mocking laughter.

"Oh, don't do it again, Tom, it is too horrid," said Becky.

"It is horrid, but I better, Becky; they *might* hear us, you know," and he shouted again.

The "might" was even a chillier horror than the ghostly laughter, it so confessed a perishing hope. The children stood still and listened; but there was no result. Tom turned upon the back track at once, and hurried his steps. It was but a little while before a certain indecision in his manner revealed another fearful fact to Becky—he could not find his way back!

"Oh, Tom, you didn't make any marks!"

"Becky, I was such a fool! I never thought we might want to come back! No—I can't find the way. It's all mixed up."

"Tom, Tom, we're lost! Oh, why *did* we leave the others!"

She sank to the ground and burst into such a frenzy of crying that Tom was appalled. He sat down by her and put his arms around her; she buried her face in his bosom, she clung to him, she poured out her terrors, and the far echoes turned them all to jeering laughter. Tom begged her to pluck up hope again, and she said she could not. He fell to blaming and abusing himself for getting her into this situation; this had a better effect. She said she would try to hope again, she would get up and follow wherever he might lead if only he would not talk like that anymore. For he was no more to blame than she, she said.

So they moved on again—simply at random. Moving, in some direction, in any direction, might at least bear fruit; to sit down was to invite death. But at last Becky's frail limbs refused to carry her farther. She sat down. Tom rested with her, and they talked of home, and the friends there, and the comfortable beds and, above all, the light! Fatigue bore so heavily upon Becky that she drowsed off to sleep. Tom was grateful. He sat looking into her drawn face and saw it grow smooth and natural under the influence of pleasant dreams; and by and by a smile dawned and rested there. The peaceful face reflected somewhat of peace and healing into his own spirit, and his thoughts wandered away to dreamy memories. While he was deep in his musings, Becky woke up with a little laugh—but it was stricken dead upon her lips, and a groan followed.

"Oh, how *could* I sleep! I wish I never, never had waked! No! No, I don't, Tom! Don't look so! I won't say it again."

They rose up and wandered along, hand in hand and hopeless. A long time after this—they could not tell how long—Tom said they must go softly and listen for dripping water—they must find a spring. They found one presently, and sat down, and Tom fastened his candle to the wall in front of them with some clay.

Becky said, "Tom, I am so hungry."

Tom took something out of his pocket. "Do you remember this?"

Becky almost smiled. "It's our wedding cake, Tom."

"Yes—I wish it was as big as a barrel, for it's all we've got."

"I saved it from the picnic for us to dream on, Tom, the way grown-up people do with wedding cake—but it'll be our—"

She dropped the sentence where it was. Tom divided the cake and Becky ate with good appetite, while he nibbled at his moiety. There was abundance of cold water to finish the feast with. By and by Becky suggested that they move on again. Tom was silent a moment. Then he said:

"Becky, can you bear it if I tell you something?"

Becky's face paled, but she thought she could.

"Well, then, Becky, we must stay here, where there's water to drink. That little piece is our last candle!"

Becky gave loose to tears; but at length she said, "Tom, they'll miss us and hunt for us! Maybe they're hunting now."

"I reckon maybe they are. I hope they are."

"When would they miss us, Tom?"

"When they get back to the boat, I reckon."

"Tom, it might be dark—would they notice we hadn't come?"

"I don't know. But anyway, your mother would miss you as soon as they got home."

A frightened look in Becky's face made Tom see that he had made a blunder. Becky was not to have gone home that night! The Sabbath morning might be half spent before Mrs. Thatcher discovered that Becky was not at Mrs. Harper's.

The children fastened their eyes upon their bit of candle and watched it melt pitilessly away; saw the half inch of wick stand alone at last; saw the feeble flame rise and fall, climb the thin column of smoke, linger at its top a moment, and then—the horror of utter darkness reigned!

After what seemed a mighty stretch of time, both awoke out of a dead stupor of sleep and resumed their miseries once more. Tom said it might be Sunday, now—maybe Monday. He said that they must have been missed long ago, and no doubt the search was going on. He would shout and maybe someone would come. He tried it; but in the darkness the distant echoes sounded so hideous that he tried it no more.

The hours wasted away, and hunger came to torment the captives again. A portion of Tom's half of the cake was left; they divided and ate it. But they seemed hungrier than before.

By and by Tom said, "*Sh!* Did you hear that?"

Both held their breath and listened. There was a sound like the faintest, far-off shout. Instantly Tom answered it, and, leading Becky by the hand, started groping down the corridor in its direction. Presently he listened again; again the sound was heard, and apparently a little nearer. "It's them!" said Tom. "Come along, Becky—we're all right now!"

The joy of the prisoners was almost overwhelming. Their speed was slow, however, because pitfalls were common, and had to be guarded against. They shortly came to one and had to stop. It might be three feet deep, it might be a hundred—there was no passing it, at any rate. Tom got down on his breast and reached as far as he could. No bottom. They must stay there until the searchers came. They listened; evidently the distant shoutings were growing more distant! A moment or two more and they had gone altogether. Tom whooped until he was hoarse, but it was of no use.

The children groped their way back to the spring. They slept again, and awoke famished and woe-stricken. Tom believed it must be Tuesday by this time.

Now an idea struck him. There were some side passages near at hand. It would be better to explore some of these than bear the weight of the heavy time in idleness. He took a kite line from his pocket, tied it to a projection, and he and Becky started, Tom in the lead, unwinding the line as he groped along.

At the end of twenty steps the corridor ended in a "jumping-off place." Tom got down on his knees and felt below, and then as far around the corner as he could reach with his hands; he made an effort to stretch yet a little farther to the right, and at that moment, not twenty yards away, a human hand, holding a candle, appeared from behind a rock! Tom lifted up a glorious shout, and instantly that hand was followed by the body it belonged to—Injun Joe's! Tom was paralyzed. He was vastly gratified the next moment to see the "Spaniard" take to his heels out of sight. Tom wondered that Joe had not recognized his voice and come and killed him for testifying in court. But the echoes must have disguised the voice. He was careful to keep from Becky what it was he had seen. He told her he had only shouted "for luck."

But hunger and wretchedness rise superior to fears in the long run. Another tedious wait at the spring and another long sleep brought changes. The children awoke tortured with hunger. Tom proposed to explore another passage. He felt willing to risk Injun Joe and all other terrors. But Becky had sunk into a dreary apathy. She said she would wait, now, where she was, and die; but she implored him to come back every little while and speak to her, and she made him promise that when the awful time came, he would stay by her and hold her hand until it was over.

Tom kissed her, choking; then he took the kite line in his hand and went groping down one of the passages on his hands and knees, distressed with hunger and bodings of coming doom.

CHAPTER XVI

TUESDAY AFTERNOON CAME, and waned to the twilight. The village of St. Petersburg still mourned. Public prayers had been offered up for the lost children, but still no good news came from the cave. The majority of the searchers had gone back to their daily vocations, saying that it was plain the children could never be found. Mrs. Thatcher was ill. Aunt Polly had drooped into a settled melancholy, and her gray hair had grown almost white. The village went to its rest on Tuesday night sad and forlorn.

Away in the middle of the night a wild peal burst from the village bells, and in a moment the streets were swarming with half-clad people, who shouted, "Turn out! Turn out! They're found!" Tin pans and horns were added to the din, the population moved toward the river, met the children coming in an open carriage, thronged around it, joined its homeward march, and swept magnificently up the main street roaring huzzah after huzzah!

The village was illuminated; nobody went to bed again; it was the greatest night the little town had ever seen. A procession of villagers filed through Judge Thatcher's house, seized and kissed the saved ones, squeezed Mrs. Thatcher's hand, tried to speak but couldn't—and drifted out raining tears all over the place.

Aunt Polly's happiness was complete, and Mrs. Thatcher's nearly so. It would be complete, however, as soon as the messenger dispatched with the great news to the cave should get the word to her husband. Tom lay upon a sofa with an eager auditory about him and told the history of the adventure, putting in many striking additions to adorn it withal; and closed with a description of how he left Becky and went on an exploring expedition; how he followed two avenues as far as his kite line would reach; how he followed a third to the fullest stretch of the kite line, and was about to turn back when he glimpsed a far-off speck that looked like daylight; dropped the line and groped toward it, pushed his hand and shoulders through a small hole and saw the broad Mississippi rolling by! And how if it had only happened to be night he would not have seen that speck of daylight or explored that passage any more! He told how he went back for Becky and how they pushed their way out at the hole; how they sat there and cried for gladness; how some men came along in a skiff and Tom hailed them; how the men didn't believe the wild tale at first, "because," said they, "you are five miles down the river below the valley the cave is in"—then took them aboard, rowed to a house, gave them supper, made them rest, and then brought them home.

Before daydawn, Judge Thatcher and the handful of searchers with him were tracked out, in the cave, by the twine clues they had strung behind them, and informed of the great news.

Three days and nights of toil and hunger in the cave were not to be shaken off at once, as Tom and Becky soon discovered. They were bedridden all of Wednesday and Thursday, and seemed to grow more tired and worn all the time. Tom got about a little on Thursday, was downtown Friday, and nearly as whole as ever Saturday; but Becky did not leave her room until Sunday, and then she looked as if she had passed through a wasting illness.

Tom learned of Huck's sickness and went to see him on Friday, but could not be admitted to the bedroom; neither could he on Saturday. He was admitted after that, but was warned to keep still about his adventure and introduce no exciting topic. The Widow Douglas stayed by to see that he obeyed. At home Tom learned of the Cardiff Hill event; also that the "ragged man's" body had been found in the river near the ferry landing; he had been drowned while trying to escape, perhaps.

About a fortnight after Tom's rescue from the cave, he stopped at Judge Thatcher's house to see Becky. The Judge had some friends there, and someone asked Tom ironically if he wouldn't like to go to the cave again. Tom said he thought he wouldn't mind. The Judge said, "Well, there are others like you, Tom. But we have taken care of that. Nobody will get lost in that cave anymore."

"Why?"

"Because I had its big door sheathed with boiler iron two weeks ago, and triple-locked—and I've got the keys."

Tom turned as white as a sheet.

"What's the matter, boy! Here, somebody! Fetch water!"

The water was brought and thrown into Tom's face.

"Ah, now you're all right. What was the matter with you, Tom?"

"Oh, Judge, Injun Joe's in the cave!"

WITHIN A FEW MINUTES the news had spread, and a dozen skiff-loads of men were on their way to McDougal's Cave. Tom Sawyer was in the skiff that bore Judge Thatcher.

When the cave door was unlocked, a sorrowful sight presented itself. Injun Joe lay stretched upon the ground, dead, with his face close to the crack of the door, as if his longing eyes had been fixed, to the latest moment, upon the light of the free world outside. Tom was touched, for he knew by his own experience how this wretch had suffered; but nevertheless he felt an abounding sense of relief and security, now, which revealed to him how vast a weight of dread had been lying upon him since the day he lifted his voice against this bloody-minded outcast.

Injun Joe was buried near the mouth of the cave, and people flocked there from all the towns and farms for miles around; and they confessed that they had almost as satisfactory a time at the funeral as they could have had at the hanging.

The morning after the funeral Tom took Huck to a private place. Huck had grown plenty strong enough, now, to hear exciting talk. He had learned all about Tom's adventure from the Welshman and the Widow Douglas, by this time, but Tom said he reckoned there was one thing they had not told him. Huck's face saddened. He said:

"I know what it is. You got into Number Two and never found anything but whiskey. I just knowed it must 'a' ben you; and I knowed you hadn't got the money, becuz if you had, you'd 'a' got at me someway or other and told me. Tom, something's always told me we'd never get holt of that swag."

"Why, Huck, *I* never told on that tavern keeper. *You* know his tavern was all right the Saturday I went to the picnic. Don't you remember you was to watch there that night?"

"Oh, yes! It was that very night that I follered Injun Joe to the widder's."

"*You* followed him?"

"Yes—but you keep mum. I reckon Injun Joe's left friends behind him, and I don't want 'em doing me mean tricks."

Then Huck told his entire adventure in confidence to Tom, who had only heard of the Welshmen's part of it before.

"Well," said Huck, presently, "whoever nipped the whiskey in Number Two nipped the money, too, I reckon."

"Huck, that money wasn't ever in Number Two!"

"What!" Huck searched his comrade's face. "Tom, have you got on the track of that money again?"

"Huck, it's in the cave!"

Huck's eyes blazed. "Tom—honest injun, now—is it fun or earnest?"

"Earnest, Huck—will you go in there with me and help get it?"

"I will if it's where we can blaze our way to it and not get lost!"

"Huck, we can do that without the least little trouble. Are you strong enough to go right now?"

"Is it far in the cave, Tom? I ben on my pins a little, three days, now, but I don't think I could walk more'n a mile."

"It's about five mile into there the way anybody but me would go, Huck, but there's a mighty short cut that they don't anybody but me know about. Huck, I'll take you right to it in a skiff."

"Let's start right off, Tom."

"All right. We want some bread and meat, and a bag or two, and two or three kite strings, and some of these newfangled things they call lucifer matches. I tell you, many's the time I wished I had some when I was in there before."

A trifle after noon the boys borrowed a small skiff from a citizen who was absent, and got under way. When they were several miles below Cave Hollow, Tom said, "Now you see this bluff here looks all alike all the way down from the hollow—no houses, bushes all alike. But do you see that white place up yonder where there's been a landslide? Well, that's one of my marks. We'll get ashore, now."

They landed.

"Now, Huck, where we're a-standing you could touch that hole I got out of with a fishing pole. See if you can find it."

Huck searched and found nothing. Tom proudly marched into a clump of sumac and said, "Here you are! Look at it, Huck; it's the snuggest hole in this country. You just keep mum about it. All along I've been wanting to be a robber, but I knew I'd got to have a thing like this, and where to run across it was the bother. We've got it now, and we'll keep it quiet, only we'll let Joe Harper and Ben Rogers in—because of course there's got to be a gang, or there wouldn't be any style about it. Tom Sawyer's Gang—it sounds splendid, don't it, Huck?"

"Well, it just does, Tom. It's real bully. I bleeve it's better'n to be a pirate."

"Yes, it's better in some ways, because it's close to home and circuses and all that."

By this time everything was ready and the boys entered the hole, Tom in the lead. They toiled to the farther end of the tunnel, then made their spliced kite strings fast and moved on. A few steps brought them to the spring, and Tom felt a shudder quiver all through him. He showed Huck the fragment of candlewick perched on a lump of clay against the wall, and described how he and Becky had watched the flame struggle and expire.

The boys began to quiet down to whispers, now, for the stillness and gloom of the place oppressed their spirits. They went on, and presently followed Tom's other corridor until they reached the "jumping-off place." The candles revealed the fact that it was not really a precipice, but only a steep clay hill twenty feet high. Tom whispered, "Now I'll show you something." He held his candle aloft. "Look as far around the corner as you can. There, see—on the big rock over yonder—done with candle smoke."

"Tom, it's a *cross!*"

"*Now* where's your Number Two? *Under the cross*, hey? Right yonder's where I saw Injun Joe poke up his candle, Huck!"

Huck stared at the mystic sign awhile, and then said with a shaky voice, "Tom, let's git out of here!"

"What! And leave the treasure?"

"Yes—leave it. Injun Joe's ghost is round about there, certain."

"No it ain't, Huck. It would ha'nt the place where he died."

"No, Tom, it wouldn't. It would hang round the money."

Misgivings gathered in Tom's mind. But presently an idea occurred to him—"Looky here, Huck, Injun Joe's ghost ain't a-going to come around where there's a cross!"

The point was well taken. It had its effect.

"Tom, I didn't think of that. But that's so. I reckon we'll climb down there and have a hunt for that box."

Tom went first, cutting rude steps in the clay hill as he descended. Huck followed. Four avenues opened out of the small cavern where the great rock stood. The boys examined three of them with no result. They found a small recess in the one nearest the base of the rock, with a pallet of blankets in it; also an old suspender and the well-gnawed bones of two or three fowl. But there was no money box. Tom said, "He said *under* the cross. Well, this comes nearest to being under the cross. It can't be under the rock itself, because that sets solid on the ground."

They searched everywhere once more, and then sat down, discouraged. By and by Tom said, "Looky here, Huck, there's footprints and some candle grease on the clay about one side of this rock, but not on the other sides. Now, what's that for? I bet you the money *is* under the rock. I'm going to dig in the clay."

"That ain't no bad notion, Tom!" said Huck.

Tom's "real Barlow" was out at once, and he had not dug four inches before he struck wood. "Hey, Huck! You hear that?"

Huck began to dig and scratch now. Some boards were soon uncovered and removed. They had concealed a natural chasm which led under the rock. Tom got into this and held out his candle, but he could not see to the end of the rift. He stooped and passed under with Huck at his heels; the narrow way descended gradually. Then Tom turned a short curve and exclaimed, "My goodness, Huck, looky here!"

It was the treasure box, sure enough, occupying a snug little cavern, along with an empty powder keg, a couple of guns in leather cases, two or three pairs of old moccasins, a belt, and some other rubbish well soaked with the water drip.

"Got it at last!" said Huck, plowing among the tarnished coins with his hand. "My, but we're rich, Tom!"

"Huck, I always reckoned we'd get it. It's just too good to believe, but we *have* got it, sure! Say—let's not fool around here. Let's snake it out. Lemme see if I can lift the box."

It weighed about fifty pounds. Tom could lift it, but could not carry it. "I thought so," he said. "*They* carried it like it was heavy, that day at the ha'nted house. I reckon I was right to fetch the bags along."

The money was soon in the bags and the boys took it up to the cross rock.

"Now let's fetch the guns and things," said Huck.

"No, Huck—leave them there. They're just the tricks to have when we go to robbing. We'll keep them there, and we'll hold our orgies there, too. It's an awful snug place for orgies."

"What orgies?"

"*I* dono. But robbers always have orgies. Come along, Huck; it's getting late. I'm hungry. We'll eat in the skiff."

They presently emerged into the clump of sumac, looked warily out, found the coast clear, and were soon lunching in the skiff. As the sun dipped toward the horizon they got under way. Tom skimmed up the shore through the long twilight, chatting cheerily with Huck, and landed shortly after dark.

"Now, Huck," said Tom, "we'll hide the money in the loft of the widow's woodshed, and I'll come up in the morning and we'll count it and divide, and then we'll hunt up a place out in the woods for it where it will be safe. Just you lay quiet here and watch the stuff till I run and hook Benny Taylor's little wagon; I won't be gone a minute."

He presently returned with the wagon, put the sacks into it, threw some old rags on top of them and started off, dragging his cargo behind him. When the boys reached the Welshman's house, the Welshman stepped out and said, "Hello, who's that?"

"Huck and Tom Sawyer."

"Good! Come along with me, boys; you are keeping everybody waiting. Here—hurry up, trot ahead—I'll haul the wagon. Why, it's not as light as it might be. Got bricks in it? Or old metal?"

"Old metal," said Tom.

"I judged so. The boys in this town will fool away more time hunting up six bits' worth of old iron to sell to the foundry than they would to make twice the money at regular work. But that's human nature—hurry along, hurry along!"

Huck wanted to know what the hurry was about.

"Never mind; you'll see when we get to the Widow Douglas's."

A little later Huck found himself pushed, along with Tom, into Mrs. Douglas's drawing room. Mr. Jones, the Welshman, left the wagon near the door and followed.

The place was grandly lighted, and everybody that was of any consequence in the village was there. The Thatchers were there, the Harpers, the Rogerses, Aunt Polly, Sid, Mary, the minister, and a great many more, and all dressed in their best. The widow received the boys as heartily as anyone could well receive two such looking beings. They were covered with clay and candle grease. Aunt Polly blushed crimson with humiliation, and frowned at Tom. Nobody suffered half as much as the two boys did, however. Mr. Jones said, "Tom wasn't at home yet, so I gave him up; but I stumbled on him and Huck right at my door, and so I just brought them along."

"You did just right," said the widow. "Come with me, boys."

She took them to a bedchamber and said, "Now wash and dress yourselves. Here are two new suits of clothes—shirts, socks, everything. They're Huck's—no, no thanks, Huck—Mr. Jones bought one and I the other. But they'll fit both of you. Get into them. We'll wait—come down when you are slicked up enough."

Then she left, and Huck said, "Tom, we can slope, if we can find a rope. The window ain't high from the ground."

"Shucks, what do you want to slope for?"

"Well, I ain't used to that kind of a crowd. I ain't going down there, Tom."

"Oh, bother! It ain't anything. I'll take care of you."

Sid appeared. "Tom," said he, "Auntie has been waiting for you all afternoon. Say—ain't this grease and clay on your clothes?"

"Now, Mr. Siddy, you jist 'tend to your own business. What's all this blowout about, anyway?"

"It's one of the widow's parties that she's always having. This time it's for the Welshman and his sons, on account of that scrape they helped her out of. And say—I can tell you something, if you want to know."

"Well, what?"

"Why, old Mr. Jones is going to try to spring something on the people here tonight, but I overheard him tell Auntie today about it, as a secret, but I reckon it's not much of a secret *now*. Everybody knows—the widow, too, for all she tries to let on she don't. Mr. Jones was bound Huck should be here—couldn't get along with his grand secret without Huck, you know!"

"Secret about what, Sid?"

"About Huck tracking the robbers to the widow's. I reckon Mr. Jones was going to make a grand time over his surprise, but I bet you it will drop pretty flat." Sid chuckled in a contented way.

"Sid, was it you that told?"

"Oh, never mind who it was. *Somebody* told—that's enough."

"Sid, there's only one person in this town mean enough to do that, and that's you. You can't do any but mean things, and you can't bear to see anybody praised for doing good ones. There—no thanks, as the widow says"—and Tom cuffed Sid's ears and helped him to the door with several kicks. "Now go and tell Auntie if you dare!"

Some minutes later the widow's guests were at the supper table, and a dozen children were propped up at little side tables in the same room, after the fashion of that country and that day. At the proper time Mr. Jones made his little speech, in which he thanked the widow for the honor she was doing himself and his sons, but said that there was another person whose modesty—

And so forth and so on. He sprung his secret about Huck's share in the adventure in a fine dramatic manner, but the surprise it occasioned was largely counterfeit. However, the widow made a pretty fair show of astonishment, and heaped so many compliments upon Huck that he almost forgot the nearly intolerable discomfort of his new clothes in the entirely intolerable discomfort of being set up as a target for everybody's gaze and laudations.

The widow said she meant to give Huck a home under her roof and have him educated; and that when she could spare the money she would start him in business. Tom's chance was come. He said, "Huck don't need it. Huck's rich."

Nothing but a heavy strain upon the good manners of the company kept back the proper complimentary laugh at this pleasant joke. But the silence was a little awkward. Tom broke it. "Oh, you needn't smile—I reckon I can show you. You just wait a minute."

Tom ran out of doors. The company looked at each other—and looked inquiringly at Huck, who was tongue-tied.

"Sid, what ails Tom?" said Aunt Polly. "I never—"

Tom entered, struggling with the weight of his sacks, and Aunt Polly did not finish her sentence. Tom poured the mass of yellow coin upon the table and said, "There—what did I tell you? Half of it's Huck's and half of it's mine!"

All gazed, nobody spoke for a moment. Then there was a unanimous call for an explanation. Tom said he could furnish it, and he did. The tale was long, but brimful of interest. There was no interruption to break the charm of its flow.

When he had finished, Mr. Jones said, "I thought I had fixed up a little surprise for this occasion, but it don't amount to anything now. This one makes it sing mighty small, I'll allow."

The money was counted. The sum amounted to over twelve thousand dollars.

CHAPTER XVII

THE READER MAY REST satisfied that Tom's and Huck's windfall made a mighty stir in the poor little village of St. Petersburg. So vast a sum, in actual cash, seemed next to incredible. It was talked about, gloated over, glorified, until the reason of many of the citizens tottered under the strain of the unhealthy excitement. Every "haunted" house in St. Petersburg and the neighboring villages was dissected, plank by plank, and ransacked for hidden treasure—and not by boys, but men—pretty grave, unromantic men, too, some of them. Wherever Tom and Huck appeared they were courted, admired, stared at. All their sayings were treasured and repeated; everything they did seemed to be regarded as remarkable; moreover, their past history was raked up and discovered to bear marks of conspicuous originality.

The Widow Douglas put Huck's money out at six percent, and Judge Thatcher did the same with Tom's at Aunt Polly's request. Each lad had an income, now, that was simply prodigious—a dollar for every weekday in the year and half of the Sundays. It was just what the minister got—no, it was what he was promised—he generally couldn't collect it. A dollar and a quarter a week would board, lodge and school a boy in those old simple days—and clothe him and wash him, too, for that matter.

Judge Thatcher had conceived a great opinion of Tom. He said that no commonplace boy would ever have got his daughter out of the cave. The Judge hoped to see Tom a great lawyer or a great soldier someday, and he said he meant to look to it that Tom should be admitted to the national military academy and afterward trained in the best law school in the country, in order that he might be ready for either career or both. When Becky told her father, in strict confidence, how Tom had taken her whipping at school, the Judge was visibly moved; and when she pleaded grace for the mighty lie which Tom had told in order to shift that whipping from her shoulders to his own, the Judge said with a fine outburst that it was a noble, a generous, a magnanimous lie.

Huck Finn's wealth and the fact that he was now under the Widow Douglas's protection introduced him into society—no, dragged him into it, hurled him into it—and his sufferings were almost more than he could bear. The widow's servants kept him clean and neat, combed and brushed. He had to eat with knife and fork; he had to go to church; he had to talk so properly that speech was become insipid in his mouth.

He bravely bore his miseries three weeks, and then one day turned up missing. For forty-eight hours the widow hunted for him everywhere in great distress. The public were profoundly concerned; they searched high and low. Early the third morning Tom Sawyer wisely went poking among some old empty hogs-heads down behind the abandoned slaughterhouse, and in one of them he found the refugee. Huck had slept there; he had just breakfasted upon some stolen odds and ends of food, and was lying off, now, in comfort, with his pipe. He was unkempt, un-combed, and clad in his old ruin of rags. Tom routed him out, told him the trouble he had been causing, and urged him to go home. Huck's face took a melancholy cast. He said:

"Don't talk about it, Tom. I've tried it, and it don't work. It ain't for me. The widder's good to me, and friendly, but I can't stand them ways. She makes me git up at the same time every morning; she makes me wash, and wear them blamed clothes that just smothers me. I got to go to church and—I hate them ornery sermons! I can't ketch a fly in there, I can't chaw, and I got to wear shoes all Sunday."

"Well, everybody does that way, Huck."

"Tom, it don't make no difference. I ain't everybody, and I can't *stand* it. It's awful to be tied up so. And grub comes too easy—I don't take no interest in vittles, that way. I got to ask to go a-fishing; I got to ask to go in a-swimming—dern'd if I hain't got to ask to do everything! I *had* to shove, Tom. And besides, that school's going to open, and I'd 'a' had to go to it—well, I wouldn't stand *that!* Looky here, Tom, being rich ain't what it's cracked up to be. It's just worry and worry, and sweat and sweat, and a-wishing you was dead all the time. Now these clothes suits me, and this bar'l suits me, and I ain't ever going to shake 'em anymore. Tom, I wouldn't ever got into all this trouble if it hadn't 'a' been for that money. Now you just take my sheer of it along with your'n, and gimme a ten-center sometimes—not many times, becuz I don't give a dern for a thing 'thout it's tollable hard to git—and you go and beg off for me with the widder."

"Oh, Huck, you know I can't do that. 'Tain't fair; and besides, if you'll try this thing just a while longer you'll come to like it."

"Like it! Yes—the way I'd like a hot stove if I was to set on it long enough. No, Tom, I won't be rich, and I won't live in them cussed smothery houses. I like the woods, and the river, and hogsheads. Blame it all! Just as we'd got guns, and a cave, and all just fixed to rob, here this dern foolishness has got to come up and spile it all!"

Tom saw his opportunity— "Looky here, Huck, being rich ain't going to keep me back from turning robber."

"No! Oh, good licks, are you in deadwood earnest, Tom?"

"Just as dead earnest as I'm a-sitting here. But, Huck, we can't let you into the gang if you ain't respectable, you know."

Huck's joy was quenched. "Can't let me in, Tom? Didn't you let me go for a pirate?"

"Yes, but that's different. A robber is more high-toned than a pirate—as a general thing."

"Now, Tom, hain't you always ben friendly to me? You wouldn't shet me out, would you, Tom?"

"Huck, I wouldn't want to, and I *don't* want to—but what would people say? Why, they'd say, 'Mph! Tom Sawyer's Gang! Pretty low characters in it!' They'd mean you, Huck."

Huck was silent, engaged in a mental struggle. Finally he said, "Well, I'll go back to the widder for a month and see if I can come to stand it, if you'll let me b'long to the gang, Tom."

"All right, Huck, it's a whiz! Come along, and I'll ask the widow to let up on you a little."

"Will you, Tom? That's good. If she'll let up on some of the roughest things, I'll cuss private, and crowd through or bust. When you going to start the gang?"

"Oh, right off. We'll get the boys together and have the initiation tonight, maybe."

"What's that?"

"It's to swear to stand by one another, and never tell the gang's secrets, even if you're chopped all to flinders, and kill anybody and all his family that hurts one of the gang."

"That's gay—that's mighty gay, Tom, I tell you."

"Well, I bet it is. And all that swearing's got to be done at midnight, in the lonesomest, awfulest place you can find—a ha'nted house is the best, but they're all ripped up now."

"Well, midnight's good, anyway, Tom."

"Yes, so it is. And you've got to swear on a coffin, and sign it with blood."

"Now, that's something *like!* Why, it's a million times bullier than pirating. I'll stick to the widder till I rot, Tom; and if I git to be a reg'lar ripper of a robber, and everybody talking about it, I reckon she'll be proud she snaked me in out of the wet."

CONCLUSION

So ENDETH THIS CHRONICLE. It being strictly a history of a *boy*, it must stop here; the story could not go much further without becoming the history of a *man*. When one writes a novel about grown people, he knows exactly where to stop—that is, with a marriage; but when he writes of juveniles, he must stop where he best can.

THE GOOD
EARTH

THE GOOD EARTH

a
condensation
of the book
by

Pearl S. Buck

ILLUSTRATED BY JOHN BIGGERS

In March 1927, in the Chinese city of Nanking, a young American teacher lay hidden for fourteen hours while her house was looted by a revolutionary mob. She was one of the few foreigners to live through that terrible day, but it is characteristic of Pearl Buck that her love and understanding of the Chinese survived the ordeal undiminished.

The Good Earth was published four years later, and the description on the jacket of the first edition is just as true today: "The reader soon becomes unaware of distinctions of race, of period, of locale. These people are born, play, toil, suffer and dream as all humans have done under whatever sun, on whatever patch of our common earth. . . . Through Wang Lung and his children we trace the whole cycle of life. . . ."

Pearl Buck's theme is the humanity common to all peoples; but she is first of all a very great storyteller, and *The Good Earth* tells a gripping story. It has been translated into innumerable languages. It won the Pulitzer Prize for 1931, and when, in 1938, its author was awarded the Nobel Prize, she was the first American woman to be so honored.

The daughter of American missionaries, Pearl Buck grew up in a purely Chinese world. Her first playmates were Chinese children; she could speak their language even before she had mastered her own, and she made intimate friends among every sort of Chinese, from the poorest peasant to the proudest aristocrat. (From this unique experience she later wrote a memorable autobiography, *My Several Worlds*.) She attended college in America and eventually, with her first husband, Dr. John Lossing Buck, an agricultural missionary, she returned to live for a time in the region of North China so vividly described in *The Good Earth*.

Since her return to the United States some years ago, Pearl Buck has written numerous books and articles. She has also practiced what she preached. In 1949 she founded Welcome House on the Bucks County, Pennsylvania, farm where she lives. Here she provides a warm home for orphans of mixed Asian-American heritage while arranging to have them permanently adopted. She is a tireless worker for aid to retarded children. And in recent years she has created the Pearl S. Buck Foundation, devoted to rescuing children left in foreign lands by American servicemen. As a writer and humanitarian, she is one of the truly splendid women of our time.

I

IT WAS WANG LUNG's marriage day. At first, opening his eyes in the blackness of the curtains about his bed, he could not think why the dawn seemed different from any other. The house was still except for the faint, gasping cough of his old father, whose room was opposite his own across the middle room. Wang Lung usually lay listening to it, but this morning he did not wait. He sprang up and pushed aside the curtains. It was a dark, ruddy dawn, and through a square hole of a window a glimpse of bronze sky gleamed. The hole was barely large enough to admit his hand as he thrust it out to feel the air. A small soft wind blew gently from the east, a wind mild and murmurous and full of rain. Within a few days there would be water. It was good. Yesterday he had said to his father that if this brazen, glittering sunshine continued, the wheat could not fill in the ear. Now it was as if Heaven had chosen this day to wish him well.

He hurried out into the middle room, drawing on his blue outer trousers as he went, and knotting about his waist his girdle of blue cotton cloth. He left his upper body bare until he had heated water to bathe himself. He went into the kitchen, a shed leaning against the house, and out of its dusk an ox lowed at him deeply from behind the corner next the door. The kitchen was made of earthen bricks as the house was, great squares of earth dug from their own fields, and thatched with straw from their own wheat. Out of their own earth had his grandfather fashioned also the oven, baked and black with many years of meal preparing. On top of this stood a deep, round, iron caldron.

This caldron he filled partly full of water, dipping it with a half gourd from an earthen jar that stood near, but he dipped cautiously, for water was precious. Then, after a hesitation, he suddenly lifted the jar and emptied all the water into the caldron. This day he would bathe his whole body. Not since he was a child had anyone looked upon his body. Today one would, and he would have it clean. Selecting a handful of the dry grass and stalks standing in the corner of the kitchen, he arranged it delicately in the mouth of the oven. Then from an old flint and iron he caught a flame and thrust it into the straw and there was a blaze.

This was the last morning he would have to light the fire. Every morning since his mother died six years before, he had lit the fire, boiled water, and taken it in a bowl to the room where his father sat upon his bed and waited for hot water to ease him of his morning coughing. Now father and son could rest. There was a woman coming to the house. Their house had seemed half empty since his mother died. They were always having to resist relatives who were more crowded—his uncle, with his endless brood of children, coaxing,

"Now, how can two lone men need three rooms? Cannot father and son sleep together? The warmth of the young one's body will comfort the old one's cough."

But the father always replied, "I am saving my bed for my grandson. He will warm my bones in my age."

Now the grandsons were coming—grandsons upon grandsons! They would have to put beds along the walls and in the middle room. The blaze of the oven died down while Wang Lung thought of all the beds there would be, and the water began to chill in the caldron. The shadowy figure of the old man appeared in the door-

way, holding his unbuttoned garments about him. He was coughing and spitting and he gasped,

"How is it that there is not water yet to heat my lungs?"

Wang Lung stared and recalled himself and was ashamed.

"This fuel is damp," he muttered. "The damp wind—"

The old man continued to cough perseveringly until the water
boiled. Wang Lung dipped some into a bowl, and then, after a moment, he opened a glazed jar that stood upon a ledge of the stove
and took from it a dozen or so of the curled dried leaves and
sprinkled them upon the water. The old man's eyes opened greedily and immediately he began to complain.

"Why are you wasteful? Tea is like eating silver," and he grasped
the bowl in his shriveled, knotty fingers, muttering, uttering little
grunts. He watched the leaves uncurl and spread upon the surface
of the water, unable to bear drinking the precious stuff.

"It will be cold," said Wang Lung.

"True—true—" said the old man in alarm, and he began to take
great gulps of the hot tea. He passed into an animal satisfaction,
like a child fixed upon its feeding. But he was not too forgetful to
see Wang Lung dipping the water recklessly from the caldron into
a deep wooden tub. He lifted his head and stared at his son.

"Now there is water enough to bring a crop to fruit," he said.

Wang Lung continued to dip the water to the last drop. He did
not answer. He was ashamed to say to his father that he wished his
body to be clean for a woman to see. He hurried out, carrying the
tub to his own room. The door was hung loosely upon a warped
wooden frame, and the old man put his mouth to the opening and
bawled, "It will be ill if we start the woman like this—tea in the
morning water and all this washing!"

"It is only one day," shouted Wang Lung. And then he added,
"I will throw the water on the earth when I am finished."

The old man was silent at this, and Wang Lung unfastened his
girdle and stepped out of his clothing. In the light that streamed in
a square block from the hole he wrung a small towel from the
steaming water and scrubbed his dark, slender body vigorously,
passing the towel in and out of the water until from his whole

body there went up a delicate cloud of steam. Then he drew from a box a fresh suit of blue cotton cloth. He might be a little cold this day, but the covering of the wadded winter garments was torn and filthy, and he did not want this woman to see him for the first time with the wadding sticking out of his clothes. Later she would have to wash and mend, but not the first day. Then with swift fingers he unplaited the long braid of hair that hung down his back, and taking a wooden comb he began to comb out his hair.

His father again put his mouth to the crack of the door.

"Am I to have nothing to eat this day?" he complained. "At my age the bones are water in the morning until food is given them."

"I am coming," said Wang Lung, braiding his hair quickly and smoothly and weaving into the strands a tasseled, black silk cord. Then he wound his braid about his head and went out, carrying the tub of water. He had quite forgotten breakfast. He would stir a little water into cornmeal and give it to his father. For himself he could not eat. He staggered with the tub to the threshold and, as he poured the water upon the earth nearest the door, he remembered he had used all the water in the caldron for his bathing and he would have to start the fire again. A wave of anger passed over him.

"That old head thinks of nothing except his eating and his drinking," he muttered into the mouth of the oven; but aloud he said nothing. It was the last morning he would have to prepare food for the old man. He put a very little water into the caldron, drawing it in a bucket from the well near the door, and it boiled quickly and he stirred meal together and took it to the old man.

"We will have rice this night, my father," he said. "Meanwhile, here is corn."

"There is only a little rice left in the basket," said the old man, seating himself at the table in the middle room and stirring with his chopsticks the thick yellow gruel.

"We will eat a little less then at the spring festival," said Wang Lung. But the old man did not hear. He was supping loudly at his bowl.

Wang Lung went into his own room then, and drew over the blue cotton coat and trousers a long robe made of the same material—his one long robe, which he wore on feast days only, ten days or so in the year—and let down the braid of his hair. He passed his hand over his brow and his cheeks. Perhaps he had better be newly shaven? He could pass through the Street of Barbers before he went to the house where the woman waited for him.

He took from his girdle a small, greasy pouch of gray cloth and counted the money in it. There were six silver pieces and a double handful of copper coins. He had asked friends to sup that night, and he planned to bring back from the town pork, a small pond fish, and a handful of chestnuts. He might even buy a few bamboo sprouts and a little beef to stew with the cabbage from his garden. But this only if there were money left after he shaved his head.

He went out into the early morning. The sun was mounting the horizon clouds and sparkled upon the dew on the rising wheat and barley. The farmer in Wang Lung was diverted for an instant and he stooped to examine the budding heads. He smelled the air and looked anxiously at the sky. Rain was there, dark in the clouds, heavy upon the wind. He would buy incense and place it in the little temple to the Earth God. On a day like this he would do it.

He wound his way among the fields upon the narrow path. In the near distance the gray city wall arose. Within that wall stood the great house where the woman had been a slave girl since her childhood, the House of Hwang. There were those who said, "It is better to live alone than to marry a woman who has been a slave." But when he had said to his father, "Am I never to have a woman?" his father replied, "With every woman wanting gold rings and silk clothes before she will take a man, there remain only slaves to be had for the poor."

His father had stirred himself then, and gone to the House of Hwang and asked if there were a slave to spare.

"Not too young, and above all, not pretty," he had said.

Wang Lung had suffered that she must not be pretty; it would be something to have a pretty wife that other men would congratulate him upon having. His father, seeing his mutinous face, had cried out at him,

"And what will we do with a pretty woman? We must have a

woman who will tend the house and bear children as she works in the fields, and will a pretty woman do these things? She will be forever thinking about clothes to go with her face!"

Wang Lung knew his father spoke well. Nevertheless, he said violently, "At least, I will not have a woman who is pockmarked, or who has a split upper lip."

"We will have to see what is to be had," his father replied.

Well, the woman was not pockmarked, nor had she a split lip. He and his father had taken two silver rings, washed with gold, and silver earrings, to the woman's owner in acknowledgment of betrothal. This much he knew, but beyond this, he knew nothing of the woman who was to be his, except that on this day he could go and get her.

He walked into the cool dark tunnel of the city gate under the thick wall of earth and brick. Water carriers, their barrows laden with great tubs, passed to and fro, the water splashing out of the tubs upon the stones. Baskets of small, hard green peaches stood along the walls, and the vendors cried out,

"The first peaches of spring—the first peaches! Buy, eat, purge your bowels of the poisons of winter!"

Wang Lung said to himself,

"If she likes them, I will buy her a handful when we return."

He turned to the right within the gate and after a moment was in the Street of Barbers. There were few before him so early, only some farmers who had carried their produce into the town the night before in order that they might sell their vegetables at the dawn markets and return for the day's work in the fields. They had slept shivering and crouching over their baskets, the baskets now empty at their feet. Wang Lung avoided them lest some recognize him, for he wanted none of their joking on this day. All down the street in a long line the barbers stood behind their small stalls, and Wang Lung went to the farthest one and sat down upon the stool. The barber began quickly to pour hot water, from a kettle on his pot of charcoal, into his brass basin.

"Shave everything?" the barber asked.

"My head and my face," said Wang Lung.

"Ears and nostrils cleaned?"

"How much will that cost extra?" asked Wang Lung cautiously.

"Four pence," said the barber, beginning to pass a black cloth in and out of the hot water.

"I will give you two," said Wang Lung.

"Then I will clean one ear and one nostril," rejoined the barber promptly. "On which side of the face do you wish it done?" He grimaced at the next barber as he spoke and the other burst into a guffaw. Feeling inferior in some unaccountable way, as he always did, to these town dwellers, even though they were the lowest of persons, Wang Lung said quickly,

"As you will—as you will—"

Then he submitted himself to the soaping and shaving, and being after all a generous fellow enough, the barber gave him without extra charge a series of skillful poundings upon his shoulders and back to loosen his muscles. He commented upon Wang Lung as he shaved his upper forehead,

"This would not be a bad-looking farmer if he would cut off his hair. The new fashion is to take off the braid."

His razor hovered so near the circle of hair upon Wang Lung's crown that Wang Lung cried out,

"I cannot cut it off without asking my father!" And the barber laughed and skirted the round spot of hair.

When it was finished and the money counted into the barber's wrinkled, water-soaked hand, Wang Lung had a moment of horror. So much money! But walking down the street again with the wind fresh upon his shaven skin, he said to himself,

"It is only once."

He went to the market, then, and bought two pounds of pork wrapped in a dried lotus leaf. This he placed in the basket he carried, and then, hesitating, he bought also six ounces of beef. When all had been bought, even to fresh squares of bean curd, shivering in a jelly upon its leaf, he went to a candlemaker's shop and there he bought a pair of incense sticks. Then he turned his steps with great shyness toward the House of Hwang.

Once at the gates of the house he was seized with terror. He had never been in a great house before. How could he go in with his wedding feast on his arm, and say, "I have come for a woman"?

He stood for a long time, looking at the two great wooden gates, painted black and studded with iron, closed fast upon each other. Two lions made of stone stood on guard, one at either side. There was no one else.

He felt suddenly faint. He would go first and buy a little food. He had eaten nothing. He went into a small restaurant, and putting two pence upon the table, he sat down. A dirty waiting boy with a shiny black apron came near and he called out to him, "Two bowls of noodles!" And when they were come, he ate them greedily.

There was no one Wang Lung knew in the small, dark room. Only a few men sat eating or drinking tea. It was a place for poor men, and among them he looked neat and almost well-to-do, so that a passing beggar whined at him,

"Have a good heart, teacher, and give me a small cash—I starve!"

Wang Lung had never had a beggar ask of him before, nor had any ever called him teacher. He was pleased and he threw into the beggar's bowl two small cash, which are one fifth of a penny, and the beggar, grasping the cash with his black claw of a hand, fumbled them within his rags.

Wang Lung sat and the sun climbed upward. The waiting boy lounged about impatiently. "If you are buying nothing more," he said at last, "you will have to pay rent for the stool."

Incensed at such impudence, Wang Lung would have risen, except that when he thought of the great House of Hwang, sweat broke out over his whole body as though he were working in a field.

"Bring me tea," he said weakly to the boy. Before he could turn it was there and the small boy demanded sharply,

"Where is the penny?"

"It is robbery," Wang Lung muttered. Then he saw his neighbor enter, whom he had invited to the feast, and he put the penny hastily upon the table and drank the tea at a gulp and went out quickly by the side door.

"It is to be done," he said to himself desperately, and slowly he turned his way to the great gates.

This time, since it was after high noon, the gates were ajar and the keeper of the gate idled upon the threshold, picking his teeth with a bamboo sliver. He was a tall fellow with a large mole upon his left cheek, from which hung three long black hairs.

With great difficulty Wang Lung said,

"I am Wang Lung, the farmer."

"Well, and Wang Lung, the farmer, what?" retorted the gateman, who was polite to none except the rich.

"I am come—I am come—" faltered Wang Lung.

"That I see," said the gateman with elaborate patience, twisting the long hairs of his mole.

"There is a woman," said Wang Lung, his voice sinking, in spite of himself, to a whisper. In the sunshine his face was wet.

The gateman gave a great laugh.

"So you are he! I was told to expect a bridegroom. But I did not recognize you with a basket on your arm."

"It is only a few meats," said Wang Lung apologetically, waiting for the gateman to lead him within. But the gateman did not move. Wang Lung saw that he wanted money.

"I am a poor man," he said pleadingly.

"Let me see what you have in your girdle," said the gateman.

Wang Lung in his simplicity put his basket upon the stones and took out the small bag and shook into his left hand what money was left. There was one silver piece and fourteen copper pence.

"I will take the silver," said the gateman coolly, and before Wang Lung could protest the man had the silver in his sleeve and was striding through the gate, bawling loudly,

"The bridegroom, the bridegroom!"

Wang Lung, in spite of anger at what had just happened and horror at this loud announcing of his coming, could do nothing but pick up his basket and follow. With his face burning and his head bowed, he walked through court after court, hearing that voice roaring ahead of him, hearing tinkles of laughter on every side. Then suddenly when it seemed to him he had gone through a hundred courts, the gateman fell silent and pushed him into a small waiting room. The gateman went into some inner place, returning in a moment to say,

"The Old Mistress says you are to appear before her."

Wang Lung started forward, but the gateman stopped him, crying in disgust,

"You cannot appear before a great lady with a basket on your arm. How will you bow?"

"True—true—" said Wang Lung in agitation. But he did not dare to put the basket down because he was afraid something might be stolen from it. The gateman saw his fear and cried out in great contempt,

"In a house like this we feed these meats to the dogs!" and he thrust the basket behind the door and pushed Wang Lung ahead of him.

Down a long, narrow veranda they went, the roofs supported by delicate carven posts, and into a hall the like of which Wang Lung had never seen. A score of houses such as his could have been put into it, so wide were the spaces, so high the roofs. Upon a dais in the center of the room he saw a very old lady, her small, fine body clothed in pearly gray satin, and upon the low bench beside her a pipe of opium stood, burning over its little lamp. She looked at him out of small, black eyes, as sunken and sharp as a monkey's in her thin and wrinkled face. The skin of her hand that held the pipe's end was stretched over her little bones as smooth and as yellow as the gilt upon an idol. Wang Lung fell to his knees and knocked his head on the tiled floor.

"Raise him," said the old lady to the gateman. "These obeisances are not necessary. Has he come for the woman?"

"Yes, Ancient One," replied the gateman.

"Why does he not speak for himself?" asked the old lady.

"Because he is a fool, Ancient One," said the gateman, twirling the hairs of his mole.

This roused Wang Lung and he looked with indignation at the gateman. "I am only a coarse person, Great and Ancient Lady," he said. "I do not know what words to use in such a presence."

The old lady looked at him with perfect gravity and made as though she would have spoken, except that her hand closed upon the pipe which a slave had been tending for her. At once she seemed to forget him. She bent and sucked greedily at the pipe and the sharpness passed from her eyes. Wang Lung remained standing until in passing her eyes caught his figure.

"What is this man doing here?" she asked with sudden anger.

The gateman's face was immovable.

"I am waiting for the woman, Great Lady," said Wang Lung in much astonishment.

"The woman? What woman . . . ?" the old lady began, but the slave girl at her side stooped and whispered and the lady recovered herself. "Ah, yes—a small affair—he has come for the slave called O-lan. Call her quickly," said the old lady to her slave. It was as though she was suddenly impatient to be left alone.

And in an instant the slave appeared leading by the hand a rather tall figure, clothed in a clean blue cotton coat and trousers. Wang Lung glanced once and then away, his heart beating. This was his woman.

"Come here, slave," said the old lady carelessly. "This man has come for you."

The woman stood before the lady with bowed head.

"Are you ready?" asked the lady.

The woman answered slowly as an echo, "Ready."

It was a good enough voice, plain, and not ill-tempered. Wang Lung looked at her back as she stood before him, and he saw with an instant's disappointment that her feet were not bound. But this he could not dwell upon, for the old lady called Wang Lung and said, "Stand beside her while I speak." And when Wang had come forward she said to him, "This woman came into our house when she was a child of ten. Now she is twenty years old. I bought her in a year of famine. Her parents came from the north in Shantung. You see she has the strong body and the square cheeks of her kind. She will work well for you in all that you wish. She is not beautiful but that you do not need. Neither is she clever. But she does well what she is told to do and she has a good temper. Take

287

her and use her well. Had I not wished to acquire merit at the temple for my future existence by bringing more life into the world I should have kept her, for she is good enough for the kitchen. But I marry my slaves off if any will have them."

And to the woman she said, "Obey him and bear him sons and yet more sons. Bring the first child to me to see."

"Yes, Ancient Mistress," said the woman submissively.

They stood hesitating, and Wang Lung was greatly embarrassed, not knowing whether he should speak or what.

"Well, go, will you!" said the old lady in irritation, and Wang Lung, bowing hastily, turned and went out, the woman after him, and after her the gateman, carrying on his shoulder her box. This box he dropped down in the room where Wang Lung returned to find his basket, and he disappeared without another word.

Then Wang Lung turned and looked at the woman. She had a square, honest face, a short, broad nose, and her mouth was wide, a gash in her face. Her eyes were small and dull black in color, and were filled with some sadness that was not clearly expressed. It was a face that seemed habitually silent. She bore Wang Lung's look without embarrassment or response. He saw that it was true there was not beauty of any kind in her face—a brown, common, patient face. But in her ears and on her hands he saw the rings he had given her. He turned away with secret exultation. Well, he had his woman!

"Here are this box and this basket," he said gruffly.

Without a word she bent over and picking up one end of the box she placed it upon her shoulder and, staggering under its weight, tried to rise. He watched her at this and suddenly he said,

"I will take the box. Here is the basket."

And he shifted the box to his own back, regardless of the best robe he wore, and she, still speechless, took the handle of the basket. He thought of the hundred courts he had come through and of his figure, absurd under its burden.

"If there were a side gate—" he muttered. After a little thought, as though she did not understand too quickly what he said, she nodded. Then she led the way through a small unused court that was grown up with weeds, and there under a bent pine tree was an old round gate. They went through and into the street.

Once or twice he looked back at her. She plodded along steadily on her big feet, her wide face expressionless. In the gate of the wall he stopped uncertainly and fumbled in his girdle for the pennies he had left. He took out two pence and with these he bought six small green peaches.

"Take these and eat them," he said gruffly. She clutched them greedily as a child might and held them in her hand without speech. When next he looked at her as they walked along the margin of the wheat fields she was nibbling one, but when she saw him looking at her she covered it with her hand and kept her jaws motionless.

And thus they went until they reached the western field where stood the temple to the earth. This temple was not higher in all than a man's shoulder and made of gray bricks and roofed with tile. Wang Lung's grandfather, who had built it, had covered the walls with plaster, and a village artist had been hired in a good year to paint upon the plaster a scene of hills and bamboo. But rain had poured upon this painting until now there was only a faint feathery shadow of bamboos left, and the hills were almost wholly gone.

Within the temple sat two small, solemn figures, earthen, formed from the fields about the temple. These were the god himself and his lady. They wore robes of red and gilt paper, and the god had a scant, drooping mustache of real hair. Each year at the New Year, Wang Lung's father bought sheets of red paper and carefully cut and pasted new robes for the pair. And each year rain and snow beat in and the sun of summer shone in and spoiled their robes.

At this moment, however, the robes were still new, and Wang Lung was proud of their spruce appearance. He took the basket from the woman's arm and looked under the pork for the sticks of incense he had bought. When he had found them he stuck them side by side in the ashes of other sticks of incense that were heaped before the gods, for the whole neighborhood worshiped these two small figures. Then fumbling for his flint and iron he caught, with a dried leaf for tinder, a flame to light the incense.

Together this man and his woman stood before the gods of their fields. The woman watched the ends of the incense redden and turn gray. When the ash grew heavy she leaned over and with her forefinger she pushed the head of ash away. Then as though fearful for what she had done, she looked quickly at Wang Lung. But there was something he liked in her movement. It was as though she felt that the incense belonged to them both; it was a moment of marriage. They stood there in complete silence, side by side, while the incense smoldered into ashes; and then Wang Lung shouldered the box and they went home.

At the door of the house the old man stood to catch the last rays of the sun. He made no movement as Wang Lung approached with the woman. It would have been beneath him to notice her. Instead he feigned great interest in the clouds and he cried,

"That cloud which hangs upon the left horn of the new moon speaks of rain." And then as he saw the basket he cried out again,

"And have you spent money?"

"There will be guests tonight," Wang Lung said briefly, and he carried the box into the room where he slept and set it down.

The old man said volubly,

"There is no end to the money spent in this house!"

Secretly he was pleased that his son had invited guests, but he felt it would not do to give out anything but complaints before his new daughter-in-law lest she be set from the first in ways of extravagance. Wang Lung said nothing, but he went into the kitchen, and the woman followed him. He took the food piece by piece from the basket and he said to her,

"There are seven to eat. Can you prepare food?"

He did not look at the woman as he spoke. It would not have been seemly. The woman answered in her plain voice,

"I have been kitchen slave in the House of Hwang."

Wang Lung nodded and left her and did not see her again until the guests came crowding in, his uncle jovial and sly and hungry, his uncle's son an impudent lad of fifteen, and three farmers clumsy and grinning with shyness. Two of these were from the village, with whom Wang Lung exchanged seed and labor at harvest time, and one was his next-door neighbor, Ching, a small, quiet man. After they had been seated about the middle room demurring and with unwillingness to take seats, for politeness, Wang Lung went into the kitchen to bid the woman serve.

"I will hand you the bowls," she said, "if you will place them upon the table. I do not like to come out before men."

Wang Lung felt in him a great pride that this woman was his and did not fear to appear before him, but would not before other men. He took the bowls from her hands at the kitchen door and he set them upon the table in the middle room and called loudly,

"Eat, my uncle and my brothers." And they ate heartily of the good fare, and this one praised the brown sauce on the fish and that one the well-done pork, and Wang Lung said over and over in reply, "It is poor stuff—it is badly prepared."

But in his heart he was proud of the dishes, for with sugar and vinegar and a little wine and soy sauce the woman had skillfully brought forth all the force of the meat. Wang Lung had never tasted such dishes upon the tables of his friends.

That night after the guests had tarried long over their tea and their jokes, the woman still lingered behind the stove, and when Wang Lung had seen the last guest away he went in and she cowered there in the straw, asleep beside the ox. When he called her she put up her arm suddenly in her sleep as though to defend herself from a blow. When she opened her eyes at last, she looked at him with her strange, speechless gaze, and he felt as though he faced a child. He took her by the hand and led her into the room where that morning he had bathed himself for her, and he lit a red candle. In this light he was suddenly shy when he found himself alone with the woman and he was compelled to remind himself,

"This woman is mine."

And he began to undress himself doggedly. As for the woman, she crept around the corner of the curtain and began without a sound to prepare for the bed. Wang Lung said gruffly,

"When you lie down, put the light out first."

Then he lay down and drew the thick quilt about his shoulders and pretended to sleep. But he was not sleeping. He lay quivering, every nerve of his flesh awake. And when, after a long time, the room went dark, and there was the slow, silent, creeping movement of the woman beside him, an exultation filled him fit to break his body.

II

THERE WAS THIS LUXURY of living. The next morning he lay upon his bed and watched the woman who was now wholly his own. She rose and drew about her her loosened garments and fastened them closely about her throat and waist, fitting them to her body with a slow writhe and twist. Then she put her feet into her cloth shoes and drew them on by the straps hanging at the back. Her face looked unchanged. This was an astonishment to Wang Lung. He felt as though the night must have changed him; yet here was this woman rising from his bed as though she had risen from it every day of her life. The old man's cough rose querulously out of the dusky dawn and he said to her,

"Take to my father first a bowl of hot water for his lungs."

She asked, her voice exactly as it had been yesterday, "Are there to be tea leaves in it?"

The simple question troubled Wang Lung. He would have liked the woman to think that they made nothing of tea leaves in this house. In the House of Hwang even a slave, perhaps, would not drink only water. But he knew his father would be angry if on the first day the woman served tea to him. He replied negligently, therefore, "Tea? No—no—it makes his cough worse."

And then he lay in his bed warm and satisfied while in the kitchen the woman boiled the water. He would like to have slept, but his foolish body, which he had made to arise every morning so early all these years, would not sleep although it could, so he lay there, savoring his luxury of idleness. Part of the time he thought of what his harvest would be if the rains came, and of the white turnip seed he wished to buy from Ching if they could agree upon a price. But between these thoughts there ran weaving and interweaving the new thought of what his life now was, and it occurred to him to wonder if this woman of his liked him. This was a new wonder. He had questioned only of whether he would like her. He desired suddenly that she should like him as her husband.

The door opened and in her silent way she came in, bearing in both hands a steaming bowl. There were tea leaves floating upon the surface of the water. He looked up at her quickly. She was at once afraid and she said,

"I took no tea to the Old One—but to you I . . ."

Wang Lung answered before she finished, "I like it—I like it," and he drew his tea into his mouth with loud sups of pleasure.

In himself there was this new exultation, "This woman of mine likes me well enough!"

IT SEEMED TO HIM that during these next months he did nothing except watch this woman of his. In reality he worked as he had always worked. He put his hoe upon his shoulder and he walked to his plots of land and he cultivated the rows of grain, and he yoked the ox and he plowed the western field for garlic and onions. But the work was luxury, for when the sun struck the zenith he could go to his house and food would be there ready for him to eat, and the dust wiped from the table, and the bowls and the chopsticks placed neatly upon it. Hitherto he had had to prepare the meals when he came in, tired. Now whatever there was, was ready for him.

The woman, when he had gone in the morning, took the bamboo rake and she roamed the countryside, reaping here a bit of grass and there a twig, returning at noon with enough to cook the dinner. It pleased the man that they need buy no more fuel. In the afternoon she took a hoe and a basket, and she went to the main road leading into the city where she picked the droppings from the mules and donkeys and horses and carried it home for fertilizer for the fields. These things she did without being commanded. And when the end of the day came she did not rest herself until the ox had been fed and until she had dipped water to hold to its muzzle to let it drink what it would.

And with thread that she herself spun on a bamboo spindle from a wad of cotton she mended the rents in their winter clothes. Their bedding she took into the sun and ripped the coverings from the quilts and washed them and hung them upon a bamboo to dry, and the cotton in the quilts that had grown hard and gray from years she picked over, killing the vermin that had flourished in the hidden folds. Day after day she did one thing after another, until the three rooms seemed almost prosperous. The old man's cough grew better and he sat in the sun by the southern wall of the house, always half asleep and warm and content.

But she never talked, this woman, except for the brief necessities of life. Wang Lung, watching secretly the stolid, square face, the unexpressed, half-fearful look of her eyes, made nothing of her. At night he knew the soft firmness of her body. But in the day she was like a faithful, speechless serving maid. And sometimes, working over the clods in the fields, he would fall to pondering about her. What had she seen in those hundred courts? What had been her life, that life she never shared with him? And then he was ashamed of his own curiosity. She was, after all, only a woman.

But there is not that about three rooms and two meals a day to keep busy a woman who has been a slave in a great house. One day when Wang Lung was hard pressed with the swelling wheat and was cultivating it with his hoe, day after day, until his back throbbed with weariness, her shadow fell across the furrow over which he bent himself, and there she stood, with a hoe across her shoulder.

"There is nothing in the house until nightfall," she said briefly, and she took the furrow to the right of him.

The sun beat down upon them, for it was early summer, but moving together in a perfect rhythm, without a word, hour after hour, he fell into a union with her which took the pain from his labor. There was this perfect sympathy of movement, of turning this earth of theirs over and over to the sun, this earth which formed their home and fed their bodies and made their gods.

Sometimes they turned up a bit of brick, a splinter of wood. In some age, bodies of men and women had been buried there, houses had stood there, had fallen, and gone back into the earth. So would also their house, sometime, return into the earth, their bodies also. Each had his turn at this earth. They worked on, moving together—together producing the fruit of this earth—speechless in their movement together.

When the sun had set he straightened his back slowly and looked at the woman. Her face was streaked with the earth. Her wet, dark garments clung to her square body. She smoothed a last furrow slowly. Then she said, straight out, her voice more than usually plain in the silent evening air,

"I am with child."

Wang Lung stood still. What was there to say to this thing, then! It was as though she had said, "I have brought you tea." It seemed as ordinary as that to her! But to him—he could not say what it was to him. His heart swelled and stopped as though it met sudden confines.

He took the hoe suddenly from her hand and he said, his voice thick in his throat, "Let be for now. It is a day's end. We will tell the old man."

They walked home, then, she half a dozen paces behind him as befitted a woman. The old man stood at the door. He was impatient and he called out,

"I am too old to wait for my food like this!"

But Wang Lung, passing him into the room, said,

"She is with child already."

He tried to say it easily as one might say, "I have planted the western field today," but he could not. Although he spoke in a low voice it was to him as though he had shouted the words.

The old man blinked for a moment and then comprehended, and cackled with laughter. "Heh-heh—" he called to his daughter-in-law, "so the harvest is in sight!"

Her face he could not see in the dusk, but she answered evenly,

"I shall prepare food now."

"Yes—yes—food—" said the old man eagerly, following her

into the kitchen. The thought of food made him forget the child.

But Wang Lung sat by the table in the darkness and put his head upon his folded arms. Out of this body of his, out of his own loins, life!

WHEN THE HOUR FOR BIRTH drew near he said to the woman, "We must have someone to help at the time—some woman."

But she shook her head. She was clearing away the bowls after the evening food. The old man had gone to his bed and the two of them were alone in the night, with only the light that fell upon them from the flickering flame of a small tin lamp filled with bean oil, in which a twist of cotton floated for a wick.

"No woman?" he asked in consternation. He was beginning now to be accustomed to these conversations in which her part was little more than a movement of head or hand. He had even come to feel no lack in such conversing. "But it will be odd with only two men in the house!" he continued. "Is there none in the great house, with whom you were friends, who could come?"

It was the first time he had mentioned the house from which she came. She turned on him as he had never seen her, her narrow eyes widened, her face stirred with dull anger.

"None in that house!" she cried out at him.

He dropped his pipe which he was filling and stared at her. She had placed the chopsticks carefully down upon the table, and she looked at him and said,

"When I return to that house it will be with my son in my arms. I shall have a red coat on him and red-flowered trousers and a hat with a gilded Buddha on the front and on his feet tiger-faced shoes. And I will wear new shoes and a new coat of black sateen and I will go and show myself and my son to all of them."

He had never heard so many words from her before. They came forth steadily and without break. How astonishing she was! He would have said that she had scarcely thought of the child, so stilly had she gone about her work. And instead she saw this child, born and fully clothed, and herself as his mother, in a new coat! He was for once without words himself, and he pressed the tobacco diligently into a ball between his thumb and forefinger, and picking up his pipe he fitted the tobacco into the bowl.

"I suppose you will need some money," he said at last with apparent gruffness.

"If you will give me three silver pieces . . ." she said fearfully. "It is a great deal, but I will waste no penny of it. I shall make the cloth dealer give me the last inch to the foot."

Wang Lung fumbled in his girdle. The day before he had sold reeds from the pond in the western field. He put the three silver pieces upon the table. Then, after a little hesitation, he added a fourth piece which he had long kept to gamble some morning at the teahouse. But he never did more than linger and look at the dice as they clattered upon the table, fearful lest he lose if he played. He usually ended by spending his spare hours in the town at the storyteller's booth, where one may listen to an old tale and pay no more than a penny into his bowl.

"You may as well make his coat of a small remnant of silk," he said, lighting his pipe between the words, blowing quickly at the paper spill to set it aflame. "After all, he is the first."

She did not at once take the money, but she stood looking at it, her face motionless. Then she said in a half whisper,

"It is the first time I have had silver money in my hand."

Suddenly she took it and clenched it in her hand and hurried into the bedroom.

Wang Lung sat smoking, thinking of the silver. It had come out of the earth, this silver, out of his earth that he plowed and turned and spent himself upon. Drop by drop by his sweat he wrung fruit from it and from the fruit, silver. Each time before this that he had taken the silver out to give to anyone, it had been like giving a piece of his life. But now for the first time such giving was not pain. He saw the silver transmuted into something worth even more than itself—clothes upon the body of his son.

HER HOUR CAME ONE NIGHT, early, when the sun was scarcely set. She was working beside him in the harvest field. The wheat had borne and been cut and the field flooded and the young rice set, and now the rice ears were full after the warm ripening sun of early autumn. Together they cut the sheaves all day, bending and cutting with short-handled scythes. She stooped stiffly, because of the burden she bore, so that they cut unevenly, his row ahead and hers behind. She began to cut more and more slowly as noon wore on to evening, and he turned to look at her with impatience. She stopped and stood up then, her scythe dropped. On her face was a new sweat, the sweat of a new agony.

"It is come," she said. "I will go into the house. Do not come into the room until I call. Only bring me a newly peeled reed, and slit it, that I may cut the child's life from mine."

She went across the fields toward the house as though there were nothing to come, and after he had watched her he went to the edge of the pond and chose a slim green reed and peeled it carefully and slit it on the edge of his scythe. The quick autumn darkness was falling then and he shouldered his scythe and went home.

When he reached the house he found his supper hot on the table and the old man eating. She had stopped in her labor to prepare them food! He said to himself that she was a woman such as is not commonly found. Then he went to the door of their room and he called out,

"Here is the reed!"

Through the crack her hand reached out and took the reed. She said no word, but he heard her panting as an animal pants which has run for a long way.

The old man looked up from his bowl to say,

"Eat, or all will be cold! It will be a long time. I remember well when the first was born to me it was dawn before it was over. Ah, me, to think that out of all the children I begot and your mother bore, one after the other—a score or so—I forget—only you have lived!" And then he said again, as though he had just thought of it newly, "By this time tomorrow I may be grandfather to a man-child!" And he stopped his eating and sat chuckling for a long time in the dusk of the room.

But Wang Lung stood listening at the door. The panting of the woman within became quick and loud, like whispered screams, but when he could bear no more and was about to break into the room, a thin, fierce cry came out and he forgot everything.

"Is it a man?" he cried importunately, forgetting the woman. "Tell me at least this—is it a man?"

And the voice of the woman answered as faintly as an echo, "A man!"

He went and sat down at the table then. The food was long cold and the old man was asleep on his bench, but how quick it had all been! He shook the old man's shoulder.

"It is a man-child!" he called triumphantly. "You are grandfather and I am father!"

The old man woke suddenly and began to laugh as he had been laughing when he fell asleep.

"Yes—of course," he cackled, "grandfather—grandfather—" and he rose and went to his bed, still laughing.

Wang Lung took up the bowl of cold rice and began to eat. He was very hungry all at once and he could not get the food into his mouth quickly enough. He could hear the woman dragging herself about and the cry of the child was incessant and piercing.

"I suppose we shall have no more peace in this house now," he said to himself proudly.

When he had eaten he went to the door again and she called to him and he went in. She was lying neatly covered upon the bed. Beside her, wrapped in a pair of his old trousers, as the custom was, lay his son.

His heart crowded up into his breast and he leaned over the child to look at it. It had a round wrinkled face, and upon its head the hair was long and damp and black. It had ceased crying and lay with its eyes tightly shut.

He looked at his wife and she looked back at him. Her hair was still wet with her agony and her narrow eyes were sunken. Beyond this, she was as she always was. But to him she was touching, lying there. His heart rushed out to these two and he said, not knowing what else there was that could be said,

"Tomorrow I will go into the city and buy a pound of red sugar and stir it into boiling water for you to drink."

And then, looking at the child again, this burst forth from him suddenly as though he had just thought of it, "We shall have to buy a good basketful of eggs and dye them all red for the village. Thus will everyone know I have a son!"

III

THE NEXT DAY after the child was born the woman rose as usual and prepared food, but she did not go into the harvest fields; so Wang Lung worked alone until after the noon hour. Then he dressed himself in his blue gown and went into the town. He went to the market and bought fifty eggs, not new laid, but still well enough, and he bought red paper to boil in the water with them

to make them red. Then he went to the sweetshop, and there he bought a pound of red sugar. The sugar dealer smiled.

"It is for the mother of a newborn child, perhaps?"

"A firstborn son," said Wang Lung proudly.

"Ah, good fortune," answered the man.

This he had said many times to others, but to Wang Lung it seemed special and he was pleased and he bowed as he went from the shop. It seemed to him as he walked into the sharp sunshine of the dusty street that there was never a man so filled with good fortune as he.

He thought of this at first with joy and then with a pang of fear. It did not do in this life to be too fortunate. The air and the earth were filled with malignant spirits who could not endure the happiness of mortals, especially of such as are poor. He turned abruptly into the candlemaker's shop, and there he bought four sticks of incense, one for each person in his house, and he went into the small temple of the gods of the earth, and he thrust them into the cold ashes of the incense he had placed there before, he and his wife together. He watched the four sticks well lit and then went homeward, comforted.

AND THEN, ALMOST BEFORE one could realize anything, the woman was back in the fields beside him. The harvests were past, and the grain they beat out with flails in the dooryard of the house. And when the grain was flailed they winnowed it, casting it up from great flat bamboo baskets into the wind and catching the good grain as it fell, and the chaff blew away in a cloud with the wind. Then there were the fields to plant for winter wheat again, and when he had yoked the ox and plowed the land the woman followed behind with her hoe and broke the clods in the furrows.

She worked all day now and the child lay on an old torn quilt on the ground, asleep. When it cried the woman stopped and uncovered her bosom to the child's mouth, sitting flat upon the ground, and the sun beat down upon them both, the reluctant sun of late autumn that will not let go the warmth of summer until the cold of the coming winter forces it. The woman and the child were as brown as the soil and they sat there like figures made of earth, and out of the woman's great brown breast the milk gushed forth for the child in abundance. The child was fat and good-natured and ate of the inexhaustible life his mother gave him.

Winter came on and they were prepared against it. There had never been such harvests before, and the small house was bursting. From the rafters of the thatched roof hung strings and strings of dried onions and garlic, and there was even a large, salted leg of pork which Wang Lung had bought from his neighbor Ching when he killed his pig that looked as though it were sickening for a disease. There were as well two of their own chickens killed and drawn and dried with the feathers on and stuffed with salt. There were great jars made of reeds, filled full of wheat and rice. Much of this would be sold. Wang Lung was frugal and he did not spend his money at gambling or on delicate foods, and so have to sell the grain at harvest when the price was low. Instead he saved it and sold it at the New Year when people will pay well for food.

His uncle was always having to sell his grain before it was well ripened. Sometimes he even sold it standing in the field to save himself the trouble of harvesting. But then his uncle's wife was a foolish woman, fat and lazy, and forever clamoring for sweet food and for new shoes bought in the town. Wang Lung's woman made all their shoes.

In the midst of all this plenty they sat in the house, therefore, when the winds of winter came out of the desert to the northeast of them, winds bitter and biting. They had had a feast of noodles, which mean long life, on the child's month birthday, and Wang Lung had given red eggs to all those who came from the village to congratulate him. And everyone envied him his son, a great, fat, moony-faced child with high cheekbones like his mother. Now he sat on the quilt placed on the earthen floor of the house, and they opened the door to the south for the sun, and the wind on the north beat in vain against the thick earthen wall.

The leaves were soon torn from the date tree on the threshold and from the willow trees and the peach trees near the fields. Only the bamboo leaves clung to the bamboos in the sparse clump to the east of the house, though the wind wrenched the stems double. And then suddenly out of a still gray day when the wind fell and the air was quiet and warm, the rains came, and they all sat in the house filled with well-being, watching the rain fall full and straight and sink into the fields. The child stretched out his hands to catch the silver lines of the rain as it fell, and he laughed and they laughed with him and the old man squatted on the floor beside the child and said, "There is not another child like this in a dozen villages. Those brats of my brother notice nothing before they walk."

And in the fields the wheat seed sprouted and pushed spears of delicate green above the wet brown earth.

At a time like this there was visiting, because each farmer felt that for once Heaven was doing the work in the fields without their backs being broken for it, carrying buckets to and fro; and they gathered at this house and that, drinking tea, going from house to house between the fields under great oiled-paper umbrellas. But Wang Lung and his wife were not frequent at visiting. There was no house in the village of a half dozen small scattered houses which was so filled with warmth and plenty as their own, and Wang Lung felt that if he became too intimate with the others there would be borrowing. New Year was coming and who had all the money he wanted for the new clothes and the feasting? He stayed in his house, and examined his rakes of split bamboo, and where the string was broken he wove in new string made of hemp he grew himself, and where a prong was broken out he drove in cleverly a new bit of bamboo.

And what he did for the farm implements, his wife, O-lan, did for the house implements. If an earthen jar leaked she did not, as other women did, cast it aside. Instead she mixed clay and welded the crack and heated it slowly and it was as good as new.

They sat in their house, therefore, and they rejoiced in each other's approval, although their speech was never anything more than scattered words such as these:

"Did you save the seed from the large squash for the new planting?" Or, "We will sell the wheat straw and burn the bean stalks in the kitchen." Or perhaps rarely Wang Lung would say, "This is a good dish of noodles," and O-lan would answer in deprecation, "It is good flour we have this year from the fields."

From the produce, Wang Lung in this good year had a handful of silver pieces over and above what they needed and these he was fearful of keeping in his belt. So the woman dug a small hole in the wall behind their bed and into this Wang Lung thrust the silver and with a clod of earth she covered the hole, and it was as though there were nothing there. But to both it gave a sense of secret richness and reserve. And when Wang Lung walked among his fellows he walked at ease with himself and with all.

THE NEW YEAR APPROACHED and Wang Lung went into the town and he bought squares of red paper on which were brushed in gilt ink the letters for happiness and for riches; these squares he pasted upon his plow and upon the ox's yoke and upon the two buckets in which he carried his fertilizer and his water, to bring him luck in the new year. And over his doorway he pasted a fringe of red paper cunningly cut into a flower pattern. And the old man made new dresses for the gods and Wang Lung burned incense before them. And for his house he bought also two red candles to burn on the eve of the year upon the table under the picture of a god, which was pasted on the wall of the middle room.

And Wang Lung went again into the town and he bought pork fat and white sugar and the woman rendered the fat smooth and white and she took flour which the ox had ground from their own rice between their millstones, and she kneaded rich New Year's cakes, called moon cakes, such as were eaten in the House of Hwang.

When the cakes were laid out upon the table, Wang Lung felt his heart fit to burst with pride. There was no other woman in the village able to make such cakes. In some of the cakes she had put strips of little red haws and spots of dried green plums, making flowers and patterns. The old man was hovering about the table, pleased as a child with the bright colors. He said,

"Call my brother and his children—let them see!"

But the woman, her hands all dusty with the fine rice flour, said,

"Those are not for us to eat. I am preparing them for the Old Mistress. I shall take the child on the second day of the new year and carry the cakes for a gift."

Then the cakes were more important than ever, and Wang Lung was pleased that to the great hall where he had stood with so much timidity and in such poverty his wife should now go as visitor, carrying his son, dressed in red, and cakes made as these were.

All else at that New Year sank into insignificance. His new coat of black cotton cloth which O-lan had made only made him say to himself,

"I shall wear it when I take them to the great house."

He even bore carelessly the first day of the new year when his uncle and his neighbors came crowding into the house to wish his father and himself well, all boisterous with food and drink, although he found it very hard when the plain white cakes were praised not to cry out,

"You should see the colored ones!"

But he did not, for more than anything he wished to enter the great house with pride.

THEN ON THE SECOND DAY of the new year, the day for women to visit each other, they rose at dawn and the woman dressed the child in his red coat and in the tiger-faced shoes she had made, and she put on his head freshly shaven by Wang Lung himself the crownless red hat with the small gilt Buddha sewed on front, and she set him upon the bed. Then Wang Lung dressed himself quickly while his wife combed out her long black hair and knotted it with a brass pin which he had bought for her, and she put on her new coat of black that was made from the same piece as his own new robe. Then she carrying the child and he the cakes in the basket, they set out on the path across the fields.

Then Wang Lung had his reward at the great gate of the House of Hwang, for the gateman opened his eyes at all he saw and he twirled the three long hairs on his mole and cried out, "Ah, Wang the farmer, three this time instead of one! One has no need to wish you more fortune this year than you have had in the last."

Wang Lung answered negligently, "Good harvests—good harvests—" and he stepped with assurance inside the gate.

"Do you sit within my wretched room," the gateman said, "while I announce your woman and son within."

And Wang Lung stood watching them go across the court, his wife and his son, bearing gifts to the head of a great house. It was all to his honor, and when they had dwindled down the long vista of the courts, he went into the gateman's house and there he accepted from the gateman's pockmarked wife the honorable seat to the left of the table, and he accepted with only a slight nod the bowl of tea which she presented and did not drink of it, as though it were not good enough for him.

It seemed a long time before the gateman returned, bringing back the woman and child. Wang Lung looked closely at the woman's face to see if all were well, for he had learned now to detect small changes in that square countenance. She wore a look of heavy content, however, and he became impatient to hear her tell of what had happened. With short bows to the gateman and to his wife he hurried O-lan away and he took into his own arms the child who was asleep and lying all crumpled in his new coat.

"Well?" he called back to her over his shoulder. For once he was impatient with her slowness. She drew a little nearer to him and said in a whisper,

"I believe that they are feeling a pinch this year in that house."

She spoke in a shocked tone as of gods being hungry.

"What do you mean?" said Wang Lung, urging her.

But she would not be hastened. Words were to her things to be caught one by one and released with difficulty.

"The Ancient Mistress wore the same coat this year as last. I have never seen this happen before." And then after a pause she said, "I saw not one slave with a new coat like mine." And then after a while she said, "As for our son, there was not even a child among the concubines of the Old Master himself to compare to him in beauty and in dress."

A slow smile spread over her face and Wang Lung laughed aloud and held the child tenderly. How well he had done! And then as he exulted he was smitten with fear. What foolish thing was he doing, walking like this under an open sky, with a beautiful man-child for any evil spirit to see! He opened his coat hastily and thrust the child's head into his bosom and he said in a loud voice,

"What a pity our child is a female whom no one could want, and covered with smallpox as well! Let us pray it may die."

"Yes—yes—" said his wife as quickly as she could, understanding dimly what a thing they had done.

And being comforted with these precautions, Wang Lung once more urged his wife.

"Did you find out why they are poorer?"

"I had but a moment for private talk with the cook," she replied, "but she said, 'This house cannot stand forever with all the young lords spending money like waste water in foreign parts, and the Old Mistress eating enough opium every day to fill two shoes with silver.'"

"Do they indeed?" murmured Wang Lung, spellbound.

"The Old Mistress herself told me they wished to sell some of the land just outside the city wall, where they have always planted rice each year because it is good land and easily flooded from the moat around the wall."

"Sell their land!" repeated Wang Lung, convinced. "Then indeed are they growing poor. Land is one's flesh and blood."

He pondered for a while and suddenly a thought came to him and he smote the side of his head with his palm.

"What have I not thought of!" he cried, turning to the woman. "We will buy the land!"

They stared at each other, he in delight, she in stupefaction.

"Buy the land—the land—" she stammered.

"I will buy it!" he cried in a lordly voice. "I will buy it from the great House of Hwang!"

"It is better certainly than putting money into a mud wall," she said pacifically. "But why not buy a piece of your uncle's land? He is clamoring to sell that strip near the western field."

"That land of my uncle's," said Wang Lung, "I would not have it. He has been dragging a crop out of it for twenty years, and not a bit has he put back of manure. No, I will buy Hwang's land."

He said "Hwang's land" as casually as he might have said "Ching's land." He would be more than equal to these people in the foolish, great, wasteful house. He would go before the Old Lord with the silver in his hand and he would say plainly,

"I have money. What is the price of the earth you wish to sell?"

And it was as though his wife felt his thought, for again the slow smile spread over her face, the smile that never lightened the dullness of her narrow black eyes, and after a long time she said,

"Last year this time I was slave in that house."

And they walked on, silent with the fullness of this thought.

IV

THIS PIECE OF LAND greatly changed Wang Lung's life. At first, after he had dug the silver from the wall and taken it to the great house, he was visited with a depression of spirit which was almost regret. After all, this land would take hours of labor, and it was more than a third of a mile away. And again, the buying of it had not been quite so filled with glory as he had anticipated. He had gone too early to the great house. True, it was noon, but when he had said in a loud voice,

"Tell his Old Honor I have important business—tell him money is concerned!" the gateman had answered positively,

"All the money in the world would not tempt me to wake the old tiger." And then he had added maliciously, pulling at the hairs on his mole, "And do not think that silver will waken him—he has had silver under his hand since he was born."

In the end, it had had to be managed with the Old Lord's agent, an oily scoundrel whose hands were heavy with the money that stuck to them in passing. When Wang Lung had poured out his silver proudly, the agent had scraped it up carelessly and said,

"Enough for a few days of opium for the old lady, at any rate."

Well, but the land was his! Wang Lung set out one gray day in the second month of the new year to look at it, a long square of heavy black clay that lay stretched beside the moat of the town. He paced the land off carefully, three hundred paces lengthwise and a hundred and twenty across. Four stones still marked the corners, stones set with the great seal character of the House of Hwang. Well, he would have that changed. He would put his own name there—not yet, for he was not ready for people to know that he was rich enough to buy land, but later, when he was more rich, so that it did not matter what he did. And looking at that long square of land he thought to himself,

"To those at the great house it means nothing, this handful of earth, but to me it means how much!"

And the wide difference that still lay between him and the great house seemed suddenly impassable as the moat full of water, and as high as the wall beyond. He was filled with an angry determination, then, and he said to his heart that he would fill that hole with silver again and again until he had bought from the House of Hwang enough land so that this land would be less than an inch in his sight.

And so this parcel of land became to Wang Lung a sign and a symbol.

SPRING CAME WITH BLUSTERING winds and torn clouds of rain and for Wang Lung the half-idle days of winter were plunged into long days of desperate labor. The old man looked after the child now and the woman worked with the man from dawn until sunset, and when Wang Lung perceived one day that again she was with child, his first thought was that during the harvest she would be unable to work. He shouted at her, irritable with fatigue,

"So you have chosen this time to breed again, have you!"

She answered stoutly,

"This time it is nothing. It is only the first that is hard."

Beyond this nothing was said of the second child until the day came in autumn when she laid down her hoe one morning and crept into the house. He did not go back that day even for his noon meal, for the sky was heavy with thunderclouds and his rice lay ripe for gathering. Later before the sun set she was back beside him, her body flattened, spent, but her face silent and undaunted. His impulse was to say,

"For this day you have had enough. Go and lie upon your bed."

But the aching of his own body made him cruel, and he only asked between the strokes of his scythe,

"Is it male or female?"

She answered calmly,

"It is another male."

They said no more, but he was pleased, and the bending seemed less arduous, and working on until the moon rose above a bank of purple clouds, they finished the field and went home.

After his meal Wang Lung went in to look at his second son. O-lan had lain herself upon the bed after the cooking of the meal and the child lay beside her—a fat, placid child, well enough, but not so large as the first one. Wang Lung went back to the middle room well content. Another son, and another and another each year—one could not trouble with red eggs every year; it was enough to do it for the first. The house was full of good fortune—this woman brought him nothing but good fortune. He shouted to his father,

"Now, Old One, with another grandson we shall have to put the big one in your bed!"

The old man had for a long time been desiring this child to sleep in his bed and warm his chilly old flesh, but the child would not leave his mother. Now, however, staggering in with feet still unsteady with babyhood, he stared at this new child beside his mother, and seeming to comprehend with his grave eyes that another had his place, he allowed himself without protest to be placed in his grandfather's bed.

And again the harvests were good and Wang Lung again hid silver in the wall. But the rice he reaped from the land of the Hwangs brought him twice that from his own rice land. And everyone knew now that Wang Lung owned this land and in his village there was talk of making him the head.

WANG LUNG'S UNCLE began at this time to become the trouble which Wang Lung had known from the beginning that he might be. This uncle was the younger brother of Wang Lung's father, and by all the claims of relationship he might depend upon Wang

Lung if he had not enough for himself and his family. So long as Wang Lung and his father were poor the uncle made muster to scratch about on his own land and gather enough to feed his seven children and his wife and himself. But once fed none of them worked. The wife would not stir herself to sweep the floor of their hut, nor did the children trouble to wash the food from their faces. It was a disgrace that as the girls grew older they ran about the village street and left their hair uncombed, and sometimes even talked to men. Wang Lung, meeting his oldest girl cousin thus one day, was so angered for the disgrace done to his family that he dared to go to his uncle's wife and say,

"Now, who will marry a girl like my cousin, whom any man may look on? She has been marriageable these three years and today I saw an idle lout lay his hand on her arm and she answered him only with brazen laughter!"

His uncle's wife had nothing active in her body except her tongue and this she now loosed upon Wang Lung.

"Well, and who will pay for the dowry and for the middleman's fees? It is all very well for those to talk who have more land than they know what to do with, but your uncle is an unfortunate man and he has been so from the first." She fell into loud, easy tears, and began to work herself up into a fury. She snatched at her knot of hair and tore down the loose hairs about her face and she began to scream, "Ah, it is something you do not know—to have an evil destiny! Where the fields of others bear good rice, ours bear weeds; where the houses of others stand for a hundred years, the earth itself shakes under ours so that the walls crack; where others bear men, I, although I conceive a son, will yet give birth to a girl—ah, evil destiny!"

She shrieked aloud and the neighbors rushed out of their houses to see. Wang Lung stood stoutly, however, and would finish what he came to say.

"Nevertheless," he said, "although it is not for me to presume to advise the brother of my father, I will say this: it is better that the girl be married."

Having spoken thus plainly, he went away and left his uncle's wife screaming. He had it in his mind to buy more land this year from the House of Hwang, and it angered him that as he saw himself and his sons rising into a landed family, this shiftless brood should be running loose, bearing the same name as his own.

The next day his uncle came to the field where he was working. O-lan was not there, for ten moons had passed since the second child was born and a third birth was close upon her, and this time she was not so well. His uncle came slouching along a furrow, his clothes held insecurely with his girdle, so that it seemed that if a gust of wind blew at him he might suddenly stand naked. Wang Lung said maliciously without looking up,

"I ask your pardon, my uncle, for not stopping my work. These beans must, if they are to bear, be cultivated twice and thrice. Yours, doubtless, are finished. I am very slow—a poor farmer—never finishing my work in time to rest."

But his uncle answered smoothly,

"I am a man of evil destiny. This year out of twenty seed beans, one came up. There is no use in putting the hoe down. We shall have to buy beans this year if we eat them," and he sighed heavily.

Wang Lung knew that his uncle had come to ask something of him. He put his hoe down into the ground with a long even movement, breaking up the tiniest clod in the soft earth already well cultivated. The bean plants stood erect in thrifty order, casting little fringes of clear shadow in the sunshine. At last his uncle began to speak.

"The person in my house has told me," he said, "of your interest in my worthless oldest slave creature. It is wholly true what you say. She should be married. I am terrified constantly lest she bring shame to our name."

Wang Lung put his hoe down hard into the soil. He would have liked to say,

"Why do you not control her, then? Why do you not keep her decently in the house and make her sweep and cook?"

But one cannot say these things to an older generation. He remained silent, therefore, and hoed and waited.

"If it had been my good destiny," continued his uncle mournfully, "to have married a wife who could work and at the same time produce sons, instead of a woman who grows nothing but flesh and gives birth to nothing but females and that one idle son of mine, I, too, might have been rich now as you are. Then might I have, willingly would I have, shared my riches with you. Your daughters I would have wed to good men, your son would I have placed in a merchant's shop as apprentice—your house would I have delighted to repair, and you I would have fed with the best I had, you and your father and your children, for we are of one blood."

Wang Lung answered shortly,

"You know I am not rich. I have the five mouths to feed, and another mouth is being born in my house at this very moment."

His uncle replied shrilly,

"You are rich—you are rich! Is there another in the village who could have bought land from the great house?"

At this Wang Lung was goaded to anger. He flung down his hoe and he shouted suddenly, glaring at his uncle,

"If I have a handful of silver it is because I work and my wife works, and we do not, as some do, sit idling over a gambling table or gossiping on doorsteps, letting the fields grow to weeds!"

The blood flew into his uncle's yellow face and he rushed at his nephew and slapped him on both cheeks. "Now that," he cried, "for speaking so to your father's generation! Have you no religion, no morals? Have you not heard that in the Sacred Edicts it is commanded that a man is never to correct an elder?"

Wang Lung stood sullen, conscious of his fault but angry to the bottom of his heart.

"I will tell your words to the whole village!" screamed his uncle in a high, cracked voice of fury. "Yesterday you attack my house and my daughter; today you reproach me, who if your father passes on, must be as your own father to you!" And he repeated over and over, "I will tell it to the village—I will tell it to the village . . ." until at last Wang Lung said unwillingly,

"What do you want me to do?"

It touched his pride that this matter might indeed be called out before the village. After all, it was his own flesh and blood.

His uncle changed immediately. Anger melted out of him. He smiled and he put his hand on Wang Lung's arm.

"Ah, I know you—good lad—good lad—" he said softly. "A little silver in this poor old palm—say, ten pieces, or even nine, and I could begin to have arrangements with a matchmaker for that slave of mine. Ah, you are right! It is time—it is time!" He sighed and shook his head and he looked piously to the sky.

Wang Lung picked up his hoe and threw it down again.

"Come to the house," he said shortly. "I do not carry silver on me like a prince," and he strode ahead, bitter beyond speech because some of the good silver with which he had planned to buy more land was to go into this palm of his uncle's, whence it would slip onto the gambling table before night fell.

He strode into the house, brushing out of his way his two small sons who played, naked in the warm sunshine, about the threshold. His uncle, with idle good nature, called to the children and took from some recess in his clothing a copper coin for each child.

"Ah, you are two little men," he said, clasping one in either arm.

But Wang Lung went into the room where he slept. It was very dark, and except for the bar of light from the hole, he could see nothing. But he heard movement and he called out sharply,

"What now—has your time come?"

The voice of his wife answered from the bed more feebly than he had ever heard her speak,

"It is over. It is only a slave this time—not worth mentioning."

Wang Lung stood still. A sense of evil struck him. A girl! A girl was causing all this trouble in his uncle's house. Now a girl had been born into his house as well.

He went without reply then to the wall and removed the clod of earth. He fumbled among the little heap of silver and he counted out nine pieces. Then going out he thrust the money at his uncle and he walked quickly back to the field and there he fell to working as though he would tear the earth from its foundations.

It was evening before his anger was spent. And then he thought of that new mouth come into his house and it struck him with heaviness that the birth of daughters had begun for him, daughters who do not belong to their parents, but are born and reared for other families. He had not even thought, in his anger at his uncle, to stop and see the face of this small, new creature.

As he stood leaning upon his hoe he was seized with sadness and he groaned aloud.

V

IT SEEMED AS THOUGH once the gods turn against a man they will not consider him again. The rains, which should have come in early summer, withheld themselves, and day after day the skies shone with fresh and careless brilliance, and at night the stars hung out of the sky, golden and cruel in their beauty.

The fields, although Wang Lung cultivated them desperately, dried and cracked, and the young wheat stalks, which had sprung up courageously with the coming of spring, dwindled and yellowed into a barren harvest. The young rice beds were squares of jade upon the brown earth. Wang Lung carried water to them day upon day after he had given up the wheat, the heavy wooden buckets slung upon a bamboo pole across his shoulders. But though a furrow grew upon his flesh, no rain came.

At last the water in the pond dried into a cake of clay and even the water in the well sunk so low that O-lan said to him,

"If the children drink and the old man have his hot water the plants must go dry."

Wang Lung answered with anger that broke into a sob,

"Well, and they must all starve if the plants starve." It was true that all their lives depended upon the earth.

Only the land by the moat bore harvest, and this because at last Wang Lung abandoned his other fields and stayed the day out at this one, dipping water from the moat to pour upon the greedy soil. This year for the first time he sold his grain as soon as it was harvested, and when he felt the silver upon his palm he gripped it hard in defiance. He would, in spite of gods and drought, do that which he had determined. And he hurried to the House of Hwang.

Now Wang Lung had heard here and there that for the House of Hwang it had been a year verging upon poverty; there, too, there were no harvests. The old lady had not had her full dole of opium for many days and she was like an old tigress in her hunger. Each day she sent for the agent and she cursed him and struck his face with her fan, screaming at him, "And are there not acres of land left, yet?" until he was beside himself.

As if this were not enough, the Old Lord took yet another concubine, a child of sixteen. As with the Old Mistress with her opium, so there was no making him understand there was not money for jade earrings. He could not comprehend the words "no money," who all his life had but to reach out his hand to fill it.

And the young lords shrugged their shoulders and said there must still be enough for their lifetime. They united only in berating the agent, so that he who had once been unctuous, a man of plenty and of ease, was now become anxious and harried so that his skin hung upon him like an old garment. So when Wang Lung came to the agent crying, "I have silver," it was as though one came saying to the hungry, "I have food." And where before there had been dickering, now the two men spoke in eager whispers, and more quickly than they could speak whole words, the money passed from one hand to the other and papers were signed and sealed and the land was Wang Lung's.

And Wang Lung did not count the passing of silver a hard thing. He had now a vast field of good land, for the new field was twice as large as the first. But more to him than its dark fertility was the fact that it had belonged once to the family of a prince. And this time he told no one, not even O-lan, what he had done.

MONTH PASSED INTO MONTH and still no rain fell. The sky was empty and barren, and the stately sun rose each morning and made its march and set solitary each night. And the moon in its time shone like a lesser sun for brightness.

From his fields Wang Lung reaped scanty harvest of hardy beans, and from his cornfield, which he had planted in despair when the rice beds had yellowed and died, he plucked short stubby ears with the grains scattered here and there. There was not a bean lost in the threshing, and he shelled the corn in the middle room, watching sharply every grain that flew wide. When he would have put the cobs away for fuel, his wife spoke out,

"No—do not waste them. I remember when I was a child when years like this came, even the cobs we ground and ate. It is better than grass."

When she had spoken they all fell silent. There was foreboding in these strange brilliant days when the land was failing them. And then, as though there were not enough evil, O-lan was again with child, and her milk dried up, and the frightened house was filled with the sound of a child crying for food.

IF ONE HAD ASKED Wang Lung, "And how are you fed through the autumn?" he would have answered, "I do not know—a little food here and there." But in the whole countryside none asked questions of any other. None asked anything except of himself, "How shall I be fed this day?" And parents said, "How shall we be fed, we and our children?"

Now Wang Lung had cared for his ox as long as he could. He had given the beast a bit of straw and a handful of vines until winter came and these were gone. Then he turned the ox out to hunt for itself, sending the eldest boy to sit upon its back all day. But latterly he had not dared to do this, lest men from the village, even his neighbors, might overcome the lad and seize the ox for food. So he kept the ox on the threshold until it grew lean as its skeleton.

But there came a day when there were only a few beans left and a meager store of corn, and the ox lowed with its hunger and the old man said,

"We will eat the ox, next."

Then Wang Lung cried out, for it was to him as though one said, "We will eat a man next." The ox was his companion in the fields and he had walked behind and praised it and cursed it from his youth. And he said,

"How can we eat the ox? How shall we plow again?"

But the old man answered, tranquil enough,

"Well, a man can buy an ox again more easily than his own life."

But Wang Lung would not that day kill it. And the next day passed and the next and the children cried out for food and O-lan looked at Wang Lung, beseeching him for the children, and he saw at last that the thing was to be done. So he said roughly,

"Let it be killed then, but I cannot do it." And he laid himself upon the bed and he wrapped the quilt about his head that he might not hear the beast's bellowing when it died.

Then O-lan crept out and she took a great iron knife and she cut a gash in the beast's neck, and thus she severed its life. And she took a bowl and caught its blood to cook for them to eat in a pudding, and she hacked to pieces the great carcass, and Wang Lung would not come out until the thing was wholly done and the flesh was cooked. But when he tried to eat the flesh of his ox his gorge rose and he could not swallow it and he drank only a little of the soup. And O-lan said to him,

"An ox is but an ox and this one grew old. Eat, for there will be another one day."

Wang Lung was a little comforted then and they all ate. But the ox was all too quickly gone, and there was nothing left of it except the skin.

At first it was supposed in the village that he had food stored away. His uncle, who was among the first to be hungry, came importuning to his door. Wang Lung measured unwillingly into the skirt of his uncle's robe a small heap of beans and a precious handful of corn. Then he said with firmness,

"It is all I can spare and I have first my old father to consider, even if I had no children."

When his uncle came again Wang Lung cried out,

"Even filial piety will not feed my house!" and he sent his uncle empty away.

From that day his uncle turned against him like a dog that has been kicked. And as family after family finished its store and spent its last coin in the scanty markets of the town, and the winds of winter came down, cold as a knife of steel, the hearts of the villagers grew distraught with their hunger. And when Wang Lung's uncle shivered about the street like a lean dog and whispered, "There is one who has food—there is one whose children are fat, still," the men took up poles and went to the house of Wang Lung and beat upon the door. And when he had opened, his neighbors pushed him out of the doorway and they fell upon every corner, to find where he had hidden his food. Then when they found his wretched store of a few dried beans and a bowlful of dried corn they gave a great howl of disappointment, and they seized his bits of furniture, the table and the benches and the bed where the old man lay, frightened and weeping.

Then O-lan came forward and spoke, and her plain, slow voice rose above the men,

"Not that—not that yet," she called out. "You have all our food. But out of your own houses you have not sold yet your own table and benches. Leave us ours. We are even. Heaven will strike you if you take more. Now, we will go out together and hunt for grass to eat and bark from the trees, you for your children, and we for our three children, and for this fourth who is to be born in such times." She pressed her hand to her belly as she spoke, and the men were ashamed before her and went out one by one, for they were not evil men except when they starved.

One lingered, that one called Ching. He would have spoken some good word of shame, for only his crying child had forced him to evil. But in his bosom was a handful of beans he had snatched and he was fearful lest he must return them if he spoke, and so he only looked at Wang Lung with haggard, speechless eyes and he went out.

Wang Lung stood there in his dooryard where year after year he had threshed his good harvests, and which had lain now for many months idle. There was such anger in him now as he could not express. And he walked, dragging one foot after another in his famished weakness, to the temple of the earth, and deliberately he spat upon the face of the gods. There had been no sticks of incense now for many moons, and the paper clothes were tattered. But they sat there unmoved and Wang Lung gnashed his teeth at them and walked back to his house groaning and fell upon his bed.

They scarcely rose at all now, any of them. Fitful sleep took the place of the food they had not. The cobs of the corn they had dried and eaten and they stripped the bark from trees and all over the countryside people were eating what grass they could find upon the wintry hills. There was not an animal anywhere. One never saw in these days a child playing upon the village street. At most the two boys in Wang Lung's house crept to the door

and sat in the cruel, shining sun. Their once rounded bodies were angular and bony now, sharp small bones like the bones of birds, except for their ponderous bellies, swollen out with empty wind.

Although at first the angry insistence of her crying had filled the house, the girl-child lay uncomplaining, hour after hour, wrapped in an old quilt, her little sunken blue lips like a toothless old woman's, and hollow black eyes peering. This persistence of the small life in some way won her father's affection, although if she had been round and merry he would have been careless of her for a girl. Sometimes looking at her he whispered softly,

"Poor fool—poor little fool." And once when she essayed a weak smile, he broke into tears and took into his lean hard hand her small claw and held the tiny grasp of her fingers over his forefinger. Thereafter he would sometimes lift her, and thrust her inside his coat against his flesh and sit with her so by the threshold of the house, looking out over the dry, flat fields.

As for the old man, he fared better than any, for if there was anything to eat he was given it. Wang Lung said to himself proudly that none should say in the hour of death he had forgotten his father.

THERE WAS A DAY WHEN his neighbor, Ching, worn now to less than the shadow of a human creature, came to Wang Lung's door and whispered, "We have eaten the beasts and the grass and the bark of trees. What now remains for food?"

Wang Lung shook his head hopelessly, and looked down into the delicate bony face of his girl-child, and into the sharp, sad eyes that watched him unceasingly from his breast. When he caught those eyes in his glance, invariably there wavered upon the child's face a flickering smile that broke his heart.

Ching thrust his face nearer.

"In the village they are eating human flesh," he whispered. "It is said your uncle and his wife are eating. How else are they living with strength enough to walk about—they, who have never had anything?"

Wang Lung drew back from the deathlike head, afraid with a fear he did not understand. He rose quickly as though to cast off some entangling danger.

"We will leave this place," he said loudly. "We will go south! We must, lest we forget our nature and eat each other as the wild dogs do."

And then it seemed to him suddenly that what he said was very right, and he called aloud to O-lan, who lay upon the bed,

"Come, woman, we will go south!"

There was cheer in his voice such as none had heard in many moons, and the children looked up and the old man hobbled out from his room and O-lan rose feebly from her bed and came to the door of their room and clinging to the doorframe she said,

"It is a good thing to do. One can at least die walking."

The child in her body hung from her lean loins like a knotty fruit and from her face every particle of flesh was gone, so that the jagged bones stood forth rocklike under her skin. "Only wait until tomorrow," she said. "I shall have given birth by then."

Then Wang Lung saw his wife's face and he was moved with pity. "How shall you walk, you poor creature!" he muttered, and he said unwillingly to Ching, who still leaned against the house by the door, "If you have any food left, for a good heart's sake give me a handful to save the life of the mother of my sons, and I will forget that I saw you in my house as a robber."

Ching looked at him ashamed and he answered humbly,

"I have never thought of you with peace since that hour. It was that dog, your uncle, who enticed me. Before this cruel Heaven I promise you that I have only a handful of dried red beans buried beneath the stone of my doorway. This I and my wife placed there for our last hour, for our daughter and ourselves, that we might die with a little food in our stomachs. But some of it I will give to you. Tomorrow go south, if you can. I stay, I and my house. I have no son, and it does not matter whether I live or die."

And he went away and in a little while he came back, bringing tied in a cotton kerchief a double handful of small red beans, moldy with the soil. The children clambered about at the sight of the food, and even the old man's eyes glistened, but Wang Lung pushed them away for once and he took the food in to his wife as she lay and she ate a little of it, bean by bean, unwillingly except that her hour was upon her and she knew that if she had not any food she would die in the clutches of her pain.

Only a few of the beans did Wang Lung put into his own mouth and he chewed them into a soft pulp and then putting his lips to the lips of his daughter he pushed into her mouth the food, and watching her small lips move, he felt himself fed.

THAT NIGHT HE STAYED in the middle room, as he had during the birth of his firstborn son. He listened intently for the small sharp cry he knew so well, and he listened with despair.

"It would be merciful if there were no breath," he muttered, and then he heard the feeble cry—how feeble a cry!—hang for an instant upon the stillness. "But there is no mercy of any kind in these days," he finished bitterly.

There was no second cry, and over the house the stillness became impenetrable. And Wang Lung could not bear it. He was afraid. He rose and went to the door of the room and he called and the sound of his own voice heartened him a little.

"You are safe?" he called to the woman. He listened. Suppose she had died as he sat there! But he could hear a slight rustling, and at last she answered, her voice a sigh,

"Come!"

He went in, then, and she lay there upon the bed, her body scarcely raising the cover. She lay alone.

"Where is the child?" he asked.

She made a slight movement of her hand and he saw upon the floor the child's body—a wisp of bone and skin—a girl.

"Dead!" he exclaimed.

"Dead," she whispered.

He was about to say, "But I heard it crying—alive"—and then he looked at the woman's face. Her eyes were closed and the color of her flesh was the color of ashes—a poor silent face that lay there, having endured to the utmost, and there was nothing he could say. After all, during these months he had had only his own body to drag about. What agony of starvation this woman had endured, with the starved creature gnawing at her from within, desperate for its own life!

He said nothing, but he took the dead child into the other room and laid it upon the earthen floor and searched until he found a bit of broken mat and this he wrapped about it. Upon the neck he saw two dark, bruised spots, but he finished what he had to do. Then he took the roll of matting, and going as far from the house as he had strength, he laid the burden against the hollowed side of an old grave, just at the border of his western field. Now he felt his legs sinking beneath him, and covering his face with his hands he went away.

"It is better as it is," he muttered to himself, and for the first time was wholly filled with despair.

THE NEXT MORNING when the sun rose unchanging in its sky of varnished blue it seemed to him a dream that he could ever have thought of leaving his house. How could they drag their bodies over a hundred miles, even to plenty? He had no money. Long ago the last coin was gone. And who knew whether or not they would wear out all their last strength only to find more starving people and these strangers to them? Far better to stay where they could die in their beds. He sat despondent on the threshold of the door and gazed bleakly over the dried and hardened fields.

And then, as he sat there, giving up hope, some men came across the fields toward him. One was his uncle and with him three men he did not know.

"I have not seen you these many days," called his uncle with loud and affected good humor. "And how well you have fared! And your father, my elder brother, he is well?"

Wang Lung looked at his uncle. The man was thin, it is true, but not starved, as he should be. Wang Lung felt in his own shriveled body the last remaining strength of life gathering into a devastating anger.

"How you have eaten—how you have eaten!" he muttered thickly. He thought nothing of these strangers or of any courtesy. He saw only his uncle with flesh on his bones, still. His uncle opened wide his eyes and threw up his hands to the sky.

"Eaten!" he cried. "If you could see my house! Not a sparrow even could pick up a crumb there. My wife—do you remember how fat she was? Now she is like a garment hung on a pole—nothing but the poor bones, rattling together in her skin. And of our children only four are left—the three little ones gone—gone—and as for me, you see me!" He took the edge of his sleeve and wiped the corner of each eye carefully.

"You have eaten," repeated Wang Lung dully.

"I have borrowed from these good men in the town a little food," retorted his uncle briskly, "on the promise that I would help them to buy some land. And I thought of you first of all, you, the son of my brother. They have come to buy your land and to give you money—food—life!" His uncle, having said these words, stepped back and folded his arms with a flourish of his dirty and ragged robes.

Wang Lung did not rise. But he lifted his head and he saw that the men were indeed from the town, dressed in long robes of soiled silk. Their hands were soft and their nails long. He suddenly hated them with an immense hatred. Here were these men, having eaten and drunk, standing beside him whose children were starving; here they were, come to squeeze his land from him in his extremity. He looked up at them sullenly, his eyes deep and enormous in his bony, skull-like face.

"I will not sell my land," he said.

His uncle stepped forward. At this instant Wang Lung's younger son came creeping to the doorway upon his hands and knees. Since he had so little strength the child at times had gone back to crawling.

"Is that your lad?" cried the uncle, "the little fat lad I gave a copper to in the summer?"

And they all looked at the child and suddenly Wang Lung began to weep silently, the tears gathering in great knots of pain in his throat and rolling down his cheeks.

And then one of the men from the city spoke, a man with one eye blind and sunken in his face, and unctuously he said,

"My poor man, for the sake of the boy, we will give you a better price than could be got in these times anywhere. We will give you . . ." He paused and then he said harshly, "We will give you a hundred pence an acre!"

Wang Lung laughed bitterly. "Why, that is taking land for a gift. I pay twenty times that."

"Ah, but not when you buy it from men who are starving," said the other man. He was a small fellow with a high thin nose, but his voice came out of him unexpectedly large and coarse and hard.

Wang Lung looked at them. They were sure of him, these men! What will not a man give for his starving children and his old father! He sprang up and at the men as a dog springs at an enemy.

"I shall never sell the land!" he shrieked at them. "I will feed the earth itself to the children and when they die I will bury them in the land, and I and my wife and my old father, even he, we will die on the land that has given us birth!"

He was weeping violently and his anger went out of him as suddenly as a wind and he stood shaking and weeping. The men stood there smiling slightly, his uncle among them, unmoved. This talk was madness and they waited until Wang's anger was spent.

And then suddenly O-lan came to the door and spoke, her voice flat as though such things were commonplace.

"The land we will not sell, surely," she said, "else when we return from the south we shall have nothing to feed us. But we will sell the table, the beds, the benches and even the caldron. But the rakes and the hoe and the plow we will not sell, nor the land."

The calmness in her voice carried more strength than all Wang Lung's anger, and the one-eyed man spoke to the others and they muttered among themselves and the one-eyed man turned and said,

"They are poor things and fit only for fuel. Two silver bits for the lot and take it or leave it."

He spoke with contempt, but O-lan answered tranquilly,

"It is less than the cost of one bed, but if you have the silver give it to me quickly and take the things."

The one-eyed man fumbled in his girdle and dropped the silver into her hand and the men came into the house and they took out the table and the benches and the bed in Wang Lung's room, and they wrenched the caldron from the oven on which it stood. But when they went into the old man's room Wang Lung's uncle stood outside. He did not wish to be there when his older brother was laid on the floor and the bed taken from under him. When all was finished and the house was wholly empty except for the rakes and the hoes and the plow, O-lan said to her husband,

"Let us go while we have the silver and before we must sell the rafters of the house and have no hole into which we can crawl when we return."

And Wang Lung answered heavily, "Let us go."

But he looked across the fields at the small figures of the men receding and he muttered over and over, "At least I have the land—I have the land."

THERE WAS NOTHING to do but to pull the door tight upon its wooden hinges and fasten the iron hasp. All their clothes they had upon them. Into each child's hands O-lan thrust a rice bowl and a pair of chopsticks and the two little boys held them tight as a promise of food to come. Thus they started across the fields, a dreary small procession moving so slowly that it seemed they would never reach the town.

Soon Wang Lung saw that the old man would fall, and stooping under his father he lifted him on his back and carried him, staggering under the old man's dry, light frame. The bitter wind never ceased to blow against them so that the two boys cried of its cold. But Wang Lung coaxed them saying,

"You are two big men and you are travelers to the south. There is warmth there and white rice every day."

In time they reached the gate of the wall, resting continually every little way, and where Wang Lung had once delighted in its coolness now he clenched his teeth against the gust of wintry wind that swept furiously through its channel, as icy water will rush between cliffs. Beneath their feet the thick mud was speared through with needles of ice and the little boys could make no headway and O-lan was laden with the girl and desperate under the weight of her own body. Wang Lung staggered through with the old man and set him down and then went back and lifted each child and carried him through, and his sweat poured out of him like rain, spending all his strength with it, so that he had to lean for a long time against the wall, his eyes shut and his breath coming and going quickly, and his family stood shivering and waiting about him.

They were close to the gate of the great house now, but it was locked fast, and upon the steps lay cowering a few dingy shapes of men and women. When Wang Lung passed with his miserable little procession one cried out in a cracked voice,

"The hearts of these rich are hard like the hearts of the gods.

They have still rice and from the rice they do not eat they are still making wine, while we starve. A thousand curses to the parents that bore the children of Hwang!"

Wang Lung answered nothing and in silence they went on toward the south. When they had passed through the town it was evening, and they found a multitude of people going in the same direction. Wang Lung asked of one,

"Where is all this multitude going?"

And the man said,

"We are starving people and we are going to catch the fire wagon and ride to the south. It leaves from yonder house and there are wagons for such as we for less than a silver piece."

Fire wagons! Wang Lung in the tea shop had heard men tell of these wagons, chained one to the other and drawn neither by man nor beast, but by a machine breathing fire like a dragon. He had said to himself many times that he would go and see it, but with one thing and another there had never been time.

Now, however, he turned doubtfully to the woman and said,

"Shall we also then go on this fire wagon?"

They drew the old man and the children a little away from the passing crowd and looked at each other anxiously. At the instant's respite the old man and the little boys sank upon the ground. O-lan carried the girl-child still, but the child's head hung over her arm with such a look of death that Wang Lung cried out,

"Is the little slave already dead?"

O-lan shook her head. "Not yet. The breath flutters back and forth in her. But she will die this night and all of us unless—"

Then as if she could say no other word she looked at him, her square face exhausted and gaunt. And Wang Lung said with what cheer there was to be found in his voice,

"Up, my sons, and help the grandfather up. We will go on the fire wagon and sit while we walk south."

But whether or not they could have moved none knows, had there not come thundering out of the darkness a noise like a dragon's voice and two great eyes puffing fire out, so that everyone screamed and ran. In the confusion they were pushed hither and thither, but always they clung desperately together, until they were pushed somehow in the darkness into a boxlike room, and then with an incessant roaring the thing tore forth into the darkness, bearing them in its vitals.

WITH HIS TWO PIECES OF SILVER Wang Lung paid for a hundred miles of road and the officer who took his silver gave him back a handful of copper pence, and with a few of these Wang Lung bought from a vendor, who thrust his tray of wares in at a hole in the wagon as soon as it stopped, four small loaves of bread and a bowl of soft rice for the girl. It was more than they had had to eat at one time for many days, and although they were starved for food, when it was in their mouths desire left them and it was only by coaxing that the boys could be made to swallow. But the old man sucked perseveringly at the bread between his toothless gums.

"One must eat," he cackled forth, very friendly to all who pressed about him as the wagon rocked on its way. "I do not care that my foolish belly is grown lazy after all these days of little to do. It must be fed. I will not die because it does not wish to work."

And men laughed suddenly at the smiling, wizened little old man, whose sparse white beard was scattered all over his chin.

There were in the wagon some who went each year to the rich cities of the south to work and to beg. And Wang Lung, when he had grown used to the astonishment of seeing the land whirl by the holes in the wagon, listened to what these men said. They spoke with the loudness of wisdom where others are ignorant.

"First you must buy six-mats," said one, a man with coarse, hanging lips like a camel's. "These are two pence for one mat, but if you act like a country bumpkin you will be charged three. I cannot be fooled by the men in the southern cities, even if they are rich." He wagged his head and looked about for admiration. Wang Lung listened anxiously.

"And then?" he urged. He sat squatting upon his haunches on the bottom of the wagon, which was, after all, only an empty room made of wood, with the wind and the dust flying up through the cracks in the floor.

"Then," said the man, "you bind these together into a hut, and you go out to beg, first smearing yourself with filth to make yourselves piteous."

"One must beg?" Wang Lung disliked this notion.

"Ah, indeed," said the coarse-mouthed man, "but not until you have eaten. These people in the south have so much rice that each morning you may go to a public kitchen and for a penny hold as much as you can in your belly of the white rice gruel. Then you can beg comfortably and buy bean curd and cabbage and garlic."

Wang Lung withdrew a little from the others and secretly with his hand in his girdle he counted out the pence he had left. There was enough for the six mats and enough each for a penny for rice. It came over him with comfort that thus they could begin the new life. But the notion of holding up a bowl and begging continued to distress him. It was very well for the old man and for the children and even for the woman, but he had his two hands.

"Is there no work?" he asked of the man.

"Aye, work!" said the man with contempt, and he spat upon the floor. "You can rent a ricksha and pull a rich man in the ricksha if you like, and sweat your blood out. Give me begging!" And he cursed a round curse, so that Wang Lung would not ask anything of him further.

But still it was a good thing that he had heard what the man said, for when the fire wagon had carried them as far as it would and had turned them out upon the ground, Wang Lung had ready a plan. He set the old man and the children against a long gray wall of a house and he told the woman to watch them, and he went off, asking of this one and that where the market streets lay. At first he could scarcely understand what was said to him, so brittle and sharp was the sound which these southerners made. But he found the mat shop at last and he put his pennies down as one who knew the price and he carried away his roll of mats. When he returned to where he had left the others, they stood there waiting, although the boys cried out at him in relief, and he saw that they had been filled with terror in this strange place. Only the old man watched everything with pleasure and he murmured to Wang Lung,

"You see how fat they all are, these southerners, and how oily are their skins. They eat pork every day, doubtless."

But none who passed looked at Wang Lung and his family. Men came and went along the cobbled highway to the city, busy and intent, and every little while a caravan of donkeys came pattering by, their small feet fitting neatly to the stones, and they were laden with baskets of brick and with great bags of grain. The driver rode on the hindermost beast of each caravan, and no prince could have looked more haughty than these drivers as they passed by the small group of persons, standing wondering at the edge of the roadway.

Wang Lung turned away to see where he could put his hut. There were already other huts clinging to the wall behind them, like fleas to a dog's back. Wang Lung observed the huts and he began to shape his own mats this way and that, but they were stiff and clumsy, being made of split reeds, and he despaired, when suddenly O-lan said,

"That I can do. I remember it from my childhood."

And she placed the girl upon the ground and pulled the mats thus and thus, and shaped a rounded roof high enough for a man to sit under, and upon the edges of the mats that were upon the ground she placed bricks that were lying about. When it was finished they went within and with one mat she had not used they made a floor and sat down and were sheltered.

Sitting thus and looking at each other, it seemed less than possible that the day before they had left their own house and land and that these were now a hundred miles away. Then the general feeling of plenty in this rich land filled them and when Wang Lung said, "Let us go and seek the public kitchens," they rose up almost cheerfully and went out once more, and this time the small boys clattered their chopsticks against their bowls as they walked, for there would soon be something to put into them. And they soon found along the street many people carrying bowls and buckets, going to the kitchens for the poor. And with them they came at last to two great buildings made of mats.

Now in the rear of each building were earthen stoves, larger than Wang Lung had ever seen, and on them iron caldrons as big as small ponds; and there was the good white rice bubbling and boiling, and clouds of fragrant steam. Now the fragrance of rice was the sweetest in the world to their nostrils, and they all pressed forward in a great mass and people called out and mothers shouted in anger and fear lest their children be trodden upon and little babies cried; and Wang Lung caught in their midst could do nothing but cling to his father and his two sons and when he was swept to the great caldron he held out his bowl and when it was filled threw down his pence, and it was all he could do not to be swept on before the thing was done.

Then when they had come to the street again and stood eating their rice, he ate and was filled. The children tugged at Wang Lung then, and Wang Lung led them all back to the hut, and there they laid themselves down and they slept until the next morning, for it was the first time since summer they had been filled with food.

The next morning it was necessary that there be more money. Wang Lung looked at O-lan, doubtful as to what should be done, but O-lan answered him steadily, as though this were the life she had known always,

"I and the children can beg and the old man also. His gray hairs will move some who will not give to me."

And she called the two boys to her, for they had forgotten everything except that they had food again and were in a strange place, and stood staring at all that passed, and she said to them,

"Each take your bowl and hold it thus and cry out thus—"

And she held out her empty bowl and called piteously,

"A heart, good sir—a heart, good lady! Have a kind heart—a good deed for your life in Heaven! Feed a starving child!"

The little boys stared at her, and Wang Lung also. Where had she learned to cry thus? How much of this woman there was that he did not know! She answered his look saying,

"So I called when I was a child and so I was fed. In such a year as this I was sold a slave."

Then the old man, who had been sleeping, awoke, and the four of them went out on the road to beg. The woman thrust the girl-child into her naked bosom, and she cried out at every passerby,

"Unless you give, good sir, good lady—this child dies—we starve—" And indeed the child looked dead, its head shaking this way and that, and there were some, a few, who tossed her unwillingly a small cash.

But the boys after a while began to take the begging as play, and then their mother perceiving it dragged them into the hut. "And do you talk of starving, and laugh at the same time! You fools, starve then!" And she slapped them until the tears were running down their faces and she sent them out saying,

"Now you are fit to beg! That and more if you laugh again!"

As for Wang Lung, he went into the streets and asked hither and thither until he found a place where rickshas were for hire and he went in and hired one for the day and then dragged the thing out to the street.

Pulling this rickety wooden wagon on its two wheels behind him, it seemed to him that everyone looked at him for a fool. He was as awkward between its shafts as an ox yoked for the first time, and he could scarcely walk; yet must he run if he were to earn his living. He went into a narrow side street where there were no shops, and he went up and down for a while to accustom himself, and just as he said to himself in despair that he had better beg, a door opened, and an old man, spectacled and garbed as a teacher, stepped forth and hailed him.

Wang Lung began to tell him that he was too new at it to run,

but the old man was deaf, motioning to him tranquilly to lower the shafts and let him step in. Wang Lung obeyed, not knowing what else to do. Then the old man, sitting erect, said,

"Take me to the Confucian temple."

Wang had no knowledge of where the temple stood, but as he went he asked, and since the road lay along crowded streets, with vendors and carriages and many vehicles like his own, there was no possibility of running, and he walked as swiftly as he was able. To loads upon his back he was used, but not to pulling, and before the temple was in sight his arms were aching and his hands blistered. But at last he lowered the ricksha at the temple gates, and the old man stepped forth and feeling in his bosom he drew out a small coin and gave it to Wang Lung saying,

"Now I never pay more than this, and there is no use in complaint." And with this he went into the temple.

Wang Lung had not thought to complain for he had not seen this coin before, but another ricksha puller stood near and he said,

"How far did you pull that old head?" And when Wang told

him, the man cried out, "He gave you only half the proper fare. How much did you argue for before you started?"

"I did not argue," said Wang Lung. "He said come and I came."

"Now there is a country lout for you, pigtail and all!" the other man called out to bystanders. "Someone says come and he comes, and he never asks, 'How much will you give me if I come?' Know this, idiot, only white foreigners can be taken without argument. They are such fools they do not know the proper price of anything, but let the silver run out of their pockets like water."

Wang Lung felt very ignorant in all this crowd of city people, and he pulled his vehicle away without a word in answer.

He had one more passenger during the morning and with this one he argued and agreed upon a price and in the afternoon two more called to him. But at night, when he counted out his money he had only a penny above the rent of the ricksha, and he went back to his hut in great bitterness, saying to himself that for labor greater than the labor of a day in a harvest field he had earned only one copper penny. Then there came flooding over him the memory of his land. The thought of it lying back there, far away but waiting and his own, filled him with peace, and so he came to his hut.

When he entered there he found that O-lan had for her day's begging received forty small cash, which is less than five pence, and of the boys, the elder had eight cash and the younger thirteen, and with these put together there was enough to pay for the rice in the morning. Only when they put the younger boy's in with all, he howled for his own, and he loved the money he had begged, and slept with it that night in his hand, and they could not take it from him until he gave it himself for his own rice.

But the old man had received nothing at all. All day long he had sat by the roadside, but he did not beg. He slept and woke and stared at what passed him, and then he slept again. And being of the older generation, he could not be reproved. When he saw that his hands were empty he said merely,

"I have sown seed, and I have reaped harvest and thus have I filled my rice bowl. And I have beyond this begotten a son."

With this he trusted like a child that he would be fed.

NOW AFTER THE FIRST SHARPNESS of Wang Lung's hunger was over and he saw that his children had daily something to eat, and of his day's labor and of O-lan's begging enough to pay for it, the strangeness of his life passed, and he began to feel what this city was, to whose fringes he clung. Running about the streets all day long he learned that in the morning the women he drew in his vehicle went to the market, and the men to the schools and to the houses of business, and at night he drew men to big teahouses and to places of pleasure. But none of these places did Wang Lung know for himself, since his feet crossed no threshold except that of his own hut. He lived in the rich city as alien as a rat in a rich man's house.

It is true that the people who went about the streets had black hair and eyes as Wang Lung and all his family had, and it is true that if one listened well to the language of these southerners it could be understood. But in Wang Lung's country a man, if he had a roll of good wheat bread and a sprig of garlic in it, had a full meal. But here the people dabbled with pork balls and bamboo sprouts and chestnuts stewed with chicken. The very smell of garlic would make the shopkeepers in the cloth shops raise the price of cloth as they might for a foreigner.

But then the little village of sheds clinging to the wall never became a part of the city, and once when Wang Lung heard a young man haranguing a crowd at a corner, and the young man said that China must rise against the hated foreigners, Wang Lung was alarmed and slunk away, feeling that he was the foreigner against whom the young man spoke. It was only one day when he was on the street of the silk markets looking for a passenger that he learned that there were those who were more foreign than he in this city. He happened to pass a shop whence someone came out suddenly, a creature the like of whom he had never seen before. He had no idea of whether it was male or female, but it was tall and dressed in a straight black robe of some rough harsh material and there was the skin of a dead animal wrapped about its neck. As he passed, the person motioned to him sharply to lower the shafts and he did so, and when he stood erect again, dazed at what had befallen him, the person in broken accents directed that he was to go to the Street of Bridges. He began to run hurriedly, scarcely knowing what he did, and he called to another puller whom he knew casually,

"Look at this—what is this I pull?"

And the man shouted back at him,

"A foreigner—a female from America—you are rich—"

But Wang Lung ran as fast as he could for fear of the strange creature behind him, and when he reached the Street of Bridges he was exhausted and dripping with sweat.

This female stepped out then and said, "You need not have run yourself to death," and left him with double the usual fare.

Then Wang Lung knew that this was indeed a foreigner and more foreign yet than he, and that after all people of black hair and black eyes are one sort and people of light hair and light eyes of another sort, and he was no longer after that wholly foreign in the city.

At least in this great, sprawling, opulent city it seemed that there could not be any lack of food. The cobbled streets of the fish market were lined with great baskets of silver fish; at the grain markets there were such baskets of grain that a man might step into them; and at the meat markets whole hogs hung by their necks, split open the length of their great bodies, and row upon row, from the ceilings, hung brown baked ducks, white salted ducks, and geese and pheasant and every kind of fowl. As for the vegetables, there was everything which the hand of man could coax from the soil; glittering red radishes, lotus root and taro, green cabbages and celery, curling bean sprouts and garnishes of cress. There was nothing which the appetite of man might desire that was not to be found in the markets of that city. And going hither and thither were the vendors of sweets and fruits and nuts and of hot delicacies of sweet potatoes browned in sweet oils and little delicately spiced balls of pork wrapped in dough and steamed, and sugar cakes made from rice, and the children of the city ran out to the vendors with their hands full of pennies and they bought and they ate until their skins glistened with sugar and oil.

Yes, one would say that in this city there could be none who starved.

Still, every morning a little after dawn Wang Lung and his family made a small group in a long procession of people, each shivering in clothes too thin for the damp river fog, walking curved against the chill morning wind to the public kitchens. And with all Wang Lung's pulling and with all O-lan's begging, they never could gain enough to cook rice in their own hut. If there was a penny over and above the price of the rice at the kitchens, they bought a bit of cabbage. But the cabbage was dear and the boys must go to hunt for fuel to cook it between the two bricks O-lan had set up for a stove.

One night there was in the stew of cabbage a good round piece of pork. It was the first time they had had flesh to eat since they killed their own ox, and Wang Lung's eyes widened.

"You must have begged of a foreigner this day," he said to O-lan. But she said nothing. Then the younger boy, too young for wisdom and filled with his own pride of cleverness, said,

"I took it—it is mine, this meat. When the butcher looked the other way after he had sliced it off, I ran under an old woman's arm and I seized it and ran into an alley and hid in a dry water jar."

"Now will I not eat this meat!" cried Wang Lung angrily. "Beggars we may be but thieves we are not." And he took the meat out of the pot with his fingers and threw it upon the ground and was heedless of the younger lad's howling.

Then O-lan came forward in her stolid fashion and she picked up the meat and washed it off and thrust it back into the pot.

"Meat is meat," she said quietly.

Wang Lung said nothing then, but he was angry and afraid in his heart because his sons were growing into thieves, and he himself would have none of it, contenting himself with the cabbage. But after the meal was over he took his younger son into the street and there he took the boy's head under his arm and cuffed it soundly.

"There and there and there!" he shouted. "That for a thief!"

But to himself, when he had let the lad go sniveling home, he said, "We must get back to the land."

THUS DAY BY DAY beneath the opulence of this city Wang Lung lived in the foundations of poverty upon which it was laid. With the food spilling out of the markets, with rich men clothed in satin and in velvet, in that part where Wang Lung lived there was not food enough to feed savage hunger, and not clothes enough to cover bones.

Men labored all day at the baking of breads and cakes for feasts for the rich and slept all greasy and grimed as they were upon rough pallets on the floor and staggered to the ovens next day, and there was not money enough given them to buy a piece of the rich breads they made for others. And men and women labored at the cutting and contriving of heavy furs for the winter and of soft light furs for the spring and at the thick brocaded silks, to cut and shape them into sumptuous robes for the rich, and they themselves snatched a bit of coarse blue cotton cloth and sewed it hastily together to cover their own bareness.

At home in the small hovels where they lived, around Wang Lung's hovel, the women sewed rags together to make a covering for the children they were forever breeding, and they wandered about the bordering countryside, snatching at bits of cabbage from farmers' fields and stealing handfuls of rice from the grain markets, and at harvest they followed the reapers like fowl, their eyes sharp for every dropped grain. And through these huts passed children; they were born and dead and born again until mothers and fathers scarcely knew how many were living.

THE OLD MEN and the old women accepted the life they had. But there was talk among the young men, angry, growling talk. The scattered anger of their youth became settled into a fierce despair because all their lives they labored more severely than beasts, and for nothing except a handful of refuse to fill their bellies. Listening to such talk one evening Wang Lung heard for the first time what was on the other side of the great wall to which their rows of huts clung.

It was at the end of one of those days in late winter when for the first time it seems possible that spring may come again. The ground about the huts was still muddy with the melting snow and the water ran into the huts so that each family had hunted for a few bricks upon which to sleep. But with the discomfort of the damp earth there was this night a soft mildness in the air which made Wang Lung exceedingly restless, and there arose within him a mighty longing for his fields. And he said roughly to his wife,

"If I had anything to sell I would sell it and go back to the land. Or if it were not for the old head, we would walk though we starved."

O-lan had been rinsing the rice bowls, and now she piled them in a corner of the hut and looked at him.

"There is nothing to sell except the girl," she answered slowly.

Wang Lung's breath caught.

"Now, I would not sell a child!" he said loudly.

"I was sold," she answered. "I was sold to a great house so that my parents could return to their home."

"And would you sell the child, therefore?"

"If it were only I, she would be killed before she was sold. . . . But a dead girl brings nothing. I would sell this girl for you—to take you back to the land."

"Never would I," said Wang Lung stoutly, "not though I spent my life in this wilderness." And he went out to the street's edge and stood there idle.

Here his old father habitually sat squatting on his thighs and leaning against the wall and here he sat now, having taken his bowl of food there to sup it. The old man held in one hand the end of a loop of cloth which O-lan had torn from her girdle, and within this loop the girl-child staggered to and fro. Thus he spent his days looking after this child who had now grown rebellious at having to be in her mother's bosom as she begged. Wang Lung looked at the small girl, staggering persistently at the end of the loop. She had grown greatly on the food given her each day, and although she had as yet said no word at all, her lips that had been like an old woman's were smiling and red, and as of old she grew merry when he looked at her and she smiled.

"I might have done it," he mused, "if she had not lain in my bosom and smiled like that."

And then he thought again of his land and he cried out passionately, "Shall I never see it again! With all this labor and begging there is never enough to do more than feed us today."

Then out of the dusk there answered him a deep burly voice, "You are not the only one. There are a hundred hundred like you in the city."

The man came up, smoking a short bamboo pipe, and it was the father of the family in the hut next but two to Wang Lung's hut. He was a man seldom seen in the daylight, for he slept all day and worked at night pulling heavy wagons of merchandise which were too large for the streets by day. Sometimes Wang Lung saw him come creeping home at dawn, panting and spent, and his great knotty shoulders drooping, as he went out to his own ricksha pulling. And sometimes at dusk the man came out and stood with the other men who were about to go into their hovels to sleep.

"Well, and is it forever?" asked Wang Lung bitterly.

The man puffed at his pipe and spat upon the ground.

"No, and not forever. When the rich are too rich there are ways, and when the poor are too poor there are ways. Last winter we sold two girls and endured. This is one of the ways when the poor are too poor. When the rich are too rich there is a way, and if I am not mistaken, that way will come soon." He nodded and pointed with the stem of his pipe to the wall behind them. "Have you seen inside that wall?"

Wang Lung shook his head, staring. The man continued,

"I took one of my slaves in there to sell and I saw it. You would not believe it if I told you how money comes and goes in that house. I will tell you this—even the servants eat with chopsticks of ivory bound with silver, and even the slave women sew pearls upon their shoes, and when the shoes have a bit of mud upon them, they throw them away, pearls and all!"

The man drew hard on his pipe and Wang Lung listened, his mouth ajar. Over this wall, then, there were such things!

"There is a way when men are too rich," said the man, and was silent for a time; then as though he had said nothing he added indifferently, "Well, work again," and was gone into the night.

Wang Lung that night could not sleep for thinking of silver and gold and pearls on the other side of this wall against which his body rested, his body clad in what he wore day after day, because there was no quilt to cover him and only a mat upon bricks beneath him. But still he understood nothing of what the man had meant when he said, "There is a way, when the rich are too rich."

VIII

SPRING SEETHED in the village of huts. A swarm of ragged women and children issued forth each day to search the countryside for the green dandelions and shepherd's purse that thrust up feeble new leaves, the food they could get without begging and without money. And out with this swarm went O-lan and the two boys.

But the men worked on as before, although the lengthening warm days and sudden rains filled everyone with longings and discontents. In the evening when the twilight lingered they gathered out of their huts and talked together, and Wang Lung saw this one and that of the men who had lived near him and whom through the winter he had not known.

Most of these ragged men had nothing beyond what they took in the day's labor, and thought only of how they might tomorrow eat a bit of fish, or of how they might idle a bit. They talked always of money; of what they had paid for a foot of cloth, and of what they had paid for a small fish, or of what they could earn in a day, and always at last of what they would do if they had the money which the man over the wall had in his coffers. Every day the talk ended with this:

"And if I had the gold that he has and the silver and if I had the pearls his concubines wear and the rubies his wife wears . . ."

And listening to all the things which they would do if they had these things, Wang Lung cried out suddenly one night,

"If I had the gold and the silver, I would buy land with it, and I would bring forth harvests."

At this they united in turning on him.

"Now here is a pig-tailed country bumpkin who understands nothing of city life and of what may be done with money. He would go on working like a slave behind an ox or an ass!" And each one of them felt he was more worthy to have the riches than was Wang Lung, because they knew better how to spend it.

But this scorn did not change the mind of Wang Lung, and he grew more impatient every day for the land that was already his.

Being possessed continually by this thought, Wang Lung saw as in a dream the things that happened about him in the city every day. He accepted this strangeness and that without questioning. There was, for example, the paper that men gave out here and there, and sometimes even to him.

The first time he had such paper given him, it was given by a foreigner, a man, very tall, with eyes as blue as ice and a hairy face. Wang Lung, although frightened to take anything from his hand, was more frightened to refuse, seeing the man's strange eyes. Then, when he had courage to look at the paper after the foreigner had passed on, he saw on it a picture of a man, white-skinned, who hung upon a crosspiece of wood. The man was without clothes except for a bit about his loins, and to all appearances was dead, since his head drooped upon his shoulder and his eyes were closed. Wang Lung looked at the pictured man in horror. There were characters beneath, but of these he could make nothing. He carried the picture home at night and they discussed its possible meaning, he and the old man and the two boys. The old man said,

"Surely this was a very evil man to be thus hung."

But Wang Lung was fearful of the picture and pondered as to why a foreigner had given it to him, whether or not some brother of this foreigner's had not been so treated and the other brethren seeking revenge. He avoided, therefore, the street on which he had met the man and after a few days, when the paper was forgotten, O-lan sewed it into a shoe sole together with other bits of paper she picked up to make the soles firm.

But the next time one handed a paper freely to Wang Lung it was a man of the city, a young man well clothed, who talked loudly as he distributed sheets hither and thither among the crowds on the street. This paper bore also a picture of blood and death, but the man who died this time was not white-skinned but a man like Wang Lung himself, a common fellow, slight and black of hair and eye and clothed in ragged garments. Upon the dead figure a great fat one stood and stabbed the dead figure with a long knife. It was a piteous sight and Wang Lung stared at it and then listened to the young man, and what he heard was what he had never heard before.

"The dead man is yourselves," proclaimed the young man, "and the murderous one who stabs you is the rich. You are poor and downtrodden and it is because the rich seize everything."

Now, that he was poor Wang Lung knew full well, but he had heretofore blamed it on a heaven that would not rain in its season. Therefore he listened in interest to hear further what the rich men had to do with this thing. And at last when the young man said nothing of this matter, Wang Lung grew bold and asked,

"Sir, is there any way whereby the rich who oppress us can make it rain so that I can work on the land?"

At this the young man turned on him with scorn and replied,

"Now how ignorant you are! If the rich would share with us what they have, rain or not would matter to none, because we would all have money and food."

A great shout went up from those who listened, but Wang Lung turned away unsatisfied, for he desired nothing but his land under his feet again.

THEN IN THIS CITY out of which something new was always springing at him, Wang Lung saw another thing he did not understand. He saw one day, when he pulled his ricksha empty down a street, a man seized by a small band of armed soldiers, and when

345

the man protested, the soldiers brandished knives in his face, and while Wang Lung watched in amazement, the soldiers seized another and another, and it came to Wang Lung that these who were seized were all common fellows who worked with their hands, and while he stared, yet another man was seized, and this one a man who lived in the hut nearest his own against the wall.

Then Wang Lung thrust his ricksha into a side alley and darted into a hot-water shop lest he be next, and there he hid behind the great caldrons until the soldiers passed. And he asked the keeper of the shop the meaning of the thing he had seen, and the man, who was old and shriveled with the steam rising continually about him out of the caldrons, answered with indifference,

"It is but another war somewhere. Who knows what all this fighting to and fro is about?"

"But why do they seize my neighbor, who is as innocent as I who have never heard of this war?" asked Wang Lung in great consternation. And the old man clattered the lids of his caldrons and answered,

"The soldiers are going to battle somewhere and need carriers for bedding and ammunition and so they force laborers like you to go with them and do it. It is no new sight in this city."

"Well, but a man's family—" said Wang Lung, aghast.

"Well, and what do they care of that?" said the old man scornfully, peering under the lid of the nearest caldron to see if the water bubbled yet.

When the sound of the soldiers' leathern boots was gone Wang Lung darted out, and seizing his ricksha he ran with it empty to the hut. Then to O-lan, who had but just returned from gathering green stuff on the roadside, he told in broken, panting words what was happening and how nearly he had not escaped. He looked at O-lan haggardly and he said,

"Now am I truly tempted to sell the little slave and go north."

But she mused and said in her plain way,

"Wait a few days. There is strange talk about."

Nevertheless, he went out no more in the daylight, but he sent the eldest lad to return the ricksha to the place from where he had hired it. Then he waited until the night came and he went to the houses of merchandise and for half what he had earned before he pulled all night the great wagonloads of boxes, to each wagon a dozen men pulling and straining and groaning. And all night through the dark streets he strained against the ropes, his body naked and streaming with sweat. Before them to show the way ran a little lad carrying a flaming torch and in its light the faces and the bodies of the men and the wet cobbles glistened alike. And Wang Lung came home before dawn, too broken for food until he had slept. But during the day when the soldiers searched the street he slept safely in the furthermost corner of the hut behind a pile of straw O-lan gathered to make a shield for him.

With the further coming of spring the city became filled with the unrest of fear. Carriages drawn by horses pulled rich men and their possessions to the river's edge where ships carried them away. Wang Lung's sons came back with their eyes wide, crying,

"We saw a man as fat and monstrous as a god in a temple, and such boxes and boxes and when I asked what was in them one said, 'There is gold and silver in them, but the rich cannot take all they have away, and someday it will all be ours.' Now, what did he mean by this, my father?"

But when Wang Lung answered shortly, "How should I know what an idle city fellow means?" the elder lad cried wistfully,

"Oh, I wish we might go even now and get it if it is ours. I should like to taste a sweet cake with sesame seed sprinkled on the top."

And Wang Lung remembered the cakes that O-lan had once made at the New Year's feast, cakes of rice flour and lard and sugar, and his heart pained him with longing for that which was passed. Suddenly it seemed to him that not one more day could he lie in this wretched hut, nor could he another night strain the hours through, his body bent against a rope cutting his flesh, and dragging the load over the cobblestones. Each stone he had come to know now as a separate enemy, and he knew each rut by which he might evade a stone and so use an ounce less of his life.

"Ah, the fair land!" he cried out suddenly and fell to weeping so that the children were frightened and the old man twisted his face this way and that under his sparse beard, as a child's face twists when he sees his mother weep.

Then Wang Lung took his girl-child into his arms and he sat with her in the hut and he looked at her and said,

"Little fool, would you like to go to a great house where there is food and drink?"

Then she smiled, not understanding what he said, and put up her small hand to touch with wonder his staring eyes and he could not bear it and he cried out to the woman,

"Tell me, and were you beaten in that great house?"

And she answered him flatly and somberly,

"Every day I was beaten."

Wang Lung groaned and held the child to him and said over and over to her softly, "Oh, little fool—oh, poor little fool."

Then suddenly as he sat there came a noise like the cracking of heaven and every one of them fell unthinking on the ground and hid their faces, for it seemed as though the hideous roar would catch them all up and crush them. And Wang Lung covered the girl-child's face with his hand.

But O-lan, when silence had fallen as suddenly as it had gone, lifted her head and said, "Now that which I have heard of has come to pass. The enemy has broken in the gates of the city." And before any could answer her there was a shout over the city, a rising shout of human voices, at first faint, as one may hear the wind of a storm approaching, and gathering in a deep howl, louder and more loud as it filled the streets.

Wang Lung sat erect then, on the floor of his hut, and a strange fear crept over his flesh, so that he felt it stirring among the roots of his hair, and everyone sat erect and they all stared at each other waiting for something they knew not. But there was only the noise of the gathering of human beings and each man howling.

Then they heard the sound of a great door groaning upon its hinges, and suddenly the man who had talked to Wang Lung once at dusk thrust his head in at the hut's opening and cried out,

"Now do you still sit here? The hour has come—the gates of the rich man are open to us!" And as if by magic of some kind O-lan was gone, creeping out under the man's arm as he spoke.

Then Wang Lung rose up, half dazed, and he set the girl-child down and he went out and there before the great iron gates of the rich man's house a multitude of clamoring common people pressed forward, howling together the deep, tigerish howl that he had heard, rising and swelling out of the streets, and he knew that at the gates of all rich men there pressed this howling multitude of men and women who had been starved and imprisoned and now were for the moment free to do as they would. And the great gates were ajar and the people pressed forward so tightly packed together that foot was on foot and body wedged tightly against body so that the whole mass moved together as one.

Thus was Wang Lung forced along over the threshold of the great gates, his feet scarcely touching the ground. Through court after court he was swept, and of those men and women who had lived in the house he saw not one. It was as though here were a palace long dead except that early lilies bloomed among the rocks of the gardens and the golden flowers of the early trees of spring blossomed upon bare branches. But in the rooms food stood upon a table and in the kitchens fire burned. In the inner courts, where the lords and ladies have their dainty beds and where stand their lacquered boxes of black and red and gold, their boxes of silken clothing, the crowd fell upon the treasures, seizing from each other what was revealed in every newly opened closet, so that clothing and bedding and curtains and dishes passed from hand to hand, each hand snatching that which another held, and none stopping to see what he had.

Only Wang Lung in the confusion took nothing. He had never in all his life taken what belonged to another, and not at once could he do it. So he stood in the middle of the crowd at first, dragged this way and that, and then coming somewhat to his senses, he pushed with perseverance toward the edge and found himself at the back of the innermost court where the ladies of the rich dwell. The back gate was ajar, that gate which the rich have for centuries kept for their escape in such times, and therefore called the gate of peace. Through this gate doubtless they had escaped this day and were hidden through the streets, listening to the howling in their courts. But one man, whether because of his size or because of his drunken heaviness of sleep, had failed to escape. He had hidden in an empty inner room, and now, thinking he was alone, he crept out to escape. And thus Wang Lung, drifting away from the others until he too was alone, came upon him.

He was a great fat fellow, neither old nor young, and his naked body gaped through a purple satin robe he held about him, and in the mountains of his cheeks his eyes were small and sunken as a pig's. When he saw Wang Lung he shook all over and fell upon his knees and knocked his head on the floor and he cried,

"Save a life—save a life—do not kill me. I have money for you—much money—"

It was this word "money" which suddenly brought to Wang Lung's mind a piercing clarity. Money! Aye, and he needed that! The child saved! *The land!*

He cried out in a harsh voice such as he did not himself know was in his breast,

"Give me the money then!"

And the fat man rose to his knees, sobbing and gibbering, and feeling for the pocket of the robe, and he brought forth his yellow hands dripping with silver and Wang Lung held out the end of his coat and received it. And again Wang Lung cried out in that strange voice that was like another man's,

"Give me more!"

And again the man's hands came forth dripping with silver and he whimpered,

"Now there is none left and I have nothing but my wretched life," and he fell to weeping, his tears running like oil down his hanging cheeks. Wang Lung, looking at him as he shivered and wept, suddenly loathed him as he had loathed nothing in his life and he cried,

"Out of my sight, lest I kill you for a fat worm!"

And the man ran past him like a cur and was gone.

Then Wang Lung was left alone with the silver. He did not

stop to count it, but went out of the open gate of peace and across the small back streets to his hut. He hugged to his bosom the silver that was yet warm from the other man's body and to himself he said over and over,

"We go back to the land—tomorrow we go back to the land!"

IX

BEFORE A HANDFUL of days had passed it seemed to Wang Lung that he had never been away from his land, as indeed in his heart he never had. With six pieces of the silver he bought good seed from the south, full grains of wheat and of rice and of corn, and for very recklessness of riches he bought seeds the like of which he had never planted before, celery and lotus for his pond and great red radishes and fragrant red beans. And before ever he reached his own land, he bought an ox from a farmer plowing in a field. He saw the man plowing and he stopped and they all stopped, the old man and the children and the woman, eager as they were to reach the house and the land, and they looked at the ox. Wang Lung had been struck with its great strong neck and he called out,

"That is a worthless ox! What will you sell it for, seeing that I have no animal and am hard put to it and willing to take anything?"

And the farmer called back,

"I would sooner sell my wife than this ox which is but three years old and in its prime," and he plowed on and would not stop for Wang Lung.

Then it seemed to Wang Lung as if out of all the oxen the world held he must have this one. He had set his heart on it because of its sturdy pulling of the soil and because of its smooth yellow coat and its full dark eye. With this ox he could plow his fields and cultivate them, and with this ox tied to his mill he could grind the grain. And he said to the farmer,

"I will give you enough to buy another ox and more, but this ox I will have."

At last after bickering and quarreling the farmer yielded for half again the worth of an ox. But silver was suddenly nothing to Wang Lung when he looked at this ox, and he led it away with a rope through its nostrils, his heart burning with his possession.

When they reached the house they found the door torn away and the thatch from the roof gone, and their hoes and rakes were also gone, so only the bare rafters and the earthen walls remained. But after the first astonishment all this was as nothing to Wang Lung. He went to the town and he bought a plow of hard wood and two rakes and two hoes and mats to cover the roof until they could grow thatch again from the harvest.

Then in the evening he stood in the doorway of his house and looked across the land, his own land, lying loose and fresh from the winter's freezing, and ready for planting. It was full spring and in the shallow pool the frogs croaked drowsily. Through the twilight he could see dimly the fringe of trees at the border of the near field. They were peach trees, budded most delicately pink, and willow trees thrusting forth tender green leaves. And up from the quiescent, waiting land a faint mist rose, silver as moonlight, and clung about the tree trunks.

At first it seemed to Wang Lung that he wished only to be alone on his land, and when they came to him, those who were left of the winter's starving, he was surly with them.

"Which of you have my rake and my hoe and which of you burned my roof in his oven?" Thus he bawled at them.

And they shook their heads, full of virtue, and said, "Nay, in these evil times, how can it be said that this one or that stole anything? Hunger makes thief of any man."

Then Ching, his neighbor, came creeping forth from his house to see Wang Lung and he said, "Through the winter a band of robbers lived in your house and preyed upon the town. Your uncle, it is said, knows more of them than an honest man should. But who knows what is true in these days?"

This man was nothing but a shadow indeed, so close did his skin stick to his bones and so thin and gray had his hair grown, although he had not yet reached forty-five years of his age. Wang Lung stared at him and then in compassion he said suddenly,

"Now you have fared worse than we and what have you eaten?"

And the man sighed forth in a whisper,

"What have I not eaten? Offal from the streets like dogs; my woman brewed some soup from flesh I dared not ask what it was. Then she died, having less strength than I, and I gave the girl to a soldier because I could not see her die also." He fell silent and after a time he said, "If I had a little seed I would plant once more."

"Come here!" cried Wang Lung roughly and dragged him into the house by the hand. There he bade the man hold up the ragged tail of his coat and into it Wang Lung poured from the store of seed he had brought from the south, and he said,

"Tomorrow I will come and plow your land with my ox."

Then Ching began to weep and Wang Lung rubbed his own eyes and cried out as if he were angry, "Do you think I have forgotten that you gave me that handful of beans?" But Ching could answer nothing, only he walked away weeping without stop.

It was joy to Wang Lung to find that his uncle was no longer in the village and where he was none knew certainly. Some said he had gone to distant parts with his wife and his son. But his uncle's daughters, and this Wang Lung heard with stout anger, had been sold, the prettiest first, for the price they could bring.

Then Wang Lung set himself robustly to the soil and he begrudged even the hours he must spend in the house for food and sleep. He loved rather to take his roll of bread and garlic to the field and stand there eating, planning and thinking, "Here shall I put the black-eyed peas and here the young rice beds." And if he grew too weary in the day he laid himself into a furrow, and there with the good warmth of his own land against his flesh, he slept.

And O-lan in the house was not idle. With her own hands she lashed the mats firmly to the rafters and took earth from the fields and mixed it with water and mended the walls of the house, and she built again the oven and filled the holes in the floor that the rain had washed. Then she went into the town one day with Wang Lung and together they bought beds and a table and six benches and a great iron caldron and then they bought for pleasure a red clay teapot with a black flower marked on it in ink and six bowls to match. Last of all they went into an incense shop and bought a paper god of wealth to hang on the wall over the table in the middle room, and they bought two pewter candlesticks and two red candles to burn before the god, thick red candles of cow's fat having a reed through the middle for wick.

And with this, Wang Lung thought of the two small gods in the temple to the earth and on his way home he went and peered in at them, and they were piteous to behold, the clay of their bodies naked and sticking through the tatters of their paper clothes. None had paid any heed to them in this dreadful year and Wang Lung looked at them grimly and with content and he said aloud, as one might speak to a punished child,

"Thus it is with gods who do evil to men!"

Nevertheless, when the house was itself again, and the pewter candlesticks gleaming and the candles burning in them shining red, and the teapot and the bowls upon the table and the beds in their places once more, Wang Lung was afraid of his happiness. O-lan grew great with the next child; his children tumbled like brown puppies about his threshold and against the southern wall his old father dozed and smiled as he slept; in his fields the young rice sprouted as green as jade and more beautiful, and the young beans lifted their hooded heads from the soil. And out of the silver there was still enough left to feed them until the harvest. Looking at the blue heaven above him and the white clouds driving across it, feeling upon his plowed fields as upon his own flesh the sun and rain in proportion, Wang Lung muttered unwillingly,

"I must stick a little incense before those two in the small temple. After all, they have power over earth."

ONE NIGHT AS WANG LUNG lay with his wife he felt a hard lump the size of a man's closed hand between her breasts and he said,

"Now what is this thing you have on your body?"

He put his hand to it and he found a cloth-wrapped bundle. She drew back violently at first but then she yielded and said,

"Well, look at it then, if you must," and she broke the string which held it to her neck and gave him the thing. It was wrapped in a bit of rag and he tore this away. Suddenly into his hand fell a heap of jewels. Wang Lung gazed at them stupefied. There were such jewels as one had never dreamed could be together, jewels red as the flesh of watermelons, golden as wheat, green as young leaves in spring, clear as water trickling out of the earth. What the names of them were Wang did not know, but holding them there in the hollow of his hand, he knew from the glittering in the half-dark room that he held wealth. Motionless, drunk with color and shape, he and the woman stared at what he held. At last he whispered to her, breathless,

"Where—where—"

And she whispered back as softly,

"In the rich man's house. I saw a brick loosened in the wall and I slipped there carelessly so no other soul could see. I pulled the brick away, caught the shining, and put them into my sleeve. I have lived in a rich man's house. I knew the meaning of a loosened brick."

Again they fell silent, staring at the wonder of the stones. Then after a time Wang Lung drew in his breath and said resolutely,

"Now treasure like this one cannot keep. It must be sold and put into safety—into land, for nothing else is safe. If any knew of this we should be dead by the next day."

As he wrapped the stones in the rag again by chance he saw the woman's face. She was sitting cross-legged upon the bed and her heavy face that never spoke of anything was moved with a dim yearning of open lips.

"Well, and now what?" he asked, wondering at her.

"Will you sell them all?" she asked in a hoarse whisper.

"And why not?" he answered, astonished. "Why should we have jewels like this in an earthen house?"

"I wish I could keep two for myself," she said with such helpless wistfulness that he was moved as he might be by one of his children longing for a toy.

"Well, now!" he cried in amazement.

"If I could have two," she went on humbly, "only two small ones—the two small white pearls even . . . I would not wear them." And she dropped her eyes and fell to twisting a bit of the bedding where a thread was loosened. "I could hold them in my hand sometimes," she added, as if she thought to herself.

Then Wang Lung, without comprehending it, looked for an instant into the heart of this dull and faithful creature, who had labored all her life at some task for which she had won no reward and who in the great house had seen others wearing jewels that she had never even felt in her hand once. And, moved by something he did not understand, he handed the jewels to her in silence, and she searched among the glittering colors, her hard brown hand turning over the stones delicately and lingeringly until she found the two smooth white pearls. Then she tore a bit of the corner of her coat away and wrapped the pearls in this and hid them between her breasts and was comforted.

But Wang Lung watched her astonished, and afterward during the day and on other days he would stop and stare at her and say to himself, "Well now, that woman of mine, she has those two pearls between her breasts still, I suppose." But he never saw her take them out or look at them and they never spoke of them at all.

As for the other jewels, he decided he would go to the great house and see if there were more land to buy. To the great house he now went, but there was in these days no gateman standing at the gate, twisting the long hairs of his mole. Instead the great gates were locked. Wang Lung pounded against them with both fists and no one came. But at last he heard slow footsteps coming, slow wandering footsteps that halted and came on by fits, and then he heard the slow drawing of the iron bar and the gate creaked and a cracked voice whispered, "Who is it?"

Wang Lung answered loudly, "It is I, Wang Lung!"

Then the voice said peevishly,

"Now who is an accursed Wang Lung?"

And Wang Lung perceived that it was the Old Lord himself, because he cursed as one accustomed to servants. Wang Lung answered, therefore, more humbly than before.

"Sir and lord, I am come not to disturb your lordship, but to talk a little business with the agent."

Then the Old Lord answered through the crack,

"Now curse him, that dog left me many months ago—may his mother and his mother's mother be cursed for him—he took all that I had. No debts can be paid."

"No—no—" called Wang Lung hastily, "I came to pay out, not to collect debt."

At this there was a shrill scream from a voice Wang Lung had not yet heard and a woman thrust her face out of the gates.

"Now that is a thing I have not heard for a long time," she said sharply. "Come in," and she opened the gates wide enough to admit him, and then behind his back, while he stood astonished in the court, she barred them securely again.

The Old Lord stood there coughing and staring, a dirty gray satin robe wrapped about him, from which hung an edge of bedraggled fur. Wang Lung stared back, curious, yet half afraid, for it seemed impossible that the Old Lord, of whom he had heard so much, was this old figure, no more dreadful than his old father, and indeed less so for his father was a cleanly and smiling old man, and the Old Lord, who had been fat, was now lean, and his skin hung in folds about him and he was unwashed and unshaven and his hand was yellow and trembled as he passed it over his chin and pulled at his loose old lips.

The woman was clean enough. She had a sharp face, handsome with a sort of hawk's beauty of high-bridged nose and keen bright black eyes and pale skin stretched too tightly over her bones, and her cheeks and lips were red and hard. Her black hair was like a mirror for smooth shining blackness, but from her speech one could perceive she was but a slave, sharp-voiced and bitter-tongued. And beside these two, the woman and the Old Lord, there was not another person in the court where before men and women and children had run to and fro.

"Now about money," said the woman sharply. But Wang Lung hesitated. He could not well speak before the Old Lord and this the woman instantly perceived, and she said to the old man shrilly, "Now off with you!"

And the aged lord, without a word, shambled silently away, his old velvet shoes flapping on and off at his heels. As for Wang Lung, left alone with this woman, he was stupefied with the silence everywhere. And about the court he saw heaps of refuse and scattered straw and branches of bamboo and dried pine needles, as though not for a long time had anyone taken a broom to sweep it.

"Now then, woodenhead!" said the woman with exceeding sharpness, and Wang Lung jumped at the shrill sound of her voice. "What is your business? If you have money, let me see it."

"Well, but I cannot speak with a woman," objected Wang Lung mildly. He could make nothing of the situation in which he found himself, and he was still staring about him.

"Well, and why not?" retorted the woman with anger. Then she shouted at him suddenly, "Have you not heard, fool, that there is no one here?"

Wang Lung stared at her, unbelieving, and the woman shouted at him again, "I, Cuckoo, and the Old Lord—there is no one else!"

"Where then?" asked Wang Lung, too much aghast to make sense in his words.

"Have you not heard how bandits swept into the house and how they carried away what they would? And they hung the Old Lord up by his thumbs and beat him and the Old Mistress they tied in a chair and everyone ran. But I hid. And when I came out they were gone and the Old Mistress sat dead in her chair, not from any touch they had given her but from fright."

"And the servants and the slaves?" gasped Wang Lung.

"Oh, those," she answered carelessly, "they were gone long ago—all those who had feet to carry them away, for there was no food and no money by the middle of the winter."

The woman fell silent and the silence of the courts was heavy as silence is after life has gone. Then she said, "But all this was not a sudden thing. The fall of this house has been coming. In the last generation the lords ceased to see the land and spent the moneys carelessly as water. And the strength of the land has gone from them and bit by bit the land has begun to go also."

"Where are the young lords?" asked Wang Lung, still staring about him, so impossible was it for him to believe these things.

"Hither and thither," said the woman indifferently. "The elder young lord when he heard what had befallen sent a messenger to take his father, but I persuaded the old head not to go. I said, 'Who will be in the courts, and it is not seemly for me, who am only a woman.'" She pursed her narrow red lips virtuously as she spoke these words, and cast down her bold eyes, and again she said, "Besides, I have been my lord's faithful slave for these several years and I have no other house."

Wang Lung looked at her closely then. He began to perceive what this was, a woman who clung to an old and dying man because of what last thing she might get from him. He said with contempt, "Seeing that you are only a slave, how can I do business with you?"

At that she cried out, "He will do anything I tell him."

Wang Lung pondered. Well, and there was the land. Others would buy it through this woman if he did not.

"How much land is there left?" he asked her unwillingly, and she saw instantly what his purpose was.

"If you have come to buy land," she said, "there are a hundred acres to the west and to the south two hundred that he will sell."

This she said so readily that Wang Lung perceived she knew everything the old man had left, even to the last foot of land. But still he was unbelieving and not willing to do business with her.

"Into whose hand would I put the money?" he asked.

"Into the Old Lord's hand, and whose else?" replied the woman smoothly. Wang Lung knew that the Old Lord's hand would open into hers. But all this time here were these jewels hot and heavy against his body. He could not rest now until they were changed into land, and he said to her,

"Will the Old Lord set his own seal to the deeds of sale?"

And the woman answered eagerly,

"He will—he will—on my life!"

Then Wang Lung said plainly,

"Will you sell the land for silver or for jewels?"

And her eyes glittered as she spoke.

"I will sell it for jewels!"

Now WANG LUNG had more land than one man with an ox can plow and harvest, and so he built another small room to his house and he said to his neighbor, Ching,

"Sell me the little land you have and come into my house and help me with my land." And Ching was glad to do it.

The heavens rained in season then; and when the wheat was harvested in heavy sheaves, the two men planted the young rice, more rice than Wang Lung had ever planted he planted this year, for the rains came in abundance, so that lands that were before dry were this year fit for rice. Then when this harvest came he and Ching alone could not harvest it, so great it was, and Wang Lung hired as laborers two other men who lived in the village.

He remembered also the idle young lords of the fallen great house as he worked on the land he had bought from the House of Hwang, and he bade his two sons sharply each morning to come into the fields with him and he set them at what labor their small hands could do, guiding the ox and the ass, and making them, if they could accomplish no great labor, at least to know the heat of the sun on their bodies and the weariness of walking back and forth along the furrows.

But O-lan he would not allow to work in the fields, for he was no longer a poor man, but a man who could hire labor if he would, seeing that never had the land given forth such harvests as it had this year. He was compelled to build yet another room to the house to store his harvests in. And he bought three pigs and a flock of fowls to feed on the grains spilled from the harvests.

Then O-lan worked in the house and made new clothes for each one and new shoes, and she made coverings of flowered cloth stuffed with warm new cotton for every bed, and when all was finished they were rich in clothing and in bedding as they had never been. And once more she laid herself down upon her bed and gave birth again; and though she could hire whom she chose, she chose to be alone.

This time she was long at labor and when Wang Lung came home at evening he found his father standing at the door and laughing and saying,

"An egg with a double yolk this time!"

And when Wang Lung went in there was O-lan upon the bed with two newborn children, a boy and a girl as alike as two grains of rice. He laughed boisterously at what she had done.

"So this is why you bore two jewels in your bosom!"

And he laughed again at what he had thought of to say, and O-lan, seeing how merry he was, smiled her slow, painful smile.

Wang Lung had, therefore, at this time no sorrow of any kind, unless it was this sorrow, that his eldest girl-child neither spoke nor did those things which were right for her age. Whether it was the desperate first year of her life or the starving or what it was, month after month went past and Wang Lung waited for the first words to come from her lips, even for his name which the children called him, "Da-da." But no sound came, only the sweet, empty smile, and when he looked at her he groaned forth,

"Little fool—my poor little fool."

And as if to make amends, he made much of her and she followed him silently about, smiling when he noticed her.

In these parts, where Wang Lung had lived all his life and his father and his father's father had lived upon the land, there were famines once in five years, or, if the gods were lenient, once in seven or eight or even ten years. This was because the heavens rained too much or not at all. Time after time men fled from the land and came back to it, but Wang Lung set himself now to build his fortunes so securely that through the bad years to come he need never leave his land again but live on the fruits of the good years.

For seven years there were harvests, and every year Wang Lung hired more laborers and he builded a new house behind his old one, a large room behind a court and two small rooms on each side of the court beside the large room. The house he covered with tiles, but the walls were still made of the hard tamped earth from the fields, only he had them brushed with lime and they were white and clean. Into these rooms he and his family moved, and the laborers, with Ching at their head, lived in the old house.

Wang Lung had set Ching to be his steward over the men and over the land and he paid him well, two silver pieces a month besides his food. But with all Wang Lung's urging Ching to eat, the man still put no flesh on his bones, remaining always a small, spare man of great gravity. Nevertheless he labored gladly, pottering silently from dawn until dark, speaking if there was anything to be said, but happiest if he could be silent. But still Wang Lung knew that if any one of the laborers slept too long or ate more than his share of the bean curd in the common dish or if any bade his wife or child come secretly at harvest time and snatch handfuls of the grain, Ching would, at the end of the year when master and man feast together after the harvest, whisper to Wang Lung,

"Such an one do not ask back for the next year."

And it seemed that the handful of beans and of seed which had passed between these two men had made them brothers, except that Ching never wholly forgot that he was hired.

By the end of the fifth year Wang Lung worked little in his fields himself, having indeed to spend his whole time upon the marketing of his produce. He was greatly hampered by his lack of book knowledge, and it was a shame to him when he was in a grain shop that when a contract was written he must say humbly to the haughty dealers in the town,

"Sir, and will you read it for me, for I am too stupid."

And it was a shame to him that when he must set his name to the contract another, even a paltry clerk, lifted his eyebrows in scorn and, with his brush pointed on the wet ink block, brushed hastily the characters of Wang Lung's name.

It was on such a day one harvest time after he had heard the shout of laughter which went up from the clerks in the grain shop that he went home angrily saying to himself,

"Now, not one of those town fools has a foot of land and yet each feels he can laugh a goose cackle at me because I cannot tell the meanings of brushstrokes over paper." But as his indignation wore away, he said in his heart, "I will take my eldest son from the fields and he shall go to a school and when I go into the grain markets he will read and write for me so that there may be an end of this hissing laughter against me, who am a landed man."

That very day he called to him his eldest son, a straight tall lad of twelve years now, looking like his mother for his wide face bones and his big hands and feet but with his father's quickness of eye, and Wang Lung said,

"Come out of the fields from this day on, for I need a scholar in the family."

The lad flushed a high dark red and his eyes shone.

"My father," he said, "so have I wished for these last two years that I might do, but I did not dare to ask it."

Then the younger boy when he heard of it came in crying and complaining, a thing he was wont to do, and now he whined forth to his father,

"It is not fair that my brother can sit at leisure and learn something and I must work like a hind, who am your son as well as he!"

Then Wang Lung could not bear his noise and he would give him anything if he cried loudly enough for it, and he said hastily,

"Well and well, go the both of you, and if Heaven in its evil take one of you, there will be the other one with knowledge to do the business for me."

Then arrangements were made to send the boys to a small school near the city gate kept by an old man who had in past years gone up for government examinations and failed. For a small sum he taught boys in the classics, beating them with his large fan, folded, if they were idle. And hearing the cracks of his stout fan and the cries of the pupils, the neighbors said,

"It is a worthy old teacher." And this is why Wang Lung chose the school for the one where his sons should go to learn.

On the first day when he took them there he walked ahead of them, for it is not meet that father and son walk side by side, and he carried a blue kerchief filled with fresh eggs and these eggs he gave to the old teacher when he arrived. And Wang Lung was awed by the old teacher's great brass spectacles and by his long loose robe of black and by his immense fan, which he held even in winter, and Wang Lung bowed before him and said,

"Sir, here are my two worthless sons. If anything can be driven into their thick brass skulls it is only by beating them, and therefore if you wish to please me, beat them to make them learn."

But going home again alone, having left the two lads, Wang Lung's heart was fit to burst with pride, and meeting a neighbor as he passed through the town gate, he answered the man's inquiry,

"This day I am back from my sons' school." And to the man's surprise he answered with seeming carelessness, "Now I do not need them in the fields and they may as well learn a stomachful of characters."

But to himself he said, passing by, "It would not surprise me at all if the elder one should become a prefect with all this learning!"

And from that time on the boys were no longer called Elder and Younger, but the old teacher erected names for them; for the elder, Nung En, and for the second Nung Wen, and the first word of each name signified one whose wealth is from the earth.

X

THUS WANG LUNG BUILDED the fortunes of his house, and when the seventh year came, the great river to the north was swollen with excessive rains and snows, and burst its bounds and came sweeping and flooding all over the lands of that region. All through the late spring and early summer the water rose and at last it lay like a great sea, lovely and idle, mirroring cloud and moon and willows and bamboos. Here and there an earthen house fell slowly back into the water and the earth. And so it was with all houses that were not, like Wang Lung's, built upon a hill, and these hills stood up like islands. And men went to and from town by boat and by raft, and there were those who starved as they ever had.

But Wang Lung was not afraid. His storerooms were yet filled full with harvests of the last two years. But since much of the land could not be planted he was more idle than he had ever been in his life. There were, besides, the laborers, whom he hired for a year at a time, and it was foolish for him to work when there were those who ate his rice while waiting day after day for the waters to recede. So after he had bade them mend the hoes and the rakes and the plows and to feed the cattle and to twist hemp into ropes—all those things which in the old days he did himself when he tilled his land alone—his own hands were empty and he did not know what to do with himself.

Now a man cannot sit all day and stare at a lake of water covering his fields. The house, as he wandered about it impatiently, was too silent for his vigorous blood. The old man grew very feeble now, half blind and almost wholly deaf, and there was no need of speech with him except to ask if he were warm and fed. There was no telling the old man anything for he forgot it at once. And it made Wang Lung impatient that the old man could not see how rich his son was and would always mutter if there were tea leaves in his bowl, "A little water is well enough and tea like silver."

The old man and the elder girl, who never spoke at all but sat beside her grandfather hour after hour, twisting a bit of cloth, folding and refolding it and smiling at it, these two had nothing to say to a man prosperous and vigorous. When Wang Lung had poured the old man a bowl of tea and had passed his hand over the girl's cheek and received her sweet, empty smile, which passed with such sad swiftness from her face, he always turned away from her with a moment's stillness, which was his daughter's mark of sadness on him, and he looked to his two youngest children. But a man cannot be satisfied with the foolishness of little children and after a brief time of laughter and teasing they went off to their own games and Wang Lung was alone.

Then it was that he looked at O-lan, his wife, as a man looks at the woman who has lived beside him so closely that there is nothing he does not know of her and nothing new which he may expect from her. And it seemed to Wang Lung that he looked at O-lan for the first time in his life and he saw for the first time that she was a woman whom no man could call other than a dull and common creature. He saw that her hair was rough and unoiled and that her face was large and flat and coarse-skinned. Her eyebrows were scattered and the hairs too few, and her lips were too wide, and her hands and feet were large and spreading. Looking at her thus with strange eyes, he cried out at her,

"Now anyone looking at you would say you were the wife of a common fellow. Cannot you buy a little oil for your hair and make yourself a new coat of black cloth? And those shoes you wear are not fit for a land proprietor's wife, such as you now are."

She sat upon a bench threading a long needle in and out of a shoe sole and she stopped and held the needle poised and her mouth gaped open and showed her blackened teeth. Then as if she understood at last that he had looked at her as a man at a woman, a thick red flush crept up over her high cheekbones. But she only looked at him humbly, and she hid her feet under the bench on which she sat. Then, although in his heart he was ashamed that he reproached this creature who through all these years had followed him faithfully as a dog, and although he remembered that when he was poor and labored in the fields she left her bed even after a child was born and came to help him in the harvest fields, yet he could not stem the irritation in his breast and he went on ruthlessly, although against his inner will,

"I have labored and have grown rich and I would have my wife look less like a hind. And those feet of yours—" He stopped, and looked with anger at her big feet in their loose cotton-cloth shoes, so that she thrust them yet farther under the bench.

And at last she said in a whisper, "My mother did not bind them, since I was sold so young. But the younger girl's feet I will bind."

But he flung himself off because he was ashamed that he was angry and angry because she would not be angry in return but only frightened. And he drew on his new black robe, saying fretfully, "Well, I will go to the tea shop and see if I can hear anything new. There is nothing in my house except fools and children."

His ill temper grew as he went to the town because he remembered suddenly that all these new lands of his he could not have

bought in a lifetime if O-lan had not given him the handful of jewels from the rich man's house. But he said as if to answer his own heart rebelliously, "Well, but she did not know what she did. She seized them for pleasure as a child may seize a handful of red and green sweets, and she would have hidden them forever in her bosom if I had not found it out."

Then he wondered if she still hid the pearls between her breasts. But where before it had been a thing to picture in his mind, now he thought of it with contempt, for her breasts had grown flabby and pearls between them were foolish and a waste.

All this might have been nothing if Wang Lung were still a poor man. But he had money. There was silver hidden in the walls of his house and there was a sack of silver buried under the floor, and silver sewed into the mat under their bed, and his girdle was full of silver. So that now he began to be careless of it and to think what he could do to enjoy the days of his manhood.

Everything seemed not so good to him as it was before. The tea shop which he used to enter timidly now seemed dingy and mean to him, and people nudged each other when he came in and he could hear a man whisper to another,

"There is that man Wang, he who bought the land from the House of Hwang. He is rich, now."

And Wang Lung, hearing this, sat down with seeming carelessness, but his heart swelled with pride. But on this day when he had reproached his wife even the deference he received did not please him and he sat gloomily drinking his tea. Then he thought suddenly to himself,

"Now why should I drink my tea at this shop, I who have land and whose sons are scholars?"

And he rose up quickly, threw his money on the table and wandered forth without knowing what it was he wished.

Now there was in the town a great tea shop newly opened by a man from the south, who understood such business, and Wang Lung had before this passed the place by. But now he was compelled by his restlessness to see something new. Thus he stepped across the threshold of the new tea shop into the great, glittering room, full of tables and open to the street as it was, and he went in, bold enough in his bearing and trying to be the more bold because he remembered that only in the last few years was he more than a poor man who had even labored at pulling a ricksha.

He bought his tea quietly and looked about him with wonder. This shop was a great hall and the ceiling was set about with gilt and upon the walls there were scrolls of white silk, painted with the figures of women. These women Wang Lung looked at secretly and it seemed to him they were women in dreams, for none on earth had he seen like them.

Now this tea shop was the only building in all that town which had an upper floor, except the pagoda outside the West Gate, and at night the high singing of women's voices and light laughter floated out of the upper windows, and the sweet strumming of lutes. But where Wang Lung sat the noise of many men drinking tea and the sharp bony click of dice and dominoes muffled all else.

Thus it was that Wang Lung did not hear behind him the footsteps of a woman creaking upon the narrow stair which led from the upper floor; so he started violently when one touched him on the shoulder, not expecting that any would know him here. When he looked up it was into the narrow, handsome face of Cuckoo, the woman who had helped him to buy the land from the Old Lord. She laughed when she saw him, and her laughter was a sort of sharp whispering.

"Well, and Wang the farmer!" she said, lingering with malice on the word farmer. "And who would think to see you here!"

It seemed to Wang Lung then that he must prove at any cost to this woman that he was more than a mere country fellow, and he laughed and said too loudly,

"Is not my money as good to spend as another man's? And money I do not lack in these days."

Cuckoo stopped at this, her eyes narrow and bright as a snake's eyes, and her voice smooth as oil flowing from a vessel.

"And who has not heard it? And how shall a man better spend extra money than in a place like this, where rich men and elegant lords gather to take their joy? There is no such wine as ours—have you tasted it, Wang Lung?"

"I have only drunk tea as yet," replied Wang Lung, half ashamed.

"Tea!" she exclaimed after him, laughing shrilly. "But we have tiger-bone wine and wine of fragrant rice—why need you drink tea?" And as Wang Lung hung his head she said softly and insidiously, "And I suppose you have not looked at anything else, have you, eh? No pretty little hands, no sweet-smelling cheeks?"

Wang Lung hung his head yet lower and the red blood rushed into his face; and the woman laughed again and pointed to the painted scrolls and said,

"There they are, their pictures. Choose which one you wish to see and put the silver in my hand and I will place her before you."

"Those!" said Wang Lung, wondering. "I thought they were pictures of dream women such as the storytellers speak of!"

"So they are dream women," rejoined Cuckoo, with mocking good humor, "but dreams such as a little silver will turn into flesh." And she went on her way.

But Wang Lung sat staring at the pictures with a new interest. Up this narrow stairway then, there were these women in flesh and blood. Before this they had all seemed equally beautiful, but now there were clearly some more beautiful than others, and out of the score and more he chose three most beautiful, and out of the three one, a small, slender thing, with a body light as a bamboo and a little face as pointed as a kitten's face, and one delicate hand clasping the stem of a lotus flower.

"She is like a flower on a quince tree," he said suddenly aloud, and hearing his own voice he was alarmed and ashamed and he rose hastily and put down his money and went out into the darkness that had now fallen and so to his home.

But over the fields and the water the moonlight hung, a net of silver mist, and in his body his blood ran hot and fast.

Now if the waters had at this time receded from Wang Lung's land, leaving it wet and smoking under the sun, so that it would need to have been plowed, Wang Lung might have forgotten the pointed face upon the scroll. But the waters lay placid and unmoved except for the slight summer wind that rose at sunset, and in his house O-lan looked at Wang Lung miserably as he went here and there and flung himself down in a chair and rose from it without drinking the tea she poured and without smoking the pipe he had lit. At the end of one long day, when the twilight lingered murmurous and sweet with the breath of the lake, he stood at the door of his house, and suddenly without a word he turned abruptly and went into his room and put on his new coat that O-lan had made for feast days, and with no word to anyone he went over the narrow paths along the water's edge and through the city gate until he came to the new tea shop.

There every light was lit, bright oil lamps which are to be bought in the foreign cities of the coast, and men sat under the lights drinking and talking, their robes open to the evening coolness, and everywhere fans moved to and fro and good laughter flowed out like music into the street.

Wang Lung hesitated upon the threshold and he stood in the

bright light which streamed from the open doors. And he might have stood there and gone away, for he was fearful still, although his blood was rushing through his body fit to burst his veins, but there came out of the shadows on the edge of the light a woman who had been leaning idly against the doorway and it was Cuckoo. But when she saw who it was, she shrugged her shoulders and said,

"Ah, it is only the farmer!"

Wang was stung with the sharp carelessness in her voice, and his sudden anger gave him a courage he had not otherwise, so that he said, "Well, and may I not do as other men?"

And he thrust his hand into his girdle and brought it out full of silver.

She stared at the silver and said then without further delay,

"Come and say which one you wish."

And Wang Lung, without knowing what he said, muttered,

"Well, and I do not know that I want anything." And then his desire overcame him and he whispered, "That little one—that one with the pointed chin and a face like a quince blossom for white and pink, and she holds a lotus bud in her hand."

The woman nodded easily and beckoning him she threaded her way between the crowded tables, and Wang Lung followed her at a distance. At first it seemed to him that every man watched him but when he took courage to see he saw that none paid him any heed. By this time they were walking up the narrow stairway, and this Wang Lung did with difficulty, for it was the first time he had ever climbed steps in a house. Nevertheless, when they reached the top, it was the same as a house on the earth, except that it seemed a mighty way up when he passed a window and looked into the sky. The woman led the way down a close dark hall, and at last struck a closed door harshly with the flat palm of her hand and went in and there, upon a bed covered with a flowered red quilt, sat a slender girl.

Now if one had told him there were small hands like these he would not have believed it, hands so small and fingers so pointed with long nails stained the color of lotus buds, deep and rosy; nor feet like these, little feet thrust into pink satin shoes no longer than a man's middle finger and swinging childishly over the bed's edge.

He sat stiffly on the bed beside her, and he looked at her as he had looked at the picture, and he saw the figure slender as bamboo in its tight short upper coat; he saw the small pointed face set in its painted prettiness above the high collar lined with white fur; he saw the round eyes the shape of apricots, so that at last he understood what the storytellers meant when they sang of the apricot eyes of the beauties of old. And he would not have dreamed that she was to be touched.

Then he heard laughter, light, quick, tinkling as a silver bell upon a pagoda shaking in the wind, and a little voice like laughter said, "Oh, you great fellow! Shall we sit here the night through while you stare?"

And at that he seized her hand between both of his.

Now WANG LUNG became sick with the sickness which is greater than any man can have. He had suffered under labor in the sun and he had suffered from starvation and he had suffered from the despair of laboring without hope in a southern city. But under none of these did he suffer as he now did under this slight girl's hand.

Every day he went to the tea shop; every evening he waited till she would receive him, and every night he went in to her. All during the hot summer he loved her thus. Yet he had never enough of her, and he went back to his house every night dazed and unsatisfied, and his days were endless, and his breast was filled with a sweet sick pain which he could not understand.

If any spoke to him, his wife or his children, or if Ching came to him and said, "The waters will soon recede and what is there we should prepare of seed?" he shouted and said,

"Why do you trouble me?"

All the time his heart was like to burst. And as the days went on he would not look at the grave faces of O-lan and of the children, suddenly sober in their play when he approached, nor even at his old father who peered at him and asked,

"What is this sickness that turns you full of evil temper and your skin as yellow as clay?"

And all this time the girl Lotus did what she would with him. When she laughed at the braid of his hair and said, "Now the men of the south do not have these monkey tails!" he went without a word and had it cut off.

When O-lan saw what he had done she burst out in terror, "You have cut off your life!"

But he shouted at her,

"And shall I look an old-fashioned fool forever?"

And he would have cut off his life if the girl Lotus had commanded it or desired it, because she had every beauty which had ever come into his mind to desire in a woman.

His good brown body that he washed but rarely he now washed every day. He bought red scented soap from foreign parts, and he rubbed it on his flesh, and not for any price now would he eat a stalk of garlic. He bought also new stuffs for clothes, and although O-lan had always cut his robes, making them wide and long for good measure, now he was scornful of her cutting and sewing and he took the stuffs to a tailor and he had his clothes made as the men in the town had theirs, light gray silk for a robe, cut neatly to his body, and over this a black satin sleeveless coat. And he bought black velvet shoes such as the Old Lord had worn. And beyond this he bought a silver ring washed with gold for his finger, and as his hair grew where it had been shaved above his forehead, he smoothed it with a fragrant foreign oil.

O-lan did not know what to make of all this, except that one day after staring at him for a long time she said heavily,

"There is that about you which makes me think of one of the lords in the great house."

Wang Lung laughed loudly then, but in his heart he was greatly pleased, and for that day he was more kindly with her than he had been for many days.

Now THE MONEY, the good silver, went streaming out of his hands. There was not only the price he must pay for his hours with the girl, but there was the pretty demanding of her desires for this or that jewel or trinket. And O-lan, who in the old days might have said to him easily enough, "And why do you take the money from the wall?" now said nothing, only watching him in misery, knowing that he was living some life apart from her, but not knowing what life it was. But she was afraid to ask him anything, because of his anger that was always ready for her now.

There came a day when Wang Lung returned over the fields and he drew near to her as she washed his clothes at the pool. He stood there silent for a while and then he said to her roughly, because he was ashamed and would not acknowledge his shame,

"Where are those pearls you had?"

And she answered timidly, looking up from the clothes she was beating upon a smooth flat stone,

"The pearls? I have them."

And he muttered, not looking at her but at her wrinkled, wet hands,

"There is no use in keeping pearls for nothing." And then after an instant's silence he cried out suddenly, "Give them to me—I have need of them!"

Then slowly she thrust her hand into her bosom and she drew forth the small package and she gave it to him and watched him as he unwrapped it; and the pearls lay in his hand and they caught softly the light of the sun, and he laughed.

But O-lan returned to the beating of his clothes and when tears dropped slowly and heavily from her eyes she did not put up her hand to wipe them away; only she beat the more steadily with her wooden stick upon the clothes spread over the stone.

XI

AND THUS IT MIGHT have gone forever until all the silver was spent had not that one, Wang Lung's uncle, returned suddenly without explanation. He stood in the door as though he had dropped from a cloud, his ragged clothes unbuttoned and girdled loosely as ever about him. He grinned widely at them all as they sat about the table at their early morning meal, and Wang Lung sat agape, for it was like a dead man returning to see him. His father blinked and stared and did not recognize the one who had come until he called out,

"Well, my elder brother and his son and his sons and my sister-in-law."

Then Wang Lung rose, dismayed in his heart but upon the surface of his face and voice courteous,

"Well, my uncle, and have you eaten?"

"No," replied his uncle easily, "but I will eat with you."

He sat himself down, then, and ate as though he were very hungry and none spoke until he had supped down loudly three bowls of rice gruel, cracking between his teeth the bones of the fish and the kernels of the beans. And when he had eaten he said simply,

"Now I will fetch my wife and my son. In this great house of yours it will never be missed what we eat."

Wang Lung, in great consternation, could do nothing but answer with sullen looks, for it is a shame to a man when he has enough and to spare to drive his own father's brother from the house. And that very evening his uncle came, bringing his wife and his son. And Wang Lung was exceedingly angry and the more angry because he must answer with smiles and welcome his relatives. And for three days he did not go into the town because of his anger.

Then when they were all accustomed to what had taken place and when O-lan had said to him, "Cease to be angry. It is a thing to be borne," and Wang Lung saw that his uncle and his uncle's wife and son would be courteous enough for the sake of their food and their shelter, then his thoughts turned more violently than ever to the girl Lotus and he muttered to himself,

"When a man's house is full of wild dogs he must seek peace elsewhere."

Now what O-lan had not seen in her simplicity nor the old man because of the dimness of his age, the wife of Wang Lung's uncle saw at once and she cried out to O-lan, the laughter slanting from her eyes,

"Now Wang Lung is seeking to pluck a flower somewhere."

And when O-lan looked at her humbly, not understanding, she laughed and said again, "The melon must always be split wide open before you can see the seeds, eh? Well, then, plainly, your man is mad over another woman!"

This Wang Lung heard his uncle's wife say in the court outside his window as he lay dozing one early morning. He was quickly awake, and he listened further, aghast at the sharpness of this woman's eyes. The thick voice rumbled on, pouring like oil from her fat throat,

"When a man smooths his hair and buys new clothes, then there is a new woman and that is sure."

There came a broken sound from O-lan, what it was she said he could not hear, but his uncle's wife said again,

"You, poor fool, have never been fit for a man's fancy and little better than an ox for his labor. And it is not for you to repine when he buys himself another to bring her to his house, for all men are so, and so would my old do-nothing also, except the poor wretch has never had enough silver in his life to feed himself even."

No more than this did Wang Lung hear upon his bed, for now suddenly did he see how to satisfy his thirst after this girl he loved. He would buy her and bring her to his house and make her his own. And he rose up at once from his bed and he went out and motioned secretly to the wife of his uncle, and when she had followed him outside the gate he said,

"I listened and heard what you said in the courts and you are right. I have need of more than that one and why should I not, seeing that I have land to feed us all?"

She answered volubly and eagerly,

"And why not, indeed? It is only the poor man who must needs drink from one cup." Thus she spoke, knowing what he would say next, and he went on as she had planned,

"But who will negotiate for me and be the middleman? A man cannot go to a woman and say, 'Come to my house.'"

To this she answered instantly,

"Now do you leave this affair in my hands. Only tell me which woman it is and I will manage the affair."

Then Wang Lung answered unwillingly and timidly, for he had never spoken her name aloud before to anyone,

"It is the woman called Lotus, in the great tea shop on the main street of town."

She mused awhile, fingering her lower lip, and said at last,

"I do not know anyone there. Who is the keeper of this woman?"

And when he told her, she laughed and said,

"Oh, Cuckoo? But it is a simple matter, indeed. That one would do anything, even to making a mountain, if she could feel silver enough in her palm for it."

And Wang Lung, hearing this, felt his mouth suddenly dry and parched and his voice came from him in a whisper,

"Silver, then! Silver and gold! Anything to the very price of my land!"

THEN FROM A STRANGE and contrary fever of love Wang Lung would not go again to the teahouse until the affair was arranged. Thus there was nothing to do except to gnaw his fingers and to see the house suddenly as Lotus might see it and he hurried O-lan into this and that, sweeping and washing and moving chairs, so that she, poor woman, grew more and more terror-stricken for well she knew by now, although he said nothing, what was to come to her.

Now Wang Lung said to himself that with two women in the house there must be another court where he could go with his love and be separate. So while he waited for his uncle's wife to complete the matter, he called laborers and commanded them to build another court behind the middle room, and around the court three rooms. He superintended the laborers himself, so that he need not talk with Ching of what he did. And in the little new court he built a pool and he went into the city and bought five goldfish for it. And he bought red cloth to hang at the doors for curtains and he bought a new table and two carved chairs and painted scrolls of hills and water to hang upon the wall, and then he bought a wide carven bed, and he bought flowered curtains to hang about it.

During all this time he said nothing to anyone except to scold the children if they were filthy at their noses or to roar out at O-lan that she had not brushed her hair for three days, so that at last one morning O-lan burst into tears and wept aloud, as he had never seen her weep before. He said harshly, therefore,

"Now what, woman? Cannot I say comb out your horse's tail of hair without this trouble over it?"

But she answered nothing except to say over and over, moaning,

"I have borne you sons—I have borne you sons—"

And he was silenced and uneasy and he muttered to himself for he was ashamed before her and so he let her alone.

Thus it went until one day his uncle's wife came and said,

"The thing is complete. The girl will come for jade earrings and

a ring of jade and a ring of gold and two suits of satin clothes and two suits of silk and a dozen pairs of shoes and two silken quilts."

Of all this Wang Lung heard only, "The thing is complete—" and he cried out,

"Let it be done—let it be done—" and he ran and got out silver and poured it into her hands, and to his uncle's wife he said, "And for yourself take a good ten pieces of silver."

Then she made a feint of refusal, drawing up her fat body and crying in a loud whisper,

"No, we are one family and this I do for you and not for silver." But Wang Lung saw her hand outstretched as she denied, and into it he poured the silver and he counted it well spent.

Then he bought pork and beef and mandarin fish, and he bought a snarl of dried birds' nests from the south to brew for soup, and he bought every delicacy he knew and then he waited. And at last on a shining fiery day in the eighth moon, which is the last end of summer, she came to his house.

From afar Wang Lung saw her coming. She rode in a closed sedan chair borne upon men's shoulders, and behind the sedan followed the figure of Cuckoo. Then for an instant he knew fear and he said to himself,

"What am I taking into my house?"

And scarcely knowing what he did he went quickly into the room where he had slept for these many years with his wife and he shut the door and there in the darkness he waited in confusion until he heard his uncle's wife calling loudly for him to come out, for one was at the gate. Then abashed he went slowly out, hanging his head over his fine clothes, and his eyes looking here and there but never ahead. But Cuckoo hailed him merrily,

"Well, I did not know we would be doing business like this!"

Then she went to the chair which the men had set down and she lifted the curtain and clucked her tongue and she said,

"Come, my Lotus Flower, here is your house and your lord."

Then the curtain was lifted and before he knew what he did he looked and he saw sitting in the shadowy recess of the chair, painted and cool as a lily, the girl Lotus. He forgot everything, everything but that she had come to his house forever, and he stood stiff and trembling, watching as she rose, graceful as though a wind had passed over a flower. Then she took Cuckoo's hand and stepped out, keeping her eyelids dropped as she walked, tottering and swaying upon her little feet. And as she passed him she did not speak to him, but she whispered only to Cuckoo, faintly,

"Where is my apartment?"

Then his uncle's wife came forward to her other side and they led the girl into the court that Wang Lung had built for her.

Then after a time Wang Lung's uncle's wife came out, laughing a little maliciously, and she dusted her hands together as though to free them of something that clung to them.

"She reeks of perfume and paint, that one," she said, still laughing. "Like a regular bad one she smells." And then she said with a deeper malice, "She is not so young as she looks, my nephew!" And then seeing the anger on Wang Lung's face she added hastily, "But I have never seen another more beautiful and it will be as sweet as a feast after your years with the thick-boned slave."

But Wang Lung answered nothing, only at last he dared to lift the red curtain and to go into the court he had built.

All this time O-lan had not come near the house. At dawn she had taken a hoe and she had called the children and gone out and had not returned. But when night came on she entered, silent and earth-stained, and the children silent behind her, and she went into the kitchen and prepared food as she always did, and she called the old man and put the chopsticks in his hand and she fed the poor fool. Then when the children slept at last she went into her room and slept alone upon her bed.

Then did Wang Lung eat and drink of his love night and day. Day after day he sat beside Lotus and watched her at all she did. She never came forth in the heat of the early autumn days, but lay while Cuckoo bathed her slender body with lukewarm water and perfume and rubbed oil into her hair. For Lotus had said,

"Let me have this woman for my servant, seeing that I am altogether alone in the world, for my father and my mother died when I could not yet talk and my uncle sold me as soon as I was pretty to a life such as I have had, and I have no one." This she said with her tears, always abundant and ready and glittering in the corners of her pretty eyes, and Wang Lung could have denied her nothing when she looked up at him so. Besides, it was true that the girl would be alone in his house, for it was plain enough that O-lan would not serve the second one or notice that she was in the house at all. So Cuckoo and Lotus, her mistress, dwelt apart from the others in the new court that Wang Lung had made.

And he ate and drank of his love and he feasted alone and he was satisfied.

IT WAS NOT TO BE SUPPOSED that the coming of Lotus and of her servingwoman Cuckoo into Wang Lung's house could be accomplished altogether without stir of some sort, since more than one woman under one roof is not for peace. And Wang Lung was prepared for O-lan to hate Lotus, having heard many times of such things. Some women will even hang themselves when a man takes a second woman into the house, and others will scold, and he was glad that O-lan was a silent woman for at least she could not think of words against him. But he had not foreseen that whereas she would be silent of Lotus, her anger would find its vent against Cuckoo.

Cuckoo was willing enough to be friends, albeit she did not forget that in the great house she had been in the lord's chamber and O-lan a kitchen slave, and she called out to O-lan when first she saw her,

"Well, and my old friend, here we are in a house together again, and you mistress and first wife—how things are changed!"

But O-lan only stared at her and answered nothing. Then she put down the jar of water she carried and she went to Wang Lung and she said to him plainly,

"What is this slave woman doing in our house?"

Wang Lung would have liked to say in a surly voice, "It is my house and whoever I say may come in, she shall come in, and who are you to ask?" But he could not because of some shame in him when O-lan was there before him and he only looked east and west and feigned to have mislaid his pipe. But O-lan stood there solidly on her big feet and waited. Then Wang Lung, seeing she would have an answer, said feebly,

"And what is it to you?"

And O-lan said,

"I bore her haughty looks all during my youth in the great house and her running into the kitchen a score of times a day crying out, 'Now tea for the lord'—'Now food for the lord'—and it was always this is too hot and that is too cold, and that is badly cooked, and I was too ugly and too slow and too this and too that . . ."

Then O-lan waited and when he did not speak, the hot, scanty tears welled slowly into her eyes, and at last she crept away, feeling for the door because of her tears that blinded her.

Wang Lung watched her as she went and he was glad to be

alone, but still he was ashamed and he was angry that he was ashamed and he said to himself restlessly,

"Well, and I have been good enough to her, and there are men worse than I." And he said at last that O-lan must bear it.

But O-lan was not finished with it, and she went her way silently. In the morning she heated water and presented it to the old man, and to Wang Lung if he were not in the inner court she presented tea, but when Cuckoo went to find hot water for her mistress the caldron was empty, and O-lan would go steadily to her cooking, answering nothing to Cuckoo's loud crying,

"And is my delicate lady to lie thirsting and gasping in her bed for a swallow of water in the morning?"

But O-lan would not hear her. Then Cuckoo went complaining to Wang Lung and he was angry that his love must be marred by such things and he went to O-lan to reproach her and he shouted, "And cannot you add a dipperful of water to the caldron?"

But she answered with sullenness deep upon her face,

"I am not slave of slaves in this house at least."

Then he was angry beyond bearing and he seized O-lan's shoulder and he shook her and said,

"Do not be yet more of a fool. It is not for the servant but for the mistress."

And she bore his violence and she looked at him and she said,

"And to that one you gave my two pearls!"

Then his hand dropped and he was speechless, and he went away ashamed.

And so he bade the laborers build another kitchen, and Cuckoo was pleased because he said, "You shall cook what you please in it." And he said to himself that at last his affairs were settled. And it seemed to him freshly that he could never tire of Lotus and of the way she pouted at him with the lids drooped like lily petals over her great eyes, and at the way laughter gleamed out of her eyes when she glanced up at him.

But after all this matter of the new kitchen became a thorn in his body, for Cuckoo went to the town every day and she bought this and that of expensive foods imported from the southern cities.

These all cost more money than he liked to give out, but still not so much, he was sure, as Cuckoo told him, and yet he was afraid to say, "You are eating my flesh," for fear it would displease Lotus, and so there was nothing he could do except to put his hand unwillingly to his girdle.

There was yet another small thorn that sprang from the first, and it was that his uncle's wife went often into the inner court at mealtimes, and she grew free there, and Wang Lung was not pleased that Lotus chose this woman for friend. But when he said gently, "Now, Lotus, my flower, do not waste your sweetness on an old fat hag like that one," Lotus was fretful and she answered peevishly, hanging her head away from him,

"Now I am used to a merry house and in yours there is no one except the first wife who hates me. You do not love me for if you did you would wish me to be happy."

Then Wang Lung was humbled and anxious and he said,

"Let it be only as you wish and forever."

Then she forgave him royally, but after that when he came to her, if she were drinking tea with his uncle's wife, she would bid him wait and was careless with him, and he strode away, angry. And so his love was not whole and perfect as it had been before. It was pierced through and through with small angers which were the more sharp because he could no longer go even to O-lan freely for speech, seeing that now their life was sundered.

Then like a field of thorns spreading from one root here and there, there was yet more to trouble Wang Lung. One day his father, who one would say saw nothing so drowsy with age he was, woke suddenly out of his sleeping in the sun and he tottered, leaning on his dragon-headed staff which Wang Lung had bought for him on his seventieth birthday, to the doorway where a curtain hung between the main room and the court where Lotus walked. It happened that it was at an hour when Wang Lung walked with Lotus in the court, and they stood beside the pool and looked at the fish. Then when the old man saw his son standing beside a slender painted girl he cried out in his shrill voice,

"There is a harlot in the house!" and he would not be silent although Wang Lung, fearing lest Lotus grow angry—for this small creature could shriek and scream and beat her hands together if she were angered at all—led the old man away, saying,

"Now calm your heart, my father. It is not a harlot but a second woman in the house."

But the old man would not be silent and whether he heard what was said or not no one knew, only he said suddenly, "And I had one woman and my father had one woman and we farmed the land." And again he cried out, "I say it is a harlot!"

And so the old man, with a sort of cunning hatred against Lotus, would go to the doorway of her court and shout into the air,

"Harlot!"

And one day Wang Lung heard a shriek from the inner court and he ran and there he found the two younger children, and between them his elder daughter, his poor fool. Now the children were constantly curious about this lady who lived in the inner court. The two elder boys were shy and knew well enough why she was there, although they never spoke of her. But the two younger children could never be satisfied with their peepings and exclamations. On this day, they had conceived the notion that the fool must also see the lady, and they had dragged her into the court and she stood before Lotus. Now when the fool saw the bright silk of the coat Lotus wore, she put out her hands and she laughed aloud, a laugh that was only sound and meaningless. And Lotus was frightened and screamed out, so that Wang Lung came running in, and Lotus shook with her anger and leaped up and down and shook her finger at the poor laughing girl and cried out,

"I will not stay in this house if that one comes near me. If I had known that I should have accursed idiots to endure I would not have come," and she pushed the little gaping boy who stood nearest her, clasping his twin sister's hand.

Then the good anger awoke in Wang Lung, for he loved his children, and he said roughly,

"I will not hear my children cursed, no and not by anyone!" And he gathered the children together and said to them, "Now go out, my son and my daughter, and come no more to this woman's court, for she does not love you." And to the elder girl he said with great gentleness, "And you, my poor fool, come back to your place in the sun." And he took her by the hand and led her away.

For he was most angry of all that Lotus dared to curse this child of his and call her idiot, and a load of fresh pain for the girl fell upon his heart, so that for two days he would not go near Lotus, but he played with the children and he went into the town and he bought a circle of barley candy for his poor fool and he comforted himself with her baby pleasure in the sweet stuff.

And when he went in to Lotus again, she took special trouble to please him. But he, although he loved her again, loved her not so wholly as before.

THERE CAME A DAY when summer was ended and the sky in the early morning was clear and cold and blue as seawater and a clean autumn wind blew hard over the land, and Wang Lung woke as from a sleep. He went to the door of his house and he looked over his fields. And he saw that the waters had receded.

Then a voice cried out in him, a voice deeper than love cried out for his land. And he tore off the long robe and his velvet shoes and he rolled his trousers to his knees and he stood forth robust and eager and he shouted,

"Where is the hoe and the plow? And where is the seed for the wheat planting? Come, Ching, my friend—call the men—I go out to the land!"

XII

As he had been healed of his sickness of heart when he came from the southern city, so now again Wang Lung was healed of his sickness of love by the good dark earth of his fields. For he stood first behind the oxen and saw the deep curl of earth turning as the plow went into the soil, and then he himself took a hoe and broke up the soil into fine loamy stuff, soft as black sugar, and still dark with the wetness of the land upon it. This he did for the sheer joy he had in it, and when he was weary he lay down upon his land and the health of the earth spread into his flesh and he was healed of his sickness.

When night came, he strode into his house, his body aching and weary and triumphant, and he tore aside the curtain to the inner court, and when Lotus saw him she cried out at the earth upon his clothes. But he laughed and he seized her small, curling hands in his soiled ones and he laughed again and said,

"Now you see that your lord is but a farmer and you are a farmer's wife!"

Then she cried out with spirit,

"A farmer's wife am I not, be you what you like!"

And he laughed again and went out from her easily, and he laughed because he was free. All stained as he was with the earth he ate well of the food which O-lan prepared for him, good rice and cabbage and bean curd, and fresh garlic rolled into wheat bread.

So these two women took their place in his house: Lotus for his toy and his pleasure, and O-lan for the mother who had borne his sons and who kept his house and fed him. And it was a pride to Wang Lung that men mentioned with envy the woman in his inner court; it was as though men spoke of a rare jewel that was useless except that it was sign and symbol of a man who had passed beyond the necessity of caring only to be fed and clothed and could spend his money on joy if he wished. And the men of the village now looked upon Wang Lung no more as one of themselves, but they came to borrow money of him at interest and to ask his advice concerning marriages, and if any two had a dispute over the boundary of a field, Wang Lung was asked to settle the dispute and his decision was accepted, whatever it was.

Then the year turned to winter and Wang Lung took his harvest to the markets, and this time he took with him his eldest son. Now there is a pride a man has when he sees his eldest son reading aloud the letters upon a paper, and this pride Wang Lung now had. He would not pretend it was anything out of the common, although when the lad said sharply, "Here is a letter that has the wood radical when it should have the water radical," Wang Lung's heart was fit to burst with pride, so that he was compelled to turn aside and cough. And when a murmur of surprise ran among the clerks at his son's wisdom he called out merely,

"Change it then! We will not put our name to anything wrongly written."

And when it was finished and his son had written his father's name on the deed of sale, the two walked home together.

The year deepened into snow and the New Year's festival came, and now not only from the countryside but from the town also men came to see Wang Lung to wish him fortune, and they said,

"There is no fortune we can wish you greater than you have, sons in your house and women and money and land."

And Wang Lung, dressed in his silken robe with his sons in good robes beside him, and sweet cakes and watermelon seeds and nuts upon the table, knew that his fortune was good.

But the year turned to spring and the willow trees sprouted their leaves fully and unfolded them, and the earth was moist and steaming and pregnant with harvest, and the eldest son of Wang

Lung changed suddenly and ceased to be a child. He grew moody and would not eat this and that and there was no correction that could be made of the lad at all, for if his father said to him with anything beyond coaxing, "Now eat of the good meat and rice," the lad turned stubborn, and if Wang Lung was angry at all, he burst into tears and fled from the room.

Moreover, he would not in the mornings rise out of his bed to go to school unless Wang Lung bawled at him, and then he went sullenly and sometimes he spent whole days idling about the streets, and Wang Lung only knew it when the younger boy said spitefully,

"Elder Brother was not in school today."

Wang Lung was angry at his eldest son then and he shouted, "And am I to spend good silver for nothing?"

And in his anger he fell upon the boy with a bamboo and beat him until O-lan heard it and rushed in from the kitchen and stood between her son and his father. And she said,

"It is useless for you to beat the lad. I have seen this melancholy come upon the young lords in the great house."

"It need not be so," answered Wang Lung in argument. "When I was a lad I had no such melancholy and no such weepings."

O-lan answered slowly, "I have not indeed seen it thus except with young lords. You worked on the land."

After he had pondered awhile, Wang Lung saw truth in what she said. When he himself was a lad there was no time for melancholy, for he had to be up at dawn and out with the plow, and if he wept he could weep for no one heard him, and he could not run away, for if he did there was nothing for him to eat on return. He remembered all this and he said to himself,

"But my son is not thus. He is more delicate than I was, and his father is rich, and there is no need for his labor. Besides, one cannot take a scholar and set him to the plow."

And he was secretly proud that he had a son like this and so he said to O-lan,

"Well, and if he is like a young lord it is another matter. I will betroth him and we will marry him early."

Then he went into the inner court.

Now Lotus, seeing Wang Lung thinking of things other than her beauty, pouted and said,

"If I had known that in a short year you could look at me and not see me, I would have stayed in the teahouse." And she looked at him out of the corner of her eyes so that he laughed and seized her hand and he answered,

"Well, and a man cannot always think of the jewel he has sewn on his coat, but if it were lost he could not bear it. These days I think of how my eldest son is restless with desire and he must be wed and I do not know how to find the one he should wed, and I am loath to go to a professional matchmaker, lest there be some bargain she has made with a man who has a daughter deformed."

Now Lotus, since the eldest son had grown tall and graceful with young manhood, looked on the lad with favor and she was diverted with what Wang Lung said to her and she replied, musing,

"There was a man who used to come to the great teahouse, and he often spoke of his daughter, because he said she was such an one as I, small and fine, but still only a child."

"What sort of man was this?" asked Wang Lung.

And she answered,

"I do not know except he was named Liu and I think he was master of a grain market in the Street of the Stone Bridge."

Before she finished the words Wang Lung struck his hands together in delight and he said,

"Now then, that is where I sell my grain, and it is a propitious thing."

"That is true," Lotus said gaily, "and Cuckoo shall go and ask Liu, and she shall have the matchmaker's fee if it is well done."

But the matter was not to be decided so quickly as this, and Wang Lung said,

"No, for I have decided nothing. I must think of the matter for some days."

And so he might have waited for many days, thinking, had not one early morning the lad come home with his face hot and red with wine drinking. Wang Lung heard him stumbling in the court and he ran out to see who it was, and the lad was sick and vomited, and he fell and lay on the ground in his vomit like a dog. Wang Lung was frightened and he called for O-lan, and together they lifted the lad and laid him upon the bed in O-lan's room. The lad was asleep and heavy as one dead, and O-lan brought vinegar in warm water and washed him gently, as they used to wash the young lords in the great house when they drank too heavily.

Then seeing the delicate childish face and the drunken sleep that even the washing would not awaken, Wang Lung went into the room where the two boys slept together. The younger was yawning and tying his books in a cloth to carry to school, and Wang Lung said to him,

"Where was your elder brother gone?" And when the boy would not answer, he took him by the neck and shook him and cried, "Now tell me all, you small dog!"

The boy was frightened at this, and he broke out sobbing and said between his sobs,

"He has been away to the town three nights now. He goes with the son of your uncle, our cousin."

Then Wang Lung flung the boy aside and he strode forth and he said to Lotus, "Let it be as we have said. Let Cuckoo go to the grain merchant and arrange the marriage. Let the dowry be good but not too great if the girl is suitable."

When he had said this he went in his anger to his uncle's room, and shouted,

"Now I have harbored an ungrateful nest of snakes and they have bitten me!"

His uncle was sitting eating his breakfast, and he looked up at these words and he said lazily,

"How now?"

Then Wang Lung told him, half choking, what had happened, and his uncle only laughed.

When Wang Lung heard this laughter he remembered in one crowded space of time all that he had endured because of his uncle; how his uncle had tried to force him to sell his land, how they lived here, these three, eating and drinking and idle, and how his uncle's wife ate of the expensive foods Cuckoo bought for Lotus,

and now how his uncle's son had spoiled his own lad, and he bit
his tongue between his teeth and he said,

"Now out of my house, you and yours. I will burn the house
down rather than have it shelter you, who have no gratitude even
in your idleness!"

But his uncle sat where he was and ate on, now from this bowl
and now from that, and then he turned and said,

"Drive me out if you dare."

And his uncle opened his coat.

Then Wang Lung stood still and rigid, for he saw against its
lining a false beard of red hair and a length of red cloth, and the
anger went out of him like water and he shook because there was
no strength left in him.

Now these things, the red beard and the red length of cloth,
were sign and symbol of a band of robbers who marauded toward
the northwest, and many houses had they burned and women they
had carried away, and good farmers they had bound with ropes
to the threshold of their own houses and men found them there

next day, raving mad if they lived and burned and crisp as roasted meat if they were dead. And Wang Lung stared and his eyes hung out of his head, and he turned and went away without a word. And as he went he heard his uncle's whispered laughter as he stooped again over his rice bowl.

Now WANG LUNG found himself in such a coil as he had never dreamed of. His uncle came and went as before, grinning a little under the sparse and scattered hairs of his gray beard, and Wang Lung dared not speak anything except courteous words. It was true that during all these years of prosperity, never had bandits come to his house, although he had many times been afraid and had barred the doors stoutly at night. And now suddenly he saw why he had been safe and why he would be safe so long as he fed the three of his uncle's house. When he thought of this he sweated heavy cold sweat, and he dared to tell no one what his uncle hid in his bosom.

Then as if this were not enough Cuckoo came back with news that although the affair of the betrothal had gone well, the merchant Liu was not willing that anything should take place now, for the maid was too young for marriage, being but fourteen years old, and it must wait for another three years.

Wang Lung was dismayed at three more years of this lad's anger and idleness and mooning eyes. The next morning he tore off his long robes, and as was his wont when the affairs of his house became too deep for him, he took a hoe and he went out to his fields. And he went out to his land day after day for many days.

Then the good land did again its healing work and the warm winds of summer wrapped him about with peace. And as if to cure him of his ceaseless thought of his own troubles, there came out of the south one day a small slight cloud. Except it did not come hither and thither as clouds blown by the wind do, but it stood steady until it spread fanwise up into the air.

The men of the village watched it and talked of it, for they feared that locusts had come out of the south to devour what was planted in the fields. Wang Lung stood there also, and he watched, and at last a wind blew something to their feet, and one stooped and picked it up and it was a dead locust, dead and lighter than the living hosts behind.

Then Wang Lung forgot everything that troubled him. Women and sons and uncle, he forgot them all, and he rushed among the frightened villagers, and he shouted at them,

"Now for our land we will fight these enemies from the skies!"

But there were some who shook their heads and said,

"No, Heaven has ordained that this year we shall starve, and why should we waste ourselves in struggle against it?"

And women went weeping to the town to buy incense to thrust before the earth gods in the little temple, and some went to the big temple in the town, where the gods of Heaven were, and thus Earth and Heaven were worshiped.

But still the locusts spread up into the air and on over the land.

Then Wang Lung called his own laborers and Ching stood ready beside him, and there were others of the younger farmers, and with their own hands these set fire to certain fields and they burned the good wheat and they dug wide moats and ran water into them from the wells, and they worked without sleeping. O-lan and the women brought them food, and the men ate standing and in the field.

Then the sky grew black and the air was filled with the deep still roar of many wings, and upon the land the locusts fell, flying over this field and leaving it whole, and falling upon that field, and eating it as bare as winter. And men sighed and said, "So Heaven wills," but Wang Lung was furious and he beat the locusts and trampled on them and his men flailed them with flails and the locusts fell into the fires that were kindled and they floated dead upon the waters of the moats that were dug. And many millions of them died, but to those that were left it was nothing.

Nevertheless, for all his fighting Wang Lung had this as his reward: the best of his fields were spared and when the cloud moved on and they could rest themselves, there was still wheat that he could reap and his young rice beds were spared and he was content. Then many of the people ate the roasted bodies of the locusts, but Wang Lung himself would not eat them, for to him

they were a filthy thing because of what they had done to his land.

Nevertheless, the locusts did this for him. For seven days he thought of nothing but his land, and he was healed of his troubles and his fears, and he said to himself calmly,

"Well, every man has his troubles and I must make shift to live with mine as I can, and my uncle is older than I and he will die, and three years must pass as they can with my son."

And he reaped his wheat and the rains came and the young green rice was set into the flooded fields and again it was summer.

ONE DAY AFTER WANG LUNG had said to himself that peace was in his house, his eldest son came to him as he returned from the land, and said, "Father, if I am to be a scholar, there is no more that that old head in the town can teach me."

Wang Lung had dipped from the caldron in the kitchen a basin of boiling water and into this he dipped a towel and wrung it and holding it steaming against his face he said,

"Well, and how now?"

The lad hesitated and then he went on,

"I would like to go to the south to the city and enter a great school where I can learn what is to be learned."

Wang Lung rubbed the towel about his eyes and he answered his son sharply, for his body ached with his labor in the fields,

"What nonsense is this? You have learning enough for these parts." And he dipped the cloth in again and wrung it.

But the young man stood there and he muttered something and Wang Lung was angry for he could not hear what it was, and he bawled at his son,

"Speak out what you have to say!"

Then the young man flared at his father's voice and he said,

"Well, and I will, then, for go south I will, and I will not stay in this stupid house and be watched like a child, and in this little town which is no better than a village!"

Wang Lung looked at his son, and his son stood there in a pale, long robe of silver-gray linen, thin and cool for the summer's heat, and his skin was smooth and golden and his hands under his long sleeves were soft and fine as a woman's. Then Wang Lung looked at himself and he was thick and stained with earth and he wore only trousers of blue cotton cloth, and one would have said he was his son's servant rather than his father. And this thought made him scornful, and he was brutal and he shouted out,

"Now then, get you into the fields and rub a little good earth on yourself lest men take you for a woman!"

And Wang Lung forgot that he had ever had pride in his son's cleverness, and he flung himself out, stamping his bare feet as he walked and spitting upon the floor coarsely. And the lad stood and looked at him with hatred, but Wang Lung would not turn back to see what the lad did.

Then for many days there was nothing said and the lad seemed suddenly content again, but he would not go to school anymore; he read in his own room. This Wang Lung allowed him, and

Wang Lung was content and he thought to himself, "It was a whim of his youth and he does not know what he wants and there are only three years—it may be a little extra silver will make it two."

Then Wang Lung forgot his son, for the harvests, except what the locusts had consumed, were fair enough. But one night when he sat late and alone, reckoning on his fingers what he could sell of his corn and of his rice, O-lan came softly into the room. This one with the passing of the years had grown gaunt and the rocklike bones of her face stood forth and her eyes were sunken. If one asked her how she did she said no more than this,

"There is a fire in my vitals."

Her belly was as great as though with child these three years, only there was no birth. But Wang Lung saw her only as he saw his chair or a tree in the court, never even so keenly as he might see one of the oxen drooping its head or a pig that would not eat. And she did her work alone and spoke no more than she could escape speaking. She worked at her cooking and at the washing at the pool even in the winter when the water was stiff with ice. But Wang Lung never thought to say,

"Well, and why do you not hire a servant?"

On this evening, then, when he sat alone with only the red candles in the pewter stands alight, she stood before him and looked this way and that, and at last she said in a harsh whisper,

"When you are away, the eldest son goes too often into the inner court."

Now Wang Lung could not at first grasp what she said and he leaned forward with his mouth agape.

"You dream!" he said finally.

She shook her head at this, and, the difficult speech halting on her lips, she said further,

"My lord, come home unexpectedly." And again, after a silence, "It is better to send him away, even to the south." And then as she had come she went, silent, and left him sitting there agape.

Well, and this woman, she was jealous, he said to himself. Well, and he would not trouble about this, and he rose, laughing at the small thoughts of women.

But when he went in that night to Lotus she was petulant and she pushed him away. Then the words of O-lan stood out sharply and he flung himself out of the room and he walked among the bamboos beside the house wall. And at last he watched the dawn come ruddy over his land, and he went in and he ate, and then he went out to oversee his men as his custom was in times of harvest, and he shouted loudly, so that anyone in his house might hear,

"Now I am going to the piece by the moat and I shall not be back early," and he set his face to the town.

But when he had gone halfway he turned. He strode back to his house and he went in and stood at the curtain that hung in the door to the inner court. And listening, he heard the murmuring of a man's voice, and it was the voice of his own son.

Now the anger that arose in Wang Lung's heart was an anger he had not known in all his life before, although as things had prospered with him and as men came to call him rich, he had lost his early timidity of a country fellow, and had grown full of small sudden angers, and he was proud even in the town. But this anger now was the anger of one man against another who steals away the loved woman, and when Wang Lung remembered that the other man was his own son, he was filled with a vomiting sickness.

He set his teeth then, and he went out and chose a slim, supple bamboo from the grove and he stripped off the branches. Then he went in softly, and suddenly he tore aside the curtain and there was his son, standing in the court, and looking down at Lotus, who sat on a small stool at the edge of the pool. At that Wang Lung leaped forward and he fell on his son, lashing him. When Lotus screamed and dragged at his arm he shook her off, and beat her also until she fled and he beat the young man until he stooped cowering to the ground, and covered his torn face in his hands.

Then Wang Lung paused, and he was weak as though with an illness. He threw down his bamboo and he whispered to the boy, panting, "Now get you to your room, put your things in the box and tomorrow go south to what you will and do not come home until I send for you."

And the boy rose without a word and left. Then wearily he

himself went out. O-lan was sitting sewing some garment, and when he passed she said nothing, and if she had heard the beating and the screaming, she made no sign of it. And he went on and out to his fields, spent as with the labor of a whole day.

XIII

When the eldest son was gone Wang Lung said to himself that it was a good thing, and now he could look to his other children, for what with his troubles, he hardly knew what he had for children after this eldest son.

Now the second son of Wang Lung was as unlike the eldest as two sons in a house may be. Where the eldest was big-boned and ruddy-faced and like his mother, this second one was short and slight and yellow-skinned, and there was that in him which reminded Wang Lung of his own father, a crafty, sharp, humorous eye, and a turn for malice if the moment came for it. And Wang Lung said, "Well, and this boy will make a good merchant and I will see if he can be apprenticed to Liu in the grain market. It will be a convenient thing to have a son there where I sell my harvests and he can watch the scales and tip the weight a little in my favor. And the youngest boy I will keep for the land."

Therefore Wang Lung washed himself and put on his silk coat and he set out across the fields. He went first to the Street of Bridges, and there before a gate which bore the name of Liu he stopped. Not that he knew the word himself, but he asked one who passed. It was a respectable gate built plainly of wood, and Wang Lung struck it with the palm of his hand.

Immediately it opened and a woman servant stood there, asking who he was, and when he answered his name, she led him into the first court and bade him seat himself. Then she went out to call her master. Wang Lung examined the curtains, and the table, and he was pleased, for there was evidence of good living but not of extreme wealth. He did not want a rich daughter-in-law lest she be haughty and cry for this and that.

Suddenly there was a heavy step and a stout elderly man entered and Wang Lung rose and they both bowed, looking secretly at each other, each respecting the other for what he was, a man of worth and prosperity. Then they seated themselves and drank of the hot wine which the servant woman poured out for them, and talked slowly of crops and prices. And at last Wang Lung said,

"Well, and I have come for a thing and if it is not your wish, let us talk of other things. But if you have need for a servant in your market, there is my second son, and a sharp one he is."

Then the merchant said with great good humor, "And so I have such need of a sharp young man, if he reads and writes."

And Wang Lung answered proudly, "My sons are both good scholars and they can each tell when a letter is wrongly written."

"That is well," said Liu. "Let him come, and his wages are his food until he learns the business, and then if he do well, he may have a piece of silver at the end of every moon, and at the end of three years three pieces, and after that he is no longer apprentice, but he may rise as he is able in the business. And besides this wage, there is whatever fee he may extract from this buyer and that seller, and this I say nothing about if he is able to get it."

Wang Lung rose then, well pleased, and he laughed and said,

"Now we are friends, and have you no son for my second daughter?"

Then the merchant laughed richly, for he was fat and well fed, and he said,

"I have a second son of ten whom I have not betrothed yet. How old is the girl?"

Wang Lung laughed again and answered,

"She is ten on her next birthday and she is a pretty flower."

Then Wang Lung said no more, for it was not a thing that could be discussed face to face beyond this. But after he had bowed and gone away well pleased, he said to himself, "The thing may be done," and he looked at his young daughter when he came home and she was a pretty child and she moved about with small graceful steps.

But when Wang Lung looked at her thus closely he saw the

marks of tears on her cheeks, and her face was a shade too pale for her years, and he drew her to him by her little hand and he said,

"Now why have you wept?"

Then she hung her head and toyed with a button on her coat and said, shy and half murmuring,

"Because my mother binds a cloth about my feet more tightly every day and I cannot sleep at night."

"I have not heard you weep," he said, wondering.

"No," she said simply, "my mother said I was not to weep aloud because you are too kind and you might say to leave me as I am, and then my husband would not love me even as you do not love her."

This she said as simply as a child recites a tale, and Wang Lung was stabbed at hearing it, because with all her dimness O-lan had seen the truth in him.

And in the near days after this he sent his second son away into the town and he signed the papers for the second girl's betrothal. He would have been content except that now, whether he would or not, he fell to thinking of his life and of how O-lan had been the first woman he had known and how she had been a faithful servant beside him. He saw now that she had grown thin and her skin was sere and yellow. She moved slowly and more slowly about, and he remembered, now that he thought of it, that sometimes he heard her groaning when she stooped to feed the oven, and only when he asked, "Well, and what is it?" did she cease suddenly. So, looking at her, he was stricken with remorse, although he did not know why, and he argued with himself,

"Well, and it is not my fault if I have not loved her as one loves a concubine, since men do not. I have not beat her and I have given her silver when she asked for it."

But still he could not forget what the child had said, and he kept looking at her as she brought in his food or as she moved about. And when she stooped to sweep the floor one day, he saw her face turn gray with some inner pain, and she opened her lips and panted softly, and she put her hand to her belly. He asked her sharply,

"What is it?"

But she averted her face and answered meekly,

"It is only the old pain in my vitals."

Then he stared at her and he said to the younger girl,

"Take the broom. Your mother is ill." And to O-lan he said more kindly than he had spoken to her in many years, "Go in and lie on your bed, and I will bid the girl bring you hot water."

She obeyed him slowly and without answer, and she went into her room and he heard her dragging about it, and at last she lay down and moaned softly. Then he sat listening until he could not bear it, and he rose and went into the town to a doctor's shop.

The doctor sat idle over a pot of tea. He was an old man with a long gray beard and brass spectacles large as an owl's eyes over his nose. When Wang Lung told him what his wife's signs were, he pursed his lips and said,

"I will come."

When they came to O-lan's bed she had fallen into a light sleep, and the sweat stood like dew on her forehead, and the old doctor shook his head to see it. He put forth a hand as dried and yellowed as an ape's and he felt for her pulse, and then he shook his head again gravely, saying,

"The spleen is enlarged and the liver diseased. There is a rock as large as a man's head in the womb; the stomach is disintegrated. It is a difficult case. For ten pieces of silver I will give you a prescription of herbs and a tiger's heart. But if you wish complete recovery guaranteed, then five hundred pieces of silver."

Now when Wang Lung heard this all his old remorse smote him and he answered fiercely,

"I will have no death in my house and I can pay the silver."

The old doctor's eyes shone greedily, but he knew the penalty of the law if the woman died, and so he said, although with regret,

"Nay, and as I look at the color of the whites of her eyes, I see I was mistaken. Five thousand pieces of silver must I have if I guarantee full recovery."

Then Wang Lung looked at the doctor in silence and in sad understanding; it was simply that the doctor said, "The woman will die."

He went out with the doctor, therefore, and he paid him the ten pieces of silver, and when he was gone Wang Lung went into the dark kitchen where O-lan had lived her life for the most part, and he turned his face to the blackened wall, and he wept.

BUT THERE WAS no sudden dying of life in O-lan's body. She was scarcely past the middle of her span of years, and her life would not easily pass from her body. All through the long months of winter she lay dying and upon her bed, and for the first time Wang Lung and his children knew what she had been in the house, and how she made comfort for them all and they had not known it.

It seemed now that none knew how to light the grass in the oven, and none knew how to turn a fish in the caldron without breaking it, and none knew whether sesame oil or bean were right for frying this vegetable or that. Dropped food lay under the table and none swept it unless Wang Lung grew impatient and called in a dog from the court to lick it up or shouted at the younger girl to scrape it up and throw it out.

The youngest lad did this and that to fill his mother's place with his grandfather, who was helpless as a little child now and could not understand why O-lan no longer came to bring him hot water and to help him, and he was peevish because he called her and she did not come, and he threw his bowl of tea on the ground like a willful child.

Only the poor fool knew nothing. Yet one had to think of her to bring her in at night and to feed her and to set her in the sun and to lead her in if it rained. And once they left her outside through a whole night, and the next morning the poor wretch was shivering and crying in the dawn, and Wang Lung cursed his son and daughter that they had forgotten their sister. Then he saw that they were but children trying to take their mother's place, and he forbore, and after that he saw to the poor fool himself night and morning.

Wang Lung turned over the work to Ching, and Ching labored faithfully, and night and morning he came and he asked how O-lan did. At last Wang Lung could not bear it because he could only say, "Today she drank a little soup," or "Today she ate a little thin gruel of rice." So he commanded Ching to ask no more but to do the work and it would be enough.

All during the cold dark winter Wang Lung sat beside O-lan's bed, and if she were cold he lit an earthen pot of charcoal and set it beside her bed. At last one day he burst forth,

"I cannot bear this! I would sell my land if it could heal you."

She smiled at this and said in gasps, whispering,

"No, and I would not—let you. For I must die—sometime anyway. But the land is there after me."

But he would not talk of her death and he rose and went out when she spoke of it.

Nevertheless because he knew she must die and it was his duty, he went one day into the town and chose a good black coffin made from heavy and hard wood. Then the carpenter said cunningly,

"The price is a third off for two. Why do you not buy one for yourself and know you are provided?"

"No, for my sons can do it for me," answered Wang Lung, and then he thought of his own father and he said, "I will take the two."

And Wang Lung told O-lan what he had done, and she was pleased that he had provided well for her death.

Thus he sat by her, and they did not talk much for she was faint, and besides there had never been talk between them. Often she forgot where she was and she murmured of her childhood, and for the first time Wang Lung saw into her heart.

"I will bring the meats to the door only—and well I know I am ugly and cannot appear before the great lord—" And again she said, panting, "Do not beat me—I will never eat of the dish again—" And she said over and over, "My father—my mother—my father—my mother—" and again and again, "Well I know I am ugly and cannot be loved—"

When she said this Wang Lung could not bear it and he took her hand and he soothed it, a big hard hand, stiff as though it were dead already. And he wondered and grieved at himself most of all because what she said was true, and even when he took her hand, he was ashamed because he could feel no tenderness, no melting of the heart such as Lotus could win from him with a pout of her lips.

But because of this, he was more kind to her and he bought her special food and delicate soups. Moreover, when he went in to Lotus to distract his mind from its despair, he could not forget O-lan, and even as he held Lotus, he loosed her, because of O-lan.

THERE WERE TIMES when O-lan woke to herself and to what was about her, and once she said to him,

"After I am dead that slave nor her mistress, neither is to come into my room or touch my things, and if they do, I will send my spirit back for a curse." Then she fell into her fitful sleep, and her head dropped upon the pillow.

But one day before the new year, she was suddenly better, as a candle flickers brightly at its end, and she was herself as she had not been and she sat up in bed and twisted her hair for herself, and she asked for tea to drink, and when Wang Lung came she said,

"There is a thing before I can die."

To this he replied angrily,

"You cannot speak of dying and please me!"

She smiled slowly then, the same slow smile that ended before it reached her eyes, and she answered,

"Die I must, for I feel it in my vitals waiting, but I will not die before my eldest son comes home and weds, so that I may die easily, knowing your grandson is stirred into life and a great-grandson for the old one."

Now Wang Lung was cheered at the strength in her voice, and he would not cross her, although he would have liked more time for a great wedding for his eldest son. He only said heartily to her therefore,

"Well, and we will do this thing, and today I will send a man south and he shall search for my son, and bring him home to be wed. And then you must promise me that you will gather your strength again and grow well, for the house is like a cave for beasts without you."

This he said to please her and it pleased her, although she did not speak again, but lay back and closed her eyes, smiling a little.

And as Wang Lung said, so he did, and he bade Cuckoo provide a feast and call in cooks from the town, and he poured silver into her hands and he said,

"Do as it would have been done in the great house."

Then he went into the village and into the town and invited everyone whom he knew. And he said to his uncle,

"Ask whom you will for my son's marriage, any of your friends or any of your son's friends."

This he said because he remembered always who his uncle was.

On the night of the day before his marriage, Wang Lung's eldest son came home, and Wang Lung forgot that the young man had troubled him. For two years had passed since he had seen this son, and here he was and no longer a lad, but a tall man and a goodly one, with a great square body and short black hair, shining and oiled. And he wore a long dark-red gown of satin such as one finds in the shops of the south, and a short black velvet jacket without sleeves, and Wang Lung's heart burst with pride.

Then the young man sat beside his mother's bed and the tears stood in his eyes to see her thus, but he would not say anything except cheerful things such as, "You look twice as well as they said." But O-lan said simply,

"I will see you wed and then I must die."

Now the maid who was to be wed must not of course be seen by the young man, so when her mother brought her from the town Lotus took her into the inner court to prepare her for marriage, and none could do this better than Lotus and Cuckoo. And on the morning of her wedding day they washed her and dressed her in garments she had brought from her home: white-flowered silk, a light coat of sheep's wool, and then the red satin garments of marriage. And they rubbed lime upon her forehead and pulled out the hairs of her virginity, the fringe over her brow, and they made her forehead high and smooth and square for her new estate. Then they painted her with powder and with red paint, and with a brush they drew out in two long slender lines her eyebrows, and they set upon her head the bride's crown and the beaded veil.

To everything the maid was acquiescent, but reluctant and shy as was proper for her.

Then Wang Lung and the guests waited in the middle room and the maid came in supported by her own slave and by the wife of Wang Lung's uncle, and she came in modestly and correctly with her head bowed, and she walked as though she were unwilling to wed and must be supported to it. This showed her great modesty and Wang Lung was pleased.

After this Wang Lung's eldest son came in dressed in his red robe and his black jacket. Behind him came his two brothers, and Wang Lung, seeing them, was fit to burst with pride at this procession of his goodly sons, who were to continue after him the life of his body. Then the old man, who had not understood at all what was happening, now suddenly understood and cackled out with cracked laughter and he said over and over in his piping old voice,

"There is a marriage and a marriage is children again and grand-children!"

And he laughed so heartily that the guests all laughed to see his mirth and Wang Lung thought to himself that if only O-lan had been up from her bed it would have been a merry day.

All this time Wang Lung looked sharply at his son to see if he glanced at the maid, and the young man did glance secretly from the corner of his eyes, but it was enough, for he grew pleased and merry in his ways and Wang said proudly to himself,

"Well, and I have chosen one he likes for him."

Then the young man and the maid together bowed to the old man and to Wang Lung, and then they went into the room where O-lan lay, and she had caused herself to be dressed in her good black coat and she was sitting up. And the two young persons bowed to her and she patted the bed and said,

"Sit here and drink the wine and eat the rice of your marriage, for I would see it all."

The two sat down side by side, shy of each other and in silence, and the wife of Wang Lung's uncle came in fat and important with the occasion, bearing two bowls of hot wine, and the two drank separately, and then mingled the wine of the two bowls and drank again, and they ate rice and mingled the rice. This signified that their life was now one, and thus they were wed. Then they bowed again to O-lan and to Wang Lung and then they went out and together they bowed to the assembled guests.

Then the feasting began and the rooms and the courts were filled with the smell of cooking and with the sound of laughter, for the guests came from far and wide, those whom Wang Lung had invited and with them many whom Wang Lung had never seen, since it was known he was a rich man and food would never be missed in his house at such a time.

O-lan would have all the doors open so that she could hear the laughter and could smell the food, and she said again and again to Wang Lung, who came in often to see how she did,

"And has everyone wine? And is the sweet rice dish in the middle of the feast very hot and have they put full measure of lard and sugar into it and the eight fruits?"

He assured her that everything was as she wished.

Then it was over and the guests were gone and night came. And with the silence over the house and with the ebbing of merriment strength passed from O-lan and she grew weary and she seemed to fall into a fitful sleep, and when she spoke it was as though she did not know where she was, for she said, muttering and turning her head this way and that,

"Well, and if I am ugly, still I have borne a son." And again she said, "How can that one care for him as I do?"

Then Wang Lung sat beside her while she slept, and he looked at her. And as he looked she opened her eyes and it seemed there was some strange mist over them, for she stared at him full, as though she wondered who he was. Suddenly her head dropped off the round pillow where it lay, and she shuddered and was dead.

ONCE SHE LAY DEAD it seemed to Wang Lung that he could not bear to be near her. But to comfort himself he busied himself, calling men to seal the coffin according to custom, and he went and found a geomancer and asked him for a lucky day for burials. He found a good day three months hence. Then he caused mourning to be made for himself and for his children, and their shoes were made of coarse white cloth, which is the color of mourning, and about their ankles they bound bands of white cloth, and the women in the house bound their hair with white cord.

After this Wang Lung could not bear to sleep in the room where O-lan had died and he took his possessions and moved altogether into the inner court where Lotus lived, and he said to his eldest son, "Go with your wife into that room where your mother lived and died, and beget there your own sons."

So the two moved into it and were content.

Then as though death could not easily leave the house where it had come once, the old man, Wang Lung's father, who had been distraught ever since he saw them putting the stiff dead body of O-lan into the coffin, lay down on his bed one night for sleeping, and when the second daughter came in the morning to bring him his tea, there he lay on his bed, his scattered old beard thrust up into the air, and his head thrown back in death.

She cried out at the sight and ran to her father, and Wang Lung came in and found the old man so; his light, stiff old body was dry and cold and thin as a gnarled pine tree. Then Wang Lung washed the old man himself and he laid him gently in the coffin he had bought for him and he had it sealed and he said,

"On the same day we will bury these two dead from our house and I will take a good piece of my hill land and we will bury them there together and when I die I will be laid there also."

So he did what he said he would do. And on the day appointed by the geomancer in the full of the spring Wang Lung called priests from the Taoist temple and they came dressed in their yellow robes, and he called priests from the Buddhist temples and they came in their long gray robes, and these priests beat drums and chanted the whole night through for the two who were dead. And whenever they stopped their chanting Wang Lung poured silver into their hands and they took breath again and chanted and did not cease until dawn rose.

Now Wang Lung had chosen a good place in his fields under a date tree upon a hill to set the graves, and Ching had had the

graves dug and a wall of earth made about the graves. This land Wang Lung did not begrudge, even though it was high land and good for wheat, because it was a sign of the establishment of his family. Dead and alive they would rest upon their own land.

Then after the priests had finished the night of chanting, Wang Lung stood beside the two graves and watched the burial. His grief was hard and dry, and he would not cry out loud as others did, because it seemed to him that there was nothing to be done more than he had done. But when the graves were covered over, he turned away silently and walked home alone. And out of his heaviness there stood out strangely but one clear thought and it was a pain to him: he wished he had not taken the two pearls from O-lan, and he would never bear to see Lotus put them in her ears again. And he said to himself,

"There in that land of mine is buried the first good half of my life and more. It is as though half of me were buried there."

And suddenly he wept a little, and he dried his eyes with the back of his hand, as a child does.

XIV

DURING ALL THIS TIME did Wang Lung know that if it had not been for his uncle's power he would have been robbed and sacked for his money and for the women in his house. So his uncle and his uncle's son and his uncle's wife were like guests in his house and they drank tea before others and dipped first with their chopsticks into the bowls at mealtime. And these three saw that Wang Lung was afraid of them and they grew haughty and demanded this and that and complained of what they ate and drank.

Now Wang Lung's eldest son had been engrossed in his marriage and he scarcely saw what happened except that he guarded his wife jealously from the gaze of his cousin so that now these two were no longer friends but enemies. But when he saw these three doing as they would with his father he grew angry, for he was of a quick temper, and he said,

"If you care more for these three tigers than you do for your son and his wife, it is a strange thing and we had better set up our house elsewhere."

Wang Lung told him plainly then what he had told no one,

"I hate these three worse than my life. But your uncle is lord of a horde of wild robbers, and if I coddle him we are safe."

Now when the eldest son heard this he stared until his eyes hung out of his head, and the two of them fell silent, each thinking heavily what to do. And Wang Lung spoke aloud at last, musing,

"If there were a way that we could keep them here but make them harmless and undesiring what a thing it would be."

Then the young man struck his two hands together and cried out,

"Well, and you have told me! Let us buy them opium to enjoy, and let them have their will of it as rich people do."

But Wang Lung, since he had not thought of the thing first himself, was doubtful.

"Opium is as dear as jade," he said.

"It is dearer than jade to have them at us like this," the young man argued, "and to endure besides their haughtiness and the young man peeping at my wife."

So Wang Lung went the next day into the town, to a tobacco shop. He went in to buy himself a little shredded tobacco to put in his water pipe in the evenings, and as the clerk had it on the scales, he said half unwillingly to the man,

"And how much is your opium if you have it?"

And the clerk said,

"It is not lawful in these days to sell it over the counter, but if you wish to buy it and have the silver, it is weighed out in the room behind this, an ounce for a silver piece."

Then Wang Lung would not think further what he did, but he said quickly,

"I will take six ounces of it."

Then one day Wang Lung said to his uncle,

"Since you are my father's brother, here is a little better tobacco for you."

And he opened the jar of opium and Wang Lung's uncle smelled it, and he laughed and was pleased and he said,

"Well now, I have smoked it a little but not often before this, for it is too dear, but I like it well enough."

And Wang Lung answered him, pretending to be careless,

"It is only a little I bought once for my father when he could not sleep at night and I found it today unused and I thought, 'There is my father's brother, and why should he not have it before me, who am younger and do not need it yet?'"

Then Wang Lung's uncle took it greedily, for it was sweet to smell and a thing that only rich men used, and he smoked the opium, lying all day upon his bed. And Wang Lung saw to it that there were pipes bought and left here and there and he pretended to smoke himself, but he only took a pipe to his room and left it there cold. His sons and Lotus he would not allow to touch the opium, saying as his excuse that it was too dear, but he urged it upon his uncle and upon his uncle's wife and son, and the courts were filled with the sweetish smell of the smoke, and the silver for it Wang Lung did not begrudge because it bought him peace.

NOW AS THE WINTER WORE AWAY it happened one day that his eldest son followed him and said to him proudly,

"There will soon be another mouth in the house."

Then Wang Lung, when he heard this, turned himself about and he laughed and he rubbed his hands together and said,

"Here is a good day indeed!"

And he laughed again, and went to find Ching and tell him to go to the town to buy fish and good food and he sent it in to his son's wife and said,

"Eat, make strong the body of my grandson."

All during the spring Wang Lung had this knowledge for his comfort. And thinking constantly of the child to come and of others to come from his sons when they were all wed, he bought six slaves, two about twelve years of age with big feet and strong bodies, and three younger to wait upon them all, and one, a small, delicate maid of seven years, to wait on the person of Lotus, for Cuckoo grew old.

And summer came and the land was to be planted, and he walked hither and thither and discussed with Ching the quality of each piece of soil and what change there should be of crops for the fertility of the land. And when everything was planned Wang Lung went back to his house well content and he said to his own heart,

"I am no longer young and it is not necessary for me to work anymore with my hands since I have men on my land and my sons and peace in my house."

Yet although he had given his son a wife and although he had bought slaves to serve them all, and although his uncle and his uncle's wife were given enough opium for their pleasure all day, still his uncle's son did not yield to opium easily as the two old ones did, and there was yet no peace.

For when Wang Lung entered from the fields, his eldest son drew his father aside and he said,

"I will not endure that fellow my cousin in the house anymore with his peepings and his lounging about with his eyes on the slaves."

Wang Lung had come in from the fields in high humor, and he answered, angry at this fresh trouble,

"Well, and you are a foolish child to be forever thinking of this. You have grown too fond of your wife; it is not seemly for a man to love his wife with a foolish love, as though she were a harlot."

Then the young man was stung with this rebuke, for more than anything he feared any who accused him of behavior that was not correct, and he answered quickly,

"It is not for my wife. It is because it is unseemly in my father's house. I wish that we could go into the town and live. It is not meet that we go on living in the country like hinds. We could go and we could leave my uncle and his wife and my cousin here and we could live safely in the town behind the gates."

Wang Lung laughed bitterly and shortly, and he threw the desire of the young man aside for something worthless.

"This is my house," he said stoutly, "and you may live in it or not. My house and my land it is, and if it were not for the land you could not walk about in your dainty robes."

And Wang Lung tramped about loudly and spat upon the floor and acted as a farmer may, although one side of his heart triumphed in his son's fineness.

But the eldest son was not ready to give over. He followed his father saying,

"Well, and there is the old great house of the Hwangs. The front part of it is rented out and is filled with this and that of common people. But the inner courts are locked and we could rent them and live there peacefully." And then he forced the tears to come into his eyes and he did not wipe them away and he said again, "Well, and I try to be a good son and I do not gamble and smoke opium and I am content with the woman you have given me and I ask a little of you and it is all."

Now whether the tears would have alone moved Wang Lung he did not know, but he was moved by the words of his son when he said "the great house of the Hwangs."

Never had Wang Lung forgotten that once he had gone crawling into that great house and stood ashamed in the presence of those who lived there so that he was frightened of even the gateman, and this had remained a memory of shame to him all his life and he hated it. So when his son said, "We could live in the great house," the thought leaped into his mind as though he saw it actually before his eyes, "I could sit on that seat where that old one sat and so call another into my presence." And he mused and he said to himself again, "This I could do if I wished."

Therefore, although he did not answer his son to say that he would go, yet thereafter he thought about it. And one day when he went into the town to see his second son at the grain market he asked him,

"Well, my second son, what say you of the thing your elder brother desires, that we move into the town to the great house if we can rent part of it?"

The second son was grown a young man by now and he had grown smooth and neat although still small of stature and with crafty eyes, and he answered smoothly, "It is an excellent thing and it would suit me well, for then I could wed and have my wife there also and we would all be under one roof as a great family is."

Wang Lung said in some shame, for he knew he had not done well by his second son, "I have said to myself this long time that you should be wed, but what with this thing and that I have not had time—but now the thing shall be done."

And he cast about secretly in his mind where he should find a maid. The second son said then,

"Well, and wed I will then, for it is right for a man to have sons. But do not get me a wife from a house in town, such as my brother has, for she will talk forever of what was in her father's house and make me spend money."

Wang Lung heard this with astonishment, for he had not known that his daughter-in-law was thus, seeing only that she was a woman careful to be correct in her behavior and fair enough in her looks. But it seemed to him wise talk and he rejoiced that his son was sharp and clever for the saving of money. This lad he had, indeed, scarcely known at all, for he grew up weak beside the vigor of the elder brother, and except for his piping tales he was

not a youth to whom one would pay great heed. And he said,
"What sort of a maid would you have, then?"

Then the young man answered as smoothly and steadily as if he
had had the thing planned,

"I desire a maid from a village, of good landed family and without poor relatives, neither plain nor fair to look upon, and a good
cook, so that even though there are servants in the kitchen she
may watch them. And she must be such an one that if she buys
cloth the garment will be well cut so that the scraps of cloth left
over should lie in the palm of her hand."

Now Wang Lung was astonished, for it was not such blood
as this that ran in his own lusty body when he was young, nor
in the body of his eldest son; yet he admired the wisdom of the
young man and he said laughing,

"Well, and I shall seek such a maid and Ching shall look for
her among the villages."

Still laughing, he went away and he went down the street of the
great house and he hesitated between the stone lions and then,
since there was none to stop him, he went in. And in the front
courts the trees were hung with drying clothes and women sat
everywhere gossiping, and children rolled naked and dusty upon
the tiles of the courts and the place reeked with the smell of common people who swarm into the courts of the great when the
great are gone.

Now Wang Lung in the old days would have felt himself one
of these common people and against the great. But now that
he had land and silver, he said to himself that they were filthy and
he picked his way among them with his nose up and breathing
lightly because of the stink they made, as though he himself belonged to the great house.

Still he went on through the courts, although it was for idle
curiosity and not because he had decided anything, and at the
back he found a gate locked and beside it an old woman drowsing,
and he saw that this was the pockmarked wife of the man who had
been gateman. This astonished him, for she whom he had remembered as buxom and middle-aged was now haggard and wrinkled

and white-haired, and thus he saw in a full moment how many and how swift were the years that had passed since he was a young man coming with his firstborn son in his arms, and for the first time in his life Wang Lung felt his age creeping upon him. Then he said somewhat sadly to the old woman,

"Wake and let me into the gate."

And the old woman started up blinking and said,

"I am not to open except to such as may rent the courts."

And Wang Lung said,

"Well, and so I may, if the place please me."

But he did not tell her who he was, only he went in after her and he remembered the way well, for there stood the little room where he had left his basket; here the long verandas supported by the delicate, red-varnished pillars. He followed her into the great hall itself, and there before him was the great carven dais where the old lady had sat, her fragile, tended body wrapped in silvery satin.

And moved by some strange impulse he went forward and he sat down where she had sat and he looked down on the bleary face of the old hag who blinked at him and waited in silence for what he would do. Then some satisfaction he had longed for all his days without knowing it swelled up in his heart and he struck the table with his hand and he said suddenly,

"This house I will have!"

In these days when Wang Lung had decided a thing he could not do it quickly enough. So he told his eldest son to arrange the matter, and he sent for his second son to help with the moving and on a day when they were ready they moved, first Lotus and Cuckoo and their slaves, and then Wang Lung's eldest son and his wife and their slaves.

But Wang himself, when the moment came for leaving the land whereon he was born, could not do it so quickly as he had thought and he said to his sons when they urged him,

"Well then, prepare a court for me and on a day that I wish I will come, and it will be a day before my grandson is born."

And when they urged him yet again, he said, "I will come when the maid is found who is to wed the second son, for it is easier to stay here where Ching is until the matter is completed."

There was left in the house, then, none but the uncle and his wife and son and Ching and the laboring men, besides Wang Lung and his youngest son and the fool. His second daughter was now wed to the son of Liu, and Wang Lung stirred himself to bid Ching find a maid for his second son.

Now Ching grew old and withered and lean as a reed, but there was the strength of an old and faithful dog in him yet, although Wang Lung would no longer let him lift a hoe or follow the plow. Still he was useful for he watched the labor of others and he stood by when the grain was weighed. So when he heard what Wang Lung wished he put on his good blue cotton coat and he went to this village and that and he looked at many maidens and at last he came back and he said,

"Now would I liefer have to choose a wife for myself than for your son. But if it were I and I young, there is a maid three villages away, a buxom, careful maid with no fault except a ready laugh, and her father is glad to be tied to your family by his daughter. And the dowry is good for these times."

It seemed to Wang Lung then that this was good enough and he was relieved and he said,

"Now there is but one more son and I am finished with all this marrying and I am glad I am so near my peace."

And when it was done and the wedding day set, he rested and sat in the sun and slept even as his father had done before him.

Then, as if the gods were kind for the once his uncle's son grew restless and he said to Wang Lung,

"It is said there is a war to the north. I will go and join it for something to do, if you will give me silver to buy more clothes and a foreign fire stick to put over my shoulder."

Then Wang Lung's heart leaped with pleasure but he hid his pleasure artfully as he gave him the silver, and he said to himself,

"If he likes it there is an end to this curse in my house, for there is always a war somewhere in the nation." And again he said to himself, "He may even be killed, if my good fortune holds, for sometimes in wars there are those who die." He was in high good humor, then, although he concealed it, and he comforted his uncle's wife when she wept to hear of her son's going, and he lit her opium pipe for her and he said,

"Doubtless he will rise to be a military official and honor will come to us all through him."

Now Wang Lung, as the hour drew near for the birth of his grandson, stayed more and more in the house in town and he could never have his fill of wonder at this, that here in these courts where the great family of Hwang had once lived now he lived with his sons, and now a child was to be born of a third generation.

And nothing was too good for his money to buy and he bought lengths of satin and of silk for them all for it looked ill to see common cotton robes upon the carved chairs of southern blackwood, and he was pleased when the friends that his eldest son had found in the town came into the courts and proud that they should see all that was. And Wang Lung himself, who once had been well satisfied with good wheaten bread wrapped about a stick of garlic, now tasted winter bamboo and shrimps' roe and shellfish and pigeons' eggs and all those things which rich men use to force their lagging appetites. And Cuckoo, seeing all that had come about, laughed and said,

"It is like the old days when I was in these courts."

So with this idle and luxurious living and rising when he would and sleeping when he would, Wang Lung waited for his grandson. Then one morning he heard the groans of a woman, and his eldest son said,

"The hour is come, but Cuckoo says it will be long, for the woman is narrowly made and it is a hard birth."

So Wang Lung sat and listened to the cries, and for the first time in many years he felt the need of some spirit's aid. He rose and he bought incense and he went to the temple in the town where the goddess of mercy dwells in her gilded alcove and he summoned an idling priest and gave him money and bade him thrust the incense before the goddess saying,

"It is ill for me, a man, to do it, but my first grandson is about to be born and the mother of my son is dead, and there is no woman to thrust in the incense."

Then, as he watched the priest thrust it in the ashes of the urn before the goddess he thought with sudden horror, "And what if it be not a grandson but a girl!" and he called out hastily,

"If it is a grandson I will pay for a new red robe for the goddess, but nothing will I do if it is a girl!"

He went out in agitation because he had not thought of this thing, that it might be not a grandson but a girl. And then having done all he could, he went back to the courts, very spent, and he sat down and he wished for a slave to bring him tea, but though he clapped his hands none came. There was running to and fro, but he dared to stop no one to ask what sort of a child had been born. He sat there dusty and spent and no one spoke to him.

Then at last when it seemed to him it must soon be night, so long he had waited, Lotus came in leaning upon Cuckoo, and she laughed and said loudly,

"Well, and there is a son in the house of your son. And it is fair and sound."

Then Wang Lung laughed also and he rose and he slapped his hands together. And then when Lotus had gone on to her room and he sat again he fell to musing and he thought to himself,

"Well, and I did not fear like this when that other one bore her first, my son." And he sat silent and he remembered how she had gone alone into the small dark room and how alone and silently she had borne him sons, and how she had come then to the fields and worked beside him again. And here was this one who cried like a child with her pains, and who had all the slaves running in the house, and her husband there by her door. And he remembered as one remembers a dream long past how O-lan fed the child richly out of her breast.

Then his son came in smiling and important and he said loudly,

"The man-child is born, my father, and now we must find a woman to nurse him, for I will not have my wife's beauty spoiled with the nursing. None of the women of position in the town do so."

And Wang Lung said sadly, although why he was sad he did not know,

"Well, and let it be so, if she cannot nurse her own child."

When the child was a month old its father gave the birth feast. He had many hundreds of eggs dyed scarlet, and these he gave to every guest, and there was feasting and joy, for the child was a goodly fat boy and he had passed his tenth day and lived.

And when it was over Wang Lung's son said to his father,

"Now that there are the three generations in this house, we should have the tablets of ancestors that great families have, for we are an established family now."

This pleased Wang Lung greatly, and there in the great hall the tablets were set up, his grandfather's name on one and then his father's, and the spaces left for Wang Lung's name and his son's when they should die. And Wang Lung's son bought an incense urn and set it before the tablets.

When this was finished Wang Lung remembered the red robe he had promised the goddess of mercy and so he went to the temple to give the money for it.

And then, on his way back, as if the gods cannot bear to give freely, one came running from the harvest fields to tell him that Ching lay dying suddenly. And although his noon meal stood ready, and although Lotus called loudly to him to wait until after the evening sun, he would not stay. Then Lotus sent a slave after him with an umbrella of oiled paper, but so fast did Wang Lung run that the stout maid had difficulty in holding the umbrella over his head.

Wang Lung went at once to the room where Ching had been laid and he called out loudly,

"Now how did all this come about?"

The room was full of laborers and they answered in confusion,

"He would work himself at the threshing . . ." "We told him not at his age . . ." "There was a laborer who could not hold the flail rightly and Ching would show him. . . ."

Then Wang Lung called out in a terrible voice,

"Bring me this laborer."

And they pushed the man in front before Wang Lung, and he stood there trembling and his bare knees knocking together, a great, ruddy, coarse, country lad, with his teeth sticking out in a shelf over his lower lip and round dull eyes like an ox's eyes. But Wang Lung had no pity on him. He slapped the lad on both his cheeks and he took the umbrella from the slave and he beat the lad, and none dared stop him lest his anger go into his blood and at his age poison him. And the bumpkin stood it humbly, blubbering a little and sucking his teeth.

Then Ching moaned from the bed where he lay and Wang Lung threw down the umbrella and he cried out,

"Now this one will die while I am beating a fool!"

And he sat down beside Ching and took his hand and held it. Ching's face was dark and spotted with his scanty blood, and his half-opened eyes were filmed and his breath came in gusts. Wang Lung leaned down to him and said loudly in his ear,

"Here am I and I will buy you a coffin second to my father's only!"

But Ching's ears were filled with his blood, and if he heard Wang Lung he made no sign, but he only lay there panting and dying and so he died.

When he was dead Wang Lung leaned over him and he wept as he had not wept when his own father died. He hired priests for the funeral and he walked behind wearing white mourning. And if Wang Lung had had his way he would have buried Ching inside the earthen wall. But his sons would not have it and said,

"Shall our mother and grandfather lie with a servant?"

Then Wang Lung, because at his age he would have peace in his house, buried Ching at the entrance to the wall and he said,

"It is meet, for he has ever stood guardian to me against evil." And he directed his sons that when he himself died he should lie nearest to Ching.

Then less than ever did Wang Lung go to see his lands. Now Ching was gone it stabbed him to go alone and his bones ached when he walked over the rough fields. So he rented out all his land that he could and men took it eagerly, for it was known to be good land. But Wang Lung would never talk of selling a foot of any piece, and he would only rent for a year at a time. Thus he felt it all his own and still in his hand.

And he appointed one of the laborers and his wife to live in the country house and to care for his uncle and his uncle's wife, the two old opium dreamers. Then seeing his youngest son's wistful eyes, he said,

"Well, and you may come with me into the town, and I will take my fool with me too, for now that Ching is gone I am not sure that they will be kind to her. And there is no one now to teach you concerning the land, now that Ching is gone."

So Wang Lung took his youngest son and his fool with him and thereafter he came scarcely at all to the house on his land.

XV

Now to Wang Lung it seemed there was nothing left to be desired; he could sit in the sun beside his fool and he could smoke his water pipe and be at peace. And so it might have been if it had not been for that eldest son of his, who came to his father saying,

"We must not think we can be a great family just because we live in these inner courts. It is a shame to ask guests to come through that common swarm with their stinks; and with my brother to wed and his children and mine to come we need the outer courts also."

Then Wang Lung looked at his son standing there in his handsome raiment and he shut his eyes and drew on his pipe and he growled, "Do as you like, only do not trouble me with it!"

Hearing this, the son went away quickly lest his father change and he went well pleased. And when the feast came when rents are decided upon the common people found that the rent for the courts where they lived had been greatly raised, because another would pay that much for them. They knew it was Wang Lung's eldest son who had done this, although he said nothing and did it all by letters to the son of the old Lord Hwang in foreign parts, who cared for nothing except how he could get the most money for the old house. Then the common people had to pack their tattered possessions, and they went away swelling with anger and muttering that one day they would come back even as the poor do come back when the rich are too rich.

But all this Wang Lung did not hear, since he was in the inner courts and seldom came forth. And his son called carpenters and masons and they repaired the rooms and the courts that the common people had ruined with their coarse ways of living, and he built again the pools and he bought flecked and golden fish to put in them. And it was all made beautiful as far as he knew beauty, and he planted lotus and lilies in the pools, and the scarlet-berried bamboo of India and everything he could remember he had seen in southern parts.

Wang Lung saw this and he spoke to his eldest son, saying,

"Have done with all this painting and polishing. It is enough. We are, after all, countryfolk."

But the young man answered proudly,

"That we are not. Men in the town are beginning to call us the great family Wang."

Now Wang Lung had not known that men so called his house, but it pleased him secretly and so he said,

"Well, even great families are from the land and rooted in the land."

But the young man answered smartly,

"Yes, but they do not stay there. They branch forth and bear flowers and fruits."

Wang Lung would not have his son answering him too easily like this, so he said,

"I have said what I have said. Have done with pouring out silver. And roots, if they are to bear fruit, must be kept well in the soil of the land."

Then since evening came on, he wished his son would go away. But there was no peace for him with this son of his for he began again,

"Well, let it be enough, but there is another thing. It concerns my youngest brother. It is not fit that he grow up so ignorant. He should be taught. For this he weeps in the night."

Now Wang Lung had never thought to ask his youngest son what he wished to do with his life, since he had decided one son must be on the land, and this that his eldest son had said struck him between the brows and he was silent, pondering about his third son. He was a lad not like either of his brothers, a lad as silent as his mother, and because he was silent none paid any attention to him.

"Well, but one lad must be on the land," said Wang Lung suddenly in argument and his voice was very loud.

"But why, my father?" urged the young man. "You are a man who need not have any sons like serfs. People will say, 'There is a man who makes his son into a hind while he lives like a prince.'"

Now the young man knew that his father cared mightily what people said of him; and Wang Lung said at last,

"Send him here to me."

The third son came and Wang Lung looked at him to see what he was. And he saw a tall and slender lad, who had his mother's gravity and silence. But there was more beauty in him than there had been in his mother, and for beauty alone he had more of it than any of Wang Lung's children except the second girl. But across the lad's forehead and almost a mar to his beauty were his two black brows, too heavy and black for his young, pale face, and when he frowned these brows met, heavy and straight.

And after Wang Lung had seen him well, he said,

"Your eldest brother says you wish to learn to read."

And the boy said, scarcely stirring his lips,

"Aye."

Wang Lung shook the ash from his pipe and pushed fresh tobacco in slowly with his thumb.

"Well, and I suppose that means I shall not have a son on my own land, and I with sons and to spare."

This he said with bitterness, feeling that these sons of his were too much for him in his old age. But the boy said nothing. He stood there straight and still in his long white robe of summer linen, and at last Wang Lung was angry at his silence and he shouted at him,

"What is it to me what you do? Get away from me!"

Then the boy went away swiftly and Wang Lung sat alone and he said to himself that his two girls were better after all than his sons; one, poor fool that she was, never wanted anything more than a bit of food and her length of cloth to play with, and the other one married and away from his house. And the twilight came down over the court and shut him into it alone.

But as Wang Lung always did when his anger passed, he let his sons have their way, and he called his eldest son and he said,

"Engage a tutor for the third one if he wills it, and let him do as he likes, only I am not to be troubled about it."

And he called his second son and said,

"Since I am not to have a son on the land it is your duty to see to the rents. You shall be my steward."

The second son was pleased, for this meant the money would pass through his hands and he would know what came in and he could complain to his father if more than enough was spent in the house.

Now this second son of his seemed more strange to Wang than any of his sons, for even at the wedding day, which came on, he was careful of the money, and kept the best meats for his friends in the town who knew the cost of the dishes, and to the tenants and the country people he gave only the second best, since they daily ate coarse fare, and to them a little better was very good. And he gave to the slaves and servants the least that could be given them, so that Cuckoo sneered, and she said in the hearing of many,

"Now a truly great family is not so careful of its silver and one can see that this family does not belong in these courts."

The eldest son heard this, and he was ashamed and angry with his second brother. Thus there was trouble between them even on the wedding day, and when the bride's chair was entering the courts, the eldest son stood aside scornfully, and he said,

"My brother has chosen an earthen pot when he might, from my father's position, have had a cup of jade."

And he was scornful and nodded stiffly when the pair came and bowed before him and his wife as their elder brother and sister. And the wife of the eldest son was correct and haughty and bowed only the least that could be considered proper for her position.

Now of all of them who lived in these courts it seemed there was none wholly at peace there except the small grandson who had been born to Wang Lung. And to this small one this great house was neither great nor small but only his house, and here was his mother and here his father and grandfather and all those who lived but to serve him. And from this one did Wang Lung secure peace, and he could never have enough of watching him and laughing at him and picking him up when he fell. He remembered also what his own father had done, and he delighted to take a girdle and put it about the child and hold him thus from falling, and they went from court to court, and the child pointed at the darting fish in the pools and jabbered this and that and snatched the head of a flower and was at his ease in the midst of everything, and only thus did Wang Lung find peace.

Nor was there only this one. In the space of five years Wang Lung had four grandsons and three granddaughters and the courts were filled with their laughter and their weeping. And when one said to him, "There is to be another mouth again," he only laughed and said,

"Eh—eh—well, there is rice and enough for all since we have the good land."

Now FIVE YEARS IS NOTHING in a man's life except when he is very young and very old, and if it gave to Wang Lung these others, it took away also that old dreamer, his uncle, whom he had almost forgotten except to see that he and his old wife were fed and clothed and had what they wished of opium. Wang Lung's uncle and his wife had long since smoked all the flesh off their bones and they lay day in and day out on their beds like two old dry sticks. Then Wang Lung heard that his uncle lay dead one evening when the serving woman went in to take him a bowl of soup. And Wang Lung buried him beside his father, only a little lower than his father's grave but above the place where his own was to be. He moved his uncle's wife into the town, and he gave her a room for her own, and the old woman sucked her opium pipe and lay on her bed in great content. And Wang Lung marveled to think that once he had feared her, this woman who had once been a great fat blowsy countrywoman and who lay there now as shriveled and yellow as the Old Mistress had been in the fallen House of Hwang.

Now Wang Lung's second son came home from the market one day for his noon rice and he said to his father,

"The war is to the south of us now and nearer every day, and we must hold our stores of grain until later for the price will go higher and higher as the armies come nearer to us."

Wang Lung listened to this as he ate and he said,

"Well, and it is a curious thing and I shall be glad to see a war for what it is, for I have heard of it all my life and never seen it."

He remembered that once he had been afraid because he would have been seized, but now he was too old for use and besides he was rich and the rich need not fear anything. So he paid no great heed to the matter beyond this.

And in the days to come he played with his grandchildren, and he slept and ate and smoked and sometimes he went to see his poor fool who sat in a far corner of his court.

Then sweeping out of the northwest like a swarm of locusts there came one day in early summer a horde of men. Wang Lung's small grandson stood at the gate with a manservant to see what passed and when he saw the long ranks of gray-coated men, he ran back to his grandfather and he cried out,

"See what comes, Old One!"

Then Wang Lung went back to the gate with him to humor him, and there the men were filling the street, and Wang Lung felt as though air and sunlight had been suddenly cut off because of the numbers of gray men tramping heavily through the town. Then Wang Lung looked at them closely and he saw that every man held a fire stick with a knife sticking out of the end and the face of every man was wild and fierce and coarse. And Wang Lung drew the child to him hastily and he murmured,

"Let us lock the gate. They are not good men, my little heart."

But suddenly, before he could turn, one saw him from among the men and shouted out at him,

"Ho there, my old father's nephew!"

Wang Lung looked up, and he saw the son of his uncle, and he was clad like the others and dusty and gray, but his face was wilder and more fierce than any. And he laughed harshly and called out to his fellows,

"Here we may stop, my comrades, for this is a rich man and my relative!"

Before Wang Lung could move in his horror, the horde was pouring past him into his own courts, like evil filthy water, filling every corner and crack. They laid themselves down on the floors and they dipped with their hands in the pools and drank, and they clattered their knives down upon carven tables and they spat and shouted at each other. Then Wang Lung in despair ran back with the child into his eldest son's courts and there his son sat reading a book; and when he heard what Wang Lung gasped forth, he began to groan and he went out.

But when he saw his cousin he did not know whether to curse him or to be courteous. But he looked and he groaned forth to his father who was behind him,

"Every man with a knife!"

So he was courteous then and he said,

"Well, my cousin, welcome to your home again."

And the cousin grinned widely and said,

"I have brought a few guests."

"They are welcome, being yours," said Wang Lung's eldest son, "and we will prepare a meal so that they may eat before they go."

Then the cousin said, still grinning,

"Do, but make no haste afterward, for we will rest a handful of days or a moon or a year or two, for we are to be quartered on the town until the war calls."

Now when Wang Lung and his son heard this they could scarcely conceal their dismay, but still it must be concealed because of the knives, so they smiled what poor smiles they could muster and they said, "We are fortunate—we are fortunate!"

And the eldest son pretended he must go to prepare and he took his father's hand and the two of them rushed into the inner court and the eldest son barred the door, and then father and son stared at each other in consternation, and neither knew what to do.

Then the second son came running and he beat upon the door and when they let him in he fell in his haste and he panted,

"There are soldiers everywhere in every house—and I came running to say you must not protest, for today a clerk in my shop—I knew him well—went to his house and there were soldiers in the very room where his wife lay ill, and he protested and they ran a knife through him as though he were made of lard—as smoothly as that—and it came through him clean to the other side! Whatever they wish we must give, but let us only pray that the war move on."

Then the three of them looked at each other heavily, and thought of their women and of these lusty, hungry men. And the eldest son said,

"We must put the women in the innermost court and we must keep the gates barred and the gate of peace ready to be opened."

Thus they did. They put the women and children all into the court where Lotus lived, and there in discomfort and crowding they lived. And Wang Lung and his sons watched the gate day and night.

But there was that one, the cousin, and because he was a relative none could lawfully keep him out and he would come in and he walked about at will, carrying his knife glittering and open in his hand. The eldest son followed him about, his face full of bitterness, but still not daring to say anything, and the cousin looked at this and that and appraised each woman.

Then when the cousin had seen everything he went to see his mother and Wang Lung went with him to show where she was. There she lay on her bed, asleep so her son could hardly wake her, but wake her he did, clapping the thick end of his gun upon the tiles of the floor. Then she woke and stared at him out of a dream, and he said impatiently,

"Here is your son and yet you sleep on!"

She raised herself then in her bed and stared at him again and she said wondering,

"My son—it is my son—" and she looked at him for a long time and at last as though she did not know what else to do she proffered him her opium pipe.

Wang Lung was afraid lest this man should turn on him and say, "What have you done to my mother that she is sere and yellow like this?" So Wang said hastily himself,

"I wish she were content with less, for her opium runs into a handful of silver a day, but at her age we do not dare to cross her." And he sighed as he spoke, and he glanced secretly at his uncle's son, but the man only stared to see what his mother had become, and when she fell back and into her sleep again, he rose and clattered forth, using his gun as a stick in his hand.

NONE OF THE HORDE of idle men did Wang Lung and his family hate and fear as they did this cousin of theirs; this, although the men tore at the trees and the flowering shrubs, and though they crushed the delicate carvings of chairs with their great boots, and though they sullied the pools with filth so that the fish died and floated on the water with their white bellies upturned.

For the cousin ran in and out as he would and he cast eyes at the women and Wang Lung and his sons looked at each other out of eyes haggard and sunken because they dared not sleep. Then Cuckoo saw it and she said,

"Now there is only one thing to do, he must be given a slave while he is here, or else he will be taking where he should not."

And Wang Lung seized eagerly on what she said, and he bade her ask the cousin what slave he would have. So Cuckoo did, then, and she came back and she said,

"He says he will have the little pale one who sleeps on the bed of the mistress."

Now this pale slave was called Pear Blossom and because she was delicate they had petted her and allowed her only to do the lesser things about Lotus, filling her pipe and pouring her tea, and it was thus the cousin had seen her.

When Pear Blossom heard this as she poured the tea for Lotus, she dropped the pot and it broke into pieces and the tea all streamed out, but the maid did not see what she had done. She only threw herself down before Lotus and she knocked her head on the tiles and she moaned,

"Oh, my mistress, not I—I am afraid of him for my life—"

And Lotus was displeased and she answered pettishly,

"He is only a man, and what is this ado?" And she turned to Cuckoo and said, "Take this slave and give her to him."

Then the young maid put her hands together piteously and cried and her little body was all trembling with her fear, and she looked from this face to that, beseeching with her weeping.

Now the sons of Wang Lung could not speak against their father's wife. And the youngest son stood there staring at her, his hands clenched on his bosom and his brows drawn down over his eyes, straight and black. But he did not speak. And there was only the sound of this dreadful, frightened weeping.

Wang Lung looked at the young girl doubtfully, not caring to anger Lotus but still moved, because he had always a soft heart. Then the maid saw his heart in his face and she ran and held his feet. And he looked down at her and saw how small her shoulders were and how they shook and he remembered the great, coarse body of his cousin, now long past his youth, and a distaste for the thing seized him and he said to Lotus,

"Well now, it is ill to force the maid. Let me buy for you another slave, or what you will, but let me see what can be done."

Then Lotus, who had long been minded for a foreign clock and a ruby ring, was silent and Wang Lung said to Cuckoo,

"Go and tell my cousin the girl has a vile and incurable disease, and if he fears it as we all do, then tell him we have another and a sound one."

And he cast his eyes over the slaves who stood about and they turned away their faces, all except one stout wench, and she said with her face red and laughing,

"Well, he is not so hideous a man as some."

Then Wang Lung answered in relief,

"Well, go then!"

And Cuckoo said,

"Follow close behind me." And they went out.

But Lotus was still angry, and she rose and went into her room. Then Wang Lung raised the maid gently and she stood before him, and he saw that she had a little, soft, oval face, exceedingly delicate, and a little pale-red mouth. And he said kindly,

"Now keep away from your mistress for a day or two, my child, until she is past her anger, and when that other one comes in, hide, lest he desire you again."

And she lifted her eyes and looked at him full and passionately, and she passed him, silent as a shadow, and was gone.

THE COUSIN LIVED THERE for a moon and a half and the stout wench conceived by him and boasted of it. Then suddenly the war called and the horde went away quickly as chaff driven by the wind, and there was nothing left except the filth and destruction they had wrought. And Wang Lung's cousin stood before them with his gun over his shoulder and he said mockingly,

"Well, if I come not back I have left you my second self and a grandson for my mother. It is one of the benefits of the soldier's life—his seed springs up behind him and others must tend it!"

And laughing at them all, he went his way with the others.

XVI

WHEN THE SOLDIERS WERE GONE Wang Lung and his two elder sons for once agreed and it was that all trace of what had just passed must be wiped away, and they called in carpenters and masons. And within a year the place was fresh and flowering again and there was order once more everywhere.

The slave who had conceived by the son of Wang Lung's uncle he commanded to wait upon his uncle's wife as long as she lived, which could not be long now. And it was a matter for joy to Wang Lung that this slave gave birth only to a girl, for if it had been a boy she would have been proud and have claimed a place in the family, but being a girl it was only slave bearing slave, and she was no more than before.

Nevertheless, Wang Lung was just to her, and he gave her a little silver, and the woman was content except for one thing.

"Hold the silver as dowry for me, my master," she said, "and if it is not a trouble to you, wed me to a farmer."

Wang Lung promised easily, "When the old dreamer dies, I will find a man for you." And he was struck with a thought and it was this. Here was he promising a woman to a poor man, and once he had been a poor man come into these courts for his woman. And he had not for long thought of O-lan, and now he thought of her with sadness that was heaviness of memory and things long gone.

And the woman came to him one morning and said,

"Now redeem your promise, my master, for the old one died in the early morning, and I have put her in her coffin."

And Wang Lung remembered the blubbering lad who had caused Ching's death, and he said,

"Well, and he did not mean the thing he did, and he is as good as any and the only one I can think of now."

So he sent for the lad and he came, and he was a man grown now, but still he was rude and still his teeth were as they were. And it was Wang Lung's whim to sit on the dais in the great hall and to call the two before him and he said slowly, that he might taste the whole flavor of the strange moment,

"Here, fellow, is this woman, and she is yours if you will have her, and none has known her except the son of my own uncle."

And the man took her gratefully, for she was a good-natured wench, and he was too poor to wed except to such an one.

Then Wang Lung came down off the dais and it seemed to him that now his life was rounded off and he had done more than he would ever have dreamed he could, and that peace could truly come to him and he could sleep in the sun. It was time for it, also, for he was close to sixty-five years of his age and his grandsons were like young bamboos about him. Well, and there was the third son to wed one day soon, and with that over there was nothing left to trouble him in his life, and he could be at peace.

Now his youngest son had lived among the soldiers when they were there, and he had listened to their tales of war and battle, and he had begged novels of his tutor, and had read stories of the wars of the Three Kingdoms, and his head was full of dreams. So now he went to his father and he said,

"I know what I will do. I will go to be a soldier."

When Wang Lung heard this, he cried out in great dismay,

"Now what madness is this, my son! It is said from ancient times that men do not take good iron to make a nail nor a good man to make a soldier, and you are my little son. How shall I sleep and you wandering over the earth here and there in a war?"

But the boy was determined and he looked at his father and drew down his black brows, and his eyes were alight under his brows.

"There is to be a war such as we have not heard of," he said. "There is to be a revolution and our land is to be free!"

Wang Lung listened to this in the greatest astonishment he had yet had from his three sons.

"Now what all this stuff is, I do not know," he said wondering. "Our land is free already—all our good land is free. You are clothed and are fed with it, and I do not know what freedom you desire more than you have."

But the boy only muttered bitterly, "You do not understand—you are too old—you understand nothing."

And Wang Lung pondered and he looked at this son of his and he saw the suffering young face, and he saw that he was tall as a man already, though still reedy with youth, and he said, doubtfully, muttering and half aloud,

"Well, it may be he needs one thing more." And he said aloud then and slowly, "If there is a woman you desire—"

And the boy answered with lofty looks and with dignity, folding his arms on his breast,

"I am not the ordinary young man. I wish for glory. There are women everywhere." And then as though he remembered something he had forgotten, he suddenly broke from his dignity and his arms dropped and he said in his usual voice, "Besides, there never were an uglier set of slaves than we have. If I cared—but I do not—well, there is not a beauty in the courts except perhaps the little pale maid who waits on the one in the inner courts."

Then Wang knew he spoke of Pear Blossom and he was smitten with a strange jealousy. Until the day when he had protected her from the son of his uncle, Wang Lung had not thought of the girl except as a child. But since that day he had thought of the pretty pale young maid more than he himself would believe he did. And he suddenly felt himself older than he was—a man too thick of girth and with whitening hair, and he saw his son a man slim and young, and it was not for this moment father and son, but two men, one old and one young, and Wang Lung said angrily,

"Now keep off the slaves—I will not have the rotten ways of young lords in my house."

Then the boy lifted his black brows and shrugged his shoulders. "You spoke of it first!" he said, and he turned and went out.

Then Wang Lung sat there alone in his room, confused with many angers, but, although he could not understand why, this anger stood forth most clearly; his son had looked on a little pale young maid in the house and had found her fair.

AFTER THAT HE COULD NOT CEASE from his thought of what his youngest son had said of Pear Blossom, and he watched the maid incessantly as she came and went. The thought of her filled his mind and he doted on her.

One night in the early summer of that year, at the time when the night air is thick and soft with the mists of warmth and fragrance, he sat in his own court alone under a flowering cassia tree and the sweet heavy scent of the flowers filled his nostrils and his blood ran full and hot like the blood of a young man. So he stayed away from Lotus, because well she knew when a man was restless. And he remembered that he himself would before many years be seventy and he was ashamed of his coursing blood, and he thought,

"It would be a good thing to give the maid to the lad," and this he said to himself again and again, and every time he said it the thing stabbed like a thrust on flesh already sore, and yet he could not but stab. And so he sat in his court alone and there was not one in all his house to whom he could go as friend.

Then as he sat there in the darkness one passed the gate of his court, and he looked quickly and it was Pear Blossom.

"Pear Blossom!" he called, and his voice came in a whisper.

She stopped suddenly, her head bent in listening.

Then he called again and his voice would scarcely come from his throat, "Come here to me!"

Then hearing him she crept timidly through the gate and stood before him and he put out his hand and laid hold of her little coat and he said, half choking, "Child—!"

There he stopped with the word. He said to himself that it was a disgraceful thing for a man with grandsons nearer to this child's age than he was. Then she, waiting, caught from him the heat of his blood and she bent over and slipped, like a flower crumpling upon its stalk, to the ground, and she clasped his feet and lay there. And he said slowly,

"Child—I am an old man—a very old man. A little maid like you should have a tall straight youth."

And she said, and her voice came out of the darkness like the very breath of the cassia tree, "I like old men—they are so kind—young men are only fierce—"

And hearing her small childish voice quavering up from about his feet his heart welled up in a great wave of love, and he raised her gently, and then he led her into his own courts.

Now the eye of Cuckoo marked first what Wang Lung had done; she saw the maid slipping at dawn out of his court and she laid hold of the girl and laughed, and her old hawk's eyes glittered.

"Well!" she said. "And so it is the Old Lord over again!"

And Wang Lung in his room, hearing her, girded his robe about him quickly and he came out and smiled sheepishly and half proudly and he said muttering,

"Well, and I said she had better take a young lad and she would have the old one!"

"It will be a pretty thing to tell the mistress," Cuckoo said, then, and her eyes sparkled with malice.

Wang Lung, fearing the anger of Lotus more than anything, begged Cuckoo, "Do you tell her, and if you can manage it without anger to my face I will give you a handful of money."

So Cuckoo, still laughing and shaking her head, promised, and Wang Lung went back to his court and he would not come forth until Cuckoo came back and said,

"The thing is told, and she was angry enough until I reminded her she has wanted this long time the foreign clock you promised her, and she will have ruby rings and other things as she thinks of them and a slave to take Pear Blossom's place, and Pear Blossom is not to come to her anymore, and you are not to come soon either, because the sight of you sickens her."

And Wang Lung promised eagerly and he said,

"Get her what she wills and I do not begrudge anything."

And he was pleased that he need not see Lotus until her anger was cooled with the fulfillment of her wishes.

That night, Wang Lung sat in his middle room on the court and the red candles were lit on the table and he sat there smoking, and Pear Blossom sat silently on the other side of the table from him, and her hands were folded and quiet in her lap. Sometimes she looked at Wang Lung, fully and without coquetry as a child does, and he watched her and shame went out of him and he was proud of what he had done.

Then suddenly there was his youngest son standing before him, sprung out of the darkness of the court. Wang Lung was reminded in a flash of a panther he had once seen the men of the village bring in from the hills, and the beast had been tied but he crouched for a spring, and his eyes gleamed, and the lad's eyes gleamed and he fixed them upon his father's face. And those brows of his he gathered fierce and black above his eyes. Thus he stood and at last he said in a low and surcharged voice,

"Now I will go for a soldier—I will go for a soldier—"

But he did not look at the girl, only at his father, and Wang Lung was suddenly afraid of this son, whom he had scarcely considered from his birth up. He would have spoken, but when he took his pipe from his mouth, no sound came. And his son repeated again and again,

"Now I will go—now I will go—"

Suddenly he turned and looked at the girl once, and she looked back at him, shrinking, her two hands at her face. Then the young man tore his eyes from her and he went in a leap from the room, out through the door into the black summer night, and he was gone and there was silence everywhere.

At last Wang Lung turned to the girl and he said humbly and gently and with a great sadness,

"I am too old for you, my heart, and well I know it."

But the girl dropped her hands from her face and she cried more passionately than he had ever heard her cry,

"Young men are cruel—I like old men best!"

When the morning came of the next day Wang Lung's youngest son was gone and where he was gone no one knew.

THEN, AS AUTUMN FLARES with the false heat of summer before it dies into the winter, so was it with the quick love Wang Lung had for Pear Blossom. With the passing of the flame out of him he was suddenly cold with age and he was an old man. Nevertheless, he was fond of her, and it was a comfort to him that she was in his court and she served him faithfully and with a patience beyond her years, and he was kind to her with a perfect kindness, and his love for her was the love of father for daughter.

And for his sake she was even kind to his poor fool and this was comfort to him. Now Wang Lung had thought many times of what would come of his poor fool when he was dead; so he bought a little bundle of white poisonous stuff at the medicine shop, and he called Pear Blossom to him one day and he said,

"There is none other but you to whom I can leave this poor fool of mine when I am gone, and she will live on after me, seeing that her mind has no troubles of its own to kill her. And well I know that no one will think when I am gone to feed her or to bring her out of the rain. Now here is a gate of safety for her in this packet, and when I die you are to mix it in her rice and let her eat it, that she may follow me where I am. And so shall I be at ease."

But Pear Blossom shrank from the thing he held and she said in her soft way,

"I can scarcely kill an insect and how could I take this life? No, my lord, but I will take this poor fool for mine because you have been kind to me—the only kind one."

And Wang Lung could have wept for what she said because no one had ever requited him like this, and he said,

"Nevertheless, take it, my child, for even you must die one day and after you there is none—no, not one."

So when she saw his meaning, Pear Blossom took the packet from him and said no more and Wang Lung trusted her and was comforted for the fate of his poor fool.

Then Wang Lung withdrew more and more into his age and he lived much alone except for these two in his courts, his poor fool and Pear Blossom. Sometimes he roused himself a little and he looked at Pear Blossom and he was troubled and said,

"It is too quiet a life for you, my child."

But she always answered gently and in great gratitude,

"It is quiet and safe."

Once when she said this Wang Lung was curious and he asked,

"What was it in your tender years that made you thus fearful of men? Now I should have said you had lived quietly and easily in my courts."

And looking at her for answer he saw a great terror in her eyes and she covered them with her hands and she whispered,

"Every man I hate except you—I have hated every man, even my father who sold me."

And she would say nothing more, and he mused on it, but then he sighed and gave over his questions, because above everything now he would have peace, and he wished only to sit in his court near these two.

XVII

So Wang Lung sat, and so his age came on him day by day and year by year, and he slept fitfully in the sun as his father had done.

Sometimes, but seldom, he went into the other courts and sometimes he saw Lotus, and she never mentioned the maid he had taken, but she greeted him well enough, for she was old too now and satisfied with the food and the wine she loved. She and Cuckoo sat together now as friends and no longer as mistress and servant, and they talked and ate and slept, and woke to gossip again.

And when Wang Lung went, and it was very seldom, into his sons' courts, they treated him courteously and they ran to get tea for him.

Then he would sit awhile and look at the children gathering around him to stare. His grandsons were tall lads now, and he looked at them, peering at them, and he muttered to himself,

"Now that one has the look of his great-grandfather and there is a small merchant Liu, and here is myself when young."

And he asked them, "Do you go to school?"

"Yes, Grandfather," they answered in a scattered chorus, and he said again,

"Do you study the Four Books?"

Then they laughed with clear young scorn at a man so old as this and they said,

"No, Grandfather, and no one studies the Four Books since the Revolution."

And he answered, musing,

"Ah, I have heard of a revolution, but I have been too busy in my life to attend to it. There was always the land."

But the lads snickered at this, and at last Wang Lung rose, feeling himself after all but a guest in his sons' courts.

Then after a time he went no more to see his sons, but sometimes he would ask Cuckoo,

"Does any ever hear from that youngest son of mine where he is gone this long time?"

And Cuckoo answered, for there was nothing she did not know in these courts,

"It is said he is a military official and great enough in a thing they

441

call a revolution, but what it is I do not know—perhaps some sort of business."

And Wang Lung said, "Ah?"

And he would have thought of it, but the evening was falling and his bones ached in the chill air. For his mind now went where it would and he could not hold it long to any one thing. And the needs of his old body for food and for hot tea were more keen than for anything.

THUS SPRING WORE ON again and again, and as these years passed still one thing remained to him and it was his love for his land. He had gone away from it and he had set up his house in a town, but his roots were in his land and although he forgot it for months together, when spring came each year he must go out onto the land; and he went. Sometimes he took a servant and his bed and he slept again in the old earthen house where he had begotten children and where O-lan had died. When he woke in the dawn he went out and with his trembling hands he reached and plucked a bit of budding willow and a spray of peach bloom and held them all day in his hand.

Thus he wandered one day in a late spring, and he went over his fields a little way and he came to the place on the low hill where he had buried his dead. He stood trembling on his staff and he looked at the graves and he remembered them every one. They were more clear to him now than the sons who lived in his own house. Then he mused and he thought suddenly,

"Well, and I shall be the next."

Then he stared at the bit of earth where he was to lie and he muttered,

"I must see to the coffin."

This thought he held fast and painfully in his mind and he went back to the town and he sent for his eldest son, and he said,

"There is something I have to say."

"Then say on," answered the son, "I am here."

But when Wang Lung would have spoken he suddenly could not remember what it was, and the tears stood in his eyes because he had held the matter so painfully in his mind and now it had slipped away from him. So he called Pear Blossom and he said to her, "Child, what was it I wanted to say?"

And Pear Blossom answered gently,

"Where were you this day?"

"I was upon the land," Wang Lung replied. Then suddenly the thing flew into his mind again and he cried, laughing out of his wet eyes,

"Well, and I do remember. My son, I have chosen my place in the earth, and it is below my father and his brother and above your mother and near to Ching, and I would see my coffin before I die."

Then Wang Lung's eldest son cried out dutifully and properly,

"Do not say that word, my father, but I will do as you say."

Then his son bought a carven coffin hewn from a great log of fragrant wood that is as lasting as iron, and Wang Lung was comforted, and he said,

"Well, and I would have it moved out to the earthen house and there I will live out my few days and there I will die."

And when they saw how he had set his heart they did what he wished and he went back to the house on his land, he and Pear Blossom and the fool, and what servants they needed; and Wang Lung took up his abode again on his land, and he left the house in the town to the family he had founded.

Spring passed and summer passed into harvest and in the hot autumn sun Wang Lung sat where his father had sat against the wall. And he thought no more about anything now except his food and his land. And he stooped sometimes and gathered some of the earth up in his hand, and it seemed full of life between his fingers. And he was content, holding it thus, and he thought of it fitfully and of his good coffin; and the kind earth waited without haste until he came to it.

His sons were proper enough to him and they came to him every day or so, and they sent him delicate food fit for his age, but he liked best to have one stir up meal in hot water and sup it as his father had done.

But one day after his two sons had greeted him courteously they went out and they walked about the land. Now Wang Lung followed them silently, and they did not hear the sound of his footsteps or his staff on the soft earth, and Wang Lung heard his second son say,

"We will sell the land, and we will divide the money between us evenly, for now with the railroad straight through I can ship rice to the sea . . ."

But the old man heard only these words, "sell the land," and he cried out and he could not keep his voice from trembling with his anger,

"Now, evil, idle sons—sell the land?" He choked and would have fallen, and they caught him and held him up, and he began to weep.

Then they soothed him and they said, soothing him,

"No—no—we will never sell the land—"

"It is the end of a family—when they begin to sell the land," he said brokenly. "Out of the land we came and into it we must go— and if you will hold your land you can live—no one can rob you of land—"

And the old man let his scanty tears dry upon his cheeks and they made salty stains there. And he stooped and took up a handful of the soil and he muttered,

"If you sell the land, it is the end."

And his two sons held him, one on either side, and he held tight in his hand the warm loose earth. And they soothed him and they said over and over, the eldest son and the second son,

"Rest assured, our father. The land is not to be sold."

But over the old man's head they looked at each other and smiled.

The
Merry Adventures
of
ROBIN HOOD

THE MERRY ADVENTURES OF ROBIN HOOD

a condensation of the book by

HOWARD PYLE

illustrated by

JEAN LEON HUENS

IN THE ENGLAND of the Middle Ages many a daring tale was told, many a romantic ballad sung about Robin Hood—the gallant outlaw who stole boldly from the rich that he might give generously to the poor. Like King Arthur, he is a legendary figure. But whereas Arthur was a hero of the knightly classes, Robin was the beloved champion of the peasantry.

Howard Pyle has chosen the best of the Robin Hood stories for this book. He has placed Robin in the twelfth century during the successive reigns of Henry II with his beautiful queen, Eleanor of Aquitaine, of their chivalrous son, Richard the Lion-Hearted, and of Richard's tyrannical brother, John. This was a time when the land was tilled by Saxon serfs but owned by Norman noblemen and wealthy churchmen. The forests, which abounded in game, were royal property, with heavy penalties for poaching therein, even when famine stalked the countryside. The common folk were often oppressed, and it was only natural they should dream of a hero of their very own—a young man who freely roamed the forests, who laughed merrily at the hated authorities, who revered God but played pranks on pompous clergymen.

Whether Robin was real, imaginary, or a composite of several men, no one knows. But Sherwood Forest in Nottinghamshire was—and is—a real place. Much of it has been destroyed to make way for farms and factories, but part of it has been preserved. Here the sunlight still filters through great trees to fall on grassy glades, and one can almost hear the call of Robin's horn, the twang of his bowstring in the leafy quiet. Here, as in the pages of Howard Pyle's book, he seems very much alive.

Mr. Pyle also wrote and illustrated *King Arthur and His Knights*, *Otto of the Silver Hand* and *Men of Iron*. Born in Wilmington, Delaware, in 1853, he attended school there, and began to study art while helping his father in the leather business. Later he devoted all his time to writing, painting and teaching. In 1900 he started an art school, and his pupils included many who later became famous, such as N. C. Wyeth and Maxfield Parrish. He died in 1911.

IN MERRY ENGLAND in the time of old, when good King Henry the Second ruled the land, there lived within the green glades of Sherwood Forest, near Nottingham Town, a famous outlaw whose name was Robin Hood. No archer ever lived that could speed a shaft with such skill as his, nor were there ever such yeomen as the sevenscore merry men that roamed with him through the greenwood, passing their time in games of archery or bouts of cudgel play, and living upon the King's venison washed down with draughts of ale. Not only Robin himself but all the band were outlaws and dwelt apart from other men, yet they were beloved by the country people round about, for no one ever came to jolly Robin for help in time of need and went away with an empty fist.

And now I will tell how it came about that Robin Hood fell afoul of the law.

When Robin was a youth of eighteen, stout of sinew and bold of heart, the Sheriff of Nottingham proclaimed a shooting match and offered a prize of a butt of ale to whosoever should shoot the best shaft in Nottinghamshire. "Now," quoth Robin, "will I go too, for fain would I draw a string for a butt of good October brewing." So he took his good stout yew bow and a score of broad cloth-yard arrows, and started off from his home in Locksley Town through Sherwood Forest to Nottingham.

It was at the dawn of day in the merry Maytime, when hedge-rows are green and flowers bedeck the meadows; when apple buds blossom and birds sing, the lark, the throstle cock and cuckoo; when lads and lasses look upon each other with sweet thoughts; when housewives spread their linen to bleach upon the grass. Sweet was the greenwood, and blithely Robin whistled as he trudged along its paths.

Suddenly he came upon some foresters beneath a great oak tree. Fifteen there were in all, feasting and drinking as they sat around a huge pasty, each thrusting his hands into the pie and washing down that which he ate with great horns of ale. Then one of them, with his mouth full, called out to Robin, "Halloa, where goest thou, little lad, with thy one-penny bow and thy farthing shafts?"

Then Robin grew angry, for no stripling likes to be taunted with his green years. "Now," quoth he, "my bow and mine arrows are as good as thine. I go to the shooting match at Nottingham Town."

"Ho! Listen to the lad!" said one. "Why, boy, thy mother's milk is yet scarce dry upon thy lips, and yet thou pratest of standing up with good stout men at Nottingham butts."

"I'll hold you twenty marks," quoth Robin, "that I hit the clout at threescore rods."

Then all laughed aloud, and one said, "Well boasted, thou fair infant, well boasted! And well thou knowest that no target is nigh to make good thy wager."

At this Robin grew right mad. "Hark ye," said he, "yonder, at the glade's end, I see a herd of deer, even more than threescore rods distant. I'll hold you twenty marks that, by leave of Our Lady, I cause the best hart among them to die."

"Now done!" cried he who had spoken first. "I wager that thou causest no beast to die, with or without the aid of Our Lady."

Then Robin took his bow in his hand, and placing the tip at his instep he strung it right deftly; then he nocked an arrow and, raising the bow, drew the gray goose feather to his ear; the next moment the bowstring rang and the arrow sped down the glade as a sparrow hawk skims in a northern wind. High leaped the noblest hart of all the herd, only to fall dead on the path.

"Ha!" cried Robin. "How likest thou that shot, good fellow?"

Then all the foresters were filled with rage, and he who had lost the wager was more angry than all. "Knowest thou not," cried he, "that thou hast killed the King's deer, and, by the laws of King Harry, thine ears should be shaven close to thy head?"

Never a word said Robin Hood, but he looked at the foresters with a grim face; then, turning on his heel, he strode away from them down the forest glade.

Now, he who had first spoken sprang to his feet and seized upon his bow. "I'll hurry thee anon," cried he. And he sent an arrow whistling after Robin.

It was well for Robin that the forester's head was spinning with ale, or else he would never have taken another step. As it was, the arrow whistled within three inches of his head. Then he turned and quickly drew his own bow, and sent an arrow in return. "Ye said I was no archer," cried he, "but say so now again!"

The shaft flew straight; the archer fell forward with a cry and lay on his face upon the ground, his arrows rattling about him from out of his quiver, the gray goose shaft wet with his heart's blood. Then Robin Hood was gone into the depths of the greenwood. Some started after him, but not with much heart, for each feared to suffer the death of his fellow; so presently they all came back and bore the dead man away to Nottingham.

Meanwhile Robin ran through the greenwood. Gone was all the joy and brightness, for his heart was sick. "Alas," cried he, "I would that my right forefinger had been stricken off ere this had happened. In haste I smote, but grieve I sore at leisure."

And so he came to dwell in the greenwood, never again to see the happy days with the lads and lasses of Locksley Town. For he was outlawed: he had killed a man, and he had poached upon the King's deer, and two hundred pounds were set upon his head.

Now the Sheriff of Nottingham swore that he himself would bring this knave to justice; first, because he wanted the two hundred pounds, and next, because the forester that Robin Hood had killed was of kin to him. But Robin hid in Sherwood Forest, and there gathered around him many others like himself. Some had shot deer in hungry wintertime, when they could get no other food, and had been seen in the act by the foresters, but had escaped; some had been turned out of their inheritance, that their farms might be added to the King's lands; some had been despoiled by a great baron or a rich abbot.

So, in one year, fivescore or more good stout yeomen gathered about Robin Hood, and chose him to be their chief. They vowed that even as they themselves had been despoiled they would despoil their oppressors, and that from each they would take that which had been wrung from the poor by unjust taxes, or in wrongful fines. But to the poor folk they would give help in need and trouble. Besides this, they swore never to harm a child nor to wrong a woman; so that, after a while, the people came to praise Robin and his men, and to tell many tales of him and of his doings.

ONE MORN WHEN ALL THE BIRDS were singing blithely among the leaves, up rose Robin Hood and all his merry men, each washing his head and hands in the brook that leaped laughing from stone to stone. Then said Robin, "Today I will go abroad to seek adventures. But tarry ye all in the greenwood; only see that ye mind well my call. Three blasts upon the bugle horn I will blow in my hour of need; then come quickly, for I shall want your aid."

So saying, he strode away through the leafy forest glades until he had come to the verge of Sherwood. There he wandered through highway and byway. Now he met a buxom lass in a shady lane, and each gave the other a merry word and passed his way; now he saw a fair lady upon an ambling pad, to whom he doffed his cap, and who bowed sedately in return; now he saw a fat monk on a pannier-laden ass; now a gallant knight, with spear and shield and armor that flashed brightly in the sunlight; and now a stout burgher from Nottingham Town, pacing along with serious footsteps; but adventure he found none. At last he took a bypath that dipped toward a broad, pebbly stream spanned by a narrow bridge made of a log of wood. As he drew nigh this bridge he saw a tall stranger coming from the other side. Thereupon Robin quickened his pace, as did the stranger, each thinking to cross first.

"Now stand thou back," quoth Robin, "and let the better man cross first."

"Nay," answered the stranger, "then stand back thine own self, for the better man, I wot, am I."

"Stand thou," quoth Robin, "or else, by the bright brow of Saint Ælfrida, I will show thee right good Nottingham play with a cloth-yard shaft betwixt thy ribs."

"Thou pratest like a coward," answered the stranger. "Thou standest there with a bow, while I have naught but a staff."

"By my faith," quoth Robin. "Never have I had a coward's name. I will lay by my bow, and if thou darest abide my coming, I will go and cut a cudgel to test thy manhood withal."

"Aye, marry, that will I abide and joyously," quoth the stranger.

Then Robin Hood stepped quickly to the coverside and cut a staff of ground oak, straight, without flaw, and six feet in length, and came back trimming away the tender stems from it, while the stranger leaned upon his staff and whistled as he gazed round about. Robin observed him furtively as he trimmed his staff, measuring him from top to toe from out the corner of his eye, and thought that he had never seen a stouter man. Tall was Robin, but taller was the stranger by a head, for he was seven feet in height. Broad was Robin across the shoulders, but broader was the stranger by twice the breadth of a palm.

Nevertheless, said Robin to himself, I will baste thy hide, my good fellow. Then aloud, "Lo, here is my staff. Now meet an thou darest. We will fight until one of us tumble into the stream by dint of blows."

"Marry, that meeteth my whole heart!" cried the stranger, twirling his staff above his head betwixt his fingers and thumb.

Never did the knights of Arthur's Round Table meet in a stouter fight than did these two. Robin stepped quickly upon the bridge where the stranger stood; first he made a feint, and then delivered a blow at the stranger's head that, had it met its mark, would have tumbled him speedily into the water. But the stranger turned the blow right deftly and in return gave one as stout, which Robin also turned. So they stood, each in his place, neither moving

a finger's breadth back, for one good hour, and many blows were given and received, till here and there were sore bones and bumps, yet neither thought of crying "Enough," or seemed likely to fall from off the bridge. At last Robin gave the stranger a blow that made his jacket smoke like a damp straw thatch in the sun; but he regained himself right quickly and thwacked Robin so fairly that he fell heels over head into the water.

"And where art thou now, my good lad?" shouted the stranger, roaring with laughter.

"Oh, floating adown with the tide," cried Robin, nor could he forbear laughing himself at his sorry plight. He waded to the bank, the little fish speeding hither and thither, all frightened at his splashing. "Give me thy hand. I must needs own thou art a brave soul and a good one with the cudgels. My head hummeth like to a hive of bees." Then he clapped his horn to his lips and winded three blasts that went echoing down the forest paths.

"And thou," quoth the stranger, "takest thy cudgeling like a stout yeoman."

But now the distant twigs and branches rustled, and suddenly a score or two of men, all clad in Lincoln green, burst from out the covert, with Will Stutely at their head.

"Good master," cried Will, "how is this? Truly thou art all wet from head to foot, and that to the very skin."

"Why, marry," answered Robin, "yon stout fellow hath tumbled me into the water and given me a drubbing besides."

"Then shall he not go without a ducking and a drubbing himself!" cried Will Stutely. "Have at him, lads!"

Then the yeomen leaped upon the stranger, but they found him ready and felt him strike right and left with his staff, so that, though he went down with press of numbers, some of them rubbed cracked crowns before he was overcome.

"Nay, forbear!" cried Robin, laughing until his sore sides ached again. "He is a right good man and true. Now hark ye, good youth, wilt thou be one of my band? Three suits of Lincoln green shalt thou have each year, and share with us whatsoever good shall befall us. Thou shalt eat sweet venison and quaff the stoutest ale, and mine own good right-hand man shalt thou be, for never did I see such a cudgel player in all my life before."

"That know I not," quoth the stranger surlily, for he was angry at being so tumbled about, "if ye handle yew bow no better than ye do oaken cudgel; but if there be any man here that can shoot a better shaft than I, then will I join with you."

"Now by my faith," said Robin, "thou art a saucy varlet. Good Stutely, cut thou a white piece of bark four fingers in breadth, and set it fourscore yards distant on yonder oak. Now, stranger, hit that with a gray goose shaft and call thyself an archer."

"Aye, marry, that will I," answered he. "And if I hit it not, strip me and beat me blue with bowstrings."

Then he chose the stoutest bow among them all, next to Robin's own, and a straight shaft, well feathered and smooth, and, stepping to the mark, drew the arrow to his cheek and loosed the shaft right deftly, sending it so straight that it clove the mark in the very center. "Aha!" cried he. "Mend thou that if thou canst," while even the yeomen clapped at so fair a shot.

"That is a keen shot indeed," quoth Robin. "Mend it I cannot, but mar it I may, perhaps." Then taking up his own stout bow, he shot with his greatest skill. So true flew the arrow that it lit fairly upon the stranger's shaft and split it into splinters.

"By the lusty yew bow of good Saint Withold," cried the stranger, "never saw I the like! Now truly will I be thy man."

"Then have I gained a right good man this day," quoth jolly Robin. "What name goest thou by, good fellow?"

"Men call me John Little whence I came," answered the stranger.

Then Will Stutely, who loved a jest, spoke up. "Nay, fair stranger, little art thou indeed, and small of bone and sinew, therefore shalt thou be christened Little John."

Then all the band laughed until the stranger grew angry. "An thou make a jest of me," quoth he, "thou wilt have sore bones."

"Nay, good friend," said Robin Hood, "bottle thine anger, for the name fitteth thee well. So come, my merry men, we will prepare a christening feast for this fair infant."

So through the forest they traced their steps till they reached the spot where they dwelt. There had they built huts of bark and branches of trees, and made couches of sweet rushes spread over with skins of fallow deer. Here stood a great oak tree with branches spreading broadly around, beneath which was a seat of green moss where Robin Hood was wont to sit. Here they found the rest of the band, some of whom had come in with a brace of fat does. They built great fires and roasted the does and broached a barrel of humming ale. Then they all sat down, but Robin placed Little John at his right hand, for he was henceforth to be the second in the band.

When the feast was done Will Stutely spoke up. "It is now time, I ween, to christen our bonny babe. Seven sponsors shall we have." And he chose the seven stoutest men, and together they ran upon Little John, seizing him by his legs and arms and holding him tightly in spite of his struggles. Then one came forward who had been chosen to play the priest because he had a bald crown. "Now, what name callest thou this babe?" asked he right soberly.

"Little John call I him," answered Will Stutely.

"Now Little John," quoth the mock priest, "thou hast not lived heretofore, but henceforth thou wilt live indeed. When thou lived not thou wast called John Little, but now that thou dost live, Little John shalt thou be called, so christen I thee." And at these words he emptied a pot of ale upon Little John's head. Then all shouted with laughter as the ale trickled from his nose and beard, his eyes blinked with the smart of it, and he too laughed. Then Robin clothed him from top to toe in Lincoln green, and gave him a good stout bow, and so made him a member of the band.

The Shooting Match at Nottingham Town

NOW IT WAS TOLD BEFORE how two hundred pounds were set upon Robin Hood's head, and how the Sheriff of Nottingham swore that he would seize Robin. Now the Sheriff did not know what a force Robin had about him, but thought that he might serve a warrant as he could upon any other man that had broken the laws; therefore he offered fourscore golden angels to anyone who would serve this warrant. But men of Nottingham Town knew more of Robin than the Sheriff did, and laughed to think of serving a warrant upon the bold outlaw. So a fortnight passed, in which time none came forward to do the Sheriff's business.

Then it came to the Sheriff's ears that the people made a jest of him, and he was very wroth, because a man hates nothing so much as being made a jest of. Not a word did the Sheriff speak to anyone, but all the time he was devising a plan to take Robin Hood.

Then of a sudden it came to him that were he to proclaim a great shooting match and offer some grand prize, Robin Hood might be overpersuaded by his spirit to come to the butts, even within the walls of Nottingham Town; and the Sheriff cried, "Aha!" and smote his palm upon his thigh.

So he sent messengers north and south, and east and west, to proclaim through town, hamlet and countryside this grand shooting match, and the prize was to be an arrow of pure beaten gold.

When Robin Hood first heard this news he called his men about him and spoke to them thus: "Now hearken all. Our friend the Sheriff of Nottingham hath proclaimed a shooting match, and the prize is to be a bright golden arrow. Now I fain would have one of us win it, both because of the fairness of the prize and because our friend the Sheriff hath offered it. What say ye, lads?"

Then young David of Doncaster spoke up and said, "I have come straight from our friend Eadom o' the Blue Boar Inn, good master, and there I heard that the Sheriff hath but laid a trap for thee in this match. So go not lest we all meet dole and woe."

"Now," quoth Robin, "thou art a wise lad and keepest thine ears open, as becometh a crafty woodsman. But shall we let it be said that the Sheriff did cow bold Robin Hood and sevenscore as fair archers as are in all England? Nay, good David, what thou tellest me maketh me desire the prize even more. But we must meet guile with guile. Now some of you clothe yourselves as friars, and some as peasants, and some as tinkers, but see that each man taketh a good bow or broadsword, in case need should arise. As for myself, I will shoot for this golden arrow, and should I win it, we will hang it to the branches of our greenwood tree."

Then, "Good, good!" cried all the band right heartily.

A fair sight was Nottingham Town on the day of the shooting match. All along the meadow beneath the town wall stretched a row of benches, one above the other, which were for knight and lady, squire and dame, and rich burghers and their wives. The range was twoscore paces broad, and sevenscore and ten paces in length. At one end, near the target, was a raised seat, bedecked with ribbons and garlands, for the Sheriff of Nottingham and his dame; at the other a tent of striped canvas, from the pole of which fluttered many colored flags and streamers.

Already, while it was early, the benches were beginning to fill, the people arriving in little carts or upon palfreys that curvetted gaily to the tinkle of silver bells at bridle reins. With these came also the poorer folk, who sat or lay upon the grass behind a railing. In the great tent the archers were gathering, some talking loudly of the fair shots each man had made in his day, some looking well to their bows, drawing a string betwixt the fingers to see that there was no fray upon it, or peering down a shaft to see that it was straight and true. And never was such a company of yeomen as had come to this shooting match. There was Gill o' the Red Cap, the Sheriff's own head archer, and Diccon Cruikshank of Lincoln Town, and Adam o' the Dell, a man of Tamworth, of threescore years and more, yet hale and lusty still, and many more.

At last the Sheriff came with his lady, he riding with stately mien upon his milk-white horse and she upon her brown filly. He wore a purple velvet cap, and purple velvet was his robe, all trimmed with ermine; his jerkin and hose were of sea-green silk, and his shoes of black velvet, the pointed toes fastened to his garters with golden chains. A golden chain hung about his neck, and at his collar was a great carbuncle set in red gold. His lady was in blue velvet, all trimmed with swansdown. And so they came to their place, where men-at-arms in chain mail awaited them.

Then the Sheriff bade his herald wind upon his silver horn, who thereupon sounded three blasts that came echoing back from the walls of Nottingham. The archers stepped to their places, while all the folks shouted with a mighty voice, each man calling upon his

favorite. "Red Cap!" "Cruikshank!" "Hey for William o' Leslie!"
And the ladies waved silken scarfs to urge each yeoman to do his best.

Then the Sheriff leaned forward, looking keenly among the
archers to find whether Robin Hood was among them; but no one
was there clad in Lincoln green. Nevertheless, said the Sheriff to
himself, he may still be there among the crowd. Let me see when
the ten best men shoot, for I wot he will be among them.

And now the archers shot, one arrow each in turn, and the good
folk never saw such archery as was done that day. Then ten men
were chosen of all those that had shot before, and of these, six
were famous throughout the land: Gilbert o' the Red Cap, Adam o'
the Dell, Diccon Cruikshank, William o' Leslie, Hubert o' Cloud
and Swithin o' Hertford. Two others were yeomen of Yorkshire,
another was a stranger in blue, who said he came from London
Town, and the last was a tattered stranger in scarlet, who wore a
patch over one eye.

"Now," quoth the Sheriff to a man-at-arms who stood near him,
"see'st thou Robin Hood among those ten?"

"Nay, your worship," answered the man. "Six of them I know
right well. Of those Yorkshire yeomen, one is too tall and the
other too short for that bold knave. Robin's beard is as yellow
as gold, while yon beggar in scarlet hath a beard of brown,
besides being blind of one eye. As for the stranger in blue, Robin's
shoulders, I ween, are three inches broader than his."

"Then," quoth the Sheriff, smiting his thigh angrily, "yon knave
is a coward as well as a rogue, and dares not show his face."

Then those ten stepped forth to shoot again. Each shot two arrows, and all the crowd watched with scarce a sound; but when
the last had shot a great shout arose for such marvelous shooting.

And now but three men were left. One was Gill o' the Red Cap,
one the tattered stranger in scarlet, and one Adam o' the Dell.
Then some of the people called aloud, "Ho for Gilbert o' the Red
Cap!" and some, "Hey for stout Adam o' Tamworth!" But not a
single man called upon the stranger in scarlet.

First to shoot was Gill o' the Red Cap. Straight flew his arrow
and lit fairly in the clout, a finger's breadth from the center. "A

Gilbert, a Gilbert!" shouted the crowd. And, "Now, by my faith," cried the Sheriff, smiting his hands together, "that is a shrewd shot."

Then the tattered stranger stepped forth, and all the people laughed as they saw a yellow patch that showed beneath his arm when he raised his elbow to shoot. He drew the good yew bow quickly, and so quickly loosed a shaft that no man could draw a breath betwixt the drawing and the shooting; yet his arrow lodged nearer the center than the other by twice the length of a barleycorn.

"Now by all the saints in paradise!" cried the Sheriff. "That is a lovely shaft in very truth!"

Adam o' the Dell shot, carefully and cautiously, and his arrow lodged close beside the stranger's. Then after a short space they all three shot again, and once more each arrow lodged within the clout, and again the stranger's shot was the best. And after another time of rest, they all shot for the third time. Gilbert took great heed to his aim. Straight flew the arrow, and all shouted till the very flags shook with the sound, for the shaft lodged close beside the spot that marked the center.

"Well done, Gilbert!" cried the Sheriff joyously. "Now, thou ragged knave, let me see thee shoot a better shaft than that."

Naught spoke the stranger but took his place, holding his bow in his hand while one could count five; then he drew his trusty yew, holding it drawn but a moment, then loosed the string. So true flew the arrow that it smote a gray goose feather from off Gilbert's shaft, which fell fluttering through the sunlit air as the stranger's arrow lodged close beside his of the Red Cap, and in the very center. And no one shouted, but each looked into his neighbor's face amazedly.

"Nay," quoth old Adam o' the Dell, drawing a long breath and shaking his head, "twoscore years and more have I shot shaft, and maybe not all times bad, but I shoot no more this day, for no man can match with yon stranger, whosoe'er he may be."

Then the Sheriff came down from his dais and drew near to where the stranger stood, while the folk crowded around to see the man who shot so wondrously well. "Here, good fellow," quoth the Sheriff, "take thou the prize, and fairly hast thou won it. What may be thy name, and whence comest thou?"

"Men do call me Jock o' Teviotdale," said the stranger.

"Then, by Our Lady, Jock, thou art the fairest archer that e'er mine eyes beheld. I trow thou drawest better bow than that same coward knave Robin Hood, that dared not show his face here this day. Say, good fellow, wilt thou join my service? I will clothe thee with a better coat than that thou hast upon thy back, and at every Christmastide fourscore marks shall be thy wage."

"Nay," quoth the stranger roughly. "I will be mine own, and no man in all England shall be my master."

"Then get thee gone, and a murrain seize thee!" cried the Sheriff, and his voice trembled with anger. "By my faith, I have a good part of a mind to have thee beaten for thine insolence!" Then he turned upon his heel and strode away.

It was a motley company that gathered about the greenwood tree in Sherwood that same day: a score of barefoot friars, and some that looked like tinkers, and some that seemed to be rustic hinds. And on a mossy couch was one clad in tattered scarlet, with a patch over one eye; and in his hand he held a golden arrow. Then, amid the talking and laughter, he took the patch from his eye and stripped the rags from his body and showed himself all clothed in Lincoln green; and quoth he, "Easy come these things away, but walnut stain cometh not so speedily from yellow hair." Then all laughed louder than before, for it was Robin himself.

Then all sat down to the woodland feast and talked of the jest that had been played upon the Sheriff. But when the feast was done, Robin took Little John apart and said, "Truly am I vexed in my blood, for I heard the Sheriff say today, 'Thou drawest better bow than that coward knave Robin Hood.' I would fain let him know who it was who won the golden arrow from out his hand."

Then Little John said, "Good master, take thou me and Will Stutely, and we will send yon fat Sheriff news of all this by a messenger such as he doth not expect."

That day the Sheriff sat at meat in the great hall of his house at Nottingham Town. Long tables stood down the hall, at which sat men-at-arms and household servants, in all fourscore and more.

The Sheriff sat at the head of the table upon a raised seat under a canopy, and beside him sat his dame. "By my troth," said he, "who could that saucy knave be who answered me so bravely? I wonder that I did not have him beaten; but there was something about him that spoke of other things than rags and tatters."

Even as he finished speaking, something fell rattling among the dishes on the table, startling those that sat near. It was a blunted gray goose shaft, which had been shot through the window, with a fine scroll tied near to its head. The Sheriff opened the scroll and read it, while the veins upon his forehead swelled and his cheeks grew ruddy with rage, for this was what he saw:

> *Now heaven bless thy Grace this day,*
>   *Say all in sweet Sherwood,*
> *For thou didst give the prize away*
>   *To merry Robin Hood.*

Will Stutely Rescued by His Companions

NOW WHEN THE SHERIFF found that neither law nor guile could overcome Robin Hood, he was much perplexed, and said to himself, I will try what may be done with might.

So he called his constables together. "Now take ye each four men, all armed in proof," said he, "and get ye to the forest, at different points, and lie in wait. To him that first meeteth with Robin Hood shall one hundred pounds of silver money be given if he be brought to me dead or alive; and to him that meeteth with any of his band shall twoscore pounds be given if such be brought to me."

So they went in threescore companies of five to Sherwood Forest, to take Robin Hood. For seven days they hunted, but never saw so much as a single man in Lincoln green; for tidings of all this had been brought to Robin Hood by trusty Eadom o' the Blue Boar, and Robin had said, "If the Sheriff dare send force to meet force, blood will flow. But fain would I not deal sorrow to women-folk and wives because good stout yeomen lose their lives. Once I slew a man, and never do I wish to slay a man again."

So Robin and his men hid in the depths of Sherwood for seven days; but early on the eighth day Robin Hood said to Will Stutely, "Now go you and find what the Sheriff's men are at. For I know right well they will not bide forever within Sherwood shades."

Then Will Stutely clad himself in a friar's gown, and underneath the robe he hung a good broadsword. Thus clad, he set forth, until he came to the Sign of the Blue Boar. For, quoth he to himself, our good friend Eadom will tell me all the news.

Now no sweeter inn could be found in all Nottinghamshire than the Blue Boar. None had such lovely trees standing around, or was so covered with trailing clematis and woodbine; none had such good beer; nor, in wintertime, when the north wind howled and snow drifted around the hedges, was there to be found such a roaring fire as blazed upon the hearth. There had Robin Hood and his merry companions often gathered. As for mine host, he knew how to keep a still tongue in his head, for he knew very well which side of his bread was spread with butter, for Robin and his men were the best of customers and paid their scores without having them chalked up behind the door.·

Here Will Stutely found a band of the Sheriff's men drinking right lustily. He sat down upon a distant bench, his staff in his hand, and his head bowed as though he were meditating, until he might see the landlord apart. As Stutely sat thus, a house cat came and rubbed against his knee, raising his robe a palm's breadth high. Stutely pushed his robe quickly down again, but the constable who commanded the Sheriff's men saw fair Lincoln green beneath the friar's robe. Yon is no friar of orders gray, he said to himself; and also, I wot, no honest yeoman goeth about in priest's garb. Now I think in good sooth that is one of Robin Hood's own men. So, presently, he said aloud, "Whither goest thou, holy friar?"

"I go a pilgrim to Canterbury Town," answered Will Stutely, speaking gruffly, so that none might know his voice.

Then the constable said, "Now tell me, holy father, do pilgrims to Canterbury wear Lincoln green beneath their robes?" And he flashed forth his bright sword and leaped upon Will Stutely; but Stutely held his own sword in his hand beneath his robe, so he drew it forth before the constable came upon him. Then the constable struck a mighty blow; but Stutely, parrying the blow right deftly, smote the constable back again. Then he would have escaped, but that the constable, all dizzy with the wound, seized him by the knees as he reeled and fell. The others rushed upon him, and one smote him a blow upon the crown so that the blood ran down his face and blinded him. Then, staggering, he fell, and all sprang upon him, and bound him with hempen cords.

Now Robin Hood stood under the greenwood tree, thinking of Will Stutely and how he might be faring, when suddenly he saw running down the forest path the serving lass of the Blue Boar.

"Will Stutely hath been taken," cried she, "and I fear he is wounded sore. They have taken him to Nottingham Town, and I heard that he should be hanged tomorrow day."

"He shall not," cried Robin. "Or, if he be, full many a one shall have cause to cry alackaday!" Then he clapped his horn to his lips and blew three blasts, and presently sevenscore bold blades were gathered around him. "Now hark you all!" cried Robin. "Will Stutely hath been taken by that vile Sheriff's men, therefore doth it behoove us to take bow and brand in hand to bring him off again. Is it not so?" Then all cried "Aye!" with a great voice.

So the next day they wended their way from Sherwood Forest, but by different paths, in twos and threes, to meet in a tangled dell near to Nottingham Town. There Robin spoke thus: "Now we will lie here until we get news, for it doth behoove us to be wary."

They lay hidden until the sun stood high in the sky. The day was warm and the dusty road was bare of travelers, except an aged palmer. Robin called young David of Doncaster and said, "Now get thee forth and speak to yonder palmer, for he cometh from Nottingham Town, and may tell thee news of good Stutely."

So David strode forth and saluted the pilgrim and said, "Good morrow, holy father. Canst thou tell me when Will Stutely will be hanged upon the gallows tree? I fain would not miss the sight."

"Now, out upon thee, young man," cried the palmer, "that thou shouldst speak so when a good man is to be hanged!" And he struck his staff upon the ground in anger. "Even this day, toward evening, he shall be hanged, fourscore rods from the town gate of

Nottingham, where three roads meet; there the Sheriff sweareth he shall die as a warning to all outlaws. Alas! I say. Though Robin Hood and his band be outlaws, he taketh only from the rich and the dishonest." And the palmer went upon his way, muttering.

When David told Robin what the palmer had said, Robin called the band and spoke thus: "Now let us get to Nottingham Town and mix with the people there; but keep ye one another in sight, pressing near the prisoner and his guards when they come outside the walls. Strike no man without need, but if ye do strike, strike hard. Then keep together until we come again to Sherwood."

The sun was low in the western sky when a bugle note sounded from the castle wall. Then crowds filled the streets of Nottingham Town, for all knew that the famous Will Stutely was to be hanged. The castle gates opened wide and a great array of men-at-arms came forth with noise and clatter, the Sheriff riding at their head. In the midst of the guard, in a cart, with a halter about his neck, rode Will Stutely. His face was pale, and his fair hair was clotted where the blood had hardened. He looked up and he looked down, but though he saw some faces that showed pity and some that showed friendliness, he saw none that he knew.

At last they came to the great town gate, through which Stutely saw the fair country beyond. When he saw the slanting sunlight on field and fallow, on cot and farmhouse, and when he heard the birds singing their vespers, and the sheep bleating upon the hillside, there came a fullness to his heart so that salt tears blurred his sight, and he bowed his head lest the folk should think him unmanly. But when they were outside the walls he looked up again, and his heart leaped within him, for he saw upon all sides his own dear companions crowding closely upon the men-at-arms.

"Now, stand back!" cried the Sheriff in a mighty voice. "What mean ye, varlets, that ye push upon us so?"

Then came a bustle and a noise, and one strove to push between the men-at-arms, and Stutely saw that it was Little John.

"Now stand thou back!" cried one of the men-at-arms.

"Now stand thou back thine own self," quoth Little John, and smote the man a buffet beside his head that felled him as a butcher

fells an ox, and then he leaped to the cart. With one stroke he cut the bonds that bound Stutely's arms and legs, and Stutely leaped straightway from the cart.

"Now as I live," cried the Sheriff, "yon varlet is a sturdy rebel! Take him, I bid you all, and let him not go!"

So saying, he spurred his horse upon Little John, and rising in his stirrups smote with might and main, but Little John ducked underneath the horse and the blow whistled over his head.

"Nay, good Sir Sheriff," cried he, leaping up again when the blow had passed, "I must e'en borrow thy sword." Thereupon he twitched the weapon deftly from out the Sheriff's hand. "Here, Stutely," he cried, "the Sheriff hath lent thee his sword! Back to back with me, man, and defend thyself, for help is nigh!"

Even as he spoke, a bugle horn sounded shrilly, and a cloth-yard shaft whistled within an inch of the Sheriff's head. Then came a swaying hither and thither, and oaths, cries and groans, and clashing of steel, and a score of arrows whistled through the air. And some cried, "Help!" and some, "A rescue, a rescue!"

"Treason!" bellowed the Sheriff. "Bear back! Bear back! Else we be all dead men!" Thereupon he reined his horse backward through the thickest of the crowd.

Now Robin Hood and his band might have slain half of the Sheriff's men had they desired to do so, but they let them push out of the press and get them gone.

"Oh, stay!" shouted Will Stutely after the Sheriff. "Thou wilt never catch bold Robin if thou dost not stand to meet him." But the Sheriff, bowing along his horse's back, only spurred the faster.

Then Will Stutely turned to Little John and wept aloud; and kissing his friend's cheeks, "Oh Little John!" quoth he. "Little did I reckon to see thy face this side of paradise."

Then Robin Hood gathered his band together in a close rank, with Will Stutely in the midst, and they moved slowly away toward Sherwood.

Thus the Sheriff of Nottingham tried thrice to take Robin Hood and failed each time; and the last time he was frightened for his life; so he said, "These men fear neither God nor man, nor king nor king's officers. I would sooner lose mine office than my life, so I will trouble them no more." So he kept close within his castle for many a day, and all the time he was gloomy and would speak to no one, for he was ashamed of what had happened that day.

Robin Hood Turns Butcher

NOW AFTER ALL THIS, Robin Hood said to himself, If I have the chance, I will make our worshipful Sheriff pay right well for that which he hath done to me. Maybe I may bring him to Sherwood to have a merry feast with us. For when Robin Hood caught a baron or a fat abbot or bishop, he brought him to the greenwood tree and feasted him before he lightened his purse.

But for nearly a year Robin Hood and his band lived quietly in Sherwood Forest, for Robin knew that it would not be wise for him to be seen in the neighborhood of Nottingham. At last he began to fret at his confinement; so one day he took up his cudgel and set forth to seek adventure. As he rambled along the sunlit road at the edge of Sherwood, he met a young butcher driving a fine mare and riding in a stout new cart, all hung about with meat. Merrily whistled the butcher as he jogged along.

"Good morrow to thee, jolly fellow," quoth Robin, "thou seemest happy this merry morn."

"And why should I not be so?" quoth the butcher. "Am I not hale in wind and limb? And am I not to be married to the bonniest lass in all Nottinghamshire on Thursday next?"

"Ha," said Robin, "and where goest thou with thy meat?"

"I go to the market at Nottingham Town," answered the butcher. "But who art thou, my fair friend?"

"A yeoman am I, and men do call me Robin Hood."

"Now, by Our Lady's grace," cried the butcher, "many a time have I heard thy deeds both sung and spoken of. But heaven forbid that thou shouldst take aught of me! An honest man am I."

"Not so much as one farthing would I take from thee, for I love a fair Saxon face—especially when the man that owneth it is to marry

469

a bonny lass on Thursday next. But come"—and Robin Hood plucked the purse from his girdle—"here in this purse are six marks. Now, I would fain be a butcher for the day. Wilt thou take six marks for thy meat and thy horse and cart?"

"Now may the blessing of all the saints fall on thy head!" cried the butcher right joyfully, as he leaped down from his cart and took the purse that Robin held out to him.

"Now get thee gone back to thy lass, and give her a sweet kiss from me," quoth Robin, laughing. Then he donned the butcher's apron, climbed into the cart, took the reins and drove off.

When he came to Nottingham, he entered that part of the market where butchers stood, and opened his stall and spread his meat upon the bench. Then, taking his cleaver and steel and clattering them together, he sang:

> *"Lamb have I that hath fed upon naught*
> *But the dainty daisies pied,*
> *And the violet sweet, and the daffodil*
> *That grow fair streams beside.*
>
> *"And beef have I from the heathery wolds,*
> *And mutton from dales all green,*
> *And veal as white as a maiden's brow,*
> *With its mother's milk, I ween."*

Then he shouted lustily, "Now, who'll buy? Four prices have I. Three pennyworths of meat I sell to a fat friar or priest for sixpence, for I want not their custom; stout aldermen I charge threepence, for it doth not matter to me whether they buy or not; to buxom dames I sell three pennyworths for one penny, for I like their custom well; but to the bonny lass I charge naught but one fair kiss, for I like her custom the best of all."

Then all began to stare and wonder and to crowd around, and when they came to buy they found it as he had said, for he gave dames as much meat for one penny as they could buy elsewhere for three, and when a merry lass gave him a kiss, he charged not one penny for his meat; and many such came to his stall, for his eyes were as blue as the skies of June, and he gave to each full measure.

Thus he sold all his meat so fast that no butcher that stood near him could sell anything.

Then they began to talk among themselves, and some said, "This must be some thief who has stolen meat." But others said, "When did ye ever see a thief who parted with his goods so freely? This must be some prodigal who hath sold his father's land."

Then some of the butchers came to make his acquaintance. "Come, brother," quoth one, "we be all of one trade, so wilt thou go dine with us? For this day the Sheriff hath asked all the Butcher Guild to feast with him at the Guild Hall."

"Now, right joyously," quoth Robin, "will I go dine with you, my sweet lads, and that as fast as I can hie."

The Sheriff had already come in state to the Guild Hall, and with him many butchers. When Robin came in, those that were near the Sheriff whispered to him, "Yon is some prodigal that meaneth to spend his silver and gold right merrily."

Then the Sheriff called Robin, not knowing him in his butcher's dress, and made him sit on his right hand; for he loved a rich young prodigal—especially when he thought he might lighten that prodigal's pockets into his own most worshipful purse. So he made much of Robin. "Thou art a jolly blade," he said. "I love thee mightily." And he smote Robin upon the shoulder.

"Yea," quoth Robin. "I know thou dost love a jolly blade, for didst thou not have Robin Hood at thy shooting match and didst thou not give him a bright golden arrow for his own?"

At this the Sheriff laughed, but not as though he liked the jest. "Now thou art a merry soul," quoth he, "and I wot thou must have many a head of horned beasts and many an acre of land."

"Aye," quoth Robin, "five hundred and more horned beasts have I and my brothers, and none of them have we been able to sell, else I might not have turned butcher. As for my land, I have never asked my steward how many acres I have."

The Sheriff's eyes twinkled. "Nay, good youth," quoth he, "if thou canst not sell thy cattle, it may be I will lift them from thy hands myself. How much dost thou want for them?"

"Well," quoth Robin, "they are worth five hundred pounds."

"Nay," answered the Sheriff slowly. "Fain would I help thee, but I have not five hundred pounds. Yet I will give thee three hundred for them all."

"Now thou old miser!" quoth Robin. "Well thou knowest that so many cattle are worth seven hundred pounds, and yet I will take thine offer, for I and my brothers do need the money."

"I will bring thee the money," said the Sheriff. "But what is thy name, good youth?"

"Men call me Robert o' Locksley," quoth bold Robin.

"Then, good Robert o' Locksley," quoth the Sheriff, "I will come this day to see thy horned beasts."

"So be it," said Robin Hood, laughing, and smiting his palm upon the Sheriff's hand.

Thus the bargain was closed, but many of the butchers talked among themselves of the Sheriff, saying that it was but a scurvy trick to beguile a poor spendthrift youth in this way.

That afternoon the Sheriff and Robin Hood set forth, the Sheriff upon his horse and Robin running beside him, for he had sold his horse and cart to a trader. Thus they traveled till they came within the verge of Sherwood Forest. Then the Sheriff looked up and down and to the right and to the left. "Now," quoth he, "may heaven and its saints preserve us from that rogue Robin Hood."

"Nay," said Robin, laughing, "thou may'st set thy mind at rest, for well do I know Robin Hood and well do I know that thou art in no more danger from him this day than thou art from me."

At this the Sheriff looked askance at Robin, saying to himself, I like not that thou seemest so well acquainted with this outlaw.

But still they traveled deeper into the forest, and the deeper they went, the more quiet grew the Sheriff. At last they came to where the road took a sudden bend, and before them a herd of dun deer went tripping across the path. Then Robin came close to the Sheriff and, pointing his finger, he said, "These are my horned beasts, good Master Sheriff. Are they not fat and fair?"

At this the Sheriff drew rein quickly. "Now fellow," quoth he, "I would I were well out of this forest, for I like not thy company. Go thou thine own path, and let me but go mine."

But Robin caught the Sheriff's bridle rein. "Nay," cried he, "stay awhile, for I would thou shouldst see my brothers." So saying, he winded three notes upon his bugle and presently up the path came fivescore good stout yeomen with Little John at their head.

"What wouldst thou have, good master?" quoth Little John.

"Why," answered Robin, "dost thou not see our good master, the Sheriff, hath come to feast with us?"

Then all doffed their hats humbly, without smiling or seeming to be in jest, while Little John took the bridle rein and led the palfrey still deeper into the forest, all marching in order, with Robin Hood walking beside the Sheriff, hat in hand.

The Sheriff said never a word but his heart sank. So they came to the greenwood tree, and Robin sat down, placing the Sheriff at his right hand. "Now busk ye, my merry men," quoth he, "and bring forth meat and wine, for his worship feasted me in Nottingham Guild Hall today, and I would not have him go back empty."

Then, while bright fires crackled and savory smells of roasting venison filled the glade, did Robin Hood entertain the Sheriff right royally. First, couples stood forth at quarterstaff, and so quickly did they give stroke and parry that the Sheriff clapped his hands, forgetting where he was and crying aloud, "Well struck! Well struck!" Then all feasted together until the sun was low.

At last the Sheriff arose and said, "I thank you all, good yeomen, for the entertainment ye have given me. But I must away before darkness comes, lest I lose myself within the forest."

Then Robin said to the Sheriff, "If thou must go, worshipful sir, go thou must; but thou hast forgot something. We keep a merry inn here, but our guests must pay their reckoning."

The Sheriff laughed, but the laugh was hollow. "Well, jolly boys," quoth he, "we have had a merry time, and even if ye had not asked me, I would have given you a score of pounds."

"Nay," quoth Robin, "it would ill beseem us to treat your worship so meanly. By my faith, I would be ashamed to show my face if I did not reckon the King's deputy at three hundred pounds."

"Think ye that your beggarly feast was worth three pounds," roared the Sheriff, "let alone three hundred?"

"Speak not so roundly, your worship," quoth Robin gravely, "for there be those here who love thee not so much. Look down the cloth and thou wilt see Will Stutely. Now pay thy score without more ado, or it may fare ill with thee."

As he spoke the Sheriff's ruddy cheeks grew pale, and slowly he drew forth his purse.

"Now, Little John," quoth Robin, "see that the reckoning be right. We would not doubt our Sheriff, but he might not like it if he should find he had not paid his full score."

Little John counted the money and found that the bag held three hundred pounds in silver and gold. But to the Sheriff it seemed as if every clink of the bright money was a drop of blood from his veins. And when he saw it all counted out in a heap, he turned away and silently mounted his horse. Then Robin, taking the bridle rein, led him into the main forest path. "Fare thee well," he said, "and when next thou thinkest to despoil some poor prodigal, remember thy feast in Sherwood Forest." He clapped his hand to the horse's back, and off went nag and Sheriff.

Then bitterly the Sheriff rued the day that first he meddled with Robin Hood, for all men laughed at him and many ballads were sung of how the Sheriff went to shear and came home shorn.

How Robin Hood Found New Recruits

ONE FINE DAY, ROBIN HOOD and two chosen fellows of his band, Little John and Arthur a Bland, were traveling along a sunny road when Robin waxed thirsty; so, there being a fountain of water just behind the hedgerow, they crossed a stile and came to where the water bubbled up from beneath a mossy stone. Kneeling and making cups of the palms of their hands, they drank their fill, and then, the spot being shady, they stretched their limbs and rested.

"Heyday!" quoth Robin, who had been gazing around him. "Yon is a gaily feathered bird."

The others looked and saw a young man walking slowly down the highway. His doublet was of scarlet silk and his stockings also;

a handsome sword hung by his side, the embossed leathern scabbard being picked out with fine threads of gold; his cap was of scarlet velvet, and a broad feather hung down behind one ear. His hair was long and yellow and curled upon his shoulders.

"Truly, his clothes have overmuch prettiness," quoth Arthur, "but his shoulders are broad and his arms dangle not down like spindles, but hang stiff and bend at the elbow. I take my vow, there be no bread-and-milk limbs in those fine clothes."

"Pah!" quoth Robin Hood. "I take it thou art wrong. Were a furious mouse to run across his path, he would cry, 'La!' and fall straightway into a swoon. I wonder who he may be."

"Some great baron's son, I doubt not," answered Little John, "with good and true men's money lining his purse."

"Aye, marry, that is true, I make no doubt," quoth Robin. "What a pity that such men should have good fellows, whose shoes they are not fit to tie, dancing at their bidding. Now, lie ye both here, while I show you how I drub this fellow." So saying, Robin Hood crossed the stile and stood in the road, with his hands on his hips, in the stranger's path.

Meantime the stranger neither quickened his pace nor seemed to see that such a man as Robin Hood was in the world.

"Hold!" cried Robin, when the other had come close to him. "Hold! Stand where thou art!"

"Wherefore should I hold, good fellow?" said the stranger in a gentle voice. "Ne'ertheless, as thou dost desire that I should stay, I will abide for a short time."

"Then," quoth Robin, "I would have thee deliver to me thy purse, fair friend, that I may look into it, and judge whether thou hast more wealth about thee than our law allows."

"Alas," said the youth with a smile, "I do love to hear thee talk, thou pretty fellow, but I have nothing to give thee. Let me go my way, I prithee."

"Nay, thou goest not," quoth Robin, "till thou hast shown me thy purse." So saying, he raised his quarterstaff above his head.

"Alas!" said the stranger sadly. "I fear much that I must slay thee, thou poor fellow!" So saying, he drew his sword.

"Put by thy weapon," quoth Robin. "It cannot stand against my staff. Yonder is a good oaken thicket; take a cudgel thence and defend thyself fairly."

Then the stranger stepped to the little clump of ground oaks Robin had spoken of. Presently he found a sapling to his liking. Rolling up his sleeves, he laid hold of it, placed his heel against the ground and, with one mighty pull, plucked the young tree up by the roots. Then he came back, trimming away the roots and stems with his sword as quietly as if he had done naught to speak of.

When Little John and Arthur saw the stranger drag the sapling up from the earth, and heard the rending and snapping of its roots, Arthur pursed his lips together, drawing his breath between them in a long inward whistle.

"By the breath of my body!" said Little John. "I think our poor master will stand but an ill chance with yon fellow."

Whatever Robin Hood thought, he stood his ground, and now he and the stranger stood face to face. Back and forth they fought, the dust of the highway rising about them like a cloud. Thrice Robin struck the stranger, but at last the stranger struck Robin's cudgel so fairly in the middle that he not only beat down Robin's guard, but gave him such a rap that down he tumbled in the road.

"Hold!" cried Robin Hood, when he saw the stranger raising his staff once more. "I yield me!"

"Alas!" cried Little John, bursting from his cover, with a twinkle in his eye. "Thou art in an ill plight, good master. Thy jerkin is all befouled with the dust of the road. Let me help thee to arise."

"A plague on thy aid!" cried Robin angrily. "I can get to my feet without thy help." Then, turning to the stranger, he said, "What may be thy name, good fellow?"

"My name is Gamwell," answered the other.

"Ha!" cried Robin. "Is it even so? I have near kin of that name. Whence camest thou, fair friend?"

"From Maxfield Town I come," answered the stranger, "to seek my mother's young brother, whom men call Robin Hood."

"Will Gamwell!" cried Robin, placing both hands upon the other's shoulders. "Dost thou not know me, lad?"

"Now, by the breath of my body!" cried the other. "I do believe that thou art mine own Uncle Robin." And each flung his arms around the other, kissing him upon the cheek.

"Why, how now," quoth Robin, "what change is here? Verily, some ten years ago I left thee a stripling lad, with great joints and ill-hung limbs, and lo! Here thou art, as tight a fellow as e'er I set mine eyes upon. Dost thou remember, lad, how I showed thee the proper way to throw out thy bow arm?"

"Yea," said young Gamwell, "and I thought thee so above all other men that, I make my vow, had I known who thou wert, I would never have dared to lift hand against thee this day. I trust I did thee no great harm."

"No, no, thou didst not harm me," quoth Robin hastily. "Yet thou art the strongest man that ever I laid eyes upon. But tell me, how camest thou to leave Sir Edward and thy mother?"

"Alas!" answered young Gamwell. "It is an ill story, Uncle. My father's steward was a saucy varlet, and I know not why my father kept him, saving that he did oversee with great judgment, and that my father was ever slow to anger. Well, one day that saucy fellow sought to berate my father, I standing by. I could stand it no longer, good Uncle, so I gave him a box o' the ear, and—wouldst thou believe it?—the fellow straightway died o't. I think they said I broke his neck. So off they packed me to seek thee and escape the law."

"Well, by my faith," quoth Robin, "for anyone escaping the law, thou wert taking it the most easily that ever I beheld."

"Nay, Uncle," answered Will Gamwell, "overhaste never churned good butter. Moreover, I do verily believe that this overstrength of my body hath taken the nimbleness out of my heels."

"In truth," quoth Robin, "I am glad to see thee, Will. But thou must change thy name, for warrants will be out against thee; so, because of thy clothes, thou shalt be called Will Scarlet."

"Will Scarlet," quoth Little John, stepping forward and reaching out his great palm, which the other took, "the name fitteth thee well. Thou art like to achieve fame, Will, for there will be many a merry ballad sung about the country of how Robin Hood bit off so large a piece of cake that he choked on it."

"Nay, good Little John, let us keep this day's doing among ourselves," cried Robin, biting his nether lip, while the others could not forbear laughing. "Come, we will return to Sherwood."

So, turning their backs, they retraced their steps. Now, when the four had traveled for a long time, "How now!" quoth Robin suddenly. "Who may yon fellow be coming along the road?"

"Truly," said Little John, "I think he is a certain young miller I have seen now and then around the edge of Sherwood."

As the young miller came near they could see that his clothes were dusted with flour, and over his back he carried a great sack of meal, and across the sack was a thick quarterstaff. His limbs were stout and strong, and his cheeks ruddy as a winter hip; his hair was flaxen, and on his chin was a downy growth of beard.

"Now let us have a merry jest with this good fellow," quoth Robin Hood. "We will pretend to rob him of his honest gains. Then will we give him a feast in the forest and send him home with crowns in his purse for every penny he hath." Whereupon all four of them ran out and surrounded the miller.

"Hold, friend!" cried Robin. "We be good Christian men and would fain help thee by carrying part of thy heavy load."

"I give you all thanks," said the miller, "but my bag is none that heavy that I cannot carry it e'en by myself."

"Nay, thou dost mistake," quoth Robin. "I meant that thou mightest have some heavy farthings or pence about thee, not to speak of silver."

"Alas!" cried the miller, throwing the great sack to the ground. "I have not about me so much as a groat. Let me depart in peace, I pray you. Moreover, let me tell you that ye are upon Robin Hood's ground, and should he find you seeking to rob an honest craftsman, he will clip your ears to your heads."

"In truth I fear Robin Hood no more than I do myself," quoth jolly Robin. "Good Arthur, empty that fat sack upon the ground; I warrant thou wilt find a shilling or two in the flour."

"Spoil not my good meal!" cried the miller, falling upon his knees. "Spare it, and I will give up the money in the bag."

Slowly and unwillingly the miller untied the mouth of the bag,

and slowly thrust his hands into the flour. The others gathered
around him, looking and wondering what he would bring forth.
But while he pretended to be searching for the money, the miller
gathered two great handfuls of meal. "Ha," quoth he, "here they
are, the beauties." As the others leaned still more forward to see
what he had, he suddenly cast the meal into their faces, filling their
eyes and noses and mouths with the flour. Then, while all four
stumbled about, roaring with the smart of it, and rubbed their
eyes till the tears made great channels on their faces through the
meal, the miller threw another handful of flour and another and another, till their hair and beards and clothes were white as snow.

Then, catching up his great staff, the miller began laying about
him as though he were clean gone mad. This way and that skipped
the four, like peas on a drumhead, but they could see neither to
defend themselves nor to run away. Thwack! Thwack! went the
miller's cudgel across their backs, and at every blow great white
clouds of flour rose in the air and went drifting down the breeze.

"Stop!" roared Robin at last. "Give over! I am Robin Hood!"

"Thou liest, knave," cried the miller. "Stout Robin never robbed
an honest tradesman." And he gave him another blow. "Nay, thou
art not getting thy share, thou long-legged knave." And he smote
Little John so that he sent him skipping half across the road. "It is
thy turn now, black beard." And he gave Arthur a crack. "How
now, red coat, let me brush the dust from thee!" cried he, smiting
Will Scarlet. And so he gave them merry words and blows until
at last Robin found his horn and blew three blasts upon it.

Now it chanced that Will Stutely and a party of men were in the
glade not far away. So they dashed forward with might and main
and burst from the covert into the highroad. But what a sight they
saw! Five men stood there white with meal from top to toe, for
much of the flour had fallen back upon the miller.

"What is thy need, master?" cried Will Stutely. "And what doth
all this mean?"

Hereupon, while he and the others rubbed the meal from their
eyes and brushed their clothes clean, Robin told them all.

"Quick, men, seize the vile miller!" cried Stutely, who was nigh choking with laughter. Whereupon several seized the stout fellow, and bound his arms behind his back with bowstrings.

"Ha!" cried Robin, when they brought the miller to him. "Thou wouldst murder me, wouldst thou? By my faith—" Here he stopped and stood glaring upon the miller grimly. But Robin's anger could not hold, so in spite of all he broke into a laugh. And when they saw their master laugh, the yeomen could contain themselves no longer, and a mighty shout of laughter went up.

"What is thy name, good fellow?" said Robin.

"Alas, sir, I am Midge, the Miller's son," said the miller.

"I make my vow," quoth Robin, "thou art the mightiest Midge that e'er I beheld. Now wilt thou leave thy dusty mill and join my band? By my faith, thou art too stout a man to spend thy days betwixt the hopper and the till."

"Then truly, if thou dost forgive me for the blows I struck, I will join with thee right merrily," said the miller.

"Then have I gained this day," quoth Robin, "the two stoutest yeomen in all Nottinghamshire. We will get us away to the greenwood tree, and there hold a feast in honor of our new friends." So saying, he turned and led the way into the forest.

Robin Hood and Allan a Dale

Two DAYS HAD PASSED BY, yet still, when Robin moved of a sudden, pain here and there would, as it were, jog him, crying, "Thou hast had a drubbing, good fellow." The day was bright and jocund, and he sat under the greenwood tree; on one side was Will Scarlet, lying upon his back, gazing up into the clear sky, with hands clasped behind his head; upon the other side sat Little John, fashioning a cudgel out of a stout crab-tree limb. Elsewhere upon the grass sat many others of the band.

"By my faith," quoth Robin, "our money groweth low in the purse, for no one hath come to pay a reckoning for many a day. Now choose thee six men, good Stutely, and get thee to Fosse Way, and bring rich guests to eat with us this evening."

"Truly, my limbs do grow slack through abiding idly here," quoth Stutely, springing to his feet. "As for two of my six, I will choose Midge the Miller and Will Scarlet, for, as well thou knowest, good master, they are stout fists at the quarterstaff."

At this all laughed but Robin, who twisted up his face. "I can speak for them," said he.

So, having chosen four more stout fellows, Will Stutely and his band set forth. For all the livelong day they abided near Fosse Way, but no guest such as they desired showed his face. At last the sun began to sink. Then Stutely arose. "A plague of such ill luck!" quoth he. "Come, lads, let us pack up and home again, say I."

Accordingly, the others arose, and they all turned back to Sherwood. After they had gone some distance, Will Stutely suddenly stopped. "Hist!" quoth he. "Methinks I hear a sound." At this all stopped and listened with bated breath; and they heard a faint and melancholy sound, like someone in lamentation.

"Ha!" quoth Will Scarlet. "This must be looked into." Thus saying, he led the way to an opening in the woodland, whence a brook spread out into a glassy-pebbled pool. By the side of this pool, and beneath a willow, lay a youth, weeping aloud. From the branches overhead hung a beautiful harp inlaid with gold and silver. Beside him lay a stout ashen bow and half a score of arrows.

"Halloa!" shouted Will Stutely. "Who art thou, fellow, that liest there killing the green grass with salt water?"

Hearing the voice, the stranger sprang to his feet and, snatching up his bow and fitting a shaft, held himself in readiness for whatever ill might befall him.

"Pah!" cried Will Stutely. "Wipe thine eyes, man! I hate to see a tall, stout fellow sniveling like a girl of fourteen over a dead tomtit. Put down thy bow! We mean thee no harm."

But Will Scarlet, seeing how the young stranger was stung by Stutely's words, came up to him and put his hand upon his shoulder. "Nay, thou art in trouble, poor boy!" said he kindly. "Mind not these fellows. They are rough, but they mean thee well. Thou shalt come with us, and perchance we may find a certain one that can aid thee in thy perplexities."

"Yea, truly," said Will Stutely gruffly, "I meant no harm. Take down thy singing tool, and away with us."

With bowed head and sorrowful steps, the youth did as he was bidden. A glimmering gray fell over all things, and the strange whispering sounds of nighttime came to the ear. At last they came to the open glade, now bathed in pale moonlight. In the center crackled a great fire, throwing a red glow all around; and the air was filled with the sweet smell of good things cooking.

So, with Will Scarlet upon one side and Stutely upon the other, the stranger came to where Robin sat under the greenwood tree.

"Good even, fair friend," said Robin. "And hast thou come to feast with me this day?"

"Alas! I know not," said the lad, looking around him with dazed eyes. "Truly, I know not whether I be in a dream."

"Nay, marry," quoth Robin, laughing, "thou art awake, as thou wilt presently find, for a fine feast is a-cooking for thee."

Still the stranger looked about him. "Methinks," said he at last, "I know now where I am. Art not thou the great Robin Hood?"

"Thou hast hit the bull's-eye," quoth Robin, clapping him upon the shoulder. "Sin' thou knowest me, thou knowest also that he who feasteth with me must pay his reckoning."

"Alas!" said the stranger. "I have no money, saving only the half of a sixpence, the other half of which mine own dear love doth carry, hung about her neck by a silken thread."

At this Robin turned sharply to Will Stutely. "How now," quoth he, "is this the guest thou hast brought to fill our purse?"

Up spoke Will Scarlet, and told how they had found the lad in sorrow, and how they had brought him to Robin, thinking that he might aid him. Then Robin Hood placed his hand upon the youth's shoulder and held him off at arm's length, scanning his face.

"A young face," quoth he in a low voice, "a fair face. But, if I may judge, grief cometh to young as well as to old." At these words, spoken so kindly, the lad's eyes brimmed up with tears. "Nay," said Robin hastily, "cheer up, lad. I warrant thy case is not so bad that it cannot be mended. What may be thy name?"

"Allan a Dale is my name, good master."

"Allan a Dale," repeated Robin, musing. "Surely thou art the minstrel of whom we have been hearing lately, whose voice so charmeth all men. Dost thou not come from Rotherstream?"

"Yea, truly," answered Allan, "I do come thence."

"How old art thou, Allan?" said Robin.

"I am but twenty years of age."

"Methinks thou art overyoung to be perplexed with trouble," quoth Robin kindly. Then, turning to the others, he cried, "Come, lads, busk ye and get our feast; only thou, Will Scarlet, and thou, Little John, stay here." Then Robin turned once more to the youth. "Now, lad," said he, "sit thou beside me, and tell us thy troubles. A flow of words doth ever ease the heart of sorrows."

Then the youth told all that was in his heart; at first in broken words and phrases, then freely when he saw that all listened closely to what he said. He told them how he had come from York to the vale of Rother, traveling the country through as a minstrel, stopping now at castle, now at hall; and how one evening in a certain farmhouse he sang before a stout franklin and a maiden as pure and lovely as the first snowdrop of spring; and how sweet Ellen had listened to him and had loved him. He told how he had watched for her when she went abroad, but was all too afraid to speak to her, until at last, beside the banks of Rother, he had spoken of his love, and she had whispered that which had made his heartstrings quiver for joy. Then they broke a sixpence between them, and vowed to be true to one another forever.

Next he told how her father had discovered what was a-doing, and had taken her away from him; how this morn, only one short month and a half from the time that he had seen her last, he had heard that she was to marry old Sir Stephen of Trent two days hence, for Ellen's father thought it would be a grand thing to have his daughter marry so high, albeit she wished it not.

"By the breath of my body," burst forth Little John. "I have a mind to go straightway and cudgel the nasty life out of that same vile Sir Stephen. Does an old weazen think that tender lasses are to be bought like pullets o' a market day?"

Then up spoke Will Scarlet. "Methinks it seemeth but ill done of the lass that she should so quickly change at others' bidding. I like it not in her, Allan."

"Nay," said Allan hotly, "thou dost wrong her. She is as gentle as a stockdove. She may do her father's bidding, but if she marries Sir Stephen, her heart will break and she will die."

While the others were speaking, Robin had been sunk in thought. "I have a plan might fit thy case, Allan," said he. "If thy true love's father be the man I take him to be, he shall give you both his blessing as wedded man and wife, in the place of old Sir Stephen and upon his wedding morn. But stay, there's one thing reckoned not upon—the priest. Those of the cloth do not love me overmuch, and in such a matter they are like to prove stiff-necked."

"So far as that goeth," quoth Will Scarlet, "I know of a certain friar that would do thy business, couldst thou but get on the soft side of him. He is known as the Curtal Friar of Fountain Dale. A stout pair of legs could carry a man to his cell and back in a day."

"Then give me thy hand, Allan," cried Robin, "and I swear by the bright hair of Saint Ælfrida that this time two days hence Ellen a Dale shall be thy wife."

But now one came to say that the feast was ready; so, Robin leading the way, the others followed to where the meal was spread upon the grass. When they had eaten, Robin Hood turned to Allan. "Now, Allan," quoth he, "so much has been said of thy singing that we would fain have a taste of thy skill ourselves."

"Surely!" answered Allan readily, and, taking up his harp, he ran his fingers lightly over the strings. Then, backing his voice with music on his harp, he sang many a sweet ballad.

Not a sound broke the stillness while Allan a Dale sang; so sweet was his voice that each man sat with bated breath.

"By my faith and my troth," quoth Robin when at last the minstrel had done, "thou must not leave our company, Allan! Wilt thou not stay with us here in the forest?"

Then Allan took Robin's hand and kissed it. "I will stay with thee always, dear master," said he, "for never have I known such kindness as thou hast shown me this day."

And thus Allan a Dale became one of Robin Hood's band.

THE YEOMEN OF SHERWOOD were ever early risers of a morn, more especially when the summertime had come, for then the dew was the brightest, and the song of the birds the sweetest.

Quoth Robin, "Now will I go to seek this same Friar of Fountain Dale of whom we spoke yesternight, and I will take with me Little John, Will Scarlet, David of Doncaster and Arthur a Bland. Bide the rest of you here, and Will Stutely shall be your chief while I am gone." Then straightway Robin Hood donned a fine steel coat of chain mail, over which he put on a light jacket of Lincoln green. His head he covered with a cap of soft white leather, in which stood a nodding cock's plume. By his side he hung a good broadsword of bluish tempered steel. A gallant sight was Robin so arrayed, the glint of steel showing here and there as the sunlight caught the links of polished mail that showed beneath his green coat.

So he and the four yeomen set forth, Will Scarlet taking the lead, for he knew whither to go. Thus they strode mile after mile, now along a sunlit road, now adown some sweet forest path, till at last they came to a wide, glassy and lily-padded stream. Here a path stretched along the banks, on which labored the horses that tugged slow-moving barges, laden with barley meal, from the countryside to the town. But now, in the hot silence of the midday no horse was seen nor any man besides themselves.

"Now, good Uncle," quoth Will Scarlet, "just beyond yon bend is a ford no deeper than thy mid-thigh, and on the other side is the friar's little hermitage."

"Had I thought I should have to wade water," quoth Robin, "I had donned other clothes. But no matter, now, for a wetting will not wash the skin away. But bide ye here, lads, for I would enjoy this merry adventure alone." So saying, he strode onward.

Now Robin had walked no farther than where the bend of the path hid his men from his view when he stopped suddenly, for he thought that he heard voices. The sound came from over behind the bank, that here dropped steep a half a score of feet to the verge of the river. Robin laid him softly down upon the grass and peered over the edge.

All was cool and shady beneath the bank. A stout willow leaned across the water. All around grew feathery ferns, and up to Robin's nostrils came the tender odor of the wild thyme that loves the moist verges of streams. Here, with his back against the trunk of the tree, sat a brawny fellow, but no other man was there. His head was as round as a ball, and covered with a mat of close-clipped, curly black hair that grew low on his forehead. But his crown was shorn as smooth as the palm of one's hand, which, together with his loose robe, cowl, and string of beads, showed that which his looks never would have done, that he was a friar. His cheeks were nearly covered with a curly black beard, and his shoulders were e'en a match for those of Little John himself. Beneath his black brows danced a pair of little gray eyes that could not stand still for very drollery of humor. By his side lay a steel cap, and betwixt his knees he held a great pasty. In his right fist he held a piece of brown crust at which he munched sturdily, and every now and then he thrust his left hand into the pie and drew it forth full of meat.

The friar, all unknowing that he was overlooked, ate his meal placidly. At last he was done, and, having first wiped his hands upon the thyme (and sweeter napkin ne'er had king in all the world), he took up a flask that lay beside him and began talking to, and answering, himself as though he were another man.

"Dear lad, thou art the sweetest fellow; I do love thee as a lover loveth his lass. La, thou dost make me shamed to speak so to me in this solitary place, and yet if thou wilt have me say so, I do love thee as thou lovest me. Nay then, wilt thou not take a drink of good malmsey? After thee, lad, after thee. Nay, I beseech thee, sweeten the draught with thy lips. [Here he took a long, deep draught.] And now, sweet lad, 'tis thy turn. [Here he passed the bottle from his left hand to his right.] I take it, and here's wishing thee as much good as thou wishest me." Saying this, he took another draught, and truly he drank enough for two.

All this time Robin listened, while his stomach so quaked with laughter that he was forced to press his palm across his mouth to keep it from bursting forth; for, truly, he would not have spoiled such a goodly jest for the half of Nottinghamshire.

Having gotten his breath from his last draught, the friar began talking again in this wise: "Now, sweet lad, canst thou not sing me a song? La, I am in but ill voice this day; dost thou not hear how I croak like a frog? Nay, nay, thy voice is as sweet as any bullfinch. Come, methinks that thou and I might sing together; dost thou not know a dainty little catch called 'The Loving Youth and the Scornful Maid'? Methinks that thou couldst take the lass's part if I take the lad's? I know not but I will try."

Then, singing first with a voice deep and gruff, and anon in one high and squeaking, he blithely trolled the merry catch of "The Loving Youth and The Scornful Maid":

"HE: *Ah, it's wilt thou come with me, my love?*
And it's wilt thou, love, be mine?
For I will give unto thee, my love,
 Gay knots and ribbons so fine.
I'll woo thee, love, on my bended knee,
And I'll pipe sweet songs to none but thee.
  Then it's hark! hark! hark!
   To the winged lark,
  And it's hark to the cooing dove!
   And the bright daffodil
   Groweth down by the rill,
  So come thou and be my love.

"SHE: *Now get thee away, young man so fine;*
 Now get thee away, I say;
For my true love shall never be thine,
 And so thou hadst better not stay.
Thou art not a fine enough lad for me,
So I'll wait till a better young man I see."

Here Robin could contain himself no longer but burst forth into a mighty roar of laughter; then, as the friar did not seem to have heard him but kept on with the song, he joined in the chorus, and together they sang, or as one might say, bellowed:

> *"For it's hark! hark! hark!*
> *To the joyous lark,*
> *And it's hark to the cooing dove!*
> *For the bright daffodil*
> *Groweth down by the rill,*
> *Yet never I'll be thy love."*

But no sooner had the last word been sung than the holy man clapped his steel cap on his head, and springing to his feet cried in a great voice, "What spy have we here? Come forth, thou limb of evil, and I will carve thee into as fine pudding meat as e'er a wife cooked of a Sunday." Hereupon he drew from beneath his robe a great broadsword full as stout as Robin's.

"Nay, put up thy pinking iron, friend," quoth Robin. "Folk who have sung so sweetly together should not fight thereafter." Hereupon he leaped down the bank. "I tell thee, friend," said he, "my throat is as parched with that song as e'er a barley stubble in October. Hast thou haply any malmsey left?"

"Truly," said the friar, "thou dost ask thyself freely where thou art not bidden. Yet I am too good a Christian to refuse any man drink that is athirst." And he held the bottle out to Robin.

Putting it to his lips, Robin tilted his head back, while that which was within said *glug! glug! glug!* for more than three winks, I wot. When Robin was done, the friar took the bottle quickly. He shook it, looked reproachfully at the yeoman, and straightway placed it at his own lips. When it came away again there was naught within it.

Then said Robin, laughing, "Dost thou know of one hereabout who goeth by the name of Curtal Friar of Fountain Dale?"

"Yea, somewhat," answered the other dryly.

"I do wish," quoth Robin, looking thoughtfully at the priest, "to cross yon ford and find this friar. But I fain would not get my fine clothes wet. Methinks thy shoulders are stout and broad. Couldst thou not find it in thy heart to carry me across?"

"Now, by the white hand of the holy Lady of the Fountain!" burst forth the friar in a mighty rage. "Dost thou, thou poor puny stripling, ask me, the holy Tuck, to carry thee? Now I swear—" Here he paused suddenly, then the anger passed from his face, and his little eyes twinkled once more. "But why should I not?" quoth he piously. "Did not the holy Saint Christopher ever carry the stranger across the river? And should I, poor sinner that I am, be ashamed to do likewise? Come with me, stranger, and I will do thy bidding in an humble frame of mind." So saying, he led the way to the shallow pebbly ford.

Having come to the ford, he girded up his robes about his loins, tucked his good broadsword beneath his arm and stooped his back to take Robin upon it. Suddenly he straightened up. "Methinks," quoth he, "thou'lt get thy weapon wet. Let me tuck it beneath mine arm along with mine own, for I would carry it as a penance to my pride."

So Robin handed his sword to the other. Then once more the friar bent his back and, Robin having mounted, he stepped into the water and so strode onward, splashing in the shoal and breaking the surface into ever widening rings. At last he reached the other side and Robin leaped lightly from his back.

"Many thanks, good father," quoth he. "Prithee, now, give me my sword and let me away, for I am in haste."

At this the stout friar looked upon Robin, with head on one side, and slowly winked his right eye. "Nay, good youth," said he. "I doubt not that thou art in haste with thine affairs, yet thou dost think nothing of mine. Thine are of a carnal nature; mine are of a spiritual nature. Moreover, mine affairs do lie upon the other side of this stream. I see by thy quest of this holy recluse that thou art a good man. I did get wet coming hither, and am sadly afraid that should I wade the water again I might get certain cricks i' the joints that would mar my devotions for many a day to come. I know that since I have so humbly done thy bidding thou wilt carry me back again. Thou see'st how Saint Godrick, that holy hermit whose natal day this is, hath placed in my hands two swords and in thine never a one."

"Thou cunning friar," quoth Robin, biting his lips, "thou hast me fair enow. I might have known from thy looks that thou wert no such holy man as thou didst pretend to be. Yet give me my sword and I do promise to carry thee back straightway. I will not lift the weapon against thee."

"Marry," quoth the friar, "I fear thee not. Here is thy skewer; and get thyself ready, for I would hasten back."

So Robin took his sword again and buckled it at his side; then he bent his stout back and took the friar upon it.

Now I wot Robin Hood had a heavier load to carry in the friar than the friar had in him. Moreover he did not know the ford, so he went stumbling among the stones while the sweat ran down his face in beads. Meantime, the friar dug his heels into Robin's sides and bade him hasten, calling him many ill names the while. To all this Robin answered never a word, but softly felt around till he found the buckle of the belt that held the friar's sword. So, when Robin stood on dry land and the friar leaped from his back, the yeoman gripped hold of the friar's sword so that it came away from the holy man.

"Now," quoth Robin, panting, "I have thee, fellow. This time that saint of whom thou didst speak hath delivered two swords into my hand. If thou dost not carry me back, and speedily, I will prick thy skin till it is as full of holes as a slashed doublet."

The friar looked at Robin with a grim look. "I knew not that thou wert so cunning," said he. "Truly, thou hast me upon the hip. Give me my sword, and I promise not to draw it save in self-defense; also, I promise to take thee upon my back."

So Robin gave him his sword, which the friar buckled to his side more securely; then tucking up his robes once more, he took Robin upon his back and stepped into the water, while Robin sat there laughing. At last he reached the middle, where the water was deepest. Here he stopped and, with a sudden heave of his shoulders, shot Robin over his head as though he were a sack of grain.

Down went Robin into the water with a mighty splash. "There," quoth the holy man, calmly turning back again to the shore, "let that cool thy hot spirit, if it may."

Robin got to his feet, the water running from him in little rills. He shot the water out of his ears and spat some out of his mouth, and, gathering his scattered wits, saw the stout friar laughing on the bank. "Stay, thou villain!" roared Robin. "I am after thee straight, and if I do not carve thy brawn for thee, may I never lift finger again!" So saying, he dashed, splashing, to the bank.

"Thou needst not hasten," quoth the friar. "I will abide here."

And now Robin began to roll up his sleeves. The friar, also, tucked his robes more about him, showing a great, stout arm on which the muscles stood out like humps of an aged tree. Then Robin saw that the friar had also a coat of chain mail beneath his gown.

"Look to thyself," cried Robin, drawing his good sword.

"Aye, marry," quoth the friar, who held his already in his hand. And thereupon began a mighty battle. The swords flashed in the sun and then met with a clash that sounded far and near. For an hour or more they strove, yet neither harmed the other.

At last Robin cried, "Hold thy hand, good friend! I crave a boon of thee, ere we begin again." For he began to think that it would be an ill thing either to be smitten or to smite so stout a fellow.

"What wouldst thou have of me?" asked the friar.

"Only that thou wilt let me blow upon my horn."

The friar bent his brows. "Now I do think that thou hast some cunning trick in this," quoth he. "Ne'ertheless, I will let thee have thy wish, providing thou wilt let me blow upon my whistle."

"With all my heart," quoth Robin. So saying, he raised his silver horn to his lips and blew thrice upon it, clear and high.

Scarcely had the echo of the last note of Robin's bugle come winding back from across the river when four tall men in Lincoln green came running around the bend of the path, each with a bow in his hand and an arrow ready nocked upon the string.

"Ha! Is it thus, thou traitor knave!" cried the friar. "Then, marry, look to thyself!" So saying, he clapped a little silver whistle to his lips and blew a shrill blast. And now there came a crackling of the bushes that lined the path, and forth from the covert burst four great, shaggy hounds. "At 'em," cried the friar, pointing to where the yeomen were standing stock-still with wonder.

As the hawk darts upon its quarry, so sped the dogs at the yeomen; and it would have been an ill day had not Will Scarlet stepped forth and met the dogs as they came rushing. "How now, Fangs!" cried he sternly. "Down, Beauty! What means this?"

At the sound of his voice each dog came to him straightway and licked his hands, as is the wont of dogs that meet one they know. "Why, how now!" cried the stout friar. "Art thou a wizard to turn those wolves into lambs? Ha! Can I trust mine eyes? What means it that I see young Master Gamwell in such company?"

"Nay, Tuck," said the young man, as the four came forward, "my name is no longer Will Gamwell, but Will Scarlet; and this is my good uncle, Robin Hood."

"Truly, good master," said the friar, reaching out his great palm to Robin, "I ha' oft heard thy name. I crave thy forgiveness, and wonder not that I found so stout a man against me. But, Master Will, how is it that thou dost abide in Sherwood?"

"Why, Tuck, dost thou not know of my ill happening with my father's steward?" answered Scarlet.

"Yea, truly, yet I knew not that thou wert in hiding because of it. Marry, the times are all awry when a gentleman must lie hidden for so small a thing."

"But we are losing time," quoth Robin, "and I have yet to find the Curtal Friar of Fountain Dale."

"Why, Uncle," said Will Scarlet, "he stands beside thee."

"How?" quoth Robin to the friar. "Art thou the man I have been at such pains to seek all day, and have got such a ducking for?"

"Why, truly," said the friar demurely, "some do call me the Curtal Friar of Fountain Dale; others call me simply Friar Tuck."

"I like the last name best," quoth Robin, "for it doth slip more glibly off the tongue. But why didst thou not tell me?"

"Why, truly, thou didst not ask me, good master," quoth stout Tuck. "But what didst thou desire of me?"

"Nay," quoth Robin, "the day groweth late. Come back with us to Sherwood, and I will unfold all to thee as we travel."

So they all departed, with the dogs at their heels; but it was long past nightfall ere they reached the greenwood tree.

AND NOW HAD COME the morning when fair Ellen was to be married, and on which Robin Hood had sworn that Allan a Dale should, as it were, eat out of the platter that had been filled for Sir Stephen of Trent. Up rose Robin, blithe and gay, up rose his merry men, and up rose last of all Friar Tuck, winking the smart of sleep from out his eyes.

"Now," quoth Robin, when they had broken their fast, "it is time to set forth upon the undertaking that we have in hand. I will choose one score of my good men to go with me; thou, Will Scarlet, wilt be the chief here while I am gone." Then Robin called Little John and Will Stutely and other famous lads of whom I have told you. And after the score were chosen, Robin donned a gay, beribboned coat such as might have been worn by some minstrel, and slung a harp across his shoulder; and the band stared and laughed, for never had they seen their master in such a fantastic guise before.

"Truly," quoth Robin, holding up his arms and looking down at himself, "I do think it be somewhat of a gaudy grasshopper dress; but it doth not ill befit my looks. But stay, Little John, here are two bags of gold that I would have thee carry in thy pouch." Then gathering his men together in a close rank, in the midst of which were Allan and Friar Tuck, Robin led them forth.

So they walked on for a long time till they came to a certain little church that belonged to the rich Priory of Emmet. Here it was that fair Ellen was to be married. On the other side of the road from where the church stood, with waving fields of barley around, ran a stone wall covered by a mass of blossoming woodbine. Behind the wall, in the tall soft grass, the yeomen sat them down, and glad they were to rest after their long tramp.

"Now," quoth Robin, "I would have young David of Doncaster watch and tell me when he sees anyone coming to the church. So get thee upon the wall, David, and hide beneath the woodbine."

Accordingly young David did as he was bidden. Then all was quiet save only for the low voices of those that talked together, and for the mellow snoring of Friar Tuck, who enjoyed his sleep with a noise as of one sawing soft wood very slowly, and saving also for Allan's restless footsteps pacing up and down, for his soul was so full of disturbance that he could not stand still. And so a long time passed.

Then up spoke Robin, "Now, David, what dost thou see?"

Then David answered, "I see three black crows flying over the wold; but naught else do I see, good master."

So another time passed till Robin, growing impatient, spoke again. "Now tell me, David, what dost thou see by this?"

And David answered, "I see the windmills swinging and three tall poplar trees swaying against the sky; but naught else do I see."

So another time passed, till Robin asked young David once more what he saw; and David said, "I see how the wind makes waves in the barley field; and now over the hill to the church cometh an old friar, and he carries a great bunch of keys."

Then Robin shook Friar Tuck awake. "Come, rouse thee, holy man!" cried he. "For yonder is one of thy cloth. Go, get thee into the church, that thou may'st be there when thou art wanted."

So with much grunting the stout Friar Tuck clambered over the wall and came to the church where the old friar was laboring with the key, the lock being rusty and he somewhat feeble.

"Halloa, brother," quoth Tuck, "let me aid thee." So saying, he took the key from the other's hand and quickly opened the door.

"Who art thou, brother?" asked the old friar, in a high, wheezing voice. And he blinked at Tuck like an owl at the sun.

"My name is Tuck," said the other, "and I come from Fountain Dale. But, if I understand aught, there is to be a wedding here today and I would fain see this fine sight."

"Truly, thou art welcome, brother," said the old man, leading the way within. Meantime, Robin Hood, in his guise of harper, with Little John and Will Stutely, had come to the church. Robin sat him down on a bench beside the door, but Little John, carrying the bags of gold, went within, as did Will Stutely.

So Robin looked up and down the road till he saw six horsemen come riding sedately. The first was the Bishop of Hereford, and a fine figure he cut. His vestments were of the richest silk, and around his neck was a chain of gold, and around his black velvet cap were rows of jewels that flashed in the sunlight. His hose were of flame-colored silk, and his shoes of black velvet, and on either instep was embroidered a cross in gold thread. Beside the Bishop rode the Prior of Emmet upon a mincing palfrey. Rich were his clothes also, but not so gay as the Bishop's. Behind these were two of the higher brethren of Emmet, and behind these again two retainers belonging to the Bishop; for the Lord Bishop strove to be as like the great barons as was in his power.

When Robin saw this train drawing near, quoth he to himself, Yon Bishop is overgaudy for a holy man. I do wonder whether his patron, Saint Thomas, was given to wearing golden chains, silk clothing and pointed shoes, the money for which, God wot, hath been wrung from the sweat of poor tenants. Bishop, Bishop, thy pride may have a fall ere thou wottest of it.

So the holy men came to the church and dismounted; and the Bishop caught sight of Robin. "Halloa, good fellow," quoth he in a jovial voice, "who art thou that struttest in such gay feathers?"

"A harper am I from the north country," quoth Robin, "and I can touch the strings, I wot, as never another man in all merry England. Many a knight and burgher have danced to my music, and most times greatly against their will; such is the magic of my harping. Now, my Lord Bishop, if I may play at this wedding, I will cause the fair bride to love the man she marries with a love that shall last as long as that twain shall live."

"Ha! Is it so?" cried the Bishop. "Now, if thou wilt cause this maiden (who hath verily bewitched my poor cousin Stephen) thus to love, I will give thee whatsoever thou wilt ask me in due measure. Look, Prior, hither cometh our cousin and his ladylove."

And now, around the bend of the road, came riding Sir Stephen, a tall, thin man, dressed in black silk, with a black velvet cap upon his head. Beside him rode a stout Saxon franklin, Ellen's father, Edward of Deirwold; behind those two came a litter borne by two horses, and therein was a maiden. Behind this litter rode six men-at-arms, the sunlight flashing on their steel caps. So these also came to the church, and there Sir Stephen leaped from his horse and handed Ellen out from the litter. She was the fairest maiden that ever Robin had beheld. But she was pale and drooping, like a lily snapped at the stem; and so, with bent head and sorrowful look, she went within the church, Sir Stephen leading her by the hand.

"Why dost thou not play, fellow?" quoth the Bishop, looking sternly at Robin.

"Marry," said Robin calmly, "I will play in greater wise than your lordship thinks; but not till the right time hath come."

And now fair Ellen and Sir Stephen stood before the altar, and the Bishop came in his robes and opened his book, whereat Ellen looked up and about her in bitter despair. Then, in all his fluttering tags and ribbons of red and yellow, Robin Hood strode forward and stood between the bride and bridegroom.

"Let me look upon this lass," he said in a loud voice. "Why, what have we here? Here be lilies in the cheeks, and not roses such as befit a bonny bride. This is no fit wedding. Thou, Sir Knight, so old, and she so young. I tell thee it may not be, for thou art not her own true love."

At this everyone looked at Robin as though changed to stone. Then he clapped his horn to his lips and blew three blasts that echoed from floor to rafter, as though sounded by the trump of doom. Then straightway Little John and Will Stutely came leaping and stood on either side of Robin Hood, and quickly drew their broadswords, the while a mighty voice rolled over the heads of all: "Here be I, good master, when thou wantest me"; for it was Friar Tuck that so called from the organ loft.

Stout Edward strode forward raging, and would have dragged his daughter away, but Little John stepped between them. "Stand back, old man," said he, "thou art a hobbled horse this day."

"Down with the villains!" cried Sir Stephen, and felt for his sword, but it hung not beside him on his wedding day.

Then the men-at-arms drew their swords, and it seemed like that blood would wet the stones; but suddenly came a bustle at the door and loud voices, steel flashed in the light, and up the aisle came leaping eighteen stout yeomen clad in Lincoln green, with Allan a Dale at their head. In his hand he bore Robin's yew bow, and this he gave to him, kneeling the while upon one knee.

Then up spoke Edward of Deirwold in a deep voice of anger, "Is it thou, Allan a Dale, that hath bred this coil in a church?"

"Nay," quoth merry Robin, "that have I done, and I care not who knoweth it, for my name is Robin Hood."

At this a sudden silence fell. Those of Emmet gathered together like a flock of frightened sheep when the scent of the wolf is nigh, while the Bishop crossed himself devoutly. "Now heaven keep us this day," said he, "from that evil man!"

"Nay," quoth Robin, "I mean you no harm; but here is fair Ellen's betrothed husband, and she shall marry him."

Then up spoke stout Edward in a loud and angry voice, "Now I say nay! I am her father, and she shall marry Sir Stephen."

"Nay, fellow," said Sir Stephen, "I would not marry thy daughter after this day's doings could I gain all England thereby. I loved her, old as I am, and would have taken her up like a jewel from the sty, yet, truly, I knew not that she did love this fellow, and was beloved by him. Maiden, if thou dost rather choose a beggarly minstrel than a highborn knight, take thy choice." Thus saying, he gathered his men about him and walked proudly down the aisle.

Then the Bishop spoke hastily, "I, too, have no business here, and so will depart." But Robin laid hold of his clothes and held him. "Stay, my Lord Bishop," said he, "I have yet somewhat to say to thee." The Bishop's face fell, but he stayed.

Then Robin Hood turned to stout Edward of Deirwold, and said he, "Give thy blessing on thy daughter's marriage to this yeoman and all will be well. Little John, give me the bags of gold. Look, farmer. Here are two hundred bright golden angels; give thy blessing, as I say, and I will count them out to thee. Give not thy blessing, and she shall be married all the same, but not so much as a cracked farthing shall cross thy palm."

Then Edward looked upon the ground with bent brows; but he was a shrewd man and one, withal, that made the best use of a cracked pipkin; so at last he looked up and said, but in no joyous tone, "If the wench will go her own gait, let her go. I had thought to make a lady of her. Ne'ertheless, I will give her my blessing."

"But the wedding may not be," spoke up one of those of Emmet. "The banns have not been duly published, neither is there any priest here willing to marry them."

"How say'st thou?" roared Tuck from the organ loft. "No priest? Marry, here stands as holy a man as thou art. As for the question of banns, stumble not over that straw, brother, for I will publish them." So saying, he called the banns; and, lest three times should not be enough, he published them nine times o'er. Then he came down from the loft and forthwith performed the marriage service; and so Allan and Ellen were duly wedded.

And now Robin counted out two hundred golden angels to Edward of Deirwold, and he gave his blessing, yet not, I wot, with overmuch goodwill. Then the stout yeomen crowded around and grasped Allan's palm, and he, holding Ellen's hand within his own, looked about him all dizzy with happiness.

Then at last Robin turned to the Bishop. "My Lord Bishop," quoth he, "thou didst promise me that did I play in such wise as to cause this fair lass to love her husband, thou wouldst give me whatsoever I asked in reason. I have played my play, and she loveth her husband, which she would not have done but for me; so now give me, I prithee, thy golden chain as a wedding present for this fair bride."

Then the Bishop's cheeks grew red with rage, but he saw in Robin's face that which bade him pause. Slowly he took the chain from about his neck and handed it to Robin, who flung it over Ellen's head so that it hung glittering about her shoulders.

Now Robin Hood gathered his men together, and, with Allan and his bride, they turned their steps toward the woodlands. On the way Friar Tuck came close to Robin and plucked him by the sleeve. "Thou dost lead a merry life," quoth he, "but dost thou not think it would be for the welfare of all your souls to have a good stout chaplain, such as I, to oversee holy matters?" At this Robin laughed amain, and bade him become one of the band.

That night there was such a feast in the greenwood as Nottinghamshire never saw before. To that feast you and I were not bidden; so, lest we should both feel the matter more keenly, I will say no more about it.

Robin Hood Aids a Sorrowful Knight

So PASSED THE SUMMER with its quivering heat, its long twilights and its mellow nights, through which the frogs croaked and fairy folk were said to be out on the hillsides. The time of fall had come; now, when the harvest was gathered home, bands of gleaners roamed the country, singing along the roads in the daytime and sleeping beneath hedgerows and hayricks at night. Now the hips burned red in the thickets and the haws waxed black in the hedgerows, the stubble lay all crisp and naked to the sky, and the leaves were fast turning russet and brown.

Quoth Robin, snuffing the air, "Here is a fair day, Little John, and one that we can ill waste in idleness. Choose such men as thou dost need, and go thou east while I will wend to the west, and see that each of us bringeth back some goodly guest to dine beneath the greenwood tree."

"Marry," cried Little John, clapping his palms together for joy, "I'll bring thee a guest, or come not back mine own self."

Now, you and I cannot go two ways at the same time, so we will e'en let Little John and his men follow their own path while we trudge after Robin. And here is good company: Robin Hood, Will Scarlet, Allan a Dale, Midge, the Miller's son, and others.

Robin followed his fancy and the others followed Robin. Passing by fair Mansfield Town, with its towers and battlements and spires all smiling in the sun, they came at last out of the forest lands. Onward they journeyed, until they came over beyond Alverton in Derbyshire. By this time high noontide had come; so, coming to a shrine at the crossing of two roads, Robin called upon them to stop, for on either side was shelter of high hedgerows, behind which they could watch the roads. Here, where the grass was soft, they sat them down. Then each drew from his pouch that which he had brought to eat. In front of them, one of the roads crawled up the steep hill and then dipped suddenly over its crest. Over the top of the hill showed a windmill, the sails slowly rising and dipping against the clear blue sky as the light wind moved them with creaking and labored swing.

After a time, a man came riding over the hill and down the road toward where Robin and his band lay hidden. No chain of gold hung around his neck, and no jewel was about him; yet no one could mistake him for aught but one of proud and noble blood. But his head was bowed and his hands drooped limp on either side; and even his horse, the reins loose upon his neck, walked with hanging head, as though he shared his master's grief.

Quoth Robin, "Yon is verily a sorry-looking gallant; nevertheless, there may be some pickings. Bide ye here till I look into this matter." So, when the knight came riding slowly along, Robin stepped forward and laid his hand upon the bridle rein.

"What art thou, friend, who dost stop a traveler in this manner upon his most gracious Majesty's highway?" said the knight.

"Marry," quoth Robin, "that is hard to answer. One man calleth me kind, another cruel; this one calleth me honest fellow, and that one, vile thief. Truly, the world hath as many eyes to look upon a man as there are spots on a toad; with what eyes thou regardest me lieth with thine own self. My name is Robin Hood."

"Truly," said the knight, a smile twitching at the corners of his mouth, "thou hast a quaint conceit. As for the eyes with which I regard thee, they are as favorable as may be, for I hear much good of thee and little ill. What is thy will of me?"

"Now, I make my vow, Sir Knight," quoth Robin, "thou hast spoken fair words. If thou wilt go with me this day to Sherwood Forest, I will give thee a merry feast. We keep an inn, as it were, but so far from highroads that guests do not often come nigh us; so I and my friends set off merrily and seek them when we grow dull of ourselves. Yet I will furthermore tell thee, Sir Knight, that we count upon our guests paying a reckoning." Then, still holding the horse by the bridle rein, he put his fingers to his lips and blew a shrill whistle, whereupon fourscore yeomen came running to where he stood. "These," said Robin, "are some of my merry men. They share and share alike with me all joys and troubles, gains and losses. Now, Sir Knight, I prithee tell me what money thou hast about thee."

A slow red arose into the knight's cheeks, and he said, "I know not why I should be ashamed; but, friend, I pledge my knightly word that in my purse are ten shillings, and that that is every groat that Sir Richard of the Lea hath in all the world." And he held his purse out to Robin.

"Put up thy purse, Sir Richard," quoth Robin. "Far be it from me to doubt the word of so gentle a knight. The proud I strive to bring low, but those that walk in sorrow I would aid if I could. Come, Sir Richard, go with us to the greenwood. I may perchance aid thee, if thou dost find it in thy heart to tell me of thy sorrows."

"Truly, friend," said Sir Richard, "methinks thou meanest kindness; nevertheless my troubles are such that it is not likely thou canst cure them. But I will go with thee."

As they traveled, the knight spoke of his sorrows thus: "My castle and my lands are in pawn for a debt. Three days hence the money must be paid or else all mine estate falls into the hands of the Priory of Emmet."

Quoth Robin, "I understand not why those of thy kind live in such a manner that all their wealth passeth from them like snow beneath the springtide sun."

"Thou wrongest me, Robin," said the knight, "for listen: I have a son but twenty winters old. Last year the jousts were held at Chester, and thither my son went, as did I and my lady wife. I wot it was a proud time for us, for he unhorsed each knight that he tilted against. At last he ran a course with a great knight, Sir Walter of Lancaster. My son kept his seat, albeit both spears were shivered to the haft; but a splinter of my boy's lance ran through the visor of Sir Walter's helmet, so that he died. Sir Walter had great friends at court, so, to save my son from prison, I had to pay a ransom of six hundred pounds. All might have gone well even yet, only that, by ins and outs and crookedness of laws, I was shorn like a sheep. I had to pawn my lands to the Priory of Emmet, and a hard bargain they drove."

"But where is thy son now?" asked Robin.

"In Palestine," said Sir Richard, "battling like a brave Christian soldier for the Cross and the Holy Sepulcher. England was an ill place for him because of the hate of Sir Walter's kinsmen."

"Truly," said Robin, much moved, "thine is a hard lot. But tell me, what is owing to Emmet for thine estates?"

"Only four hundred pounds," said Sir Richard.

At this, Robin smote his thigh in anger. "Oh the bloodsuckers!" cried he. "A noble estate to be forfeit for four hundred pounds!"

"Yet it is not mine own lot that doth trouble me," said the knight, "but my dear lady's; for should I lose my land she will have to betake herself to some kinsman and there abide in charity. As for me, I will go to Palestine to join my son."

Then up spoke Will Scarlet, "But hast thou no friend that will help thee in thy dire need?"

"Never a man," said Sir Richard. "While I was rich enow, I had friends. But when the oak falls in the forest the swine run from beneath it lest they should be smitten down also."

Then Robin said, "Thou say'st thou hast no friends. I make no boast, but many have found Robin Hood a friend in their troubles. Cheer up, Sir Richard, I may help thee yet."

The day was well-nigh gone when they came to the greenwood tree, and whom should they find that Little John had brought but the Lord Bishop of Hereford! Up and down the Bishop walked like a fox caught in a hen coop. Behind him were three Black Friars standing close together, like three black sheep in a tempest. Hitched to the trees close at hand were six horses, one of them a barb with gay trappings upon which the Bishop was wont to ride, and the others laden with divers packs.

When the Bishop saw Robin he made as though he would have run toward the yeoman, but the fellow that guarded him thrust his quarterstaff in front, so that his lordship was fain to stand back.

"Stay, my Lord Bishop," cried Robin. "I will come to thee with all speed, for I would rather see thee than any man in England."

"How now," quoth the Bishop in an angry voice, "is this the way thy band treats the Church? I and these brethren were passing peacefully along the highroad with a halfscore of guards, when up comes a fellow full seven feet high, with fourscore or more men back of him, and calls upon me to stop—me, the Lord Bishop of Hereford! Whereupon my guards—beshrew them for cowards!—straight ran away. But look ye; not only did this fellow stop me, but he called me such vile names as fat priest, man-eating bishop and money-gorging usurer."

"Alas! my lord," said Robin, "that thou hast been so ill-treated! Little John, didst thou call his lordship a fat priest?"

"Aye," said Little John sorrowfully.

"And a man-eating bishop, and a money-gorging usurer?"

"Aye," said Little John, more sorrowfully than before.

"Alas, that these things should be!" said Robin, turning to the Bishop. "For I have ever found Little John a truthful man."

At this, a roar of laughter went up, whereat the blood rushed into the Bishop's face till it was cherry-red; but he swallowed his words, though they well-nigh choked him.

"Nay, my Lord Bishop," said Robin, "we are rough fellows, but there is not a man here that would harm a hair of thy reverence's head. Come, my merry men, get the feast ready."

Then, when the feast was spread, Robin brought forward Sir Richard of the Lea. "My Lord Bishop," said he, "here is another guest that we have with us this day. I wish that thou mightest know him better." Then Robin bade his guests be seated. "I have a story to tell you all, so listen to what I have to say," quoth he. Then the Bishop's heart sank within him with grim forebodings, as he told them all about Sir Richard, and how his lands were in pawn. "Now, my Lord Bishop," said Robin, "dost thou not think this is ill done of anyone, much more of a churchman, who should live in charity? And, as thou art the richest bishop in all England, canst thou not help this needy brother?"

To this the Bishop answered not a word but looked upon the ground with moody eyes.

Then Robin said to Little John, "Go thou and Will Stutely and bring forth those packhorses yonder." Then asked he of the friars, "Who hath the score of the goods?"

Then up spoke the smallest of the Black Friars in a trembling voice—an old man he was, with a gentle, wrinkled face. "That have I; but, I pray thee, harm me not."

"Nay," quoth Robin, "I have never harmed harmless man yet; but give it to me, good father." So the old man handed Robin the tablet on which was marked down the account of the various packs. This Robin handed to Will Scarlet, bidding him to read the same. So Will began:

"*Three bales of silk to Quentin, the mercer at Ancaster.*"

"That we touch not," quoth Robin, "for this Quentin is an honest fellow, who hath risen by his own thrift."

"*One bale of silk velvet for the Abbey of Beaumont.*"

"What do priests want of silk velvet?" quoth Robin. "Nevertheless, I will not take all. Measure it off into three lots, one to be sold for charity, one for us, and one for the abbey."

"*Twoscore of wax candles for the Chapel of Saint Thomas.*"

"They belong fairly to Saint Thomas," said Robin. So the list was gone through, and the goods adjudged according to what Robin thought fit; and so they came to the last line upon the tablet—"*A box belonging to the Lord Bishop of Hereford.*"

At these words the Bishop shook as with a chill, and a box heavily bound with bands of iron was set upon the ground.

"My Lord Bishop, hast thou the key of this box?" asked Robin. The Bishop shook his head.

"Will Scarlet," said Robin, "cut this box open." Then up rose Will Scarlet and he smote that ironbound box with a great two-handed sword. At the third blow it burst open and a heap of gold came rolling forth, gleaming red in the torchlight. At this sight a murmur went all around among the band.

Quoth Robin, "Thou, Will Scarlet, thou, Allan a Dale, and thou, Little John, count it over."

When all the money had been scored up, Will Scarlet called out that there were fifteen hundred golden pounds. But among the gold they found a paper, and this he read in a loud voice, that this money was the rental and forfeits from estates belonging to the Bishopric of Hereford.

"My Lord Bishop," said Robin Hood, "thou shalt take back one third of thy money. One third of it thou canst well spare to us for thy entertainment; and one third of it for Sir Richard of the Lea. The Church seemed like to despoil Sir Richard, therefore some of the overplus of Church gains may well be used in aiding him."

Sir Richard looked at Robin until something arose in his eyes that made all the lights and the faces blur together. At last he said, "I thank thee, friend, from my heart; yet, think not ill if I cannot take thy gift freely. But I will take the money and pay my debts, and in a year and a day hence will return it safe either to thee or to the Lord Bishop of Hereford. For this I pledge my most solemn knightly word. I feel free to borrow, for I know no man that should be more bound to aid me than one so high in that church that hath driven such a hard bargain."

"Sir Knight," quoth Robin, "it shall be as thou dost wish. But thou hadst best bring the money to me at the end of the year, for mayhap I may make better use of it than the Bishop." Thereupon he ordered that five hundred pounds be tied up in a leathern bag for Sir Richard.

Then Sir Richard arose. "I cannot stay later, good friends," said he, "for my lady will wax anxious if I come not home."

Then up spoke Will Stutely, "Let us give Sir Richard yon bale of rich velvet to take to his noble lady."

At this all clapped their hands for joy, and Robin said, "Thou hast well spoken, and it shall be done."

Then Sir Richard of the Lea said in a husky, trembling voice, "Ye shall all see, good friends, that Sir Richard o' the Lea will ever remember your kindness this day. And if ye be at any time in dire trouble, come to me and my lady, and the walls of Castle Lea shall be battered down ere harm shall befall you."

But now Little John led forward Sir Richard's horse, and the knight mounted. He looked down at Robin for a little time, then stooped and kissed his cheek; and all the forest glades rang with the shout that went up as the knight rode off.

Then up spoke the Bishop of Hereford in a mournful voice, "I, too, must be jogging, good fellow, for the night waxes late."

"Be not so hasty, Lord Bishop," said Robin. "Three days hence Sir Richard must pay his debts to Emmet; until that time thou must abide with me. I promise thee that thou shalt have great sport, for I know thou art fond of hunting the dun deer."

So the Bishop and his train abided with Robin for three days, and much sport his lordship had in that time, so he was sorry when the time came to go. And Robin sent him forth, with a guard to keep freebooters from taking what was left of the packs. But, as the Bishop rode away, he vowed within himself that he would make Robin rue the day that he stopped him in Sherwood.

THE AFTERNOON SUN was streaming in through the arched windows of the refectory at Emmet Priory; it lay in broad squares of light upon the stone floor and across the board covered with a snowy linen cloth. At the head of the table sat Prior Vincent of Emmet all clad in soft robes of fine cloth; on his head was a black velvet cap picked out with gold, and around his neck hung a heavy chain of gold, with a great locket pendant therefrom. On the arm of his chair roosted his favorite falcon. On his right hand sat the Sheriff of Nottingham in robes of purple trimmed with fur, and on his left a famous doctor of law in dark and sober garb.

The wizened face of the man of law was twisted into a wrinkled smile, for in his pouch were fourscore golden angels that the Prior had paid him in fee for the case betwixt him and Sir Richard of the Lea. The learned doctor had been paid beforehand, for he had not overmuch trust in the holy Vincent of Emmet.

Quoth the Sheriff of Nottingham, "But art thou sure, Sir Prior, that thou hast the lands so safe?"

"Aye, marry," said Prior Vincent, smacking his lips after a deep draught of wine, "I have kept a close watch upon Sir Richard and I know right well that he hath no money to pay me withal."

"Aye, true," said the man of law in a dry, husky voice, "and his land is surely forfeit if he cometh not to pay this day."

But even as the doctor spoke, there came a sudden clatter of horses' hoofs and a jingle of iron mail in the courtyard below.

Then a door at the lower end of the refectory swung open, and in came Sir Richard, with folded hands, and head bowed upon his breast. Thus humbly he walked up the hall, while his men-at-arms stood about the door. When he had come to where the Prior sat, he knelt upon one knee. "Save and keep thee, Sir Prior," said he, "I am come to keep my day."

"Hast thou brought my money?" the Prior said.

"Alas! I have not so much as a penny upon me," said the knight. "As thou hopest for heaven's mercy, show mercy to me. Strip me not of my lands and so reduce a true knight to poverty."

"Thy day is broken and thy lands forfeit," said the man of law, while the Prior's eyes sparkled.

Still the knight knelt upon the hard stone. "Wilt thou not be my friend, Sir Sheriff?" said he.

"Nay," quoth the Sheriff, "this is no business of mine; yet . . . wilt thou not ease him of some of his debts, Sir Prior?"

At this the Prior smiled grimly. "Pay me three hundred pounds, Sir Richard," said he, "and I will give thee quittance of thy debt."

"Thou knowest, Sir Prior, that it is as easy for me to pay four hundred pounds as three hundred," said Sir Richard. "But wilt thou not give me another twelvemonth to pay my debt?"

"Not another day," cried the Prior. "Either pay thy debt as I have said, or release thy land and get thee gone."

Then Sir Richard arose to his feet. "Thou false priest! Hast thou so little courtesy that thou wouldst see a true knight kneel for all this time, and never offer him meat or drink?"

Then turning to his men-at-arms, he called, "Come hither"; whereupon the tallest came forward and handed him a leathern bag. Sir Richard took the bag and shot from it upon the table a glittering stream of golden money. "Bear in mind, Sir Prior," said he, "that thou hast promised me quittance for three hundred pounds. Not one farthing above that shalt thou get." So saying, he counted out three hundred pounds and pushed it toward the Prior.

But now the Prior's hands dropped at his sides and his head hung upon his shoulder, for not only had he lost all hopes of the land, but he had forgiven the knight one hundred pounds of his debt and had paid the man of law fourscore angels. To him he turned, and quoth he, "Give me back my money that thou hast."

"Nay," cried the other shrilly, "it is but my fee that thou didst pay me." And he hugged his gown about him.

"Sir Prior," quoth Sir Richard, "I have paid my dues; there is no more betwixt us." So saying, he turned and strode away.

Now a twelvemonth and a day passed since Prior Vincent sat at feast, and once more the mellow fall had come. But the year had brought great change to the lands of Sir Richard of the Lea; for, where before shaggy wild grasses grew, now all stretched away in golden stubble. In the castle, also, where were empty moats and the crumbling of neglect, all was now orderly and well kept.

Bright shone the sun on battlement and tower, and in the blue air overhead a flock of clattering jackdaws flew around the gilded weather vane and spire. Then the drawbridge fell across the moat with a rattle and clank of chains, the gate of the castle swung open, and a goodly array of steel-clad men-at-arms, with a knight all clothed in chain mail, as white as frost on brier of a winter morning, came flashing out from the castle courtyard. In his hand the knight held a great spear, from the point of which fluttered a blood-red pennant. And in the midst of the troop walked three packhorses laden with parcels of divers shapes. Thus rode forth good Sir Richard of the Lea to pay his debt to Robin Hood.

As they marched onward, Robin stood in the greenwood with his stout yeomen around him, awaiting Sir Richard's coming. At last a glint of steel was seen through the brown forest leaves, and into the open rode Sir Richard at the head of his men.

"Why, how now," said Robin, "methinks thou art a gayer bird than when I saw thee last."

"Yes, thanks to thee, Robin," said the knight, leaping from his horse and laying his hand upon the yeoman's shoulder. "But for thee I would now have been wandering in misery in a far country. But I have brought back the money that thou didst lend me, and which I have doubled four times over again, and so become rich once more. Along with this money I have brought a gift to thee and thy brave men from my dear lady and myself." Then one of the men brought the knight a strongbox from which he took a bag and counted out five hundred pounds.

Then Sir Richard had the packs opened and lo, there were tenscore bows of finest Spanish yew, all inlaid with fanciful figures in silver. Beside these were tenscore quivers of leather embroidered with golden thread, and in each quiver were a score of shafts with burnished heads; each shaft was feathered with peacock's plumes, nocked with silver. Sir Richard gave to each yeoman a bow and a quiver of arrows, but to Robin he gave a stout bow inlaid with the cunningest workmanship in gold, while each arrow in his quiver was nocked with gold. Then all swore that they would die if need be for Sir Richard and his lady.

At last, after a merry feast, the time came for Sir Richard to go, whereupon each of the yeomen took a torch to light the way through the forest. So they came to the edge of Sherwood, and there the knight kissed Robin upon his cheek and left him.

Little John Turns Barefoot Friar

COLD WINTER HAD PASSED and spring had come again. The budding leaves hung like a tender mist about the trees, and in the open country the cornfields were thick and soft with growing blades. The plowboy shouted in the sun, and in the new-turned furrows flocks of birds hunted for fat worms.

On a deer's hide, stretched out in front of the greenwood tree, sat Robin Hood basking in the sun. Leaning back with his hands clasped about his knees, he lazily watched Little John rolling a stout bowstring from long strands of hempen thread, wetting the palms of his hands ever and anon, and rolling the cord upon his thigh. Nearby sat Allan a Dale fitting a new string to his harp.

Quoth Robin, "Methinks I would rather roam this forest than be king of all merry England."

"Yea," quoth Little John, as he rubbed his new-made bowstring with yellow beeswax, "the life we lead is the life for me. Even the winter hath its joys. Dost thou remember that night thou and Friar Tuck and I passed at the Blue Boar with the two beggars and the strolling friar?"

"Yea," quoth Robin, "that was a goodly song that the strolling friar sang. Friar Tuck, thou hast a quick ear for a tune. Dost thou remember it?"

"Let me see," said Tuck, and he touched his forefinger to his forehead in thought, humming to himself, and stopping ever and anon to fit what he had got to what he searched for in his mind. At last he cleared his throat and sang in a mellow voice:

> *"Good is the life of the strolling friar,*
> *With aplenty to eat and to drink;*
> *For the goodwife will keep him a seat by the fire,*
> *And the pretty girls smile at his wink.*
> *Then he lustily trolls,*
> *As he onward strolls,*
> *A rollicking song for the saving of souls.*
> *When the wind doth blow,*
> *With the coming of snow,*
> *There's a place by the fire*
> *For the fatherly friar,*
> *And a crab in the bowl for his heart's desire."*

"It is a goodly song," quoth Little John, "and, were I not a yeoman of Sherwood Forest, fain would I be a strolling friar."

"Yea," said Robin, "but methought those two burly beggars led a merrier life. What say'st thou, Little John, to an adventure? Don thou a friar's gown from our chest of strange garments, and I will stop the first beggar I meet and change clothes with him. Then let us wander the country about, and see what befalls us."

"That fitteth my mind well," quoth Little John.

Thereupon Little John went to the storehouse of the band, and chose the robe of a Gray Friar. When he came forth again, a mighty roar of laughter went up, for the robe was too short for him by a good palm's breadth. But Little John's hands were folded in his sleeves, and Little John's eyes were cast upon the ground, and at his girdle hung a long string of beads.

And now Little John took up his stout staff, at the end of which hung a little leathern bottle, such as palmers carry; but in it was something, I wot, more like good malmsey than cold spring water, such as godly pilgrims carry. Then up rose Robin and took his stout staff in his hand, likewise, and slipped ten golden angels into his pouch, and the two yeomen set forth. They walked down the forest path and then along the highway till it split in twain.

Quoth Robin, "Take thou this road, and I will take that. So, fare thee well, holy father, and may'st thou not ha' cause to count thy beads in earnest ere we meet again."

"Good den, good beggar that is to be," quoth Little John. "May'st thou have no cause to beg for mercy ere I see thee next."

Up hill and down dale walked Little John, the fresh wind blowing in his face and his robes fluttering behind, and at last he came to a crossroad. Here he met three pretty lasses, each bearing a basket of eggs. Quoth he, "Whither away, fair maids?"

Then they huddled together and nudged one another, and one said, "We are going to the Tuxford market, holy friar."

"Now out upon it!" quoth Little John. "Surely, it is a pity that such fair lasses should be forced to carry eggs to market. An I had the shaping of things in this world, ye should all have been clothed in silk, and ride upon milk-white horses, and feed upon nothing but whipped cream and strawberries."

At this speech the pretty maids blushed and simpered. One said, "La!" another, "Marry, a' maketh sport of us!" and the third, "Listen, now, to the holy man!"

"Now, look you," said Little John, "I cannot see such dainty damsels carrying baskets along a highroad. Let me take them, and one of you may carry my staff for me."

"Nay," said one of the lasses, "but thou canst not carry three baskets all at one time."

"Yea, but I can," said Little John. "Look ye, now. Here I take this great basket, so; here I tie my rosary around the handle, thus; and here I slip the rosary over my head and sling the basket upon my back, in this wise." And the basket hung down behind him like a peddler's pack; then, giving his staff to one of the maids, and taking a basket upon either arm, he stepped forth merrily toward Tuxford Town, a pretty maid on either side, and one walking ahead, carrying the staff. In this wise they journeyed along, and everyone they met stopped and looked after them, laughing.

When they came nigh to Tuxford, Little John set down the baskets, for he did not care to meet some of the Sheriff's men. "Alas! sweet chucks," quoth he, "here I must leave you. Now, ere we part, we must drink sweet friendship." So saying, he unslung the leathern bottle from the end of his staff, and, drawing the stopper therefrom, he handed it to the lass who had carried his staff. Then each lass took a fair drink of what was within, and Little John finished what was left. Then, kissing each lass sweetly, he wished them all good den, and left them. But the maids stood looking after him as he walked away whistling. "What a pity," quoth one, "that such a lusty lad should be in holy orders."

"Marry," quoth Little John, as he strode along, "yon was no such ill happening; Saint Dunstan send me more of the like."

After a time he began to wax thirsty again in the warmth of the day. He shook his leathern bottle beside his ear, but not a sound came therefrom! Then he placed it to his lips and tilted it aloft, but not a drop was there. Little John, Little John, said he sadly to himself, woman will be thy ruin yet!

At last he came to a little inn. Beside the door stood two stout cobs with broad soft-padded saddles, speaking of rich guests. In front of the door three merry fellows, a tinker, a peddler and a beggar, were seated on a bench in the sun quaffing ale.

"I give you good den, sweet friends," quoth Little John.

"Give thee good den, holy father," quoth the beggar. "But look thee, thy gown is too short. Thou hadst best cut a piece off the top and tack it to the bottom. But come, sit beside us and take a taste of ale, if thy vows forbid thee not."

"Nay," quoth Little John, "the blessed Saint Dunstan hath given me a dispensation for all indulgence in that line."

"Truly," quoth the tinker, "without thy looks belie thee, holy

515

friar, the good Saint Dunstan was wise, for without such dispensation his votary is like to ha' many a penance to make. Ho, landlord, a pot of ale!"

So the ale was brought and given to Little John. Then, blowing the froth a little way to make room for his lips, he tilted the bottom of the pot higher and higher till it pointed to the sky, and he had to shut his eyes to keep the dazzle of the sunshine out of them. Then he heaved a full deep sigh.

"Ho, landlord!" cried the peddler. "Bring this good fellow another pot of ale, for truly it is a credit to us all to have one among us who can empty a cannikin so lustily."

So they talked among themselves merrily, until after a while quoth Little John, "Who rideth those two nags yonder?"

"Two holy men like thee, brother, from Fountain Abbey, in Yorkshire," quoth the beggar. "They are now having a goodly feast within. But come, good friar, has not thy holy Saint Dunstan taught thee a song or two?"

"Why," quoth Little John, grinning, "mayhap he lent me aid to learn a ditty or so." And, after a word or two about a certain hoarseness that troubled him, he sang thus:

> "*Ah, pretty, pretty maid, whither dost thou go?*
> *I prithee, prithee, wait for thy lover also,*
> *And we'll gather the rose*
> *As it sweetly blows,*
> *For the merry, merry winds are blo-o-o-wing.*"

Now he had got no farther than this when out of the inn came the two brothers of Fountain Abbey. The one was as fat as a suet pudding, the other lean as an old wife's spindle. When they saw who it was that sang, the fat little brother drew his heavy eyebrows together. "How, now," he roared, his voice coming from him like loud thunder from a little cloud, "is this a fit place for one in thy garb to tipple and sing profane songs?"

"Nay," quoth Little John, "sin' I cannot tipple and sing, like your worship's reverence, in such a goodly place as Fountain Abbey, I must e'en tipple and sing where I can."

"Now, out upon thee," cried the thin brother, "that thou shouldst so disgrace thy cloth by this talk and bearing."

"Marry," quoth Little John, "methinks it is more disgrace to wring hard-earned farthings out of poor lean peasants."

The tinker and the peddler and the beggar nudged one another, and the friars scowled blackly; but they could think of nothing further to say, so they turned to their horses. Then Little John arose. "Truly, your words have smitten my sinful heart," quoth he. "I will abide no longer in this den of evil, but will go with you. No vile temptation will fall upon me in such holy company."

Now, at this all the good fellows on the bench grinned till their teeth glistened. As for the friars, they knew not what to do. It made them feel sick with shame to think of riding along the high-road with a strolling friar, in robes all too short for him. Then up spoke the fat brother, but more mildly than before. "Nay, good brother," said he, "we will ride fast, and thou wilt tire to death at the pace."

"Truly, I am grateful to thee for the thought," quoth Little John, "but have no fear, brother; my limbs are stout."

So the two brethren, as they could do naught else, mounted their nags, turned their noses toward Lincoln and rode away.

"Off we go, we three," quoth Little John, as he pushed in betwixt the two cobs. And swinging his stout staff over his shoulder, he trudged off, measuring his pace with that of the two nags.

The two brothers drew as far away from Little John as they could, so that he walked in the middle of the road while they rode on the footpath on either side. As they so went away, the tinker, the peddler and the beggar ran skipping out into the highway, each with a pot in his hand, and looked after them laughing.

While they were in sight of those at the inn, the brothers walked their horses soberly, not caring to make ill matters worse by seeming to run away from Little John; but when they had crossed the crest of the hill, quoth the fat brother to the thin brother, "Brother Ambrose, had we not better mend our pace?"

"Why truly," spoke up Little John, "methinks it would be well to boil our pot a little faster, for the day is passing on."

At this the two friars glared on Little John with baleful looks, and clucked to their horses. Both broke into a canter, and for a mile and more Little John ran betwixt them as lightly as a stag. At last the fat brother drew his horse's rein with a groan, for he could stand the shaking no longer. "Alas," said Little John, with not so much as a catch in his breath, "I did sadly fear that the pace would shake thy poor old fat paunch."

At this the fat friar stared straight before him and gnawed his nether lip. And now they traveled forward more quietly. Presently they met three minstrels, who stared amain at so strange a sight.

"Make way!" Little John cried, waving his staff. "For here we go, we three!" Then how the minstrels laughed! But the fat friar shook as with an ague, and the lean friar bowed his head over his horse's neck.

Next they met two knights in rich array, with hawk on wrist, and two fair ladies in silks and velvets, all a-riding on noble steeds. These all made room, staring, and Little John bowed humbly. "Give you greetings, lords and ladies," said he. "But here we go, Big Jack, Lean Jack, and Fat Jack-pudding." The ladies laughed, and the fat friar seemed as if he were like to fall from his saddle for shame; the other brother looked grimly before him.

Soon they came to a crossroad. "Look ye, fellow," quoth the lean friar, in a voice quivering with rage, "we care no longer to be made sport of. Go thy way, and let us go ours in peace."

"La there!" quoth Little John. "Methought we were such a merry company, and I can ill spare you, for I am a poor man and ye are rich. I pray you, brothers, give me a penny or two to buy me bread and cheese at the next inn."

"We have no money, fellow," said the lean friar harshly.

"Ha' ye, in holy truth, no money?" Little John asked. "Then get both of you down from off your horses, and we will kneel here in the middle of the crossroads and pray the blessed Saint Dunstan to send us some money to carry us on our journey."

"Thou limb of evil," cried the lean friar, "dost thou bid me, the high cellarer of Fountain Abbey, to kneel in the dirty road to pray to some beggarly Saxon saint?"

"Now," quoth Little John, "I ha' part of a mind to crack thy head for thee for speaking thus of the good Saint Dunstan! But get down straightway; my patience will not last much longer." So saying, he twirled his staff till it whistled.

At this both friars grew as pale as dough, and down they slipped from off their horses.

"Now, brothers, down on your knees and pray," said Little John; thereupon, putting his heavy hands upon the shoulder of each, he forced them to their knees, he kneeling also. Then Little John began to pray, somewhat in this wise: "O gracious Saint Dunstan! Send some money straightway to these poor folk; but send them only ten shillings apiece, lest they grow puffed up with pride. Any more than that that thou sendest, send to me."

"Now," quoth he, rising, "let us see what each man hath." Then he thrust his hand into his own pouch and drew thence four golden angels. "What have ye, brothers?" said he.

Then each friar slowly thrust his hand into his pouch, and brought it out with nothing in it.

"Have ye nothing?" quoth Little John. "Nay, I warrant there is somewhat that hath crept into the seams of your pouches, and so ye ha' missed it. Let me look." So he went first to the lean friar, and, thrusting his hand into the pouch, he drew forth a leathern bag and counted therefrom one hundred and ten pounds of golden money. Then he thrust his hand into the pouch of the fat friar and drew thence a bag like the other and counted out from it threescore and ten pounds. "Look ye now," quoth he, "I knew the good saint had sent some pittance ye had missed."

Then, giving them one pound between them, he slipped the rest into his own pouch, saying, "Ye pledged me your word that ye had no money. Therefore I know the good Saint Dunstan hath sent this. But as I only prayed for ten shillings to be sent to each of you, all over and above belongeth by rights to me. I give you good den, brothers." The friars looked at one another woefully, and sadly they mounted their horses and rode away.

But Little John turned his footsteps back again to Sherwood Forest, and merrily he whistled as he strode along.

Robin Hood Turns Beggar

AFTER ROBIN HAD LEFT Little John at the forking of the roads, he walked merrily onward for a long distance until he came to where a stout fellow was sitting upon a stile, swinging his legs. All about this lusty rogue dangled pouches and bags of different sizes and kinds, with great, gaping mouths, like a brood of hungry daws. His coat was patched with as many colors as there are stripes upon a maypole, and on his head he wore a tall leathern cap. Across his knees rested a heavy quarterstaff of blackthorn. His eyes twinkled with merriment, and as jolly a beggar was he as ever trod the lanes of Nottinghamshire.

"Halloa, good fellow," quoth Robin, "what art thou doing here this merry day?"

Then the other winked one eye and straightway trolled forth:

> *"I sit upon the stile,*
> *And I sing a little while*
> *As I wait for my own true dear, O,*
> *For the sun is shining bright,*
> *And the leaves are dancing light,*
> *And the little fowl sings she is near, O.*

And so it is with me, bully boy, saving that my doxy cometh not."

"Now that is a right sweet song," quoth Robin, "and, were I in the mind to listen, I could bear well to hear more; but I have two things of seriousness to ask of thee. First, I have come a long way and fain would know where I shall get somewhat to eat and drink."

"Marry," quoth the beggar, "I make no such serious thoughts upon the matter. I eat when I can get it, and munch my crust when I can get no crumb; likewise, when there is no ale to be had I wash the dust from my throat with water."

"Now, in good sooth," quoth Robin, laughing, "hast thou truly naught but a dry crust about thee? Methinks thy bags and pouches are fat and lusty for such thin fare."

"Why, mayhap there is some other cold fare therein," said the beggar slyly.

"And hast thou naught to drink but cold water?" said Robin.

"Never so much as a drop," quoth the beggar. "Over beyond yon clump of trees is a sweet inn, but I go no more thither. Once, when the good Prior of Emmet was dining there, the landlady set a dear little tart upon the windowsill to cool, and I, fearing it might be lost, took it with me till I could find the owner. Since then they have acted very ill toward me; yet truth bids me say that they have the best ale there that ever rolled over my tongue."

"Marry," quoth Robin, "they did ill toward thee for thy kindness. But tell me truly, what hast thou in thy pouches?"

"Why," quoth the beggar, peeping into the mouths of his bags, "I find here a piece of pigeon pie, wrapped in a cabbage leaf to hold the gravy. Here I behold four oaten cakes and a cold knuckle of ham. Insooth, 'tis strange; but I find six eggs that must have come by accident from some poultry yard hereabout. Roasted upon the coals and spread with a piece of butter that I see—"

"Peace, good friend!" cried Robin. "Thou makest my poor stomach quake with joy. If thou wilt give me to eat, I will straightway hie me to that inn and bring back a skin of ale."

"Friend, thou hast said enough," said the beggar, getting down from the stile. "I will feast thee with the best I have."

So Robin straightway left the beggar, who, upon his part, went to a budding lime bush back of the hedge, and there spread his feast upon the grass and roasted his eggs upon a little fagot fire with a deftness gained by long labor in that line. After a while back came Robin bearing a skin of ale upon his shoulder. Then the one seized upon the ale and the other upon the pie, and nothing was heard for a while but the munching of food and the gurgle of ale as it left the skin.

At last, Robin pushed the food from him and heaved a sigh of deep content. "And now, good friend," quoth he, leaning upon one elbow, "I would have at thee about the other serious matter of which I spoke. I have taken a liking to thy craft and would fain have a taste of a beggar's life. Methinks I shall change clothes with thee, and I will give thee two golden angels to boot. I have brought my staff, thinking that I might have to rap someone of the brethren of thy cloth over the head by way of argument in this matter, but I love thee so much for the feast thou hast given me that I would not lift even my little finger against thee."

"Lift thy finger against me, forsooth! Art thou out of thy wits?" cried the beggar, rising and taking up his staff. "My name is Riccon Hazel, and I come from Flintshire. I have cracked the head of many a better man than thou. Thou shalt not have so much as one tagrag of my coat. So take up thy club and defend thyself."

Then up leaped merry Robin and snatched up his staff also; and, ere you could count three, Riccon's staff was over the hedge, and Riccon himself lay upon the grass. Then Robin, seeing that he was stunned with the blow, brought the skin of ale and poured some of it on the beggar's head and some down his throat, so that presently he opened his eyes and looked around.

"Now, good fellow," Robin said, "wilt thou change clothes with me, or shall I tap thee again?"

Then Riccon sat up and rubbed the bump on his crown. "If I must give up my clothes, I must," quoth he. "But first promise me that thou wilt take naught from me but my clothes."

"I promise on the word of a true yeoman," quoth Robin.

Thereupon the beggar drew a little knife and, ripping up the lining of his coat, took thence ten golden pounds, which he laid beside him with a wink at Robin. "Now thou may'st have my clothes and welcome," said he, "and thou mightest have had them without the cost of a farthing, far less two golden angels."

"Marry," quoth Robin, laughing, "thou art a sly fellow. Had I known thou hadst so much thou might'st not have carried it away, for I warrant thou didst not come honestly by it."

Then each put on the other's clothes, and as lusty a beggar was Robin Hood as e'er you could find. But Riccon skipped and danced for joy of the fair suit of Lincoln green. Quoth he, "Thou may'st keep the cold pieces of the feast, friend, for I mean to live well while my money lasts and my clothes are gay."

So he left Robin and, crossing the stile, was gone. Then Robin strolled onward until he came to where a little grass-grown path left the road and, for no reason but that his fancy led him, he took the path and so came to a little dingle, where four lusty fellows sat with legs outstretched around a goodly feast.

Four merry beggars were they, and each had slung about his neck a little board that rested upon his breast. One board had written upon it, *I Am Blind*, another, *I Am Deaf*, another, *I Am Dumb*, and the fourth, *Pity the Lame One*.

The deaf man was the first to hear Robin, for he said, "Hark, brothers, I hear someone coming." And the blind man was the first to see him, for he said, "He is an honest man, and one of like craft to ourselves." Then the dumb man called to him in a great voice, "Welcome, brother; come and sit while there is still a little malmsey in the bottle." At this, the lame man, who had taken off his wooden leg and unstrapped his own leg, and was sitting with it stretched out upon the grass so as to rest it, made room for Robin and held out the flask of malmsey.

"Marry," quoth Robin, laughing, "methinks it is no more than seemly of you all to be glad to see me, seeing that I bring sight to the blind, speech to the dumb, hearing to the deaf, and a lusty leg to a lame man. I drink to your happiness, as I may not drink to your health, seeing ye are already hale."

At this all grinned, and the blind beggar smote Robin upon the shoulder, swearing he was a right merry wag.

"Whence comest thou, lad?" asked the dumb man.

"Why," quoth Robin, "I came this morning from sleeping overnight in Sherwood."

"Is it even so?" said the deaf man. "I would not for all the money we are carrying sleep one night in Sherwood. If Robin Hood caught one of our trade in his woodlands he would, methinks, clip his ears."

"Methinks he would, too," quoth Robin, laughing. "But what money is that that ye speak of?"

Then up spoke the lame man. "Our king, Peter of York," said he, "hath sent us to Lincoln with those moneys that—"

"Stay," quoth the blind man, "I would not doubt our brother

here, but bear in mind we know him not. What art thou, brother? Upright-man, Jurk-man, Clapper-dudgeon or Abraham-man?"

At these words Robin looked from one man to the other with mouth agape. "Truly," quoth he, "I am an upright man, at least, I strive to be; but I know not what thou meanest by such jargon."

A silence fell on all. "Thou dost surely jest when thou sayest that thou dost not understand," quoth the blind man. "Answer me this: Hast thou ever fibbed a chouse quarrons in the Rome pad?"

"Now out upon it," quoth Robin Hood testily. "Ye make sport of me by pattering such gibberish. I have the best part of a mind to crack your heads, and would do so, too, but for the sweet malmsey ye have given me."

But the four beggars leaped to their feet and snatched up their cudgels. Then Robin, albeit he knew not what the coil was about, leaped to his feet also and clapped his back against a tree. "How, now!" cried he, twirling his staff betwixt his fingers. "Would you four fellows set upon one man? Stand back, or I will score your pates till they have as many marks upon them as a pothouse door! Are ye mad? I have done you no harm."

"Thou liest!" quoth the one who pretended to be blind. "Thou hast come as a spy. But thine ears have heard too much for thy body's good, and this day thou shalt die!" Then, whirling up his cudgel, he rushed upon Robin. But Robin struck two blows as quick as a wink, and down went the blind man on the grass.

At this the others bore back and stood at a little distance scowling upon Robin. Then, seeing them so hesitate, Robin leaped upon them, striking even as he leaped. Down went the dumb man, and away flew his cudgel as he fell. At this the others took to their heels as though they had the west wind's boots upon their feet. Robin looked after them, laughing, and thought that never had he seen so fleet a runner as the lame man.

Then Robin turned to the two upon the ground. Quoth he, "These fellows spoke somewhat about certain moneys; methinks it were a pity to let sound money stay in the pockets of such thieving knaves." So saying, he stooped over the blind man and searched among his rags, till presently his fingers felt a leathern pouch. In it were four round rolls wrapped up in sheepskin; and in each one Robin found fifty bright new-stamped golden pounds. His mouth gaped. Quoth he, "I have oft heard that the Beggars' Guild was overrich, but never did I think they sent such sums as this to their treasury. I shall take it with me, for it will be better used for charity." So saying, he thrust the pouch into his own bosom. Then taking up his staff, he went merrily on his way.

He strode along, singing as he went; and so blithe was he and so fresh and clean, that every lass he met had a sweet word for him, while the dogs, that most times hate a beggar, wagged their tails; for dogs know an honest man by his smell, and honest Robin was— in his own way. Thus he went till he came to the wayside cross nigh Ollerton. Being somewhat tired, he sat him down upon the grassy bank, and after a time he saw someone drawing near, riding upon a horse. The traveler was a thin, wizened man, and, to look upon him, you could not tell whether he was thirty years old or sixty. As for the nag, it was as thin as the rider.

Robin laughed at the droll sight, but he knew the wayfarer to be a certain rich corn engrosser, who more than once had bought all the grain in the countryside and held it till it reached famine prices, thus making much money from poor people's needs.

So, after a while, the corn engrosser came riding up to where Robin sat; whereupon Robin stepped forth and laid his hand upon the horse's rein, calling upon the other to stop.

"Now, out upon thee!" snarled the other. "Such rogues as thou art are better dancing upon nothing, with a hempen collar about the neck, than strolling the highways so freely."

Then Robin looked up and down, as if to see that no one was nigh, and coming close to the corn engrosser stood on tiptoe and spoke in his ear. "Thinkest thou insooth that I am as I seem to be? Look upon me. There is not a grain of dirt upon my hands or face. Didst thou ever see a beggar so? Look, friend." Here he took the purse from his breast and showed to the dazzled eyes of the corn engrosser the bright golden pieces. "These rags but hide an honest rich man from the eyes of Robin Hood."

"Put up thy money, lad," cried the other quickly. "Art thou a fool, to trust to beggar's rags to shield thee from Robin Hood? If he caught thee, he would strip thee to the skin, for he hates a lusty beggar as he doth a fat priest or those of my kind."

"Is it indeed so?" quoth Robin. "Had I known this, I had not come in this garb. But I must go forward now, as much depends upon my journeying! Where goest thou, friend?"

"I go to Newark," said the corn engrosser.

"Why, I myself am on the way to Newark," quoth Robin, "so that, as two honest men are better than one in roads beset by such as this Robin Hood, I will jog along with thee."

"Why, as thou art an honest fellow and a rich fellow," said the corn engrosser, "I mind not thy company."

"Then forward," quoth Robin, "for the day wanes and it will be dark ere we reach Newark." So off they went, the lean horse hobbling along as before, and Robin pacing beside.

So they traveled along till they reached a hill on the outskirts of Sherwood. Here the lean man turned in his saddle and spoke to Robin for the first time since they had left the cross. "Here is thy greatest danger, friend," said he, "for here we are nighest to where that vile thief dwells."

"Alas!" quoth Robin, "I would that I had as little money by me as thou hast, for I fear this Robin Hood."

Then the other winked cunningly at Robin. Quoth he, "I tell thee, friend, I have nigh as much as thou hast, but it is hidden. See thou these clogs upon my feet?"

"Yea, truly, they are large enough for any man to see."

"The soles are not what they seem to be," said the corn engrosser. "Each is a little box, and the upper of the shoe lifts up like a lid, and within each shoe are fourscore and ten bright golden pounds, all wrapped in hair to keep them from telling tales of themselves."

When the corn engrosser had told this, Robin broke into a roar of laughter and stopped the sad-looking nag. "Stay, good friend," quoth he, "on second thoughts I go no farther. Thou may go forward if thou list, but thou must go forward barefoot, for I have taken a great fancy to thy shoon."

At these words the corn factor grew pale as a linen napkin. "Who art thou that talkest so?" said he.

Then Robin laughed, and quoth he, "Men hereabout call me Robin Hood; so thou hadst best do my bidding, and hasten, I prithee, or thou wilt not get to Newark Town till after dark."

At the sound of the name of Robin Hood, the corn factor quaked with fear, so that he had to seize his horse by the mane to save himself from falling off its back. Then, without more words, he stripped off his clogs and let them fall upon the road. Then Robin said, "Take a fool's advice of me, sweet friend, and come no more so nigh to Sherwood, or mayhap someday thou may'st of a sudden find a cloth-yard shaft betwixt thy ribs." Hereupon he clapped his hand to the horse's flank and off went nag and rider.

When he was fairly gone, Robin turned, laughing, and entered the forest carrying the shoes in his hand.

That night in Sherwood the fires glowed brightly, and all around sat the stout fellows of the band to hear Robin Hood and Little John tell their adventures. When all was told, Friar Tuck spoke up. "Good master, thou hast had a pretty time, but still I hold that the life of the barefoot friar is the merrier of the two."

"Nay," quoth Will Stutely, "I hold with our master, that he hath had the pleasanter doings of the two, for he hath had two stout bouts at quarterstaff this day."

So some of the band held with Robin Hood and some with Little John. As for me, I think— But I leave it with you to say for yourselves which you hold with.

Robin Hood Shoots Before Queen Eleanor

THE HIGHROAD STRETCHED white and dusty in the hot summer afternoon sun, and the trees stood motionless along the roadside. All across the meadowlands the hot air quivered, and in the limpid waters of the lowland brook the fish hung motionless above the yellow gravel.

Along the road a youth came riding upon a milk-white barb, and folk stopped and looked after him, for never had so lovely a lad been seen in Nottingham before. He could not have been more than sixteen years of age. His long yellow hair flowed behind him, and he was clad in silk and velvet, his dagger jingling against the pommel of the saddle. Thus came the Queen's Page, young Richard Partington, from famous London Town to Sherwood Forest.

His journey had been long, and young Partington was right glad when he saw before him a little inn with a sign bearing the picture of a blue boar. Five lusty fellows sat drinking beer upon a bench, two of the stoutest clothed in Lincoln green.

Here the fair lad drew rein and called loudly for Rhenish wine, for stout country ale was too coarse a drink for this young gentleman. The landlord brought a bottle of wine and a long narrow glass upon a salver, which he held up to the page as he sat upon his horse. Young Partington poured forth the bright yellow wine, and holding the glass aloft cried, "Here is to the health and happiness of the noble Queen Eleanor; may my journey and her desirings soon have end, and I find a certain stout yeoman men call Robin Hood."

At these words, the two in Lincoln green began whispering. Then one of the two, whom Partington thought to be the tallest fellow he had ever beheld, spoke up: "What does our good Queen Eleanor wish of Robin Hood, Sir Page? Methinks I and my friend here might safely guide thee to him. Yet I tell thee plainly, we would not for all merry England have aught of harm befall him."

"Set thy mind at ease; I bring naught of ill," quoth Partington. "I bring a kind message to him from our Queen."

Then the tall yeoman said, "Surely it were safe, Will"; whereat the other nodded. Thereupon Partington paid his score, and, the yeomen coming forward, they all departed on their way.

Robin Hood and many of his band were lying upon the grass under the greenwood tree when Little John and Will Stutely came into the open glade, young Richard Partington riding between them. Then Robin arose and stepped forth to meet him, and Partington leaped from his horse and doffed his cap.

"Now, welcome fair youth!" cried Robin. "And tell me, I

prithee, what bringeth one clad in such noble garb to our forest?"

Then young Partington said, "If I err not, thou art the famous outlaw Robin Hood. To thee I bring greetings from our noble Queen Eleanor. Oft hath she heard thee spoken of, and fain would she behold thy face; therefore she bids me tell thee that if thou wilt presently come to London Town, she will do all in her power to guard thee against harm, and will send thee back safe to Sherwood. Four days hence, in Finsbury Fields, our good King Henry holdeth a grand shooting match, and all the most famous archers of England will be there. Our Queen would fain see thee strive with these, knowing that if thou come thou wilt, with little doubt, carry off the prize. She sends thee, as a sign of great goodwill, this golden ring, which I give herewith into thy hands."

Then Robin Hood kissed the ring and slipped it upon his little finger. Quoth he, "Ere this ring departs from me, my hand shall be cold in death. Sir Page, I will do our Queen's bidding."

"If there be any of thy band that thou wouldst take with thee," said the page, "our Queen will make them right welcome."

"I will choose three," quoth Robin, "and these three shall be Little John, Will Scarlet and Allan a Dale. Thou, Will Stutely, shalt be the chief of the band while I am gone."

Then they prepared themselves for the journey, and a right fair sight they made, for Robin was clad in all blue, and Little John and Will Scarlet in good Lincoln green, and Allan a Dale was dressed in scarlet from the crown of his head to the toes of his pointed shoes. Each wore beneath his cap a little head covering of burnished steel, and underneath his jerkin a coat of linked mail as fine as carded wool, yet so tough that no arrow could pierce it. Then young Partington mounted his horse again, and the five departed. For four days they traveled, and on the fifth morning they came at last to the towers and walls of London Town.

Queen Eleanor sat in her bower, and about her stood her ladies-in-waiting chatting in low voices. She herself sat dreamily where the air came drifting into the room laden with the perfumes of the roses that bloomed in the royal garden. To her came one who said that Partington and four yeomen waited her pleasure in the court below. Then Queen Eleanor arose joyously and bade them be shown into her presence.

Thus Robin Hood and Little John and Will Scarlet and Allan a Dale came before the Queen. Robin knelt before her with his hands folded upon his breast, saying, "Here am I, Robin Hood. Lo, I am thy true servant, and will do thy bidding, even if it be to the shedding of the last drop of my life's blood."

Good Queen Eleanor smiled pleasantly upon him; then she made them all be seated to rest. Rich food was brought and noble wines, and after they had eaten, she questioned them of their adventures. They told her all of the lusty doings herein spoken of, and among others that concerning Sir Richard of the Lea, and how the Bishop had abided three days in Sherwood Forest. At this, the Queen and her ladies laughed again and again; and the time passed till the hour drew nigh for the great archery match.

A gay sight were famous Finsbury Fields on that sunny morning. The King's yeomen were divided into ten companies of fourscore men, and each company had a captain over it. Along the end of the meadow stood booths of striped canvas, one for each band, and at the peak of each fluttered a flag. From the center booth hung the yellow flag of Tepus, the famous bow bearer of the King; next to it, on one hand, was the blue flag of Gilbert of the White Hand, and on the other the blood-red pennant of young Clifton of Buckinghamshire; for these were the most famous of all. On each side of the range were rows upon rows of seats, and in the center of the north side was a raised dais for the King and Queen. All the benches were full of people, rising head above head high aloft till it made the eye dizzy to look upon them.

At last a blast of bugles sounded, and into the meadow came riding six trumpeters with silver trumpets, from which hung velvet banners heavy with rich workings of silver and gold thread. Behind these came King Henry upon a dapple-gray stallion, with his Queen beside him upon a milk-white palfrey. On either side of them walked the yeomen of the guard, the sunlight flashing on their steel halberds. Then came the court in a great crowd, so that all the lawn was alive with waving plumes and flashing jewels.

Then all the people arose and shouted, so that their voices sounded like the storm upon the Cornish coast, when the dark waves run upon the shore and leap and break amid the rocks; so the King and Queen came to their place, and there were seated on thrones bedecked with purple silks and cloths of silver and of gold.

When all was quiet a bugle sounded, and straightway forty-score stalwart archers came marching in order from their tents and stood in front of King Henry. The King looked up and down their ranks right proudly; then his herald, Sir Hugh de Mowbray, proclaimed the rules governing the game, and that the first prize was to be twoscore and ten golden pounds, a silver bugle horn inlaid with gold, and a quiver with ten white arrows tipped with gold and feathered with the white swan's wing. The second prize was to be fivescore of the finest harts that run on Dallen Lea, to be shot when the yeoman that won them chose. The third prize was to be two tuns of good Rhenish wine.

When Sir Hugh had done, each band marched in order back to its place. And now the shooting began, the captains first taking stand, each speeding seven shafts and then making room for the men who shot, each in turn, after them. When the shooting was done each target looked like the back of a hedgehog when the farm dog snuffs at it. Then the judges came forward, looked carefully at the targets, and proclaimed which three had shot the best in each band. Then ten fresh targets were brought forward, and these archers took their places once more.

This time three shafts were shot by each archer. Then the judges again called aloud the best bowman of each band. Of these Gilbert of the White Hand led, for six of the ten arrows he had shot had lodged in the center; but stout Tepus and young Clifton trod close upon his heels. And now those fellows that were left went back to their tents to rest and change their bowstrings.

Then while a deep buzz of talking sounded all around, the King turned to Queen Eleanor, and quoth he, "Truly these yeomen are the very best archers in all the wide world."

"Yet," said the Queen, "I know of three yeomen that I would not fear to match against the best three from among thy guard, and, moreover, I will match them here this day, but only providing thou wilt grant a free pardon to all that come in my behalf."

The King laughed loud and long. "Truly," said he, "thou art taking up with strange matters for a queen. If thou wilt bring those three I promise to give them free pardon for forty days. Moreover, if they shoot better than my yeomen, man for man, they shall have the prizes for themselves. But as thou hast so taken up with sports, hast thou a mind for a wager?"

"Why, insooth," said Queen Eleanor. "I know naught of such matters, but I will strive to pleasure thee. What wilt thou wager?"

Then the King laughed again, for he loved a goodly jest. "I will wager thee ten tuns of the stoutest ale," he said, "and tenscore bows of tempered Spanish yew, with quivers and arrows to match."

All that stood around smiled at this, for it seemed a merry wager for a king to give to a queen; but Queen Eleanor said quietly, "I will take thy wager, for I know right well where to place those things. Now, who will be on my side in this matter? Wilt thou, my Lord Bishop of Hereford?"

"Nay," quoth the Bishop, who sat nearby, "it ill befits one of my cloth to deal in such matters. Moreover, there are no such archers as his Majesty's in all the world; I would but lose my money."

"Methinks the thought of thy gold weigheth more heavily with thee than the wrong to thy cloth," said the Queen, smiling. Then she turned to a knight who stood near, whose name was Sir Robert Lee. "Wilt thou back me?" said she. "Thou art surely rich enough to risk so much for the sake of a lady."

"To pleasure my Queen I will do it," said Sir Robert, "but for the sake of no other in all the world would I wager a groat, for no man can stand against Tepus and Gilbert and Clifton."

Then Queen Eleanor said to the King, "I want no such aid as Sir Robert giveth me; but against thy beer and bows I wager this girdle all set with jewels from around my waist; and surely that is worth more than thine."

"Now, I take thy wager," quoth the King. "Send for thine archers. But here come forth the others; let them shoot, and then I will match those that win against all the world."

"So be it," said the Queen. Thereupon, beckoning to Richard Partington, she whispered something in his ear, and the page bowed and crossed the meadow to the other side of the range, where he was lost in the crowd. At this, all that stood around whispered to one another, wondering what it meant.

And now the ten archers of the King's guard took their stand again. Carefully each man shot three shafts, and so deep was the silence of the crowd that you could hear every arrow rap against the target. Then, when the last shaft had sped, a great roar went up. Once again Gilbert had lodged three arrows in the white; Tepus came second with two in the white and one in the black ring next to it; but stout Clifton had gone down and Hubert of Suffolk had taken the third place.

All the archers around Gilbert's booth shouted for joy, tossing their caps aloft, and shaking hands with one another.

In the midst of all the hubbub four strangers came across the lawn toward the King's pavilion. The first was a yeoman clad in blue, and behind came two in Lincoln green and one in scarlet. This last carried three stout bows of yew, inlaid with silver and gold. And all the folk leaned forward to see what was toward.

When they came before the King and Queen, the four yeomen bent their knees and doffed their caps. King Henry leaned far forward and stared at them closely, but the Bishop of Hereford started as though stung by a wasp.

Then the Queen leaned forward and spoke in a clear voice. "Locksley," said she, "I have made a wager with the King that thou and two of thy men can outshoot any three that he can send against you. Wilt thou do thy best for my sake?"

"Yea," quoth Robin Hood, to whom she spoke, "and, if I fail, I make my vow never to finger bowstring more."

Now, although Little John had been somewhat abashed in the Queen's bower, when the soles of his feet pressed green grass he felt himself again; so he said boldly, "Now, blessings on thy sweet face. An there lived a man that would not do his best for thee— I would like to have the cracking of his knave's pate!"

"Peace, Little John!" said Robin Hood hastily, in a low voice;

but good Queen Eleanor laughed aloud, and a ripple of merriment sounded all over the booth.

The Bishop of Hereford did not laugh; neither did the King, but he turned to the Queen, and quoth he, "Who are these men?"

Then up spoke the Bishop hastily, for he could hold his peace no longer: "Your Majesty, yon fellow in blue is a certain outlawed thief of the mid-country named Robin Hood; yon tall, strapping villain goeth by the name of Little John; the other in green is a certain backsliding gentleman known as Will Scarlet; the man in red is a rogue of a northern minstrel named Allan a Dale."

At this speech the King's brows drew together blackly, and he turned to the Queen. "Is this true?" said he sternly.

"Yea," said the Queen, smiling, "and truly the Bishop should know them well, for he spent three days in merry sport with Robin Hood in Sherwood Forest. But bear in mind that thou hast promised the safety of these good yeomen for forty days."

"I will keep my promise," said the King, in a deep voice that showed his anger, "but when these forty days are gone let this outlaw look to himself." Then he turned to Gilbert, Tepus and Hubert, who stood nearby. Quoth he, "I have pledged myself that ye shall shoot against three of these knaves. If ye outshoot them I will fill your caps with silver pennies; if ye fail ye shall lose your prizes that ye have won so fairly. Do your best, lads, and if ye win ye shall be glad of it to the last of your life."

Then the archers of the King went and told their friends all that had passed; and from the archers the news was taken up by the crowd, so that at last everybody stood up, craning their necks to catch sight of the famous outlaws.

Six fresh targets were now set up, one for each man; whereupon Robin Hood and Gilbert of the White Hand tossed a farthing aloft to see who should lead in the shooting, and the lot fell to Gilbert's side; thereupon he called upon Hubert of Suffolk to lead.

Hubert took his place, planted his foot firmly, and fitted an arrow; then, breathing upon his fingertips, he drew the string slowly and carefully. The arrow sped true, and lodged in the white; again he shot, and again he hit the clout; a third shaft he sped, but this time failed of the center, and but struck the black, yet not more than a finger's breadth from the white.

Then Will Scarlet took his place; but, because of overcaution, he spoiled his target with the very first arrow that he sped, for he hit the next ring to the black, the second from the center. "Lad, lad," quoth Robin, "hold not the string so long! Have I not often told thee overcaution spilleth the milk?" To this Will Scarlet took heed, so the next arrows he shot lodged fairly in the center ring; but, for all that, Hubert had outshot him. Then all that looked on shouted with joy, because Hubert had overcome the stranger.

Quoth the King grimly to the Queen, "If thine archers shoot no better than that, thou art like to lose thy wager, lady." But Queen Eleanor smiled, for she looked for better things from Robin Hood and Little John.

Now Tepus took his place. The first arrow struck the center ring, but then he, also, took overheed, and the second smote the black; the last arrow was tipped with luck, for it smote the very center of the clout. Quoth Robin, "That is the sweetest shot that hath been sped this day; but, nevertheless, friend Tepus, thy cake is burned, methinks. Little John, it is thy turn next."

Little John shot his three arrows quickly; yet all three smote the center. But at this no shouting was heard, for the folk of London Town did not like to see stout Tepus overcome by a fellow from the countryside.

And now stout Gilbert took his place and shot with the greatest care; and again he struck all three shafts into the clout.

"Well done, Gilbert!" quoth Robin, smiting him upon the shoulder. "I make my vow, thou art one of the best archers that ever mine eyes beheld."

Then the King muttered in his beard, "Now, blessed Saint Hubert, if thou wilt but jog that rogue's elbow, I will give eight-score waxen candles to thy chapel nigh Matching." But it may be Saint Hubert's ears were stuffed with tow, for he seemed not to hear the King's prayer this day.

Having gotten three shafts to his liking, Robin looked carefully to his bowstring ere he shot. "Yea," quoth he to Gilbert, who

stood nigh him to watch his shooting, "thou shouldst pay us a visit at merry Sherwood." Here he drew the bowstring to his ear. "In London"—here he loosed his shaft—"thou canst find naught to shoot at but rooks and daws; there one can tickle the ribs of the noblest stags in England." So he shot even while he talked, yet the shaft lodged not more than half an inch from the very center.

"By my soul!" cried Gilbert. "Art thou the devil in blue, to shoot in that wise?"

"Nay," quoth Robin, laughing, "not quite so ill as that, I trust." And again he shot, and again he smote his arrow close beside the center; a third time he dropped his arrow betwixt the other two and into the very center, so that the feathers of all three were ruffled together, seeming from a distance to be one thick shaft.

And now a low murmur ran among the crowd, for never before had London seen such shooting as this. Stout Gilbert clapped his palm to Robin's, owning that he could never hope to draw such a bowstring as Robin Hood. But the King was full of wrath. "Nay!" cried he, clenching his hands upon the arms of his seat. "Gilbert is not yet beaten! Did he not strike the clout thrice? Go thou, Sir Hugh, and bid them shoot another round, and another, till either he or that knave Robin Hood is overcome." Then Sir Hugh went straightway and told them what the King had said.

So Gilbert took his place once more, but this time he failed, for, a sudden little wind arising, his shaft missed the center ring, but by not more than the breadth of a barley straw.

"Thine eggs are cracked, Gilbert," quoth Robin, laughing; and once more he smote the white circle of the center.

Then the King arose; not a word said he, but looked around with a baleful look. Then he and his Queen and all the court left the place, but the King's heart was brimming full of wrath.

After the King had gone, all the yeomen of the archer guard came crowding around Robin, and Little John, and Will, and Allan, to snatch a look at these famous fellows from the mid-country; and with them came many onlookers.

Then the chief judge came forward and said to Robin, "The first prize belongeth rightly to thee; so here I give thee the silver bugle, here the quiver of arrows, and here a purse of twoscore and ten golden pounds." And he handed those things to Robin. Then he said to Little John, "To thee belongeth the second prize, to wit, fivescore of the finest harts that run on Dallen Lea. Thou mayest shoot them whensoever thou dost list." Last of all he said to stout Hubert, "Thou hast held thine own, and so thou hast kept the prize duly thine, to wit, two tuns of good Rhenish wine. These shall be delivered to thee whensoever thou dost list."

Then up spoke Robin: "This silver bugle I keep in honor of this shooting match; but thou, Gilbert, art the best archer of all the King's guard, and to thee I freely give this purse of gold. Would it were ten times as much, for thou art a right yeoman, good and true. To each of the ten that last shot I give one of these golden shafts. Keep them always by you, so that ye may tell your grandchildren that ye are the stoutest yeomen in all the world." At this all shouted aloud, for it pleased them to hear Robin speak so.

Then up spoke Little John. "Good friend Tepus," said he, "I want not those harts of Dallen Lea, for we have more than enow in our own country. Twoscore and ten I give to thee for thine own shooting, and five I give to each band for their pleasure."

At this many tossed their caps aloft, and swore that no better fellows ever walked the sod than Robin Hood and his yeomen.

Then a burly yeoman of the King's guard came forward and plucked Robin by the sleeve. "Good master," quoth he, "a young peacock of a page, one Richard Partington, was seeking thee without avail in the crowd, and told me that he bore a message to thee from a certain lady that thou wottest of. This message he bade me tell thee privily. Let me see—I trust I have forgot it not—yea, thus it was: 'The lion growls. Beware thy head.'"

"Is it so?" quoth Robin, starting, for he knew right well that it was the Queen sent the message, and that she spoke of the King's wrath. "Now, I thank thee, good fellow, for thou hast done me greater service than thou knowest of this day." Then he called his three yeomen together and told them privately that they had best be jogging. So, without tarrying, they made their way through the crowd; then they left London Town and started northward.

NOW IT HAPPENED that after the King left the archery ground, he went straightway to his cabinet, and with him went the Bishop and Sir Robert Lee; but the King said never a word, but sat gnawing his lip, for his heart was galled within him. At last the Bishop spoke, in a sorrowful voice: "It is a sad thing, your Majesty, that this knavish outlaw should be let escape; for, let him but get back to Sherwood, and he may snap his fingers at king and king's men."

"Say'st thou so?" quoth the King grimly. "Nay, when the forty days are past, I will seize upon this thieving outlaw, if I have to tear down all of Sherwood to find him."

Then the Bishop spoke again, in his soft, smooth voice: "Forgive my boldness, your Majesty, and believe that I have naught but the good of England at heart; but what would it boot though my gracious lord did root up every tree of Sherwood? There are many other woodlands in Nottingham and Derby, Lincoln and York, amid any of which your Majesty might as well think to seize upon Robin Hood as to lay finger upon a rat among the dust and broken things of a garret. Nay, if he doth once plant foot in the woodland, he is lost to the law forever."

The King tapped his fingertips upon the table beside him with vexation. "What wouldst thou have me do, Bishop?" quoth he. "Didst thou not hear me pledge my word to the Queen?"

"Far be it from me," said the cunning Bishop, "to point the way to one so clear-sighted as your Majesty; but, were I the King of England, I should look upon the matter in this wise. Suppose I had promised to do her Majesty's bidding, whereupon she bade me to slay myself; should I, then, run blindly upon my sword? I would say unto myself, A woman knoweth naught of state government; and, likewise, a woman is ever prone to take up a fancy, even as she would pluck a daisy from the roadside and then throw it away when the savor is gone; therefore, though she hath taken a fancy to this outlaw, it will soon be forgotten. As for me, am I to let the greatest villain in England slip from my grasp?" So the Bishop talked, and the King lent his ear to his evil counsel, until, after a while, he turned to Sir Robert Lee and bade him send six yeomen of the guard to take Robin and his three men prisoners.

Now Sir Robert Lee was a gentle knight, and he felt grieved to see the King so break his promise; nevertheless, he said nothing, for he saw how bitterly the King was set against Robin Hood; but he did not send the yeomen of the guard at once; he went first to the Queen, and bade her send word to Robin of his danger. This he did, not for the well-being of Robin, but because he would save his lord's honor. Thus it came about that when the yeomen of the guard went to the archery field, they found not Robin.

The afternoon was well-nigh gone when Robin Hood, Little John, Will and Allan set forth upon their homeward way, and the great round moon was floating in the eastern sky when they saw before them the twinkling lights of Barnet Town, some twelve miles from London. Down they walked through the stony streets and past the cozy houses, and so came at last to a little inn. The spot pleased Robin well, and he said, "Here will we rest, for we are well away from London Town and our King's wrath."

"I could wish that we were farther, Uncle," quoth Will Scarlet. "Nevertheless, if thou thinkest best, let us in for the night."

So in they went and called for the best that the place afforded. But when they were done eating, the landlord came in of a sudden, and said that there was at the door a certain Richard Partington, who wished to speak with the lad in blue.

So Robin arose quickly, and found young Richard sitting upon his horse in the moonlight. "What news bearest thou, Sir Page?" said Robin. "I trust that it is not of an ill nature."

"Why," said young Partington, "it is ill enow. The King hath been bitterly stirred up against thee by that vile Bishop of Hereford. Not finding thee at Finsbury Fields, he hath gathered together fiftyscore and more armed men, and is sending them in haste along this very road, to prevent thy getting back to Sherwood. He hath given the Bishop command over all these men, and thou knowest what thou hast to expect of him—short shrift and a long rope. So thou hadst best get thee gone from this place. This word the Queen hath bidden me bring to thee."

"Now, Richard Partington," quoth Robin, "I thank thee. Thou may'st tell the good Queen that I will leave this place without delay, and will let the landlord think that we are going to Saint Albans; but when we are upon the highroad again, I will go one way to Sherwood and will send my men the other, so that if one falleth into the King's hands the others may haply escape. And now, Sir Page, I wish thee farewell."

"Farewell, thou bold yeoman," said young Partington, "and may'st thou reach thy hiding in safety."

So each shook the other's hand, and the lad turned back toward London, while Robin entered the inn once more. There he found his yeomen waiting his coming; likewise the landlord was there, for he was curious to know what Master Partington had to do with the fellow in blue. "Up, my merry men!" quoth Robin. "There are those after us with whom we will stand but an ill chance. So we will go forward to Saint Albans." Hereupon he paid the landlord his score, and so they left the inn.

When they had come without the town, Robin told them all that had passed. Then he told them that they three should go to the eastward and he would go to the westward, and so, skirting the main highroads, they would come by devious paths to Sherwood. Then Robin kissed the three upon the cheeks, and so they parted.

Not long after this, a score of the King's men came clattering up to the inn at Barnet Town. They leaped from their horses and surrounded the place, but found that the birds had flown.

"Methought that they were naughty fellows," said the host. "But I heard that blue-clad knave say they would go to Saint Albans; so, an ye hurry, ye may catch them betwixt here and there." At this the band set forth again, galloping toward Saint Albans.

Little John and Will Scarlet and Allan a Dale traveled eastward, until they came to Chelmsford, in Essex. Thence they turned northward, and came through Cambridge and Lincolnshire, to the good town of Gainsborough. Then, striking to the westward and the south, they came at last to the northern borders of Sherwood.

Eight days they journeyed thus; but when they got to the green-wood glade they found that Robin had not yet returned.

For Robin was not as lucky as his men had been. Having left the great north road and turned his face to the west, he came to Wood-stock, in Oxfordshire. Thence he traveled northward, till he came to Dudley, in Staffordshire. Seven days it took him to journey thus far, and then, turning toward the eastward, shunning the main roads, he went by way of Litchfield until he came to a place called Stanton. Now Robin thought that his danger had gone by; but there is many a slip betwixt the cup and the lip, and this Robin was to find. For thus it was:

When the King's men found themselves foiled at Saint Albans, they knew not what to do. Presently another band of horsemen came, and another, until all the moonlit streets were full of armed men. Betwixt midnight and dawn came the Bishop of Hereford also. He gathered his bands together and pushed northward with speed. On the evening of the fourth day he reached Nottingham Town, and there divided his men into bands of six or seven, and sent them all through the countryside, blocking every highway and byway to the eastward and the southward and the westward of Sherwood. The Sheriff of Nottingham called forth all his men likewise, for he saw that this was the best chance that had ever be-fallen of paying back his score to Robin Hood.

But of all this Robin knew not a whit; so he whistled merrily as he trudged along the road beyond Stanton. At last he came to where a little stream spread across the road in a shallow sheet, tinkling and sparkling as it fretted over its bed of golden gravel. Here Robin stopped and, kneeling down, he made a cup of the palms of his hands, and began to drink. On either side of the road stood tangled thickets, and it pleased Robin's heart to hear the little birds singing therein. But of a sudden a gray goose shaft hissed past his ear, and struck with a splash into the water beside him. Robin sprang to his feet, and, at one bound, crossed the stream and the roadside and plunged headlong into the thicket. Then up the road came riding some of the King's men at headlong speed. They leaped from their horses and plunged into the thicket after Robin. But Robin, crawling here, stooping there and running across some little open, soon left them far behind, coming out upon another road about eight hundred paces distant. For a moment he stood listening to the shouts of the men as they beat in the thickets like hounds that had lost the scent of their quarry. Then, buckling his belt more tightly, he ran fleetly down the road toward Sherwood.

But Robin had not gone more than three furlongs when he came to the brow of a hill, and saw another band of the King's men in the valley beneath him. Seeing that they had not caught sight of him, he turned back, knowing that it was better to run the chance of escaping those fellows that were yet in the thickets than to rush into the arms of those in the valley. He ran with all speed, and had gotten safely past the thickets, when the seven men came forth into the open road. They raised a great shout when they saw him, but Robin was then a quarter of a mile and more away from them, coursing over the ground like a greyhound. He never slackened his pace till he had come nigh to Mackworth, over beyond the Derwent River. Here, seeing that he was out of present danger, he sat down beneath a hedge to catch his wind.

Now along that road came plodding a certain cobbler, one Quince, of Derby, who had been to take a pair of shoes to a farmer nigh Kirk Langly. Good Quince was an honest fellow, but his wits were somewhat of the heavy sort, like unbaked dough, so that the only thing that was in his mind was, Three shillings sixpence ha'penny for thy shoon; and this traveled round and round inside of his head, as a pea in an empty pot.

"Halloa, good friend," quoth Robin, from beneath the hedge, when the other had gotten nigh. "Whither away so merrily?"

The cobbler stopped, and, seeing a well-clad stranger in blue, he spoke to him in seemly wise. "Give ye good den, fair sir, and I would say that I come from Kirk Langly, where I ha' sold my shoon for three shillings sixpence ha'penny. But, an I may be so bold, what dost thou there beneath the hedge?"

"Marry," quoth merry Robin, "I sit beneath the hedge here to drop salt on the tails of golden birds."

At these words the cobbler's eyes opened big and wide with

wonder. "Alackaday," quoth he, "I ha' never seen those same golden birds. And dost thou insooth find them in these hedges?"

"Aye, truly," quoth Robin, "they are as thick here as fresh herring in Cannock Chase."

"And dost thou insooth catch them by dropping salt on their pretty tails?" said the cobbler, all drowned in wonder.

"Yea," quoth Robin, "but this salt is of an odd kind, for it can only be gotten by boiling down a quart of moonbeams, and then one hath but a pinch. But tell me, thou witty man, hast thou a mind to sell thy clothes and leathern apron? I will give thee these gay clothes of blue and ten shillings to boot."

"Nay, thou dost jest," said the cobbler, "for my clothes are coarse and patched, and thine are of fine stuff and very pretty."

"Never a jest do I speak," quoth Robin. "I tell thee I like thy clothes well." At these words he began slipping off his doublet, and the cobbler, seeing him so in earnest, began pulling off his clothes also, for Robin Hood's garb tickled his eye. So each put on the other fellow's clothes, and Robin gave the cobbler ten bright new shillings.

Then of a sudden six horsemen burst upon them, and seized roughly upon the honest craftsman. "Ha!" roared the leader. "Have we then caught thee at last, thou blue-clad knave? Now, blessed be the name of Saint Hubert, for the good Bishop of Hereford hath promised fourscore pounds to the band that shall bring thee to him. Oho! Thou wouldst look so innocent, forsooth! We know thee, thou old fox. But off thou goest with us to have thy brush clipped forthwith." At this the poor cobbler's mouth gaped as though he had swallowed all his words.

Robin also gaped, just as the cobbler would have done in his place. "Alackadaisy, me," quoth he. "What meaneth all this stir i' th' pot, dear gentlemen? Surely this is an honest fellow."

" 'Honest fellow,' say'st thou, clown?" quoth one of the men. "Why, this is that same rogue that men call Robin Hood."

At this speech there was such a threshing of thoughts going on within the cobbler's poor head that his wits were befogged with the dust thereof. Moreover, as he saw Robin looking so like what he knew himself to be, he began to think that mayhap he was the great outlaw in real sooth. Said he in a slow, wondering voice, "Am I in truth that fellow? Now I had thought—but nay, Quince, thou art mistook—yet—am I? Nay, I must indeed be Robin Hood!"

"Alas!" quoth Robin Hood. "Look ye there, now! See how your ill-treatment hath curdled his poor wits!"

Then they tied the cobbler's hands behind him and led him off with a rope, as a farmer leads off a calf from the fair. When they were gone Robin laughed till the tears rolled down his cheeks; for he knew that no harm would befall the honest fellow, and he pictured to himself the Bishop's face when good Quince was brought before him as Robin Hood.

But Robin's journey had been hard and long, and in a se'ennight he had traveled sevenscore and more of miles. He had not gone far ere he felt his strength giving way. So, coming to an inn, he entered and bade the landlord show him to a room, although the sun was only then just sinking in the western sky. There were but two bedrooms besides his own in the place, and to the meanest one the landlord showed Robin Hood, but little Robin cared, for he could have slept that night upon a bed of broken stones. So, stripping off his clothes, he rolled into the bed and went to sleep.

Not long after, a great cloud peeped blackly over the hills to the west. Higher and higher it rose until it piled up into the night like a mountain of darkness. All around beneath it came ever and anon a dull red flash, and presently a short grim mutter of thunder was heard. Then up rode four stout burghers. Leaving their nags to the stableman, they entered the inn, and, having eaten, they bade the landlord show them to his best rooms. Then off they went, grumbling at having to sleep two in a bed; but their troubles on this score were soon lost in the quietness of sleep.

And now a gust of wind rushed past the place, banging the doors and shutters. As though the wind had brought a guest with it, the door opened and in came a rich friar of Emmet Priory. He bade the landlord first have his mule well fed and bedded in the stable, and then to bring him the very best in the house. So presently a savory stew of tripe and onions, with sweet little fat dumplings, was set before him, and the holy friar fell to with great heartiness, so that in a short time naught was left but a little pool of gravy not large enow to keep the life in a starving mouse.

Presently the rain came rattling down, beating against the casements like a hundred little hands; bright flashes of lightning lit up every raindrop, and with them came cracks of thunder. At last the holy friar bade the landlord show him to a room. When he heard that he was to bed with a cobbler, he was ill contented; he went off, grumbling like the thunder. When he came to the room, he slipped off his clothes and huddled into the bed where Robin, grunting in his sleep, made room for him. Robin was more sound asleep, I wot, than he had been for many a day, else he would never have rested so quietly with one of the friar's sort beside him. As for the friar, had he known who Robin was, you may well believe he would almost as soon have slept with an adder.

So the night passed comfortably enough, but at the first dawn of day Robin opened his eyes. Then how he stared, for there beside him lay one all shaven and shorn. Robin arose softly, and looking about the room he espied the friar's clothes upon a bench. First he looked at the clothes, with his head on one side, and then he looked at the friar and slowly winked one eye. Quoth he, "Good Brother Whate'er-thy-name-may-be, as thou hast borrowed my bed so freely I'll e'en borrow thy clothes in return." So saying, he straightway donned the holy man's garb, but kindly left the cobbler's clothes in the place of it. Then he went forth into the freshness of the morning, and the stableman asked Robin whether he wanted his mule brought from the stable.

"Yea, my son," quoth Robin—albeit he knew naught of the mule, "and bring it forth quickly, for I am late and must be jogging." So presently the stableman brought forth the mule, and Robin mounted it and went on his way rejoicing.

As for the holy friar, when he arose he raged and swore like any layman, for his rich, soft robes were gone, likewise his purse with ten golden pounds in it, and naught was left but patched clothes and a leathern apron. But as he was forced to be at Emmet

Priory that very morning, he was fain either to don the cobbler's clothes or travel the road in nakedness. So he put on the clothes and set forth afoot; but his ills had not yet done with him, for he had not gone far ere he fell into the hands of the King's men, who marched him off, willy-nilly, to Tutbury Town. In vain he swore he was a holy man, and showed his shaven crown; off he must go, for nothing would do but that he was Robin Hood.

Meanwhile Robin rode along contentedly. Now and then he passed bands of the King's men, but none of those bands stopped him, and so, at last, he reached the sweet, leafy woodlands.

Robin Hood and Guy of Gisbourne

A LONG TIME HAD PASSED since the great shooting match, and great changes had fallen in this time; for King Henry had died and King Richard had come to the crown that fitted him so well. But in Sherwood's shades Robin Hood and his men dwelt as merrily as they had ever done; for the outside world troubled them but little.

The dawning of one summer's day was fresh and bright, and the birds sang in such a tumult of sound that it awakened Robin Hood. So he rose and walked down a forest path till he came of a sudden to where a man was seated upon the mossy roots of a great oak. Robin saw that the stranger had not caught sight of him, so he stopped and looked at the other a long time. And the stranger, I wot, was well worth looking at, for from his head to his feet he was clad in a horse's hide, dressed with the hair upon it. Even the cowl that hid his face was made of the horse's skin, the ears whereof stuck up like those of a rabbit. By his side was a heavy broadsword and a double-edged dagger. A quiver of arrows hung across his shoulders, and his yew bow leaned against the tree.

"Halloa, friend," cried Robin at last, "who art thou? I make my vow I ha' never seen such a sight in all my life before."

The other answered not a word, but he pushed the cowl back from his head and showed a knit brow, a hooked nose and fierce, restless black eyes, which made Robin think of a hawk. But besides this there was something about the lines on the stranger's face, and his thin cruel mouth, that made one's flesh creep.

"What is thy name, rascal?" said he at last in a loud voice.

"As for my name," quoth Robin, "it may be this or it may be that; but methinks it is more meet for thee to tell me thine, seeing that thou art the greater stranger in these parts. Prithee, tell me, sweet chuck, why wearest thou that dainty garb?"

At these words the other broke into a short, harsh roar of laughter. "I wear this garb, thou fool, to keep my body warm," quoth he. "Likewise it is near as good as a coat of steel. As for my name, it is Guy of Gisbourne. I come from Herefordshire, upon the lands of the Bishop of that ilk. I am an outlaw, and get my living in a manner it boots not now to tell of. Not long since the Bishop sent for me, and said that if I would do a certain thing for the Sheriff of Nottingham, he would get me a free pardon, and tenscore pounds to boot. And what thinkest thou my sweet Sheriff wanted? Why, to come here to hunt up one Robin Hood and take him alive or dead. It seemeth they have no one here to face that bold fellow, and so sent all the way to Herefordshire, and to me, for thou knowest the old saying, 'Set a thief to catch a thief.' As for the slaying of this fellow, it galleth me not a whit, for I would shed the blood of my own brother for the half of two hundred pounds."

To all this Robin listened, and his gorge rose. Well he knew of this Guy of Gisbourne, and of all the bloody deeds that he had done in Herefordshire. Yet he held his peace, for he had an end to serve. "Truly," quoth he, "I have heard of thy gentle doings. Methinks there is no one in all the world that Robin Hood would rather meet than thee."

At this Guy of Gisbourne gave another harsh laugh. "Why," quoth he, "it is a merry thing to think of one stout outlaw meeting another. Only in this case it will be an ill happening for Robin Hood, for the day he meets Guy of Gisbourne he shall die."

"But, thou merry spirit," quoth Robin, "dost thou not think that mayhap this same Robin Hood may be the better man? Many think that he is one of the stoutest hereabout."

"He may be the stoutest hereabout," quoth Guy of Gisbourne,

"yet this sty of yours is not the wide world. I lay my life upon it I am the better man. Why, I hear that he hath never let blood, saving when he first came to the forest. Some call him a great archer; marry, I would not be afraid to stand against him with a bow."

"Truly, some do call him a great archer," said Robin, "but we of Nottinghamshire are famous hands with the longbow. Even I, though but a simple hand, would not fear to try a bout with thee."

"Now," quoth Guy of Gisbourne, "thou art a bold fellow. I like thy spirit in so speaking up to me, for few men have dared to do so. Put up a garland, lad, and I will try a bout with thee."

"Tut, tut," quoth Robin, "only babes shoot at garlands hereabout. I will put up a good Nottingham mark for thee." So saying, he cut a hazel wand about twice the thickness of a man's thumb. From this he peeled the bark, and stuck it up in the ground fourscore paces from where the other sat. "There," quoth he. "Now let me see thee split that wand."

Then Guy of Gisbourne arose. "Now out upon it!" cried he. "The devil himself could not hit such a mark as that."

"That we shall never know till thou hast shot," quoth Robin.

At these words Guy of Gisbourne looked upon Robin with knit brows, but, as the yeoman looked innocent of any ill meaning, he bottled his words and strung his bow in silence. Twice he shot, but neither time did he hit the wand.

"Good fellow," quoth Robin, "if thou art no better with the broadsword than with the bow, thou wilt never overcome Robin Hood."

Then twice shot Robin Hood, the first time hitting within an inch of the wand, and the second time splitting it fairly in the middle. "There, thou bloody villain!" cried he, flinging his bow upon the ground. "Let that show thee how little thou knowest of manly sports. And now look thy last upon the daylight, for the good earth hath been befouled long enough by thee! This day, Our Lady willing, thou diest—I am Robin Hood." So saying, he flashed forth his bright sword in the sunlight.

"Art thou indeed?" cried Guy of Gisbourne in a wild rage. "Now I am glad to meet thee, thou poor wretch! Shrive thyself, for

thou wilt have no time for shriving when I am done with thee."
So saying, he also drew his sword.

And now came the fiercest fight that ever Sherwood saw; for
each man knew that either he or the other must die. Up and down
they fought, till at last Guy of Gisbourne made a thrust at Robin
Hood, from which Robin leaped back lightly. But in so leaping he
caught his heel in a root and fell heavily upon his back. "Now,
Holy Mary aid me!" muttered he, as the other leaped at him.
Fiercely Guy of Gisbourne stabbed with his great sword; but Robin
caught the blade in his naked hand, and, though it cut his palm, he
turned the point so that it plunged deep into the ground beside
him. Then he leaped to his feet, with his good sword in his hand,
and struck Guy of Gisbourne a backhanded blow beneath the
sword arm. Down fell the sword from Guy of Gisbourne's grasp
and back he staggered at the stroke, and, ere he could regain himself, Robin's sword passed through his body. Around he spun, and,
flinging his hands aloft with a shrill, wild cry, fell upon his face.

Then Robin wiped his sword and thrust it back into the scabbard, and he stood over Guy of Gisbourne with folded arms, talking to himself: This is the first man I have slain since I shot the
King's forester in the hot days of my youth. I think bitterly, even
yet, of that first life I took, but of this I am as glad as though I had
slain a wild boar. Since the Sheriff hath sent such a one as this
against me, I will put on the fellow's garb and go to find his worship, and perchance pay him the debt I owe upon this score.

So saying, Robin put on the hairy garments, all bloody as they
were. Then, strapping the other's sword and dagger around his
body and carrying his own in his hand, together with the two yew
bows, he drew the cowl of horse's hide over his face and set forth
toward Nottingham Town. As he strode along the country roads,
men, women and children hid away from him, for the terror of
Guy of Gisbourne's doings had spread far and near.

Now while these things were happening, Little John also had
been walking through the forest paths, until he had come to the
highroad where a little thatched cottage stood back of a cluster

of twisted crab-apple trees. Here he thought that he heard the sound of someone in sorrow; so he pushed open the wicket and entered the cottage. There he saw a gray-haired dame rocking herself to and fro and weeping bitterly.

Now Little John had a tender heart for the sorrows of other folk, so, patting the old woman kindly upon the shoulder, he bade her tell him her troubles. So the good dame told him all that bore upon her mind. That that morning she had three as fair, tall sons beside her as one could find in all Nottinghamshire, but that they were now taken from her, and were like to be hanged; that, want having come upon them, her eldest boy, the night before, had slain a hind in the forest; that the King's rangers had followed the blood upon the grass until they had come to her cottage, and had there found the deer's meat in the cupboard; that, as neither of the younger sons would betray their brother, the foresters had taken all three away, in spite of the eldest's saying that he alone had slain the deer; that, as they went, she had heard the rangers saying that the Sheriff had sworn that he would put a check upon the slaughter of deer that had been going on of late by hanging the first rogue caught thereat upon the nearest tree, and that they would take the three youths to the King's Head Inn, near Nottingham Town, where the Sheriff was abiding that day.

"Alas," quoth Little John, "this is indeed an ill case. No time may be lost if we would save their lives. Tell me, hast thou any clothes hereabout that I may put on in place of these? Marry, if our Sheriff catcheth me without disguise, I am like to be run up more quickly than thy sons."

Then the woman brought some of the clothes of her husband, who had died only two years before; and Little John, doffing his garb of Lincoln green, put them on in its stead. Then, making a wig and false beard of uncarded wool, he covered his own brown hair and beard, and, putting on a tall hat that had belonged to the old peasant, he took his staff in one hand and his bow in the other, and set forth.

At the cozy inn bearing the Sign of the King's Head there was a great bustle and stir, for the Sheriff and his men had come there to await Guy of Gisbourne's return from the forest. The Sheriff sat within, feasting merrily, and the Sheriff's men sat upon the bench before the door, quaffing ale. All around stood the horses of the band, with a great noise of stamping feet and a great switching of tails. To this inn came the King's rangers, driving the widow's sons before them. The hands of the three youths were tied tightly behind their backs, and a cord from neck to neck fastened them all together. So they were marched to where the Sheriff sat at meat, and stood trembling before him.

"So," quoth he, in an angry voice, "ye have been poaching upon the King's deer? Now I will hang up all three of you as a farmer would hang up three crows to scare others of the kind."

Then the Sheriff bade the rangers to take the poor youths away till he had done his eating. So they were marched outside, where they stood with bowed heads and despairing hearts, till after a while the Sheriff came forth. Then he called his men about him, and quoth he, "We will take these three villains over yonder to that belt of woodlands, for I would fain hang them upon the very trees of Sherwood itself, to show those vile outlaws therein what they may expect of me if I ever have the good luck to lay hands upon them." So saying, he mounted his horse, as did his men-at-arms, and all together they set forth for the woodlands, the poor youths walking in their midst. So they came at last to the spot, and here nooses were fastened around the necks of the three, and the ends of the cords flung over the branch of a great oak tree.

While all this had been going forward, an old man had drawn near and stood leaning on his staff, looking on. His hair and beard were all curly and white, and across his back was a bow of yew that looked much too strong for him to draw. The Sheriff's eyes fell upon this strange old man, and he beckoned to him. So Little John, for it was none other, came forward, and the Sheriff, thinking there was something strangely familiar in the face, said, "Methinks I have seen thee before. What may thy name be, father?"

"Please your worship," said Little John, in a cracked voice like that of an old man, "my name is Giles Hobble."

"Giles Hobble, Giles Hobble," muttered the Sheriff. "I remember not thy name, but it matters not. Hast thou a mind to earn sixpence this bright morn?"

"Aye, marry," quoth Little John, "for money is not so plenty with me that I should cast sixpence away an I could earn it by an honest turn. What is it your worship would have me do?"

"Why, this," said the Sheriff. "Here are three men that need hanging as badly as any e'er I saw. If thou wilt string them up I will pay thee twopence apiece for them. I like not that my men-at-arms should turn hangmen. Wilt thou try thy hand?"

"Insooth," said Little John, "I ha' never done such a thing before; but an a sixpence is to be earned I might as well ha' it as anybody. But, your worship, are these fellows shrived?"

"Nay," said the Sheriff, laughing, "never a whit; but thou may'st turn thy hand to that also if thou art so minded."

So Little John came to where the youths stood trembling, and, putting his face to the first fellow's cheek as though he were listening to him, he whispered softly, "Stand still, brother, when thou feelest thy bonds cut, but when thou see'st me throw aside my woolen wig and beard, cast the noose from thy neck and run for the woodlands." Then he slyly cut the cord that bound the youth's hands; who, upon his part, stood still as though he were yet bound. Then he spoke to the second fellow in the same way, and also cut his bonds. This he did to the third likewise.

Then Little John turned to the Sheriff. "Please your worship," said he, "will you give me leave to string my bow? For I would fain help these fellows along the way, when they are swinging, with an arrow beneath the ribs."

"With all my heart," said the Sheriff, "only make haste."

Little John put the tip of his bow to his instep, and strung the weapon so deftly that all wondered to see an old man so strong. Next he drew an arrow from his quiver and fitted it to the string; then he cast away the wool from his head and face, shouting in a mighty voice, "Run!" Quick as a flash the three youths flung the nooses from their necks and sped across the open to the woodlands. Little John also flew toward the covert, while the Sheriff and his men gazed after him all bewildered with the sudden doing. But ere the yeoman had gone far the Sheriff roused himself. "After him!" he roared; for he knew now who it was.

When Little John heard the Sheriff's words, he stopped and turned suddenly, holding his bow as though he were about to shoot. "Stand back!" cried he fiercely. "The first man that cometh a foot forward dieth!"

At these words the Sheriff's men stood as still as stocks. In vain the Sheriff urged them forward; they would not budge an inch, but watched Little John as he moved slowly toward the forest, keeping his gaze fixed upon them. But when the Sheriff saw his enemy thus slipping betwixt his fingers he grew mad with rage. So, plunging his spurs into his horse's sides, he gave a great shout, rose in his stirrups and came down upon Little John like the wind. Then Little John raised his bow and drew the gray goose feather to his cheek. But alas! Ere he could loose the shaft, the good bow that had served him so long split in his hands, and the arrow fell harmless at his feet. Seeing this, the Sheriff, leaning forward, struck Little John a mighty blow. Little John ducked and the Sheriff's sword turned in his hand, but the flat of the blade struck the other upon the head and smote him down, senseless.

"Now, I am right glad," said the Sheriff, when the men came up and found that Little John was not dead, "that I have not slain this man in my haste! I would rather lose five hundred pounds than have him die thus instead of hanging." Presently Little John opened his eyes and looked around him, all dazed and bewildered. Then they tied his hands behind him, and set him upon the back of one of the horses, with his face to its tail and his feet strapped beneath its belly. And so they took him back toward the inn.

Now the Sheriff's heart rejoiced. Quoth he to himself, This time tomorrow the rogue shall hang upon the gallows tree in front of the great gate of Nottingham Town. But then the Sheriff shook his head and muttered to himself, Should his master escape Guy of Gisbourne, there is no knowing what he may do. Belike I had better not wait until tomorrow. So he said to his men, "This rogue shall be hanged forthwith, and that from the very tree whence he saved those three young villains."

So, one leading the horse whereon Little John sat and the others riding around him, they went back to that tree from the branches of which they had thought to hang the poachers. Here one of the men spoke to the Sheriff of a sudden. "Your worship," cried he, "is not yon fellow coming toward us that same Guy of Gisbourne whom thou didst send to seek Robin Hood?"

The Sheriff shaded his eyes and looked. "Why, certes," quoth he, "yon fellow is the same. Now, heaven send that he hath slain the master thief, as we will presently slay the man!"

When Little John heard this speech he looked up, and straightway his heart crumbled within him, for not only were the man's garments all covered with blood, but he wore Robin Hood's bugle horn and carried his bow and broadsword.

"How now!" cried the Sheriff, when Robin Hood, in Guy of Gisbourne's clothes, had come nigh to them. "What luck hath befallen thee? Why, man, thy clothes are all over blood!"

"An thou likest not my clothes," said Robin in a harsh voice like that of Guy of Gisbourne, "thou may'st shut thine eyes. Marry, the blood upon me is that of the vilest outlaw that ever trod the woodlands, and one whom I have slain this day."

Then out spoke Little John, for the first time since he had fallen into the Sheriff's hands. "Oh thou bloody wretch! Is it by such a hand as thine that the gentlest heart that ever beat is stilled? Truly, thou art a fit tool for this coward Sheriff. Now care I not how I die, for life is naught to me!"

But the Sheriff laughed for joy. "This is a good day!" cried he. "The great outlaw dead and his right-hand man in my hands! Ask what thou wilt, Guy of Gisbourne, and it is thine!"

"Then this I ask," said Robin. "As I have slain the master I would now kill the man. Give this fellow's life into my hands."

"Now thou art a fool!" cried the Sheriff. "Thou might'st have had money enough for a knight's ransom if thou hadst asked for it. I like ill to let this fellow pass from my hands, but as I have promised, thou shalt have him."

"I thank thee right heartily," cried Robin. "Take the rogue down from the horse, men, and lean him against yonder tree."

While the Sheriff's men were doing this Robin strung both his bow and that of Guy of Gisbourne, albeit none of them took notice of his doing so. Then, when Little John stood against the tree, Robin drew Guy of Gisbourne's dagger. "Fall back! Fall back!" cried he. "Would ye crowd so on my pleasure, ye unmannerly knaves? Back, I say! Farther yet!"

"Come!" cried Little John. "Here is my breast. It is meet that the hand that slew my dear master should butcher me also!"

"Peace, Little John!" said Robin in a low voice. "Couldst thou not tell me beneath this beast's hide? Just in front of thee lie my bow and arrows, likewise my broadsword. Take them when I cut thy bonds. Now!" So saying, he cut the bonds, and Little John, quick as a wink, caught up the bow and arrows and the broadsword. At the same time Robin Hood threw back the cowl from his face and bent Guy of Gisbourne's bow, with a keen, barbed arrow fitted to the string. "Stand back!" cried he sternly. "The first man that toucheth finger to bowstring dieth! I have slain thy man, Sheriff; take heed that it is not thy turn next." Then, seeing that Little John had armed himself, he clapped his horn to his lips and blew three blasts both loud and shrill.

Now when the Sheriff saw whose face it was beneath Guy of Gisbourne's hood, and when he heard those bugle notes ring in his ear, he felt as if his hour had come. "Robin Hood!" roared he, and without another word he wheeled his horse and went off in a cloud of dust. The Sheriff's men, seeing their master thus fleeing, clapped spurs to their horses and dashed away after him. But though the Sheriff went fast, he could not outstrip a cloth-yard arrow. Little John twanged his bowstring with a shout, and when the Sheriff dashed in through the gates of Nottingham Town it was with a gray goose shaft sticking out behind him, like a molting sparrow with one feather in its tail. For a month afterward the poor Sheriff could sit upon naught but the softest cushions.

Thus it was that when Will Stutely and a dozen yeomen burst from out the covert, they saw the Sheriff and his men scurrying away in the distance. Then they all went back into the forest, where they found the widow's three sons, who ran to Little John and kissed his hands. But it would not do for them to roam the forest at large anymore; so they promised that, after they had told their mother of their escape, they would return to the greenwood tree and thenceforth become men of the band.

King Richard Comes to Sherwood Forest

NOT MORE THAN TWO MONTHS after these adventures all Nottinghamshire was in a mighty stir and tumult, for King Richard of the Lion's Heart was making a royal progress through merry England, and his Majesty was to stop in Nottingham Town, as the guest of the Sheriff. A rapping of hammers and a babble of voices sounded through the place, for the folk were building great arches across the streets, and were draping these arches with banners and streamers of many colors. A grand banquet was to be given in the Guild Hall to the King and his nobles.

At last the day came that should bring the King into the town, and bright shone the sun down into the stony streets. On either side of the way great crowds of folk stood packed as close as dried herring in a box, so that the Sheriff's men could hardly press them back to leave space for the King's riding.

And now a gallant array of men came into sight, and the cheering of the people ran down the crowd as the fire runs in dry grass. Eight and twenty heralds in velvet and cloth of gold came riding forward, each herald bearing in his hand a long silver trumpet, which he blew musically. From each trumpet hung a heavy banner with the royal arms of England emblazoned thereon. After these came riding fivescore noble knights, two by two, all fully armed, saving that their heads were uncovered. In their hands they bore tall lances, from the tops of which fluttered pennons of many colors and devices. By the side of each knight walked a page, bearing in his hands his master's helmet, from which waved long, floating plumes of feathers. Behind the knights came the barons and the nobles of the mid-country; behind these again came menat-arms, with spears and halberds in their hands, and, in the midst of these, two riders side by side. One was the Sheriff of Nottingham in his robes of office. The other, who was a head taller than the Sheriff, was clad in a rich but simple garb, with a heavy chain about his neck. His hair and beard were like threads of gold, and his eyes were as blue as the summer sky. As he rode along he bowed to the right and the left, and a mighty roar of voices followed him as he passed; for this was King Richard.

Then, above the tumult, a great voice was heard. "Heaven, its saints bless thee, our gracious King Richard!" Then the King, looking toward the spot whence the sound came, saw a tall, burly priest standing in front of all the crowd with his legs wide apart.

"By my soul, Sheriff," said King Richard, laughing, "ye have here the tallest priests that e'er I saw in all my life."

At this all the blood left the Sheriff's cheeks, and he caught at the pommel of his saddle to keep himself from falling; for he knew the tall priest to be Friar Tuck; and behind Friar Tuck he saw the faces of Robin Hood and others of the band.

"How now," said the King hastily, "art thou ill, Sheriff, that thou growest so white?"

"Nay, your Majesty," said the Sheriff, "it was but a sudden pain that will soon pass by." For he was ashamed that the King should know that Robin Hood feared him so little that he thus dared to come within the very gates of Nottingham Town.

Thus rode the King into Nottingham; and none rejoiced more than Robin and his men to see him come so royally unto his own.

EVENTIDE HAD COME; the great feast in the Guild Hall at Nottingham Town was done, and the wine passed freely. At the head of the table, upon a throne all hung with cloth of gold, sat King Richard with the Sheriff beside him. Quoth the King, laughing as he spoke, "I have heard much spoken concerning the doings of certain outlaws hereabout, one Robin Hood and his band. Canst thou not tell me somewhat of them, Sir Sheriff?"

At these words the Sheriff looked down gloomily. "I can tell your Majesty but little concerning those fellows," quoth he, "saving that they are the boldest lawbreakers in all the land."

559

Then up spoke young Sir Henry of the Lea, a favorite with the King, under whom he had fought in Palestine. "May it please your Majesty," said he, "I have heard ofttimes from my father of this Robin Hood." Then he told how Robin had aided Sir Richard with money borrowed from the Bishop of Hereford. The King roared with laughter, while the Bishop, who was present, waxed cherry-red in the face. Then others, seeing how the King enjoyed this tale, told other tales of Robin and his men.

"By the hilt of my sword," said King Richard, "this is as merry a knave as ever I heard tell of. Marry, I must do what thou couldst not do, Sheriff, to wit, clear the forest of his band."

That night the King sat in the place that was set apart for his lodging while in Nottingham Town. With him were young Sir Henry of the Lea and two other knights and three barons of Nottinghamshire; but the King's mind still dwelt upon Robin Hood. "Now," quoth he, "I would give a hundred pounds to meet this fellow, and to see somewhat of his doings."

Then up spoke Sir Hubert of Bingham, laughing. "Such a desire is not so hard to satisfy, if your Majesty is willing to lose one hundred pounds. Let us put on the robes of the Order of Black Friars, and let your Majesty hang a purse of one hundred pounds beneath your gown; then let us ride from here to Mansfield Town tomorrow, and, without I am much mistaken, we will both meet with Robin Hood and dine with him."

"I like thy plan, Sir Hubert," quoth the King merrily, "and tomorrow we will try it and see whether there be virtue in it."

So it happened that when early the next morning the Sheriff came to his liege lord to pay his duty to him, the King told him what merry adventure they were set upon undertaking. "Alas!" said the Sheriff. "My gracious lord, you know not what you do! This villain hath no reverence either for king or king's laws."

"But did I not hear aright that this Robin Hood hath shed no blood since he was outlawed, saving only that of that vile Guy of Gisbourne, for whose death all honest men should thank him?"

"Yea, your Majesty," said the Sheriff. "Nevertheless—"

"Then," quoth the King, breaking in on the Sheriff's speech, "what have I to fear in meeting him, having done him no harm? But mayhap thou wilt go with us, Sir Sheriff."

"Nay," quoth the Sheriff hastily. "Heaven forbid!"

But now seven habits such as Black Friars wear were brought, and the King and those about him having clad themselves therein, and his Majesty having hung a purse with a hundred golden pounds in it beneath his robes, they all mounted on mules and so set forth upon their way. Onward they traveled till they came within the heavy shade of the forest itself.

"By the holy Saint Martin," quoth the King. "Here have we come away and brought never a drop of anything to drink. Now I would give half a hundred pounds for somewhat to quench my thirst."

No sooner had the King so spoken, than out from the covert at the roadside stepped a tall fellow with yellow beard and hair and a pair of merry blue eyes. "Truly, holy brother," said he, laying his hand upon the King's bridle rein, "it were unchristian not to give fitting answer to so fair a bargain. We keep an inn hereabout, and for fifty pounds we will not only give thee a good draught of wine, but will give thee as noble a feast as ever did tickle thy gullet." So saying, he put his fingers to his lips and blew a shrill whistle. Then straightway threescore yeomen in Lincoln green burst out of the covert.

"How now," quoth the King, "who art thou, thou naughty rogue? Hast thou no regard for such holy men as we are?"

"Not a whit," quoth the merry fellow, "for insooth, all the holiness belonging to rich friars, such as ye are, one could drop into a thimble and the goodwife would never feel it with the tip of her finger. As for my name, it is Robin Hood."

"Now out upon thee!" quoth King Richard. "Thou art a bold and lawless fellow, as I have often heard tell. Now, prithee, let me, and these brethren of mine, travel forward in peace."

"It may not be," said Robin, "for it would look but ill of us to let such holy men travel onward with empty stomachs. But I doubt not that thou hast a fat purse to pay thy score at our inn, since thou offerest freely so much for a poor draught of wine. Show me thy purse, reverend brother, or I may perchance have to strip thy robes from thee to search for it myself."

"Nay, use no force," said the King sternly. "Here is my purse, but lay not thy lawless hands upon our person."

"Hut, tut," quoth Robin, "what proud words are these? Art thou the King of England, to talk so? Here, Will, take this purse and see what there is within."

Will Scarlet took the purse and counted out the money. Then Robin bade him keep fifty pounds, and put fifty back into the purse. This he handed to the King. "Here, brother," quoth he, "take this and thank Saint Martin, on whom thou didst call, that thou hast fallen into the hands of such gentle rogues. But wilt thou not put back thy cowl? For I would fain see thy face."

"Nay," said the King, drawing back, "for we seven have vowed that we will not show our faces for four and twenty hours."

"Then keep them covered in peace," said Robin, "and far be it from me to make you break your vows."

So he bade seven of his men each take a mule by the bridle; then they journeyed on until they came to the greenwood tree, where Friar Tuck and twoscore or more stout yeomen abided them.

"By my soul," quoth King Richard, looking about him, "thou hast in truth a fine lot of young men about thee, Robin. Methinks King Richard himself would be glad of such a bodyguard."

"These are not all of my fellows," said Robin proudly, "for threescore more of them are away on business. But, as for King Richard, I tell thee, brother, there is not a man of us all but would pour out our blood like water for him. Ye churchmen cannot rightly understand our King; but we yeomen love him for the sake of his brave doings."

But now Friar Tuck came bustling up. "Gi' ye good den, brothers," said he. "I am right glad to welcome some of my cloth in this naughty place. Methinks these rogues of outlaws would stand but an ill chance were it not for the prayers of holy Tuck." Here he winked slyly and stuck his tongue into his cheek.

"Who art thou, mad priest?" said the King in a serious voice, albeit he smiled beneath his cowl.

At this Friar Tuck gazed around. "Look you now," quoth he, "never let me hear you say again that I am no patient man. Here is a knave of a friar calleth me a mad priest, and yet I smite him not. My name is Friar Tuck, fellow—the holy Friar Tuck."

"There, Tuck," said Robin, "cease thy talk and bring some wine. These reverend men are athirst, and sin' they have paid so richly for their score they must e'en have the best."

Friar Tuck bridled at being so checked; nevertheless he went. So presently a great crock was brought, and wine was poured out for all. Then Robin held his cup aloft. "Here is to good King Richard," cried he, "and may all enemies to him be confounded!"

Then all drank to the King, even the King himself. "Methinks," said he, "thou hast drunk to thine own confusion."

"Never a whit," quoth Robin, "for I tell thee that we are more loyal than those of thine order. We would give up our lives for the King while ye lie snug in your abbeys, let reign who will."

At this the King laughed. Quoth he, "Perhaps King Richard's welfare is more to me than thou wottest of. But enough of that matter. I have oft heard that ye are wondrous archers. Wilt thou not show us somewhat of your skill?"

"With all my heart," said Robin. "Ho, lads! Set up a garland at the end of the glade, and each of you shoot three arrows thereat. If any fellow misseth, he shall have a buffet of Will Scarlet's fist."

"Why, master," quoth Friar Tuck, "thou dost bestow buffets from thy strapping nephew as though they were love taps from some bouncing lass."

First David of Doncaster shot, and lodged all of his arrows within the garland. Next Midge, the Miller's son, shot, and he also lodged his arrows in the garland. Then followed Wat, the Tinker, but one of his shafts missed by the breadth of two fingers.

"Come hither, fellow," said Will Scarlet, in his gentle voice. Then Wat stood in front of Will Scarlet, screwing up his face, and as though he already felt his ears ringing with the buffet. Will Scarlet rolled up his sleeve, and, standing on tiptoe, struck with might and main. *Whoof!* came his palm against the tinker's head, and down went stout Wat to the grass, heels over head.

Then, as the tinker sat up upon the grass, blinking at the bright stars that danced before his eyes, the yeomen roared with mirth. As for King Richard, he laughed till the tears ran down his cheeks. Thus the band shot, each in turn, some getting off scot-free, and some winning a buffet that always sent them to the grass. And now, last of all, Robin took his place. The first shaft he shot split a piece from the stake on which the garland was hung; the second lodged within an inch of the other. And now, for the third time Robin shot; but alas for him! The arrow was ill feathered, and, wavering to one side, it smote an inch outside the garland.

At this the yeomen shouted with laughter, for never before had they seen their master miss his mark; but Robin flung his bow upon the ground. "Now, out upon it!" cried he. "That shaft had an ill feather. Give me a clean arrow, and I will engage to split the wand with it."

"Nay, good Uncle," said Will Scarlet, "I swear the arrow was as good as any that hath been loosed this day. Come hither; I owe thee somewhat, and would fain pay it."

"Go, good master," roared Friar Tuck, "and my blessing go with thee. Thou hast bestowed Will Scarlet's love taps with great freedom. It were pity an thou gottest not thine own share."

"It may not be," said Robin. "I am king here, and no subject may raise hand against the king. But even great King Richard may yield to the holy Pope without shame; therefore I will yield myself to this holy friar." Thus saying, he turned to the King. "I prithee, brother, wilt thou take my punishing into thy hands?"

"With all my heart," quoth King Richard, rising. "I owe thee somewhat for having lifted a heavy weight from my purse."

"An thou makest me tumble," quoth Robin, "I will freely give thee back thy fifty pounds."

"So be it," said the King. Thereupon he rolled up his sleeve and showed an arm that made the yeomen stare. But Robin, with his feet wide apart, stood firmly planted, waiting the other, smiling. Then the King swung back his arm, and delivered a buffet that fell like a thunderbolt, and down went Robin headlong upon the grass. Then how the yeomen laughed, for never had they seen such a buffet given. As for Robin, he presently sat up and looked all around him, as though he had dropped from a cloud and had lit in a place he had never seen before. After a while, he put his fingertips softly to his ear and felt all around it tenderly. "Will Scarlet," said he, "count this fellow out his fifty pounds; I want nothing more either of his money or of him. I would that I had taken my dues from thee, for I verily believe he hath deafened mine ear from ever hearing again."

Then Will Scarlet counted out the fifty pounds, and the King dropped it into his purse again. "I give thee thanks, fellow," said he, "and if ever thou shouldst wish for another box of the ear, come to me and I will fit thee with it for naught."

Even as the King ended, there came suddenly the sound of many voices, and out from the covert burst Little John and threescore men, with Sir Richard of the Lea in the midst. "Make haste, dear friend," Sir Richard shouted to Robin, "gather thy band together and come with me! A rumor has reached me that King Richard left Nottingham Town this very morning, and cometh to seek thee in the woodlands. Therefore hasten to Castle Lea, for there thou may'st lie hidden till thy present danger passeth. Who are these strangers that thou hast with thee?"

"Why," quoth Robin, rising from the grass, "these are certain gentle guests that I met with on the highroad. I know not their names."

Sir Richard looked keenly at the tall friar, who, drawing himself up to his full height, looked fixedly back at the knight. Then Sir Richard's cheeks grew pale, for he knew who it was that he looked upon. Quickly he leaped from off his horse and flung himself upon his knees before the other. At this, the King threw back his cowl, and all the yeomen knew him also, for there was not one of them but had seen him riding in Nottingham with the Sheriff. Down they fell upon their knees, nor could they say a word. Then the King looked all around right grimly, and, last of all, his glance rested again upon Sir Richard.

"How is this, Sir Richard?" said he. "How darest thou offer thy knightly castle for a refuge to these outlaws?"

Then Sir Richard raised his eyes to the King's face. "Far be it from me," said he, "to do aught that could bring your Majesty's anger upon me. Yet, sooner would I face your Majesty's wrath than suffer aught of harm to fall upon Robin Hood and his band; for to them I owe life, honor, everything."

Ere the knight had done speaking, one of the mock friars came forward and knelt beside Sir Richard, and throwing back his cowl showed the face of young Sir Henry of the Lea. Then Sir Henry grasped his father's hand and said, "Here kneels one, King Richard, who hath stepped between thee and death in Palestine; yet here I say also, that I would freely give shelter to this noble outlaw, even though it brought thy wrath upon me, for my father's honor and welfare are as dear to me as mine own."

King Richard looked from one to the other of the kneeling knights, and the frown faded from his brow. "Sir Richard," quoth he, "thou art a bold-spoken knight, and thy son taketh after his sire in boldness of speech and of deed, for, as he sayeth, he stepped one time betwixt me and death; wherefore I would pardon thee for his sake even if thou hadst done more than thou hast. Rise all of you, for ye shall suffer no harm through me this day; it were pity that a merry time should end in a manner as to mar its joyousness."

Then the King beckoned to Robin Hood and said, with something of sternness in his voice, "Take not thy sins lightly, good Robin; but now come, look up. I hereby give thee and all thy band free pardon. I will take thee at thy word, when thou didst say thou wouldst give thy service to me, and thou shalt go back to London with me. We will take that bold knave Little John also, and thy cousin, Will Scarlet, and thy minstrel, Allan a Dale. As for the rest of thy band, we will have them duly recorded as royal rangers; for methinks it were wiser to have them changed to law-abiding caretakers of our deer in Sherwood than to leave them to run at large as outlawed slayers thereof. But now get a feast ready; I would see how ye live in the woodlands."

So straightway great fires were kindled and burned brightly, at which savory things roasted sweetly. While this was going forward, Allan a Dale sang and played upon his harp for the King. Then

King Richard feasted and drank, and when he was done he swore roundly that he had never sat at such a lusty repast in all his life.

That night he lay in Sherwood Forest upon a bed of sweet green leaves, and early the next morning he set forth for Nottingham Town, Robin Hood and all of his band going with him. You may guess what a stir there was in the town when all these famous outlaws came marching into the streets. As for the Sheriff, he knew not what to say when he saw Robin Hood in such high favor with the King, and all his heart was filled with gall.

The next day Robin Hood and Little John and Will Scarlet and Allan a Dale shook hands with all the rest of the band, kissing the cheeks of each man, and swearing that they would come often to Sherwood. Then each mounted his horse and they rode away in the train of the King.

EPILOGUE

THUS END THE MERRY ADVENTURES of Robin Hood; for, in spite of his promise, it was many a year ere he saw Sherwood again.

After a year or two at court Little John came back to Nottinghamshire, where he lived in an orderly way, though within sight of Sherwood, and where he achieved fame as the champion of all England with the quarterstaff. Will Scarlet after a time came back to his own home, whence he had been driven by his unlucky killing of his father's steward. The rest of the band did their duty as royal rangers right well. But Robin (and Allan a Dale) did not come again to Sherwood so quickly, for Robin, through his great fame as an archer, speedily rose in rank to be the chief of all the yeomen, and the King, seeing how faithful he was, created him Earl of Huntingdon; so Robin followed the King to the wars, and had no chance to come back to Sherwood.

And now, dear friend, I will tell as speedily as may be of how that stout fellow died as he had lived, not at court, but with bow in hand, and his heart in the greenwood.

King Richard died upon the battlefield, in such a way as properly

became a lionhearted king; so, after a time, the Earl of Huntingdon—or Robin Hood, as we still call him—finding nothing for his
doing abroad, came back to England. With him came Allan a
Dale and his wife, the fair Ellen, for these two had been chief of
Robin's household ever since he had left Sherwood Forest.

It was in the springtime when they landed on the shores of
England. The leaves were green and the small birds sang blithely,
just as they used to do in Sherwood when Robin roamed the forest, so that a great longing came upon him to behold the woodlands once more. So he went to King John and besought leave to
visit Nottingham. The King gave him leave, but bade him not stay
longer than three days. So Robin and Allan a Dale set forth.

At Nottingham Town they took up their inn, yet they did not
pay their duty to the Sheriff, for his worship's bitter grudge had
not been lessened by Robin's rise in the world. The next day they
set forth for the woodlands. As they rode along it seemed to Robin
that he knew every stick and stone that his eyes looked upon.
Yonder was a path that he had ofttimes trod of a mellow evening,
with Little John beside him; here was one, now nigh choked with
brambles, along which he and a little band had walked when they
went forth to seek a certain curtal friar.

At last they came to the open glade, and the widespreading
greenwood tree which was their home for so many years. Robin
looked all about him at the well-known things, so like what
they used to be and yet so different; for where once was the
bustle of many busy fellows was now the quietness of solitude;
and, as he looked, the woodlands, the greensward and the sky all
blurred together in his sight through salt tears.

That morning he had slung his good old bugle horn over his
shoulder, and now came a longing to sound his bugle once more.
He raised it to his lips; he blew a blast. *Tirila, lirila*, the sweet, clear
notes went winding down the forest paths, coming back again
from the more distant bosky shades in faint echoes, *Tirila, lirila,
tirila, lirila*, until it faded away and was lost.

Now it chanced that on that very morn Little John was walking
through a spur of the forest upon a matter of business when the

faint, clear notes of a distant bugle horn came to his ear. All the blood in Little John's body seemed to rush like a flame into his cheeks as he bent his head and listened. Again came the bugle note, thin and clear, and yet again it sounded. Then Little John gave a wild cry of joy and yet of grief, and putting down his head, he dashed into the thicket. Onward he plunged, through the under-brush, little recking he of thorns and briers that scratched his flesh and tore his clothing, for all he thought of was to get, by the shortest way, to the greenwood glade whence the sound of the bugle horn came. Out he burst from the covert, at last, a shower of little broken twigs falling about him, and rushed forward and flung himself at Robin's feet. Then he clasped his arms around the master's knees, and all his body was shaken with sobs; neither could Robin nor Allan a Dale speak, but stood looking down at Little John, the tears rolling down their cheeks.

While they thus stood, seven royal rangers rushed into the open glade and raised a great shout of joy at the sight of Robin; and at their head was Will Stutely. Then, after a while, came four more, and one was Midge, the Miller's son; for all of these had heard the sound of Robin Hood's horn.

Robin looked around him and said, in a husky voice, "Now, I swear that never again will I leave these dear woodlands. I have been away from them and from you too long. Now do I lay by the name of Robert, Earl of Huntingdon, and take upon me once again that nobler title, Robin Hood, the Yeoman." At this all the yeomen shouted and shook one another's hands for joy.

The news that Robin Hood had come back to dwell in Sher-wood as of old spread like wildfire all over the countryside, so that ere a se'ennight had passed nearly all of his old yeomen had gathered about him again. But when the news of this reached King John, he swore both loud and deep and took a solemn vow that he would not rest until he had Robin Hood in his power, dead or alive. Now there was a certain knight, Sir William Dale, who was head keeper over that part of Sherwood Forest that lay nigh to Mansfield Town; so the King bade him take an army of men, and the Sheriff also, and go straightway to seek Robin Hood. So Sir

William and the Sheriff set forth to do the King's bidding; and for seven days they hunted Robin up and down, and yet found him not.

Now, had Robin Hood been as peaceful as of old, everything might have ended in smoke, as other such ventures had always done before; but he had fought for years under King Richard, and it galled his pride thus to flee, as a chased fox flees from the hounds; so it came about, at last, that Robin and his yeomen met Sir William and the Sheriff and their men in the forest, and a bloody fight followed. The first man slain was the Sheriff of Nottingham, for he fell from his horse with an arrow in his brain ere half a score of shafts had been sped. Many a better man than the Sheriff kissed the sod that day, but at last, Sir William Dale being wounded and most of his men slain, he withdrew, beaten, and left the forest. Scores of good fellows were left behind him, stretched out all stiff beneath the sweet green boughs.

But though Robin Hood had beaten off his enemies in fair fight, all this lay heavily upon his mind, so that he brooded over it until a fever seized upon him. For three days it held him, and though he strove to fight it off, he was forced to yield at last. On the morning of the fourth day, he bade Little John go with him to his cousin, the prioress of the nunnery near Kirklees, in Yorkshire, who was a skillful leech; he would have her open a vein in his arm and take a little blood from him, for the bettering of his health. Little John and he took their leave of the others, and Robin Hood bade Will Stutely be the captain of the band until they should come back. Thus they came by easy stages and slow journeying to Kirklees.

Now Robin had done much to aid this cousin of his; for it was through King Richard's love of him that she had been made prioress of the place. But there is naught in the world so easily forgot as gratitude; so, when the Prioress of Kirklees had heard how her cousin, the Earl of Huntingdon, had thrown away his earldom and gone back again to Sherwood, she feared lest her cousinship with him should bring the King's wrath upon her also. Thus it happened that when Robin came to her and told her how he wished her services as leech, she began plotting ill against him in her mind, thinking that by doing evil to him she might find favor with his enemies. Nevertheless, she received Robin with seeming kindness. She led him up the winding stone stair to a room which was just beneath the eaves of a high, round tower; but she would not let Little John come with him.

So the poor yeoman left his master in the hands of the women. But he did not go far away; for he laid him down in a glade nearby, where he could watch the place, like some great, faithful dog turned away from the door where his master had entered.

After the women had gotten Robin Hood to the room beneath the eaves, the Prioress sent all of the others away; then, taking a little cord, she tied it tightly about Robin's arm, as though she were about to bleed him, but the vein she opened was not one of those that lie close and blue beneath the skin; but one of those through which the bright red blood runs leaping from the heart.

Having done this vile deed, the Prioress left her cousin, locking the door behind her. All that day the blood ran from Robin's arm, nor could he check it, though he strove in every way to do so. Again and again he called for help, but no help came, for his cousin had betrayed him, and Little John was too far away to hear his voice. So he bled and bled until he felt his strength slipping away from him. Then he arose, tottering, and bearing himself up by the palms of his hands against the wall, he reached his bugle horn at last. Thrice he sounded it, but faintly, for his breath was fluttering through loss of strength; nevertheless, Little John heard it where he lay in the glade, and, with a heart all sick with dread, he came running toward the nunnery. Loudly he knocked at the the door, and shouted for them to let him in; but the door was of massive oak, strongly barred, and studded with spikes, so they felt safe, and bade Little John begone.

Then Little John looked wildly about him, and his sight fell upon a heavy stone mortar, such as three men could not lift nowadays. Little John took three steps forward, and, bending his back, heaved the stone mortar up from where it stood deeply rooted. Staggering under its weight, he came forward and hurled it against the door. In burst the door, and away fled the frightened nuns, shrieking. Then Little John strode in, and up the winding stone steps he ran to the room wherein his master was. Here he found the door locked also, but, putting his shoulder against it, he burst the locks as though they were made of brittle ice.

There he saw his own dear master leaning against the stone wall, his face all white and drawn, and his head swaying to and fro with weakness. Then, with a great cry of grief and pity, Little John caught Robin Hood in his arms. Up he lifted him as a mother lifts her child, and laid him tenderly on the bed.

And now the Prioress came in hastily, for she was frightened at what she had done, and dreaded the vengeance of Little John and the band; then she stanched the blood by cunning bandages, so that it flowed no more. And after she had done, Little John sternly bade her to begone, and she obeyed, pale and trembling.

Then Little John spoke cheering words, saying that no stout yeoman would die at the loss of a few drops of blood.

But Robin smiled faintly where he lay. "Mine own dear Little John," whispered he, "heaven bless thy kind, rough heart. But we will never roam the woodlands together again."

"Aye, but we will!" quoth Little John loudly. "No more harm shall come upon thee! Am I not by? Let me see who dares touch—" Here he stopped of a sudden, for his words choked him. At last he said, in a husky voice, "Now, if aught of harm befalls thee because of this day's doings, I swear by Saint George that hot flames shall lick every crack and cranny of this house. As for these women—it will be an ill day for them!"

But Robin Hood took Little John's rough, brown fist in his white hands, and chid him softly, asking him since what time Little John had thought of doing harm to women, even in vengeance. Thus he talked till at last the other promised that no ill should fall upon the place, no matter what happened. Then a silence fell, and Little John sat with Robin's hand in his. The sun dropped slowly to the west, till all the sky was ablaze with a red glory. Then Robin Hood, in a faltering voice, bade Little John raise him, that he might look out once more upon the woodlands; so the yeoman lifted him in his arms, and Robin's head lay on his friend's shoulder. Long he gazed, while the other sat with bowed head, the hot tears rolling from his eyes, for he felt that the time of parting was near at hand. Presently, Robin Hood bade him string his stout bow for him, and choose a smooth fair arrow from his quiver. This Little John did, though without disturbing his master or rising from where he sat. Robin Hood's fingers wrapped lovingly around his bow, and he smiled faintly when he felt it in his grasp; then he nocked the arrow. "Little John," said he, "mine own dear friend, mark, I prithee, where this arrow lodges, and there let my grave be digged. Lay me with my face toward the east, Little John, and see that my resting place be kept green, and that my weary bones be not disturbed."

As he finished speaking, he raised himself of a sudden and sat upright. His old strength seemed to come back to him, and, drawing the bowstring to his ear, he sped the arrow out the open casement. As the shaft flew, his hand sank slowly with the bow till it lay across his knees, and his body likewise sank back again into Little John's loving arms; but something had sped from that body, even as the winged arrow sped from the bow.

For some minutes Little John sat motionless, but presently he laid that which he held gently down, then, folding the hands upon the breast and covering up the face, he turned upon his heel and left the room without a word or a sound.

Upon the steep stairway he met the Prioress and some of the chief among the sisters. To them he said in a deep, quivering voice, "An ye go within a score of feet of yonder room, I will tear down your rookery over your heads so that not one stone shall be left upon another." So saying, he left them, and they presently saw him running across the open, through the falling of the dusk, until he was swallowed up by the forest.

The early gray of the coming morn was just beginning to lighten the black sky toward the eastward when Little John and six more of the band came rapidly across the open toward the nunnery. They saw no one, for the sisters were all hidden away from sight. Up the stone stair they ran, and a great sound of weeping was presently heard. After a while this ceased, and then came the scuffling and shuffling of men's feet as they carried a heavy weight down the steep and winding stairs. So they went forth from the nunnery, and, as they passed through the doors thereof, a great, loud sound of wailing arose from the glade that lay all dark in the dawning, as though many men, hidden in the shadows, had lifted up their voices in sorrow.

Thus died Robin Hood, at Kirklees Nunnery, with mercy in his heart toward those that had been his undoing; for thus he showed pity for the weak through all the time of his living.

His yeomen were scattered henceforth, but no great ill befell them thereafter, for, a more merciful sheriff succeeding the one that had gone, and they being separated here and there throughout the countryside, they abided in peace and quietness, so that many lived to hand down these tales to their children and their children's children.

A certain one sayeth that upon a stone at Kirklees is an old inscription. This I give in the ancient English in which it was written, and thus it runs:

> *Hear undernead dis laitl stean*
> *Lais Robert Earl of Huntingtun*
> *Nea arcir ver as hie sae geud*
> *An pipl kauld im Robin Heud*
> *Sick utlaws as hi an is men*
> *Vil England nidir si agen.*
> *Obiit 24 Kal. Dekembris 1247.*

And now, dear friend, we also must part, for our merry journeyings have ended, and here, at the grave of Robin Hood, we turn, each going his own way.